The Rod of Wind and Iron

by

Mikko Azul

Copyright © 2022 by Mikko Azul

All rights reserved.

Published in the United States by
Not a Pipe Publishing, Independence, Oregon.
www.NotAPipePublishing.com

Trade Paperback Edition

ISBN-13: 978-1-956892-03-1

Dedication

To Jared,
whose love and encouragement
fill my days with joy
and make the dark times bearable

The Rod of

Wind and Iron

Contents

MAP OF MURALIA
TA'VORAN MARSH
DÚLNAT
TÁMON
SPÁSTI RIVER
NURKIAK'S CAULDRON
SINHARKON RANGE
THOROMOBERK FORTRESS
MOLONARK
CHARKNAN CEYSERS
BRONÄEN SEA
LAKE JULÁNI
TAWALOTH CHASM
RABE'EN PLAINS
SURIYÄEH
ZÓNAI
ZOHÁRI
ZIC'ORMAN MARSH
ASKARI-BAI
TÁDIM PASS
DÁCON VALLEY
SAMSHÄELI
SHARÄEDAN RIVER
SHALAEN FALLS
TÁKSABAI
RONDÄDI RANGE
KHA'SAN VALLEY
CINÄEYI FOREST
SILÄERI
MAREN COVE
ZUDIAN CORGE
RÄENETTI RIVER
DATÍNAI
ZAVEEN
ZAROON QUARRY
ZAHILI DESERT
YEZMARANTHA
BRÁNON SEA
TÁLIA JUNGLE
TABORIZ

chapter 1: Abduction

Scóurj never came through the front door. Sénna felt a chill run up the back of her neck, watching from the window seat in her room as the Gróshan spy entered her father's home in the early morning light. The filthy little man brought the stench of the sewers with him, the key to his success as a spy for her father, Syrán Kráal. Being dismissed as street trash - virtually invisible to most - enabled the old man access to the places where conspiracies thrived and dark plans were hatched.

Despite her father's express instructions to the contrary, Sénna eased out of her room, glancing down the corridor, making sure nobody spotted her. Sprinting to the left, she careened into her eldest brother Murádit, bouncing off his muscular chest and landing on her bottom.

"Hey, where do you think you're going in such a hurry?" Murádit chuckled and reached a hand down to help her up. "And what are you wearing?"

Sénna grasped his hand and pulled herself to her feet. She glanced at the loose trousers and shirt she'd pilfered from her next-closest brother Myknèt's chest and blushed.

"Um, can't you smell the fresh bread from the kitchens? How could we be expected to wait until supper to try it?" Sénna gave her brother her most innocent expression.

"Uh-huh," Murádit narrowed his eyes at his little sister. "Perhaps I'll leave some for you. I need to fill my pack before heading to the Falls Watchtower for duty."

Sénna gasped and punched her brother in the arm. "You'll end up fat as a cochäera, greedy guts," she laughed and put her hands on her hips, looking her brother up and down. "I thought you said you were headed for duty."

Myknét held his arms out and twirled once. "Yes, in full uniform, as you see."

Sénna arched one eyebrow. "Your best uniform," she said, circling her brother as she inspected him. "And you've braided your hair. What's the occasion?"

Myknét's hand reached up self-consciously to tuck the braid into his hauberk. "I, uh, the wind is stronger at the Falls Watchtower. I get tired of my hair whipping my eyes."

Sénna snorted and crossed her arms over her chest. "You are the bravest and strongest legionnaire in your unit. Hair whipping your eyes? Really?"

Myknét chuckled. "Nothing gets past you, does it?" He ruffled his sister's hair. "How about you worry less about me and more about not getting caught in Murádit's old clothes. Whatever you're up to, I hope it's worth the trouble you'll be in if you get caught."

Sénna stuck out her tongue. Myknét grinned before

turning his back on his sister and making his way down the stairs to the front door. She watched him stride down the street toward the husan paddock where he kept his mount. Sénna shook her head. The youngest child of the Kráal family and the only girl, the family tried to force Sénna into being a docile, obedient pawn to her father's political machinations. At least, that's what some of them thought they were doing.

Syrán Kráal led the Gróshan, Askári-bai's vast network of spies. Her father's interests included what information he could use to his advantage and not what his errant daughter wanted. She snorted, creeping down the hall to the large painting of the glass gardens of Taboriz hanging on the wall. A wooden gold-leafed plaque with her family's crest of a rook sitting on a three-pronged crown inlaid with three gemstones clung to the wall next to the painting.

Sénna pressed the gemstones, first the right, then the left, and then the center releasing the locking mechanism behind the painting. The gears whirred, then clicked. The frame slid sideways, exposing an archway that led into the secret spaces between walls that riddled the house. Sénna was not waiting demurely in her room for her father's pleasure. She had to know what was going on.

The latch of the hidden trap door squeaked as she eased it up, echoing throughout the rafters. Sénna winced. She glanced down into her father's study below to see if anyone heard her. She spread her body along the top of the rough-hewn beam that stretched across the thirty-foot open ceiling of her father's office. Sliding slowly, she kept her breathing shallow and even to match her pace.

Sénna hooked her right boot onto the dusty plank behind her, stabilizing her body. Her left leg hung over the side for balance. She looked down and felt a twinge of vertigo. The twisting in her stomach was less about the height and more about the trouble she knew she'd be in if her father caught her spying on him *again*.

The open-beam ceiling allowed the young servant boys to shimmy out onto the rafters to the ropes that lowered the chandeliers so that they could be dusted and polished. It wasn't the first time Sénna thanked the deities for her slim, boyish frame. Her figure allowed her to wear her older brother Múradit's old clothes and access the narrow crawl spaces reserved for the nimblest of young servants.

Sénna held her breath, pinching her nose to avoid sneezing while the dust she stirred up settled. She sat up slightly and billowed the thin fabric of Múradit's threadbare linen shirt, sending cool drafts of air onto her sweating back. The sound of approaching voices drifted upwards. Sénna froze, then inched back down across the beam as the door to her father's study opened. Below, Syrán entered, followed by Scóurj, whose filth flaked off his crusted shoes soiling the carpet.

"…heard from the longshoremen that them sailors cut out quick from Zaveen afore them warrior priestesses could get at them. Dunno what was took, but bet it's important." The little man scratched his head, then examined his nails, flicking something to the floor.

Syrán sat down behind his desk and nodded to his companion. "Mmm-hmm, yes. Ah, anything else?" Sénna held her breath as her father raised his head and massaged one side of his neck and shoulder.

Scóurj sat down in the heavy gilded chair opposite Syrán, eyeing his leader. He leaned forward and narrowed his eyes.

"There's smoke floatin' down from the north. I hear tell it's from Garanth fires. Them brutes been laying waste to everything south of the mountains," he breathed, shaking his head.

"Hmm, yes, well, keep an eye on that, will you?" Syrán murmured as he shuffled through the sheaves of paper on his desk, pulling out a scroll and frowning at it.

Sénna's mouth dropped open. Scóurj announced that the Garanth, terrifying and vicious warriors who had once ravaged their lands, were again burning the northlands. Her father sloughed that information off like he'd been told how many husan were purchased for the races. She squinted down at her father's desk but couldn't read the scroll he held.

Scóurj rose from his chair and slammed both hands on the front of the desk. Syrán jolted to attention. His forehead wrinkled, and he took a breath, but his spy spoke before he could.

"M'lord, I just told you them Garanth is bringing war. We need to prepare!" Scóurj insisted, glaring at his Master.

Syrán shook his head, rubbing at his right temple. "That is grave news indeed, Scóurj. I'm sorry, I was distracted," he said, glaring at the scroll before setting it aside. "Do you know how many Garanth are marching south?"

"More than the whole Harmólin Legion," the little man said. "An' all them soldiers in the northern quadrant are waitin' for orders from them arrogant fárocs that run the Merchants Guild. By the time them cowards make a move, the Garanth'll overrun the whole city." Scóurj spat.

Sénna's breath hitched. Her eldest brother Myknét was a captain in the legion. The idea of him facing the monstrous Garanth bulls marching on their city made her ill. He was a fearless and capable soldier, but the Garanth were enormous brutes that stood nearly twice the size of a man, with thick hides and horns in addition to their formidable axes and hammers. The relatively feeble arrows and swords of the legion would crumple beneath the northerner's onslaught.

Syrán dropped his head into his hands and sighed. He scrubbed at his thinning hair and then his face. Sénna watched as her father picked up a stylus from the table and tapped it rapidly. He appeared lost in thought.

"Myknét and his squad are headed to patrol up north near the Shalaen Falls. They will be the first to see the horde as they make their way south through the Dágon Valley." Her father stuck the end of the stylus in his mouth and chewed thoughtfully on it. "At least he *should* be the first to spot them if he's not distracted by Cybél."

Scóurj chuckled. "Him's a lucky man. An' it's a smart match, her being pretty and the granddaughter of the apothecarist."

Syrán frowned. "Yes, but she spends a lot of time distracting my son from his duties with picnics and filling his head with ideas for physic and health. He's a warrior and needs to focus on his patrol. Smart match or not, that girl is almost more trouble than she's worth. I want you to get this information to your contacts at the Merchants Guild. Prepare them for what's coming." Syrán rubbed his eyes and picked up the scroll with the Mages Guild seal again. He frowned.

Scóurj eyed the scroll and scratched the scraggly hairs on his chin. "What does the Mages Guild want with the Gróshan?"

Syrán groaned, sliding back in his chair. "It is an offer of marriage between Red Mage Bín Nétar and my daughter. I'm still trying to figure out how to handle it."

Above the two men, Sénna gasped, clapping her hand over her mouth. Her father couldn't possibly be serious. How dare he consider marrying her off – and to a mage, no less. He knew the dangers of dealing with mages.

Heat flushed over her body, making her grip on the wood slippery. She ground her teeth to keep from screaming. Her father often chastised her for being difficult, but marrying her off to a mage was ridiculous. Sénna clenched her teeth and shook her head. Difficult wouldn't begin to describe her response to this news. She leaned down to hear how her father planned to justify this.

"...would be an alliance that would solidify the Gróshan as the legitimate guild into which I've been shaping it. Making the transition from the Thieves' Guild to Gróshan hasn't been easy. I'd hoped for an offer from the Merchants Guild, which still might be forthcoming, but—"

"You can't think them merchants would ally themselves

with the Thieves' Guild, do you?" Scóurj barked a laugh, then sobered and cleared his throat. "M'lord, your father was the King of Thieves. He was ruthless, brutal an' respected, but you…" he spread his hands wide and shrugged.

Syrán stood, shoving his chair back and leaning his hands on the front of his desk. He glared at his spy. "I know my family's history," he growled. "And I'll not have my sons face the same ridicule I do." He strode across the room to the row of portraits hanging along the wall. "I've spent my adult life building a new sort of guild, one that barters in information rather than violence. I've worked hard to change the perception of the Thieves' Guild and its *king*."

Syrán stared up at the portraits of his forefathers, his face twisted in bitter lines. He turned to face his spy. "Although I've forbidden thievery and exchanged coin for information as our currency, I've heard that I'm now called the *Gróshan King*. Can I never get out from under the scourge of my forebears?" He stepped back from the wall and walked over to Scóurj, gripping the man's bony shoulder. "I mean no disrespect to you, my friend."

Scóurj dug at his nails with the small knife he'd pulled from deep inside his coat and wiped the dirt on his trousers. "Your sons will keep doin' the good work; if they survive."

Syrán stiffened. He glanced down at Scóurj sharply. "What do you mean *if they survive*?"

The vile man shrugged. "Well, there's them Garanth coming south and other rumors. I'll check 'em out while you figure out what to do wi' that second daughter of yours."

Syrán rubbed his forehead and temple with one hand. "Shh, not so loud. Not everyone in this household knows about my eldest." Syrán gave a weak smile and shook his head. "What *am* I going to do with that girl?" he sighed. "Well, that's my problem. You, my friend, have your own problems."

"How 'bout visiting Urléen's apothecary?" Scóurj suggested with a raised eyebrow. "She'll have somethin' for that headache."

"Indeed," Syrán barked a laugh.

Syrán strode across the room to a tall bureau with interlocking gears securing the doors together. He pulled a strand of leather from beneath his shirt on which a brass key dangled. Sticking the key into the center of the locking mechanism, he turned and waited as the gears ground and turned, unhinging each strap of metal holding the doors closed. The bureau's doors opened, and Syrán reached inside for a small, heavy bag that jingled.

"Payment for your information and a little extra for you to get a warning to the legion and check out those rumors," Syrán said. He tossed the bag to Scóurj, who caught it nimbly and tucked it beneath his coat with a slight bow.

Syrán waved his hand at his spy, dismissing him from the room. Scóurj wasted no time in taking his leave, scratching his head as he left his master to his thoughts. High in the rafters, Sénna fumed. She couldn't decide what boiled her blood more: that her father was considering marrying her off to a *mage* (her mind spat the word), learning she had an older sister, or her father ignoring Scóurj's warning about the Garanth army.

Father couldn't just leave Myknét and his small patrol to fend for themselves against the approaching Garanth. She pulled the strands of long dark hair that escaped her braid and tucked them behind her ears. Sénna eased herself slowly back towards the trap door, using her hooked ankle to slide her body backward. She'd get more information about her mysterious older sister later. She knew where she could get information for the cost of a few pints of ale.

The heat was stifling in the close rafters, and Sénna was perspiring freely from the exertion of crawling. A bead of sweat dripped from her temple and dropped straight into her father's silvering hair. Sénna held her breath, not daring to move. Syrán ran a bony hand through his hair and leaned back in his chair. He lifted his gaze upwards. Sénna was sure her father heard her heart pounding in her chest.

As her father looked towards the rafters, Sénna felt more sweat pooling in the small of her back. If he spotted her, he'd lock her in her room for at least a sennight. She wouldn't have a chance to argue against him marrying her off to that ambitious mage, or anyone else for that matter. She had only sixteen Tides and was far too young for a permanent commitment.

Sénna closed her eyes and waited for her father's wrath to explode. Instead of his voice, she heard her grandmother Am'aranth.

"Is Sénna here with you?" Sénna heard her ask.

The silver raven, Nek'ka, perched on the top of her grandmother's staff cawed and ruffled her feathers. The bird was the last vestige from the Meq'qan tribe her grandmother kept when she married Sénna's grandfather. Nek'ka gripped the round stone set into the top of the staff as Am'aranth swept into the room.

"No, I haven't seen her," Syrán sighed, giving his mother a wan smile.

Am'aranth's yellow Meq'qan eyes flashed as she looked around the room. She banged her staff on the hard floor, causing Nek'ka to flap her wings and squawk. "She needs to be fitted for her gown, preferably *before* the Autumntide Festival."

Syrán shoved his chair back and stood. Walking around his desk, he took the older woman's hand and tucked it into the crook of his elbow. "Let's see if we can find her."

Sénna exhaled and wiped her face with the damp sleeve of her shirt. She scooted backward as quickly as she could and ducked into the trap door. She knew her father and grandmother would be heading for her room, so she crawled into the tight space between the walls and scooted sideways towards the servant's quarters.

Sénna passed the hidden doors that opened behind the faux walls. When she reached the wall at the end, she pulled the lever above her head and eased the paneling aside. Sénna scanned the corridor but saw nobody. The servants would all be preparing for the midday meal. She slipped from the hidden passageway and tore down the back stairs towards the kitchen. She hit the kitchen at a full run, skidding to a halt at the sight of the cook.

The tall, rawboned woman had her back turned and was plucking the feathers of a large fároc. The fat bird's mate stared with clouded eyes from the counter; his bright feathers dimmed by splattered blood. Sénna snatched a small loaf of bread as she slipped through the pantry.

"And just what do you think you're doing, young man?" The cook turned and rounded on the intruder, brandishing a wooden spoon.

Sénna hunched her shoulders. She cleared her throat and smiled at the cook.

"It's just me," she bobbed a quick curtsey and took a bite of the loaf. "I couldn't resist the smell of your fresh bread, and I missed the morning meal."

Cook glared down at Sénna, one hand on her hip and the other still threatening with the spoon. "Don't try your sass with me, m'girl. Your grandmother is looking for you and will be sore to see you in breeches again."

Sénna laughed feebly and shifted from one foot to the other. "Yes, well, I'm headed to the dressmaker, and I'm late, so I need to run. Heavy skirts aren't practical for making good time, you know."

Cook rolled her eyes and grunted, jutting her chin towards the door before turning back to her grisly task. Sénna swiped a juicy redfruit as she exited the kitchens and made her escape. She sped towards the waterfront and The Lotril's Cave, the pub all the sailors eventually passed through. Her father hated her spending time in the pubs listening and spying instead of learning music and embroidery. Still, if she could glean what was happening in Zaveen and find a way to warn Myknét about the Garanth, maybe her father would forgive her. If her informant was there, Sénna could ask her about this mysterious sister her father mentioned. Perhaps she'd been born of her father's first marriage. That wife died young, and Syrán never spoke of her.

Sénna settled herself into a shadowy corner with a pint of dark ale and darker thoughts. The leather pouch at her side still had a few flecksun coins, but not enough to make her a target. Still fuming over her father's intention to marry her to a mage and ruminating over the danger to the city, she drummed her fingers on the table so loudly that she nearly missed the low conversation around the corner to her right. Sénna clenched her fingers and eased back, adjusting the cap on her head and peeking around the corner.

A stranger was scolding two seamen dressed in thin, loose-fitting breeches and billowy shirts with colorful sashes at the waist. The stranger was no sailor. He wore black from the tightly-wound turban, laced shirt, and trousers to his scuffed boots. Even the sash around his waist was black and held a wickedly-curved blade nestled against his left hip. Around his neck was a large amulet with a red stone set amidst a complicated silver knotwork setting.

Sénna gave a sharp inhale, then leaned over her pint, hiding her face. She'd seen an amulet like that one before. Only once, but she'd never forgotten it. Her heart raced. She knew the man was a magic wielder but not necessarily attached to the Mages Guild. She also knew that a bearer of an identical amulet was responsible for her mother's death.

"I told you, we were only stopping for provisions," the man in black growled, his hands on his hips.

The sailors shifted and glanced at each other. "But ale *is* a provision," the sailor on the left spoke up.

"Yes," agreed the second sailor. "We'll need a few kegs for the trip north. I know it's a short jaunt to the Falls Watchtower, but the crew doesn't like having their ale rationed."

The turbaned man's face darkened, and he leaned over the sailors. "You and your men won't live to get your rations if you don't get the cargo loaded so we can get underway. We have a rendezvous to make and a relic to deliver. Death will be the least of our problems if we fail. Now, round up the crew and get that sloop loaded."

The black-clad man turned and strode out of The Lotril's Cave, his boots clicking on the plank floor. The sailors muttered together for a moment, then went to the tables where their shipmates sat nursing their pints. Sénna took one last gulp of her ale and slipped out the back of the pub. These men were headed north to where her brother was on patrol. With whom would they have a secret rendezvous? What relic? Could it be the stolen one Scóurj mentioned? She had so many questions and nobody else to find the answers.

If Sénna could get on board their ship, she might get the information she needed; information that could be critical to her father. The Falls Watchtower trip wouldn't take more than a couple of hours, as the Tímin Sea waters were calm. She felt her blood racing in her veins. There was a good chance she would get caught. Well, she'd lied her way out of many situations before. Besides, Myknét would be on patrol and nearby to help her if she got into trouble.

Tucking her hair beneath her cap, Sénna scurried towards the pier and slipped in with the gang of young men loading a sloop flying the Támonan flag. As she passed the small keg up the gangplank, she saw the man with the black turban on deck. She nudged the boy next to her to help her with the heavy crate coming up the line. The two of them grunted and heaved, lifting the carton over the side of the railing and setting it on the deck.

Sénna fished out a coin from her pouch and dropped it. The sparkling blue disc bearing the compass rose stamp of the Askári ruling family rolled towards the port side of the ship. Chasing after it, Sénna scanned the deck. Nobody paid her any attention; they were all hurrying to get the sloop loaded and out to sea. She grabbed her coin and thrust it into her pouch.

One last glance around, and Sénna grasped the bulwark railing. She found a pile of coiled ropes and nets and buried herself among them. The shadows behind the lines and netting would hide her until she could find a better place.

The daytime deity Lord Shamar's light warmed her skin as he arched above the boat. His rays filtered through the spaces in the woven netting, beating down on Sénna. Her left shoulder and hand were numb from lying in one position. She shifted to return the blood flow and to ease a cramp in her leg. The Támonan flag above her snapped in the breeze.

The scent of the salt air mixed with the decaying net reminded her of the games she used to play with Múradit when they were younger. Sénna would hide among the shipments of offloaded goods, and Múradit would seek her while their father negotiated with the guild leaders in his efforts to legitimize the Gróshan's dealings. Not even her eldest brother Myknét could find her if she'd put her mind to it, a fact which had always ended with her father locking her in her room.

Often, her father scolded that her place was with the guild's ladies and not snooping about like one of his spies. She scowled. She certainly hoped he'd appreciate her spying now, especially if these men were stealing sacred relics from the priestesses in Zaveen and giving them to the cursed mages. As the leader of the Gróshan, information was the cornerstone of her father's success.

Unable to see more than a few feet around her through the netting, Sénna kept her ears alert and memorized every word she'd overheard as the men lashed down their cargo and prepared to set sail. Harsh, angry sounds came from the men sorting through crates just beyond her hiding place. Cocking her head to one side, she tried to catch the words that the bearded man nearest her had begun grunting as he threw aside another empty crate.

"Curse that old fool," he snarled, throwing the lid to another crate aside. "Oy," he yelled. "The shipment from Zaveen, right?"

Another man nodded his head. "That's what the mage said. It's a long, flat box and should have the temple's symbol branded on the lid."

The turbaned man stood supervising the others and fingering the amulet that hung around his neck. His garment was different from most mages, who wore long, flowing white, red, or black robes, depending on their level. Sénna wondered what connection the Mages Guild had with the priestesses of Zaveen, the remote settlement in the Zahili Desert, and home to the famed Temple of Orwaena.

The priestesses there studied only the martial arts of war, abstaining from marriage and family. They were renowned for their skill and craftsmanship in designing zolenium armor and weapons. It made sense for shipments to go from the temple to the Hármolin Legion, but mages didn't fight. Sénna couldn't think what the priestesses made that would be valuable to the Mages Guild. Mages were cowards who fought with magic, not bravely with weapons like her brother Myknét and the other Hármolin Legionnaires that protected the city.

"This is it."

Sénna heard the gravelly voice of the bearded man behind her and much closer than she'd expected. She held her breath.

"Good," said the turbaned leader. "Put it in our packs with the husan in the hold. We'll need to ride inland to meet the mage and deliver the box."

Sénna eased her breath out at the mention of husan. She loved riding the large equines. Their midnight blue coats were soft and inviting, directly contrasting the dangerous horns that curved wickedly from above and below their long snouts. There were stables in the hold, which would also be an excellent hiding place for the short duration of this journey if she could only get down there without being seen.

Sénna knew she'd have to wait until the crew went belowdecks for their meal. Then there would only be one or two left on watch, and she could get to the husan. She was comfortable around the beasts and knew how to handle them. She began to plan for how she'd take one and escape once the sloop landed.

Slowly, the sloop tacked across the crowded port toward the breakwater and open sea. The southerly winds picked up once they left Táksabai's harbor, eliciting curses from the sloop's crew as they furled the sails. Sénna felt the rumbling and thumping of oars extending into the water as the slaves began the arduous task of rowing the ship up the coastline. Sénna nodded, her eyelids heavy in the warmth of the late morning despite the cramping of her long limbs. The fresh scent of sea air blended with the creaking ropes and timbers of the ship, lulling her mind.

The loud rumble of her belly startled her into alertness. Sénna sensed something else was different. Something other than hunger gnawed at her guts. She shifted so that she could scan the skies. No clouds, but she was sure that it had grown darker. A blast of frigid air swept across the deck, followed by the turbaned leader.

"You have the scepter's sheath?" The voice came from nowhere and everywhere at once, surrounding the ship in its frozen depths.

Ice tore through Sénna's veins with jagged edges as the frigid voice permeated her senses. The sound seemed to emanate from the very bowels of the world. She felt the tendrils of panic whispering in her mind, then screaming for her to run while simultaneously rooting her in place. There was no escape. There was no word for the thing that froze the deck of the ship, no horror from childhood nightmares that came close.

"Yes, Master," the turbaned man said, gripping his

amulet with white knuckles. The red stone in the center pulsed with an eerie glow. "We'll meet with the mage inland above the Dágon Valley. The ship is making good time, and our husan are fresh."

"Excellent," the icy voice grated. "But do not deliver it to the mage. I have sent another who will not disappoint me as the mage has."

Sénna felt the boards bend as the turbaned man shifted his feet. "Uh, a-another?"

"He travels with the Garanth army coming down from the north. Do not try to betray him, or you will answer to me."

Sénna's heart stopped. If the Garanth army was already in the Dágon Valley, it would reach her city of Táksabai in days. She had to warn the Hármolin Legion. Sénna thought of Myknét and prayed to Orwaena, the warrior goddess, to watch over him.

"No, of course not, my Master," the turbaned man's breathing became labored. "We have only done your bidding."

"Ah, but you have been careless," the wintry voice chilled the marrow in Sénna's bones. "Your men are lazy, and you have become complacent."

The turbaned man fell to his knees, gasping. His voice raised an octave. "No, Master. I have taken every precaution. The crew—" The man screamed in pain, clutching his sides.

"Fool! You were followed. You have a stowaway."

Sénna watched the ice form across the top of the netting, freezing her bones in place. Only her eyes moved as she saw the turbaned man reach for the rope coils that had kept her hidden.

Chapter 2: Captives

Pain. Sénna's mind roared from oblivion into the red haze of torment. Searing, raw agony cut into her wrists. Dull throbbing filled her body from her pounding head to her bound ankles. She groaned and opened her eyes. She was no longer on the sloop but in a small chamber on land.

Rough timbers framed the ceiling and door. Two narrow crenels for archers filtered in Lord Shamar's light as he angled towards the horizon. The walls were weathered wood framing stonework with chipped mortar. The chill of the flagstone floor seeped into her body through her thin homespun shirt and trousers. She'd lost her woolen cap, and her long dark hair spilled around her head in a halo.

Sénna inhaled slowly. The damp, stale air of the room mixed with the reek of drying seaweed and rotting shellfish. She could hear the shush of waves against rocks and the steady roar of distant falls. Sénna fought through the pain to think. The sloop she was aboard traveled north and bore the Támonan flag. How far had they sailed? How long had she been unconscious after her captors had found and beaten her?

The roar of the falls pushed through the haze in her mind. There was only one place in all of Askári-bai that had such a large waterfall. The old abandoned coastal watchtower above the Shalaen Falls; that must be where they'd taken her. Sénna exhaled, relaxing her shoulders. Myknét patrolled this area from the newer Falls Watchtower less than a league away down the coast. She wondered if he spotted the sloop landing or the men bringing her ashore.

Sénna tried to roll over and gasped as a sharp pain in her side robbed her of breath. She took inventory of the damage to her body. Bound at the wrists and ankles with bruised or broken ribs and a throbbing headache. If she ever got back to her father in one piece, he was going to kill her. She'd always managed to slip away undiscovered – or at least unscathed – on her spying jaunts, but this time she hadn't been so fortunate.

Sénna tried to picture who'd captured and beaten her. She remembered swiping bread from the kitchen and sitting in The Lotril's Cave. The memory of a red amulet and the terrible, icy voice chilled her more than the stone. The man in black had found her hiding and bound her securely before beating her senseless.

A tunnel snake slithered across Sénna's ankles. She shivered, shaking her head clear of the memories. Her guts twisted, and her lips tightened at the recall of earlier events. She'd been so careful – but never would she have expected a demon. That was the only answer that made sense.

The deities banished all demons to the abyss millennia

ago, and that was undoubtedly where that horrible voice had originated. Somehow, demons had escaped their prison; there was no other explanation. Sénna had to warn her family and the legion. The city wasn't prepared for the Garanth army, let alone the terrifying threat of demons.

Sénna twisted her feet back and forth, trying to loosen the twine binding her ankles. She pried at the knot with her fingers, but the rope was so tight that her fingers had little feeling and no strength. She clawed at the knot feverishly, swearing as her nails tore and bled. Through the crumbled ceiling above her, she could hear men's voices raised in argument. Sénna strained her ears to catch their words.

"…should just kill her and get going…" rumbling and murmuring.

"…run straight into the Varkáras Caravan that's camped just over the hill…" a higher voice pitched in.

Then a smooth baritone voice commanded, "…cause a distraction, we could attack the caravan from behind…" murmurs of agreement and heavy footsteps.

Outside, the melancholy wail of gulls competed with the crashing of waves upon the shore. The gnawing of her empty belly compounded the discomfort in her bruised and aching body. A tear escaped Sénna's eye, and she swiped it away savagely with the back of her bound hands. She would not show any weakness in front of her captors, who she could hear stomping down to her level. She took a steadying breath and closed her eyes, whispering a prayer to Hamra, the moon goddess who presided over births and deaths.

"Well, young lady, we seem to be in some disagreement about what to do with you," the leader said in his deep, resonant voice.

He knelt in front of her, displaying piercing brown eyes beneath heavy brows and his black turban. He reached for her face and lifted her chin, forcing her to look directly at him.

"Ha, you're right; she *is* the daughter of the Gróshan

king," he said. His thin lips twisted as he leaned closer to her. "Your Meq'qan eyes betray you, or they've saved you, depending on your perspective." He stood and faced his men. "We'll keep her with us and ransom—" his mouth snapped shut as he heard voices outside.

Sénna twisted to see around the men whose bodies were instantly still but taut as bowstrings. Their glances and nods conveyed instructions that Sénna could only guess at, but it didn't look promising for the new arrivals. She heard a woman laughing and then a man's voice.

"…stunning when Lord Shamar relinquishes the sky to his moon daughters, the colors…."

Sénna froze. Her breath caught in her throat. Myknét! She recognized her brother's voice, but who was with him? The woman trilled again with laughter, and Sénna closed her eyes. Only one woman had that laugh. Cybél Láhta, the apothecarist's granddaughter. Myknét captured the attention of the loveliest eligible girl in Táksabai and was wooing her right into the hands of these villains.

"Myknét, run!" Sénna screamed. "Get out—" Pain exploded in the back of her head.

"Shut up, girl," the turbaned man snarled. "Or I'll kill you now. No ransom is worth this hassle."

Turning to his men, he pointed to a swarthy, short man whose thick, russet beard couldn't hide the sneer on his face. "Keep an eye on her. If she squeaks again, slit her throat."

The bearded man nodded and loosened the blade tucked into the sash at his waist. Sénna's jaw snapped shut, her eyes wide as she watched the rest of the men sneak up the worn steps and out of the watchtower door, which hung slightly ajar. She waited, praying her brother had heeded her warning. Silence. She could hear the sound of her blood pounding in her ears, marking the endless moments of stillness. She noted the song of a blade being pulled from its sheath.

"Sénna, is that you?" Myknét called.

Silence.

"Who's there?" Myknét called again, this time closer to the tower. "Come out and face me."

A scream rent the air, sending a shiver down Sénna's spine. She tugged again at her bonds and felt the sharp edge of the blade caress her neck.

"Go ahead," the man urged in a voice that grated like rusted hinges. "Your throat is so smooth I might accidentally slip."

The sounds of a skirmish came from outside. There were grunts and the clash of blades. Sénna heard her brother's voice raised in a challenge, and her heart broke. More clashing and guttural calls. Another scream cut short. Silence. Tears coursed down Sénna's cheeks from wide, unblinking eyes. She knew her life was over. She felt the tranquility of the doomed and knew she wouldn't be alone. Myknét's soul would fly into the bosom of Lady Muralia, and she would follow him.

Sénna jerked her head up at the sound of running feet. The rest of her captors were returning, with Myknét right behind them swinging his blade. Her brother caught one of the sailors across the calf with the tip of his sword. The man screamed and fell as Myknét leaped past him. Her brother plunged into the doorway of the tower and immediately faced two more men. He sliced the man on his right through the arm, forcing him to drop his weapon.

Myknét spotted Sénna as the second man brought his blade down towards the soldier's head. Myknét had been a legionnaire for many Tides. He blocked the man's downward blow with his sword and swung his left fist up into the man's jaw. The assailant's eyes rolled up, and he crumpled to the floor.

Myknét turned and strode to his sister. "Sénna, what happened to you? Are you hurt?"

Then he saw the man hovering in the shadows behind his sister with the knife held to her throat.

"Let her go," he ordered and lowered his blade towards the man's eye.

Sénna felt the bite of steel along her throat and the warmth of blood running along her collar bone. She swallowed hard and shook her head. "Myknét, take Cybél, and get out of here!"

The man behind her pulled her hair, tipping her head backward. His blade slid further along her neck. Myknét's eyes widened, and he froze. From the doorway, the turbaned leader shoved Cybél into the tower. Her hair was torn from its ornate plaits and clung to her face. She was pale and whimpered as the man pulled her arm up behind her back. The basket of food she'd carried hung in the crook of her elbow, squeezed protectively against her body.

"Drop your sword, legionnaire," the man holding Cybél barked. "And I will kill you quickly."

Sénna saw Myknét glance at Cybél and swallow hard. He gritted his teeth. The knuckles clenching the sword hilt were white. Sénna's chest inflated with pride. Myknét had never backed down from a challenge and had never lost a fight. She looked at the remaining men and nodded to her brother. He could take them. She might die in the process, but he would kill them all before he was through.

Cybél cried out as the turbaned man viciously wrenched her arm behind her. Myknét tensed, then dropped his shoulders. He hung his head and dropped his sword.

"Let the girls go," he said and looked up. He held Sénna's gaze for a moment and opened his mouth to speak.

"Ha, the legion is as weak as we thought," one of the wounded men behind Myknét laughed and thrust his sword into her brother's back.

Sénna heard the sudden grunt and release of air as the blade sank into her brother's body. Myknét's mouth worked soundlessly. He dropped to his knees and reached towards her face. With a roar, the wounded sailor shoved the blade entirely through Myknét's chest. The tip of the blade pierced the blue and silver fabric of Myknét's uniform. Red blossomed below the point and spread across his chest. Myknét fell to the floor.

"No!" Sénna screamed and wriggled against her captor. She jerked her head backward and smashed the man's nose.

Cybél screamed and twisted against the man with the turban. She wrenched herself free and flung herself on Myknét's body, sobbing. The forgotten basket rolled on the floor, spilling meat pies, a round of cheese, and corked bottles of ale. The leader grabbed her around the waist, but she clung to Myknét with the fierceness of an asátto, the large grassland feline.

"I don't have time for this!" the black-turbaned man roared. He kicked Cybél in the stomach. She groaned and rolled away.

One of the remaining men picked Cybél up and carried her away from Myknét's corpse towards where Sénna had been knocked forward by the captor with the broken nose. The man grunted as he swung Cybél's body off his shoulders and onto the floor. Bile filled Sénna's mouth at the sickening crack of the young woman's skull hitting the stone floor.

Blood oozed from a gash down Cybél's left temple, and a bruise on her cheekbone swelled her left eye nearly shut. Cybél lay still. Her face paled beneath the tendrils of hennaed hair plastered to her skin.

Sénna looked around the room at the remaining men. One of them was dripping blood from a deep gash in his leg. Two more supported each other as they limped down the stairs, one with his arm hanging loosely at his side. Sénna's lips curved. Her brother had proven that the Hármolin Legion was *not* weak. These men would not forget him. She sent a prayer of thanks to Orwaena for blessing her brother with an honorable death.

One of the men walked over to where Cybél lay and whistled. "This one's got ample curves. Maybe we should take her instead? I'm sure she could provide a lot more entertainment than that spindly thing," he stuck his thumb towards Sénna, licking his meaty lips.

"We don't have time for that. Leave the girls and grab the box," the leader ordered his men. "The Varkáras Caravan is camped between us and our contact. We'll need to create a diversion for the men of the caravan to investigate so we can slip past them."

The leader scanned the room, puckering his lips in and out as he considered. He gazed up towards the rotted wooden beams that framed the ceiling, door, and crenels as he walked the length of the room. Nodding, he turned and faced his men and his prisoners.

"Get a jar of Yezman oil from the pack," he said, pointing to the man with the limp. He then walked over to the man with the slashed arm and stuck his fingers into the man's pouch. "I'll need to borrow this."

Sénna gasped. Her throat went dry when she saw the tinderbox.

chapter 3: Shalean Falls

"No!" Sénna screamed as the turbaned man struck the flint.

Sparks spilled from his fingers, hitting the flammable oil that trailed along the doorframe and around the room. The *whoosh* of fire following the fuel's ignition blew her hair back and singed her eyebrows.

"This will keep men from the caravan occupied for a bit," the leader said. "They won't notice us riding around their perimeter." He cracked his knuckles as he surveyed the flames licking at the rotted timbers of the door frame.

The turbaned man turned to the girls who lay on the floor,

surrounded by the rising flames. "They may be in time to find you," he said, his grin widening. "But I doubt they'll find more than your charred, fire-ravaged bodies," he said, clicking his tongue and shaking his head in mock regret. "Perhaps ravaging by us would have been preferable had you only cooperated. Alas, that is not your fate."

The leader tucked his amulet underneath his cloak and motioned for his remaining men to follow him. Sénna could hear the nervous husan stamping and blowing outside the watchtower. They didn't like the flames any better than she did, but at least they would soon gallop away.

Dread gripped Sénna's chest with tightening fingers. Images surged to the surface of her mind, memories she'd locked away and tried to forget. She pictured her mother's terrified expression, the explosion, and the chilling laugh as the mage with a similar red amulet flew away from the burning guild halls astride his enormous, black raptor.

A loud crack followed the crash of supports over the doorway, returning Sénna to the fire now burning around her. The terror of her memories spurred her into action. She twisted around, searching for anything that would dampen the flames. The room was bare save for herself, Myknét's body, and Cybél, who was still prone and bleeding. Sénna remembered her grandmother telling her that corpses didn't bleed and felt a twinge of hope.

Sénna rolled over on her back and scooted across the floor, wincing as the movement jarred her injuries. Reaching Cybél, Sénna pulled the hood of Cybél's cloak away from her face and laid her cheek over the other girl's nose and mouth. She felt Cybél's breath stir the short hairs near her temple. Sénna sobbed her relief and clutched Cybél by the shoulder.

"Wake Cybél, you must wake!" Sénna punctuated her words with sharp shakes.

Cybél's brow creased, and she uttered a low moan. Her eyelids fluttered before she squinted them open halfway.

"What happened?" she croaked. Cybél raised a manicured hand to the wound on her head. She sat up, reaching for Sénna, and froze. "Myknét! Where is he? I saw that sword...."

Sénna stared at Cybél, unable to speak. She tried to swallow, but her throat constricted. Her eyes stung, and she dropped her head, her tears splashing onto the stone floor. Cybél gasped and clapped her fist to her mouth, her eyes wide.

"Oh, my Myknét," she gasped, shaking her head and looking around. "He fought so bravely."

"And now he's dead," Senna's voice was thick as she shook the older girl's shoulder again with her bound hands. "We need to get out of here. Can you untie my hands and feet?" Sénna coughed and swung her legs around so that they lay next to the skirts crumpled around Cybél's legs.

The smoke thickened, burning Sénna's throat, and blurring her vision. The fire raced through the tower, crackling above them, devouring the wooden floor and shingled roof above in its fierce hunger. Cybél coughed and reached for the knot on Sénna's legs. Sénna twisted her ankles together, giving some slack to the twine.

A crash from upstairs shook the tower. It sounded like the roof collapsed. Sénna felt her heart beat faster, feeling the heat seeping through the rotted beams. She brought her wrists to her mouth and started to tear at the knot with her teeth. The blood from the chaffing on her wrists made the rope slippery, and the knot pulled apart.

"Hurry!" Sénna coughed, struggling to breathe in the acrid air.

"Almost got it," Cybél grunted. "There!" She pulled the knot loose.

Sénna rolled to her feet and stood, then wobbled into the wall. She felt the painful tingling of blood flowing back into her feet and lurched toward the blazing doorway.

"Quick," she said, keeping low to the ground. "Throw

your cloak over your head and follow me."

Cybél's face was pale, and her hands shook, but she nodded and threw her cloak up over her head. The two girls crawled through the inferno raging around them. They picked their way around the burning debris that fell through the crackling ceiling above. They nearly reached the door when there was a crash.

The color drained from Cybél's already ashen face. She wavered for a moment, then plopped on the flagstones, her cloak framing her auburn hair. "Myknét's dead," she said in a small voice. She looked up at Sénna. "And we're going to die with him. This building will be our pyre," her voice rose slightly. "I should be grateful not to have to grieve long for him, but…."

Cybél stared at the ring on her hand and coughed, her breathing becoming shallow and rapid. "I don't want to die! Not like this!"

Cybél grasped her hair with both hands, her fingers tangling in the long locks as she shook her head and sobbed. The tower shook. A blast of heat washed over the young women, blowing them back into the stairwell.

"The roof of the tower has collapsed," cried Sénna. She wiped soot from her eyes and peered at the pile of smoldering wood and cracked stone piled against the door. "We're trapped!" She sprang up and grasped at the fallen timbers blocking the door, burning her hands as she tossed them aside. "We have to get out of here!"

Sénna's chest squeezed until she had to force air in and out. The echoes of her mother's screams tormented her mind and blended with Cybél's weeping. She stomped her foot and turned on Cybél.

"You are not helping," she snarled.

Sénna turned away from the crying young woman and resumed pulling at the crumbled stones and smoking embers. Picking up a long, burning beam, she squatted and roared as she flung herself back from the door using what strength she had left to pull the wood free.

Sénna sagged against the wall, her breaths scorching her throat and lungs raw. Cybél's sobs had become more guttural as her throat strained in the smoky air. In the silence between breaths, Sénna heard another sound. Men's voices and shouting. She stood alert, then Cybél's wailing began again.

She turned to Cybél and slapped her across the face. "Be quiet! Someone's outside!"

Cybél's eyes were red and swollen. A hand-shaped welt bloomed on her cheek, but she was silent. Sénna pulled Cybél to her feet and dragged her towards the blocked opening. They listened and could make out voices above the crackling of the fire. The women looked at each other. Cybél wiped her eyes, smearing her porcelain cheek with dirt, and raised her brows. Sénna pursed her lips, then nodded.

"Help! We're trapped!" they cried in unison, both scrabbling at the debris preventing their escape as they coughed and choked on the smoke.

The voices came closer to the tower.

"How many are inside?" Sénna heard a man's voice yell.

Tears filled Sénna's eyes, but she refused to let them fall. "Two, there are two of us!"

Cybél stared at Sénna. "There are three of us!"

Sénna glanced back through the smoke to the back of the chamber at her brother's body and closed her eyes. She shook her head. "I am not ready to follow him, and he cannot come with us. You know that as well as I do."

The young women could hear the men talking, their voices raised in argument.

"Please…help us!" Sénna coughed. "The smoke…we can't breathe."

The argument broke off, and a man called out. "Get back from the door."

Sénna grasped Cybél by the upper arm and propelled her back into the stairwell as the front door exploded inward.

The blast knocked them down on the hard, stone steps. Sénna picked splinters of smoking timbers out of her hair and rose to her feet. She picked up Cybél and took her hand. They made slow, cautious steps toward the now-opened space that was once the tower door and part of its wall.

Beyond the opening stood two young men. One of them had dark hair and wore what looked like ragged elements of a legionnaire's uniform. Sénna gasped when she saw the other young man. His golden hair gleamed in the firelight. He stood several inches taller than his companion, and his translucent skin seemed to have an inner glow. He held a staff made of bones with a red stone glowing in its tip. The macabre talisman gave Sénna a twinge of unease.

Sénna pulled Cybél through the demolished door and skirted around the wall away from the blonde young man. She could tell he was at least part Shäeli, and she didn't want to go near him. She looked at the dark man, whose beardless chin contradicted the harsh lines in his face, making it impossible to guess his age. They were both reasonably young, though gangly and awkward.

"Who are you?" Sénna asked, keeping a narrow gaze on the pale Shäeli. "And how did you do that?" She waved at the gaping hole in the side of the burning tower several yards away.

The young men looked at each other, their expressions blank. The legionnaire shrugged and pulled his dark braid back over his shoulder, grinning at the young women. The Shäeli stepped forward and gave a slight bow, his green eyes wary.

"I am Cédron Varkáras of Dúlnat, son of Regent Kásuin and Lady Maräera." A bleak look flickered over his face, and he cleared his throat, turning to his companion. "May I present Anéton Bessínos, Harmólin Legionnaire also of Dúlnat."

Anéton stepped forward and made a courtly bow. "Pleased to be of service, ladies."

Sénna scowled. She'd heard the unbelievable tale that the heir of the famed Varkáras Caravan had taken a Shäeli bride and settled down in Dúlnat. This Cédron must be the spawn of that union. She didn't trust either of these young men, and giving them information could provide the strangers with an unfair advantage. She inclined her head towards Anéton.

"My name is Sénna, and this is Cybél," she said. Sénna pulled Cybél forward, hissing as she scraped her burned hands across Cybél's sleeve.

Another crash from the tower caused them all to flinch and turn to face the building. Sénna felt the blood drain from her face. The back wall of the tower collapsed, leaving Myknét's body open to the sky. Lord Shamar's fading light glinted off the hilt of his sword, lying just beyond the reach of his outstretched arm. The fire raged, smoke billowed around the tower, but her brother's body sprawled open to the elements and clear of both.

Cybél cried out and reached her hand toward her fallen love. She fell back into Sénna and fainted. Sénna buckled under the unexpected burden. Anéton jumped forward and helped ease the young woman to the ground.

"Is she injured or burned?" Anéton asked, his brows creased as he smoothed her hair out of her face.

Sénna swallowed hard and shook her head, her eyes not leaving her brother's body. "He was her betrothed and my...."

Sénna's legs were heavy as if she were wading through deep mud to reach her brother's body. She scrambled over the debris and stumbled to his side. Falling to her knees, silent tears coursed down her smudged cheeks. Blood pooled around the wound, where the blade pierced his body. Myknét's empty golden eyes stared towards the heavens. She reached down to close his lids, then kissed his brow. Her heart shattered in her chest. She bent over him and sobbed.

"He was your brother?" a soft voice spoke behind her.

Sénna was in no mood for compassion. All the terror,

rage, and helplessness of the past several hours boiled up inside her. She jumped to her feet and whirled around.

"Get away from us, you Shäeli demon!" Sénna hissed, her fists clenched at her sides and shaking.

Cédron raised his hands, palms open. "I just want to help. I won't hurt you." He took a tentative step forward. "I don't have anything to dig with, but we can't leave the body here. The caravan isn't far. We could get a wagon and take him with us if you like."

Sénna clenched her teeth and hung her head. "There isn't time for that," she said, her voice cracking. "The men who captured us said that the Garanth army was coming down from the north."

A shiver ran down her spine. She needed to warn the legion before it was too late. She glanced down at her brother's waxen face. She needed to get back to Táksabai before she lost what little family she had left.

Cédron glanced at her sharply. "These men, what did they look like?"

Sénna shrugged. "They were seamen, mostly. Their leader wasn't, though. I think he belonged to a guild, but I don't know which one."

"How was he different?" Cédron asked, his body tensing next to her as if he were getting ready to spring.

Sénna looked at him with one eyebrow raised. "He wore black clothes and a turban," she said. She remembered the frigid voice from the ship and shuddered. "He had a strange knotted amulet."

Cédron paled and looked at Anéton.

"He spoke to a demon through the firestone in its center," Sénna swallowed against the lump of terror, choking on the memories.

"Hazzara!" Cédron spat. He reached out for Sénna's hand. "We need to get back to the caravan now."

Sénna jerked her hand out of his reach and turned back to the corpse. "But, my brother, we can't just leave him like this."

"I can burn him," Cédron said softly. "It's faster than a pyre and cleaner."

Sénna gaped at him. "How are you going to do that?"

Cédron pursed his lips, then shrugged. "The same way I blasted the door open; I'm Shäeli, as you so eloquently pointed out."

Cédron hefted the staff. A pulsing, cabochon firestone, the size of her fist, nestled in the finger bone crown atop the skull.

A wave of nausea crashed over Sénna. She swallowed, her face twisting at the bitterness rising in the back of her throat. "Stay away from me and get away from Myknét!" She stood protectively in front of her brother, her arms outstretched to prevent the demon from getting any closer.

Cédron's strange green eyes flashed in the light of the throbbing stone. "Shall we leave your brother to the carrion birds then? They will enjoy picking out his eyes first, then move on to the rest of his soft parts, slowly until he is picked clean."

Sénna screamed and launched herself at him, beating his wiry chest with her fists. He grabbed her wrists and held them down.

"What's your problem? Mine is the same energy that connects all of us to the deities," Cédron growled.

Sénna wriggled free. "There is no connection to the deities. I won't let you defile him with your Shäeli magic!"

Sénna swung a fist at Cédron's head. He grabbed her wrist as it arched towards him and spun her into him, twisting her arm up behind her back.

"Look, we don't have time for this," he hissed into her ear. "Let me honor your brother's noble death and send his spirit freely to Lady Muralia so we can get back to the caravan before it's too late."

Sénna twisted to get free, but despite his slender frame, the young Shäeli was very strong. After a few moments, she sagged her shoulders and stopped fighting. She hated magic wielders more than anything, but not more than she loved her brother. She couldn't bear the thought of his body ravaged by birds and animals. She looked at Cybél, who was being lifted to her feet by the legionnaire.

Anéton held out his arm and guided Cybél to Sénna's side. He then stepped over the smoldering door frame to pick up the discarded basket and round up its contents. Cybél looked at Myknét for a long moment, then grabbed Sénna's arm.

"Please, Sénna," Cybél's voice shook, but there was no mistaking the plea in her eyes. "Let him honor Myknét properly. He died a warrior's death. We can do no better for him."

Sénna snarled as she wrenched herself free of Cédron's grip but stood aside so that he could reach her brother's body. She watched him raise the staff above his head, the fiery glow of the firestone brightening in the fading light.

"Wait!" Sénna cried, running to her brother's side. She pulled the knife and sheath from his belt and cut the dark braid from his head. Sénna walked back to Cybél, touching the coil of hair to her own forehead before handing it to Cybél. Silent tears coursed down Cybél's cheeks. She kissed the keepsake and tucked it gently into the basket. Sénna slid the knife and sheath onto her belt. She grabbed Cybél's hand and nodded at Cédron.

Cédron raised the staff again and closed his eyes. The glow of the firestone spread to cover Myknét's body in a blanket of vermillion heat. Steam rose, and Sénna hoped that Myknét wasn't going to burn up in front of her. The gruesome thought of watching his skin char and fall away from bone made her chest ache.

The glow intensified, and Myknét's body shimmered in the billowing smoke. Sénna squinted against the bright light and heat. As she watched, her brother's body slowly changed. Tiny particles of glowing light separated from his skin. They floated upward in the sparkling light until his entire body blended with the smoke of the burning tower, causing the hilltop to radiate ethereal light.

Sénna caught the scent of heliotrope, her brother's favorite flower, drifting in the air. The vanilla-anise fragrance filled her mind with memories of his kind smile. She blinked, freeing the cascade of tears to flow like a river of grief.

Cédron raised the staff towards the darkening sky, guiding the essence of Myknét home to Lady Muralia. When the last of the glowing lights disappeared, Cédron lowered the darkened talisman and slung it across his back. Sénna felt an unfamiliar pang when she noticed the tears on the demon's cheeks. She closed her eyes. She said her final farewell to her brother and sent a prayer to Hamra to watch over him. Taking several deep breaths to get her feelings under control, Sénna wiped the crook of her elbow over her face, erasing the tears.

She turned toward the tower and the silent group. "I'm ready."

Sénna watched the gigantic Caravan Master as he assisted his men in gathering supplies. He stood nearly a full head above the tallest of the other men, the sable skin of his bald head reflecting the firelight. He pointed with fingers that reminded her of the long, dried sausages hanging in the butcher's window. The caravan men quickly executed their Master's orders, dousing fires and gathering supplies to be loaded into a long wagon hitched to a team of four husan. Their midnight blue manes and horns gleamed in the firelight.

Caravan Master Shozin Chezak listened gravely to Sénna's story, interrupting her only occasionally with questions. Sénna was wary of the man who stood nearly seven feet tall, with a voice as deep as the sea. He took her hand in his, hers dwarfed inside his plate-sized palms, and thanked her for the information. He then set the men to work, loading the water barrels aboard the two carts and removing all traces of their fire. Master Chezak's voice boomed throughout the clearing as he bellowed his orders.

Sénna and a still-shaken Cybél were returned to the care of Cédron and Anéton. The young men escorted the ladies to a smaller, wooden wagon filled with water barrels and firewood. A lone husan harnessed to the wagon tossed its blue mane, waiting to follow the others back to the main caravan encampment.

"I'm sorry for the rough accommodations," Cédron apologized, rubbing the back of his neck. "We were gathering supplies for the caravan when we saw the fire."

Cédron's eyes were barely visible through lowered lashes as he pulled Cybél's skirt hem from the gate hinges and tucked it beneath her ankles. Cybél nodded to him and smiled slightly as the strange young man blushed. Anéton stepped next to his friend, holding out a length of fabric.

"You l-ladies can sit on my cloak," Anéton stammered and flushed. "It would be more comfortable than the hard planks."

Cybél stared blankly at him

Sénna rolled her eyes and shook her head. She winced as she pulled the gate up against their knees and shoved the pin into the grommet to secure it in place.

"We're fine," she snapped.

Anéton's flush deepened, and he cleared his throat. "As you wish, milady." He flung the cloak over his shoulders before nodding Cédron to precede him to the front of the wagon.

The two young men climbed up behind the driver, sitting on top of the water barrels as the Caravan Master whistled for the husan to pull the wagons back to the Dágon Valley.

The driver cracked a whip over the beast's deep blue hide. The muscular equine tossed its head, its long mane twisting around the horns above and below the long snout. The husan strained in its harness, digging its curved talons into the soft dirt to gain the traction needed to pull the laden wagon forward.

Cybél looked over at Sénna and grasped her hands. She turned them over, palms up, to inspect the damage. Sénna saw the angry red blisters on the pads of her fingers and palm. She bit her tongue as Cybél prodded one with a finger.

"I have some salve that will help with the pain," she said.

Cybél snagged a leather pouch from among the items in her basket. She rummaged through the bag, pulling out a wooden puzzle box the size of her dainty hand. She then pressed three different wood sections where a square sank into the veneer. The box slid apart after the third click, revealing a pale, rose-colored gel that glimmered slightly.

"Here, let me rub some of this on the blisters. It will numb the skin. Be careful, though," Cybél admonished as she closed the box and put it back into her basket. "Just because they don't hurt doesn't mean you should use them. Give your hands time to heal."

"Thank you," Sénna nodded. "That's a fancy box for a simple ointment."

Cybél shook her head. "My grandmother uses the oil from spilánthes flowers for clients with toothaches, but some men think it an aphrodisiac." She rolled her eyes and sighed. "So, I keep it hidden from them but available for pain relief if others need it."

Sénna sniffed at her hands and smiled, remembering how her grandmother Am'aranth told her something similar when she'd rubbed a pungent gel of aloe mixed with calendula and lavender on her knees when she'd scraped them. The young ladies sat back against the water barrels and crossed their arms, both lost in their thoughts. Although Sénna was sure that being hosted by the Varkáras Caravan was better than being held hostage by the Hazzara, she wasn't certain by how much.

The bone staff Cédron carried troubled Sénna. Her grandmother's people, the Meq'qan, made talismans out of bone, but his staff felt foreign to her. There was something about it that prickled the hair on the back of her neck. Sénna drummed her fingers on her knees as the husan plodded along the narrow track towards the valley. The creaking wheels and sloshing water in the barrels joined the warnings in her mind to create a symphony of uneasiness that only increased as they entered the valley.

Sénna turned to sit on her knees and face forward as they entered the valley. She kept her eyes focused on the flurry of activity that was the Varkáras Caravan down in the valley before them. The jingling of harnesses and the whistling of riders could be heard faintly above the old wagon's rattling and creaking as it made its way down the rutted path towards the valley floor. Nervous whispers from the men in the other wagons floated back to her. Although she strained to catch their words, she was left frustrated as they lapsed into silence.

Lord Shamar bid farewell to the night sky in favor of his daughter, Orwaena, when the rider racing up from the valley reached them with an urgent message for Master Chezak. Sénna watched the Caravan Master's face turn grave as the two men spoke. Sénna felt a growing tightening in her chest. Master Chezak dismissed the messenger with a few curt instructions and then promptly encouraged the wagon drivers to push their beasts to the caravan's safety with all haste.

In the approaching twilight of Orwaena's blood-red beams, the race to their destination came to an end. The Varkáras Caravan was aglow with lanterns hanging from the ornately carved and painted wagons, bathing the entire area in their soft light. Gaily dressed women with layers of colorful skirts and embroidered bodices spoke in clipped sentences with somber expressions. Dark men with brilliantly colored sashes tying their billowing shirts to loose trousers efficiently packed up their wagons, preparing to defend themselves.

Sénna watched in fascination as shutters were locked and stairs folded up, making each delicately carved wagon a tiny fortress. Harnesses for the mighty kazan, the enormous bovines that pulled the largest wagons, and the smaller husan were switched from the decorative-belled straps to unadorned leather. The caravan was either preparing for a siege or attempting to escape, and they needed to do it in silence. Cold dread washed over her as she looked towards Táksabai and her home, knowing that she wouldn't reach that destination any time soon.

Cybél grasped Sénna's wrist and squeezed. "Tell me what's going on," she begged.

"I'm not sure," Sénna frowned and pulled her hand away, craning her head around to try and spot the Caravan Master. "From all appearances, it looks like we're either going to be attacked or—"

The gate pin grated as Cédron released it, dropping the wooden slat and freeing the young ladies from their wagon. He smiled tightly and waved for them to follow him.

"Come on; Master Chezak wants you both to ride with Sahráron," he said.

Maintaining a firm grip on Sénna's arm, Cybél raised her eyebrows. Sénna looked at the retreating Shäeli and shrugged her shoulders. The young women eased their cramped legs out of the wagon and slid to the ground. They followed Cédron as quickly as their stiff limbs would allow, Sénna's senses responding to the fear etched into the visage of every face they encountered.

Near the center of the encampment was a wagon of such exquisite beauty that Cybél gasped in delight, and even Sénna paused to marvel at its splendor. Gemstones of every color and shape lined the wagon's windows and eaves, giving the vehicle an ethereal appearance in the flickering light of the hanging lanterns. A tall, gaunt woman with greying dark hair stepped from the back of the wagon. Cédron waved to catch her attention.

"Sahráron, may I present Sénna and Cybél," Cédron said, pulling the ladies forward. "Master Chezak instructed me to leave them in your charge."

"Has he now?" Sahráron's brown eyes sparkled amidst a sea of freckles that made her face appear youthful despite the lines and wrinkles. "And just what am I supposed to do with them, I wonder?"

Cédron shuffled his feet and shrugged one shoulder. "Feed them? Keep them safe?"

Sahráron pressed her lips together, her angular features sharpening with a slight frown. Sénna felt Cybél's clammy hand in her own as the woman's stare raked over them. Sénna stuck out her chin and straightened her shoulders under the scrutiny. She returned Sahráron's gaze and was surprised at the slight twitch at the corner of the woman's mouth. A flush of anger and shame flared in her cheeks. The woman was laughing at them. Sénna released Cybél's hand and folded her arms across her chest. Cybél stepped forward hesitantly and executed a small curtsey.

"I'm very pleased to meet you in person, Mistress Sahráron," she said. "My grandmother has always spoken very highly of your wares."

Sénna belatedly recognized the esteemed gem cutter and jewelry maker. Naturally, Cybél would know of her; her grandmother was a gaudy woman who decorated herself in jewelry as if they would increase her personal value.

Sénna stepped forward and offered her palm up in the traditional greeting. "I am Sénna."

Sahráron acknowledged Cybél's courtesy with a wave and brief smile, then stepped over to Sénna and placed her hand over the offered palm.

"Sénna, is it?" The woman's eyes narrowed as she examined Sénna's face. "Am'aranth is your grandmother, is she not?"

Sénna inhaled and withdrew her hand, silently cursing her Meq'qan eyes. She lowered her gaze and nodded. Sahráron firmly grasped Sénna's chin, tilting her head up so that she could see Sénna's face.

"There is no shame in your heritage," she said softly. "Your grandmother is a remarkable woman. I am honored to meet her granddaughter."

Sahráron released Sénna's chin and beckoned both young women into her wagon. Cybél followed Sahráron meekly into the back of the wagon. Sénna didn't follow the women into the opulent wagon but stood transfixed at the base of the stairs.

Sénna still reeled from Sahráron's touch, her eyes prickling from the force and kindness of the brief statement. A lifetime of prejudice for her mixed-blood hardened her against the contempt of strangers, and this compassion was unexpected. She wondered what the connection was between her grandmother and the famed gem cutter.

Perhaps it was just professional, but Sahráron's tone had indicated a deeper relationship. Sénna was startled from her thoughts as Master Chezak strode by, accompanied by three of his advisors. She shrank into the shadows behind the wagon to avoid notice as the Caravan Master's black eyes swept the area.

"Are all the wagons and citizens secure?" he asked the man on his left.

The scarred, wiry man nodded as they continued their inspection of the caravan. "Yes, we are just waiting for you to determine which direction to go."

Master Chezak stopped, placing his left hand on his hip. He glanced at his companions, then turned to investigate the hills towards Támon and the Rónhadi Mountains. Sénna followed his gaze and was startled to see tiny pinpricks of light, thousands of them, sparkling against the hillside. She couldn't imagine what could be creating those lights, but something nagged at the back of her mind. She gulped. No, it couldn't be.

The group of men watched their leader as he rubbed the top of his shiny, sable head with one hand, taking a bite of the meatroll in his other hand. Sénna held her breath, praying that she wouldn't be spotted and would hear whether or not it was the Garanth army. She didn't think they would be able to move that quickly through the mountains, but the threat was unmistakable. With a heavy sigh, the Caravan Master finished eating and wiped his hand on his loose trousers. He turned back to his small group and shook his head, frowning.

"Rílek, what is the news from the patrol?" he asked, turning to the burly man on his right.

Rílek scratched his black goatee as he gazed towards the advancing lights. "The Garanth are moving swiftly enough to overtake us well before we reach the safety of Táksabai." He paused, taking a deep breath, then looked at the Caravan Master. "They have created Arkmuln along the way."

Sénna's breath caught in her throat at his words. *Arkmuln!* All parents terrorized their misbehaving children with the myth of Arkmuln, corpses defiled and animated by demonic spirits. She shook her head. The Garanth didn't have that kind of magic. Her breath hitched, recalling the frozen voice that emanated through the Hazzara's talisman. But demons did. And demons could spur an army faster than was usually possible. A shiver of fear rippled throughout Sénna's body at the implications of Rílek's words.

The Caravan Master slumped his shoulders. "Then, we have but one option left to us."

Shozin looked at Rílek, who nodded. Each man nodded as the Caravan Master looked to him for his answer. When they were all in accord, the Caravan Master sighed with his hands on his hips. Sénna caught the grim determination in his black eyes as he made his decision.

"Right. Let's see if we can manage to live through the night."

Chapter 4: Subterranean Fury

Cédron and Anéton returned to the healer's wagon after leaving Sénna and Cybél with Sahráron. The two young men fetched their gear and informed Cédron's Uncle Roväen of Master Chezak's desperate plan to escape the Garanth army bearing down on them from the north. The Caravan Master made the heart-wrenching decision to abandon their goods, livelihoods, and animals in the hope of saving the caravan's human members.

After a short hour of frantically gathering supplies and herding beasts, the last of the wagons rolled into a narrow ravine they hoped would preserve them from the advancing horde. They covered the wagons with green netting to hide them from a cursory inspection. They hobbled and laid their remaining bales of hay for the livestock until the danger had passed, or they could move to a safer location. Master Chezak then led the group toward the caves behind the falls.

Guided by torchlight, Cédron climbed the rocky pathway up the cliffs behind the raging waterfall. His uncle's ragged breath was the only thing spurring him into the dreaded caves. He and Rováen were the last of the one hundred plus members of the Varkáras Caravan to enter the cavern just south of the Shalean Falls. Cédron cast a glance backward out over the vast expanse of the Tímin Sea, crashing upon the shores behind him.

Azria, the second moon, was a pale blue haze on the western horizon, bathing the beach's white sands in her soft hues. Violet Hamra would begin her dance from the east in just a couple of hours. Master Chezak told the group that it would likely take the rest of the night and some of the next day to travel the underground route to Táksabai, a distance of just over two leagues by sea but an unknown amount through the caves. Some of the old aunties put up a fuss, droning on about myths and legends of guardians and sea creatures, but they were placated with cups of ale and returned to complaining about their aching joints.

Cédron now turned his attention to the task ahead, following his uncle deeper into the cavern. He shuddered. Droplets of water splashed on the top of his head, leaving a trail of raised bumps as the icy liquid coursed between his shoulder blades. Hairs on the back of his neck stiffened when he passed into the gloom of caves and tunnels behind the Shalean Falls.

The stench of rotting shellfish struck his nostrils first, followed by the more subtle smell of dried seaweed. The stone floor and walls were worn nearly smooth with the erosion from Tides of water crashing and snaking through the network of caves and tunnels. Cédron inhaled cautiously, flaring his nostrils at the gleam of slime that slid down the walls and stalactites.

It was dark. Cédron's breath came shallow and fast. Shadows of his companions danced eerily across the walls in the torchlight. Flinching at the imaginary crawlers landing in his hair and skulking along his shoulders, he shook his head to dispel the tingling water and his morbid thoughts.

Cédron wasn't convinced that the underground passage from the falls to Táksabai was the safest path. He hesitated. The last time he'd walked into a cave, it tried to devour Anéton. Plus, his terror of crawlers caused his breath to hitch. Sweat prickled along his hairline.

Cédron handed his feeble torch to Anéton, then pulled the bone staff from his back and red firestone from his pouch. Placing the firestone into the crown atop the skull made of finger bones, he willed the stone to glow, covering the ground with its rosy light. Holding the staff always made him feel powerful, focused, and calm. He appreciated the presence inside the talisman. With her, he was not alone.

The staff pulsed gently in his hands, recognizing his discomfort. The talisman had once been his cousin Räesha, an elite Sumäeri warrior. Cédron remembered how she intimidated him when he first met her. She was strong, confident, and persistent. Räesha was so invested in his quest that even death couldn't stop her. She'd fallen in battle protecting him, but her spirit hadn't completed its mission and still sought the revenge she desired for her slain family.

Orwaena heard Räesha's fervent prayer and returned her to Cédron in the form of a staff, made of her bones and imbued with her living essence. Orwaena's action was the first direct intervention by a deity in hundreds of Tides, and those who met Räeshun, the name Räesha took to represent her staff form, were awed.

Cédron glanced down at the pale bones that bore the etching of her Sumäeri tattoos along their lengths and smiled. No, he was not alone. Räeshun was with him, offering guidance, courage, and wisdom as he continued to seek the sacred stones of Muralia. But first, he had to get clear of these miserable caverns and past the Garanth army.

Rováen leaned against the cavern wall, panting a moment before taking the lead. Cédron took a steadying breath and followed his uncle deeper into the cavern.

"You're not fooling anyone, you know," Cédron said, nudging his uncle gently in the shoulder.

Rováen grunted and frowned. "It's just bruised ribs. There was no reason for you to waste your Árk'äezhi on such a triviality. As I said, the sacred stones' powers are greater than you realize. You must use their energies mindfully and with restraint, else they can overwhelm you and those around you."

Cédron felt a flush of heat in his cheeks. He'd abused their power once before, and the memory still haunted him. He ground his teeth and swallowed the bitterness in his mouth. Räeshun would prevent that sort of thing from happening again. Both the slender young man and his staff learned as they faced each new challenge. He sighed, caressing the smooth curve of bone in his hand.

"Algarik blasted you into a stone wall yesterday," Cédron retorted with a scowl. "You've got more than bruising, and you know it. Let us help you. You can't help my quest if you're weak and injured."

Rováen stopped and placed a hand on his nephew's shoulder. He sighed with what little breath he had and nodded.

"My old bones aren't healing like they did when I was young. One minute, that's all I need," Rováen said, leaning against the cavern wall and closing his eyes.

Cédron grinned and held Räeshun toward Rováen, placing the firestone in her crown against his uncle's chest. The glow of the stone bathed Rováen in its healing light, speeding up the blood flow in his veins and knitting any fractures back together. The increased blood flow would also improve any muscle soreness and bruising. After one minute, Rovaen opened his eyes and took a deeper breath.

"See, good as new," Rovaen chuckled. He squeezed Cédron's shoulder. "Now, let's get moving before Anéton gives us any grief."

One side of Cédron's mouth twitched as Anéton shoved past his shoulder, nudging his taller friend. The legionnaire pulled the leather thong from his long braid and handed it to Cédron.

"Here, pull your hair back with this," he smirked, holding out the tie. "I don't want you blasting anyone with your magic because you think you've got crawlers hanging in your face."

Cédron pursed his lips. "I don't know what you're talking about."

Anéton barked a laugh and placed the thong in Cédron's hands. "Uh-huh. Are you telling me that you waved your torch around the tunnels from Dúlnat to the Zig'orman Marsh because you wanted the exercise?" he drawled, tucking his thick braid into the back of his jerkin. "Because if so, I'll let you carry my pack as well as yours to improve your endurance."

"I didn't realize it was that obvious."

Cédron felt the heat burning the tips of his ears. He took the leather strip and pulled his fair hair back off his face, tying it securely behind his head. He looked around to see if anyone else had noticed and leaned in closer to Anéton.

"I've faced a Garanth patrol, mulark dogs, a cave roknaar, and a flying rinzar, but I'm terrified of crawlers. How can I hope to face the Great Demon?" He exhaled through puffed cheeks.

Anéton grinned at his friend, his dark eyes dancing in the flickering light of the torches. "Because you've faced a Garanth patrol, mulark dogs, a cave roknaar, and a flying rinzar, not to mention saving my life on all of those occasions and the lives of others." He clapped his friend on the shoulder and whispered conspiratorially. "Don't worry; I'll protect you from the crawlers as long as you stand up to whatever terrible nasties come at us from the bowels of these tunnels."

Cédron nodded and grinned, grasping Anéton's shoulder. "You're my hero."

The friends stepped further back into the large cavern. Cédron marveled at the sheer size of the hidden landscape that comfortably housed the entire Varkáras Caravan. The torchlight reached the ceiling, displaying the hanging stalactites from which the icy water dripped. Littered haphazardly around the cave floor were varying lengths of stalagmites that glittered in the soft light cast by glowstones and torches. Cédron wandered over to the pedestal closest to his uncle and bent over to inspect it.

"Looks like róhiti scales," Rováen said, his hands caressing the stalagmite. "Though they must have dried to the stone a long time ago, the shimmer is barely discernible."

Cédron laid Räeshun on the ground and knelt, scrutinizing the rock. The magical properties of róhiti scales were legendary. He pulled out a knife from his belt and tried to pry the ancient fish scales that had dried onto the stone. Lady Muralia had created the colorful fish as the keepers of the source of water magic.

Maräera, Cédron's mother, told him stories when he was young of how their scales could stop a wound from bleeding or be sewn together to make garments that would create the illusion of invisibility. The pang of grief and shame that always accompanied thoughts of his mother wrenched his guts. The explosion that killed her wasn't his fault, but the pain of her death still tormented him.

Cédron focused his mind on the last image he had of his beautiful mother, saw Räeshun's pulse of reassurance, and returned his thoughts to the scales. He couldn't remember, but he knew that they had other valuable properties that could be beneficial. He scraped at the edges of the dried scales with his knife, tearing away the stone with little success.

Roväen chuckled. "I doubt you'll be able to harvest the scales that way. You'll dull your knife."

Cédron halted his efforts and stood, placing his hands on his hips and frowning at the gouges in the stone. "Róhiti scales are so rare; I've got to try." He bent down again, but Roväen stopped him with a hand on his shoulder.

Sighing, the old Shäeli pulled his nephew to his feet and shook his head. "The róhiti were nearly annihilated during the War of Betrayal. I don't know if any still exist, but if you seek viable scales, they will be in the tide pools in the caves down below sea level."

Roväen gave Cédron a wan smile. Cédron wiped his dulled blade on his trousers and tucked it back into the sheath on his belt. He glanced over at Anéton, who returned his gaze and shrugged.

"We could do some exploring, but I'd rather see how our new friends are doing in Sahráron's care." Anéton shuffled his feet, then laughed at Cédron's grimace.

Cédron looked at his uncle, his eyebrows raised.

Roväen smiled and nodded. "I'm fine," he said. "You two go charm the ladies."

"Are you sure?" Cédron asked.

Roväen nodded and waved them away. "I'll stay close to the healer in case my old carcass threatens to expire."

Anéton laughed, and Cédron gasped, initially misinterpreting his uncle's sarcasm. The young man grinned belatedly and grabbed Räeshun from the cavern floor.

"Just stay out of trouble, ok?" Cédron's brows were heavy over his moss-green eyes.

"I always do - try, that is."

Cédron opened his mouth with a retort, but Anéton grabbed him by the arm and dragged him away from his uncle.

"Come on, there they are," Anéton nodded at the women

bunched together near the back of the cave.

Cédron looked around at the groups of people that Master Chezak and his second-in-command Rílek Zúhn had marshaled. The women and children were in a large, guarded group near the back, with the most experienced fighting men stationed at the cave entrance. Master Chezak spoke animatedly with his leaders, the sweat on his bald head glittering in the torchlight like black diamonds. Cédron fervently hoped that the Caravan Master knew what he was doing. He looked away and caught up to Anéton, who presented himself to Sahráron and the young ladies they'd rescued.

"May we offer ourselves as your escorts?" The swarthy legionnaire bowed awkwardly to Sahráron, Sénna, and Cybél.

Cédron rolled his eyes, shifting his weight from one foot to the other. He nodded curtly to the three women, then clasped his hands behind his back. Although Cybél had a little color back in her cheeks, she barely acknowledged them. Sénna pursed her lips and glared. Cédron's insides squirmed. He knew what it felt like to be different, despised for the sin of being impure.

Sénna's golden eyes betrayed her Meq'qan heritage, and he knew how the Askári treated those of mixed blood. The thinly-veiled tolerance of his Shäeli legacy by his father's people had very nearly killed him. Watching her, Cédron recognized the strength of character and rigid control that Sénna embodied. In the few hours he'd known her, her behavior informed him that she was used to giving orders, not taking them, despite her differences from the Askári. Overcoming such prejudice with confidence indicated a wealthy and influential family.

"Forgive my friend," Cédron nodded, shoving Anéton in the shoulder and catching Sénna's eyes. "He means well, even if he's a bit obnoxious."

Cédron interpreted the disdain on Sénna's face as Anéton

stumbled over his words to Cybél and Sahráron. He shook his head and ignored the weight in his guts. "I think he is a lost cause."

Sénna crossed her arms over her chest. "We should all be paying attention to the Caravan Master. That giant fool may have saved us from the Garanth, but he's only swapped one death for another by bringing us into these caves."

Cédron turned his attention to Master Chezak, standing at the front of the cavern and calling for everyone's attention.

"…will go ahead and scout the various options. We are not sure of the shortest route through the tunnels, but if we keep a southerly direction, we should reach the city eventually." The Caravan Master's dark eyes glittered in the flickering light as he scanned the room.

Cédron noticed Sénna's scowl deepen and strained to catch the words she was muttering under her breath.

"…has no idea…lead clear to Táksabai…no way out…?"

"Um, do you know your way through these caverns?" he asked in Sénna's ear, startling the girl from her private tirade.

Sénna turned to him, the full weight of her gleaming golden eyes boring into his. "What difference does it make if I do?" she hissed. "We'll never make it past the guardian with this rabble." She waved her arm wildly, indicating the room full of people. "We'll all be dead before Lord Shamar's first light."

"What do you know about these caves," Cédron demanded, his eyes darting around the cavern.

Sénna began pacing back and forth. "I know that we're trapped. What I know about these caves is a moot point."

"Moot point?" Cédron gaped. "You mean, it doesn't matter, or you don't deign to share it?"

Sénna glared at him. "What difference does it make when we're all going to die anyway?"

Cédron's eyes hardened to spheres of green ice. He grabbed Sénna by her wiry upper arm and propelled her toward the back of the tunnel.

"Let's just have a word with Master Chezak, shall we?"

Walking through the semi-darkness of the cavern tunnels, Cédron ran through their plan again. It was risky and didn't feel right. He didn't trust Sénna or her stories. She had been too evasive when asked how she'd acquired her extensive knowledge of the guardian Wézija. He certainly didn't trust her suggestion for distracting the beast.

As they walked, Cédron ruminated. The caverns seemed interminable, giving him time to find endless holes in their strategy. A thousand things could go wrong. There were too many questions, too many unknowns. Still, Master Chezak had devised the illogical course of action after listening to this strange girl. Nobody offered any alternatives, so they moved forward despite his misgivings.

Roväen attached glowstones to his belt and stood at the front of their short line, casting a feeble light along the corridors that felt both alien and hostile as Cédron trod down them. The decline of the passage sharpened as they continued south. Master Chezak was hesitant about sending Cédron ahead with a small group of guards, considering the risk involved. If something went wrong and he or Räeshun were lost, the world would fall to the Great Demon Laylur. Cédron had only narrowly thwarted the demon's first attempt at escaping his prison.

Cédron inhaled deeply. No, they had to be the ones to seek Wézija, for they were the only magic wielders. Behind him, he heard Anéton whispering encouragement to Cybél. The young woman had panicked at the thought of being separated from Sénna. He understood that Sénna was Cybél's friend, but he hoped she wouldn't hinder their progress. He also hoped that the young woman wouldn't panic if they encountered Wézija and compromise the entire group.

What Cédron still didn't understand was why Shozin had insisted they take an armed escort. He should have kept all his men back to protect Sahráron and the rest of those under his care. Worst case, they would have to choose between the guardian and the Garanth, and Cédron wanted the caravan, and all those he loved, to have the best chance of survival. He sent a prayer to Hamra for the success of Sénna's plan.

Sénna disclosed that she had navigated these passages with her grandmother, who had brought a small herd of mijáko to appease the guardian. She could find her way through but couldn't say if or where Wézija would appear or if the guardian would let them pass without a blood sacrifice.

Glancing back toward the three guards bringing up the rear, Cédron saw Anéton catch Cybél's elbow as she stumbled along the roughly hewn passageway. His friend's distraction with the young women could prove problematic, should they need to fight the guardian. Cédron gritted his teeth and returned his attention to Sénna and Roväen and their heated but whispered discussion ahead of him.

"…should be safe until high tide."

Cédron couldn't catch Roväen's reply but saw Sénna knit her brows together.

"No, I don't," she hissed, crossing her arms across her chest. "I don't have any idea what time of day it is."

Cédron rummaged through the pouch slung over his shoulder and pulled out the diptych compass that Sahráron had made and given him when he left Dúlnat. Opening the lapis lazuli-encrusted ivory box, he touched the polished beryl inside the lid and concentrated on Lord Shamar.

The compass either showed him the direction to where he wanted to go or a visual image of whatever he needed to see or find. The smooth surface remained dark. Cédron tried again, concentrating on the Hamra. This time, the right edges of the box slowly turned plum and bled lavender as the image of the violet moon sank behind the trees above the cliffs.

"Hamra's just set," he whispered to the figures in front of him.

Sénna stopped in her tracks and whirled around to face him. "How do you know that?"

The rest of the group stopped to watch the exchange between the three, who now blocked their progress. Cédron cast his eyes downward and held out his compass for the young woman to see.

"It's a device Sahráron designed for me," he mumbled. "It shows the way…whatever way I need to see."

Sénna's eyes gleamed in the soft light of the glowstones as she examined the tool.

"It's like a compass, but…." She grabbed the instrument and turned it over in her hands. "Tell me how this works," she demanded.

Cédron looked at Rováen for guidance, and the older man shrugged, the smile hidden in his silvery beard.

"The inside of the lid shows me what I'm looking for," he instructed, pointing at the configuration. "The bottom shows me where it is relative to my location."

Sénna held the device gingerly in her hands, her eyes wide. Cédron wasn't sure if she was afraid because of its magical aspect or because she wasn't sure what she wanted to see.

Sénna's eyes narrowed, and she glared at him. "So, the magic you used on my brother wasn't from your staff; it was you; you're the common denominator," she said, shoving the compass into his hands before backing up several steps. "And just how are you any different from your Uncle Algarik?"

Behind him, Cybél gasped. Cédron turned to find the girl pale and edging back away from him. He turned his attention back to Sénna. The two stood at an impasse, green glare to gold, for several seconds. Cédron felt the tension among the companions rise to a palpable level.

Cédron's eyes darted to Rováen, then Anéton. They alone knew the true nature of the relationship between Cédron and his rogue mage uncle, who had become a pawn of the Great Demon Laylur. Together, the two stepped in front of Cédron to shield him from the hostile stares of his feminine Askári companions. Cédron slowly closed the lid on the compass and placed it in his pouch, keeping his movements slow and deliberate.

"What makes you think Algarik is my uncle?" Cédron asked, not taking his eyes off Sénna.

"I listen, and I hear. More than one has commented on the battle you had earlier with him and the abominable rinzar he created. More than one watches to see how you'll handle your power. More than one doesn't trust you," Sénna sneered.

Cédron's heart sank, and he felt the blood drain from his face. He understood his mistake too late. In his naïve wish to be helpful, he just jeopardized his entire quest. He didn't know who these girls were or who they might tell of their meeting with him, should they all escape.

There was no point in explaining what they were doing; their reactions to magic were unexpected and unsettling. Should Sénna understand the extent of his abilities, she might send him and his entire group into Wézija's lair to squelch so much dangerous magic. He exhaled slowly through his nose and looked to his uncle for guidance.

Rováen placed a hand on Cybél's shoulder and captured her attention. "We are Shäeli, the lad and I, and are not bound by the same laws as you Askári. We each have our particular talent in using our Árk'äezhi energies, and it's not something you need to fear."

Cybél's lips trembled, then she looked at Anéton, who was still hovering between her and the offending companion. Cédron watched his shoulders rise in a shrug, the legionnaire's hand relaxing from the hilt of his sword.

Although Cybél seemed to accept his uncle's explanation, Sénna continued to glare at him.

"I'm not going another step with—" she began.

"We need to keep going," Rováen interrupted. "We have a long way to go and unknown dangers still to face."

Cédron held his breath as Sénna's shoulders tensed, and her mouth opened to protest. She pursed her lips in a thin, angry line but didn't argue further. Sénna's eyes bored into Cédron, then Rováen and back before jutting her sharp chin.

"What is going on here?" she asked Rováen. "I'm not a fool; I can see that there is more here than you've told us."

Cédron caught his uncle's resigned glance and exhaled the breath he'd been holding. He sagged against the cave wall.

"You wouldn't believe us if we told you," he said.

Sénna placed her hands on her hips and faced the young man. "Try me."

"There's no time," Rováen said, turning back down the tunnel. "We have to get through these caves before high tide."

"You'll never make it without my help," Sénna snapped. She turned to Anéton and shoved her index finger into the startled young man's chest. "You. Talk. Now."

Anéton's eyes flitted from Sénna to Cédron then to Rováen and back several times. Cédron felt his throat constrict but swallowed and shrugged his shoulders. He nodded to the legionnaire.

"The Garanth army isn't out there on a whim," Anéton sighed. "It is annihilating everything and everyone in its path. The Meq'qan of the Ta'voran Marshes, Támon, and possibly Dúlnat, have already fallen," Cédron watched Anéton's face pale as he continued. "The Hazzara that kidnapped you two and the demons that have been pursuing us, they're all part of a plan to destroy us, to destroy Cédron."

"Hazzara," Sénna's mouth twisted as if she'd tasted

something foul. "They are responsible for more crimes than kidnapping Cybél and me. You say they are pursuing him?" Sénna's glare raked Cédron from top to toe; the curl of her lips let the Shäeli know that her opinion of him was not flattering. "What do they want with you? What makes you so important?" she asked.

Cédron felt the walls of the tunnel squeeze inward. It became difficult to breathe as the enormity of his mission hit home. He didn't know how to answer that without frightening her further. His cursed Uncle Algarik had forced him into this quest to fulfill a prophecy that he was only beginning to believe, but Sénna wouldn't care about that.

Cédron thought of all those who had already perished: his dearest friend, his mother, Räesha, and her family. He clenched his jaw. Anger boiled up in Cédron's body at the thought of Algarik's manipulation and destruction, causing the tattoos beneath his linen shirt to glow as the Árk'äezhi activated. He looked down in horror at his luminous markings in response to the girls' sudden gasps.

"Laylur's beast, you're like a beacon!" Sénna's shrill cry echoed through the tunnel. "Turn it off!"

Cédron flushed and snapped. "I can't just turn it off; it's reacting to my feelings. Besides, it's just my Árk'äezhi – it won't hurt you."

Sénna's eyes scanned the walls of the tunnel wildly as if expecting something terrifying to appear at any moment. "Turn off your magic; it's like a siren!" she cried and tore down the corridor away from him.

Cédron took a step to follow her, but his Uncle Roväen blocked him.

"Wait," he said softly, uncertainty flickering in his blue eyes. "Take a few breaths and get your emotions under control. I'll go after Sénna." The old Shäeli turned and trotted gingerly down the tunnel after the fleeing young woman.

"Mijáko piles!" Cédron roared, expelling the frustration

from his body through the waves of sound that echoed throughout the caverns. The walls shook slightly, and Cybél stared at him with wide eyes. "Come on," he waved to Anéton and the three guards from the caravan. "We have to stay together."

Cédron turned and ran down the tunnel after Sénna and his uncle. His heart thudded in his chest as the blood seared through his veins. If he didn't control his emotions, his wild magic would cause another cave-in. He'd had enough of those for one lifetime. Gasping for air, Cédron clamped down on the roiling emotions and tried to focus on the words his mother's spirit had given to him when he'd mastered the aquastone.

Cédron reached into his pouch and grasped the aquastone. He felt the cool, soothing caress of water flowing over his body. The markings on his skin receded as if with the tide. His mind calmed, and he slowed his pace.

Ahead, the light from the glowstones Roväen wore dimmed. When Cédron and the remaining five in the group caught up to the old Shäeli, he saw the light dispersed throughout the enormous cavern they entered. Cédron felt the gentle breeze on his damp forehead and tasted the tinge of salt on the air from the waves crashing against the rocks below. Dawn had arrived, and Lord Shamar's light spilled in from the opening only a hundred paces away.

Shallow pools dotted the floor just yards from where they stood, huddled around each other. A few steps away, Roväen stood next to Sénna, who was shivering, her haunted eyes searching the obscure depths of the cavern beyond where the glow stones reached with their feeble light.

Cédron stared at Sénna's face. Wide eyes and waxen skin replaced her usual expression of haughty disdain. He glanced around the cavern, wondering what could have frightened her. A slight scrape along the back wall caused them all to jump and stare across the rising pools.

Cédron pulled Räeshun from his back and held her across

his body defensively, her smooth bones comforting in his palms. Cybél grasped Anéton's hand with white knuckles. Behind him, the three guards unsheathed their swords. They stepped in front of Cédron, facing the blackness.

"She's here," Sénna gasped, scrabbling back against the far wall. "Your magic has summoned her."

Roväen stepped back to her and grabbed her shoulders, shaking her slightly. "Who's here? What is it?" he urged.

A splash and a whistle were all the warning Cédron had. A gigantic blue tentacle covered in glowing white circles swung through the air towards his head. Cédron heard Cybél's screams reverberating off the cavern walls and deep into his mind. The guard standing next to him didn't have time to swing his sword before the arm grasped him around the middle and pulled him into the pool. Anéton and the remaining two guards shoved Cédron and the women against the far wall and ranged themselves in front.

"Whatever it is," Anéton shouted, "it's coming from all directions!"

Cédron looked at Sénna and saw the calm knowledge of hopeless despair in her eyes.

"We're doomed," she whispered. "It's Wézija in all her fury."

Chapter 5: Tóran's Pursuit

Tóran crawled on his belly through the thick gorse brambles, avoiding the bushes' spiky thorns as he wormed his way beneath the yellow flowers. The sweet scent of the blossoms was layered with an acrid overtone of scorched earth and grass. Reaching the top of the hill, Tóran peered down over the outcropping of rock and scanned the smoldering wasteland below that had once been the fertile Dágon Valley.

For as long as the Askári populated this land, the sativa that fed the people and their livestock had been grown in these now-barren fields. Tóran's father had always instilled in him the value of preparing for lean times. Dúlnat had several granaries and underground storages where food was preserved and held for long winters and dry summers. Tóran didn't know if the ruling guilds could agree long enough to enact such a life-saving policy for their people. Such was the danger of Táksabai's oligarchy.

Tóran felt a twinge in his guts as echoes of his father's words whispered in his ear. He remembered the history and economics discussion around Táksabai's governing guilds and his father's disgust with their self-serving inaction. Due to such political short-sightedness, Kásuin had relocated to Dúlnat and taken up the regency. As Regent, he passed along his values of serving people first to his sons.

Looking back over the fields, Tóran sighed and shook his head. It wasn't likely that the Merchants Guild, currently the strongest of Táksabai's guilds, would have made any preparations for the general populace. With nothing to harvest and the growing season nearly at an end, the people faced starvation. Although the fires the Garanth patrols started no longer raged with flames, the smoking remnants cut a swath in the land to ease the main army's passage as it moved inexorably towards the capital.

Billowing ash still clung to the ground in the fresh morning air. Tóran blinked back tears formed from both the sting of caustic smoke and the mounting devastation he and his companions witnessed in their efforts to catch the marauding army. The weight of his impossible task pressed down on his young shoulders.

The young Askári legionnaire and his small force of Meq'qan warriors followed the Garanth's trail of destruction for nearly a week after their exhaustive crossing of the Rónhadi Mountains from the Zig'orman Marshes. Always days behind, they were too late to prevent the wanton death and destruction the savage northerners visited on the smaller cities of Askári-bai. Tóran debated with himself over whether or not to engage the thousand-strong Garanth patrol now before they reached Táksabai or to wait and attempt to slow down the following army.

The outcropping he crouched behind stood high above the Sharäedan River, which flowed rapidly down to the Shalaen Falls to the west and into the Tímin Sea. He listened from his perch for the roar of the falls, but he was too far. He did hear the crackle of charred grass that heralded the end of life in the valley.

Glancing back over his shoulder, Tóran could see the advance lines of the Garanth horde as it wended its way south from the ruins of Tamón, its numbers swelling exponentially with every conquest. They must be nearly one-hundred-thousand strong now. It was hard for him to get a breath.

Tóran sat frozen with indecision. High Priestess Zale'en gave him the job of leading the surviving Meq'qan warriors from their devastated homes in the Zig'orman Marshes into his homeland of Askári-bai in a failed attempt to prevent the Garanth army from similarly destroying his lands and peoples.

Even mounted upon a herd of armored watowren, the massive, horned bovines of the marshlands, the three-hundred odd men were too late. Tóran pounded the ground with his fist. Horrific memories of Dúlnat surfaced while he watched the Garanth raze their way through the valley towards Askári-bai's capital.

Dúlnat was his home and a shining jewel of Askári-bai. Built deep in the Rónhadi Mountains, his father, Kásuin Varkáras chose to flout traditional conventions and bring in artisans from all lands. Together, they rebuilt the forsaken mining town as a haven for his Shäeli bride. It was a remote location, which allowed Kásuin and his demon wife Maräera some peace away from the ancient hatred and prejudice that the Askári populace held for the Shäeli.

Together, Kásuin and Maräera established a thriving town where artisans of all races could practice their craft.

They reopened the mines and found rich veins of both gemstones and precious metals. Their most significant achievement was the exquisite gardens that pilgrims traveled from all lands to see. All that and the thousands of families that had made Dúlnat their homes were now gone, wiped out by the Garanth plague that left the reek of death and decay in its wake.

When Tóran and his Meq'qan warriors first entered the city to find its white walls scarred and blackened, they held onto the feeble hope that perhaps some of the city's inhabitants, and the Regent, survived by hiding in the mining tunnels that ran beneath the city. They scoured the warren of tunnels for hours before the Meq'qan forced Tóran to accept the inevitable. His father and all of his people were gone. They found very few corpses, which verified the reports that a demon traveled with the Garanth, performing the grisly task of converting prisoners into Arkmuln.

Arkmuln were bodies infused with demonic spirits that could live without food, without rest, and felt no pain like the walking dead. It was one thing to turn corpses into Arkmuln, but it was beyond comprehension to know healthy individuals also fell to the demons' spirits. Tóran felt sick at the thought of having to face comrades, friends, or worst of all, his father in the coming battle. He didn't know if he'd be able to strike them down, even though he knew that they would no longer be themselves.

It took only a few hours to round up the remaining bodies, which Tóran and his Meq'qan warriors buried with cursory prayers in a makeshift cemetery that was once the staging area for the Varkáras Caravan. As Tóran and his companions offered their prayers to the goddess Hamra for the souls of the dead, he swore vengeance upon the Garanth tribes for their destruction of the only home he had ever known.

Now, as Tóran gazed out at the swarming horde of Garanth, the ember seething in the pit of his stomach flared.

He gripped the edge of the stone that obscured him from his quarry until his knuckles turned white. Tóran wished that he had an army mighty enough to crush the Garanth before they reached the capital. He wondered if Táksabai's Harmólin Legion would be formidable enough to fend them off. If not, the entire Askári culture would fall. He thought of the Mages Guild and wondered if their magic could - his mind shifted mid-thought. Cédron!

A stinging breath caught in Tóran's throat. His brother Cédron left the marshes for Táksabai just ahead of him with only two companions. Tóran prayed the small group made it to the safety of the capital. The thought of his brother tangled up with the Garanth, or their demons, made him cringe. Cédron and his quest were the only things preventing the end of their world. His brother had to survive to restore the balance of magical energy in their world and keep the Great Demon imprisoned in the abyss.

Tóran's musings were interrupted as Chaq'ta and Ta'riq crawled through the gorse to the outcropping on either side of him and looked out upon the Garanth. Chaq'ta, the hot-headed leader of the Zig'orman Meq'qan, jutted his chin at the advancing army and nudged Tóran's shoulder.

"They are moving more quickly now that the fires are low," Chaq'ta said. His perpetual scowl deepened as he studied the army's progress. "They will reach Táksabai soon if we don't slow them down."

Tóran regarded the Meq'qan leader coolly. He had no intention of letting Chaq'ta rouse his warriors into a suicidal frenzy. Even if they could slow down their quarry and inflict some damage, it would ultimately waste resources.

High Priestess Zale'en had warned him before they left to keep Chaq'ta's aggressive impulses in check, lest he charge recklessly into a losing battle. Tóran rolled over onto his back and closed his eyes, breathing as deeply as he could in the poisoned air while he considered his words carefully.

"What course of action would you suggest?" Tóran

asked, glancing over at the warrior, still staring out at the Garanth army.

Chaq'ta's yellow eyes gleamed brighter than the braided amber necklace around his neck. He grinned, the space between his front teeth whistling with his exhalation.

"We could bring the watowren through their encampment tonight. It would cause them enough trouble to at least scatter them before they reach the city's gates. That might slow them down enough, especially if we could set fire to their supply wagons," Chaq'ta grinned.

Tóran nodded noncommittally. He turned his head to Ta'riq, his other Meq'qan companion. "How many Garanth are out there, do you think?"

Ta'riq scanned the valley, looked at his two companions with haunted eyes, and touched his protective necklace convulsively. Ta'riq was one of only three surviving Meq'qan of the Ta'voran Marshes. The Garanth army swept through his tribes at the beginning of Suntide, slaughtering all who opposed them and creating Arkmuln from those caught trying to flee. Only his blood debt to Cédron and Anéton compelled him to accompany Tóran on this quest.

"Engaging the entire Garanth horde with our paltry force on an open battlefield is akin to insanity," Ta'riq's eyes showed white around the golden irises as he glanced from Tóran to Chaq'ta and back again. He shook his head and slumped down further below the bushes of the outcropping, hissing as the long gorse thorns scraped his shoulders.

Tóran's eyes softened as he nodded at Ta'riq. "What would you recommend, my friend?"

Ta'riq swallowed, stroking the amber stones in his necklace. "We must find a way to maximize our effect without unduly risking our men and beasts." Ta'riq's said, his voice trembling.

Chaq'ta smirked and dismissed the idea with a wave of his hand. "We are not like those fároc Hazzara, content to hide and strike from behind bushes or in tall grass. The

Garanth have flattened all the land in their wake; there is no cover to fight from," he said. He crossed his arms across his chest and glared at Tóran. "Well, what do you suggest, Askári?"

Tóran smiled inwardly. He knew it rankled Chaq'ta that Caf'iq Mak'ki had placed him, a foreigner, in the position of leader of this endeavor. The chieftain succumbed to his mate Zale'en's directive after much-heated debate and no small amount of protestations by Chaq'ta himself. Zale'en convinced the Caf'iq, based on her status as High Priestess of Lady Muralia, and telling him that it was the deity's desire. She and Tóran knew it was common sense that placed the reckless Chaq'ta as subordinate to the much-younger and foreign legionnaire. Tóran pulled the several strands of his dark hair that escaped his braid and tucked them behind his ear, pretending to ponder Chaq'ta's question.

"We are all warriors," he began, catching Chaq'ta's eyes as well as Ta'riq's frightened pale gaze. "Regardless of what we call ourselves or who we pray to, we are brothers in this."

Tóran rolled back over onto his stomach, scanning the horizon. He could see the spires of Táksabai's four guilds' towers in the far distance, peeking just above the smoky haze. The tall peaks of the Tádim Pass, Zóhir and Zóhari rose in the east just beyond the edge of the Dágon Valley. An idea formed in his mind.

"If we bring the watowren back around and down through the Tádim Pass, we can catch the Garanth between the Harmólin Legion and our beasts. The only possible route they'll have will be towards the sea, and they won't like that." Tóran's full lips curved.

"But that will give them time to reach the city and lay siege to it!" Chaq'ta sputtered, his golden eyes darkening. "We cannot be so cowardly as to allow them to breach the city walls and kill more innocents when we can engage them now! The people have no idea what's heading their direction."

Tóran placed his hand on Chaq'ta's arm. "There is no way someone hasn't raised the alarm. They've already burned the valley and the crops. The city must be preparing for the invasion as we speak."

Ta'riq grasped Tóran's shoulder and turned him around, his tawny eyes wide. "You know this?"

Tóran glanced down briefly, then met Ta'riq's hopeful expression with his own. "I have every reason to believe it, but no, I have no proof. Cédron was headed to Táksabai when he left us in the marshes. He should have arrived several days ago, validating any reports made from patrols outside the city."

"Then he could have warned the Mages Guild and the Harmólin Legion already!" Ta'riq's face lit up. "They could be preparing to march out and meet them as we speak. Then we could do as you say and bring our men upon them from the east, forcing the Garanth towards the sea." Ta'riq nodded, satisfied with their new plan.

"Mijáko piles," snorted Chaq'ta. He drummed his fingers along his biceps and furrowed his brow so deep that Tóran thought he'd have a permanent trench on his forehead. "It's also possible that your brother ran into this Garanth patrol before we caught up to them." Chaq'ta's face reddened, and he stabbed a finger into Tóran's chest. "If he did, we're all doomed, and you have no way of knowing either way, do you, Askári?"

Tóran's insides knotted with the truth of Chaq'ta's words. He gazed out towards the direction of the falls and pondered what had become of his brother. The tall, awkward boy who looked up to him with such adoration had become the catalyst to global conflict.

Cédron was rejected and hunted by both of his peoples for his mixed heritage. Except for the Mages Guild, the Askári wanted him dead. The Shäeli were divided, with the Näenji Council denouncing Cédron as an abomination, and the Sumäri warriors hailing him as the next savior of the land.

Tóran clenched his jaw and glared at Chaq'ta, his eyes blazing in Lord Shamar's early morning light. "My brother's fate is far from decided. We can't know yet what has happened to him or how the Askári have received him. Our job now is to determine how to challenge the Garanth and—"

"Laylur's beast! What's that out there?" Ta'riq interrupted, pointing north towards the Shalaen Falls.

The tension in the air between Chaq'ta and Tóran broke with the flash of scarlet light shooting from the falls out to sea. The three men looked at each other and forgot the Garanth scouting party entirely as they scanned the horizon for more clues to the strange phenomenon. After a few moments, more fiery balls of light shot out to sea. This time, they also captured the attention of the Garanth scouts. Half of them moved towards the sea and the fiery lights.

That was Cédron; it had to be. He hadn't made it past the Shalaen Falls. Tóran clenched his fists. He knew that if Cédron was using his magic openly to defend himself, he was in grave danger. Tóran scratched the stubble prickling his cheeks. Who could he be fighting? Had the Askári turned on him, or was there some other threat? Tingles in his hands and fingers caused Tóran to clench his fists as he stared at the fireballs shooting out to sea.

"That's your brother's power," Ta'riq said in a quiet voice. "He didn't make it to Táksabai after all, did he?"

Tóran turned to see Ta'riq's face become a bleak mask of despair. The lump in his throat prevented him from speaking, so he responded with a silent shake of his head. The coming battle may be in vain if Cédron couldn't stop Laylur. Without Cédron, the Garanth army was the least of their worries.

"We can assume the Harmólin Legion has seen the burning fields and are preparing to engage the Garanth," Tóran said, after getting his emotions and his voice under control. He slithered back down the hill from the outcropping, cursing as the sharp gorse thorns pricked his arms and hands.

Ta'riq and Chaq'ta emerged from the bushes just behind him and waited for his orders. Both Meq'qan bled from gorse scratches, but neither seemed aware of their minor injuries. Tóran looked them over to ensure that neither had scrapes that needed tending. These stoic Meq'qan warriors were much more formidable than his legion in Dúlnat. They seemed to find confidence in the necklaces of protective amber that Zale'en's priestesses had woven for all of them, and Tóran wondered if the stones had some unseen power.

Perhaps it was the recent battle against the Hazzara that hardened these men. Tóran was glad he was leading them and not his former regiment. He nodded and began to make his way down the hill toward the waiting Meq'qan on the watowren when Ta'riq grabbed his shoulder and stopped his descent.

"What about your brother?" Ta'riq asked, his eyes returning to the red lights launching skyward from the falls.

Tóran stopped. The Garanth patrol had noticed the fireballs too. Some of them were already headed in that direction and would find Cédron. The main body of the patrol continued toward the capital. Tóran put his hands on his hips and paced a few steps. They had a chance to circle the valley and pinch the Garanth army between the mountains and the city, but Cédron was also in danger.

If his brother were killed or converted to Arkmuln, then he would lose his last remaining family. Although Tóran was an orphan adopted by Kásuin and Maräera, they were the only family he'd ever known. He shared no blood with Cédron, but Tóran loved his family and felt the bonds of brotherhood. He couldn't betray his brother now. If Cédron's quest failed, their entire world would fall to Laylur and his minions. Tóran looked at his companions. While Ta'riq's pale eyes reflected compassion, there was no compromise in

Chaq'ta's stony gaze.

"Your brother is a lost cause," Chaq'ta spat, his eyes flashing. "You know that our duty lies in helping the Askári and exacting our vengeance upon the Garanth. You cannot risk our entire force to rescue your brother. The patrol will reach him long before we can, regardless of your feelings about it."

Tóran felt the heat rising in his cheeks at Chaq'ta's insubordination. The Meq'qan warrior didn't hide his distrust of Cédron's powers. It didn't matter that Cédron used his abilities to save Chaq'ta's family, along with several others stricken with fatal toxins during the attack on their village.

It was as Zale'en said. Chaq'ta didn't grasp the broader perspective of what was happening. The warrior understood bitterness and vengeance and the need to crush his enemies. The subtleties of the power struggle between the deities and Cédron's role were beyond Chaq'ta's limited scope. Tóran saw that, although Chaq'ta had a valid point. He couldn't leave his brother alone and unprotected against the Garanth patrol that was heading in his direction.

"We must split our forces," Tóran began, nodding first at Ta'riq, then at Chaq'ta. "I will follow the Garanth patrol to Cédron and offer him what assistance I can. I will hold them until you get there with the rest of the Meq'qan warriors. You," he pointed at Chaq'ta, "will bring a score of mounted warriors to the Shalaen Falls where we will engage the patrol." Tóran turned to Ta'riq. "I want you to lead the remainder of the Meq'qan through the foothills below the peak Zóhir. We will rendezvous above the plains and meet the Garanth after they reach Táksabai."

Ta'riq shook his head. "We should not splinter our numbers. Our only strength lies in our combined effort. We should not separate your leadership and our passion for retribution."

Tóran pursed his lips. He'd expected trouble from

Chaq'ta, but not Ta'riq. The survivor of the Ta'voran Marsh slaughter had been his staunchest supporter throughout this venture, and Tóran hated to risk that. On the other hand, Cédron was in danger and needed him. Tóran's honor and promise to their father to help his brother succeed in his quest bound him.

"I am not abandoning you or the warriors, my friend. I am just taking a side trip. The Garanth army is far enough behind us to allow the watowren to get around to the valley. Chaq'ta and I will not let any of the patrol escape," Tóran said. He gripped Ta'riq's forearm in a gesture of farewell and reinforced his commitment. "We will meet you by Lord Shamar's first light day after tomorrow."

Chaq'ta grinned and hammered his chest once with his right fist in salute. "Be quick, little Askári, for we will be riding on your heels!"

Tóran allowed a faint smile and nodded at his two commanders. They would follow his orders to the letter, of that he had no doubt. Chaq'ta would waste no time choosing twenty of his best warriors and marshaling them into the valley to engage the patrol. Although Ta'riq was leery of the pending battle, he always did what Tóran asked of him without complaint. With a clear conscience, Tóran shifted his sword belt from his waist to over his shoulder and began sprinting down the hill and into the valley below.

Tóran tore through the smoldering grasslands, fear propelling him faster forward than he thought possible. Tóran chanted a mantra to keep his brother safe, the passion of his desire lending him the strength and stamina to catch up with his quarry.

The Garanth had quite a lead on him, but they were massive and slow-moving creatures. It was just over a league from his perch above the valley to the Shalaen Falls, according to Tóran's best judgment. The legionnaire figured he would traverse the valley and reach the falls before mid-morning at his pace.

Training with the legion had prepared him for efforts like this, but he never expected to be grateful for the endurance runs. As he reached the central valley, the smoke layer forced him to slow his pace to a trot. His eyes teared, and his nostrils burned from the smoke.

Tearing off a wide strip from the hem of his shirt, Tóran tied the fabric over his nose and mouth and picked up his pace once more. The fireballs increased in number, an indication to Tóran that Cédron's situation was more critical. He forced his protesting legs to pump faster, ignoring the hitch in his side and the burning of his throat and lungs from the smoke.

Tóran kept his eyes forward, focusing on where he placed his feet to avoid stepping on any fuming branches that could erupt into flame by stirring them up. His shadow shortened before him as Lord Shamar rose higher in the sky, but still, the Garanth remained elusive. Tóran felt the familiar stirrings of panic that he'd be too late to help his brother.

The sweat, already coursing down his cheeks and back, chilled with the image of finding Cédron dead, or worse, transformed into Arkmuln. Tóran clamped down on his morbid thoughts and forced himself to find a high place from which he could check his bearings.

Tóran spied a small hill off to his right, and he angled toward it. Racing to the top of the rocks, the young man stopped short. He reached the cliff's edge without realizing it in the smoke-filled air. The rumbling background noise soon became the full-blown roar of the falls. Tóran scoured the rocky area, searching desperately for any sign of Cédron or the patrol he was pursuing.

Scanning out over the frothing waves, Tóran saw a tiny boat with grey sails making its way south along the shoreline but nothing else remarkable in the water near the beach below him. Jumping down from the outcropping, Tóran charged to the edge of the cliffs and began looking for a way down.

The falls pounded the rocks far below him on the right. Tóran leaned out over the cliff's edge and looked up and down the sand and rock beach below him. He saw nothing; no Garanth and no sign of Cédron. It was as if all traces of life had disappeared. Tóran headed north towards the center of the falls. He tried to remember everything he'd learned about the Shalaen Falls, but only the old stories of whirlpools filled with the magical róhiti fish came to mind.

Tóran paced along the edge of the falls, minding the slippery rocks, his body taut as a bowstring. He jumped at every shape in the billowing mists and residual smoke, sure that the Garanth patrol had spotted him. They could sneak up behind him while his attention was on finding signs of his brother.

Tóran's ears strained for any sound, human or otherwise, above the falls' roaring and crashing, but there was nothing. The fireballs had ceased to fly out to sea some time ago, leaving him with no guide towards his brother. Tóran felt a wave of despair sucking and tugging at his soul, the horrors of the past fortnight rising unbidden into his imagination. He wavered between calling out and remaining silent. If he called and the Garanth heard him, he could be risking discovery and capture for both himself and his brother.

Indecision rooted him to the edge of the falls. He didn't dare leave, but he couldn't find a route down. The wind from offshore blew across his face, tangling the dark strands of hair that had again escaped his braid. Tóran yanked out the offending hair, his eyes watering in the process. He blinked, and when his eyes cleared, he gasped.

The breeze cleared away some of the smoke and mist surrounding the falls. A large cave materialized below, just to the south of the falls. Tóran squinted to make sure his eyes were not deceiving him. His vision sharpened and, as his gaze encompassed the surrounding area, he spied the narrow path that led from the cave up to the cliffs. He had a way down.

Tóran hurried over to the lip of the cliffside that obscured the trailhead and carefully made his way down the narrow path to the cave entrance. He crept as quickly as he dared, keeping his boot heels silent by stepping only on his toes. There were scorch marks all over the walls and the cave's mouth. Tóran's stomach clenched. All of the signs pointed to his brother's magic, but where was Cédron?

A breeze coursed along the cliffs as Tóran inched his way into the cavern. The onslaught of smells emanating from the recesses of the cavern assailed his senses. The familiar scents of dried seaweed and decaying shellfish were the undertones for the metallic scent of fresh blood and a pungent, burnt smell lingering on the back of his tongue that he couldn't identify. Tóran made his way past the first smattering of stalagmites rising from the cavern floor that obscured the darker interior. As he rounded the largest in his path, he froze.

Littering the floor between the shallow tide pools and broken stones were scattered pieces of Garanth warriors. Whatever killed them had not left, or he would have spotted it. Tóran held his breath, straining to hear anything that would alert him to the position of his enemy, but the crashing of the falls on the rocks below him drowned out all other sounds. His eyes darted around the darkened cavern, picking out the scattered sections of Garanth limbs and their weapons nearby. Nothing lived in this cave, and there was no sign of Cédron.

Tóran drew his weapon from its sheath. Whatever creature slaughtered the Garanth had done so quickly. If it had killed the entire patrol, then Cédron and his party were likely its previous victims. Tóran dropped his sword and sank to his knees. He closed his eyes and wept. He wept for his adopted parents Kásuin and Maräera Varkáras and all the people of Dúlnat that he'd been too late to save. He wept for his brother Cédron who, despite being a magic-wielding demon, was the closest thing that their world had to a weapon against the inevitable. Finally, he wept for the future their beautiful land of Muralia would not have. The deities had sacrificed so much for this world, and it was all a loss.

When his grief ran dry, Tóran sat back on his haunches and stared desolately at the carnage around him. The massacre of these hundred warriors was just the beginning of the slaughter that he would face.

"Argh!"

The growl startled Tóran, and he fell onto his backside. From further back in the cave, the rising shape of a Garanth warrior loomed up and staggered towards him. Tóran sprang to his feet, grasping for his sword. He brandished the weapon, but he'd never been faced with an adversary so enormous before.

Even wounded, the Garanth was a fearsome creature. He stood twice as tall as Tóran and was easily double his width. Two curved horns grew from the top of his forehead and arched back over his skull like a protective shield. The long nose and pointed chin curved towards each other, drawing the eyes towards the sharp, pointy teeth that leered at him.

Tóran noted the wet slicks of blood staining the Garanth's dark skin and saw that the pain in the creature's eyes had pushed it beyond sanity. He could not face this enemy and win, but perhaps he could die fighting.

"Askáriii!" Tóran cried and charged forward with his sword over his head.

The blade struck the Garanth bull on the left thigh, leaving a gash in the beast's leather trousers and skin. Blood welled from the wound, but the Garanth didn't seem to notice. He had no weapon. Tóran saw the heavy fist swing towards his head and ducked but was struck in the jaw by the Garanth's knee. The impact tossed him back into the wall, and he reeled. Bright lights popped in front of his eyes.

The Garanth stepped forward, grunting but inexorable. Tóran shook his head and slid to the floor as the bull's fist struck where his head had been a moment before. The Garanth roared, and Tóran scrambled between his opponent's legs, swinging his blade at the bull's neck. The blade bounced off the metal gorget around the Garanth's throat, making Tóran's hands vibrate. It took all his will to maintain his grip on the hilt.

The Garanth turned, bringing his backhand with him. He struck Tóran's right cheek, knocking him to the ground and causing his ears to ring. Tóran remembered taking a similar hit from Aréon Kírsis at the Warriors Challenge. He rolled away and lurched to his feet, planning to make for the cave entrance and escape. He took four steps before the bull caught him.

The Garanth grasped his long dark braid and pulled Tóran onto his back. Tóran swallowed against the blade held firmly against his throat as the Garanth studied him. Tóran refused to show fear or beg for his life. He closed his eyes and waited for the inevitable, but the killing stroke never came.

Instead, the Garanth bull lifted Tóran by his braid and slung the legionnaire over his shoulder. The northerner began his slow hike back up the cliffside towards the main army. Tóran swallowed the scream that threatened to expose his terror to his enemy but did nothing to lessen his dread. The Garanth lumbered toward their camp and the demon that would make Tóran an Arkmuln.

Chapter 6: Dark Discoveries

The melancholy wail of a seabird swooping past the mage's window roused Gérand Kiél from the remnants of his disturbing dreams. His bones ached, and he shivered in the predawn chill. The white mage wasn't sure whether the tremors were from the cold or of the sense of unease seeping deeper into his awareness.

Gérand looked up from his rush pillow and glanced out at the early morning sky. Hamra, the violet moon, exited the heavens in the west, bathing the skies in the pale lavenders and plums of her farewell as her father, Lord Shamar, heralded the dawn with his golden hues from the east. He sighed heavily and closed his eyes, trying to determine the origin of this pervasive sense of foreboding. The harder he tried, the more elusive the answer became.

The misty chill of morning was brutal on Gérand. His joints protested as he rolled out of bed and lit the fire already laid in the fireplace. He rummaged through the piles of junk scattered in disarray across his desk, seeking his silken shoulder knot of office. Gérand pulled the coiled rope over his head and attached the knot to the flap on his right shoulder, then slid the large ruby ring of his office over his arthritic knuckle. Decked in full guild raiment, Gérand stared into the looking glass at the stranger with wiry gray hair and the deeply lined face that had once been jovial. He grimaced at the reflection.

Once, he'd have sought the counsel of the High Mage to interpret the dark dreams, but these days—

His thoughts were interrupted by a knock at his door. Gérand rose from his dressing table and opened the door. He welcomed the aroma of adzuki tea originating from the steaming mugs on a platter with food held by his red-robed journeymage, Óren Fár.

"Ah, you bring the elixir to quicken the heart and warm the bones," Gérand said. He smiled at the dark, curly-haired red mage, brushing the filaments of his early morning musings to the back of his mind. He beckoned the younger man to join him at his table. "And to what do I owe this very early morning visit?"

"You have a visitor, sir," Óren began, blowing on his hot drink before sipping it. "I told him you would be able to see him directly."

Adzuki tea was Gérand's favorite. The sweet, nutty beverage warmed his belly and stimulated his exhausted mind. He inhaled and sighed, closing his eyes as the glow spread from his stomach through his chest.

Óren paused mid-sip, hesitating as his eyes took in his Master's rumpled appearance and the room's disarray.

"You're up very early this morning, sir. Is everything all right?"

Gérand snorted. "I find that the older I get, the less sleep I require. And the less sleep I get, the more time I have to worry about other things. Who is it that awaits me?"

The red mage shifted in his chair and lowered his brown eyes. "Well, he's a rather disgusting creature. He said his name was Scóurj, but he didn't look like the type of person you would normally invite to break your fast."

Scóurj! The heat in Gérand's belly turned cold. He took a deep breath and smiled wanly at his journeymage.

"Alas, my young friend, these are changing times, and we must not be hasty in the judgment of our associates. I will see him. However, his arrival here doesn't bode well, for he is a Gróshan spy that I planned to meet in secret a fortnight hence."

A knot of apprehension tied itself around Gérand's chest. The implication of such a public meeting between himself and the spy made him uneasy. Gérand had recognized the value of the Gróshan's abilities and had kept Scóurj well-paid and himself well-informed of all activities of importance over the Tides.

Due to this relationship, Gérand had progressed rapidly through the ranks of the Mages Guild. Information was essential in politics. However, the two made sure that their relationship's true nature could never become public, for that would undermine their success. The spy's unexpected appearance, coupled with his early morning discomfort, caused a feeling of doom to settle over Gérand's mind. He pasted on a genial smile at the tapping on his door and welcomed the spy as an old friend, offering him the chair closest to the fire.

Scóurj was indeed a repugnant little man who bore the appearance of one who spent a lifetime in the gutters with the rodents and filth. However, his sharp eyes and accounting of the information requested directly contrasted his decrepit outward appearance. Gérand realized Tides ago that nobody knew what occurred in the streets of the various towns and cities better than those who lived in them. He justified utilizing this objectionable resource to himself, and it had never let him down.

"My guttersnipes 'n Zaveen saw that ancient silver staff fitting 'n the dirty hands of them what get paid to do the nasty deeds of their betters," the wizened little man began. "My men says the cripple who saw it had his tongue split an' he passed on afore he could tell us who them was what did it."

Gérand raised his bushy eyebrows. Zaveen was the settlement on the edge of the Zahili Desert that housed the great temple of the goddess Orwaena.

"What about the priestesses?" Gérand asked, sipping the adzuki tea.

Óren leaned forward, his nostrils flaring, but his eyes alert, and his hands balled into fists.

Scóurj shrugged and slowly drew a finger across his throat.

Gérand closed his eyes and sent a silent prayer to Hamra for the souls of the murdered priestesses. He had feared dark tidings but hadn't expected such a devastating tragedy. The Sceptre of Kulari, created to destroy Laräeth the Betrayer by the mages of all races, had been disassembled after Laräeth's defeat. The sacred stones went back to their lands, and the wooden sceptre returned to Auräevya, the Tree of Life in Samshäeli.

The warrior priestesses in Zaveen guarded the silver sheath that held the stones onto the sceptre. The wilds of the Tália Jungle were challenging to navigate, and the desert temple was hard to access. All assumed the sheath would be safe there. Scóurj's message was the first Gérand had of any unrest from that part of the world.

"This is appalling news," Gérand said.

Gérand frowned as he paced back and forth in front of his

table, where the little Gróshan was picking through the tray of delicacies with his grimy fingers. He glanced over at his journeymage and stifled a chuckle at the disgust on Óren's face. He looked back at Scóurj and watched with morbid fascination as the filthy little man picked at a piece of meat caught in his yellowed teeth with his talon-like fingernails. Óren's face took on the pallor of one about to vomit.

"I get what you're trying to do, Kiél," Scóurj began while sucking more food from his crooked teeth, "and I'm willing to do my part...for a price." He glanced sideways at Gérand and winked.

"You have more to divulge?" asked Gérand, interpreting Scóurj's gesture.

"Aye, there's more for them what's quick enough to know the value of it," the spy nodded. "Unlike my Master."

Gérand nodded to Óren. "Go to my vault. Bring me two of the bags you'll find there. Make sure nobody sees you."

Óren nodded and rose, turning on his heel. The red mage held his breath and exited the room, exhaling loudly in the corridor. Gérand chuckled again, knowing it would take his journeymage time to get used to the idea of associating with the more odiferous elements of Askári society.

"It is unlike your Master to ignore important information," Gérand mused. He sat on the chair opposite his guest.

Scóurj clucked his tongue and shrugged. "He has more immediate problems to deal with."

"Alright, then tell me, greedy one, what great doom is upon us?" Gérand picked up his stone pipe and tapped out the ash, then filled it with fresh leaves.

The lice-ridden man scratched his head and grimaced. "These is bad times, very bad. Them Garanth razed the Dágon Valley an' are just above the Shalaen Falls. Them patrols came first, but the main army'll reach Táksabai 'n a day or so."

Gérand dropped the pipe he'd begun to light, the panic

brought on by Scóurj's statement causing his fingertips to tingle.

"What of the legion?" the mage asked, turning to his companion. "Have they realized the danger yet? Hasn't anyone warned them?"

Scóurj picked up the mage's pipe and lit it, taking a couple of long pulls before answering. "They was warned days ago and haven't done nothin'. Them officers sit 'n committee with the leaders of the Merchants Guild an' gripe about money. By tomorrow, Táksabai'll be under siege. Even if the Merchants Guild orders 'em to mobilize, it'll be too late."

Gérand felt the band of pressure squeeze tighter around his chest.

"There's more," Scóurj sighed, the blue smoke exiting his nostrils in twin streams. "My spies seen the Várkaras Caravan headin' down from Támon. Them Garanth patrols trapped the folk 'tween the valley and falls."

Gérand knew that the legion wouldn't muster to assist the caravan even if they were right outside the city's gates. Once the Merchants Guild took control of Táksbai, the Várkaras Caravan was tolerated with thinly-veiled hatred by the guild's members because of their ability to bring wares that nobody else could acquire. The caravan provided the resources for many of the other guilds' wares because they were the only entity allowed to travel unmolested across the various lands and closed borders of Muralia. If the Garanth destroyed the Varkáras Caravan, not only would they lose their supplier of magical ores and gemstones, but the world would lose their only beacon of tolerance. Gérand could not condone such a loss if he had any ability to intervene.

"What can I do?" Gérand asked the filthy Gróshan, who continued to smoke without a care in the world.

The agent sat still for a moment, his eyes glittering in the tiny light of the embers. "Them Garanth don't like water," he said finally. "I would try to get some of them caravanners that way if any survive."

Gérand ran gnarled fingers through his wiry hair and pondered his options. If he took a small sailboat up the coast, he could probably reach the falls before midmorning and survey the situation. But Gérand knew that there were at least one hundred members in the caravan. To bring as many as possible back to the temporary safety of Táksabai, he would need to take one of the two-masted schooners. A boat that size would also require at least two other people to operate her. Looking at the vile little man seated before him, Gérand made his decision.

"Wait here. I'll be right back."

Scóurj bowed his head, his lips twisted on his scarred face. "Like I got anywhere better to go?"

Gérand snorted and slipped into the hall where Óren was returning.

"Go and wake one of your trusted peers," Gérand whispered. He grabbed the bags of coin from Óren. "Get one of the schooners ready to launch; we have a caravan to rescue."

Óren nodded and turned away, racing down the hall to his quarters. Gérand Kiél took a deep breath and returned to his room and his guest. Handing the full bags of flecksun coins to the Gróshan, Gérand charged the little man with the most important task of his depraved life. The significance of which wasn't lost on the man, despite its simplicity.

"It will be done," Scóurj said.

Chapter 7: Arkmuln

The scream, raw and primal, tore through the blackness that blanketed Tóran's mind. The sound raked along his nerves, causing him to clench his jaw. Whoever was making that sound passed the threshold of human tolerance and crossed into pure animalistic torment. Tóran tried to open his eyes but couldn't. He raised his eyelids with his fingers but still couldn't see.

A taut, stretching sensation in his cheeks gave Tóran pause while he reasoned it out. A bitter seed of despair took root in his bowels and burst into a flower of fear as it reached his heart. He was blind! His eyes were damaged or worse, taken.

Tóran's whimper was overshadowed by yet another agonized scream not far away. He clamped down on his mounting fear and, although unable to see, tried to get his bearings. The tortured creature was near but muffled, likely in a different room.

The air smelled of smoke and unwashed bodies. There was no breeze, so Tóran reasoned he was in some sort of enclosure. He knew he'd been brought back to the Garanth encampment by the wounded warrior who abducted him from the cavern. The beast must have put him inside one of their tents.

Tóran racked his brain to remember what had happened after being thrown over the Garanth's shoulder. The journey had been slow, the warrior severely wounded by whatever attacked the patrol in the cavern. Tóran developed a grudging respect for the creature's stamina, bearing his prisoner's weight, being grievously injured, and trekking across the entirety of the Dágon Valley towards the main army.

Tóran remembered his only thought at the time was figuring out how to take his own life to avoid being converted into Arkmuln. The realization that he still had his own thoughts struck him like a lightning bolt. He leaned, ever so slightly, in the direction of hope.

Taking a deep breath, Tóran tried to calm his ravaged nerves. The screaming stopped, and in its place, the sound of approaching footsteps. Tóran could hear the clink of heavy boot clasps striking the dirt. Someone was heading in his direction, someone big.

The tent flap to his left raised, causing light to burst through the dark tent. Tóran feigned unconsciousness but winced involuntarily at the shock of light and cold air. A Garanth bull entered the tent and, with a grunt, lobbed a hefty object to the ground behind him. The tent flap cracked as it closed. The Garanth lumbered away, leaving behind only silence.

Tóran strained to hear any sound from behind him where the heavy object lay. All he heard was the sound of his heartbeat and breathing. Moving his head slowly from side to side, Tóran let out a long breath. He still had his eyes! They reacted to the light, and he could feel them rolling around behind his lids.

Reaching his hands to his face, he felt his eyes and head. His eyes were swollen, and a crust of what he assumed was his blood sealed them closed. Tóran scratched and picked at the scabs, gritting his teeth against the pain. He'd suffered a severe beating after being knocked unconscious. Every muscle ached, but he was grateful for no broken bones.

Tóran peeled away the layers of grime and blood that caked his eyes and peered through watery lenses at the layout inside the tent. To his left were the closed flaps, with daylight glowing around the seams. In front of him were more prisoners, some sleeping, some unconscious, others watching with haunted eyes. All were Askári, probably from Tamón, the city directly to the north.

None of the tent's occupants were Meq'qan. That meant either Chaq'ta's warriors had avoided capture, or the Garanth had killed them outright in battle. Either way, Tóran would get no assistance from his men. He stared at his fellow prisoners. Nobody spoke, nobody moved. Tóran pulled himself up to his knees and turned around. His breath caught in his throat.

Piled along the back wall of the tent was a mass of bodies, limbs, and torsos twisted into positions they couldn't have achieved in life. Eyes stared unseeing but reflecting the torment of their final moments. Blinking away the burning tears, Tóran was horrified that most of the bodies were smaller than his; women and children.

Why would the Garanth not send women and children against the Askári? They would be difficult for his people to face. Tóran shook his head, abhorred at the train of his thoughts. His legion training required him to put himself in his enemy's position to discern their likely strategy, but he couldn't fathom why they only kept the men.

Tóran considered what he would do if he were laying siege to the city. He would infiltrate the city with local citizens. The Hármolin Legion wouldn't suspect Askári men. The young soldier turned back around and closed his eyes, the air forced from his lungs as if he'd been struck. Táksabai and her people were lost.

Outside the tent, the unmistakable sound of approaching footsteps caused Tóran's fellow prisoners to whimper and huddle together. Some of the prone bodies stirred, rousing from the bliss of unconsciousness to the nightmare of their captivity. Footsteps stopped just outside the tent. The flap opened, blinding the prisoners with the daylight. A mammoth Garanth bull stepped in and pulled two men close to the opening to their feet.

The Garanth caught Tóran's eye and grunted something in his guttural language. Tóran didn't move. The beast grunted at him again, jutting its pointed chin toward the door. He knew the Garanth wanted him to go out the door but feigned ignorance.

Snarling, the Garanth grasped Tóran by his shirt front. Tóran's world spun as he was raised high, his feet dangling above the ground. It flung him outside the tent and into the arms of another waiting Garanth. The enormous bull then exited the tent, carrying the two men, one over each of his shoulders.

The first two men began struggling against their captors. Tóran was impressed to see some fight left in the beaten Askári men. They pounded the warrior with their fists and kicked with their bare feet, but to no avail. The Garanth bull snorted and shook them like rag dolls. There was a loud snap, and the man in the brute's left hand went limp, his neck broken.

An anguished cry rose from the other man. He clasped

both hands together, swinging his fists at the bull's face. The blow landed, but it only annoyed the giant warrior. Roaring his indignation, the Garanth dropped the dead man and slammed his left fist into the second man's face, crushing his skull.

The bull then picked up the two corpses and threw them back into the tent along the wall before grabbing two new candidates, a young man no older than Tóran and a middle-aged man. The Garanth carrying Tóran grunted and turned, making his way deeper into the center of the camp.

Tóran's survival instincts took over as soon as he exited the tent, despite hanging upside down over the Garanth's shoulder. He scanned the area, fixing the location of his tent within the surrounding hills. His tent was at the center of the encampment and was one of only a few tents scattered throughout the area. The Garanth warriors gathered around fires, roasting meat on sticks or lying down to enjoy the early morning coolness.

Separated from the main army's campfires stood a horde of people, corralled by ropes. Tóran watched them for a moment, intrigued by their docile behavior; they all just stood silently. They were Askári; their dark hair and clothing gave that much away, but the legionnaire couldn't determine whether or not they were prisoners or −Tóran swallowed hard. He scoured the sea of dark heads for any indication of life and found none.

Thousands of his kinsmen stood behind their rudimentary fences and waited for the command to destroy their brethren. One of the nameless masses looked his way, and Tóran's eyes locked onto the milky-white irises of the man who could have been anybody's brother. His face was utterly devoid of expression. All that remained of his once-vibrant humanity was the pale emptiness of death. Tóran swallowed. He was about to join their ranks.

The three prisoners were carted like sacks of root vegetables over their enemies' shoulders toward a tent triple the other tents' size. It sprawled across the middle of the camp. The shelter itself was unremarkable, made of black canvas that blended in easily with the scorched fields. As Tóran got closer to the tent, a feeling of uneasiness plagued him.

Energy, malignant and powerful, radiated outwards from the tent and infiltrated his heart and mind as if the barriers of bone and flesh were nonexistent. Tóran felt bumps rise on his flesh. The black pavilion sat amid a barren swath of ground where nothing grew, and none of the Garanth ventured to build their fires. Even they kept their distance from whatever horror dwelt inside the looming tent.

Ahead of him, the two prisoners began to struggle. They started screaming and kicking to get away, but the bull simply roared and squeezed them more tightly about the middle, cutting off their air. Tóran felt a similar panic rush over him. His mind screamed to get away from the dark force that threatened to overwhelm his senses. His breath became labored, and he felt his heart pounding in his chest. Tóran closed his eyes and sent a fervent prayer to Orwaena, but it was no use. He felt the Garanth carrying him bend as he ducked inside the black awning.

Almost against his will, Tóran wrenched his eyes open. He gasped. Languishing across a pile of jewel-hued cushions was the most striking man he'd ever seen. Tóran felt the compulsion to drink in the man's beauty war with the sickening knowledge that the creature was unnatural. The man's skin was like alabaster, with no blemish marring its pale perfection. His limbs were long and supple; his sculpted body gracefully relaxed across the pillows. His silver hair spilled across his shoulders.

What captured Tóran's full attention was the man's face. Amidst the planes and angles of his features were sapphire eyes so blue they were nearly black. Their depth spoke of eternity and glittered dark among the stars of forever. Tóran shuddered. This man was the demon that traveled with the

Garanth. Tóran studied the creature and swallowed the thick lump of guilt and shame that filled his throat. The devil looked like a Shäeli.

The demon's eyes bored into Tóran's, laying bare all of his thoughts and emotions. Never had Tóran felt so exposed, so vulnerable. He tried not to think of the Meq'qan warriors he hoped were moving towards the valley to engage the Garanth from the east. The harder he tried to hide his thoughts, the more transparent they became.

The creature's mouth tugged slightly upwards as Tóran struggled, then it gestured carelessly to the cages lined up along the left side of the tent. The bull carrying the two men flung them unceremoniously into the first cage while Tóran tumbled into the second. He scrambled to a corner, then curled up into a ball with his hands around his knees—the whimpers from the two men adjacent to him the only sound.

Tóran's eyes darted around the room. Except for the metal cages he and his companions occupied, the tent's decorations were opulent. Thick carpets blanketed the floor. Ornately cast brass lanterns hung throughout the pavilion, dangling on tasseled ropes and filled with glowstones, giving a warm ambiance to the room.

Plush pillows lay scattered around low tables filled with delicacies from all realms of Muralia. Tóran recognized the cambar shellfish and flaky white shadfish, both found in the lakes and rivers around Dúlnat, surrounded by exotic dishes he didn't recognize. His mouth watered despite the danger of his situation. If this was to be his last meal, he couldn't complain about the food.

The demon shifted on the pillows and turned to face the cages.

"Well now, aren't you a delectable morsel?" The demon asked, his eyes gleaming as he smiled at his prisoner.

Tóran shifted uncomfortably in his cage, pulling his knees tighter around his body. He didn't think Shäeli demons ate people, but he felt a need to protect himself.

"It's too bad I need strong men for my minions to lead that mindless rabble out there," he said, jutting his chin towards the horde of Arkmuln standing behind their ropes. "Your passion and determination are positively mouthwatering." The demon rose, moving languidly towards Tóran's cage. "Come closer," he purred, reaching into the cage for Tóran's face.

Unable to resist the demon's power, Tóran's legs betrayed his internal command. He rose and walked haltingly to the edge of the cage. The creature placed his hand on Tóran's cheek, caressing it. White heat burned Tóran's skin with an intensity he'd never experienced before. It was a heat that burned with a painful yearning, a yearning that confused him.

"Wh-what do you want of me?" Tóran asked, trying to muster as much courage as he could under the intoxicating spell of the demon's proximity.

The demon smiled, eying the young man hungrily. "What I want from you and what I shall take are, sadly, two very different things." The demon sighed. "You are going to—"

A commotion outside the pavilion's awning halted the demon's explanation. The creature tore its gaze from Tóran and turned to face the group of men that had just entered the tent. His eyes widened in recognition. Their dark skin and all-black clothing gave them away instantly. Hazzara. In league with the Garanth and a demon at the helm.

All Tóran's hopes faded. Even if Cédron succeeded in his quest to stop Laylur, there wouldn't be much left of their beloved Muralia to salvage once the demons got through. The Meq'qan were all but eradicated already, and Askári-bai would fall next. Tóran sank back down to the floor. He curled into a tight ball and rested his head between his knees. He wept.

The demon hissed at the intrusion. "You had better have a good reason for this interruption," the demon spat, looming over the leader of the Hazzara.

The Hazzara leader waved his men forward. They brought a three-foot-long, flat box forward. The leader cleared a space off one of the low tables and motioned for the men to lay the box upon it. As the leader bent down over the box, his torus knot amulet slipped from between the folds of his shirt. The ruby at its center glinted in the light of the glowstones. The leader of the Hazzara waved his men back and opened the box with a flourish.

"Behold," he announced. "The silver sheath of the Sceptre of Kulari. We are one step closer to bringing the deities to their knees."

Tóran raised his head and watched, fascinated, as the demon reached for the silver ornament and held it in his delicate hands. The sheath of silver sprouted four branches that folded out from metal joints. The end of each component had four prongs meant to hold the sacred stones. The demon twirled it between his long fingers.

"Excellent! My Master will be most pleased to have this in his possession. Once we finish creating our army of Arkmuln from the Askári, we can march towards Samshäeli. Without the sceptre, their prophecy is as worthless as their blasted tree," he chuckled.

The scorn in his voice echoed in the gruff laughter of the men around him. The knot that settled in Tóran's bowels festered and made him nauseous. Räesha had said that the tree of life, Auräevya, was withering. That was why she'd come from Samshäeli for Cédron. If he couldn't fulfill the prophecy by activating the Sceptre of Kulari, then there indeed was no hope.

Tóran wallowed in self-pity for another moment before a spark of anger flared briefly in his heart. He pounded a fist on his knee. No! Cédron had survived so much already. That he might fail was unthinkable. The deities had intervened on his behalf.

Tóran didn't understand how this Shäeli demon was different from Räesha and Trilläen, or the intricacies of

Shäeli politics, but he recognized the need to escape and warn his friends. He sprang to his feet, rattling the wooden bars of his cage, desperate to find a weakness that he could exploit. The men huddled in the cell next to him whimpered and cried, casting terrified glances at the demon and his guests.

"What are you doing?" the older man hissed. "Do not bring their attention back to us, you fool!"

Their host and Hazzara looked up from their conversation. The demon reverently placed the silver sheath back into the box and closed the lid, locking the clasps and caressing the wood before turning his attention to the captives.

"Ah, my enthusiastic one!" the demon crooned. "Are you so anxious to join me?"

The demon circled the table and stopped before the cages, his dark blue eyes sparkling in the soft light. Tóran held his breath and swallowed. If his captor released him, he might be able to buy himself some time to figure out a way to escape.

Tóran straightened, pulling his dark hair back out of his face and meeting the demon's gaze straight on. It took every ounce of willpower he had not to wilt beneath the intensity of the demon's eternal eyes. Tóran thought of his father, always proud and confident in his capacity as Regent of Dúlnat. The lad drew in a deep breath and reached for the demon's arm.

"We have a common enemy," he said tightly. "I would gladly join a war against the Shäeli. Long have they held my people in contempt, killing our soldiers and poisoning us with their magic."

The demon licked his lips, the sharp tongue a stain of red against his even white teeth. "And so you shall, my pet," he murmured. "So you shall, …but not yet."

The demon turned his attention to the adjacent cage, his eyes on the younger man huddled in the older man's partial embrace.

"Father!" came the younger man's strangled cry. "Don't let him take me!" The young man grabbed his father's free hand, squeezing until their skin showed white.

The leader of the Hazzara grasped one of the bars, smiling genially at the pair of terrified prisoners. "Don't worry, my friends," he said with an oily voice. "Eternal bliss is only a few short moments of torture away."

The Hazzara stepped back, and the demon held out his hand, palm up. Straining slightly, he pulled at a bump that rose in the palm of his hand. Tóran gasped as the lump turned, twisting upwards into a corkscrew-shaped shell. The form spiraled until it was as long as a man's hand. Spiny ridges poked along the outside of the surface, giving it a sinister appearance. The enamel sparkled with the same timeless blue of the demon's eyes.

From the base of the spiral-shaped shell emerged a soft, silvery substance. As it grew, it spread out like a slug made of molten metal. Tóran had visited the mines of Dúlnat with his father and was well-versed in heating metals to their melting points to pour the liquid into forms. This silvery slug slithered forward, carrying the blue shell on its back. Tendrils of silver stretched out from the slug, searching. Tóran couldn't tear his eyes away.

The demon bent down and laid his hand on the carpet. The offspring slithered onto the cage floor. Its silvery tentacles reached out towards the men as the slimy body with its sparkling shell inched across the cage bottom. The creature worked its way to the young man's leg and pulled itself along the lad's body.

Tóran clamped his hands over his ears and gritted his teeth to shut out the young man's screams of terror, but it was impossible. The older man held his grown son with skin taut over his knuckles, but the bleak look in the man's eyes told Tóran that he had succumbed to the inevitable. The sparkling creature made its way around to the back of the young man's neck and wormed its silvery tentacles around the base of his head.

The shrieks reached a fevered pitch as the demon slug burrowed into the young man's scalp with its molten appendages, pulling itself further into the skull until the corkscrew shell had lodged itself securely in his brain. Tóran watched as his companion's eyes rolled back, leaving only the whites showing. His jaw went slack, and the screams stopped.

Tóran's stomach roiled. He knew that once the father transitioned, he'd be next. The young man turned to face his father, his eyes now the glittering deep blue of the shell. The Arkmuln outside had milky-white eyes. Perhaps this identified him as a leader of the mindless Arkmuln, the slug a connection to the demon. The father stood, pulling his son up with him. With tears streaming down his anguished face, the older man held out his hand for the bane that would end his life and begin his new existence alongside his son.

Tóran turned his face away and retched.

chapter 8: Wézija

Sénna tried to swallow the panic that rose along with the bile souring her mouth. Only once before had she felt the dread of Wézija's presence. The memories of the guardian's barbaric demand for tribute had haunted her for Tides. A wave of nausea overwhelmed her, remembering the mijáko herd's screams of terror when her grandmother sacrificed them to the guardian.

Sénna remembered the splatters of blood arching across the cave walls and the coppery smell of entrails. Her breath quickened into a shallow pant as her memories invaded her mind. Their plan had failed. This small group would be a tribute to Wézija's voracious appetite. Her mind went numb. She retched.

To her left, a tentacle larger and longer than a caravan wagon caught one of the guards around the waist. The man swung his curved sword but only grazed Wézija's tough hide. Cybél screamed and buried her face in her hands.

The doomed man's strangled cry ended as a second arm snaked around his throat and ripped his head from his shoulders. Gore painted the walls and the group indiscriminately. The guardian pulled the pieces of her tribute towards the rows of grinding teeth that surfaced above the center pool's deep water.

Sénna gritted her teeth against the sound of Wézija grinding the man's bones deep within her cavernous mouth. Behind her, the group recovered from their initial paralysis. She could hear barked orders and shuffling feet.

"Quick, run back down the tunnel," she heard the young legionnaire call over Cybél's screams.

"Shut that girl up!" growled another male voice.

Someone grabbed Sénna's wrist and jerked her backward. Her feet slipped in the spilled contents of her stomach as she retreated from Wézija's fury. Footsteps shifted, and boots hammered against the stone floor as the remaining members jostled back down the narrower corridor that they had just exited. Sénna heard a loud crack, and Cybél's wails suddenly muted to a whimper. The group raced back to the previous small cavern to regroup, their eyes wide as they caught their breath.

"Laylur's beast," the last of the guards swore. "That thing tore Járrik apart like it was plucking a flower!"

Sénna's breath caught in her throat as she returned the guard's wide-eyed stare. It happened so fast she didn't have time to distinguish between her memories and what she just witnessed. The guardian would slaughter them all as she'd done with the herd of mijáko. There was no escaping her hunger now that she'd roused from her slumber.

"W-Wézija ha-has," Sénna stuttered, her voice shaking. "She has accepted us as her tribute." She closed her eyes and slumped against the wall, sliding down until her backside hit the cold stone floor.

"No, that isn't how it is supposed to happen."

"We're going to be shredded like Járrik?"

Squeezing her eyes shut, Sénna winced from her pinched shoulders and the cloying smell of death assaulting her nose. She opened her eyes to the elderly Shäeli bending over her. He shook her, rousing her from her stupor.

"What else can you tell me of this Wézija? Now that she's here, is there any way to get past her?" Rováen implored.

Sénna thought back to her previous visit with her grandmother. Her grandmother had herded the mijáko into the caves behind the falls, their bleating echoing off the walls. The guardian fell on her prey with terrifying ferocity, paralyzing Sénna. Am'aranth pulled her deeper into the caves, and they escaped while Wézija enjoyed her tribute. Sénna's voice was as hollow as her eyes as she shared her memories.

Rováen listened to her without speaking. After Sénna told him all she could remember, he sat back against the wall next to her and let out a slow breath. The remaining group members glanced uneasily at each other and shifted their feet as if preparing to run back to Shozin Chezak and the caravan.

Sénna ignored them and retreated further into herself. Her death would spare her father the indignity of having to ransom her. That was a small consolation. He wouldn't have to suffer from the compromising position she'd put him in again by sneaking out. He'd never know the details of her death unless Am'aranth found their bones on one of her future trips through the caves.

"We have to get past Wézija to the beach outside," Rováen mused.

Sénna watched him as he stood and began to pace back and forth along the side of the cavern, pulling on his silvery beard. "If we can entice the Garanth patrol to our location, then Wézija may—"

"And just how do you propose we get past her?" Anéton hissed. "Did you see those enormous tentacles? I didn't count them, but there appeared to be more of them than there are of us, not to mention the rows of teeth and—"

"I know!" Rovåen cried, clutching his head in his hands and grasping handfuls of silver hair. "I know."

Cédron stepped next to his uncle. "Do you think Wézija could sense us if we were invisible? Do you think we could slip past her?"

Sénna's head snapped up, her lips curling in a sneer. "Ah, the arrogance of the magic wielder. Do you think you can fool the guardian with your tricks?"

Sénna felt a tiny bit of satisfaction at their surprised looks. Her behavior was petty in light of their current peril, but those Shäeli demons should know that they hadn't fooled her. They could not be trusted.

Cédron sighed and turned his attention from her and back to Rovåen.

"It's worth a try. Even if just one of us makes it," Cédron whispered. He glanced back towards the terror of the guardian.

Sénna snorted, then smiled up at him. "That's a marvelous idea. Why don't you give it a try?"

"What's your problem?" Cédron frowned at her. "We're just trying to help you and everyone else to survive."

"You're a magic wielder, aren't you?" Sénna responded, getting to her feet and poking Cédron in the chest. "That means you're out for yourself and will sacrifice the rest of us."

Sénna swallowed to prevent the ball of grief that threatened to choke her. The memory of her mother's gentle touch and kind eyes mocked her. Her mother had been so trusting, so forgiving, to her detriment.

"Never mind," Sénna scowled. "One less magic wielder in the world is a good thing. Go, see how Wézija enjoys the taste of your flesh."

Cédron opened his mouth to speak, his eyes reflecting hurt and confusion. Sénna didn't care. She couldn't care for this lanky young man who'd shown her nothing but kindness. He'd used his power to give Myknét's body a proper, even beautiful, release to Lady Muralia. She clamped down on that train of thought. No matter how kind these two Shäeli appeared to be, softening towards them was too dangerous.

Rovärn sighed and eased himself to his feet, grunting with the movement. He placed an arm on Cédron's shoulders and nodded. "Let's give it a try."

Sénna watched as Cédron dug into his pouch, producing two gemstones the size of her palm. One was pale blue, and the other a deep red. He pulled the strange bone staff from across his back, placing the stones in the phalanges of the crown. Sénna marveled at how the talisman seemed alive as it grasped the rocks.

Cédron then pulled out a bloodstone from the pouch, holding the rock in his free hand. He swallowed, then nodded to his companions with a determined glint in his eyes. Rovärn stepped in front as the two made their way back down the corridor towards the guardian.

Cybél stood beside Anéton with wide eyes, her chest heaving with shallow breaths. The strain on the young man's face was evident in the waning glow as he patted her hand.

"I'm going too," he said huskily, nodding at the remaining two guards.

Cybél grasped at Anéton's shirt as he moved away, but he shook his head. Taking her wrists in his hands, he propelled her towards Sénna. Cybél's mouth formed into an O, but she didn't fight him.

"Watch out for each other," the legionnaire instructed the

young women. "Both of you stay back where it's safe." Nodding to the guards, the three men turned and followed Cédron and Rovӓen down the corridor.

Sénna sat stone-faced against the wall while Cybél rummaged through her leather hip bag. Her ears strained to catch the sound of Wézija's arms whistling through the air and capturing her prey, but the long moments of silence screamed at her, propelling her into action. If Wézija left her pool, she could easily make her way through the caves without being heard. Remaining behind no longer felt safe. Sénna sprang to her feet and roughly hoisted Cybél under the arm against her feeble protests.

"Get up; we have to go," Sénna said.

Cybél nodded and grabbed Sénna's arm. "Here, chew this. It'll help calm the nerves," Cybél handed her a pinch of brown Valerian roots, then grabbed a few for herself. "We may not survive, but at least we won't panic when that *thing* eats us."

Sénna smiled grimly. "That *thing* is a guardian that is sensitive to Árk'äezi. She won't even notice us if she gets those Shäeli first. Come on; it's our only chance to get out of here."

The two young women inched forward in the dim light. Sénna kept one hand on the left wall while holding onto Cybél's upper arm with her right. Creeping as quickly as they could without tripping on the uneven floor, they both jumped at the clash of metal on stone, echoing back from the cavern ahead of them. Cries followed as the men engaged Wézija, and the guardian bellowed her response. Cybél sucked in a breath, inhaling the juice from her roots. She choked then coughed.

"Try not to give our position away," Sénna whispered, holding Cybél's arm as they crept towards the battle.

Shadows danced on the walls as they approached the cavern. Rounding the corner, glowstones held aloft by one of the guards illuminated the terrifying scene. Wézija had emerged from the pool in the cavern center, and her immense, pale blue bulk filled the room. Two muscular trunks of legs supported her ample female form. Arms sprouted down the sides of the body, two on each side and all ending in taloned claws.

Sénna's heart pounded in her chest. She squeezed her eyes shut against the sight of the long tentacles that sprouted from the back of Wézija's head like thick, coiling braids. The guardian's bellow shook her from her frozen terror. Sénna opened her eyes and took a deep breath.

Maintaining her hold on Cybél's arm, she pulled them both along the outer edge of the cavern wall. The two inched their way past an obstacle course of stalagmites protruding up from the floor and threatening to catch their hair and clothing. Across the cavern, Anéton and one of the guards dodged the long tentacles whizzing towards them from Wézija's enormous head.

In the center of the guardian's face, a circular orifice gnashed its long teeth at the insolent prey beneath her. Both of Wézija's milky eyes fixed on the men scurrying around the cavern, thrusting swords impudently at her legs and torso while dodging her arms and tentacles. Sénna scanned around the room but couldn't see RovÄen or Cédron. So far, their luck at remaining unseen held.

"No sudden moves," Sénna whispered into Cybél's ear. "And for our Lady's sake, keep silent."

With her heart in her throat, Sénna picked her way across the cavern toward the opening that led to the beaches and freedom. The stench of rotten seaweed and decaying shells assailed her nostrils as she passed one of the shallower pools. Cybél coughed and gagged, causing Wézija's terrifying head to spin in their direction. The milky eyes fastened on their crouched forms, and the beast let out a ferocious yell.

Cybél's eyes grew wide at the thunderous approach of the guardian. She let out a squeak and turned to flee. Wézija was quicker. The monstrous guardian grasped Cybél firmly about the middle with one of her clawed arms and raised the woman above her head. With a second arm, she plucked Sénna from where she crouched behind a stalagmite. Sénna's stomach dropped as she was lifted high into the air, the guardian's talons digging painfully into her hips. Below her, she could see the men scurrying around, trying to engage the beast without hurting its captives.

Bellowing her rage, Wézija swept up one guard and Anéton in her remaining arm. She raised them closer to her mouth. The reek of carrion and rot from Wézija's gullet made Sénna gag.

Tipped upside-down, the strap of Cybél's pouch slid off her shoulders. Sénna watched it fall, spilling its contents across the stone floor. She fought down the urge to scream. As the grinding teeth inched closer to her ankles, a piercing shriek escaped her lips, followed by the bile that filled her stomach.

Across Wézija's body, Anéton stabbed savagely at the guardian's arm with his sword, but it only seemed to ignite her anger. Sénna spotted Cybél's body clutched in the claw below her. She wasn't moving. Sénna didn't know if Cybél was unconscious or dead. Either way, she wouldn't see the end coming. Sénna closed her eyes and waited for the gnashing teeth to rip her legs apart. The pain, when it came, was of a different sort and from an unexpected quadrant.

Heat seared up her legs and across her body as scarlet light flashed into her eyes beneath the closed lids. Without warning, Wézija flung her quarry to the ground. Sénna opened her eyes only when the sensation of falling registered in her mind. She rolled to a stop against the bottom of a slender stalagmite and propped herself up. She glanced around to get her bearings. One of her arms stung, gashed by a stalagmite when she fell.

Wézija stood, screaming and writhing in pain near the outside opening of the cavern. To her left, Cédron blasted a red light into Wézija's torso. The red jewel he placed in the starburst crown was a powerful firestone. Sénna had never seen such a potent stone.

Watching Cédron challenge Wézija reminded Sénna of the torched Laborers Guild and the watchtower. Her sense of helplessness, while an inferno raged around her, again filled her with terror. Sénna wasn't sure which was the more frightening, the guardian or Cédron.

Holding the staff aloft, a sort of inner light surrounded Cédron, revealing the skin beneath his clothing. Markings covered his body, pulsing through his shirt and giving him an ethereal glow. Balls of flame burst forth from the firestone and struck Wézija, forcing the guardian away from her prey. Occasionally, Cédron missed his target, launching fireballs out of the cavern to shoot over the water.

The chamber shook with Wézija's screams of pain, threatening to collapse it. Rock chunks and smaller stalactites rained down upon the group as the guardian thrashed her arms into the walls. Sénna ducked closer to Cybél's body and spotted her open satchel. She reached for the pouch, gathering pieces of roots, dried flowers, and sachets. Rovä en was still nowhere to be seen.

"Run!" Anéton screamed, stumbling over to the inert Cybél. "We have to get out of here!"

Sénna nodded wordlessly to the legionnaire and, with her free hand, helped him lift the unconscious girl onto his shoulders. Her hand slipped on the slick blood that oozed down her arm from the gash she received in her fall. Wincing, Sénna wiped her hands on her trousers and pulled Cybél's body across Anéton's like a cloak. The sturdy legionnaire grabbed onto Cybél's left wrist and ankle, keeping the bulk of her weight across his shoulders. Once Anéton was sure he had her secure in his grasp, the three of them made their way across the cavern to the opening.

Glancing back, Sénna saw the caravan guard assisting Rovä en to his feet. The rope lines that the old Shä eli wove between the stalagmites cast an intricate pattern against the cavern wall behind them. It was an ingenious idea, but Wézija wouldn't fall for it.

The light of the glowstones wavered as the two men stumbled towards them, making for the beach outside. In front of her, Anéton grunted with the effort of navigating through the cavern while carrying his burden. She knew that if they moved quickly, it would only return Wézija's attention to them, but every nerve in her body screamed at her to run. Sénna sent a prayer to Azria, begging that they reach the beach. She concentrated on placing one foot in front of the other, inching her way closer to the mouth of the cavern.

Despite Cédron's best efforts, the guardian moved to block their escape. Wézija divined their intentions of slipping past her even through her haze of torment. She planted her feet, refusing to pursue the pest that hammered her with blasts of hot light. As if reading her thoughts, Cédron changed his tactic. He turned the staff, facing the aquastone toward Wézija. The cavern filled with the soft caress of its pale glow.

Wézija's angry shrieks calmed to frustrated snarls as the guardian watched the aquastone with narrowed eyes. Cédron's lower body glowed more brightly now, and Sénna's breath caught in her chest as the temperature in the cavern shifted dramatically. Mist formed as the colder air hit the warm rock and water of the cavern. Thicker and denser, the mist seemed to coalesce from the very tide pools lining the cavern floor.

"Come on," Rovaen whispered. "Let's slip this way before she gets a fix on our location."

Sénna followed Anéton as he staggered forward, sliding her feet along the floor to avoid stubbing her toes on the stalagmites. Wézija's growls thrummed deep in her throat as she stalked the holder of the blue light towards the north side of the cavern.

"Quickly now, we can get around her and outside,"

Rovãen urged. He grabbed Sénna's wiry arm and propelled her toward the cave entrance.

Cédron continued to entice Wézija towards the far wall of the cavern, leaving the group a clear route. Rovãen and the two guards lurched out of the cavern's entrance towards the beach, and Anéton had a firm hold on Cybél's inert body. Sénna grabbed onto a stalagmite and turned back to check Cédron's progress. A pang of guilt struck her for her harsh words towards him when she realized that Cédron had probably saved them precisely as he said he would. There was no way Cédron could survive Wézija's fury, and she'd bear the burden of guilt for his death.

Just as the thought reached her brain, Cédron caught her gaze. She saw fear in his eyes, but she didn't know if it was for himself or her and the group. Cédron lifted his chin and pointed it towards the cave opening. Interpreting his signal, Sénna nodded. She slapped her right hand over her heart, then extended her palm up in a symbol of respect. Shock registered on Cédron's face; then, a determination settled over his features. He nodded once to her in farewell as Sénna turned to leave the cavern. Behind her, Wézija's crow of triumph resounded in her ears as she ran the last few feet to freedom.

chapter 9: Forging Alliances

Cédron was trapped. The netting Rovären wove around the cave isolated him into a corner. He watched Sénna leave with his companions and closed his eyes, sending a prayer to Hamra. Wézija crowed in triumph, pounding her chest and thighs with her many fists. She bellowed her challenge and lumbered toward him.

There was no way Cédron could win this battle with the guardian, but it was a sacrifice he was willing to make. At least everyone else had gotten out of the cave and down to the beach. He confused Wézija with his combination of fireballs and cooling mist, but that only allowed him time to scurry behind the webbing at the back of the cavern. It was a good idea, but it hadn't gone according to plan. Now that he was back there, Cédron had only one way out, which was through the raging guardian.

Wézija didn't notice the trip line that Rovään had also strung across the stalagmites. She hit the trigger at a full run. The guardian bellowed like a kazan bull as she crashed to the floor, her arms and tentacles tangled in the ropes. Cédron stood frozen, the immortal's eyes fixed on him from her lower vantage point. He'd never seen such hatred. His legs turned to jelly, and he knew that his final moments were upon him. Wézija reached for him. Cédron closed his eyes, seeing his mother's face one last time.

The squeeze of Wézija's lethal tentacles never came. Outside, on the edge of the cavern, came a challenging yell. Cédron opened one eye, then the other. Garanth bulls slid down the rocks and poured into the cavern. There were scores of them, all roaring their challenge and charging toward the immense blue guardian that turned to face them. Hesitating for only a few seconds, Cédron took his opportunity to activate the bloodstone and become invisible.

Cédron slipped around the back of the cavern, skirting the grisly tableau between the Garanth and Wézija. The guardian accepted the Garanth patrol as a tribute and wasted no time slaughtering the scores of warriors, taking only minor damage herself. Cédron hurried down the path to the cliff before either the Garanth or Wézija could spot him. He was lucky he'd put the stones back into his pouch when he exited the cavern as the tremors from the raging battle above caused the eroding path to give way.

The rocks were sharp and slippery. Cédron grasped at them, hoping to slow his descent before crashing into the rocky shoreline. He tore a hole in the worn sole of his boots before his toes caught hold in a fissure that halted his downward momentum. Cédron clung to the cliff, his fingertips raw from grasping at the sharp rock face. The fragile shale broke from the constant battering of waves against their surface, making his progress slow and dangerous.

Cédron eased his right foot across the surface, seeking purchase for his toes. His foot tore a chunk of cliff away beneath his feet. His grip slipped. Cédron flattened his body against the bluff and slid a few feet before catching himself on an outcropping. A continuous spray from the falls soaked the cliff face. Sharp stones tore his fingers, and they bled, adding moisture to the already slippery surface.

Lord Shamar's rays beat down. Cédron squinted in the glare, the heat and exertion sapping his diminishing strength. Blinking droplets of sweat and waterfall mist from his eyes, Cédron hazarded a glance downward. There was no sign of Roväen or the rest of his group, but he was sure they had all escaped Wézija's wrath. Grunting, Cédron grasped at a piece of tree root embedded in the rock.

Cédron's hand closed around the root, and the toehold on his left foot gave way. He dangled from his right hand and slammed into the wall, losing his focus. He stopped swinging, but his hold on the root was slipping. He shook his hair out of his eyes; the dripping sweat stung the gash in his cheek as it rolled into the torn skin. His time and strength were waning. If he couldn't scale his way down to the beach, he'd plunge to his death on the sharp boulders below.

It fitted that his bones should shatter on the rocks beneath the cliff. Cédron grunted, gritting his teeth. Two men already died protecting him from the guardian. He wasn't quick enough, and his magic wasn't powerful enough to challenge Wézija. His muscles yearned to give up, but his thoughts drove him on.

What good were powers if all he could accomplish was the death of innocents? Cédron closed his eyes. The two caravan guards' deaths were on his head, and he accepted responsibility for them. They were younger men, likely with families. He couldn't leave those who loved the guards to wonder what happened to them. He had to bring them closure and provide for them.

Before he could make reparations to the men's families, he would have to get himself off the cliffside and back to the caravan and his friends. His strength was ebbing, and his hands slipped. Cédron knew that if he didn't make a move soon, he wouldn't have the opportunity to make amends with anyone.

A shadow swept across the rock face causing Cédron to duck. For a brief moment, he thought that perhaps Wézija had come for him, sending her fearsome tentacles after the prey that had gotten away. A gull screeched overhead. Cédron resumed breathing, easing the band that had constricted around his chest.

It was unlikely that Wézija would pursue him after the abrupt arrival of the Garanth. The guardian terrified him, and he flinched at every sound. Cédron doubted he would ever forget the first harrowing glimpse of the creature's snaking tentacles as she tore the first man to pieces. Another pang of guilt assailed him.

Cédron gripped the root harder and swung his right leg over to a promising ledge. It held. He inched his body across the stone's surface towards the ridge, maintaining a death grip on the root. The screams of the fallen echoed in his mind. It wasn't just the men his group had lost, but the patrol of Garanth that had stormed the cave shortly after his friends had escaped.

Cédron never imagined being so happy to see Garanthian warriors. They must have been investigating the fireballs. They had no idea that they would face the rage of an immortal. Cédron felt something close to pity for the unsuspecting patrol.

The roars of both Wézija and the Garanth receded into the back of Cédron's thoughts as he fought his protesting body and weary mind for the stamina to reach and grab, push and hold. Cédron strained to hear any signs of pursuit, but the cavern above him was eerily silent now. Only the sounds of his ragged breathing and grunts as he continued his descent interrupted the constant roar of the falls.

Cédron's hands began to shake. His sweaty fingers lost their tenuous grip on the rocks. Looking down, Cédron spotted a sandy break in the boulders. It was too far to jump and not hurt himself, but it was better than falling onto the sharp rocks below. He took a deep breath and willed his Árk'äezhi to obey his command. Whispering a desperate prayer to Orwaena, he shaped the intention of what he wanted in his mind.

The gentle breeze caressing his skin snapped like a pennant in a storm, swirling around him. Heat stirred in Cédron's fingertips as the power coursed through his body and down into his hands. He took one last look at the patch of sand he aimed for and released his hold on the jagged stone. Blowing his lungs as powerfully as he could, Cédron waved his hands in circles, catching the wind and forcing it to remain just below his body. He cushioned his fall with the pillow of air he'd created.

Cédron grinned despite his exhaustion. He floated gently away from the cliff and downward. Cédron felt the last of his reserves draining from his body and out his fingers. His depleted Árk'äezhi sputtered and died. Cédron fell the last few feet to the ground, landing with a thud on his back. The impact knocked all breath from his lungs. He lay in shock while his body registered the effects of the landing and tried remembering how to inhale.

"Pull those jibs taut," Gérand ordered from the tiller of the two-masted ship. "We need all the wind we can get with this load."

Salt-tinged spray lashed against the sleek hull as the

mages sailed away from the dangers lurking below the falls. Lord Shamar's rays shortened the shadow of the boat as the deity rose in the sky. The white mage wondered if the celestial being had any idea of what was about to befall his people as he gazed down on them benignly from his place in the heavens. Gérand wasn't sure if the father of the skies even cared.

Óren and a novice mage he'd recruited had spent the early morning hours supplying and rigging the schooner they had commandeered for their rescue mission. Racing against time they didn't have, they captured favorable winds and all but flew up the coast. Gérand pondered the strange balls of light arching from the cliffs over the water, visible from a couple of leagues away.

By the time they reached the strong currents swirling around the Shalaen Falls, the colorful lights had ceased flying. A small group of people exited a large cave and made their way down to the beach. Óren hailed the group and took the tender ashore to pick them up.

The mages continued up the coast to just below the falls and were relieved to find the rest of the caravan folk safe but frightened in the large cavern. Gérand was assisted by Rováen in convincing Master Chezak to sail his people to Táksabai rather than attempt the caverns. It took most of the morning and more than a bit of cajoling to persuade the caravan members to leave their wagons and escape the invading army by sea.

Although the refugees were packed into the schooner so tightly that none had room to move, Óren hadn't hesitated when he saw the young lad fall from the cliffs. The red mage swam back to shore and, after making sure the young man was alive and sound enough to swim, had brought him aboard.

Gérand strained to keep the sluggish ship on course and watched this newest addition with keen interest. The strange young man piqued his curiosity. There was something about him, something powerful and, at the same time, vulnerable. It was an unusual group traveling together in Askári-bai, but then again, being with the Várkaras Caravan provided a tolerance for diversity that didn't exist elsewhere.

Gérand recognized the daughter of the Gróshan king and the apothecarist Urléen's granddaughter. He wondered briefly how the young ladies ended up in the company of the caravan this far north. Most prestigious families kept their womenfolk under close supervision. Gérand's wasn't the only jaw to drop upon learning of the Hazzara kidnapping and burning of the watchtower.

"Can you describe the amulet that the Hazzara agent wore?" Óren asked Sénna when she finished her tale.

Sénna finished braiding her dark hair and nodded. "It was a torus knot woven around a cabochon ruby. The chain was fairly heavy silver, as was the amulet."

Óren's brows furrowed, and he leaned toward his mentor. "I've seen a similar if not identical amulet before. Algarik wears it," he said in an undertone.

The young man and his Shäeli companion both started at the comment, their sharp ears having picked up on the journeymage's accusation.

"You know Algarik?" the gangly youth asked, getting up from his spot. "Has he returned to the Mages Guild then?"

Gérand and Óren exchanged glances. Óren shrugged.

"It appears that Algarik has left the Mages Guild for the time being," the journeymage answered. "Why do you ask?"

The young man's eyes hardened to green ice, his lips compressing into a thin line. "My uncle has many things to account for."

"Uncle?" Gérand asked, looking harder at the young man but seeing no family resemblance. "That would make you whom?"

The awkward young man stood straight, pulling back his narrow shoulders and jutting his chin forward slightly. "I am Cédron Varkáras, son of Regent Kásuin Varkáras of Dúlnat and Maräera Angäersol of Samshäeli." He gestured to his companions in order. "This is my Uncle Roväen Angäersol from Samshäeli and Anéton Bessínos of the Hármolin Legion of Dúlnat. We fought Algarik above the falls two days ago and thwarted his efforts to free Laylur from the abyss, but he got away."

Gérand raised his eyebrows at the revelation. "That's quite a mouthful, young Cédron," he said. "But your father and his caravan are well-known and respected in the Mages Guild. You are welcome to whatever aid we can offer."

Cédron bowed, and Gérand watched the young man's shoulders relax. Cédron exchanged a look with Roväen, who nodded.

"That Algarik Muhr is the brother of Kásuin Varkáras puts several missing pieces of his history into perspective," Gérand continued, fingering the talisman at his chest. "I was also not aware he was in league with the Great Demon."

Roväen shifted sideways and shaded his eyes against Lord Shamar's light. "We believe he's been using the Mages Guild as a base for both operations and information. We don't know who else is working with him, but he has significant resources."

Gérand stared out to sea. It would take him another couple of hours to steer the boat back to the Mages Guild. By then, the Garanth army would be well into the Dágon Valley and preparing to lay siege to Táksabai. He would have to deal with Algarik's transgressions later.

"You said Algarik tried to free Laylur from the abyss," Gérand turned back to Cédron. "How?"

Cédron's eyes flashed, and he bared his teeth. "He is behind all of this." He swept his hands around, encompassing his companions. "Laylur poisoned the waters of the world. That weakened Lady Muralia's control of the abyss and caused the increasing ground shakes. I have restored the purity of the waters, but there has been a great cost." Cédron swallowed hard before continuing.

"His Hazzara agents stole the sacred firestone from the Garanth, inciting them to war. They've already slaughtered the Meq'qan tribes of the Ta'voran Marshes, and Our Lady only knows what they've done to Dúlnat and Tamón on their way south." Cédron's eyes glazed, and he took a deep breath. "I have no idea if my father is still alive or..." he trailed off.

Gérand cast a dark look at Óren, who shook his head. Turning back to Cédron, Gérand placed a hand on his shoulder. "I'm so sorry to hear of your troubles. Your father is a strong and resourceful man, and I'm sure he's led his people to safety somewhere in the Ronhádi Mountains." Gérand turned Cédron to face him, giving his shoulders a shake. "I have to ask you again; do you know how Algarik will try to free Laylur?"

Cédron shot a quick look at Roväen, who nodded, then shifted to make himself more comfortable. Cédron reached behind his back and pulled off the bone staff.

"Algarik is after the Sceptre of Kulari. He is acquiring all the scattered pieces and will either assemble it himself or destroy the pieces so that nobody can use it against him." Cédron held Räeshun up, turning her so that the mage could see both stones set into either side of the starburst crown. "I have earned the sacred firestone and aquastone. I am headed to Molonark to convince the Towaki to relinquish their terrastone to me."

Gérand's eyes widened, and he heard Óren gasp next to him. "But, you must stay here and stop the Garanth army from destroying Táksabai."

Cédron shifted his weight from side to side, his shoulders hunched. "I can't do that," he said, shoving the staff into the sling on his back.

"Laylur's beast, why not?" Gérand cried, grunting as he fought the wheel in the wind. "If you don't, the Garanth could wipe out the entire population of Táksabai." Turning to Óren, he jutted his chin toward Cédron. "Convince him."

Roväen leaped up in front of Cédron, blocking him from the advancing mage. Anéton had his hand on the pommel of his sword and stepped to the Shäeli's other side.

"You will have to forgive us," Roväen said, his blue eyes narrowed. "Cédron can't give up the stones or fight against the Garanth. Auräevya, the Tree of Life in Samshäeli, is withering, and Laylur's prison weakens. Already, his freed minions have infiltrated councils and scourged the land. Arkmuln have swollen the Garanth ranks with the undead," Roväen said, looking over at Cédron with a sad smile. "This lad here is our only hope for reviving Auräevya and restoring the demon's prison."

Gérand blinked rapidly, taking in all this information. He knew the histories; every mage studied them during their first Tide at the guild. He'd taught novices the story of how Laylur betrayed Lord Shamar's trust and wooed his youngest daughter Hamra. Their forbidden love tore the deities apart, launching a celestial war. Only the grievous sacrifice by Lady Muralia and her three daughters ended the destruction of their brethren. Lady Muralia tricked Laylur into negotiations and captured his essence.

With her daughters' help, Lady Muralia transformed herself into the Terran planet bearing her name, keeping the demon Laylur trapped within the abyss in the core. Her daughters became the moons that continue to watch over their mother at night while their father, Lord Shamar, patrols the daytime in all his fiery glory. If Auräevya's weakness allowed a breach in the abyss, then the very foundations of their world could be compromised.

"But the only way to imprison Laylur—" Gérand began.

"Is with the Sceptre of Kulari," Óren finished, crossing his arms over his chest. "Now, your little spy's report makes more sense."

Gérand felt his knees weaken. Scóurj's disturbing news of the attack on Zaveen and the silver sheath's theft meant Laylur and his minions were already doing everything in their power to prevent the Sceptre from being re-assembled. Without the Sceptre and the four sacred stones, Auräevya would weaken and die. His temples pounded from the pressure in his head, and he ground his thumbs into them, trying to rub the pain away.

"Why you?" Óren asked Cédron, still standing behind the cover of Roväen and Anéton. "Why not a trained mage?"

Mute, Cédron stared back at him with defiant eyes. Anéton puffed up his chest and leaned toward Óren, his fists clenching and unclenching at his sides.

Gérand placed a hand on his journeymage's arm. "Let them finish their story."

Roväen pulled Cédron close to him. "A prophecy was revealed to my people after Laräeth's Betrayal. In essence: 'A Child of Muralia, born of all the lands, will come and restore balance to the world.' Cédron's heritage, abilities, and connection to the deities have placed this burden upon him. He must gather the sacred stones and the silver sheath and bring them to Auräevya so that the tree can release the Sceptre of Kulari to him."

Gérand's brows knotted together. Taking a deep breath, he sighed. "That is going to be impossible. I've learned this morning that someone stole the silver sheath from the temple in Zaveen. We don't know how, by whom, but we do know they killed all the priestesses of Orwaena in the process. This is grim news, indeed."

Anéton turned to Cédron. "Do you think you can assemble the Sceptre without the sheath?"

Cédron shrugged. "I don't know; I've never seen it. It may not be like Räeshun, who could hold them in her fingers."

Gérand closed his eyes and let out a long breath. "Well, I don't know where Algarik is, but I have a good idea of how to find him. I can't make any promises of the Mages Guild, but Óren and I will do everything in our power to help you on your way."

Cédron nodded. Rová̈en clasped Gérand's forearm. "Just get us all safely to Táksabai."

Chapter 10: Ta'riq's Betrayal

Ta'riq watched Tóran race down the hill towards the valley before turning back to Chaq'ta. He knew that the impulsive warrior had been itching to get his spear into Garanthian hide from the beginning. Chaq'ta would risk everything for the glory of battle, but those were risks Ta'riq was not willing to take.

Ta'riq had already witnessed the extermination of his entire tribe. Only one other of Ta'riq's kinsmen and their tribe's Seer survived the carnage of the Ta'voran Marsh attack. Betraying Chaq'ta was a risk, but letting the warrior follow this plan was just too dangerous. Steeling himself,

Ta'riq turned to his distant cousin.

"Watch out!" Ta'riq cried, swinging the butt of his spear upwards and cracking Chaq'ta underneath the chin.

Chaq'ta's eyes rolled up, and he crumpled backward to the ground. Ta'riq knelt by Chaq'ta's side and placed his cheek above the warrior's mouth. Chaq'ta's breathing was shallow. Touching the warrior's neck, Ta'riq felt Chaq'ta's blood pulsing strong beneath the skin.

Running back up the hillside to the dense gorse bushes, Ta'riq dug beneath the fragrant yellow blossoms to the two-inch thorns that ringed the shrubs' thick base. Using his knife to slice through three of them, the lean tribesman slid back down the hillside and raked them along Chaq'ta's shoulders and back. Ta'riq scored three long stripes across each shoulder.

The wounds looked like an asátto attack. The feline predators of the grasslands were ferocious predators. He sliced through Chaq'ta's jerkin, the thorns catching in the dense, tightly woven fibers the Meq'qan made into their clothing. Ta'riq hadn't appreciated how tough the fibers were until he tried to saw through them. Sweat dripped down the side of his head and onto his neck, causing the amber necklace to stick uncomfortably to his skin.

Ta'riq flinched as a low moan escaped Chaq'ta's lips. He would rouse soon, and Ta'riq was running out of time. Abandoning the carving on Chaq'ta's arms, Ta'riq turned the thorns onto himself. He wedged a thorn in between each finger and made a fist, gripping the barbs as if they were claws. Gritting his teeth, he gouged them across his neck and chest, leaving himself drenched in blood and sweat.

Chaq'ta rolled his head slowly as his groans grew louder. Ta'riq glanced over at the man and tossed the thorns aside. Grasping his spear, he raced away from Chaq'ta, then threw himself onto the ground.

Chaq'ta's eyes fluttered open, and the warrior wobbled to a sitting position. As he looked around, Ta'riq crawled towards him.

"Chaq'ta, help me!" Ta'riq cried out, his voice shaking.

Chaq'ta scrambled to his feet, staggered a few steps before using his spear to steady his progress as he lurched towards Ta'riq.

"What happened?" Chaq'ta gasped, using both hands to hold his body upright along his spear.

Ta'riq continued to slither towards his companion, the pain from his exertions masking the deception in his voice.

"The asátto, is it gone?" Ta'riq gasped, looking around with wild eyes.

Chaq'ta squinted, confused. "Asátto? What asátto? What happened?"

Ta'riq pulled himself to his knees, making a great show of inspecting his wounds and panting. He raised haunted eyes to Chaq'ta and pointed to the warrior's chest.

"The great feline charged out of the tall grass and knocked me over before turning on you. I saw you strike its chest. The beast must have decided on easier prey," Ta'riq said. He prostrated himself at Chaq'ta's feet, his arms outstretched. "I am indebted to you for saving my life, my cousin."

Chaq'ta sputtered, blinking his eyes as he touched the ring of protective stones around his neck.

"I don't remember the asátto," Chaq'ta said, scratching his head. "I fought it off?"

Ta'riq lifted his head and nodded. "You fought with the speed of a serpent, the fierceness of an urluk."

Chaq'ta moved his hand from his head to the back of his neck. He then stretched and rotated his injured shoulders. Ta'riq got to his feet as Chaq'ta paced back and forth. Ta'riq assumed the warrior wouldn't deny the proclamation of his heroism. Ta'riq appeared to win that gamble, at least for now. Chaq'ta staggered to Ta'riq and put his arm around the other man's shoulders so that they could support one another.

"The stones of our priestesses appear to have succeeded

in keeping us alive. Come, let's return to camp and decide what our next move should be," Chaq'ta said, his eyes still glazed.

Chaq'ta limped slowly down the hill with Ta'riq's help. Together, the Meq'qan cousins made their way back to the encampment and their brethren. Shouts and cries for help reached their ears when the patrol spotted them. Ta'riq shared the story of the asátto attack with the men who swarmed around them, clamoring for news.

Ta'riq made sure that Chaq'ta's role was apparent, for Ta'riq knew that Chaq'ta would never rescind or challenge a story in which he featured so prominently as the hero. Despite Chaq'ta's confused look and inability to keep his facts straight, the Meq'qan warriors never doubted their leader's ability to fend off the dreaded grassland felines. Ta'riq knew that by the next day, the story would grow, crediting Chaq'ta with slaying five asáttos before succumbing to his wounds.

"But what of Tóran?"

"Yes, where is he?"

Ta'riq's pulse raced. He felt his heart pounding in his chest as he took a breath and stared out at the sea of pale-yellow eyes that looked to him for answers.

"Tóran left early this morning to scout ahead," Ta'riq said, the bitter taste filling his mouth as the lie left his lips. He hated deceiving his brethren, but he knew that this was the only way he could save them. "He wants us to stay here until he returns. No fires, but we can rest this day and night to recover our strength. Tomorrow we will march into the Tádim Pass and meet the Garanth on the outskirts of Táksabai. Tóran will follow us and should catch up shortly after we make camp tomorrow."

Ta'riq's announcement was met with silence and confused stares, most notably from Chaq'ta. However, the burly warrior shrugged his shoulders and made his way to the healer to clean his wounds. Ta'riq released the breath he was holding. Relief washed over him at Chaq'ta's acceptance of the story, even though he knew it would be short-lived.

Ta'riq heard the clicking above his head and opened his eyes. A tiny white shape fluttered in the air around him, bobbing and weaving as it tried to stay aloft with its load. Slowly, he reached out his arm to let the leathery diclurue land on his palm. He angled his hand carefully to avoid the poisonous stinger on the end of the creature's narrow tail, his eyes darting around the campsite to see whether anyone else had noticed his pre-dawn visitor.

To the west, the last pale hues of lavender fled the skies as Hamra retired beneath the sea, and Lord Shamar's golden glory outlined the twin peaks of Zóhir and Zóhari to the east. A soft breeze caused Ta'riq to shiver, startling the diclurue clinging to his hand.

The tiny creature wrapped its long tail around the Meq'qan's thumb, resting its triangular head between the man's third and fourth fingers. Ta'riq eased himself out of his blanket and crept away from the camp. He slunk away from the valley's edge and into the forest, where thick evergreen trees would keep him hidden from spying eyes.

Ta'riq pulled a glowstone from the pocket of his woven jerkin and charged it with his free hand. The small stone cast a feeble light after just a few moments, and Ta'riq paused again. The amber beads around his neck gleamed, so he tucked them back beneath his jerkin, dimming their brilliance. Ta'riq listened for any signs of pursuit before continuing further into the forest.

Chaq'ta was suspicious of his story about the asátto, particularly after Tóran hadn't returned last night, as Ta'riq promised. The Meq'qan warrior's instincts were not wrong, but Ta'riq was not going to admit to any falsehoods if he didn't have to. He hadn't slept well since he'd deceived his kinsman, and he knew that his eyes would eventually betray him.

Not only had he lied to Chaq'ta, but the scouts had reported seeing Tóran carried into the main encampment of the Garanth army by one of the bulls. Nobody knew what happened to the rest of the advance patrol, but the fact that Tóran was a prisoner did not bode well for the young Askári legionnaire.

Ta'riq held up his glowstone and scanned the body of the diclurue resting in his hand. The beast had exhausted itself, carrying the inch-long scroll of parchment attached to the underside of its narrow form. Ta'riq carefully untied the leather string and unrolled the message, careful of the diclurue's delicate membrane wings.

This note was the reply to his panicked message to Zale'en, the Meq'qan's high priestess the day before. She put Tóran in charge of their remaining warriors, much to Chaq'ta's frustration, and with Tóran gone, Ta'riq was at a loss. He needed guidance to keep the overzealous warrior restrained and from charging into the Garanth camp on a suicide mission with their remaining warriors.

Gently, Ta'riq lifted the diclurue off the message and read the short note written in Priestess Zale'en's sprawling script. *YOU MUST SAVE THE ASKÁRI.* Guilt gnawed at his innards. Tóran had left to pursue his brother Cédron with the expectation that Chaq'ta would bring warriors mounted upon their armored wakazan behind him to engage the Garanth patrol.

Although the Askári legionnaire had trusted Chaq'ta to follow his orders, Ta'riq had been skeptical. While the Meq'qan warrior was keen to lead his men into battle, following a usurper to his position had not been a priority. Now that their leader was a captive, Zale'en put her faith in him to set things right.

Ta'riq sighed, shaking his head. He had no idea how to

get into that camp unseen, let alone rescue a guarded prisoner of the Garanth. The entire valley was crawling with Garanth bulls bristling with weapons and hordes of Arkmuln. He shuddered.

Their scouts warned him that many of the Arkmuln had been members of his tribe. Ta'riq had no desire to come face to face with friends or family whose bodies now fought in a war with no other purpose than to destroy life. Ta'riq gently laid the diclurue down on the ground and turned to go back to camp. Off to his left, he heard a stick crack. Ta'riq froze.

"Sneaking off now, are you?" Chaq'ta sneered, not attempting to hide his approach. "Give me the message." The warrior held out his hand, his face hard and uncompromising.

Ta'riq swallowed. He held out the scroll, his mind racing through reasons he could give for communicating with the priestess behind the warrior's back, but none of them were very credible. He was very much on his own in this.

Chaq'ta scanned the short note. "Who sent this?" he asked.

Ta'riq's eyes dropped to the ground. He mumbled something unintelligible, hoping Chaq'ta would let it go. The warrior lunged the last two steps and grabbed Ta'riq by the throat, forcing the amber beads of his necklace to bite painfully into the soft flesh of his neck.

"I asked you who sent this," Chaq'ta snarled.

Ta'riq struggled against the warrior's iron grip. Chaq'ta squeezed tighter, lifting Ta'riq into the air. Ta'riq felt his toes leave the ground and his blood pounding behind his eyes. Tiny spots of light danced before him as the world began to dim. Convinced his life would be over in moments, he sent a feeble prayer for forgiveness to the deitics and quit struggling.

Roaring his frustration, Chaq'ta slammed Ta'riq to the ground. "Answer me, you wingless fároc!" Chaq'ta's fury stormed across his knitted brow, his complexion deepening to a dark crimson.

Ta'riq pulled himself to all fours, gulping in deep breaths as light and pain exploded into his air-starved brain. He couldn't betray Priestess Zale'en to Chaq'ta; he knew the warrior would respond with anger and spite, rashly risking his warriors and their mounts for whatever tidbit of glory he could muster. Instead, the Meq'qan coughed and choked, buying himself time to think.

Chaq'ta would have none of it. He grasped a fist full of Ta'riq's jerkin and pulled the man to his feet. "If you won't tell me, then perhaps you will admit your treachery to the rest of the men." The warrior leered, pulling Ta'riq close enough to see the madness flicker in Chaq'ta's eyes. "Either way, the men will judge you. Then we will have to decide what to do with you."

Ta'riq's stomach clenched. He knew that the punishment for his supposed betrayal would be torturous. He glanced at Chaq'ta, and his heart sank. The man was grinning. This was the moment Chaq'ta had been waiting for, his opportunity to discredit the foreigners and seize control of their warriors.

Tóran was no longer in charge, and he had proof of Ta'riq's betrayal. Chaq'ta would be able to sway even the most level-headed of the warriors to his cause. He would force them to engage the Garanth. Ta'riq squeezed his eyes tightly against the horrific images that sprang unbidden into his mind, and he stumbled over a rock. As he lurched forward, twisting his ankle, he nudged his captor, throwing Chaq'ta off balance. Ta'riq didn't hesitate.

Twisting his body to the left, Ta'riq rolled down and out of Chaq'ta's grasp. The warrior fell forward, forgetting to brace himself in his efforts to maintain his grip on his quarry. Chaq'ta hit the ground with a thud while Ta'riq sprang to his feet and raced back to camp. He didn't know what he would do or say to his brethren, but he fervently hoped that some would see the light of insanity burning in Chaq'ta and argue for caution.

Lord Shamar's golden hues had just touched the tips of the trees encircling their makeshift camp, stirring the wakazan to greet the new day with their deep, throaty bellows resonating throughout the area. The men were waking; some were already strapping into their dense, rush grass and leather armor while others still stretched and faced east to greet the daytime deity with their arms raised.

They lit no fires due to their proximity to the Garanth army and their lurking patrols, so breakfast was a cold affair of dried fruit and meat for everyone. Men sat hunkered down on their packs in small groups eating and murmuring, while others tended the wakazan. Ta'riq scanned the entire scene in a flash as he tore through the forest and hurdled over the first few startled Meq'qan warriors just beginning their day.

Chaq'ta crashed through the trees behind him. "Grab him!" he shouted. "Ta'riq has betrayed us!"

Despite his early momentum, the fleeing man had no chance against the surging tide of bodies raised to thwart his escape. Hands grabbed every piece of clothing, every appendage. They held him fast as Chaq'ta strutted through the crowd, his head high and a cruel twist on his lips.

"You see, my brothers," the warrior walked between the line of Meq'qan spreading open before him, leaving Ta'riq and his captors at the end of the aisle. "Caf'iq Mak'ki was right – the foreigners have been conspiring against us. See for yourself!"

Chaq'ta pulled out the roll of parchment from Zale'en for all to see. "I found him sneaking off this morning to accept this message. He refuses to admit who it comes from, so we must assume the worst."

Angry mutterings from all around filled Ta'riq's ears. The men holding him gripped his arms and clothing with fierce determination. Ta'riq tested their strength as Chaq'ta swaggered forward the last few steps to stand directly in front of him. The warrior glared at him then turned to face the gathered Meq'qan warriors.

"No longer will we hide, skirting the enemy and spying on them like frightened fárocs! We will march on the Garanth. This day, they will feel our wrath, and we will have our vengeance!" Chaq'ta raised his arms in triumph, rousing the surrounding Meq'qan warriors into joining his battle cry.

Ta'riq began to sweat. He was going to lose all of them to Chaq'ta's ravings.

"But first," Chaq'ta turned to face his prisoner. "First, we deal with this traitor."

Chapter 11: Uneasy Allies

A cry went up near the rear of the encampment as shadows larger than the wakazan raced across the ground. The Meq'qan ducked as the Wing of gigantic golden läeniers swooped down from above, Lord Shamar's rays at their backs silhouetting the Shäeli raptors against the morning brightness.

The fierce war birds shrieked their challenge as they circled the Meq'qan and their wakazan. The bovines protested loudly, stomping their feet and tossing their long horns skyward while bellowing their counter-challenge. The Meq'qan held their ground; weapons were drawn as they watched the skies.

One of the beasts began spiraling down. Ta'riq's heart pounded in his chest as he strained to identify the läenier's rider. The raptor found a spot to land and tore through the ground with his long talons. The rider wore the brushed gold leather armor of the läenier Wing, but the man who jumped off and walked towards the two Meq'qan leaders wore the woven green chest plate of the Sumäeri warriors.

The man wore his silver hair cut uncharacteristically short. Foliage tattoos wound around his porcelain skin, skirting his face; Ta'riq recognized the plum-colored irises and chiseled features of the Sumäeri rebel Trilläen Villinäes. Ta'riq exhaled and sank back against his captors with a grin on his face.

Chaq'ta cursed under his breath. "Laylur's beast, what does *he* want?"

Trilläen Villinäes, the fugitive former captain of the Council Guard, surveyed the scene laid out before him with mounting frustration. In less than a sennight, he'd lost his love, been branded a traitor, and recruited the other units of Sumäeri warriors to his cause. Most were reluctant to defy their Covenant. It was only because Räesha's sisters accompanied him to corroborate his story that the läenier Wings pledged their support out of respect for their fallen comrade.

Trilläen clamped down on the wave of guilt and loss that threatened to choke him from within whenever he thought of Räesha. He'd shorn his long silver braid as much for his grief as for losing his title and rank. Trilläen ran trembling fingers through his jagged bangs, pulling them out of his eyes while he blinked back the emotions that would not lie still. The captain took another deep breath, nodded to his läenier rider, and walked towards the Meq'qan gathered in the clearing at the edge of the trees.

Wisps of mist still swirled gently in the breeze, below where the Meq'qan had set up camp. Trilläen shivered from more than the chill. Even if the Askári could somehow turn back the Garanth and Arkmuln, their troubles would just be starting. With no food in the fields to feed their animals and people, starvation and illness would finish what the savages from the north began. He allowed only a twinge of sadness for the Askári before facing the inevitable. Before this was over, the Askári could very well face the near extinction that the Meq'qan already suffered. It was a sacrifice he was willing to make.

"Well met," Trilläen said, fixing a smile on his weathered face as he approached the Meq'qan leaders. As he held out his palm in the traditional greeting, he noted Ta'riq's hands tied behind his back and Chaq'ta's menacing posture. "What's going on here? Where is Tóran? I thought he was leading your warriors?"

Ta'riq's head hung as Chaq'ta barked out a laugh.

"Ta'riq has betrayed us, and that upstart got himself captured by the Garanth," Chaq'ta jutted out his chin. "I'm taking charge of the Meq'qan now."

Trilläen's pulse quickened. He scanned the faces of the Meq'qan warriors and read smugness on some, ranging to indecision on others. Taking a breath, Trilläen raised his hand over his head and swung it down, signaling the Wings of läenier riders to land. Two pairs flew off to the southwest to reconnoiter the situation over Táksabai, and two others stayed aloft as a patrol. The rest circled down, landing in the clearing just beyond the forest. Trilläen smiled internally as Chaq'ta's visage darkened into a scowl watching the läenier Wings land.

"I see," Trilläen said, nodding to Chaq'ta and stepping closer. "Please update me on your efforts to recover Tóran."

Ta'riq's head jerked up, sudden optimism animating his dark features. "Yes, we must go after him. If he becomes

Arkmuln, the Garanth will know our plans."

Chaq'ta backhanded Ta'riq across the mouth, nearly knocking him out of his captor's grasp. "Shut up, traitor," he snarled. "I decide what we do next, not you, and not them." He gestured to the hundreds of läenier riders surrounding their camp.

Ta'riq straightened his shoulders, ignoring the blood dripping down his chin from the cut on his upper lip. He looked around at his fellow Meq'qan and took a deep breath.

"Chaq'ta is mistaken," he began in a wavering voice. "Tóran was chosen to lead our force because of his success against the Hazzara in the marshes. His tactics saved the Zig'orman tribes, where Chaq'ta would have gotten us all slaughtered."

Ta'riq's voice grew bolder. "Although I am from a different tribe, remember that my people are already dead or Arkmuln. High Priestess Zale'en herself sent me a message this day to save Tóran. I am loyal to Lady Muralia and her priestess. If we are to have any hope of salvaging our world, we must work together. If we can't rescue Tóran, then we must kill him before the demon takes over his mind and exposes us all."

Trilläen caught Ta'riq's eye and nodded imperceptibly. All around, Meq'qan warriors were muttering amongst themselves, choosing sides and evaluating their loyalties. Chaq'ta pulled out the tiny scroll from his jerkin and held it up for all to see.

"The traitor says this is from Zale'en," Chaq'ta scoffed, his eyes flashing. "But he can't prove it was from her. It could be from anyone. He could be working with the Garanth for all we know."

Trilläen groaned inwardly. He recognized the grizzled warrior's behavior, the frustration of being passed over for a younger leader who was less worthy in his eyes. The same blind jealousy led to Bräentu's madness and his lethal attack on Räesha before his demise. Chaq'ta was spiraling down the same dark path. Even if he could prove Ta'riq's innocence and loyalty, Trilläen didn't think the spurned warrior could accept it.

Turning to his Wings of läeniers, Trilläen craned his neck to find the one Sumäeri whose gift might sort this all out. After the Council Guard destroyed the Angäersol family's home and killed their parents, the Näenji Council hunted the remaining Angäersol girls. Before Bräentu killed her, Räesha had asked her Wing to protect her remaining three sisters, although it meant defying their leaders and risking their lives.

The Wings welcomed the renowned Angäersol sisters to their ranks. Läerei's talent lay in extracting toxins from plants. She also had a penchant for dying her hair in different colors. She provided a range of tips for her Wings' weapons ranging in toxicity from immobilizing to lethal. The twins, Läenshi and Säeshi, had complimentary gifts. Säeshi, the slender, willowy twin, could detect and identify Árk'äezhi energy. Her powerfully built sister, Läenshi, could enhance it. It was Säeshi he needed now.

Whistling to his riding partner, Trilläen beckoned the man over. "Please ask your beast to find Säeshi Angäersol."

The man nodded and charged over to his golden raptor, silver braid swinging as he ran. Trilläen marveled yet again at how the riders and their beasts communicated. It wasn't through words, Läerei once tried to explain to him, but through feelings and images, the läeniers and their riders connected. It wasn't two breaths before a screech echoed across the clearing.

A young woman sprinted towards him with the grace and power of an asátto. The foliage and flower tattoos covering her body flexed as she ran. Her green Sumäeri armor glittered emerald as she raced between the golden raptors and their beige-plated riders.

"You need—" She began, then suddenly stiffened. Her thin shoulders hunched to her ears, and she ducked as if warding off a blow. Crying out, she dropped to her knees.

Everyone watching the exchange flinched and scoured the skies and their surroundings, expecting some sort of attack. An Autunmntide breeze blew a few leaves from the trees, but otherwise, the day was silent. Lord Shamar crested the trees and began stripping the crispness from the morning air.

Trilläen grabbed Säeshi by the shoulders and pulled her to her feet, shaking her slightly. "What is it? What do you sense?" he urged.

Haunted eyes stared up at him. Säeshi opened her mouth to speak, but nothing came out. She began to tremble.

Chaq'ta snorted and slapped one of the men holding Ta'riq in the chest. "More Shäeli tricks to distract us. Come, let's deal with the traitor."

Chaq'ta turned and started to walk away, Ta'riq and his captors following when the woman cried out. They stopped and turned to see what had caused her distress. Säeshi stood nearly a foot taller, with broad shoulders and a muscular chest. Her eyes turned a deep, sparkling blue. Trilläen jumped back from her as if she burned his skin.

"What is this devilry?" Chaq'ta shouted, stepping back and placing Ta'riq between himself and the morphing Sumäeri.

Säeshi slumped forward, her body shrinking back to normal. Trilläen held Säeshi's shoulders and focused on her eyes, which faded to her usual aquamarine. Trilläen cleared his throat and propelled her towards Chaq'ta and the waiting Meq'qan.

"This is Säeshi Angäersol, one of Räesha's younger sisters," Trilläen said, introducing Säeshi.

"So, what," Chaq'ta growled. His eyes narrowed, and he puffed out his chest.

Trilläen closed his eyes and took a slow breath. "So, her talent is the detection and identification of Árk'äezhi. We have just seen a demonstration."

Chaq'ta shifted his stance. His eyes roamed over Säeshi. "What was that she just became?"

Trilläen looked down at the shivering Sumäeri and squeezed her arm. "What do you sense? Who or what was that?"

Säeshi shuddered. "I don't know. It's an Árk'äezhi energy I've never felt before, and yet it seems strangely familiar. It's almost as if…No, that's not possible." She shook her head and clamped her mouth shut.

"What? What's not possible?"

"It's a big feeling, like what I felt in Auräevya's presence or the temple, but at the same time, it feels different, like it's been warped or tainted." She looked at Trilläen with confused eyes. "I can't explain it. But I can tell you that he's powerful. I wouldn't want to go up against him. I-I think he may be the demon in the Garanth camp, but how can that be?"

Säeshi shook her head, wincing. "He's close but not an immediate threat. I can only feel him when his Árk'äezhi is active – Oh!" She slapped her hand over her mouth, her eyes white.

The hairs on Trilläen's arms raised as he thought about what was happening in the Garanth encampment. Arkmuln! The demon used his power to warp the Árk'äezhi of his prisoners, and Tóran was one of them!

"We're out of time," he said flatly. "We need to get Tóran out of there now."

Chaq'ta's face paled, but he thrust his chest out and stepped forward. "I don't care who she is or what kind of witchery you're using. We will deal with the traitor our way, then make our move against the Garanth."

Trilläen stepped in front of the men and held out his hand for the scroll. "Give her the scroll. She can show you who sent it. Then we can decide what to do with Ta'riq."

Chaq'ta glowered at the Shäeli. The Meq'qan murmured to themselves, and Trilläen saw several heads nodding at his suggestion. The tension in his chest relaxed. Slowly, Chaq'ta reached inside his jerkin, pulled out the rolled parchment, and untied it. He handed it to Trilläen with pursed lips.

"Alright, let's see who the traitor has been communicating with," he sneered and crossed his arms over his chest.

Trilläen handed the scroll to Säeshi, whose appearance shifted immediately. Her posture stooped, and her skin sagged. Her cheeks were hollow with age when she looked up, but her eyes were sharp and yellow.

"Foolish man, you will doom us all with your pride!" Säeshi chastised Chaq'ta with Zale'en's voice. "Save the Askári lad and get our people out of there before it's too late."

Säeshi dropped the scroll into the dried grass and sank to her knees. Trilläen waved to his rider for assistance.

"No, let me," Chaq'ta said with a sour twist to his mouth. "Zale'en is not only my priestess; she is my mother. Defying her has never worked out well for me."

Chaq'ta reached out to lift the exhausted girl to her feet. Trilläen noted his drawn features and shadowed eyes. Chaq'ta nodded at the men to release Ta'riq. One of the guards whispered something to Ta'riq, causing him to stiffen. Ta'riq's eyes shifted to Trilläen, and his mouth drew down at the corners.

"Come," Trilläen turned and walked towards the Wing of läeniers waiting in the clearing. "We must discuss our tactics and move out before it's too late. That demon is converting Arkmuln as we delay here."

Chaq'ta offered Säeshi his arm and steadied her as Trilläen waved for them to precede him. Ta'riq followed closely behind Chaq'ta, rubbing his chafed wrists to get the blood circulating back into his hands. Trilläen whistled a complicated tune and waved his hand once in the air. The majestic beasts and their riders parted for him, making a semi-circle in their midst.

Two female riders, one with a magenta streak in her silver hair and the other well-muscled and bristling with weapons, detached themselves from the others, taking Säeshi from Chaq'ta's arms and assessing their sister while Trilläen gathered his thoughts. Läerei and Läenshi Angäersol would skin him alive if they found anything amiss with Säeshi.

"Do you know which tent Tóran is in?" Trilläen asked, turning to face the two Meq'qan.

Chaq'ta scuffed the dirt with his feet; his downcast eyes focused on the ground. Ta'riq stepped forward in front of him.

"He was put into one of the tents along the outer rim yesterday afternoon. However, our scouts saw him being taken into the large black tent in the center of the encampment just a few moments ago." Ta'riq scrubbed his face with both hands. "He doesn't have much time."

"Right."

Trilläen closed his eyes and sighed. He knew that they expected him to have the plan, to lead them in whatever endeavor he chose. They had put their lives in his hands. Trilläen turned to face Säeshi, who had recovered from her ordeal, and stood between her sisters, waiting for his command.

"Are you willing to try again?" he asked her. "Can you see what else may be out there?"

Läenshi's muscles flexed, and Läerei took a half-step in front of her sister. Both women opened their mouths to protest, but Säeshi held up her hand and stepped towards Trilläen.

"I will do what I can," she said, nodding.

Säeshi reached out to each of her sisters, placing one hand on each of their shoulders for support, and closed her eyes. Trilläen held his breath. Perhaps if there was just the one demon in the Garanth encampment, they could get around him and rescue Tóran. If there were more, they would have trouble. All eyes were on the young woman whose willowy body swayed as she reached out with her gift to detect any other sources of Árk'äezhi in the area. Her head turned one way, then circled the other direction, but her eyes remained shut, relying solely on her inner vision to guide her.

Barely daring to breathe, Trilläen narrowed his eyes as he watched Säeshi closely for any changes in her movements. She stiffened, and Trilläen felt a jolt of panic burn through his body.

"What is it?" he pounced on the change. "What do you sense?"

Läerei held up a warning hand, giving Säeshi a moment to focus on the energy and identify it. All eyes waited for the Sumäeri to morph into the source of Árk'äezhi, but her body remained neutral. She took a couple of deep breaths and opened her eyes.

"There is an underlying source of energy," she said, her brows knitting as she rubbed her temples. "But I can't identify it specifically. I can tell that it is protective, but not who or where it is coming from."

Säeshi walked to the rocks that jutted out over the valley below them. Waving Trilläen to join her, she stared out toward the city.

"It seems to be emanating from the Mages Guild or at least from that general direction," she said as her silver hair blew across her face in the breeze. "It doesn't feel like an individual, but more like a protective barrier or essence and—" She inhaled sharply, grabbing Trilläen's forearm. "I feel it through the Lluric Field! The mages must have figured out a way to tap into it!"

Trilläen snorted. The guild's mages hadn't performed much magic for centuries, not since the War of Betrayal. Whatever Säeshi was sensing was ancient and dormant. A quiet argument erupted behind him. He turned and found Läenshi and Läerei standing just behind him, eavesdropping. The two were whispering and gesturing sharply. Läerei's features were rigid, her fingers twisted in her pink-streaked hair, while Läenshi's body was taut and ready to spring.

"I won't let you," Läerei stated flatly, crossing her arms over her chest.

Läenshi giggled and rolled her muscular shoulders. "You can't stop me."

The young woman turned and raced away to her läenier, her silver braid swinging across her back as she ran. Läerei started to sprint after her, but Trilläen grasped her arm.

"What is it? Where is she going?" he asked, searching Läerei's face for a hint of her source for concern.

Läerei snatched her arm away with a snarl. "She thinks she can activate and enhance the protective Árk'äezhi surrounding the Mages Guild. What she can't do is protect herself from the Garanth and that demon if she fails. Now let me go!"

"Wait!" Trilläen reached for her again, the germ of an idea sprouting in his mind. "Let her Wing go with her as an escort. They can protect her while she works her gift. If she is successful, it will cause a diversion for us. If not, they will have sufficient numbers to engage the Garanth from the west and keep their attention from the rest of us."

Läerei's deep sapphire eyes darkened. "And just what will the rest of us be doing that is worth risking my sister's life?"

Trilläen thought rapidly. As far as he could tell, the warriors from the north had only just set up their encampment and corralled their Arkmuln. Trilläen summoned his rider, Chaq'ta, and Ta'riq. The men stepped up and stood next to Säeshi and Läerei, watching the former captain.

"The Garanth have not yet begun their main attack on the city," Trilläen began, catching each of their eyes in turn. "They are digging in for a siege of the city that could last weeks. We don't have that kind of time. We need to create diversions that will disorganize and confuse them while a small group attempts to rescue Tóran. Any suggestions?"

"A direct attack would be foolish," Ta'riq began.

"*Fároc!*" muttered Chaq'ta.

Trillian saw Ta'riq's face reddened at the insult, his eyes cast down. Ta'riq scuffed at a stone buried in the dirt with his foot. He lifted his eyes to Trilläen then to Chaq'ta.

"You would have all your warriors sacrifice themselves for your pride?" He asked.

Chaq'ta's eyes flashed. "No, for *their* pride!"

Trilläen held up his hand to forestall any further argument between the two Meq'qan. He turned to the Angäersol sisters.

"Säeshi, what do you sense from the Arkmuln? Can you tell if they retain their own identities, or are they gone?"

Säeshi closed her eyes, slowing her breath as she accessed her gift. All eyes watched her slender form. Säeshi's brows creased. Beads of sweat formed along her upper lip. Trilläen waited, the knot in his stomach growing as precious time slipped away.

Most of the Arkmuln now standing in the valley were Meq'qan. Trilläen switched his attention to Ta'riq. His face was ashen, but his expression was stern. Trilläen caught Säeshi's twitch out of the corner of his eyes. He turned his attention back to her and found himself staring into her aqua eyes.

"I cannot sense the people," she said, her voice soft. "Not individual energies anyway. I feel a low-level thrum among them, but it's foreign and," she glanced up at Ta'riq. " It is separate somehow from the Arkmuln themselves."

Ta'riq's head swiveled from Trilläen to Säeshi and back. "Wait, no!" Comprehension dawned on his face as he grasped the line of the Shäeli's conversation. "Those are my people down there; you can't just destroy them."

Trilläen frowned. He paced around the clearing for a moment, both hands pulling at his ragged silver hair to massage the dull ache that throbbed at his temples. He shivered. Lord Shamar's rays were taking longer to warm the air, and the light leather armor of his Suntide uniform was no longer sufficient.

Trilläen noticed that the trees in the nearby forest began changing color as Autumntide advanced. Only three more lunar cycles of the Moon Daughters, and they would be in Dormantide's frigid grasp. It would be impossible to defend the peoples of Muralia from the demon-created hordes who felt no discomfort in the cold, barren season.

Trilläen sighed and trudged back over to the small group. Ta'riq's stance remained taut as if he were anticipating a physical blow. Chaq'ta smirked and crossed his arms over his chest. Trilläen understood the tribesmans' positions, but that didn't make his decision any easier.

Läerei's hands rewove the magenta stripe into her silver braid. Her eyes kept shifting to Läenshi, who was preparing to depart. Trilläen knew that if anything happened to Säeshi's twin, Läerei would hold him accountable. He swallowed the lump in his throat. Glancing at Säeshi, Trilläen saw her eyes soften as she shook her head slightly.

Trilläen nodded and turned to Läerei. "What do we have that could immobilize the Arkmuln? Do any of your toxins operate that way?"

Ta'riq clenched his jaw and closed his eyes but remained silent. Chaq'ta snorted. Läerei ignored them and pulled her pouch around from her back. Rummaging through it, she held up a vial of something inky black. Gingerly, she placed it in Trilläen's hands.

"Black-seed," she said softly. "Normally, it's used to remove an infection, reduce swelling, and purify the body." Läerei glanced in Läenshi's direction before turning her attention back to Trilläen and the waiting Meq'qan. "With my sister's help, we can enhance its properties to cleanse the Arkmuln of their demon infestations."

"Will it destroy them?" Ta'riq asked, a spark of hope in his eyes.

"Pfft, of course, it will," Chaq'ta snorted. "That's what these Shäeli demons do. We're just trading one set for the other." He jutted his chin out and glared, daring Läerei to contradict his claim.

Läerei raised her eyebrows and stared for a moment at Chaq'ta before turning back to Trilläen. She shrugged her shoulders.

"Perhaps the Meq'qan is right," she said, glancing briefly at Chaq'ta with a mixture of pity and contempt. "I honestly don't know exactly how it will affect the Arkmuln. We know black-seed is flammable, so my suggestion is to have the first wave of läeniers throw bags of it over the corralled Arkmuln and a second wave shoot the bags with flaming arrows."

Ta'riq gasped and jerked his head towards the plains below, where hundreds from his tribe stood like cattle. "What if they die when the demons leave their bodies?"

"Then they keel over and litter the area with their corpses," Chaq'ta growled. "I'm more worried about what happens if they survive. What do we do with them? How do we explain what happened and expect them not to despise their bodies for the defilement they've suffered?"

Säeshi surveyed the smoldering wasteland that was once lush fields and looked at Läerei with huge eyes. "How could we feed them?"

Trilläen rubbed his temples harder. He couldn't worry about the fate of the Arkmuln should Läerei's potion restore them. His job right now was to disable the Arkmuln and distract the Garanth so that he and his small band could rescue Tóran. The rest, he would have to let shake out as it would.

"Do it," he nodded to Läerei. "Ask Läenshi to enhance the black-seed before she heads off to the Mages Guild. Gather your Wing and report to me when you're ready to go. Säeshi, you stay with me."

Läerei nodded, then turned and sprinted towards her

waiting beast.

"Chaq'ta, it is time for you to engage your enemies," Trilläen tensed, expecting the Meq'qan warrior to challenge his statement, but Chaq'ta only grinned and pounded his chest once with his right hand.

"We will crash through them with the strength of a surging flood. Our armored wakazan will crush Garanth skulls under their heavy claws!" Chaq'ta turned and let out a fierce battle cry, echoed by his tribesmen as they gathered their weapons and mounted their enormous, horned bovines.

Ta'riq turned to Trilläen and grasped him by the arm. "Have you gone mad? You've sent them to their deaths!"

Trilläen grasped Ta'riq's shoulders. "No, I am giving them their pride. As much as I hate to admit it, Chaq'ta has a valid point. Your people must prove to themselves that they can face this threat and overcome it. If they hide under stumps like terrified fárocs, they have lost more than just their self-respect. Remember, they are not alone."

Trilläen whistled another complicated series of notes. Within seconds, his rider was at his side, awaiting orders.

"Instruct the Wing leaders to fly south and engage the Garanth behind their lines. The Meq'qan will strike from the east, Läerei's Wing will release the Arkmuln from their bondage, and, with any luck, the Hármolin Legion will be mounting a defense from the gates of the city," he said. "Läenshi will then lead her Wing to the Mages Guild to attempt the release of the defensive magic that lies dormant beneath the city. If we can surround their forces and pin them against Táksabai's walls, they will be too busy defending themselves to notice our little group."

The rider gave a curt nod and took off. Trilläen knew that he could trust the Wingleaders to follow his directives. That left Säeshi and Ta'riq. While the rest of the Meq'qan warriors and läenier riders prepared their attack plans, Trilläen gathered his small group away from the bustle of activity.

"I have a plan," he solemnly glanced at each of them in turn. "I can't promise that it will work, but it's the best I've got."

Chapter 12: The Gróshan King

Sénna stood facing her father, who sat behind his enormous wooden desk with hands clenched as tightly as his jaw. Sénna hated this room and the fluttering, sick feeling she had when she was in it. She much preferred skulking along the beams of the ceiling above the study and its oppressive atmosphere. The collective grief she and her family shared over the loss of Myknét smothered her, making it hard to breathe.

The room's grand opulence displayed generations of thievery, spoils, and blood upon which her family had built its wealth and power. Trinkets and treasures from across the lands lined two walls of shelves, including books of Muralian history that Sénna often filched and returned without her father's knowledge. Myknét's blade, a testament to the family's wealth, lay on her father's desk, the semi-precious gems winking accusingly at her in the glowstone's light.

Portraits of Králl ancestors scowled down at her from the walls, silent witnesses to her trespassing. Marble statues and busts below them glared at her with stony disapproval, recriminating her for her role in her brother's death. Sénna gritted her teeth and stared back, challenging the censure she felt directed towards her. Myknét's death was her fault, but she'd been trying to help her family. Her knees felt weak, but she clenched her fists, refusing to show weakness.

A cushioned chair waited for her in front of the desk, but Sénna remained standing. She was never comfortable in a room emanating so much wealth and power. Yet this was the very image her father maintained to solidify his credibility among the slippery members of his guild. Syrán strove tirelessly to shift the focus of the family enterprise from illicit to respectable, but changing perceptions required more than merely changing a name.

Sénna was proud of her father's accomplishments in leading the Thieves Guild, now called Gróshan, towards a better and more honest future of information brokerage. It rankled that he insisted on maintaining certain vestiges of their past. With this perspective, he would never accept her as one of his agents, especially given recent tragic events. She would wait until the current crisis ended before trying to convince him to break with tradition and let go of his expectations for her. The Garanth attack might provide an opportunity for her to redeem herself in his eyes.

As much as Sénna loved and admired her father, she didn't trust him, and neither had Mage Kiél. Sénna's respect for the elderly mage had grown as he'd crafted their tale of rescue from the Garanth without mention of their encounter with Wezija or any hint of Cédron's quest. She didn't know if Mage Kiel had previously known of her father's distrust of the occult and magic or not, but she was grateful that he and Master Chezak had been circumspect about their encounter with Wezija. It wouldn't do to have her father angrier than he already was.

"Why do you seek to defy me at every turn?" Sénna's father demanded, throwing his arms in the air as he stood and stormed over to the large bay windows. He thrust the heavy brocade draperies aside and stared at the manicured gardens beyond. "Your foolishness has cost Myknét's life. If that wasn't bad enough, you still want me to trust you to join my organization as a spy? Do you have any idea how badly you've already compromised the Gróshan with your escapades?"

Sénna bit her tongue. Although she had excellent answers to her father's questions, she knew that they were primarily rhetorical. She avoided looking around the room, keeping her eyes focused on her father. She forced her cramped fingers to release the pleats of fabric she'd creased in her skirts and flattened her palms on her thighs. She took a deep breath and exhaled through her nose. Sénna had only been forced into her father's study on two prior occasions.

The first time was after her father learned she'd convinced the cook she was a delivery boy from the Merchants Guild and wheedled a plate of tarts to eat while "waiting for her parcel." The second visit came after Sénna's brother Múradit spotted her lurking in the common room of the Lótril's Cave. Sénna was sure her brother was more interested in keeping her out of his husan racing schemes than her safety. Syrán had banished Sénna to her room for a week after that incident.

Sénna's attention returned to her father's rigid form as his long, slender fingers splayed and clenched into fists at his sides. Even with his back to her, she could feel the grief and tension rolling off his narrow shoulders, striking her more forcefully than a slap. Lord Shamar's late afternoon beams glinted in the gray hairs that had cropped up around Syrán's temples in the few short Tides since he had taken his place as the leader of the Gróshan.

"Father, I'm not trying to defy you," Sénna sighed, "I'm trying to help. The watchtower fire—"

"Persénia!" Syrán raised a hand, stopping her from speaking.

Sénna cringed, her mouth snapping shut. She hated it when her father used her full name. It was an indication of the depth of his annoyance with her and was a precursor to a repeat of their all-too-frequent one-sided conversations where he spoke, and she was only allowed to listen.

Syrán stepped behind the desk and sat down with a force that made the legs of the chair groan. He gripped the intricately carved arms of the wooden chair and regarded his daughter with hollow eyes. His gaunt cheeks hung slack, giving his long nose and chin the impression of exaggerated sharpness.

Sénna's heart sank to realize it had been her actions that had brought her father such misery. If she hadn't snuck onto that ship, her brother might still be alive. She hung her head. The plush carpet beneath her feet had wear marks on it as if she was only the most recent penitent to succumb to a Gróshan King's wrath. Two strips of threadbare lining showed where the boots of the room's previous visitors had scuffed their feet and shifted their weight under the fierce gaze of the guild's master.

Syrán clenched his jaw, and Sénna could see the muscles tighten around his temples. "How can you expect me to let your behavior go unpunished? My whole organization knows of your disobedience and Myknét's...." He turned his grief-stricken face away.

Sénna saw a tear at the corner of his eye and felt the full weight of what she'd done.

"I would have lost you too had the caravan not rescued

you," Syrán continued, having gathered himself. "I've heard the whispers, the rumors. How can I lead the Gróshan when I can't even get my own daughter to behave?"

"But if you'd just listen," she pleaded, taking a step closer to the polished desk that stood like a wall between the two of them. "Those men in the watchtower, the Hazzara, they only killed Myknét because he got in their way. They are working with some mage that—"

Syrán slammed his hand on the desk, startling Sénna into silence. "For Our Lady's sake, don't blame this on Myknét! If you would only behave like the lady you are, Myknét wouldn't be dead, and we wouldn't be having this conversation!"

Sénna's cheeks burned. She took a steadying breath and tried unsuccessfully to control the shame and guilt that the memory of her brother caused. "I do not want to be a lady; I cannot be like Cybél, father. Let me serve you any other way."

"I don't have time for this now," Syrán sighed, hanging his weary head in his hands and rubbing his forehead. "The Garanth army is about to lay siege to our city, and I have no idea how I'm going to keep my remaining two children safe. I must decide what to do with our guests from the caravan and keep our citizens from panicking." He steepled his fingers and brought them to his lips as he thought. "I can't worry about you making impulsive decisions right now. You will go to your room and stay there until I straighten all this out." He looked out the window at the seabirds screeching as they swooped, seeking scraps around the marketplace below. "If you disobey me again, I'll marry you off to that mage just to relieve the aggravation."

Sénna's eyes flashed, and she clenched her fists into tight balls. "If having me under your roof is too much trouble, I can go. Myknét's death means more to me than you think, and I *will* have my vengeance whether you want me to or not!"

Syrán's nostrils flared. "Don't presume to—"

A quiet knock at the door interrupted the king's argument. Syrán took a deep breath and closed his eyes, his lips compressed into a thin, white line.

"Enter."

Sénna turned around to see a dark-haired young man duck into the room.

"Murádit!" she cried, relieved at the sight of her brother and potential ally.

Only one Tide her senior, Murádit stood nearly half a head taller, but his face remained smooth with only a smattering of dark hair above his upper lip. Dust covered his weathered trousers and boots, likely from the husan racing track, but he made no move to tidy himself as he approached.

Murádit reached out one arm to hold his sister. Raising his right arm, palm up, he greeted his father and king. "Our spies have informed me that the Harmólin Legion has finally mustered. They will begin mounting a defensive around the northern perimeter of the city to face the Garanth threat."

"What of the request I sent to the legion for assistance in rescuing the Varkáras Caravan?" Syrán asked.

Murádit made a face and shook his head. "My friends from the Laborer's Guild have volunteered us the use of the husan transport barges to rescue the caravan," he said, nodding at his father. "We'll be back before supper."

Syrán regarded his second son with shrewd eyes. "Given the lack of response by the Hármolin Legion, I suppose that is the only alternative. Salvage as many of the caravan's wagons as you can. You can hide them in the underground city where they should be safe for the time being."

Sénna inhaled. "You know how to get into the underground city?" She shot her brother an accusatory glance, then looked at her father. "Why can't I—?"

"No," her father said.

"It's too dangerous," Murádit said, squeezing her

shoulder. "Our family has suffered enough loss. I can't risk losing my favorite sister."

Sénna snorted. "I'm your only sister."

Murádit inhaled to retort and choked. "Indeed you are, and that makes you precious," he coughed. "Leave the underground city to me."

Sénna had always been fascinated with stories of the underground city but was strictly forbidden to seek entrance to it. The Králl children grew up with stories of how a millennium ago, the ground had shaken, causing huge waves to cover the city. The history buried there made her mouth water.

The tsunami nearly destroyed Táksabai, and instead of clearing the debris, the surviving residents decided to build a new city on top of the old one. It took generations to rebuild it into the thriving metropolis it was now. Sénna's research uncovered traces of old streets and buildings that the current city covered, proving that it was much more extensive than she'd ever believed.

There were maps and accounts written in the books she'd taken from her father's study. Sénna's favorite stories were those of the Guardians created centuries ago by the ancient Askári mariners to protect their city when the men were at sea. How she wished those stories were true, and they could call upon the ancient guardians to protect their city against the advancing Garanth army.

"Father," Sénna pleaded, stepping forward and laying her hands on the desk. "Please let me accompany them. I promise to stay out of trouble and—"

"That's enough!" Syrán slammed his fists on the table, ending her plea. "You will go to your room now and stay there." He turned to his son, his hands on his hips. "You will take our guests into the underground city, then return home immediately. Have the Caravan Master show your friends where their wagons are. Your friends can assist with securing them. I want you to remain in the city."

Murádit nodded. "It will be done. I will report to you upon my return." With one last squeeze of his sister's shoulder, the young man turned on his heel and marched out of the room.

Sénna watched her brother go, then turned to face her father. "Let me help," she pleaded, leaning forward towards her father. "Please, give me a task…anything but sitting in my room waiting for something to happen."

Sénna stepped to the edge of the desk and reached for her father's hands. Her throat tightened as she noted the downward curve of his mouth. It had been such a long time since she'd seen him smile. "I must live my own life, father. I must feel the wind in my hair and the blood coursing through my veins. Do not force me into a role like Grandmother Am'aranth's; I would not survive it."

Syrán tensed at the mention of his Meq'qan mother. He released her hands as if she'd burned him. "You know nothing about that," he snapped, glaring at his daughter with his yellow eyes.

"I know enough."

Syrán held his head in his hands, scrubbing at the scalp around his temples. He could still hear Sénna's footsteps stomping behind her brother. She was getting harder to control. If he didn't do something drastic soon, she'd end up like – No, he wouldn't compare Sénna to *her*. He sighed, twisting the heavy gold ring on his forefinger.

"She comes by that stubbornness naturally, you know," a woman's voice called from the side door.

Syrán flinched and looked up as his mother approached, the thump of her silver staff muffled on the carpet. Nek'ka, Am'aranth's silver raven, perched atop the round silver knob with wings half-outstretched for balance.

"If that's meant to make me feel better, it doesn't," Syrán twisted his lips up on one side as he rose to greet his mother. He kissed her proffered cheek and led her to the cushioned chair in front of his desk. "I've arranged for her to marry a mage, but with the situation at hand—"

"Everything has changed. Yes," Am'aranth nodded and smoothed her skirts with a wrinkled hand. "Tell me about this Shäeli boy. Nek'ka has had a vision about him."

Syrán felt a twinge in his chest at the mention of the strange young man. He wasn't sure what to make of Cédron or his 'quest,' and he certainly didn't want Sénna entangled with him.

"There isn't much to tell. The boy has powerful Árk'äezhi at his command and is searching for the pieces of the Sceptre of Kulari. Apparently, he has met and defeated Laylur once and seeks the Sceptre to finish the job. I don't know how much of their story I believe."

Am'aranth narrowed her golden eyes. "You would be wise to believe all of it. Nek'ka has recognized his involvement with the deities. I don't know what his whole purpose is, but his fate and Sénna's are intertwined."

Syrán's head snapped up, and he regarded his mother. "Sénna has been sent to her room where I can keep her safe. Murádit is escorting the boy and the rest of the caravan to the underground city to be kept safe. There is no reason for Sénna to be entangled in this mess any further."

Am'aranth regarded him for a long moment. "You cannot keep her locked up forever. Sooner or later, she'll escape and live her life."

"Exactly," Syrán slammed his hand on the desk. "That's why I'm setting everything up for her to live a safe and happy life. I can't lose her, too."

Am'aranth reached across the desk and grasped Syrán's hand. She squeezed and said in a soft voice, "I'm sorry to learn of Myknét's death. He was a brave legionnaire, and we are all very proud of him. I supported your efforts to mold

Sénna into a young lady befitting her station, but the Garanth are at our gates. We need to get her out of the city, and she needs to go with Cédron."

Syrán shook his head and pulled his hand free. "I can't do that. Sénna cannot go into the underground city. It's too risky. What if she meets her sister?"

Am'aranth pressed her lips together. "Selénia made her choice and now has to live outside the family. Sénna doesn't even know she *has* an older sister. The chances of their meeting are slim. You must release Sénna to go with the caravan."

"Sénna is far too interested in the underground city. The fact that it has always been forbidden to her just makes it more appealing. She'll want to explore and learn everything. What if Selénia sees her? You know she'd entice Sénna with whatever might hurt me most. The girl defies me at every turn!" Syrán exploded, tossing his hands in the air and slumping back into his wing-backed chair.

Am'aranth leaned forward, one hand holding her staff and the other on the table. "Léna defies you at every turn also, undermining your authority with your own guild. She flaunts her power under your nose, and yet you do nothing about it except clamping down tighter on your remaining daughter. How is that going to fix anything?"

Syrán pinched the bridge of his nose, his eyes closed. "Léna didn't have a choice. She was abducted and forced into the life she now lives. I can't blame her for that."

A snort escaped Am'aranth's nose. "Your daughter has had ample opportunity to change her life. She has chosen this lifestyle – embraces it with a relish that turns my stomach. It would have been preferable had she died."

Syrán slammed his hands on the desk, rising to his full height. His eyes flashed, and he felt his cheeks flush with heat. "How dare you? She is your granddaughter. How can you not love her despite the choices she's made?"

Am'aranth rose to her feet with slow deliberation. She

gripped the staff with white knuckles. "Because she's a filthy whore who dredges the Králl name in the mud. Her brothel caters to those with dangerous fetishes and sinful tastes. You'll have to love her for the both of us; I cannot. Nor can I sit idly by while you ruin your remaining daughter's life chaining her to a mage, especially Bín Nétar. What were you thinking?"

"I was thinking that Bín Nétar is an ambitious mage who is likely to lead the Mages Guild when that ancient Ánderan Pól finally dies," Syrán sighed, sinking back into his chair. "He can provide for her. She doesn't have to love him."

Syrán's temples throbbed. Only the death of his wife Beréza had hurt more than learning that his eldest daughter had taken over the largest bordello in the underground city. The place was thriving under Léna's management. Am'aranth was right; the young woman did succeed in her new life, as much as it turned his stomach to think about it. Selénia had been every bit as stubborn as Sénna, and he had indulged her. Now he was paying the price, but he wouldn't make the same mistake with his youngest child.

"I suppose you have an alternative plan for my daughter?" Syrán raised his eyebrows and gave his mother his full attention.

"I do," she said. "And you would do well to follow it."

Syrán swallowed audibly. "Can I trust you to keep your knowledge of Selénia from Sénna and keep her safe?"

Am'aranth stared at her son for a long moment before giving him an enigmatic smile. "That is just one of the many secrets I carry."

Sénna sat in her window seat, absently thumping the back of her head against the stone wall. She stared out the window towards the city's perimeter where the Garanth army was bearing down and preparing for an all-out siege. The dull ache behind her eyes reminded her that she still lived despite her grief for losing her brother and her father's good graces.

The mind-numbing frustration of being locked in her room only gave her the space to wallow in her grief. Twice she'd checked the door, praying to each of the deities in turn for a change in her father's attitude, but to no avail. How could he keep her imprisoned when there were preparations to make and lives to save?

Lord Shamar's rays angled from the battlements of the city walls as the deity surveyed the preparations for the coming battle. Sénna glanced down at the streets filled with panicked townspeople abandoning their homes and livelihoods for the assumed safety of other cities. She snorted. They had nowhere to run that the Garanth wouldn't eventually find and destroy. They'd raze Táksabai to the ground, overrunning the land and slaughtering the Askári people down to the last child.

Táksabai, the capital city of Askári-bai, was a testament to the ancient seafarers who founded it. The town was laid out like a compass rose, with circular walls surrounding the city proper, and long roadways extended beyond the city walls in each of the four directions, like the spokes of a wagon wheel extending from its center. The four main routes, called radients by the locals, terminated in walled fortresses that housed each main guild's headquarters. Circular buildings with tall spires holding both watch and bell towers crowned the center of each radient's citadel, providing both guild and city with an early warning system in the case of trouble.

Built into the northern radient that extended into the Dágon Valley were the tallest watchtower and the barracks of the Hármolin Legion. The Mages Guild sat at the end of the western radient, which extended into the Tímin Sea at high tide, making access to the guild nearly impossible without a boat and an explicit invitation.

The Laborers Guild was by far the largest and took up most of the land extending beyond the southernmost radient and clear to the edges of the Tália Jungle. Sénna's mother, Beréza, had dedicated her life and work to that guild's animal husbandry program. Murádit continued her work with animals, especially the racing husan, but Sénna hadn't set foot in the southern radient since her mother died in the fire.

Shuddering at the memory, Sénna raised her eyes towards the mountains. To the east, nestled in the foothills of the Rónhadi Range, was the opulent radient dedicated to the Merchants Guild and its members. The town center had shops filled with everything anyone could ever need, but the boutiques that lined the radient leading to the Merchants Guild catered to the extremely wealthy with discerning tastes.

Sénna remembered an outing with her father to the Merchants Guild. Syrán had stopped to consult with someone in the street, so she wandered over to the glass-fronted furrier's shop. The window displayed exotic pelts made into everything from clothing to upholstered furniture. She remembered with a grimace the drinking chalices made of kazan and mijáko skulls and realized that her grandmother Am'aranth must have consigned the pieces from her collection.

Once a Meq'qan priestess to Lady Muralia, the young Am'aranth was forced to give up her calling to marry the Askári King of Thieves as a token of good faith by her Meq'qan Caf'iq. Sénna knew that her grandmother never fully embraced her life in Askári-bai, but she found one friend who shared her passion for the healing arts.

It was Am'aranth's friendship with the apothecarist Urléen, Cybél's grandmother, that brought Cybél to Myknét's attention. Sénna's heart ached for her oldest brother, who had done nothing to bring about his death besides taking the young woman he loved on a picnic. If he hadn't had to help his errant little sister, he'd still be alive. Tears rolled down her cheeks and splashed into her lap.

Sénna shook her head. Myknét was in the arms of Lady Muralia. Sénna had watched the release of his spirit and had no doubt he'd found his way to the bosom of the deities. Now she needed to quit feeling sorry for herself and figure out how to escape the prison of her chambers.

Urléen had already come and gone. After tending to Sénna's injuries, she'd begun fussing over the heartbroken Cybél and the injured half-Shäeli boy equally in her professional capacity as the town's preeminent healer. Sénna wondered what Cédron and his small group would do.

Sénna supposed they would join the rest of the Varkáras Caravan in the underground city once they'd been rounded up by her brother and his friends. But what then? Would they stay and fight the Garanth or slip away to continue the quest?

Murádit followed in their mother's footsteps and had gone into breeding and training the racing husan. He and his friends developed a large following with their sleek beasts from the hardy northern husan and the lithe runners that inhabited the Rabe'en Plains. Of course, Murádit stood to lose both his formidable racers and their potential profits should the Garanth overrun the city. He would also lose his life if he failed to escape.

Murádit's willingness to retrieve the caravan no doubt coincided with his efforts to gain their father's oblique permission to stable his legendary beasts along with the caravan's husan in the underground city where they'd have the best chance of survival. Scratching her head, she chuckled at her brother's ingenuity.

Sénna sighed and looked around the room for some sort of distraction. Her chamber was small but comfortable, with rich tapestries, bookshelves, and a latched chest for her clothing. She eased her stiff legs down and slid off the window seat, shuffling over to her writing desk. She winced as the sharp tingle of blood returned to her legs. The gilded tray holding plates of thinly sliced meats and cheeses with soft bread and a glass of red wine sat untouched on her desk.

Glancing at the sheaf of papers sitting neatly in the corner, Sénna stuck her hands on her slim hips. She had nobody to whom she wanted to write. Turning to the shelves, she perused the titles arranged in chronological order. None of the books tempted her. She'd spent so many of her youthful hours poring over the escapades of others in hopes that someday she would be able to fulfill her destiny of high adventure and a life of intrigue.

The sparkle of Lord Shamar's afternoon beams alighting on the garnet necklace hanging on the stand atop her desk captured Sénna's gaze. Her father had given it to her at birth. Syrán had given one like it to all his children. Garnet was supposed to protect children from evil, but it hadn't helped Myknét or saved her from the demon on the boat. She thought about it. The monster hadn't come after her himself, so perhaps there was something to the stone's properties.

Sighing, she crossed her arms over her chest and slumped against the wall. Pulling her dark hair back away from her face, Sénna turned away from the window towards the sounds of footsteps in the corridor outside her room. At the sound of an explosion, she leaped back to the window, aghast at what she saw.

On the north end of the city, just beyond the radient that housed the Hármolin Legion, a great ball of fire shot from the trenches dug by the advancing army and launched itself into the second watchtower that stood high above the gates. The timbers of the eastern tower on the other side were already engulfed in flames. The battle had begun.

Sénna wrapped her arms tightly around her body. Was her father planning to keep her locked in her room until the Garanth swarmed into the city? She shuddered and felt the prickle of sweat along her forehead. Sénna would prefer to take her own life than let them turn her into Arkmuln.

The footsteps in the corridor grew louder. Sénna glanced frantically around her room, seeking anything that could be a weapon. She remembered the belt knife she had strapped to her trousers beneath her dress. Sénna fumbled with her skirts, grasping at the hilt stuck in its sheath.

Sénna gripped the knife with sweaty hands and dropped her skirt. Her heart pounded faster in her chest as the handle of her door wiggled, and it began to turn. Sénna coiled below her window seat, her body blocked by the bed positioned between the window and her door. Her eyes darted about the room.

There was only one avenue for escape - the opening door. Sénna tensed, ready to spring and run towards it when the door flung open with a muffled curse. Sénna's breath caught in her throat. Her grandmother had come.

Am'aranth scanned the room with her glittering golden eyes. "Come out from there, child," she commanded with a clear voice as she entered Sénna's private chamber.

Sénna stood, her hands shaking as she sheathed the blade. Arranging her skirt, she stepped out from behind her bed. "Grandmother," she said. Sénna bobbed a quick curtsey, wiping her hands self-consciously against her thighs. "What are you doing here?"

Am'aranth stared at Sénna for a moment. Her silver hair framed her face, casting shadows into the deep lines of her cheeks and jaw. Sénna was struck by how old her grandmother seemed. At her throat, the moonstone choker gleamed dully as she fingered its smooth roundness, its power of youthful illusion spent.

"Nek'ka had a vision," Am'aranth said without preamble, nodding to her bird. "Tell me about the Shäeli boy, the one with the markings."

Sénna's mind went blank. "Um…Well, his name is Cédron. He and his company found us after Cybél and I were captured. He is a half-demon and a magic wielder. He used his power to burn Myknét's body without a pyre and to fight off Wézija. His father is Kásuin Varkáras, and his mother was a Shäeli, but that's all I know."

Am'aranth stared into her granddaughter's eyes, daring her to say more. Sénna could tell that there was something her grandmother was searching for, but she didn't know what it was. She glanced at Nek'ka, who sat perched as still as stone atop Am'aranth's silver walking stick.

The bird's milky-white eyes stared blindly at the physical world; her vision attuned sharply to the fields of energy that operated outside of the ordinary senses. Her soft, blue-grey feathers complemented the silvery sheath and cloak worn by her mistress. Sénna tore her eyes from the strange bird, reaching out for her garnet necklace and placing the protective amulet around her neck.

"What did Nek'ka see?" she asked as she hooked the clasp and pulled her hair out of the chain. She rummaged around her desk until she found the malachite bracelet that Am'aranth had always insisted she wear. Hastily, she clasped the filigreed silver ornament onto her wrist and turned to face her grandmother.

Am'aranth moved towards her granddaughter, the staff thumping on the floor with every other step. She reached out and grasped Sénna's hand in an uncharacteristic gesture of affection.

"The Goddess has touched him," she said softly. "I have felt it, myself. This makes him both powerful and vulnerable. You are both so young...." Am'aranth shook her head slightly and sighed. "This boy's fate is intertwined with yours somehow. I only know that if he is lost, we will lose you, too."

Sénna dropped her grandmother's hands. Her mouth went dry, and her lips twisted into an ironic smile. Of course, it would be the demon boy that she despised who would be the one person she'd have to find and rescue.

"Then I had better get out of here and find him before he gets himself into trouble." Sénna exhaled with a gust. "Can you help me get out of the city?"

Am'aranth's face lit with rare amusement. "Your father's Gróshan have always been extremely accommodating when I ask them nicely. Where do we need to go?"

Sénna ignored the question and grabbed a pouch full of flecksun coins from its hiding place behind a carved box on her shelf. Lifting her skirts, she tied it to the knife belt holding up her trousers, earning a disapproving glare from her grandmother. Flashing an impudent grin, she picked up her cloak and threw it over her shoulders.

"Perhaps you should leave Nek'ka here," Sénna suggested. "She may not appreciate the trek we have to make."

Am'aranth nodded, lifting the bird from its perch on the staff and placing it on the bedknob. The pale raven squawked once and tucked its head under one wing, retreating from the world and its tribulations. Am'aranth pulled her own cloak tighter around her bony frame and pointed out the door with her silver staff.

"You know where to find this Cédron?"

Sénna placed her hands on her hips and nodded, the thrill of disobedience coloring her voice.

"The underground city."

Chapter 13: The Underground City

Cédron prowled back and forth along the crowded street beneath Táksabai's Citadel Park as the legionnaires marched along the streets above him to defend the city walls. The centrally-located park was a gathering spot for folks to enjoy the beauty of Askári-bai's classic architecture and orderly landscaping. He was surprised when Sénna's brother Murádit led him and the rest of the caravan members below the delicately wrought arched bridge at the park's edge and down the tunnel that wound down into the bowels beneath the city.

The air was stale, as few vents opening to the streets

above allowed in fresh air. Glowstone baskets hung at regular intervals, casting the underground city in monochromatic sepia tones. Whispered explanations about a tsunami that destroyed the original port town, forcing survivors to build atop the ruins echoed in the closed space. Right now, Cédron didn't care. He was suffocating with the forced inaction.

The meatroll Cédron tried eating stuck in his throat, threatening to choke him. He couldn't enjoy the flaky crust or the pastry's spices; everything tasted like sand to him. He couldn't appreciate the beauty of Táksabai's people, her gardens, or architecture. His mind cycled through a repetitive loop; the Garanth attacked the city, his brother Tóran was in the middle of the siege, and Cédron was stuck in the underground city with no information and no way to contact him.

The caravan members found shelter in a row of buildings that once were warehouses and work areas. Many buildings had enormous doors and windows with locks and gears that nobody could open, while others boasted mechanized statues or artwork out front. Most of these pieces had fallen into disrepair over the lonely centuries, while others stood quietly guarding their forgotten secrets.

"How about I entertain us with a song?" Anéton said, dancing into Cédron's path with a grin.

Anéton loosened the shirt's strings at his neck and reached in, sticking his hand underneath his armpit. Pumping his other arm like a fároc wing, he squeaked out the melody of a bawdy pub song. Despite himself, Cédron grinned. Leave it to Anéton to find the ridiculous in any situation. Anéton took a deep breath to push out the song's last note, but the squeak came from the opposite direction. Anéton's eyes widened, and his cheeks turned pink.

"Now, you need to wash your hands *and* wipe your backside," Rováen chuckled as he and Sahráron approached. He sent Anéton over to the wash barrel and put his arm around Cédron's shoulders. "How are you faring?"

Cédron swallowed the last of his meatroll and shook his head. "Do you have any news? Any word from above?"

"No, not yet." Roväen sighed, leaning his back against the building. The glowstones in the basket above him shook from the vibrations of movement from the street above. "We could be down here until the battle is over, but—"

"We've got to get out of here!" Cédron pounded his fist on the decaying wall next to Roväen's shoulder. He coughed as the stone disintegrated into a gray cloud around his head. "We should be halfway to the Tawaki by now. If I don't get the terrastone soon, there won't be a world left to save."

Sahráron laid a gentle hand on Cédron's forearm, and he looked at her. Cédron's throat tightened at her drawn features. He hung his head and sighed. Anéton returned, wiping his hands on his shirt. He glanced at Cédron, then over at Roväen.

"What's our plan? Do we stick around here, or can we move on?" Anéton asked.

Sahráron let go of Cédron's hands and turned to Roväen. She dug into her pouch and pulled out a glittering mass of silver chains and stones.

"Before you do anything, I want you to have this," Sahráron fit the jewelry onto Roväen's hand. "So you remember me when we're apart."

Roväen looked down at the intricate silver bracelet Sahráron placed on his wrist and fingers. Each finger sported a ring set with fingernail-sized green peridots. Chains connected the rings to the wide bracelet, set with a large, rectangular emerald. Roväen took a deep breath and pulled Sahráron into a one-armed hug. They linked their arms and walked over to Cédron, who'd paced away several steps.

"We can't get out of the city just yet," Roväen said, gripping his nephew's shoulder. "The Garanth have already laid siege to the northern causeway, and the high tide has cut us off from the Mages Guild to the west. There are no other exits from the underground city. We have to trust that the Gróshan know what they're doing and be patient."

Sahráron grasped one of Cédron's hands in hers, capturing his attention with the warmth and strength of her grip. "Be at peace, my friend. Everything will work out; it's just hard to see when you're in the middle of it."

Cédron grimaced and took a deep breath. He squeezed Sahráron's hand and smiled weakly. He wasn't fooling her, but she didn't push him. He nodded toward Roväen's bracelet.

"Do the stones in that bracelet you gave Roväen also work as scrying stones?" Cédron asked.

"Perhaps," Sahráron answered. "I have had some success with the larger stones set in silver, but only time and testing will tell. His Árk'äezhi is strong enough to activate it without me feeling too guilty."

Roväen squeezed Sahráron's shoulders and smiled. "You have a true gift to make stones bend to your will. Not only stones, either," he winked at her.

Sahráron smiled and grabbed his wrist. "Just make sure you check in with me once in a while this time." She held up the bracelet with the scrying stone and jutted her pointed chin towards the bracelet.

Roväen chuckled and embraced the slight woman. He reached his hand around the back of her head and kissed her forehead gently. Cédron stared, his jaw dropped open. The thought of his uncle and one of his closest friends together warmed his insides. He hoped they would survive the war and find time to pursue this new aspect of their relationship.

Above, the hammering of a battering ram pounded with the beating of his heart. Who knew what kind of death and destruction the people of Táksabai faced while he waited below, helpless. These Garanth had already come through Dúlnat and Támon after laying waste to the Ta'voran Marshes. Their ranks swelled with thousands of Arkmuln made up of both Meq'qan and Askári. It wasn't out of the realm of possibilities that his father was among them.

Terrifying Cédron the most was the thought of his brother Tóran leading the Zig'orman Meq'qan into battle against the Garanth and winding up part of the growing numbers of walking dead. Cédron rubbed his sweaty hands on his trousers and returned to pacing back and forth as Rováen and Sahráron showed the caravan members how to lock and unlock the mechanical doors to the warehouse.

Cédron pulled out the compass that showed him the location of whatever he sought and opened the lid. He focused his thoughts on his brother. The compass needle glowed and pointed north directly into the center of where they believed the Garanth encampment to be. Cédron gasped.

The polished stone on the lid lightened, the outline of a face becoming clearer. The image turned Cédron's blood cold. He ground his teeth together and snapped the lid shut, shoving the compass into the pouch hanging off his shoulder.

Rováen and Anéton both hurried over to where Cédron stood, Rováen's hand on the pouch as if he were going to take the compass back out.

"What did you see?" he asked hoarsely. "What was Tóran doing?"

Cédron shook his head, and he swallowed before answering. "He was lying down. His face was beaten and bloodied. I couldn't discern anything about his surroundings, but the compass has his location deep in the Garanth encampment area."

Rováen pursed his lips. He glanced at Anéton, who gave a curt nod.

"We should see if we can help him," Rováen said.

Relief flooded Cédron's body, and he grasped his uncle's forearm in gratitude. "Yes, thank you! Let's find a way out of here to the surface."

Sahráron hurried down the steps and caught Rováen's

arm. "I'll accompany you as far as I can." She dropped her glance, then looked into Roväen's eyes. "I'm not quite ready to say goodbye."

The small group shouldered their packs and started back towards the tunnel that led to the entrance beneath Citadel Park when the mechanical gate on the door across the street groaned. The interlocking gears began to move, and slowly the gate slid into the hidden compartment inside the building walls. The gears protested and creaked before a loud clang echoed loudly, and the apparatus locking the wheels in place shot aside.

To Cédron's surprise, a filthy and rickety man walked through with a bejeweled old crone on his arm. The old woman caught his attention with her brassy red hair and gaudy attire. It was her hair that identified her as the apothecarist that tended to him upon his arrival.

The woman's gown was of emerald-green silk with a dark velvet cloak thrown over her shoulders. Gemstone rings glittered on every finger, and pearls adorned the netting holding up her coiffure. The outlandish decoration seemed so contrary to her withered skin and hunched body that Cédron thought she looked more like a hairy monsáki dressed in lady's clothes than a woman.

Despite his inner turmoil, Cédron nearly laughed out loud. Rather than embarrass himself, he focused his attention on her partner. Upon closer inspection, the wizened man was rather disgusting. Lank, unkempt hair clung to an unshaven, pockmarked face. The man grinned at the woman with gnarled yellow teeth stained from Tides of chewing blackroot. Cédron's nostrils flared, and he grimaced.

The two stepped aside just past the corridor opening as hundreds of children began streaming through the corridor. The elderly couple pointed and waved their charges towards the west. Still, only the older children and occasional adult carrying infants that followed them seemed to acknowledge their directions.

In the middle of the melee, Cédron was surprised to see Sénna and Cybél make their way through the tunnel. The girls were on either side of an imposing matron dressed in a silver cloak that accentuated her silvering hair. Meq'qan yellow eyes caught his attention, and Cédron decided she must be Sénna's grandmother. The woman stepped purposefully towards him, fixing him in place with her gaze. He spread both arms to hold Rováen and Anéton back from going any farther.

"Wait," Cédron said. "It's Sénna's grandmother. I think she wants to speak with us."

Rováen turned towards the advancing party and held his ground, placing himself slightly in front of Cédron. Sahráron hung back behind Rováen, her wise eyes surveying the newcomers. Anéton stepped in close to Cédron's side, a shy smile on his face for the girls, but Cédron could see his hands weren't far from his knives. The Meq'qan woman held a silver walking staff that she leaned on for balance, but her eyes showed no frailty. She glanced at his companions on either side, nodded at Sahráron, then turned her gaze back to Cédron.

"You, boy," she said in a clear voice raised above the screaming children, pointing her finger at Cédron. "I sense Lady Muralia's touch upon you. What is your purpose here?"

Cédron looked at Rováen. His uncle shrugged and tilted his head to the side. Cédron opened his mouth to speak, but the screaming and shouting of the hundreds of children still pouring through the underground streets echoed loudly on the ceiling and off the sides of the stone and metal buildings that surrounded them. The Meq'qan woman looked around for a moment, then nodded.

"Follow me," she ordered and struck off down a side street with Sénna attached to one arm and Cybél following meekly behind her.

Uneasiness settled in the pit of Cédron's stomach. He

didn't feel the woman was dangerous, but she had power. Anéton followed Cybél, catching her elbow as she stubbed her toe on some rocky debris and stumbled. Rováen looked back at the children and their harried chaperones.

"Looks like they're trying to salvage Askári-bai's future," Rováen mused. "I don't know how those children are going to survive a siege down here, though." He sighed and looked at the back of the woman leading the way down the narrow street. "Shall we?"

Rováen held a hand out, indicating that Cédron should precede him. Rováen stuck his elbow out for Sahráron, who tucked her arm back into it and leaned into his shoulder.

Cédron glanced down at the dark face of his compass, then back at the group getting farther away from him. He exhaled slowly. "I guess so. She may have some answers and seems to know her way around. Maybe she can tell us how to get out of the city."

The three turned their backs on the streams of noisy children being herded to the west and followed Sénna's grandmother. They walked for several blocks past ruined buildings filled with the debris of mechanical devices and worn stone foundations. Cédron marveled at the intermittent posts that held baskets of glowstones lighting their way as if the underground city were still a thriving place in need of such illumination.

Monoliths of large-breasted women stood sentry outside the only building that was in good repair. Cédron squinted toward the narrow window and saw women in sheer dresses flitting about inside. Musky incense wafted from under the polished wooden door.

"What's going on in there?" Cédron turned to Rováen and Sahráron, jutting his chin toward the well-lit and polished door.

"It is a hive of depravity," Am'aranth called from ahead, steering Sénna away from the brothel with a firm hand.

"We don't have time for dalliances, lad," Rováen said,

his cheeks flushing as Sahráron cleared her throat with a grin.

"Come," Sénna's grandmother commanded without turning.

The Meq'qan woman led them through a pair of iron gates that hung precariously on their hinges and into a large, circular area that was once a courtyard or gardens. Broken stone benches littered the ground, along with marble statues and uneven cobblestones. The building walls lining the square sported mosaic murals depicting scenes of the early Askári seafarers crewing the enormous ships that carried them off to lands unknown. Fewer baskets of glowstones lit this area, making it difficult for the group to navigate the debris-strewn ground.

The courtyard held the same musty, stale scent as the other ancient buildings, but Cédron caught the essence of something else. The sharp, burnt-orange flavor lodged in the back of his throat, and he gaped at the woman. It was the same scent that the Meq'qan high priestess Zale'en had burned as she'd prepared him to face the goddess.

Cédron had only a moment to take all this in before the woman turned to face him. "I am Am'aranth, once of the Zig'orman Meq'qan. Now, boy," she commanded. "Tell me your purpose here."

Cédron stared into Am'aranth's golden eyes and squirmed. Her appearance and manner also reminded him strikingly of high priestess Zale'en. Her intense gaze made him feel as if she could read his thoughts, seeing right through to his inadequacies and insecurities. Roväen nudged him on the shoulder, and he glanced at his uncle. Roväen nodded and leaned back against the high end of a broken bench, Sahráron nestled into his shoulder. Cédron took a breath, raised his head, and leveled his gaze at Am'aranth.

"I am Cédron Varkáras, son of Kásuin Varkáras of Dúlnat and Maräera Angäersol of Samshäeli. Lady Muralia has charged me to collect the four sacred stones of our lands and present myself to Auräevya for the Sceptre of Kulari." He inhaled, trying not to shuffle his feet in his discomfort as Am'aranth's eyes continued to bore into him. "There is a prophecy—"

Am'aranth inhaled sharply. "You! Can it be true?" She looked over at Sénna, who glanced at Cédron and pursed her lips. Then, she turned back to Cédron. "Show me."

Slowly, Cédron untucked his shirt from his trousers and raised it over his head. He heard the girls catch their breath and begin murmuring together. Blushing, he lowered his shirt to cover his tattoos and avoided their eyes as he took care to readjust his wardrobe.

"You bear the markings of fire and water," Am'aranth said in a tight voice. "You do not yet have wind and terra?"

Cédron arranged his pack and knife at his hip and shook his head. "I am headed to the Tawaki for the terrastone. We must leave, but my brother is in the midst of the Garanth army. I need to find him and—"

Am'aranth held up her hand, forestalling any further comments. "You must leave immediately. Táksabai is lost, or soon will be. My raven Nek'ka has foreseen it. You cannot get out on land; you must go by sea."

"But that will take us away from the Tawaloth Chasm and the terrastone," Cédron protested, looking to Roväen and Sahráron for support. "I have to get the other two stones before Laylur escapes."

Am'aranth shook her head firmly, pounding her silver staff. "There is no time. You must all leave this doomed city now with the rest of our children." She closed her eyes and sagged against her staff, her regal bearing gone for a moment. "You are no match for what awaits you up there. I'm sorry, but your brother is lost to you now."

Cédron felt a rush of heat and opened his mouth, but Roväen held him back. Roväen then turned to Am'aranth and bowed slightly. "Please, can you tell us what sort of demon travels with the Garanth?"

Am'aranth raked the man from top to bottom with her sharp gaze; her mouth twisted. "Even you, Sumäeri warrior, cannot hope to face him. Especially you." Her bitter, throaty chuckle took Cédron by surprise.

"What does that mean?"

Am'aranth glanced over at the youth and raised one eyebrow. "It means that facing one such as him would shred the foundations of everything you Shäeli have ever believed. You are not ready to face him. You must flee now before he finds you!"

Cédron looked at his uncle and saw a flash of disbelief before indecision settled into his features. Roväen cleared his throat and shifted his position before speaking.

"Well then, perhaps we should find a boat."

Am'aranth nodded. "Scóurj, one of my son's best Gróshan, has a fleet waiting. I will take you to them."

Cédron's nostrils flared. His father had always warned him about the Gróshan, the guttersnipes that lurked around the rougher areas of cities selling information to the highest bidder. A Gróshan with the name Scóurj didn't bode well. How could he be expected to trust this man and run? Cédron crossed his arms over his chest and planted his feet.

Roväen smacked him on the back, propelling him forward. "Come, we can argue the finer points of social evolution later. Right now, we need to get out of here."

Cédron snorted, then turned and followed the rest of the group back into the main tunnel where the last of the children, mostly toddlers and infants carried by panic-stricken adults, made their way down the westward alley. Cédron had no idea what kind of ships were moored beneath the city, but there couldn't be enough to carry the several thousand that had poured in from the city streets above.

The group retraced their steps to the now-empty bordello when a whirring sound erupted. Cédron glanced behind the building to the locked entranceway that led upward to the city. This one was further west than the Citadel Park entrance, so it must be beneath the Mages Guild. Cédron gasped. The circular Konnáras compass rose design on the door began to turn, followed by alternating rings of shells turning in opposite directions. Every few seconds, the spinning rings would clunk and reverse course. Am'aranth held up her staff, halting their progress as they all watched the antique door come to life.

It occurred to Cédron that something on the other side of the door had triggered the mechanism to open it, and whatever was coming at them might not be friendly. However, the group remained frozen in position, mesmerized by the iridescent shells spinning back and forth in their circular patterns. With a final loud clunk, the mechanism stopped spinning, and the doors creaked open.

A handful of men and women robed in red with heavy packs on their backs burst through the double doors. Most of them were armed, and they encircled Cédron's small group immediately with their weapons drawn.

"Who are you, Shäeli, and what are you doing down here?" demanded the red-robed man leveling his sword at Roväen's chest.

Roväen held his palms up, and the rest of the group followed his example. Cédron recognized the red robes of journeyman-level mages. He searched their faces for his uncle's distinctive scarred features, but none of them seemed familiar. As the rest of the red-robed men and women surrounded their group, a knot of white-robed mages exited the building.

Cédron recognized the white mage Gérand Kiél and red-robed journeymage Óren Fár who'd rescued him earlier. Mage Kiél surveyed the group and instantly waved his assistant away. He walked up to Am'aranth and took her hand in his, bending down to touch his forehead to her fingers.

"Forgive my enthusiastic journeymages, Lady Am'aranth," Mage Kiél said with a tired smile. "The guild was betrayed from within and overrun. We few are all that remain." He turned to the red mage that continued to hover close to him. "Óren, get that door secured. That may slow our pursuers down."

Óren nodded and waved at two other red mages to accompany him back up the stairs. Grunting, they shoved the doors shut and began pressing a series of shells that started the circular mechanism to lock the doors. The rest of the mages lowered their weapons, but they didn't put them away. Cédron and Roväen continued to bear the brunt of the mages' hostile stares. Cédron didn't know what either of them could say that would appease the mages.

"Gérand, call off your hounds," Am'aranth commanded in a clear voice.

Am'aranth pulled her hand free of Gérand's grasp and touched the moonstone pendant at her throat. Cédron gaped as her image blurred. She appeared taller, more commanding, and, after he rubbed his eyes, younger. The glamour of the moonstone caught the mages in its thrall, and they backed away from the group.

"Now, follow me to the boats. We must leave the city immediately," Am'aranth said.

Sahráron turned and embraced Cédron tightly. "Go, I can find my way back to the caravan from here."

Mute, Cédron nodded. She released him; then, she embraced Roväen. Cédron couldn't hear the whispered exchange between the two, but there was no mistaking the sadness and longing that lingered in their eyes as they separated. Roväen watched Sahráron turn and head back down the street that would take her back to Master Chezak and the safety of the caravan.

The red mages by the door finished locking the mechanism and raced down the steps to join their companions. The mages followed Am'aranth as she turned and led the now larger group back down the westward streets toward where the children had gone. Cédron craned his neck but couldn't see very far ahead in the dim light. He wondered what sort of outlet they might have to the sea that would house enough ships to—

Before he could finish his thought, an explosion rocked the underground city, blowing the entire group forward. Some fell to the ground, while others turned to face this new threat. The acrid scent of brimstone filled the air. Cédron whirled around and saw the beautiful iridescent doors bearing the Konnáras compass rose demolished. Pouring through the twisted metal and splintered wood came creatures that froze him in his tracks and turned his blood to ice.

Chapter 14: The Nightmare Begins

Anéton whirled to face this new threat. The blood thrummed in his ears, and his heart raced. He'd confronted Garanth alone before and beaten them, but now he had help. After days of running and hiding, it felt good to take action.

The dust and smoke from the explosion filled the air, reminding him of his victory over the mulark dogs in Dúlnat when he'd first met Cédron. A wide grin spread across his face, and he roared at the enemy. Anéton pulled his sword from the sheath and glanced around to make sure the women were all behind him.

"Keep going!" he yelled, waving them off as he turned

back towards the obliterated doorway and crouched into a defensive stance.

What lurched through the opening wiped the grin off Anéton's face, replacing it with a horror he couldn't fathom. Scores of Askári surrounded the fugitives. Their eyes were milky, and their faces slack, but their bodies moved with a single purpose. Arkmuln.

Anéton stood rooted in place. He looked around at his companions, who were similarly immobile with indecision and dreading what approached. Cédron's eyes were wide with fear, Räeshun held across his body defensively, but neither could attack.

A movement to his right caught his attention, and Anéton watched as the white mage Gérand Kíel pulled something out of the sack he carried. It looked like an enormous diclurue with its white leathery wings and long, pointed teeth.

"Óren, try this!" Mage Kíel handed the object to the journeymage, always at his side.

"What does it do?" Óren asked, frantically turning the thing over in his hands to discern its purpose.

Mage Kíel threw his hands in the air. "I don't know, just throw it! I think it activates when airborne."

Óren grasped the metallic diclurue on its mesh underside and hurled it towards the Arkmuln. The wings snapped out as it left Óren's hands. It glided smoothly over their heads and exploded when it hit the building behind the advancing Arkmuln. Showers of brilliant sparks rained down, blinding the small group and disorienting the advancing masses.

Out from the detonated body flew hundreds of tiny mechanical diclurues. Their high-pitched screeches echoed in the cavernous underground city. The whirring and clicking diclurues attacked the Arkmuln, flitting around their heads and impeding their advance. Their long, needle-like teeth and sharp tails ripped and tore flesh as they dodged and circled their prey.

Rováen stepped towards Mage Kíel and leaned over to peer inside the bag. "Do you have anything else of use in there?"

Óren pulled out a leather harness with rows of bolts strapped to it, a crossbow with tiny vials attached to the underside, a handful of small, metallic rodents with glittering eyes, and a few scrolls. Rováen pounced on the crossbow.

"This is a bit fancier than I'm used to, but it will do in a pinch," Rováen said as he grabbed the bolt harness, pulled it over his head, and adjusted it on his shoulders. He hefted the crossbow and nodded at the mages.

"Quick, this way!" Mage Kíel yelled. He turned and made his way down the street with Óren at his side.

Anéton could see the women farther down the street, moving as quickly as they could. Sénna and Cybél were on either side of Am'aranth, guiding the older woman through the obstacles littering the avenue. The mages followed their leader without a backward glance while Rováen and Cédron stepped next to the legionnaire to form a rear guard. Keeping an eye on the blinded and stumbling Arkmuln, the three of them raced down the street.

"Be careful with Räeshun," Anéton teased Cédron. "These buildings are old and unstable. I don't want one coming down on my head!"

Cédron snorted. "I wouldn't worry; it's not your head I'll be aiming for."

Anéton made a slight show of scratching his eye. "Maybe if you did aim for me, I'd be safer. Remember the last ti—"

"Watch out!" Rováen yelled, pointing towards the blasted door behind the milling Arkmuln.

A dozen Garanth bulls emerged from behind the shredded doors, roaring as they caught sight of their quarry escaping. They tore through the Arkmuln, heading straight for the three of them. Anéton's grin returned as he brandished his sword and charged toward the lead Garanth. At last, an enemy he could face gladly. The thrill of battle sang in his blood.

Dodging the Arkmuln and ducking beneath the swarm of mechanical diclurues still fluttering in clouds of clicking white wings, Anéton slid beneath the downswing of the first Garanth's heavy ax. He brought the tip of his sword up through the Garanth's abdomen and into his massive chest. The beast bellowed in pain as blood pumped through the wound, spilling entrails onto the ground.

Pulling himself up by the hilt of the blade buried in his enemy's heart, Anéton retrieved his sword as the beast sank to his knees. With a mighty swing, Anéton decapitated the Garanth. The body fell, spurting blood into the path of its companions.

The hate mirrored in the eyes of the two Garanth bulls in front of him further enflamed his desire for vengeance. These beasts destroyed his homeland and wiped out an entire nation of Meq'qan. The Garanth deserved to die painful deaths.

For the first time in his life, Anéton was glad his father had forced him into the Hármolin Legion. Tides of humiliating lessons with the Weapons Master were finally paying off. If Anéton knew there would someday be a real enemy to fight, he would have taken weapons practice more seriously, but what he had learned was working for him. Anéton spat the blood from his mouth and twirled his sword once before leveling it at the bull on his left.

"Hey there, ugly, want to dance?" Anéton grinned and feinted to the left.

The Garanth followed his feint and swung his heavy blade to where Anéton's shoulder should have gone. The swing missed, and the legionnaire twirled behind the bull, slashing his left thigh as he went past. The Garanth on the right growled and stuck out his leg as Anéton danced past.

Anéton fell flat on his back, his sword clattering away from his nerveless fingers. Bright spots danced in his eyes, and he couldn't tell if they were from hitting his head on the cobblestone street or the diclurues flitting around. Either way, neither option would stop the swing of the blade aimed for his head.

Groaning, Anéton rolled over toward the Garanth with the hope of tripping him. He didn't have enough momentum behind him. The enraged bull grasped Anéton by the throat and lifted him off his feet.

Behind them, Anéton could see Cédron using a small windstone to blow his adversaries backward. He couldn't see Roväen. A flaming bolt shot out from behind Cédron. Then another from the opposite side of the street. The bolts struck their targets, detonating into small eruptions of burning liquid that ate through leather and skin alike. The Garanth roared as they tried to find the unseen and ever-moving source of the exploding darts.

Anéton remembered Roväen's demon talent was invisibility. His friends held their own, but his predicament was becoming dire. The beast pulled him closer. Its foul breath burrowed up his nostrils, causing him to gag. The Garanth opened his mouth, revealing sharp incisors and a row of enormous molars meant for grinding meat. Anéton whispered a quick prayer to Orwaena, commending his soul to her.

"Anéton, no!" He heard Cédron shout from behind him.

A blast of wind struck him like a hurricane. The force of the gale pulled him from the Garanth's grasp as they circled into the air together. Anéton felt a tug on his boots and was surprised to find Roväen trying to extricate him from the whirling windstorm. Using every ounce of strength he had left, Anéton reached down and grasped the leather strap across Roväen's shoulder. The older man heaved on the legionnaire's legs, both of them falling backward out of the windstorm and onto the ground.

Anéton crawled to his sword and lay on top of it as the screaming winds tore at his back. Roväen inched up next to him and nodded towards Cédron. They slithered back down the street, away from the swirling vortex that caught up several more Garanth as well as many of the Arkmuln.

"Come on," Rovän yelled over the racket of whirring diclurues, screaming winds, and bellowing Garanth. "We have to get behind Cédron."

Anéton stared at Cédron, whose eyes were now closed and his arms raised. He knew Cédron couldn't kill their enemies, but he could slow them down. If they could stop the Garanth and Arkmuln long enough to reach the boats, they'd be free.

Anéton felt the rumble and vibration beneath his feet before he heard it. He glanced around to find the source and saw the buildings begin to shake.

"Cédron, your wind is bringing down the buildings!" he cried, pointing to the trembling structures. "We've got to get out of here before we're buried beneath the rubble!"

The rumbling increased, and dust filled the air. Cédron's concentration wavered, and the wind died. The diclurues tormenting the Arkmuln fell to the ground in heaps of broken gears and torn leather. Their once-sparkling jeweled eyes dimmed.

One Arkmuln let out a long, grating moan, and the others turned to face it. Anéton stared at the groaning figure. It was a young man wearing a torn legionnaire uniform. But in addition to his dress, this Arkmuln was different than the others. Anéton squinted to clear his vision in the dusty air and flinched from the Arkmuln's gaze. This one had sparkling, dark blue eyes with intelligence behind them, which sent a shiver down Anéton's spine.

"I think that one's the leader," Anéton yelled at Rovän, pointing to the blue-eyed young man directing Arkmuln in their direction. "I'm going after him."

Cédron nodded and moved to join him.

"Wait," Rovän cried, pointing over Anéton's shoulder. "Over there!"

One of the buildings behind the Arkmuln shivered wildly.

As they watched, it began to topple. The three fugitives turned and fled from the falling debris, followed closely by several Garanth and Arkmuln, including the sparkling-eyed leader.

Anéton didn't wait to see how many of their adversaries the building crushed; he just ran. Dust filled the air, making it difficult to breathe. The three of them coughed and gasped as they charged down the street towards the women. Sénna and Cybél pulled Am'aranth over fallen buildings and through the debris. In just a few short minutes, Rovãen and the two young men overtook them.

"They're right behind us!" Cédron cried as he waved his hands, using Räeshun and the firestone to detonate objects behind them, blocking the path.

The group tore down the street, racing to keep ahead of their pursuers. Anéton was surprised at how quickly Am'aranth moved, but she did have two young women pulling her. They spilled out into a four-way intersection. A crumbled building blocked the western edge, its bricks spilling into the street that led to the waterfront. The group came to a halt, heaving and panting from their sprint.

"Míjako piles! How are we going to get around?" Sénna exclaimed and stomped her foot. "Do we go north or south, Grandmother?"

Am'aranth looked up and down the street, trying to get her bearings as well as her breath. "I-am-not-sure," she gasped, looking at her granddaughter. "I think we should go—"

Cybél screamed and ran across the street toward the fallen building and cowered beneath the recessed arch above what remained of the doorway.

From the cloud of dust behind them emerged several Arkmuln, followed by half a dozen Garanth warriors. Cybél huddled with her knees pulled to her chest, but the doorway provided little concealment from the Arkmuln. The blue-eyed leader skittered around the southern end of the street and came up from the side.

Anéton's heart jumped into his throat at the vision of Cybél's vitality succumbing to the demon. He couldn't bear to watch her lose her vibrant beauty to become a slack-featured and mindless pawn of the Garanth. Not only that, but nobody knew if the Arkmuln retained their memories when the demons infiltrated their minds. If they did and the demons learned their plans—that was not an option.

"Askáriiii!" Anéton's war cry rent the air as he charged the Arkmuln bearing down on Cybél.

Bringing his sword across his left side, Anéton swung a backstroke with enough fury to behead the Arkmuln, but his blade never reached the target. The blue-eyed Arkmuln hissed and jumped backward away from Cybél and the advancing sword. Anéton nearly hit Cybél with his forward momentum, veering off and crashing into a wall at the last moment to avoid hurting her. Anéton spun around and positioned himself in front of the trembling woman, ready to protect her from anything else that advanced.

Anéton wiped the sweat from his brow and the grit out of his eyes. Their situation was hopeless. Arkmuln and Garanth surrounded the small group and herded the other four towards his position. He held his sword out at the ready, but why weren't the others fighting?

"Cédron, use Räeshun to blast them!" he ordered hoarsely. "Keep them back!"

Cédron shook his head and lowered Räeshun. He squatted down in the ample doorway, making room for the others. "I can't. There isn't enough room. They are too close. I'll end up bringing the entire intersection down upon all of us."

The buildings just to the north began to tremble slightly. The all-too-familiar roar of a ground shake started to build. Anéton looked around for cover and decided that Cybél's doorway was as good as they had time to find. Anéton huddled down to protect Cybél with his body and squeezed his eyes shut.

The ground shakes had gotten worse over the past several seasons. Anéton had seen entire sections of the land torn apart in jagged edges, and whole herds of kazan swallowed. He thought they'd healed the world of its tremors when Cédron prevented the demon Laylur from escaping his prison in the abyss beneath Lady Muralia's crust.

Perhaps they'd been mistaken. Maybe they had only slowed the demon down and not defeated him. The roaring grew louder, and the street shook with violent tremors. Above the roar of the quakes, Anéton thought he heard a whistle, then a shout.

Opening one eye, the legionnaire first thought the demons of the abyss were bearing down on him. He opened both eyes and gasped. "What in Our Lady's name is that?"

From the street to the north came barreling several massive beasts through the swirling dust. Rearing up and swiping the Garanth and Arkmuln with their long, curved talons, the enormous husan tore through the intersection, scattering enemies like straw dolls. Their eyes blazed, and they tossed their dark blue manes as the opposing horns on the top and bottom of their long snouts gored into the Arkmuln advancing upon the small group.

Anéton counted twelve of the enormous beasts harnessed to a massive flatbed wagon. Atop the bench was a young Askári man, whistling and crowing like a proud male fároc. He wheeled the wagon around, trampling more Arkmuln beneath its huge spoked wheels before coming to a halt just south of the group.

"Múradit!" cried Sénna with an enormous grin on her face.

"Come on; you've got a boat to catch!" Múradit stood and beckoned to the group.

On the back of the flatbed, Anéton whooped out loud to find Shozin Chezak and several armed guards from the caravan. The men jumped down and immediately formed a perimeter around the wagon. Cédron nudged him to help assist Am'aranth and the women into the back of the flatbed. Cybél required a little bit of coaxing, but he managed to get her up and to move fairly quickly.

Once the women were settled, Rováen and the rest of the men jumped aboard. They waited on the few stragglers from the caravan engaging the recovering Garanth, but in short order, the wagon was on its way again with a slightly puffed-up Múradit cracking his whip. Anéton and Cédron settled onto the bench right behind the driver and held onto the flimsy outside railing.

"It's a good thing I thought to keep these working husan along with my racers, or you guys would be in trouble," Múradit yelled over the roar of the galloping equines.

Anéton looked at Cédron, who shook his head in disbelief. Anéton grinned.

"He's my kind of people," Anéton nodded, grinning at Sénna's brother.

Cédron's following comment was low and lost beneath the pounding gallop of the husan. He gazed forward and let the conversation lapse. Anéton wasn't sure, but he thought Cédron had said something to the effect that he knew better than to plan into the future. A pang of guilt stabbed at his chest, but Anéton wasn't sure what his friend had said, so he let his smart rejoinder lie. For all his formidable magical talent, Anéton didn't envy Cédron's destiny.

Cédron had changed so much in the past season. They had met shortly after the festival of Nársham-vu in Suntide. Cédron had been a skinny, awkward guy who seemed afraid of his abilities. Now, with Dormantide rapidly approaching, Cédron had practiced for several weeks, and he'd faced death and the deities on multiple occasions. Cédron was harder, more confident, but behind his eyes lingered a sadness and isolation that Anéton supposed would haunt him until the end of his days. With another stab of guilt, it occurred to Anéton that there might not be that many days left for Cédron.

The wagon lurched to the right, throwing Anéton out of his musings and almost into Cédron's lap. Rovaen and Shozin held onto the women as the other caravan members righted themselves after the jolt. Grasping onto the railing, Anéton stood to see what had caused the sudden change in direction. The husan easily dodged the fallen buildings in their frenzied dash to the city's western edge, but the road became choked with more debris. The two-story statue they had just swung to avoid lay stretched behind them nearly across the entire roadway.

Múradit whistled at the husan and pulled back on the reins to slow them down a bit. He maneuvered the flatbed carefully among the rubble and holes that checkered the westbound lane. The husan screamed and tossed their midnight blue manes. Bits of foam and sweat flung from their heads as they altered their pace. The sturdy husan could easily pull the heavy load, but not at the breakneck speed at which Múradit pushed them to try and evade the Garanth.

Anéton glanced back in the direction they'd come and saw no sign of pursuit, but he knew it was on its way. Inevitably, the Garanth would lead their Arkmuln to where the boats were waiting. If the group didn't hurry, they would be trapped. Anéton hoped that the filthy little Gróshan had gotten all those children loaded up and cast off before the wagon arrived because any delay would be costly.

"Look at that!" Sénna pointed to a large opening up ahead of them.

Everyone's eyes followed her finger. A few gasped out loud. The underground road opened into an enormous cavern stretching high above the buildings, with a ceiling made of leaded glass. The walls arched around a vast harbor that housed a fleet of ships still loading the doomed city's children.

The walls had been sanded smooth ages ago and sparkled as the light of the glowstones reflected off the polished crystal fragments. The stone was light with black veins that reminded Anéton of the macabre shrines to Lady Muralia in the Meq'qan village. The walls of those shrines had blood offerings that ran and dried in similar patterns.

"I sure hope it survives the siege," Cybél sighed, clasping her hands together in her lap.

Mage Kíel, seated down from her, glanced up and nodded. "That is the floor of the old seafarer's hall." His face cracked into a smile that caused a thousand folds of skin to wrinkle up in protest. "Very few people know what lies beneath it. My Gróshan friends have been using this cavern for decades to smuggle people, information, and goods to and from the city right under the guild's nose." He chuckled softly and shook his head. "I never realized what a great debt I owe to them."

Múradit maneuvered the wagon down the street to the south and along the waterfront. The tangy smell of dried seaweed mingled with the dank aroma of rotting shellfish, the constant and familiar scents of a pier. As they pulled up near the long line of docks that jutted into the harbor, Anéton looked out at the end of the pier, where the cavern opened up to the sea. Several ships headed out of the cavern; their sails hoisted to catch the winds that blew outside the protected harbor.

Shozin rose from his seat on the flatbed and leaped over the railing, landing on the ground. Pulling the tailgate down, he ushered everyone from the wagon. "Load the rest of those people into the last boats. We must get out of here before the Garanth catch up," Shozin instructed, then pulled Anéton aside. "I need you to get the ladies out of here as quickly as they can move. I'll get the rest of our people—"

A faint bellow echoed from the east. All eyes turned to look at the way they had just come. Anéton could see nothing, but the roar of the Garanth was unmistakable. Turning back around, he nodded to Shozin and assisted Am'aranth out of the wagon.

"Come, let's get you into that boat," he smiled tightly at Sénna's grandmother, who accepted his solid hands and let him ease her to the ground.

Am'aranth wasted no time heading down the closest pier where perhaps three scores of children and a few escorts had lined up to walk the treacherous gangplank onto the deck of the boat. The younger children moved slowly as their unsteady legs navigated the narrow, bouncing board. More than once, a child nearly toppled into the water, but the crew always managed to grasp the child just in time. Anéton could feel the heat of frustration rising in his chest as the children made their way slowly onto the boat. At this rate, they would be lucky to get any of their group aboard before their pursuers reached them.

As if on cue, three Garanth bulls lumbered into view from the eastern road. A score of Arkmuln followed, shambling as quickly as their protesting bodies could move. Anéton drew his sword and called to the men of the caravan. Master Chezak nodded and spread his men out along the harbor to protect the last three boats still loading children.

Turning back, Anéton made sure the women were in the group waiting to board the closest ship. Roväen was trying to get Cédron on board, but it appeared that his friend had other ideas. He couldn't hear their words, but watching Cédron's golden hair shake as he pushed his uncle away indicated that two more would be joining the resistance. Anéton turned back around to face the onslaught of enemies racing up behind the wagon.

"Help me!" Múradit grabbed his arm and pulled him towards the wagon.

Anéton lost his balance as Sénna's brother nearly pulled him off his feet. The two hastened to the front of the wagon, where Múradit showed Anéton how to disengage the harness. After a few pointed curses at the knots, the two released the cart and swiftly began removing the straps from the dozen enormous husan. Anéton sidestepped carefully around the stomping, nervous beasts and their wicked tusks protruding from their long snouts.

"Hyah!" Múradit howled and struck the first three husan on their hindquarters.

The startled equines reared up and screamed, turning away from the source of their discomfort. They charged down the street into the oncoming Arkmuln. Following Múradit's lead, Anéton yelled and swatted at the two husan on his side.

The husan directly in front of Anéton got the curved talons of its back leg caught on the wagon wheel spokes and began pounding itself into the wagon in its confusion. The beast struck Anéton in the chest and knocked him down beneath its stomping legs. Rolling quickly underneath the flatbed, Anéton missed the first wave of the attack.

From his vantage point, Anéton could see Shozin Chezak and his men challenging the three Garanth. The group of mages was frantically emptying the sacks they'd been carrying, but Anéton saw nothing that even remotely resembled usable weapons in the piles at their feet. The dirty little Gróshan was waving to Am'aranth and the young women from the railing of the last boat.

Next to him was the gaudy woman who screeched something at the advancing Arkmuln. Sénna and Cybél pulled Am'aranth aboard the final ship as the brassy woman threw some sparkling powder into the air. When it hit the wooden planks of the dock, the Arkmuln began losing their footing. It was as if the planks had become too slippery to gain purchase. A few tried to reach out towards the ship but lost their balance on the treacherous ground and fell into the water.

Above him, the enormous husan twisted up in the spokes of the wagon wheel. It stomped and screamed in its panic. The beast was so powerful that the front half of the wagon lifted off the ground with its efforts to free itself. The sideboards slid out of their holders, splintering as they hit the ground. Anéton barked a laugh at the beast's inspiration.

Anéton crawled out from under the cart and waited until the powerful beast reared up into the air again. As the wagon wheels left the ground, Anéton shoved from beneath the vehicle, forcing it onto its side. The altered direction of the spokes allowed the husan to extricate its tangled talon. It bounded away in terror, paying no heed to the bodies of Arkmuln it trampled in its haste to escape.

"Good thinking!" Múradit grinned from his shoulder where he'd appeared. "Let's move this into the street and block the rest of them."

The two young men heaved and shoved, their muscles straining against the weight of the flatbed. The toppled wagon groaned as the wooden boards slid over the cobblestones. It might not stop the enemy from reaching them, but it would slow them down enough to allow more people to get away on the ships. Anéton felt the wood shudder as the first wave of Arkmuln struck the barricade. The wagon held its ground. Múradit grinned, his yellow eyes gleaming wickedly in the glow stone light.

"Just in time," he pointed back down the street behind the Arkmuln. "Looks like we have more company."

Anéton followed Múradit's gaze to where several mages were making their way towards the wagon. There were a few red-robed journeymages, but most of them wore the black cloaks of apprenticeship. One mage garbed in white led them. Anéton felt a flaring of hope, but something about the mages was wrong. The Arkmuln ignored them as they passed into their clusters. Anéton watched the Arkmuln give them a wide berth as if repelled by them.

Anéton turned to Múradit. "What's going on? I thought the mages were on our side?"

Múradit's face sobered. "Mage Kiél has always been our ally, but he has long been on the wrong side of Bín Nétar, the next leader of the guild." Múradit nodded towards the white mage maneuvering through the Arkmuln with his entourage behind him. "He's a bad one. It doesn't surprise me that he's involved in all of this. High Mage Andékarron Pól is ancient but refuses to give up the leadership. Bín Nétar is ambitious, and a Garanth invasion would certainly be one way to get rid of the old guy and cleanse the guild of any opposition, don't you think?" He winked and placed a finger along the side of his nose. "We'd better get out of here."

The two young men pulled back from the overturned wagon and ran over to where Mage Kiél sorted through his dumped treasures as the red journeymages kept the Arkmuln at bay. The white mage picked up a set of scrolls and tossed them aside. Muttering to himself, he then grabbed a pair of long, shimmering gauntlets.

"Óren, come take a look at these," Kiél called to his protége.

Óren shoved an Arkmuln back with a long staff before turning.

"Can you cover me?" Óren raised his eyebrows at Anéton and Múradit as the Arkmuln struggled to regain his feet.

The two young men nodded and took up defensive positions around the mages. Off to his right, Anéton saw that Rováen and Cédron were fending off a trio of Arkmuln.

"Look, Master," Óren said as he held up one of the shimmering gauntlets. "It's Orwaena's symbol."

Anéton turned to catch a glimpse of his favorite deity's relic when the Arkmuln he'd been keeping at the end of the staff tried grabbing the wood from him. He knocked the man back down with a savage growl, then turned around toward the mages.

"Ah, the fabled Konárras gauntlets," Mage Kiél nodded and examined the fabric more closely in the dim light. "Made from rohiti scales, if the legend is true. These gloves can repel fire as well as any hostile spells. Put them on quickly; I see we have more than Arkmuln to deal with."

Óren and Anéton both saw the opposing white mage home in on their general location. Óren handed the gauntlets back to his Master.

"You must wear them – you know he's coming for you."

Mage Kiél nodded, a bemused smile on his face. "I guess I should have expected that." He pulled on the gauntlets and faced his adversary. "Bín Nétar, you've gone to a lot of trouble just to take over the Mages Guild."

Bín Nétar smiled, and Anéton was shocked to see the flicker of demon possession behind his eyes.

"This isn't for the guild, you fool," Nétar hissed, his eyes darting around the cavern seeking something that he wasn't finding. "I know the child of the prophecy is here. Where is he?"

Anéton searched the cavern for Cédron. His friend crouched behind Roväen and Shozin Chezak, who were madly pushing back the three Arkmuln that continued to stalk them. They, too, hesitated to kill any converted Askári, and a little of the tension in Anéton's chest relaxed. Roväen caught his eyes and shook his head slightly, glancing over at the menacing Bín Nétar. Anéton nodded and turned to Múradit.

"I'm going to give Roväen a hand. Are you ok here?" He asked.

Murádit clasped his arm. "I've got this."

Anéton no sooner stepped away from the mages when Bín Nétar threw his first spell at Gérand Kiél. Mage Kiél threw his hands up to protect his face, and the curse glanced off the Konárras gauntlets. Several red mages to Nétar's left crumpled into heaps of slime as the spell ricocheted off the gauntlets and hit them.

"What mischief is this?" Bin Nétar raged, surveying the carnage. "Where did you get those gauntlets?"

Gérand Kiél smiled serenely and held them up. "I took it upon myself to spare as many of our treasures as I could find from the rabble you let through the front gates, traitor."

"Traitor, is it?" the rogue mage stepped past his dissolved journeymages and closer to his opponent. "That word only applies if you're on the losing side; I'm not."

Bin Nétar hurled another spell, this time toward red mage Óren Fár, hoping to catch Mage Kiél off guard. The old mage lunged over his journeymage and swept the curse back towards Bin Nétar. Screams erupted as the Arkmuln and apprentice mages incinerated as the magic took effect.

The demon behind Bin Nétar's eyes flickered wildly. "Tell me where the child is, or I will destroy the entire cavern."

Kiél shrugged. "I don't know which child you mean. We have hundreds here."

"So be it," the demon-altered mage hissed.

Bin Nétar pulled an amulet from behind his robes and let it sit on his chest. It was a ruby ensconced within a torus knot. He closed his eyes and raised the amulet in both hands. Calling out in a harsh language that Anéton didn't recognize, the demon sent a spell hurtling into one of the boats filled with children that had pulled away from the dock. The ship exploded in flames, instantly killing all aboard.

All the breath left Anéton's body, and he staggered towards the dock. He felt the blood draining from his face as he gaped at the carnage. There was nothing he could have done, no action he could have taken that would have saved any of the doomed children and their escorts. Turning back to the rogue mage, he looked more closely at the amulet. A chill went down his spine as he recognized the shape of the torus knot. *Hazzara!*

chapter 15: Engaging the Enemy

"This is it!" Läenshi whooped as she bounded to her läenier Juläen's back. Reaching around her sleek neck to grasp the riding straps, Läenshi could barely keep the thrill from her voice. "We're finally going to *do* something. Something that only we can do."

Juläen, the mighty raptor, turned her amber eyes towards her rider and clawed the ground, shaking out her wings. Läenshi grinned and nodded her head as the Wingleader blew a series of complicated whistles and motioned for her to take the point position.

The roar of the wind as the Wing of läeniers lifted from

the valley floor drowned out her older sister Läerei's final admonition to be careful and not to put herself in danger. Läenshi just shrugged and pointed to her ear, pretending not to hear. She was a Sumäeri; she didn't need her elder sister's protection.

The rush of exhilaration that Läenshi felt every time she flew with her new partner had chipped away at the block of grief that encased her heart since she'd learned of Räesha's death and the murder of her parents. Läenshi and her remaining sisters were devastated at losing their parents and their family's ancestral home.

Still, seeing Räesha's spirit ensconced in the bone staff overshadowed their earlier grief. Räesha may have lost her life, but not her determination to help the Askári boy, Cédron, finish his quest. Even in death, Räesha contributed more than any other to avenge their parents and thwart the demons threatening to take over their world. Läenshi shook her head, barely aware of her silver braid swinging between her shoulder blades, banishing the pang of inadequacy she felt whenever she thought of Räesha's sacrifice.

Läenshi's throat tightened. Well, she wasn't inadequate anymore; she was a Sumäeri and a läenier rider. She blinked back the tears that filled her eyes and swallowed the grief and doubt before it could overwhelm her. Läenshi held her head high as Juläen led the charge toward the Mages Guild of Táksabai. It was *her* turn to live up to the Angäersol family name and reputation.

Rising over the plains, Läenshi flared her nostrils as she sniffed the air. Wisps of caustic smoke still lingered above the scorched Dágon Valley, causing her nose to burn and her throat to constrict even tighter. Lord Shamar's light exposed the wanton destruction of the land from the Garanth army's passage, and a twinge of panic trickled down her spine.

The thought of Samshäeli facing a similar fate filled her with dread. Bracing herself against the acrid stench in the air, Läenshi shifted her powerful legs and guided her golden beast northwest toward the Shalaen Falls and around the eastern side of the Garanth encampment. Trilläen's plan required them to fly northwest until they saw the explosions from Läerei's black-seed bombs, then bank south over the shoreline towards the Mages Guild.

Glancing over her left shoulder, Läenshi caught a flash of light as the first of Läerei's bombs exploded. Almost instantaneously, several other sacks of black-seed detonated over the encampment. Showers of brilliant sparks filled the air as the ignited seeds coated the confined Arkmuln, making their bodies twinkle and glow as the seeds were absorbed into their hair and skin.

Läenshi held her breath, praying that Läeri's plan would work. Seconds later, the concussions from the explosions hit Läenshi's Wing. Läeniers dipped and rolled in the forceful blast, but the riders held their seats. Läenshi punched her left arm out towards the guild, her fist pointing to their destination. Pressing her right knee forward and her left knee back, she guided Juläen towards the shoreline. The radient down the spit of land permitting travel was beneath the tide, cutting off the Mages Guild from the rest of the city.

Läenshi guided her Wing of thirty-odd läenier riders towards their destination. Her whole body tensed, throwing off the shroud of helplessness that had smothered her for the past sennight. The only bright spot in this season of Autumntide had been bonding with the läenier. Although Läenshi's gift wasn't as flashy or impressive as her twin's or as practical as Läerei's, it did allow for a more profound attachment to Juläen.

Enhancing the Árk'äezhi of the läenier was, in many respects, the direct opposite of Räesha's talent of understanding and communicating with beasts. In this sense, Läenshi was the receiver of information rather than the giver. Her connection with Juläen was as stable as that of many who'd been riding their raptors for Tides.

Läenshi closed her eyes and reached out with her mind.

Even from this distance, she could feel the thrum of Árk'äezhi energy that coursed beneath the surface of the city. The Lluric Field pulsed with it. Säeshi had identified it as protective Árk'äezhi, which was as specific as she had been able to get.

Läenshi kept her thoughts focused on the dormant energy, not wanting to inadvertently strengthen the powers of the demon lurking somewhere within the encampment of the Garanth army swarming just to the east of her position. Turning her head slowly from left to right, trying to home in on the source of the Árk'äezhi, Läenshi's concentration was shattered by a piercing scream just to her right.

A läenier cut across her path as she opened her eyes. The raptor and older rider spiraled down toward the beach. She gasped as the spray of blood from the arrow sticking out of the man's shoulder splattered her. From directly behind her, Läenshi heard her Wingleader's commanding whistles. Instantly she found herself surrounded as her Wing formed a protective barrier.

"Get that protective energy activated!" the Wingleader shouted at her against the wind. "We'll cover you."

More arrows whistled past as the läeniers wove in and out, avoiding the black-shafted missiles. Läenshi's hands slipped on the reins, and she tightened her grip. Her heart was pounding so hard it nearly took her breath away. Her breath caught in her throat at the thought of their deaths. How many of her Wing would sacrifice themselves for her before she could complete her task?

Almost before she could finish her panicked thought, a wave of peace filled her mind. There were no words—just the sensation of all being well. An overtone of courageous excitement ran through it, replacing the concern. Juläen turned her head slightly and blinked an amber eye at Läenshi. She then shrieked her war cry as the Wing maneuvered towards the open ocean and out of the range of the arrows.

"Look!" The woman to her left was gesturing down to the ocean just south of the Mages Guild. "Boats are coming out from underneath the Mages Guild. There must be a hidden harbor down there."

Läenshi glanced down and saw half a dozen one- and two-masted ships with sails unfurled, making their way from the cliffs beneath the guild's stone seawall and heading south. From their height, she couldn't tell whether the ships carried friends or foes, but it didn't matter. Her job was to protect the city. She turned her attention back to the task at hand.

Patting her raptor and taking a deep, steadying breath, Läenshi closed her eyes again. Trusting Juläen to follow her brethren, she reached out once more to locate the protective energy that hummed around the Mages Guild. Juläen's strong wings beat beneath her knees, and she wrapped the reins around her knuckles to keep them secure.

Tendrils of consciousness wove through the Mages Guild, down into the terra. Questing further, Läenshi felt the stirrings of Árk'äezhi pulsing with greater force the deeper into the ground she searched. Oddly, she sensed several origins of the same type of energy. They seemed connected yet separate, like a relay. If she could trigger the primary source, it might activate the others. There! She felt a pinprick of energy in her mind, the spark that would ignite the entire string.

Läenshi's mind filled with the overwhelming sensation of a gust of wind whirling through corridors, extinguishing the life of all its enemies as it absorbed their Árk'äezhi to feed itself. Pinpoint after pinpoint of Árk'äezhi sparked to life as her talent awakened the once-dormant energy. Läenshi still had no visual idea of what she was activating, but she could sense it was big and powerful. She felt a slow stirring of life and purpose. It felt like a string attached to each piece; as one began to stir, it would tug on another, starting the process all over again.

Opening her eyes, Läenshi gazed down upon the city and the radient of the Mages Guild. Tiny pebbles of light glimmered beneath the streets of Táksabai. The buildings shivered in the ground shake that she had initiated. Below her, the water around the Mages Guild began to churn and froth.

Holding her breath, Läenshi led her Wing over the city for a closer look. Buildings tumbled, and people ran panicked through the streets. The Wing turned west and glided back down the radient extending from the city center toward the Mages Guild. The stormy water thrashed against the cliffs below the guild walls. Beyond the circular island the Mages Guild nestled on, forms rose slowly out of the water.

Scores of hundred-foot-tall metallic creatures emerged from the depths. Encrusted in barnacles and shells, the leviathans drew ever closer to shore. Their bodies were flat and oval, broad from the front but narrow from the side. They walked through the surf on four pointed appendages that curved out from the lower halves of their bodies. They had many shorter limbs ranged along the outer edge of their shell-like exoskeletons. Their heads were terrifying, with additional long, pointed antennae sprouting from each creature's center and top.

Their movements were jerky, as if unused to the fluidity of movement. Green light pulsed from deep within their bodies. The glow throbbed with life and reflected off of their neighbors' metallic exteriors. Above the roar of the crashing waves and the whooshing of the läeniers' wings, Läenshi could hear gears clashing and grinding inside the creatures. The guardians surrounded Táksabai, towering over the city's walls, and began interweaving their many limbs into a protective barrier.

Closing her eyes and focusing on the living force inside each creature, Läenshi poured her Árk'äezhi into the consciousness of the guardians. They felt empty, as if needing direction. They had created a barrier around the guild walls, but that wasn't sufficient for her purposes. She required the guardians to protect the people of Táksabai from the Garanth army.

Once the guardians reached their targets, the Askári would realize that they would protect the city and its people. Läenshi allowed herself to float on the wave of power that coursed through her into the leviathans, giving its force direction and intent. *Destroy the invaders and protect the Askári.*

Another shriek to her left jarred Läenshi from her meditation. The stricken läenier folded her wings and dropped out of the formation as more arrows whistled thickly towards them from the Mages Guild battlements. Läenshi squinted her eyes from Lord Shamar's light, trying to identify the shooters. Following the line of projectiles back to their point of origin, she gasped. The black-robed mages were firing at the läeniers. As the implications of the mage's treachery worked through her confused mind, the full impact of their deception stunned her.

If the mages of old had created the protective guardians that surrounded the guild, would they have control of them? A wave of panic crashed over Läenshi, drowning her mind in its murky depths. Trickles of cold sweat coursed down her spine, and her hands slipped from Juläen's riding straps. The band of terror around her chest squeezed the breath from her body. She had just doomed the city. If the mages had control over the guardians, there would be no escape from the sentinels she had awakened.

Trilläen looked at the sky where the Wing of läeniers vanished. Apprehension stabbed painfully in the captain's heart as he envisioned young Läenshi leading her Wing towards the Mages Guild. Would she be able to unleash the protective magic Säeshi had sensed? What form would it take? Could it be controlled once awakened?

Trilläen sent a whispered prayer to each of the Moon Daughters for Läenshi's safe passage and return. One day, he would face Räesha's shade again, and he didn't want to be the bearer of bad news when that day came. He scrubbed his face with his hands and smoothed his silver hair back.

Glancing in the opposite direction, Trilläen watched Läerei's Wing make rapid progress towards the center of the Garanth encampment. He almost pitied their Arkmuln targets. It wasn't because he was uncertain of their life status—they would be losing their lives regardless—but because they wouldn't have a chance to fight or defend themselves against Läerei's deadly gift. Trilläen shook his head. Never had he seen a more talented Sumäeri.

The Angäersol family produced generations of outstanding warriors but never had one been born with such a powerful gift or who relished finding applications for it. Where Räesha had enjoyed her work defending the borders of Samshaeli with her läenier Wing, Läerei seemed to revel in taking the offensive. Those in Läerei's path had already seen the Moon Daughter's last dance across the night skies of Muralia. This was the last day of existence for the Arkmuln and their Garanth keepers.

Turning to his small rescue team's waiting members, Trilläen watched Säeshi's eyes following her twin. The captain reached out and squeezed her thin shoulder.

"The Wing protects her," he said softly, capturing her aqua gaze with his words. "And I am sure she will be successful in her mission. She is an Angäersol, after all."

Säeshi's lips curved, but the humor didn't reach her eyes. "Yes, she is. That's what concerns me."

Trilläen opened his mouth to reassure her and clarify her meaning, but Ta'riq waylaid him.

"Captain, the Meq'qan are mounted up and ready to

move out." Ta'riq nodded toward the scores of enormous wakazan stomping and blowing in the ashy haze filtering Lord Shamar's light. "We should get ourselves into position if we are to have any hope of finding Tóran."

Trilläen hesitated for the briefest moment, torn between his duty to the mission and his desire to clarify Säeshi's cryptic remark. The urgency of his mission overrode his curiosity. Nodding to Ta'riq, the captain fingered the hilt of the short blade hanging at his hip.

"Right, let's go."

Trilläen steered Ta'riq and Säeshi behind the thundering wakazan charging down the hillside in a cloud of dust and ash towards the Dágon Valley and the Garanth army's eastern flank.

Not waiting for the air to clear, the small rescue party tore down the hillside's rocky face to a smaller outcropping of boulders halfway down the escarpment. Gasping and choking in the churning dust, the three pushed through thorny gorse bushes and scrub trees. Trilläen prayed to the deities for protection as they scrambled over the rocky terrain in full view of anyone looking in their direction.

If even one of the Garanth glanced up the hill, they would be discovered. Showers of rocks tumbled down the slope beneath their feet as they slid towards their goal, heralding their presence to everything below them. Just ahead, a small platoon of Garanth jogged from their tents toward the army's front lines. Trilläen gritted his teeth and slid down the hillside, tearing his palms on the sharp rocks in his haste to reach the next hiding place.

Behind him, Ta'riq and Säeshi grunted. Both had slid in behind him. They bumped to a halt on the high rocks that were the only cover between them and the throngs of Garanth mobilizing below them. They were still high enough to have a clear view of the encampment from their current position. They could see the effects of the diversions while remaining less than a hundred yards from the dark tent that sat ominously quiet in the center of the clearing.

The ground beneath them began to shake as the herds of mounted wakazan rounded the southern end of the pass and charged towards the eastern flank of the Garanth. Below them, the Garanth formed ranks to receive the charging Meq'qan and their enormous beasts. Trilläen glanced over at Ta'riq. The tribesman's face was pale.

"The Meq'qan are brave warriors," the Sumäeri nodded towards the oncoming beasts. "Some will fall, but Chaq'ta will retreat when they complete their mission."

Ta'riq held Trilläen's gaze for a moment before swallowing and nodding his head. "Those who fall will be honored at Lady Muralia's table for eternity. There is no shame in that."

Säeshi placed her hand on Ta'riq's and nodded in sympathy. Their common bond of loss had forged a camaraderie between the two that needed no further expression. Trilläen fervently hoped they hadn't misplaced their trust in his plan. It would take every ounce of luck, skill, and blessings from the deities for this mission to succeed. Even then, Trilläen knew that it wouldn't be without cost. He prayed that the price wouldn't be too high.

The small group's attention was diverted to the other side of the camp as a loud explosion rocked the valley, bringing with it a shower of blue-black sparks.

"Läerei was never one for subtlety," Säeshi smiled grimly at the flaming shower raining down upon the corralled Arkmuln.

Trilläen held his arms out to stop his companions, holding them back while surveying the Garanths' movements. While several of the bulls facing the Meq'qan had flinched as the wave of power from the detonation hit them, their leaders cracked whips, forcing them to hold their positions against the advancing wakazan.

More Garanth were streaming from the southern end of the camp, preparing to march on Táksabai. The scores of

Garanth bulls squared off to face this new threat from above. Garanth archers shot arrows towards the läenier Wing as the Sumäeri continued their aerial assault of flaming black-seed on the milling Arkmuln.

Thick black smoke filled the air and mingled with the remnant haze of the smoldering valley. The sparks raining down on the Arkmuln from the skies caught fire as they alighted on their targets, burning both clothing and flesh. The Arkmuln glittered brilliantly for a moment before the absorbing seeds wrought their damage. Trilläen watched in horror as thousands of Arkmuln began writhing, their mouths open in silent screams as the enhanced black-seed drove the demons from their purified bodies.

The scent of burning black-seed, clean and crisp as pine resin, filled the air. It overpowered the stink of blood and fear that permeated the valley. Enraged, the Garanth fired wantonly into the billowing smoke above them. The occasional scream of pain as errant arrows struck unlucky läeniers or their riders buoyed the Garanth's bloodlust.

The wind had picked up, causing the dense smoke to swirl hauntingly around the rocks where the three observers waited for the opportunity to get to Tóran. Keeping his eyes on the dark tent, Trilläen inched his way around the remaining boulders and motioned for his companions to follow him. They angled down the last outcropping of rocks and crouched down on the valley floor.

Linking arms to avoid getting separated in the thick smoke, Trilläen led Säeshi and Ta'riq on a zig-zagging course towards their objective. Dodging around the camp, Trilläen felt his heart leap into his throat as a dark shape loomed up in front of them. Pulling his companions back with his elbows, Trilläen circled to the left of the shadowy figure.

Trilläen held his breath as they inched their way around the dark shape. The breeze caught their hair as the menacing form leaned towards them. Peering through the swirling smoke, Trilläen heaved an audible sigh of relief as the discarded cloak hanging over the cauldron's tripod flapped innocently in the draft.

"Mijáko piles! I thought you'd led us into a trap," Säeshi punched the captain in the arm.

Trilläen winced at the blow and rubbed his bicep, grateful that the poor visibility masked his expression. Sumäeri warriors didn't show pain or weakness; they were trained to let the discomfort wash over them, channeling it into determination to complete their mission.

Säeshi would lose faith in him if she'd realized how precarious his hold on the situation was. His nerves were taut as drums as he pulled them forward slowly, straining to hear any sign of discovery. It took great willpower not to flinch at every noise.

The sounds of battle surrounded them. They could hear the bellowing of wakazans as the Meq'qan engaged the Garanth behind them. The stomping of the horned bovines' heavy hooves beat the rhythm of battle, the grunts of striking clubs, and the clashing of swords filling in the melody. Screams of pain provided the counterpoint to the roars and war cries as the three armies clashed on the barren fields outside Táksabai.

The din echoed in Trilläen's ears, disorienting him and causing him to halt and duck at every noise around him. Indecision filled his mind. He was a fool to risk the lives of his companions like this, but Tóran had to either be rescued or killed.

Before he realized it, the dark sides of the canvas structure loomed up in front of him. The tent could comfortably house a score of men. The battle sounds faded to background noise as the three rescuers skirted around the pavilion, searching for an entrance. They edged around the western edge of the tent and spotted Garanth guards posted on either side of what Trilläen assumed was the entry. The rescuers ducked back behind the curve of the canvas, where the guards couldn't see them.

"Can you throw a blade?" Trilläen asked Ta'riq, pulling out a set of flat discs.

The captain held one of the discs in the flat of his hand. He pressed the center stone of the mosaic embedded on the top. Ta'riq jumped back in surprise as the two opposing curved blades snapped out from their positions. Trilläen grinned.

"You hold it by the center disc and fling the blades sideways. They will spin right through anything in their path," Trilläen pointed his thumb towards the Garanth guards. "How's your aim?"

Ta'riq eyed the strange weapons warily. "We usually throw spears or straight blades. I'm not sure if I can hit my target—"

"We don't have time for discussion," Säeshi hissed and grabbed the second blade.

Säeshi pressed the center stone, releasing the sharp edges, and whipped it through the air toward the guards. Shivering at her efficiency, Trilläen propelled the second blade along the same trajectory. Säeshi's aim was true. The first blade sliced through the thick neck of the Garanth guard, dropping him soundlessly to the ground. The second guard turned their direction only a split second before Trilläen's blade removed his head from his muscular shoulders. Two soft thuds announced their arrival at the entrance to the demon's lair.

Ta'riq's eyes slid from the fallen guards to his companions. "I, um…never mind."

The Meq'qan slunk forward just as another gust of wind cleared the smoke from the corralled Arkmuln. He gasped, causing Säeshi and Trilläen to follow his gaze. Across the barren expanse of the scorched valley, the Arkmuln glittered in the filtered light. As the three watched, the bodies of thousands of Meq'qan and Askári Arkmuln disintegrated.

A grating, collective shriek tore from the mouths of the

Arkmuln, setting Trilläen's teeth on edge. As the bodies broke down into tiny glittering particles, puffs of smoke escaped and became immersed with the billowing embers still floating around the encampment. Trilläen looked at Ta'riq, whose pallor had gone from deathly pale to flushed pink.

"Look!" Ta'riq breathed, his eyes glowing with wonder. "Lady Muralia has claimed their souls!"

Trilläen and Säeshi stared enraptured as the glowing remains of the Arkmuln swirled up from each vaporized corpse. The tiny spirals of glittering essence rose into the sky with such purpose and direction that Trilläen did not doubt that the deities had called them. The charged particles coalesced and wafted on the breeze towards the sea. Lord Shamar's rays struck the water with a brilliant flash. The entire Arkmuln population had been released of its bondage in moments and returned to Lady Muralia's bosom.

A lump formed in Trilläen's throat at the triumphant display of the deities' powers. He turned to face his companions and noted the tears spilling down Ta'riq's angular cheeks and the glistening in Säeshi's full eyes.

Trilläen cleared his throat. "We have truly been given a great gift." He nodded to each of them. "Lord Shamar and Lady Muralia have demonstrated their participation in this world for the first time in a millennium."

"The situation must be much graver than we suspected," Säeshi interrupted. "Or else Laylur is much closer to escaping than we realized for them to intervene."

Trilläen let her words sink in. The elation of the past moment sank like a stone in his belly. He felt prickles on the back of his neck, down his arms, and into his fingertips. Rubbing his hands on his thighs, he pulled the short blade from its sheath at his hip.

"Let's see about freeing Tóran."

Ta'riq and Säeshi nodded and fell in behind him. Trilläen eased back the pavilion's flap with his right hand while holding his blade firmly at the ready in his left. The three companions gingerly stepped over the fallen guards and entered the enormous tent. Trilläen was nearly blind inside the dimly lit enclosure after witnessing the brilliance of the deities' powerful displays.

With every sense heightened, Trilläen closed his eyes to speed the adjustment of his eyes. He could smell thick, cloying incense burning somewhere deeper inside the tent, not entirely masking the unmistakable smell of death. Trilläen gripped his blade tighter.

Stepping farther into the pavilion, the three found the sumptuously decorated room nearly empty. Large pillows of every color lay scattered about the walls' edges while a long table filled with partially eaten food stood abandoned in the center of the room. Along the far wall stood two large cages, both empty.

Trilläen searched for the entity that he could sense was present even though he couldn't yet see it. Beside him, Säeshi started to shiver. He grasped her hand and advanced a few more steps.

"Welcome, my brother and sister, to my home—temporary and humble though it may be," a resonant voice greeted them from behind the table and off to their right.

Trilläen stiffened. The voice was intoxicating and compelling. He could feel the power exuding through the sound and into his mind. Stepping around the table, he noticed a long wooden box lying open on the side table. Nestled inside on a cushion of blue silk sat a silver device. He'd seen drawings of the Sceptre of Kulari before and recognized the sheath.

"Drop your weapons, and show me good manners," the voice enslaved them to its will.

Unable to control his hands, Trilläen's blade clattered to the ground. He heard Ta'riq's spear fall behind him and Säeshi's bow slip from her fingers. The presence forced them forward into the light. Sprawling across pillows on the far side of the table lounged the most striking being Trilläen had ever seen. Situated below the lean muscles of the pale man's chest lay Tóran. The Askári lad's head nestled in the man's chiseled stomach in a rather intimate pose. Trilläen saw a flicker of recognition in Tóran's eyes, but the young legionnaire didn't move a muscle.

The Sumäeri captain's mind reeled. His jaw dropped. Trilläen's mind rejected the image in front of him. He knew the creature had to be a demon, but he bore the unmistakable traits of a Shäeli. Trilläen looked over at Säeshi. Sweat sheened her skin as if a war of supreme effort raged inside her body. He tried to reach out to her, but his limbs would not obey his commands.

The demon chuckled. It was the most beautiful sound Trilläen had ever heard. It reminded him of the waterfalls of Samshäeli and Räesha when she'd teased him after saving his neck from the wild kessäeri. His body was filled with a sense of peace and contentment that contrasted with the claxon clatter of alarm bells going off in his mind.

"It's been so long since I've enjoyed the company of family," the handsome demon continued, stroking Tóran's hair. He waved his hand carelessly at his guests, indicating that they should join him on the sumptuous cushions. "Sit, eat, and enjoy yourselves!"

Trilläen's mutinous legs folded beneath him, and he found himself seated at eye level with the creature that became more enthralling and terrifying by the second. He stared into the man's sparkling dark blue eyes and realized that he wanted nothing more than to tell the demon his most intimate secrets.

chapter 16: The Black Tent

Tóran woke to the soft touch of someone caressing his hair along the temple. The contact was gentle and loving, and for a moment, he luxuriated in the blissful sensation. The thick scent of incense filled his nostrils, numbing his brain and coating his tongue with its purple-black flavor. Tóran felt weightless, peaceful, and whole. His mind wandered, remembering the Meq'qan priestesses and their healing baths, how they had kneaded his exhausted muscles and cleansed his skin after fleeing Dúlnat and the red mage pursuing Cédron...

Tóran's eyes flew open as the memories of recent events

flooded painfully into his awareness. He saw the dark canvas of the tent he was lying in and felt the soft cushions beneath his body. The fingers continued to stroke his head and along his cheek. Tóran's breath hitched, and he froze.

"Ah, my handsome warrior awakens," a melodic tenor chuckled above him.

The caresses stopped. Knees shifted, and Tóran realized that his head was nestled in someone's lap. Images of sparkling, deep blue eyes and screams of pain filled his mind. The legionnaire felt the hard thighs beneath his cheekbone. His mouth went dry. Tóran sucked in a sharp breath. He still had his own thoughts.

"I'm not Arkmuln?" he croaked, his throat parched and tight with the effort.

A laugh rolled out of the belly of the demon, the vibration tickling the back of his head where it rested against the demon's torso. "Of course not, my pet. I wouldn't waste one so delicious by turning you into Arkmuln. No," the demon sighed, "you are far too tasty a morsel for that."

Tóran's stomach clenched. His skin tingled as he tried to remember anything after arriving in the tent. He recalled watching the transformation of the other prisoners into Arkmuln. Otherwise, there was nothing except the demon's sparkling eyes. They gave him the sensation of baring his soul. Fear trickled down Tóran's spine. If he'd compromised the Meq'qan or Cédron to this fiend, he would never forgive himself.

Options raced through his brain. He was unarmed, but a likely-looking knife was on the table, and the sharp, silver sheath was still lying in the open box. A sculpture of a fabled Aruzzi graced the table, complete with wings and seven long feathered tails. From the Aruzzi's open beak curled wisps of dark smoke, a fog of incense that scattered Tóran's thoughts.

"Ah, your doomed rescue attempt has begun," the demon drawled, his voice filled with humor, his fingers resuming their stroking of Tóran's long hair. "Let's just wait here for them, shall we?"

Outside the tent, Tóran could hear the guttural shouts and grunts of the Garanth bulls as they barked orders and prepared to face the Meq'qan warriors that Chaq'ta led. Explosions caused the tent to ripple from the compressions. Shrieks, like thousands of voices raised in pain and longing, grated in Tóran's ears.

The ground rumbled beneath them, and Tóran recognized the sound of the wakazan stampeding. Sweat beaded along his hairline. If those wakazan charged into the tent, there would be nothing left in their wake. The demon stroked his hair in a slow, leisurely way as he hummed a soothing melody.

Tóran's lids were heavy and drooping. It felt like the incense was thickening and clouding his thoughts. His body felt leaden. He fought to sharpen his vision on the gleaming hilt of the knife lying on the table and focus his escape plan, but the thrumming of the demon's voice overpowered him. He struggled to sit up and realized that his host had utterly immobilized him.

Tóran could move his eyes around the room but couldn't turn his head or raise his limbs. Tendrils of panic coiled around his throat and strangled him. He grunted, trying to heave his body, any part of his body, off the demon's lap, but he was held fast in a spell as hard as iron.

"Ah, my pet," the demon crooned, lapsing into words but still wavering his voice along the soothing melodic line. "I can't have you slipping away before the big reveal now, can I? Your friends will be here shortly to get you, and I'd hate to disappoint them."

The demon stretched out his legs and continued his caresses, sliding his hands down Tóran's shoulder and curling around his muscular arm. "I have enjoyed our little dalliance," he breathed into Tóran's ear. "Your passion and purpose are so…um, fulfilling."

Gorge rose in Tóran's throat. He prayed that he could

spew across the demon's legs, distracting the monster from the binding spell that kept him incapacitated. But his body betrayed him. The acid sank back down, threatening to burn through his core as he remained rigid and helpless in the demon's lap.

More explosions and screams came from outside as the skirmish raged around them. Tóran watched the tent supports shake with the tremors caused by the wakazan as they stormed the camp. Tóran sent a prayer to Orwaena to watch over Chaq'ta, his friend Ta'riq, and the other three-hundred odd Meq'qan he'd led into this nightmare fiasco.

The demon continued to hum softly and twirl Tóran's hair around his fingers. His captor's placidity was aggravating. The vibration of the sound bored into Tóran's brain, drawing him into madness. His breathing became rapid as he strained against the invisible bonds of the spell. The demon gave him a little slap on the cheek.

"Stop that, you darling creature," he cooed, smoothing the spot where he'd struck Tóran's face. "Your friends are just arriving, and I won't have you appearing out of sorts."

True to the demon's word, he heard the tell-tale thump of guards going down and spied a ripple in the tent's canvas as someone raised the flaps. After a short moment, the demon called out a greeting to the arrivals, and Tóran heard the unmistakable sound of weapons dropping to the floor.

The demon greeted the rescue party as his family. Tóran couldn't imagine who would come to his rescue with whom this demon could claim kinship. Tóran's heart sank as he spied Ta'riq, then the Shäeli captain Trilläen Villinäes and another Sumäeri warrior. Tóran gasped. The Sumäeri looked just like Räesha. It was the eyes; the aquamarine eyes were Räesha's. That was impossible; he'd seen her fall in battle.

"Ah, the disgraced Captain Villinäes of the Council Guard," the demon said with nectar-smooth humor coloring his voice. "I do hope you haven't put too much stock in this rescue effort. It won't serve you the way you hope it will."

Turning his head, the demon nodded to the Sumäeri warrior. "And young Miss Angäersol, such an honor to have a member of your esteemed family join me in my most humble abode." The demon swept his free arm around to indicate the sumptuously decorated tent.

The demon then turned his eyes to the third member of the party. "Ta'riq, a survivor of the Ta'voran Meq'qan. I do hope you don't take offense at our little campaign against your people. It wasn't personal, you know, just this smelly business of revenge."

Tóran could see the expressions on their faces as the demon sifted through their minds, gleaning their identities and who knew what else. Each remained impassive under the demon's control, but Trilläen's eyes burned with unmistakable hate. Räesha's face seemed softer than he'd remembered it, and both sorrow and fear filled her eyes.

Ta'riq looked like he was going to faint. The legionnaire hoped that the rest of the Meq'qan were safe and engaging the Garanth under Chaq'ta's command. The alternative was too horrible to consider.

The demon waved his guests to sit down at the table and invited them to share in his repast. Tóran watched as they all moved woodenly towards the table and sat down with jerky motions. He knew that their bodies were fighting the demon's command and that it would be a losing battle.

"I'm sure you all know my companion here," the demon lifted Tóran to a sitting position but kept a possessive arm around his shoulders. "Tóran, say hello to our guests."

Tóran's mouth moved of its own accord, forming a greeting that croaked out against his will. He saw Räesha's eyes widen and Trilläen's narrow. Ta'riq's green pallor turned sheet white. Now that the demon had so conclusively demonstrated the depth of his hold upon each of them, Tóran couldn't imagine what its next move would be.

Tóran wished he knew why he hadn't been converted to Arkmuln like the rest of the captives, at least, the ones who survived the process. He wracked his brain but couldn't remember anything specific about the demon's plans for him. He recalled that the silver sheath for the Sceptre of Kulari rested in the box at the end of the table, but he couldn't remember why the demon needed it. Indeed, the sceptre was safely buried deep within Auräevya's trunk in the center of Samshäeli, where no demon could enter.

Tóran did remember Cédron's quest for all the sacred stones. They fit on the sceptre by the silver sheath. He also knew that somehow, he'd have to not only find a way to escape but to take the sheath with him. His thoughts turned away from escape as the three guests sat down across the table from him on the large cushions.

Tóran held Trilläen's gaze. He saw both fear and confusion within the Sumäeri's amethyst eyes. The warrior had a sheen of perspiration covering his forehead and cheeks, giving his skin a sickly glow in the glowstone light. Tóran glanced at Ta'riq. He could smell the sharp bitterness of the Meq'qan's sweat and terror.

"Please, eat and drink," the demon invited them with a lazy wave of his arm. "There is no need to stand on ceremony among family, and I've been so lonely with only the dull Garanth or the Arkmuln. Not a very talkative bunch, if I do say so." He chuckled at his wit.

The three guests sat stock still with only their eyes able to dart around the room. The demon unwrapped his arm from around Tóran's shoulders and leaned forward towards his guests. Tóran's torso slipped sideways down onto the seat of the chaise; his head turned upwards to watch the demon. The creature's eyes glinted, and a cold smile formed on his lips.

"I've offered you food and drink," the demon's silky voice reminded his guests. His eyes narrowed, and Tóran held his breath. "Not to accept my hospitality would be considered rude. Why would you offend me, brother?" The demon's glittering eyes fixed on Trilläen, who tensed under his gaze. "Can it be that you do not trust me? I have given you no cause—"

As the demon leaned closer towards Trilläen, a faint glow began to show through the canvas of the tent. At first, the light was weak, but it illuminated the dark shadows in the black tent's corners with bright green light within a few seconds.

Tóran felt the ground beneath him rumble as if from another ground shake, and he rolled off the chaise onto the carpeted floor. The demon rose to his feet, glancing towards the flap of the tent. The distraction loosened his grip on his captives. They sprang to life.

Ta'riq threw himself upon the table, knocking the Aruzzi incense burner to the floor. He got to his feet, stomping the clay statue and extinguishing the smoke. Tóran felt his mind clear. He rolled underneath the table and towards his friends. Trilläen whipped a knife from his belt and leaped upon the demon, both of them tumbling back onto the chaise like passionate lovers in a lethal embrace. Ta'riq reached down and pulled Tóran to his feet.

"Are you hurt?" he asked anxiously, his yellow eyes raking his friend from top to toe. "Can you walk?"

Tóran grinned and clasped Ta'riq's arm. "I can do better than that!"

With a nod to Ta'riq and Räesha, Tóran spun around and pounced on the demon's back. The creature loomed over Trilläen, who was pinned by the demon's alabaster limbs. The ground shook more forcefully now, preventing anyone from maintaining solid footing. The green light continued to burn brighter, casting the demon's features into sharp relief as it grimaced beneath the weight of his assailants.

"You cannot defeat me," the brute hissed, his dark blue eyes snapping. With a burst of energy, the demon shoved his attackers off and stood. He grasped Trilläen by the throat and reached over his shoulder for Tóran, throwing them away from himself.

Tóran found himself flying across the room, Trilläen

airborne beside him, before crashing into one of the tent poles. The entire structure shivered from the impact. The glowstone lanterns hanging from the structure's joints swung, some falling to the ground and breaking.

The fiend turned to Ta'riq. "Very clever for an ignorant Meq'qan. Dousing the incense won't save you, though. Movement only gives you the illusion of freedom. You are all still very much my prisoners."

Tóran yelled a warning to Ta'riq. Trilläen was at his side instantly, his hand out. Tóran rose shakily to his feet.

"Together then?" Trilläen handed Tóran a second dagger from his belt and jutted his sharp chin towards the demon.

Tóran gripped the long knife. He nodded at Trilläen, and they charged. The demon raised a hand and wiggled his fingers. Several hanging lanterns exploded, the shards of glass and thin metal slicing into them and slowing their advance. Outside, Tóran could hear escalations in yells and cries as the ground shake continued.

The thought of Chaq'ta's leading the wakazan and his Meq'qan warriors through the Garanth camp filled his heart with pride for a short moment, then turned it to ice. Nothing would stop them from razing the black tent. There was no way Chaq'ta would know that he and his rescuers were trapped within it.

Tóran roared and charged through the sharp, flying debris using his arm as a buffer, the blade angled to strike the demon's head the moment he was within reach. Trilläen was a half-step behind him, his war cry ringing throughout the tent. The two men circled the demon, each feinting and stabbing, looking for a distraction or weakness.

Still standing behind the table, Räesha didn't move. She stood paralyzed, staring out the flap of the tent where the green glow was brightest. Ta'riq, still pale and drawn, stared at her. His hands clenched and unclenched at his sides.

"Ta'riq!" Tóran's hoarse cry jolted the Meq'qan into action.

Ta'riq shook his head and looked around the room. The demon spun away from the advancing attack and skirted up behind the Meq'qan.

"You see," the demon hissed in Ta'riq's ear. "Your heroism was a wasted effort."

The monster stabbed a wicked blade into Ta'riq's shoulder, sliding it in hilt-deep and slicing downward. Ta'riq's eyes rolled back. He slumped over the table and slid to the floor. Dark blood pooled all around him, covering the table with its vermillion stain.

"No!" Tóran cried, his throat rasping in pain.

Ta'riq had survived the slaughter of his entire tribe and the battle against the Hazzara in the Zig'orman Marshes. He had been Tóran's staunchest supporter since leaving the Meq'qan tribes. The thought of losing his friend and ally to this beast shredded Tóran's heart. He couldn't lose Ta'riq after all they'd been through together.

Trilläen had not stopped to watch the demon strike Ta'riq. He'd found Tóran's blade on the floor of the cage behind the chaise and charged forward. The enemy turned to face this new threat, Ta'riq's blood dripping in slow, thick drops from the tip of the blade in his hand. The demon raised his hand to parry the attack.

Outside, shrieks and pounding were louder, and the ground pitched and undulated. Tóran flipped the dagger in his hand so that he was balancing the blade in his fingers. Without a second thought, he threw the knife, striking the demon's wrist at the juncture of the hand.

Howling and wringing his hand, the brute dropped his dagger just as Trilläen swung the sword. The demon twisted his wrist, and Trilläen's sword turned sideways. The blade glanced off the demon's shoulder. Tóran gasped as the monster gripped his attacker by the throat. Trilläen's feet dangled several inches off the carpet, his legs spasmodic.

"Now, is that any way to treat your family?" he hissed in Trilläen's ear. "If I didn't know better, I'd say you weren't happy to see me."

The demon slammed Trilläen to the ground with a loud crack. Trilläen screamed but maintained his hold on the sword. As he crumpled, he brought the blade up under the demon's chin and through his face. The sliver of flesh and bone fell. Only the back teeth and hollows showed where the demon's nose and eyes had been.

Although weakened and blinded, the demon inexorably rose and turned towards Trilläen again. The fiend grasped the sword by the blade and twisted it out of the captain's grip. He flung it across the tent where it landed near Ta'riq's still form.

"That wasn't very nice, little brother," the demon slurred through what remained of his mouth.

Tóran felt like retching. Ta'riq was dead, Räesha immobilized by the green light, and now Trilläen was about to be torn to shreds by this infernal creature of Laylur's. He looked around for any weapon that would be effective against his enemy and spied the silver sheath still sitting in its box from Zaveen.

An image popped unbidden into his mind. He saw the silver sheath fixed to the end of the Sceptre of Kulari with the four sacred stones in their settings, their glow painfully bright. The silver gleamed on the talisman as if it was molten, flowing down the wooden staff and reshaping into a serrated sword.

Tóran lunged for the silver sheath still resting in its box. He skidded in Ta'riq's blood as he stretched over his friend's body to grasp the sheath. Focusing on the image, he watched as the metal melted and reformed into the blade of his vision.

"Clever," rasped the demon who stood grasping Trilläen's head between his strong hands. One quick jerk and the brute would snap Trilläen's neck, Tóran had no doubt.

"But is your body as quick as your mind? Can you reach this brave young captain before I end him?" The brute grinned; at least the sides of his cheeks raised, deepening the pits behind the shorn mandible.

Räesha began to scream. At first, it was a whimper, barely audible to Tóran as he'd been in the throes of his vision, but now rose to a fevered pitch. As he turned to stare at her, she grew taller. Thick, slimy antennae sprouted from her head and arched downward over the skull behind her ears. Her face flattened, and long, spindly legs burst out all down the length of her torso. Inside the center of her flattened body, ridges began to form. They were thick and glowed with the same eerie green light that now filled the tent.

The demon gaped at her, his attention diverted from the Sumäeri within his grip. Tóran sprang into action. He threw the sheath in a high, slow arch towards the demon and flung himself over the table. His body tumbled forward in mid-air, landing with his hands on the back of the chaise lounge. He flipped himself up and over, catching the serrated blade as it spiraled down.

Tóran's feet sailed into the demon's shoulders, knocking the creature away from Trilläen. With a ferocity born from the terror of watching the prisoners become Arkmuln and the grief at the loss of Ta'riq, Tóran drew the blade across the demon's throat with such savagery that what remained of its head spun several feet away from his body. Ichor splashed the canvas walls, burning holes in the fabric.

Trilläen gripped Tóran by the shoulder in silent thanks. The two warriors cast a last glance at the demon's body and made their way across the tent. Tóran knelt by Ta'riq's side and sent a prayer to Hamra for his fallen friend. Through blurred vision, he reached down and closed the yellow eyes, now devoid of life. Tóran turned and wiped the silver blade across the sofa cushions, cleaning the demon's ichor from its polished surface. Once clean, the talisman returned to its previous form.

"You need to take this to Samshäeli," he said, holding the silver sheath to Trilläen.

The Sumäeri captain shoved it through the straps across his shoulders and nodded his thanks. "I will see that it gets safely to Cédron when he is ready."

The ground trembled again, and Tóran stood, turning towards the Shäeli woman. Her transformation informed him that she wasn't Räesha as he'd initially thought. Either she was a close family member, or perhaps the Sumäeri all resemble each other. Tóran shrugged and stepped up to Trilläen.

"Who is she, and what is she doing?" he asked, watching the young woman and keeping a distance from the waving antennae.

The woman still faced the open flap of the tent, her form slipping back to its regular shape. When her transformation was complete, she turned haunted eyes towards Trilläen.

"Whatever Läenshi has unleashed," she breathed, her eyes wide and staring. "It is not a power seen before in this world. There is no stopping it."

chapter 17: The Ancient Mariners

"Set her down here," Sénna instructed the red journeymage carrying her grandmother's unconscious and dripping form.

The exhausted journeymage bent to lay down his burden, his features straining with the effort. His grip slipped, causing the woman to hit the floor with a soft moan.

"Careful, fool!" Sénna hissed. She slipped on the floor, made wet by their sodden clothes, and nearly fell herself. "She's been through enough without you dropping her and breaking a hip."

The grim-faced mage tucked a cloak under the woman's

head. Sénna stared into Am'aranth's pale face and shivered. She couldn't lose her grandmother so soon after Myknét's death. As strong as she was, Sénna could feel the gaping chasm of grief widening, threatening to swallow her whole. Another bout of shivers took her, the result of her water-soaked clothes and the horrors she'd just witnessed.

Glancing around their temporary refuge, Sénna noted the injuries sustained by several mages and her brother Murádit. None appeared to be life-threatening other than her grandmother's, who still hadn't regained consciousness after the white mage's explosion had destroyed their boat.

Sénna closed her eyes and willed her heartbeat to slow and the shaking to stop. She took several deep breaths with little success. Images of tiny charred legs and shredded bodies floating around her filled her mind, causing her to retch. The explosion was so sudden that nobody could prepare for it. Only those few who had been in the very front of the boat made it through the initial blast. Most of the children who landed in the water couldn't yet swim and subsequently drowned. Their shrill, terrified cries still rang in Sénna's ears.

Am'aranth and Urléen had both weathered the disaster. Although Urléen maintained her faculties enough to assist the others in getting clear of the carnage, it had taken nearly all of Sénna's strength to keep her unconscious grandmother afloat. Scóurj enlisted the help of the apprentice and journeymages and got all of the survivors into the makeshift refuge. Sénna thought the building must have once been a warehouse near the underground harbor. The sounds of battle dwindled as someone shut the door, and Sénna heard footsteps approach. She opened her eyes.

"Any change?" Urléen grunted. She knelt on the opposite side of Am'aranth, her brassy curls tumbling into her eyes. She shoved them back.

Cybél hung back, pulling at her dress where it clung to her body and grimacing at the outline it revealed. Urléen's weathered face crinkled around deep-set brown eyes as Am'aranth stirred.

"Ah, she wakes." Urléen patted Sénna's hand. "I'll leave her to you then." She turned and raised a hand, beckoning Cybél to assist her to her feet. The two of them stepped a few paces away and sat down to await the end of the battle still raging along the pier outside.

Am'aranth groaned and started to sit up. Sénna leaned down and cradled her grandmother's shoulders, helping her to sit up.

"Are you hurt, Grandmother?" she asked. Sénna eyed her grandmother anxiously, her yellow eyes alert for any signs of discomfort.

Am'aranth reached out a trembling hand and wiped a stray tendril of hair off Sénna's cheek, tucking it behind her ear. She glanced over at her friend Urléen and nodded.

"I'll be fine, I just need—"

Shouts and footsteps rang out in the street just outside their haven. The door banged open, and the men from the Varkáras Caravan, the mages, and a few other stragglers spilled into the warehouse. Their faces flushed and eyes bright; even the wounded wore faint grins. The scent of dried seaweed and scorched wood followed them through the door. Sénna wrinkled her nose.

"We have sealed off the cavern and trapped our enemies on the other side," Shozin boomed as he herded the men towards the center of the warehouse. "We are safe here. We can get our wounded to the healers in the Laborers Quadrant to the south, then return to our encampment."

Sénna watched as the Caravan Master conferred with Scóurj, Mage Kiél, and a few of his journeymages. They appeared to be discussing safe locations as the men spoke animatedly with their hands, gesturing in different directions. She noticed that the group from Dúlnat stood in a tight knot across the room, speaking in hushed tones and occasionally glancing in her direction. She bent her head again to speak to

Am'aranth when Murádit bounded in front of her.

"Grandmother, are you hurt?" he asked. Concern creased Murádit's forehead and clouded his feline eyes.

Am'aranth shook her head, but Murádit's gaze then sought Sénna's. She frowned and indicated he should take Am'aranth's opposite arm. The two of them gently pulled the woman to her feet and held her steady until she could stand without swaying.

"She lost consciousness after the explosion. I helped keep her afloat until the journeymages could get us out of the water and onto the dock," Sénna informed her brother. As she spoke, her eyes studied her grandmother's pallor and stance. "She seems to have recovered fairly well."

Am'aranth's eyes flashed at her grandchildren. "I told you I am fine," she snapped and shook off their hands. She stood, listing a little to one side.

Murádit eyed her with one eyebrow raised, then glanced again at his sister. Sénna pursed her lips and shrugged. The young man nodded and grabbed his grandmother by the elbow, steering her out the back of the warehouse.

"Come on," he said as he motioned his sister to follow. "I have something to show you."

Reluctantly, Sénna followed her brother and raised her eyebrows when Urléen and Cybél moved to join them. After a moment, the group from Dúlnat followed as well. Sénna glanced over her shoulder to where the other men were still engaged in a heated discussion and hadn't seemed to notice their imminent departure.

Murádit led the small group out of the warehouse and down the back street until they reached the main thoroughfare along the northern side of the waterfront. The baskets of glowstones were dim here, their feeble light casting shadows on the crumbling walls. He stopped and turned around. Scanning the group, Murádit called back to Anéton.

"Go and tell your Caravan Master and the mages they

won't want to miss this," Murádit grinned. He turned back around and stepped toward one of the most prominent buildings lining the street.

The warehouse was longer than a city block, with a domed roof disappearing into the gloom above. Sénna had never seen such intricate locking mechanisms as those that covered the enormous double doors. Creatures with flat, rounded bodies and long, pointed appendages like tentacles guarded the entrance. They caused the skin on her arms to crawl. Murádit turned to face them with a slight half-smile on his face.

"There is no safer place in the underground city, though I doubt very much if the mages even know about it." Murádit winked at his sister and jutted his chin to the approaching group behind them. "I need Scóurj to help me open the doors. These gears require two people to activate."

Sénna turned, listening to the murmur of voices behind her. She saw the cavern's remaining survivors approaching warily, eyes darting in all directions as if expecting an attack, either from the murky streets or the city above. Her misgivings screamed in her head to flee, but she didn't know how to navigate the streets of the underground city safely or where she would go even if she could escape.

None knew what the Garanth and their Arkmuln were doing above in the city proper. There may no longer be a home where she could retreat. She turned back to her brother, who had pulled Scóurj up to the massive doors with him. Am'aranth squeezed her arm as Murádit and Scóurj began pressing a sequence of nearly imperceptible buttons in a dance that resembled a ship rolling atop the waves.

Sénna gasped, and Am'aranth's eyes widened when the gears began to turn. The rumbling voices of the crowd rose. One by one, the levers released each locking mechanism for the door like a ripple of water in a pool, flowing out from the center with gentle *snicks* until the waves faded and the door unlocked. Murádit and Scóurj pushed the doors inward and beckoned everyone forward.

Their footsteps echoed as they entered a spacious room with a vaulted ceiling covered in glass plates. The air in the room was stale and musty, but it was not the dead air of abandonment. Sénna decided that Murádit and his friends must have been there before. Lining the walls on either side of the room were rows of delicate chains hanging down with polished globes containing glowstones, filling the room with light. Behind the lamps were floor-to-ceiling shelves built into the walls and filled with scroll canisters, dusty and brittle from Tides of neglect.

In the very center of the room, covering most of the available space, was an enormous model of the heavens. In the center was Lady Muralia, resplendent as a green globe the size of a full-grown watowren, with the glimmering Lord Shamar circling her in his daily orbit. Just inside and on polar orbit from Lord Shamar were the three moon sisters, red Orwaena, blue Azria, and violet Hamra, each following the other in their protective dance across from their father.

Around the outside of the familiar celestial bodies swung a smaller object. This one, like a tiny ball with ribbons trailing out behind it, took a prolonged turn around the very outskirts of the mobile's edges. *Haeris!* Sénna recognized the comet that blazed through the sky each Tide. The whirling device squeaked as it turned, catching its gears where the teeth were dry.

Sénna pulled Am'aranth along with her, and the two reached the back of the room where a wall with a vibrant and ornate scene had caught her eye. The frieze was a rough map of Muralia. Each of the four points of the compass ended in one of the fabled four gates to the Abyss.

The western, the Shalaen Falls, was guarded by the image of Wezija in all her terrifying glory. Sénna swallowed a lump of panic; her ordeal with the guardian was still very fresh in her mind.

The northern gate rested near the volcanic Sinharkon

Range, where sulphurous fumes from Nuriak's Cauldron swirled around the image of Maftaka. He was an explosive guardian represented by plumes of smoke, flames, and wastelands. Sénna recalled only a few old tales of Maftaka told by worn travelers deep in their pints at Lótril's Cave.

To the south, deep in the Zahili Desert, rested the southern gate. Eyries of winged Aruzzi guarded it, their ornate plumage and seven-feathered tails bristling fiercely in the image. There had been speculation among the Gróshan that perhaps the Aruzzi no longer existed, for none had seen them for several generations.

The final image was of Auräevya, the Tree of Life, and the eastern gate, located in the center of Samshäeli. Even on the engraved frieze, Sénna thought the tree looked limp. If Auräevya or any other gates fell, there would be nothing between Laylur and his vengeance upon the deities who imprisoned him.

"She is failing," Am'aranth croaked in a hoarse voice, her fingers touching the image of Auräevya on the wall. "The Great Demon has focused his efforts on her because she is already weakened." She turned her golden eyes to her granddaughter and shook her head. "Such a move shows patience and cunning."

Sénna's brows raised, and she regarded her grandmother. "How so? I see no patience in his attempt on Shalaen Falls or his campaign above us."

"Ah," Am'aranth smiled and waggled a finger at her granddaughter. "But he is moving slowly, methodically." Am'aranth turned again to the frieze and placed her finger at Nuriak's Cauldron. "Laylur could have come through this gate. Maftaka is predisposed to destruction, which would have blasted all four lands into a waste like—"

"Then why didn't he?" Sénna interrupted, shrugging her shoulders. "It would have saved him time and the effort of waging war against all four lands."

Am'aranth nodded, the silver strands in her hair catching

the light of the globes. "Yes, but think about why he might not want a swift takeover. If he destroys our lands slowly and from within, we suffer. Our suffering is torture to Lady Muralia, for we are all connected. All Lord Shamar can do is watch, helpless from his vigilance in the sky, as his beloved withers and writhes in pain. That, my dear, would be fitting revenge for his interminable incarceration, don't you think?"

Sénna's brows furrowed, and her gaze returned to the frieze. She glanced around the room and spotted Cédron among the survivors milling around the marvels of the room. She wondered about his story and considered what he might have left out.

Sénna's mind raced, putting pieces together and discarding them to puzzle out Cédron's mission and role. Clearly, he was essential to all those supporting him, so he had followers who held hope. Even her grandmother had singled him out earlier—

Sénna's eyes flashed towards her grandmother. "What do you know about him?" She jerked her chin towards the fair-haired lad from the north. "You didn't believe his story about sacred stones and a prophecy, did you?"

Am'aranth regarded her granddaughter with narrowed eyes. "Yes, I did," she said and jabbed a finger into Sénna's chest. "And you had better also if you want to live. He bears the marks of fire and water already. He still needs air and terra before he can hope to wield the Sceptre of Kulari. He will need all the help he can get. You must go with him. You can guide him like no other can."

"What do you mean?" Sénna crossed her arms across her chest and frowned at her grandmother. "Why must I go? He's got companions aplenty."

Am'aranth hardened her gaze, her lips a white line across her face. "That young man has lived a sheltered life. He has no concept of the world or the people in it. You have the skills of the Gróshan that you have taught yourself, despite my best efforts to the contrary. Your ability to observe and interpret around you is a skill that could save both your lives." Sénna opened her mouth to argue, but Am'aranth raised a quelling hand. "And, somehow, your destinies are intertwined. Nek'ka has foreseen it. You must be with him when he leaves."

Am'aranth turned and made her way across the room, where Cybél sat with her grandmother. The older woman's coppery hair competed with the sparkling gemstones she'd woven in it, making her almost too painful to look at in the light of the glowstones.

Sénna shook her head. She would never understand the need for such garish adornments. Sénna turned to find her brother when she heard a thud and a grunt. She spun back around to see Urléen doubled up on the floor, struggling to breathe.

Cybél was frantically pulling at the strings of her grandmother's dress, but her cold fingers fumbled.

"A knife," she cried. "Someone help me, please!"

Sénna raced over and slid down next to the girl, pulling Myknét's dagger from her hip. She sliced through the water-tightened leather laces and helped Cybél release the binding on her grandmother's bodice. Their cries of distress had captured the attention of the Shäeli in the room. Roväen and Cédron knelt beside the wheezing woman.

Am'aranth backed away, giving the Shäeli room. Roväen's sharp blue eyes inspected every inch of Urléen in seconds, and he began rummaging through the pouch at his side. Cédron pulled his staff Räeshun from his back and looked at his uncle. Sénna and Cybél pulled off Urléen's outer bodice and gasped.

"What happened to her?" Cybél asked, eying her grandmother's swollen, blue and purple skin. "She was fine until just a few moments ago, and then…." A single tear rolled down her waxen face, and she swallowed. "She can't breathe; what can we do?"

Sénna glanced at the two Shäeli, whose grim faces

mirrored her fears. Rovӓen pulled a palm-sized green stone riddled with red veins and examined it, then pulled Urléen's shift down, exposing the woman's upper torso. Her chest heaved with effort, but her lungs were getting only a little air. The woman's eyes were wide, and her hands clawed at her granddaughter.

"She must have been struck by something when the boat exploded," Rovӓen said, running his long fingers over her chest and stomach. The swelling pulled the skin taut, and the blue-purple-black discoloration deepened at the impact site. "She is bleeding inside, and it is preventing her from breathing. I can't tell if the blood is filling up inside her lungs or just filling up her body and putting pressure on her lungs, but either way—"

"Does anyone have wine? Or water?" Cybél looked at each person as she worked the buckle of the large leather pouch she wore across her shoulder.

Anéton knelt at her side, holding out a flask. "It's not wine, but it'll take away any pain."

"Spirits work best," Cybél said, grabbing the flask and flashing a strained smile at the legionnaire. "Thank you."

Cybél pulled a small purse from the satchel and opened the drawstrings. She carefully poured a little glittering powder into the mouth of the flask. Senna heard a faint hiss as the dust hit the alcohol. A puff of red smoke rose from the tiny decanter, but Cybél bent over her grandmother before Sénna could get a good look at it.

Sénna nudged Am'aranth with her elbow. "What is that powder she's using?"

Am'aranth's golden eyes narrowed, and she pursed her lips. "I'm not sure. The Meq'qan would powder bones for tinctures, but that looked more like a powdered stone. Firestone, if I'm not mistaken."

"What good would that do? Firestone doesn't have healing properties, does it?" Sénna craned her neck to see.

Cybél lifted the drink to her grandmother's lips. "Please,

you must drink."

Urléen batted away the flask with trembling hands. "Save it for those who will live."

"No, you must live!" Cybél shook Urléen's shoulder. "You can't leave me. I'm not ready."

Urléen grasped Cybél's hand and squeezed feebly. "You must take over now. You have the skills." She wheezed and slumped back, her chest heaving with shallow pants. "Carry on our knowledge."

Cybél laid the flask on Urléen's chest. She let go of her grandmother's hand and stood, grabbing Rovään's leather jerkin. "Please, use your Shäeli magic; make her drink."

Rovään swallowed and shook his head. "The talent I have wouldn't serve her. It is her time."

"No!" Cybél's anguish echoed throughout the building. She pounded Rovään's chest, tears streaming down her cheeks. "Please, she'll die! I'll have no one left if I lose her."

Cédron pried her hands from his uncle's shirt and held them. Sénna saw him look at his uncle and acknowledge the subtle shaking of his head. Cédron glanced down at the gasping Cybél and swallowed.

"Her wounds are too great," he said, pulling Cybél into his chest and holding her as she sobbed. He stroked her hair and patted her back, then eased her away and shook her gently. "You need to be with her now. She is reaching for you."

Cybél hiccupped and nodded, kneeling at her grandmother's side and clutching her bony hands. A blue tinge painted Urléen's lips. Sénna's eyes widened when she saw Urléen's purpling fingernails. She couldn't have more than a few moments left. Sénna's chest felt tight, but she knew Cybél would need her, so she remained by the young woman's side.

"What can I do for you, grandmother?" Cybél's lips quivered, but her hands remained firmly in Urléen's grasp.

Urléen's mouth worked, but no sound came out. Urléen

pulled her right hand from her granddaughter's and grasped the ornate arm cuff on her left upper arm. She pulled it off, grimacing with the effort, and handed it to Cybél. Urléen moved her lips again.

Cybél leaned over her grandmother and put her ear to the gasping woman's lips. "What is it, grandmother?"

Senna couldn't hear everything that Urléen whispered to her granddaughter, but she thought she heard the words "key" and "past," but she couldn't be sure, and there was no time to ask. Tiny pink bubbles foamed at the corners of Urléen's mouth. Urléen gripped her granddaughter's hands with white knuckles and let go.

Cybél nodded, a sob escaping her lips as she embraced her grandmother. Urléen's wheezing became a gurgle for only a couple of breaths before she fell silent. Sénna laid a gentle hand on her friend's back. She could feel Cybél's shudders through the wet fabric of her dress. Sénna leaned in close.

"Cybél, I'm so sorry," her voice cracked, and she cleared her throat. "We will need to find a place to release her."

Cybél looked up at her with red-rimmed eyes and tear-streaked cheeks. "We have no place to bury her or light a pyre. But I can't just leave her here."

Cédron knelt to face Cybél. "We are near the sea. My uncle and I can give her a water burial. I know it's not your custom, but we don't have another choice."

Cybél looked at Sénna. The tightness in Sénna's chest worked its way higher. She still harbored misgivings, but Cédron had given Myknét a proper fire release. She shrugged her shoulders and looked down at the woman's body. The swelling had stopped, and Urléen's skin took on a gray pallor beneath all the pooled blood. Sénna wondered if her tight skin would split.

"We have to do something," she nodded to Cybél. "Perhaps he can give her the proper honors as he did—"

"With Myknét." Cybél whispered and nodded to Cédron.

"But we are too far from the sea and can't go back the way we came," Sénna frowned at the two Shäeli. "Your fire burial would burn down the building. How can you perform a water burial?"

Roväen nodded towards the mages. "I'll need their help to create a vessel. Cédron, please go tell Mage Kiél that I need to speak with him."

Despite her uneasiness around both mages and Shäeli, Sénna marveled at the quick but stunning release they'd given Urléen. At Roväen's request, Mage Kiél and his journeymages had used the Árk'äezhi energy of their terrastones to carve a depression in the bedrock and lay the woman's body within it. Cédron's staff Räeshun summoned water from the nearby sea using the aquastone affixed to her finger-bone crown.

After filling the depression deep enough to cover Urléen's body, the Shäeli stood at opposite ends of the pool, one at her head and one at her feet. Roväen held his small aquastone over Urléen's feet, and Cédron held Räeshun out with her sacred aquastone facing the pool. Then they sang.

Sénna couldn't understand the words, but she would never forget the feeling of power and joy that pulsed through her as she listened. Just like with Myknét, Urléen's body dissolved into tiny sparks of light that shimmered in the water before being absorbed into the terra and returned to Lady Muralia.

Sénna guessed that few who'd witnessed the release had ever experienced something so miraculous. It was rare indeed to see proof of the deities' involvement with and compassion for their peoples. She walked away, feeling disoriented and confused about the young Shäeli man she wanted to dislike.

"He is extraordinary," Am'aranth mused as they made their way back inside the building with the planet model and artifacts. "You know, child, I do believe he is the child of the prophecy. If our world is to survive, we must get him to safety. I will speak to Scóurj." She turned to seek the little Gróshan.

Sénna stared after her grandmother for a moment, then made her decision. She crossed the room where Cédron and his friends from Dúlnat were poking into an adjacent room filled with crates and shelves filled with objects whose purposes were lost with the ancient mariners. Along the back wall, a brown canvas covered what appeared to be more crates. Grabbing Cédron by the shoulder, she spun him around to face her. She jutted her chin, peering at him with narrowed eyes.

"Okay, you're important. I get it. We need to get you out of the city," she announced with her hands on her narrow hips. "We can't use the ships, and the city is under siege, but perhaps Scóurj and I can find a smuggler who can get us out on a wagon going south through the Laborers Guild. The Garanth army hasn't gotten beyond the northern quadrant."

Murádit and Anéton continued to scour the crates in the room for valuable items and ignored her speech. The rest of the group huddled around her as she spoke. They glanced at each other and then at the questionable little Gróshan across the room. The Caravan Master crossed his arms over his chest and looked down at the young woman.

"We'd hoped to sneak out under cover of darkness, retrieve one of our wagons from along the coast and use that," Shozin frowned. "Otherwise, we'll run out of food unless, by some miracle, these crates hold preserved stores."

Rováen stood next to the Caravan Master and shook his head. "The wagons are up the coast. I don't think we can make our way far enough north to reach them without running into the Garanth," he said, scratching the silver whiskers on his chin. "I don't know that we have any other viable options—"

A yell went up from the young men rummaging further inside the room, causing everyone to turn, braced to face this new threat. Sénna watched with pressed lips as Murádit held up several flat discs that gleamed iridescently in the light of the glowstones. A collective gasp went up from all the onlookers.

"Róhiti scales! Crates of them!" Murádit breathed, a broad grin splitting his face. "We can use these to—"

Another cry rose behind him, where Anéton unpeeled the brown canvas from the monstrous shape it covered.

Sénna bit back her annoyance and tapped her foot. "Well, what is that thing?"

"It's an air barge!" Anéton exclaimed. He pulled yards of shimmering fabric, inspecting it as he spread it out on the ground. "And look! The silks look like they're intact!"

Shozin Chezak shook his head even as he walked to the newest discovery. "Air barges haven't flown for ages, and I've only ever seen sketches of them. We don't know how to fly it even if we could get it safely up to the city."

The commotion had drawn the rest of the survivors into the large room. Murmurs and mutterings raced through the small crowd. The mages were particularly interested in the find, commandeering the silks and ship while others began rooting through the shelves for other potential items of interest. Mage Kiél held up a section of the silks to the glowstones, turning it in various ways for his inspection. Sénna watched as his expression went from the creases and frown of skeptical curiosity to raised eyebrows and smile of discovery.

"These silks were spun from lunar caterpillars and solar snails," he exclaimed, holding the shimmering fabric aloft. "They can channel energy from Lord Shamar and the Moon Daughters' energy. As long as there is light from the deities, they can raise the ship."

"Apparently, the ancient mariners of Táksabai weren't

only masters of the seas," Am'aranth muttered under her breath at Sénna's side.

Rovãen cocked his head to one side. "How is the airship steered? If the silks raise it into the air, what propels it forward?"

Mage Kíel pursed his lips and joined Rovãen. Together, they stared at the bow of the crumbling airship. At the barge's stern, Anéton pulled the rest of the tarpaulin off, calling Murádit over to assist him. There was a crash as the canvas fell to the ground. Dust plumed into the air. The two conversed over the end of the barge for several seconds, then trudged back to the group, their faces dark.

"The propeller on the back disintegrated as I pulled the canvas off," Anéton said, the anguish evident in his dark brown eyes. "Even if we could get it above ground and into the air, we'd have no way to steer it."

Chapter 18: The Guardians

The power drained from Säeshi Angäersol's body, leaving behind a shell of helpless desolation. Whatever the force was that her twin Läenshi had unleashed, it was formidable and unstoppable. Its essence had filled her body and mind, expanding her awareness beyond the confines of their small world. For a brief moment, Säeshi felt as if she'd touched the deities themselves.

Säeshi felt, from her brief moment of transformation, that the powerful creatures were both timeless and yet not quite sentient. She got the impression of there being several points of power but that none of them functioned independently. It was more like a web of energy spread out from a controlling center, but she couldn't tell where or who that center was. What she did know, without a shred of doubt, was that these creatures were guardians of Táksabai, and nothing that posed a threat to the Askári people or their lands could survive.

"We have to go," she gasped, her knees buckling as her body returned to its form. Trilläen grasped her by the elbow to hold her steady. "The guardians will destroy this encampment."

The men stared at her for a brief moment. She focused her eyes on her captain standing at her side. She noted the blood covering his green breastplate. The Askári soldier was also splattered, but neither appeared to be severely injured. The Meq'qan they traveled with was nowhere in sight. She could smell the sharp scent of fear above the sweet, metallic odor of blood.

"Where is Ta'riq?" she asked, glancing around the shaking tent. "We need to get him and go!"

Tóran's eyes lowered, and she saw Trilläen grip his shoulder. Säeshi peered around them and saw the tribesman's body, his blood soaking the woven carpet with a deep red stain. Her heart leaped into her throat as she also spied the decapitated corpse of the demon.

"You have defeated him?" she inhaled sharply, glancing from one to the other. Elation warred with terror in her chest as the implications of his defeat raced through her mind. "Then, we must go…now!"

She pulled her elbow from Trilläen's grasp and turned. Without waiting, Säeshi lurched towards the open flaps of the tent, the black canvas roiling as the ground continued to undulate beneath the advance of the guardians. She held the flap for Trilläen and Tóran, who had thrown Ta'riq's body over his shoulders. Säeshi marveled at Tóran's strength and determination. The Askári people had always seemed like ignorant kazan to her, but Tóran's integrity quickly changed her perception of their folk.

Exiting the tent, they all stopped short, their senses assaulted by the acrid pungency of the burnt black-seed, wakazan droppings, blood, and scorched grass surrounding the battlefield. The eerie green light glowed from the west, but its source was lost behind the rise of a small hill. She scanned the area. The Meq'qan's stampede of wakazan destroyed most of the camp. Säeshi glanced towards the outskirts where the throngs of Arkmuln had been corralled and saw that Läerei's black-seed bombs had done their job.

Thousands of twisted and blackened bodies lay in scattered piles behind the fences lining the camp's perimeter. Their shadows stretched across the ground as Lord Shamar angled towards the Tímin Sea. Her eyes watered for the enormous loss of life, and she sent a quick prayer to Hamra for the lost souls of the once-Arkmuln.

Over the slight rise to the west, they heard the shouts and the clash of weapons. They made their way to the top of the hill, Tóran grunting under the weight of his burden, and peered carefully over the berm. Säeshi felt the color drain from her face and panic tingle in her fingertips.

Táksabai was burning. The entire city was engulfed in flames behind its circular wall. The creatures Säeshi emulated earlier were lumbering amidst the Garanth army on the battlefield below and throughout the city. Their gargantuan bodies stood double the height of Táksabai's walls.

A score of the enormous creatures formed a protective ring around the Mages Guild. Their tentacles intertwined into a glowing and impenetrable net. Another chain encircled the city. The green aura emanating from them lit up the sky in the afternoon's fading light.

Scores more cut a swath through the Garanth army and remaining Arkmuln swarming around the northern watchtower of the besieged city. The Meq'qan astride their wakazan continued to engage the enemy, dodging the new menace that blocked their retreat behind the safety of the city's walls.

Säeshi flinched as Tóran laid Ta'riq's body down next to her and surveyed the battle raging below. She saw Trilläen glance at him, the captain's face tight with strain. Trilläen put a hand on both of their shoulders and blew out a long breath.

"We need to get the Meq'qan and their beasts to safety," he said, a deep crease forming between his brows as he considered this new challenge. "I'm not sure how we are going to get through those things." His head lifted, and he jutted his chin towards the guardians. "I don't see Läenshi's Wing anywhere." He turned his eyes to Säeshi and squeezed her shoulder. "Can you sense her?"

Säeshi stared at him numbly, the implicit question behind his words like a slap across her face. Her eyes widened, and she opened her mouth to retort, then shut it with a snap. As twins, they'd always shared a deep connection. There was never a time in her life that Läenshi's essence wasn't present in her mind. Säeshi felt her insides twist with the unbearable thought and clamped down on it before it could overwhelm her.

Facing west, where Lord Shamar was angling towards the horizon and his evening repose, she closed her eyes and stretched out her mind. She sought Läenshi's distinct essence, but the guardians' overwhelming power blocked her awareness with their green presence like a thick, impenetrable fog. She thrust her mind through the haze, seeking the familiar Árk'äezhi of her sister. Nothing.

Säeshi opened her unfocused eyes, grasping blindly towards her captain. She swayed from the effort and the heart-wrenching possibility that swam in her mind.

"It's too strong," she gasped, reeling then sinking to her knees. "The guardian's power is all I can sense. I can't tell if they are blocking Läenshi's Árk'äezhi or...."

A sob escaped Säeshi's lips. She wrapped her arms tightly around her body like the vines spiraling over her skin, holding herself together by sheer force of will. The grief of losing her parents, eldest and youngest sisters, and now maybe her twin threatened to crush her. Säeshi folded herself into a ball. Agony screamed in her head, telling her to give up, to relinquish her powers, and join the rest of her family in the peaceful embrace of Lady Muralia's arms.

Another explosion rocked the ground, and the smell of smoke and burning bodies sharpened, scorching her nostrils. Raising her head and glancing up, Säeshi and her companions watched in frozen horror as the guardians below began shooting balls of green fire from the faceted stones in the center of their chests. The Garanth and Arkmuln beneath them exploded as the blazing emerald energy struck their bodies, leaving only charred armor and thin wisps of caustic smoke.

Säeshi felt the air in her chest turn leaden. She gasped, trying to suck in air that couldn't get past her throat. The thought of losing Läenshi flayed her soul. Watching the great monsters that Läenshi had raised (and possibly been destroyed by) seared her raw mind. There was no escape, no way through, and no place to hide.

"Laylur's beast!" Tóran swore beside her, sinking to his knees. "Those things will destroy everything in their path, friend and foe alike." He turned to Trilläen, his tight lips as white as his cheeks. "We need to get Chaq'ta and the Meq'qan out of there. Do you think you can whistle loud enough for them to hear?"

"Not the Meq'qan," Trilläen scrubbed his fingers through his shorn hair, making it stand up in thick tangles. "But maybe I can get the beasts' attention."

Trilläen put fingers on either side of his mouth and blew. The piercing sound was high and sweet, well above the level of the battle raging below. He whistled again, this time raising and lowering the tone to cover several notes. He inhaled and blew harder, increasing the volume.

Roused from her stupor by the noise, Säeshi squinted

against Lord Shamar's rays. She saw several of the wakazan toss their enormous tusks from side to side, bucking and stomping at the shrill noise. Trilläen waved his arms over his head to catch the rider's attention. Säeshi saw one of them wave back and wheel his beast towards the hills where they stood.

Ignoring the wildly waving tentacles and the explosive green balls of power, Säeshi watched Chaq'ta rally his men and beasts, steering them back the way they had come. The guardians continued cutting swaths through the Garanth and Arkmuln of the army, but the small group of Meq'qan disengaged the fight and thundered towards the companions on the hill.

The breath Säeshi held released its grip on her chest, and she relaxed. There appeared to have been very few casualties among the Meq'qan as the herd pounded up the hill. She glanced back towards the city and wondered again at the impenetrable wall of leviathans surrounding Táksabai and how they were ever going to get through it.

Reaching out tentatively with her mind, Säeshi felt the rush of familiarity and cried out, sinking to the ground as her knees gave way in relief. She sensed her sister's energy and felt traces of Läenshi's excitement, but she couldn't get a fix on where her twin might be. Säeshi had the undeniable feeling that the answer lay behind the walls of the city.

Perhaps the wakazan could ram a small hole in the guardian's barricade, or maybe they could swim around the outside of the Mages Guild and find an entrance beneath it from the water's side. Just having the nearly three hundred warriors surrounding them made her feel more secure. Their dark heads tossed, and their odd, yellow eyes flashed as they greeted their recovered leader, then sobered as they saw Ta'riq's body. As one, they looked to Tóran for an explanation.

The legionnaire cleared his throat. "My friends, I bring you your kinsman Ta'riq, who fought bravely against the demon in the Garanth camp. His sacrifice saved my life and the lives of my companions." Tóran's voice shook, but it carried across the sea of somber tribesmen.

Three of the Meq'qan slid off their beasts and solemnly lifted their kinsman onto the back of the nearest wakazan. They turned to Tóran and knelt, their heads bowed. The first Meq'qan raised himself and faced Tóran, the grief cutting deep into the lines of his face.

"I will return our kinsman to the marsh," the first man croaked hoarsely, then cleared his throat. "Our high priestess can perform the ritual of passing for his sacrifice."

Tóran nodded and clasped the Meq'qan's forearm. He didn't speak, but Säeshi could see the muscles tense between his shoulders. Tóran turned away as the tribesman mounted his beast and turned its head east toward the mountain pass and the marshes beyond.

Säeshi's vision blurred as she watched the wakazan's lumbering backside. Her throat tightened, and she swallowed the wave of uncertainty that curled over her awareness. How many more would die before this war ended? Her thoughts were interrupted by the call of the leader of the Meq'qan as he reined his wakazan next to Tóran.

"Well met," Chaq'ta clasped Tóran's arm after sliding off his great beast and dodging the tusks. "We had given you up for lost or Arkmuln." Chaq'ta's brow furrowed, and he peered into Tóran's eyes.

Tóran held his gaze, his brown eyes bright and sharp. "Such little faith, my friend." He returned the arm clasp and pulled the tribesman in for a rough embrace. The two separated, and each grinned at the other, Tóran nodding at the warriors surrounding them. "You have done well, Chaq'ta. Caľiq Mak'ki will be proud of the many Garanth you and your men have slain today."

Chaq'ta's cheeks flushed, and his eyes shone, but Säeshi noticed something else flicker behind the grin. The warrior's smile faded slightly, but only for a moment. Chaq'ta turned to his men and raised his fist in a war cry, echoed by the warriors and bellowing wakazan surrounding them.

Säeshi felt her heart thump in time with the chanting and stamping of hooves. Their fierceness was contagious, but she still harbored a growing sliver of unease. What Säeshi desperately wanted was to find a quiet spot and try again to pinpoint her twin's Árk'äezhi.

Säeshi turned toward the trampled Garanth encampment, just as several shadows swept overhead. She ducked instinctively but straightened almost immediately when she saw the first of the läeniers circling its way onto the field. Her pulse quickened as she scanned the riders' faces for her sister. Her shoulders slumped. It wasn't Läenshi's Wing.

These were the riders that had destroyed the corralled Arkmuln with Läurei's black-seed bombs. She twisted her fingers together as the leader spiraled his beast down to land. The Wingleader slid off his golden raptor and smiled as he approached her. Säeshi flinched when he untied the knot of her fingers and squeezed her hand.

"We will find Läenshi," his warm tenor rising just above the thrumming of the läeniers' wings. "I don't have the same bond with her that you do, but I would know if we lost any of that group. I haven't felt any major fluxes in the Árk'äezhi field attuned to my Wing." He squeezed her hand again, then moved off to greet Trilläen and give his report.

Chapter 19: Reclamation

Cédron gripped Räeshun with sweating hands. He and his friends crept through the tunnel beneath the Mages Guild with Mage Kíel, Óren, and a few loyal apprentices leading the way to a little-used underground entrance to the guild proper. Even if they could get through the collapsed cavern, there was no getting back through the main door destroyed by Mage Bín Nétar and his Arkmuln.

The tunnel smelled like a cesspool. Cédron eyed the ground warily, not trusting any lump larger than an atoca berry. His eyes watered, and he tried breathing through his mouth. Several of his companions removed their waist sashes and tied them around their faces.

"We don't know what enemies may still wander the halls above," Mage Kíel warned the group as they approached the rusted iron gate to the staircase. "Be wary."

Sénna snorted. "How about if we see what else you have in that bag of tricks. Maybe we can find something useful."

Mage Kíel stopped and turned to face her, his raised eyebrows casting long shadows on his forehead in the flickering torchlight.

"We've been through the sack and identified everything we could," he said, narrowing his eyes at her. "Do you think you'll have more success than my trained apprentices?"

Murádit elbowed his sister in the ribs. "Shh, don't be rude."

"If you don't mind," Sénna placed her hands on her hips. "I don't want to walk into a nest of undead tribesmen when we get to the other end of this tunnel. It might make sense to prepare ourselves," she huffed.

Anéton patted his sword's pommel with one hand and fingered the knives in his sash with the other. "I'm ready."

Cédron paced back and forth, wiping one hand then the other on his trousers. "Look, while we're discussing all this, my brother is up there facing who knows what. Let's just go!" He turned and stood next to the iron door, tapping his foot.

There was no sound from the city above. The pounding of the ballista hail stopped some time ago, replaced by an eerie silence that was almost more disconcerting than the sounds of battle. The remaining ships bearing children sailed south towards Mítyon and safety. Rováen remained with Sahráron to tend the wounded and care for the caravan's animals. The rest were with Cédron in an attempt to retake the Mages Guild. Once they secured the castle, Cédron and his companions could search for Tóran.

Mage Kíel pulled at the iron key chain attached to his belt. He scanned and rejected several of the hand-sized skeletons before holding up an ancient, rusted key. He placed it in the lock and turned, creating a grating squeak that made Cédron's shoulders rise to his ears and nearly everyone else wince.

Mage Kíel held up a warning hand. Cédron held his breath as they waited. Silence. He blew the air out of his lungs as Óren waved the torch forward. They glided up the stairs toward the kitchen cellars without speaking. Óren used hand signals to wave his apprentices through the trap door and into the storage room. They spread out, weapons drawn, and circled the room before waving the rest of the group into the kitchen.

"It's clear," Óren called in a loud whisper, waving the rest of the group through the trap door.

Cédron followed Anéton, with Murádit and Sénna behind him. The larders for the guild kitchens were orderly, with stacks of crates against the walls labeled with images of their contents; tubers, greens, kassäeri eggs, and barrels lining one wall filled with redfruit, pickled greens, and salted cochäera meat. Baskets hung from beams along the ceiling filled with herbs, black Sativa rice, and braided bunches of onions. Cédron wasn't the first to pull off his face-covering and inhale the homey scents of the kitchen.

Óren and the apprentices shuffled up the stone steps toward the main keep. Mage Kíel pulled the white gauntlets from his sack and gave a low whistle to get his journeymage's attention.

"Put these on," Mage Kíel ordered, tossing the gloves to Óren. "If you insist on being the first through the door into danger, at least protect yourself."

Óren grinned, put the gauntlets on, and let his full, red sleeves fall over them. He pointed to his apprentices, and the group of them nodded in unison. Cédron felt his shoulders tense as the small group of black-robed apprentices snuck through the corridor into the main keep. He strained to hear any sounds of discovery or conflict, but all he heard was the slithering of a small tunnel snake behind the crates to his right. Seconds later, a young apprentice popped back into the doorway.

"Come on up," he grinned and waved. "It's deserted."

A collective sigh from his companions filled the room. Eyebrows unfurrowed, and hands unclenched among the group.

"Thanks be to Our Lady," Murádit murmured, touching the amber necklace at his throat.

The nearly palpable tension rolled off several sets of shoulders as the group made their way through the stone corridors into the main keep. When they reached the great hall, Cédron agreed that it appeared deserted. He'd taken only a handful of steps into the room when he felt a prickling on the back of his neck. He pulled Räeshun from her strap across his back and sensed the thrum of awareness in her bones. Cédron inhaled to call out a warning when a grating scream erupted above him.

Looking up, Cédron spied Arkmuln standing next to the pillars lining the open level above the hall. Their milky eyes turned to face the interlopers, their mouths open and fingers pointed. The screeching echoed throughout the stone chamber, rattling the windows above and making Cédron's teeth vibrate. He ground his jaws together and held Räeshun up like a shield, looking around for the reinforcements he knew the Arkmuln summoned.

"Mijáko piles," Anéton cursed as he pulled his sword from its sheath.

The group formed into a circle in the main hall center, with weapons drawn and eyes wide. Sénna pulled Mage Kíel into the center of the group and grasped the bag from his shoulder. She dumped it out and began rifling through the treasures littering the cobblestone floor.

"What are you doing?" Mage Kíel gaped at her and the pile at his feet.

"Let's see what this does," she said, holding up a metallic

disc the size of a dinner plate.

Mage Kíel reached for it, but Sénna pushed the gem embedded in the center of the disk. The stone sank into the metal, and ten curved blades sprang from around the object's circumference. There was another click. The metal lifted off Sénna's palm and spun in the air, becoming a razor-sharp wheel of death.

"Now what?" Murádit's voice quivered as he eyed the object with wide eyes.

"I'm not sure," Sénna said, raising her hand and turning it to the side. The disc followed her hand's movements. "I think if I just—"

The doors above them crashed open, and scores of black-robed mages armed with crossbows and swords poured in from the battlements above. They filled the upper-level lining the great hall's perimeter, all weapons trained on the small group. The screaming Arkmuln ceased their warning, but now the echoes were filled with male challenges.

"Hold," said one man. "Don't move."

Startled, Sénna swung her hand high and to her right. "Oops," she gasped.

The swirling disc spun erratically, forcing everyone in the circle to jump back or duck away from the flashing blades. Murádit wasn't fast enough, and the sharp edges grazed his shoulder as they spun past. He gasped and grabbed his bleeding shoulder. Cédron saw Sénna's lips press together, then raised her hand. She swung her open palm high towards the leader of the mages and into a slow arc. The disc whizzed towards the leader, who batted it out of his way with the flat of his sword. The disc wobbled and crashed to the ground, the spinning blades grinding and curling into the stone floor.

The mage leader smirked and lowered his weapon, advancing down the second-level steps towards the group.

"Mage Kíel," the young mage inclined his head in mock deference. "I thought you were dead. And here you are, big as life with your little lackey," he jutted his chin at Óren, "and insignificant friends."

Mage Kíel stepped in front of the group with his hands on his hips. "They aren't insignificant..." he scratched his head, cocking it sideways as he looked at the black mage. "I'm sorry, who are you?"

The leader's face flushed, and his grip on his sword tightened. "Someone you should have taken the time to meet, but I was always beneath your notice."

Óren snorted. Cédron turned his head to look at the red journeymage.

"You were beneath his notice. You remain beneath his notice." Óren raised his gauntleted hands, palms facing the opposing young mage, and shouted. "*Saékit!*"

The young mage continued to yell, but no sound escaped his lips. Óren grinned at the young man's discomfiture and turned to Mage Kíel.

"May I keep these for my next teaching cycle?" he asked, holding up the gauntlets.

The mage above waved at his companions, directing them to attack the small group in the main hall. Scores of voices raised the challenge as they made their way towards the sweeping staircase.

Mage Kíel turned back toward the center of the circle and his bag. "If we survive this, we can discuss it."

Cédron closed his eyes and felt his Árk'äezhi rise from deep inside. He focused on the sacred red gem and shot fireballs over the heads of the advancing mages. They ducked and cried out but continued their advance. Cédron looked into the faces of his enemies. They were all young, some younger than he, and all showed fear in their eyes. Were these young men inherently evil, or had they been led astray? Did he have the right to make that judgment?

Cédron checked himself and held Räeshun higher. The fireballs exploded over their heads, crumbling some of the walls behind them. He couldn't justify killing these young mages, but he also couldn't let them slaughter the band of friends surrounding him. Cédron squeezed his staff, asking Räeshun for guidance. She filled his mind with calm, almost as if asking him to wait.

"Got it!" Sénna cried from behind him.

Cédron spun around and watched her pull an elongated canister sideways. The foot-long container clicked and glowed with orange light. She twisted the bottom of the cartridge, and it began to whine. The iridescent light brightened, and she tossed it into the air. The glowing container spun in a slow circle as it raised toward the ceiling. A moment later, the light exploded from the cylinder, sending out a shock wave of energy. The orange power swept over the black-robed apprentice mages, freezing them into place.

"Quick, it's an immobilization spell," Sénna yelled, racing toward the stairs. "Get their weapons from them and bind them up!"

Anéton was the first of the group to recover from their momentary stasis. He sheathed his sword and tore up the stairs. Stripping the rope from the lead mage's waist, he bound the young man's wrists behind his back and shoved him to a seated position. Óren and his loyal apprentices followed suit and soon had the entire group disarmed and headed toward the cellars where they could be held safely until the crisis was over.

"How did you know what that thing was?" Murádit asked his sister with an appreciative smile.

Sénna ducked her head and grinned sheepishly. "I saw diagrams of those and similar items in some of the old books in Father's library."

Murádit shook his head. "You mean you *read* about it in a *book*?"

Sénna placed her hands on her hips. "Yes, I do read. What else do you think I do with my time when Father locks me up for sneaking out?" She huffed.

"Well, young lady," Mage Kíel stood before her and bowed. "You have saved us all today. I, for one, offer you my thanks."

Cédron felt a snigger bubble up through his chest as he watched Sénna blush and stammer, trying to accept the gratitude of the White Mage. Óren and the other mages each bowed formally to her in turn. Sénna wobbled her way through several curtseys before Murádit rescued her.

"Alright," he said, pulling her away from the group. "Don't get too big for your britches, little sister."

Sénna punched her brother's shoulder but smiled and began gathering up the treasures into the mage's pack. Cédron bent to assist her, offering to hold the folding canvas as she wedged in a bulky mechanical rodent with elongated teeth.

"What do you think this is for?" Cédron asked.

"It's a cheese grater, of course." Sénna snapped.

Cédron looked up at her, a sharp retort on his tongue, but saw her eyes twinkle and the hollow of her cheek bitten between her teeth. He grinned and shook his head. They stuffed the last of the items into the bag, and Sénna presented it to Mage Kíel.

"I don't know about you," Anéton clapped Cédron on the shoulder and shook him, "but I'm famished. Is there anything to eat in this place?"

"I think we deserve a little feast after all that," Mage Kíel nodded, scratching his chin. "Let's see if any of the kitchen staff are about."

Fortunately, most of the cooks and drudges from the kitchen were locked in the cellars. Óren found and released them, replacing the grateful men and women with his prisoners. They returned to the kitchen and began preparing a feast for their rescuers. In less than an hour, the tables in the dining hall creaked under platters of cold cuts, smoked and salted cochäera, roasted tubers and vegetables, flatbreads, and tankards of triticale ale.

Cédron returned from the battlements, where he and the rest of his small party had marveled at the enormous metallic guardians still encircling the guild and the city beyond. Their internal green lights cast a soft glow over the darkened city, competing with Orwaena's rose tones as the moon rose in the sky.

They had defeated the Garanth army, but Cédron still didn't know what had become of Tóran. There were no signs of the wakazan or the Meq'qan warriors he led in the reports coming in from the battlefield. The Gróshan spies came and went taking messages across the city, but none had any news for him. Cédron filled a tankard of ale, grabbed a piece of flatbread with smoked meat rolled in it, and sat in a corner. He didn't feel like celebrating with the others. Tóran was still out there. His compass showed only blackness when he searched for his brother's image on its surface.

Anéton stood on a bench across the hall, one boot on the table and his cup of ale waving about as he regaled the mages with tales of their adventures.

"Then out of the falls walks Cédron like he's just saved the world—which he has, mind you—and all I asked was 'did Algarik escape?' and he gives me this look...."

Roars and cat-calls erupted in the Mages Guild dining hall as Anéton's audience of apprentice mages and caravan folk listened to his rendition of recent events. Cédron's face burned, and his shoulders raised towards his ears. Anéton's retelling of their adventures took on added elements of the dramatic the more pints he drank. Soon, the apprentices would begin chucking vegetables at the legionnaire.

"That's quite a story," Gérand Kíel raised his pint towards Anéton, who was waving his arms in the air describing the fight against the rinzar. "How much of it is true?"

The white mage took a drink and sat on the bench across from him. Cédron took a deep breath and closed his eyes.

"All of it," he sighed, placing his elbows on the table and resting his chin in his hands. "But you have to remember that my friend there is prone to the dramatic."

Mage Kíel's hazel eyes twinkled. "Yes, there is that. However, his story does give some credibility to the ominous dreams I've been having of late. And to the events that have transpired."

Gérand pulled out a pipe and tapped the bowl on the edge of the table, knocking the old leaf onto the stone floor. He pinched some dried leaves from the bag at his hip and stuffed them into the bowl, lighting it with the firestone ring on his finger. Cédron watched the blue smoke circle around Mage Kíel's head, filling the room with its pleasant, sweet scent.

"What's next for you then, young Cédron?" Gérand asked, sucking on the stem of the pipe until the burning embers glowed.

Cédron looked over at his friend. "I need to find out what happened to my brother Tóran." He felt the familiar lump of grief and guilt rise from his chest to his throat. He scratched his nose and swallowed. "He led a group of over three hundred Meq'qan against the Garanth, but there is no word of what happened to them. I don't know if he survived the battle."

Mage Kíel blew smoke from the side of his mouth. "We have people seeking him and the Meq'qan. We will have word soon." The mage pointed the stem of the pipe towards Cédron. "What then is next for you in your journey? Will you head to the Tawaki?"

Cédron took a deep breath and blew it out slowly. "I don't know. I can't think beyond learning what happened to Tóran. But whether he survived or not, I still have a quest to finish. I'll have to find a way to make my way north to the

Tawaki, but I don't know if there are more Garanth lurking beyond the Sinharkon Range or if we destroyed them all here. I just don't know."

Mage Kiel listened with narrowed eyes as he blew smoke rings above his head. After a moment of silence, he put the pipe down on the table and folded his hands. He leaned towards Cédron.

"Well, regardless of the news you receive and the destination you have in mind, I have an airship that I think will help you get there." Mage Kíel raised his eyebrows. "Would that adequately demonstrate our gratitude for what you've done?"

Cédron felt a weight in his chest lift, and he nearly laughed out loud. "Yes, I believe that is a good start."

Chapter 20: The Airship

Cédron gripped Räeshun in his hand and paced along the high battlements of the Mages Guild, gazing out to sea as he skirted around the enormous airship that filled the bulk of the rooftop. The silks were raised, filled with air, and nearly ready for flight. Cédron knew they would deflate somewhat when Lord Shamar set until Orwaena rose and they inflated with the light from her moon, but they didn't plan to leave until well after dark.

The mages had spent the last two days adhering the mythical róhiti scales to the sides and bottom of the ship in an overlapping pattern, just like the fish from which they came. Sénna and Am'aranth told him that this would make the vessel nearly invisible from the ground. Watching the bulwark shimmer in the afternoon light, Cédron was inclined to believe it.

There was no rudder, but Cédron was reasonably sure he could steer the enormous craft with his windstones. Räeshun pulsed reassuringly in his hand and gave him the image of holding windstones and the resulting breeze obeying his command. Cédron squeezed the staff with gratitude and hoped that her belief in him wasn't misplaced.

Now, with his confidence buoyed by his recent success and knowledge that what remained of the city was now safe, Cédron turned his thoughts to the next step in his journey. His first hurdle was figuring out how to leave the city, then where to go. The green-glowing leviathan guardians still surrounded Táksabai, and he learned from Trilläen that it was Räesha's sister Läenshi who had awakened them.

Mage Kiél wasted no time enlisting the young twins to help him figure out how they operated and, if possible, how to control them. The enormous guardians finished what the ill-prepared Hármolin Legion had not been able to do. They destroyed both the Garanth army and the Arkmuln, but not before the enemies burned the fields and razed nearly the entire city to the ground.

Thousands of civilians lost their lives. Entire neighborhoods were flattened or burned. The followers of Hamra worked night and day, performing the releasing rites for the dead. Following the priests and priestesses, the surviving legionnaires occupied themselves with the gruesome task of burying the fallen Askári and any Meq'qan Arkmuln they could find. Three mass graves gaped like open wounds in the field outside the city, with thousands of unwrapped corpses. Cédron turned toward his companions who awaited him.

Trilläen shared the decision to have his läenier Wing follow the enormous guardians from the battlefield towards the city. Säeshi sensed the guardian's protective barrier lessened as the number of enemies dwindled. The läenier Wing was able to fly over those encircling the town without a challenge. Läenshi's Wing had already landed near the Mages Guild radient, and with the twins' reunion, the Sumäeri warriors were enjoying a well-deserved feast.

The läeniers scoured the fields for prey, picking clean the enemy corpses. The city couldn't support the provisioning of two hundred or more raptors from their depleted herds, and the wild flocks of kessäeri had fled before the Garanth's siege. Cédron shook his head. Fortunately for the surviving citizens, the Wing had no moral issue with devouring their enemies.

The legionnaires torched the remaining piles of Garanth on the field. The reek from burning bodies hung in the air, simultaneously cloying and acrid, coating the back of his tongue like bitter syrup. Cédron knew he could have been instrumental in disposing of the bodies cleanly, but Räeshun had reminded him of his more pressing obligation. He needed to move on in his quest, and he needed help.

Cédron remained awkward around the Angäersol twins. His guilt for being the cause of their many losses remained an open wound on his heart. Räeshun throbbed again, sending him soothing colors and a sense of inevitable purpose.

"Maybe," he murmured to the glowing staff, "but that doesn't make it hurt any less."

"Talking to yourself now? I knew it wouldn't take long for you to crack." A deep, familiar voice called from behind him.

Cédron whirled to find Tóran grinning at him. His breath caught in his throat, and he felt a prickle behind his eyes as chaotic feelings raged through his body. Relief that his brother was alive clashed with the shame of not having been able to rescue him. He stood, flushed and awkward, waiting for Tóran's next words.

"It's great to see you, too," Tóran smiled and embraced Cédron.

Cédron inhaled the scent of his brother's hair. Stale sweat mixed with smoke and the heavy musk of wakazan. He squeezed Tóran tight, not wanting to let him go. Tóran grunted in surprise and broke the embrace.

"I've been through too much to have you squeeze me to death now, brother," Tóran said. He grinned, gripping the back of Cédron's neck and pressing their foreheads together.

"I thought I'd lost you!" Cédron said, choking back the sob that threatened to burst from his chest. "I was trapped in the underground city and couldn't get to you, even though I could see you were injured. I've never felt so helpless."

Cédron closed his eyes and let the tension in his body relax as Tóran held the intimate greeting for another moment. He opened his mouth to speak, then clamped his jaw shut again. There were no appropriate words to express his feelings. He lifted his head and smiled through the haze hovering on his lashes.

Tóran nodded and clasped Cédron's arm, joining him in gazing out to sea. The two of them stood side by side for several minutes before Tóran turned to face his brother.

"I sent the Meq'qan home," he said.

Cédron raised his brows and regarded his brother for a moment before speaking. Tóran's expression closed; the skin stretched taut across the bones of his face. His eyes were haunted and aloof. Cédron could see the reflection of the pain and torture his brother had suffered during his imprisonment. He knew Tóran wouldn't discuss it, at least not voluntarily. Cédron felt the cold, dark chasm rise between them again and wished that he could ease his brother's mind.

Cédron cleared his throat. "What will you do now?" he asked, turning his gaze back over the water and the fading light.

Tóran fidgeted with the thong holding his hair, then

tossed the long braid over his shoulder. He took a deep breath in and let it out slowly as if measuring his words very carefully.

"I thought I'd join you on your journey," Tóran said finally, still keeping his gaze out to sea. "Trilläen has reports of another large army moving down from Molonark, but they are slow. The Meq'qan need to return home to their families and prepare to move them to safety. I don't know where or when we will need to meet this new challenge, but I feel like I can be of more use to you than in packing and evacuating the tribes."

Cédron could feel the blood pounding in his veins, and he willed his heart to cease racing. He glanced over at his brother, whose face remained pale and impassive.

"It would be my honor to have you join me," Cédron said formally, bowing slightly to his brother. Then, grinning, he pulled Tóran into another rough embrace. "I've missed having you by my side."

Tóran returned Cédron's embrace stiffly, then relaxed. They broke apart and returned to gazing out at the waves crashing against the rocks and lower walls of the Mages Guild.

"We came through Dúlnat on our way here," Tóran said, turning to face his brother. "The city was deserted, and we found very few dead." He swallowed before continuing. "I don't know what happened to Father."

Cédron closed his eyes and nodded. "Mother told me that he lived but that he was 'hidden' from her somehow. I think Algarik may have him imprisoned at Aromberk Fortress."

Tóran raised his eyebrows. "Aromberk Fortress, huh? Wait, you *spoke* with Mother?"

"When I faced the goddess to earn the aquastone," Cédron clarified. "She appeared to me as Mother so that I wouldn't fear her."

Tóran stared at his brother for another moment, then nodded. "Then we should go together and rescue him."

"Together," Cédron agreed, nodding and looking out to sea. "We can meet the Tawaki on our way north and get the terrastone."

Tóran turned and leaned his back against the merlons ringing the battlements, eying the airship skeptically. He moved towards it, testing the security of the róhiti scales and poking at the silks.

Cédron watched this demonstration, wondering if his brother shared his trepidation at flying this ancient and untested ship. He shifted away from the wall and moved to join Tóran when he caught the flashes of white and silver from the other side of the vessel. He stepped around Tóran, hoping that the intruders were friendly.

Cédron grinned at the sight of his Uncle Rováen with Trilläen, Sénna, Cybél and Mage Kiél coming around the back of the air barge towards him. Mage Kiél had some scrolls in his hands, and the other two men carried barrels of provisions for their journey. Rováen approached the brothers and laid a hand on each of their shoulders.

"It is good to see the two of you together again," he smiled and pulled the brothers in a firm embrace. "You will be joining us then, Tóran?"

Tóran hesitated, a flicker of uncertainty in his eyes, then he nodded. "I will need to gather my things. I'll be back before we cast off." He gave the ship a jaundiced look and shook his head. Excusing himself from the group with a brief bow, he headed below into the guild's main quarters.

Mage Kiél motioned for Cédron and Sénna to join him aboard the ship. They stepped through the open railing onto the ship's wooden planking. The deck was rough and worn, with old rigging, pulleys, and netting shoved into several wooden boxes scattered about the deck. The mage walked over to the helm, where a small, built-in table stood next to a man-height wheel and opened up one of the scrolls that he'd brought.

"During the siege, I learned that one of the traitors had

stolen the Rod of Shouman from our vault." The mage frowned, twisting the ruby on his finger as he spread out the scroll. "If I'm not mistaken, it was Algarik Muhr who took it. Now that he's tipped his hand, I think I know what he intends to do with it."

A sharp stab pierced Cédron's chest at the mention of his uncle. He hadn't seen Algarik since their confrontation at Shalaen Falls, but Cédron knew the rogue mage survived.

"What can he hope to accomplish with the Rod of Shouman?" Cédron's throat was thick, and he cleared it before completing his thought. "I have the firestone—"

"True," Mage Kiél interrupted with a sharp nod of his head. "But as our young friend here," he nodded and smiled towards Sénna, "has explained, this scroll instructs the user of the Rod of Shouman in how to harness the 'Fire of the Skies.' As we now know, that is Lord Shamar's power.

"I believe it's the power of the air that causes lightning to course through the clouds and strike the ground. Algarik may believe it to be the firestone that will activate the rod's power, but it clearly states here that the Rod of Shouman requires the sacred windstone to harness the power of lightning."

Mage Kíel turned to Cédron, fixing him with his piercing gaze. "I understand that you planned to travel to the Tawaki for the terrastone, but you must go to Yezmarantha and secure the sacred windstone before Algarik or any of Laylur's other servants learn of this. If Algarik finds a way to wield the Rod of Shouman before you've gotten the Sceptre of Kulari, there will be none who can stand against him."

Cédron stared at the mage, his mind racing and his breath coming in shallow pants. Algarik had the Rod of Shouman and would stop at nothing to get the firestone to wield it. He knew he couldn't avoid this confrontation, but Cédron hoped to have more experience and control of his power before he did. He'd also hoped to find his father, who could help him face his challenges. Cédron saw bright flashes at the edges of his vision as the darkness threatened to swallow him. He closed his eyes and took several deep breaths.

"I'm not ready to face him again," he said, his eyes wandering from the mage to the other men and back again. "I don't think I'm strong enough."

Rováen grasped him by the shoulders and shook him slightly. "Remember, you are not alone. We are here to help you. Sénna can read ancient languages and interpret these scrolls. You have Räeshun and your own very formidable powers. Algarik expects us to go to the Tawaki, and that is where he is leading his army. We must head southeast and find the windstone to prevent him from being able to use that talisman."

Cédron nodded. He was the only one who could challenge Algarik. The mage was responsible for the death of his mother, his dearest friend Zariun and possibly even his father. A pang of fear and guilt stabbed at his heart, but he shoved it aside. Cédron's face hardened, and he nodded to his companions.

Master Chezak pounded his way up the gangplank, his muscular bulk causing the boards and the airship to shudder. His expression was somber, and he fiddled with the sash fabric that extended down from the knot at his side.

"We've recovered the wagons and all of the beasts that were in the underground city. The caravan will be ready to leave in the morning. We will be heading back home to see what remains of Dúlnat," he said.

Cédron caught his breath and stared up at Shozin, whose black eyes were soft as he returned the young man's gaze.

"My priority is to find your father, lad. We will search for any survivors and begin whatever reconstruction is needed while we wait for your return." Shozin tried to smile, but Cédron saw the tension pulling the corners of the Caravan Master's mouth flat.

"If you find him," Cédron said, clearing the lump in his

throat and blinking. "Please have Sahráron scry on Rováen's stones. The longer I'm away, the harder it will be for me to locate him."

Rováen turned from the scrolls on the table to face Master Chezak. "Yes, please do. I will not remove the bracelet she made for me. Also, we will need your help in deciding how best to enter Taboriz when we get there. We don't necessarily need to sneak into the city, but I'm not sure what sort of reception our motley group would receive in Yezmarantha."

Shozin's laugh rumbled from deep within his chest. "The Yezman are not as paranoid as the Shäeli, for sure. That lot wouldn't let you past their borders, as I well know." He shook his head with a rueful smile at the memory. "However, you also don't want to attract a lot of attention. All that fair skin would be blinding in the desert light."

Shozin laid a broad hand on the old Shäeli's shoulder and smiled at them. "There are gates at the four quadrants of the city, but they are heavily guarded. I can give you maps of the qanats that provide water to Taboriz. You can use their system of tunnels and aqueducts to get into the city unseen. However, they are far to the east in the deep desert and will take longer to reach. Once you have entered the city, you will need to find the Market Queen. She rules the lower levels of the city where the markets and shipping industries are. There is nothing taking place within 100 leagues of Taboriz that this woman doesn't know about." The Caravan Master scratched his smooth, sable head, moving his hand lower to rub the back of his neck as he paced along the deck. "You will need to provide a tribute to the Queen. Altruism is in short supply these days, especially now."

"What sort of tribute?" Cédron asked. "Do we have to bring her a valuable gift, or will she accept a service I might provide?"

"I'm not sure," Shozin said, shaking his head. He glanced up at Lord Shamar, angling down towards the horizon where the daytime deity's light would disappear beneath the Tímin Sea in a few hours. "If you have the good fortune to arrive near Taboriz during the Zholi Festival, you could enter with all the other revelers, but that starts in less than a fortnight. You'd be hard-pressed to sail across the entire Zahili Desert in that time, even if you followed the Räenetti River the entire voyage."

Sénna looked up from the scrolls she was examining and frowned at Shozin. "I've never heard of the Zholi Festival. How would hiding with the revelers help us?"

The Caravan Master sighed and gazed towards the water, his black eyes glittering above his wistful smile. "My city is a shining gem in the desert. Lush vertical gardens climb up the walls of the buildings, and vibrant oases of color are sprinkled throughout the courtyards of homes and public spaces. During the Zholi Festival, the citizens reenact the deception the moon daughters played upon Laylur after he betrayed Lord Shamar. The entire city participates, running the parade through the streets in procession."

"We celebrate the deception played on Laylur by the handmaidens of the deities. They hid Hamra away after rescuing her from the demon's lair and raced across the world, decorating areas with brilliant mosaics of blue, red, purple, green, and gold so Laylur couldn't identify where the actual deities hid. The life-giving colors of our gods represent his defeat. The entire city explodes with colorful mosaics; they're hung on walls, woven through trees, and strung across all of the open markets, making her sparkle like a jewel."

"All Yezman travel to Taboriz for Zholi once in their lifetimes, and throngs stream through before the procession." Shozin sighed again and shook his head. "To be able to see Taboriz during the festival would be a wonder for you all."

Cédron remembered the brightly-colored murals painted on the inside of Shozin's wagon. The gardens of Taboriz were stunning, but witnessing Taboriz during the Zholi

Festival was something he hoped they could do. He glanced at Sénna, who was twisting her finger around a lock of her shoulder-length hair as she regarded the Caravan Master.

"But if people are coming into the city for the festival, won't there be additional guards at the gates?" She raised her eyebrows at Shozin.

The big man grinned, his teeth gleaming white against his skin. "That's the best part. We celebrate the deities in all their glory. Colored mosaics for each deity are hung in sections, giving the entire city quadrants various hues to confuse Laylur. Even the Zaouni guards participate. Zholi is a peaceful celebration with no expectation of trouble."

Cybél, who had been plaiting her long hair during the conversation, smiled shyly up at Shozin. "How are the colors chosen for the mosaics?"

Shozin's big grin widened as he spread his arms wide. "Most people choose the color that most aligns with the deity to whom they wish to appeal. Green for Lady Muralia, gold for Lord Shamar, and the moon sisters are, of course, red for Orwaena, blue for Azria, and purple for Hamra. It is a most wondrous sight."

Cybél smiled and sighed, flipping her thick braid over her shoulder. "I would choose blue for Azria. What are the mosaics made from?"

Shozin snorted, then exploded into another deep, rumbling laugh. "The Yezman are gifted in glassblowing, using the bountiful sands of the desert as their medium. You will find mosaics made of leaded glass, tiles, even clay. They make them from ground stone and the pigments of flowers. Revelers choose the color of the deity and sometimes spend an entire Tide perfecting their offerings."

"It sounds lovely to behold," said Mage Kíel. He rolled up the scrolls and tucked them into Sénna's satchel. "Would that I could join you, but my duty lies here where I can continue my research. I will send you updates as soon as I can."

"Updates?" Roväen asked, examining the stone array on his wrist that Sahráron had given him. "How will you get updates to us?

The white mage grinned and rummaged in his robes, triumphantly pulling out a small, white object with a large-eyed head and leathery wings. "We found these in one of the rooms beneath the Mages Guild. We knew that some mechanical diclurues could be launched and exploded over an enemy—"

"Yes, we saw you use them during the battle," Cédron interrupted, then blushed at his uncle's sharp look.

The mage nodded and continued. "Young Sénna here discovered these particular diclurues have a sort of homing device that attracts them from one person to another using a lodestone. We can use them to communicate, and I believe they will be more reliable than the live version. These are less likely to get sidetracked by juicy bugs at dusk. I've given her a set of three diclurues and a lodestone. I will continue my research and see if I can get more information to you regarding the windstone."

"What do we know right now about the whereabouts of the sacred windstone?" Cédron asked the mage.

Mage Kiél shrugged one shoulder and unrolled another scroll. "It isn't apparent, but we know that the Ancient Yezman used its power. This reference here," he touched the writing halfway down the scroll, "says 'the Aruzzi guard it with the fierceness of one of their eggs.' He looked at Sénna, who nodded. "I wouldn't want to face an Aruzzi who thought I was threatening one of its eggs."

Roväen stroked his silvery beard, brows knit together, and lips pouted in thought. "Aruzzi haven't been seen since the War of Betrayal. How do we know they still exist?"

Shozin raised one finger and cocked his head to one side. "I remember stories, more like myths, my sisters used to tell. The Aruzzi were always elusive, and the hero could never find them unless they wanted to be found."

Trilläen chuckled. "Would you make your presence known if you'd suffered as the Aruzzi had during the Great Betrayal? No, they have retreated to their eyries deep in the Zahili Desert and keep their whereabouts secret. We have heard stories of Aruzzi sightings from some of our southern patrols, but nobody knows where they make their nests."

Roväen, Shozin, and Mage Kiél all nodded their heads in agreement. "You will have to go to Taboriz and see if you can find someone who has information," Mage Kiél mused, rubbing a finger across his upper lip. "I may be able to help you in that aspect." He rummaged deep into the folds of his robes and pulled out a palm-sized, carved token. He handed it to Cédron. The object had a scalloped shell carved into it. Cédron cocked his head to one side and raised an eyebrow.

"The symbol of the traveler or, more accurately, the seeker," Mage Kíel explained. "Look for this symbol in Taboriz for those who might provide you with information and assistance. Remember these words: 'The roads to be traveled are many,' and its counter, 'The path chosen is always the Way.' Do not forget, for it may save your life."

Cédron flipped the token in the air, caught it, then stashed it in the pouch at his waist with his other treasures. He nodded his thanks after repeating both parts of the code twice to commit it to memory. Mage Kiél turned and waved toward his journeymages, who were bearing loads of provisions for the trip.

Cédron saw that they had several items from the weapons room, and the tense knot between his shoulder blades eased just a little. Few people believed in his quest; fewer still had enough confidence to support it. Cédron was exceptionally grateful for the mage's faith in him.

Trilläen nudged him and pulled open the sacks he'd brought, spilling their contents on the airship deck. Long strips of leather slithered and rolled about the floor like a den of snakes. The Sumäeri's amethyst eyes shone as he grinned.

"As we will be heading in roughly the same direction,"

he said. "I thought we'd give you a hand."

Cédron gaped at the ropes and straps that the Sumäeri captain began tying to the ship's bow. He tossed some to his other läenier riders with a barked order and nodded as they attached the ropes to the port and starboard railings.

"You may be able to steer us with your windstone powers," Trilläen pulled the knots tight and moved on to another harness. "But I don't want you exhausted when we get to Taboriz. Our läenier Wing can pull the ship across Askári-bai along the Räenetti River until we reach the outskirts of Taboriz. That will give you time to rest and work on your skills; you're going to need it."

Cédron's lips quirked up, and he nodded. Lord Shamar hovered closer to the western horizon, his exit turning the clouds above a bright orange clashing with Orwaena's early scarlet light. A similar battle was raging in his stomach.

The thrill of embarking on the next phase of his journey vied with the fear of what he knew he'd have to face. Still, he felt the warmth of Räeshun on his palm and watched his friends, both old and new, board the airship and knew he wasn't going to face his destiny alone.

The battlements were full of people, some loading the airship, others who just wanted to marvel at it, and a small group slightly apart from the rest. Cédron swallowed and felt the sting of tears as he watched Shozin, Sahráron, and Roväen clasp each other's hands. They stood close together and bowed their heads until they all touched.

The depth of love that pulsed through their bodies radiated like heat rising from the desert sands, encompassing Cédron in enfolding warmth. He would miss Shozin and Sahráron, but Roväen would suffer most from their separation. Not since his parents had Cédron seen souls so tightly knit. The thought of his parents filled his eyes further. He blinked the tears away and turned towards the desert as they rolled down his cheeks. He needed to gather his wits to face the unknown. He couldn't allow grief and sadness to overwhelm him. He turned and walked towards the pointed bow and a few moments of solitary peace before they departed.

Two hours later, the silks of the airship were full and raised with the moon Orwaena's arrival. As the ship lifted above the battlements of the Mages Guild, Cédron felt his stomach drop, and he gripped the rails. Below, his friends from the caravan and the mages waved farewell. He hoped this wouldn't be the last time he'd see Shozin and Sahráron, but he couldn't be sure. His throat felt tight as he raised his arm to return the wave.

After the airship lifted thirty feet above the battlements, the läenier riders attached their harnesses to their belts, vaulting off the sides of the ship. Cédron heard Sénna gasp, and they both raced to the railing and looked over. The riders fell for a few agonizing seconds before landing on the backs of their hovering partners.

The riders attached the harnesses to their raptors' riding straps. Cédron heard a shrill whistle from the point of the Wing. At this signal, the läeniers angled slightly away from the ship, pulling the harnesses taut. The leather creaked and groaned as the straps twisted and tightened the knots along the deck railings. The airship hovered momentarily above the Mages Guild, majestically rising above the crashing waves spraying the sides of the guild with their forceful display.

The Wing lifted the ship out and over the city of Táksabai, whose evening firelights shone as beautiful jewel points carpeting the valley floor below. The Wing of raptors turned their flight pattern from over the water towards the Dágon Valley and prepared to cross the Ronhádi Range. Cédron slipped into a comfortable trance and stretched out his mind for Räeshun. He let her strength envelop him as the smooth rhythm of the läeniers' wings lulled him into the first deep sleep he'd had in weeks.

Chapter 21: The Red Army

A lone figure sat astride his enormous winged beast on the cliffs above the Dágon Valley. The skin across his sharp features tightened as he surveyed the slaughter of both the Garanth army and his carefully laid plans by the glowing leviathans that stormed outside the city of Táksabai. The green light emitted from the guardians spread throughout the Mages Guild and blanketed the town, purging it of all who meant harm to her people.

An onshore wind blew gently, bringing with it the stench of scorched bodies and burned farmlands. A scowl twisted Algarik's features as the tic in his left cheek pulled at the scar that ran from eye to chin. He glanced toward Táksabai and its Mages Guild, situated a hundred meters into the sea. Its access was currently invisible with the high tide. Memories of the life he had made there drifted across his mind, then were lost like wisps of smoke rising from the valley. The man's scowl deepened.

Algarik had been so close to victory. Once a red mage of the guild, now he was a faithful servant of the Great Demon Laylur. All his plans had fallen into place until now. His Master was almost free of his prison in the abyss of the world. Algarik had nearly realized his dream of power second only to Laylur.

The plan would have worked but for the boy. The boy who, with his staff of fire and bone, had single-handedly reversed the damage to Lady Muralia's terra and banished Laylur again to the depths of the abyss. Cédron's triumph forced Algarik to flee with what little power he had left. He reached down to pat the long neck of the enormous rinzar he'd created.

"The boy and his staff are lost to me now," he mused. "But I'm not leaving uncompensated."

Algarik pulled at the straps holding a long, linen-wrapped article to the makeshift saddle he'd fashioned for his mount. He'd sacrificed much to acquire this item and wasn't willing to risk losing it. Algarik glared at the city and his recent failure one last time. Wheeling the black-winged raptor away from the valley, he spurred it into the skies, northeast through Tádim Pass and the next phase of his plans.

Algarik traversed the mountains, resting during the day as his nocturnal beast preferred to hunt and travel in the darkness. The rinzar's wingspan was the breadth of at least six watowren and swiftly covered the leagues once they reached the warmer air of the Rabäen Plains and turned northward. Landing at dawn on the fourth day, Algarik pulled his frozen and cramped hands from the reins and slid off the rinzar's sinewy neck. The beast launched itself into the air and angled towards the hills to the east, and the small herd of méjok-káo grazing on the prolific berry bushes that dotted the hillside.

Autumntide had come to the land, bringing with it changing leaves and the bounty of the harvest. It also brought much colder air. Algarik stamped several times to get the blood flowing back into his stiff legs and rubbed his frozen fingers. Flying at night without Lord Shamar's light to warm his bones was taking a toll. His joints ached. Shivers wracked his body, tensing his muscles and adding to the overall sense of malaise.

Algarik wrapped his cloak tighter, rubbing his arms vigorously. Glancing to the west, he spied the last deep gold gleam of Lord Shamar as the deity retreated from the skies. To the east, Orwaena kissed her father goodnight with her first pale, rose-colored rays.

Insects began their evening song as the light faded over the plains. Algarik tucked himself into a thicket of trees and swung the pack off his back. Rummaging through it, he pulled out a meatroll and hunk of cheese he'd stolen from the larder of the Mages Guild. His hands shook as he raised the pastry to his lips and took a bite.

Looking at his hands, Algarik felt a twinge in the pit of his stomach. The joints and bones were sharp under his skin. These were the hands of an older man, one who had seen more decades than he had. They were the hands of a man who had shattered his soul and paid the price of failure with his life's energy.

Laylur's anger at being thrust back into the abyss after a brief taste of freedom had been overwhelming. Upon reporting his failure to secure Cédron and take the city of Táksabai, the mage had felt the brunt of the demon's rage. Algarik's Master siphoned Tides from his Árk'äezhi, leaving him weak and barely able to control the rinzar to make his escape.

Algarik knew that one more failure would mean the end

of his physical existence and an eternity of torture in the depths of the abyss. The thought sent a shiver down his spine that even the heat from his firestone couldn't relieve. He finished his meager rations and scanned the horizon for his beast. He spotted the rinzar several hundred yards away, tearing the flesh from the shaggy ovid with his sharp beak. Algarik renewed the obedience spell he'd cast on the beast, then curled up to sleep.

The restful peace of slumber remained elusive. Algarik rolled around on the ground, long after the rinzar had tucked its grotesque head beneath its coal-black wing. Images of Laylur's eyes boring into his soul, freezing the marrow of his bones, and searing his skin filled his mind. The demon's glare produced the same green fire that demolished the Garanth, and Algarik knew he would share that fate if he failed his Master again.

Algarik clamped down on the fears that threatened to choke him and focused on the pending invasion. He couldn't leave anything to chance or Marik's ineptitude. He would meet his army of over fifty-thousand stone warriors and their Hazzara escort in two days if they kept to the pace that Marik had set for them.

Algarik only needed a quick stop at Aromberk Fortress before he could return and lead his armies to victory against the Yezman and Shäeli forces. He composed his mind for sleep after settling on plans. He took several deep breaths and tried again to relax. When the mage finally fell into an exhausted sleep, the same green glow that haunted him for the past several days filled his dreams.

Five more days of exhausting and fruitless travel found Algarik fuming and with frayed nerves. Marik had assured him that the army had left Aromberk Fortress over a fortnight ago. He had seen them in the field during his last scry, but it was impossible to discern where exactly they were. Algarik pounded a fist on his thigh, creating a rumble from deep within the rinzar's chest. The mage scrubbed his face with icy hands as if doing so could make the army appear.

Algarik finally spotted the mass of tiny dots covering the bleak countryside after he had crossed the Tawaki Chasm and was nearly through Nuriak's Cauldron. Few things grew in the barren lands of Molonark, even during the bountiful Autumntide. The volcanic action of the Sinharkon Range kept the ground in a state of perpetual upheaval. Toxic fumes from the acid pits of Nuriak's Cauldron and the Charnan Geysers poisoned the air. A few spindly trees groped at life among the boulders and scrub grasses.

Algarik urged his beast towards the standing army while he took several deep breaths to master his anger. It wouldn't do to incinerate Marik in front of the entire army, no matter how desperately the mage wanted to. Marik wasn't the only person with the soldiers; there was a contingent of Hazzara escorting them. Algarik couldn't afford to lose control of his emotions in front of them.

The deep violet sky paled to lavender as Hamra relinquished the heavens to Lord Shamar. The light glinted off the army of still black figures that blanketed the land like a swarm of insects. Algarik scanned the rows upon rows of motionless soldiers and allowed himself a smile. Exhausted though he was after several days of nighttime travel with little rest, the sight buoyed his spirits. This indestructible army of over fifty thousand, created from sheer rock by fabled stonemason Ruzik Ozan, was unstoppable. His stone soldiers would annihilate the other races and redeem Algarik in his Master's eyes.

Algarik spotted a knot of people at the massive army's forefront and urged his beast to land. The rinzar's shadow swept over the group, and each head swiveled up in their direction. Marik's knit cap wobbled dangerously on his head as the mage swung back to the group, gesturing in the short, clipped motions that always accompanied his words. The rinzar landed several yards away, stirring up whorls of dirt with the forward circle of its wings. Algarik rappelled off his colossal beast using the riding straps to get down and strode towards the group.

"You made it; how fortuitous," Marik turned to face his superior, a cold glint in his brown eyes. "But where is the boy? Weren't you supposed to have him by now?"

Algarik gritted his teeth and forced a smile. "The boy was sacrificed to Wézija and is no longer my concern." He glanced over Marik's shoulder at the army, then back. "Why do I find you not through the other side of the Tawaki Chasm as instructed, but here barely a league from the fortress?"

There was a dangerous edge to his voice, and the group of Hazzara clustered around Marik melted back toward their units. Marik's back stiffened, and he let a slow breath out his nose before answering.

"It was truly a stroke of genius reanimating the legendary Ruzik Ozan and then compelling him to create this army of indestructible stone soldiers. They are magnificent, are they not?" Marik turned to face the army, folding his arms across his chest. He stared at them for several slow breaths then turned back to Algarik.

"The only problem that we face now is moving them. Ruzik only has so much Árk'äezhi to infuse them with and still maintain enough energy to live. We can move this entire force less than half a mile each day before he needs to rest and regenerate."

Lines creased Algarik's forehead, and the tic in his cheek jumped. He glared at Marik, searching for any sign of treachery in his eyes. He found only slight amusement, which caused him to ball his hands into fists at his sides.

"Take me to him," the mage said in a tight voice.

Marik bowed slightly and turned on his heel. Algarik followed the gawky man through several ranks of inert soldiers. Algarik looked at their faces as he passed, marveling despite his anger at the individually distinct characteristics.

These soldiers were works of art. Some had facial hair carved into their chins, and others sported smooth faces— each one as unique as an army of men, only much more biddable and substantially more durable. Algarik's attention turned from the soldiers to a tall, sepia-skinned man seated cross-legged on a bare slab of marble surrounded by a ring of stone sentries. His shoulder-length black hair hung limp around his gaunt face.

The man wore baggy, loose-weave trousers and an open, embroidered vest with the high sash of the Yezman. His chest was bare despite the chill of the early morning, Lord Shamar's rays burnishing his smooth brown skin. The man's eyes were closed, and his hands splayed flat on the rock.

Algarik heard a low hum emanating from the still form. He forced a pleasant expression and gently nudged the man, swallowing his desire to throttle him.

"Ruzik," he said softly. "We need to discuss some things."

The humming continued for another moment before Ruzik opened his eyes and fixed them on the mage. One leg, then the other uncurled from its folded position, and he raised himself erect, his eyes never leaving Algarik's.

"I am, as ever, at your service, O kind and generous Master," Ruzik bowed low with a graceful flourish.

The tic in Algarik's cheek jumped once, revealing the mage's agitation despite his pleasant demeanor. He returned the bow.

"Your army is truly magnificent, Ruzik," Algarik complimented the sculptor, waving his arm to encompass the army in his praise. "There does appear to be a small flaw that we haven't anticipated."

"Indeed, O Wisest of Men?" Ruzik turned away from his army to face the mage. "I live but to do your bidding. Pray tell me of my shortcomings so that I may rectify them." The stonemason knelt at Algarik's feet, his hands outstretched in supplication.

Algarik let out a snort and pulled Ruzik to his feet, keeping his grip tight on the stonemason's arms. The mage stared into Ruzik's guileless face and narrowed his eyes.

"You know the properties of stone better than any in all of Muralia," Algarik seethed. He shook the man, squeezing his hands tighter on Ruzik's arms. "How is it that you neglected to account for the Árk'äezhi required to move them? More to the point, how do you plan to address it?"

A slight puckering of Ruzik's mouth was the only change in the man's face. Algarik didn't know if it was annoyance or amusement, but neither curbed his anger. He released the stonemason with a slight shove and turned, striding through the silent figures encircling them. Algarik caressed a cheekbone of one, then pivoted to trace the shoulder of another. He wandered through the forms surrounding Ruzik, admiring them before turning his attention back to the stonemason.

"You have created masterpieces with these soldiers," Algarik said, crossing his arms over his chest. "However, the months of delays you required to do such painstaking work have cost me Askári-bai."

Algarik's voice was low, and he forced himself to remain in control despite the heat rising along the back of his neck. He circled behind Ruzik, who stood motionless. "Now, there are more delays due to your inability to mobilize my force for more than a few minutes." Algarik returned to face Ruzik, the tic in his cheek spasming. "I'm beginning to think you are trying to thwart my plans. Is that what's going on here, Ruzik?"

The stonemason held Algarik's gaze and gave a slight shrug. Ruzik glanced around at his creations and put a hand over his chest.

"O Great Mage, you charged me with making an army for the Lord of Demons," Ruzik began, his soft, brown eyes sharp as they bored into Algarik's face. "A task that I was most humbly gratified to undertake. So, I have created an army worthy of his greatness." Ruzik spread his arms out wide, then clasped them to his chest, ducking his head. "If my work has displeased the Master, I offer him my life in recompense."

Algarik's lips pressed together. This was not the first time Ruzik had offered his life. Algarik grimaced. The stonemason seemed to have a death wish, subtle though it might be. He knew that freeing Ruzik from his crystalline resting place would have risks, but Algarik didn't think subversion would be one of them.

Perhaps Ruzik resented his freedom and subsequent return to the living. He expressed his dismay at his removal from Zaroon Quarry in Yezmarantha, but other than that, Ruzik hadn't complained. Algarik frowned. The man was clever, and not only with his hands. The mage would have to keep a closer eye on him.

"I cannot grant your death wish quite yet," Algarik said, his frown deepening. "My Master still needs you, and I doubt that you would want to disappoint him."

Ruzik's face twisted into a mask of bitterness. "I doubt, O Great Mage, that the Lord of Demons can inflict a pain greater than what I have already suffered."

Algarik looked at the man with interest. If threats wouldn't compel the man into obedience, perhaps a demonstration was in order. He nodded and wove his way around the circle of statues, rubbing his chin as if in thought. He reached with his free hand into the folds of his cloak and grasped the talisman around his neck. With a flick of his wrist, he pulled the necklace forward, the large ruby nestled among the intricate torus knot of silver glinting balefully in Lord Shamar's early rays.

Algarik called forth his Árk'äezhi and channeled it through the ruby firestone at his neck. The ball of energy coalesced in front of him as his hands shaped and contained it. Snarling his frustration, he launched the fireball into the statue closest to Ruzik, causing it to explode in a shower of marble debris.

The mage waited until the fine dust had settled, then turned to Ruzik. The stonemason's dark face blanched; his lips were bloodless. A profound sadness hovered behind the man's eyes, but he shed no tears. He exhaled and slumped his shoulders.

"What is your bidding, O Master of Destruction?" Ruzik croaked, lifting his chin and raising his gaze to Algarik.

The mage tucked his amulet back into the folds of his cloak and nodded.

"Your army needs to move much faster if we are to engage the Shäeli and Yezmen in the Rabäen Plains, and—"

"Why not engage them here?" Ruzik interrupted. He looked around at the barren land. "The toxins in the air would weaken both armies and their beasts. They would be tired from the journey, and there would be no way for them to get reinforcements or supplies."

Algarik pinched the bridge of his nose, where the headache was beginning to stab. He was too exhausted to argue military tactics with an artist who had no notion of warfare. What he needed was to get this errant sculptor back to work on the problem at hand.

"The Shäeli won't engage us up here," Algarik began, sighing. "They have too much occupying them now. To ensure a quick victory, I need this army to engage them while they're spread too thin with their other crises. That will allow me to take Samshäeli as soon as we destroy Yezmarantha."

"You," he stuck a forefinger into Ruzik's chest, "need to figure out a way to move these soldiers faster and for longer periods. Why is it that you didn't mention this particular fact before?"

"You never asked."

Ruzik's face was neutral, but Algarik was sure he caught a flicker of amusement in the man's eyes. The mage clenched his teeth and his fists tightly. Now he knew the stonemason was undermining his efforts. He inhaled and let the breath out slowly, cooling his anger and sharpening his mind.

"I'm asking now," Algarik growled, fixing the sculptor with an angry scowl. "I suggest you come up with a way of speeding them along quickly. Maybe we need to reduce their numbers to decrease the drain on your Árk'äezhi?"

Ruzik's eyes widened, and he shook his head. "No, do not destroy any more of my men." He stepped away from the mage and the remnants of his protective circle of stone troops and laid his hands on the hard ground. "There is red jasper here, beneath the terra and not too deep. I can infuse pieces of the stone with my energy then embed them into the soldiers. Red jasper is an aggressive stone; it will propel them to war and require much less of my energy to maintain. But I warn you," he stood and turned to face Algarik. "They may not be as easy to control. The jasper has its own influence on the stone used to create the army."

"You knew about this and didn't offer it before?" Algarik fumed.

Ruzik swallowed and looked bleak. "There...there are inherent dangers that you don't understand. If I animate them with red jasper, they will seek conflict. If they encounter any Maüli, the spirits could inhabit the soldiers and wreak their ferocious vengeance on all of us."

Algarik raised his brows. "Maüli can inhabit these statues? Can they be controlled?"

Ruzik shook his head, his eyes flat and expressionless.

"How do you know this?" the mage asked.

Ruzik stared beyond the mage and into the past. "I've seen it."

"Tell me," Algarik demanded.

"Her name was Zaminah," Ruzik said, his voice as toneless and hollow as his eyes. "She was my betrothed."

Ruzik returned to the flat rock he'd been meditating on earlier and sat down. He crossed his legs and clasped his hands together in his lap.

"She was the only daughter of a prosperous merchant family in Taboriz. The family was overjoyed at the match and celebrated our betrothal." He cast his eyes down to the remnants of his soldier, scattered across the ground. "Not everyone was pleased with this announcement. Another prospective suitor, Liazo Tabriz, a trader with a fleet of ships and ego as vast as the sea, also pursued her."

Algarik shifted from one foot to the other and crossed his arms over his chest. He hoped this story would get to the point before Lord Shamar reached his zenith. He watched the stonecutter's hands as he dug his fingernails into the fleshy part of the palms, drawing blood.

"Liazo's suit wasn't as advantageous as mine, and Zaminah's mother declined his offer. As for Zaminah's part...." Ruzik's voice faltered. He cleared his throat and tried again. "She truly loved me, and I loved her. We offered blessings to her mother at the Zholi Festival for supporting our match."

"How wonderful for you both," Algarik grumbled, tapping one foot on the ground.

Ruzik glared up at him, his brows thunderous. "On the eve of our wedding, my Zaminah was abducted from her home by a group of thugs. They ravaged her and dumped her torn and bloody body outside the quarry where I was living. I found her in the morning. She had just enough breath to tell me what happened before she died in my arms."

"Her Árk'äezhi emerged from her body, twisted and warped," his voice turned harsh, and his lips twisted into bitter lines. "She became Maüli, and I welcomed her destructive energy. I begged her to take my life, but she wanted vengeance and flew back to Taboriz and her attackers. Word came within a fortnight that Laizo's ships had burned in port. Her captain and crew all lost. There was an inquiry, but I knew the truth."

"Is there a point to all this?" Algarik asked. "I do have an army to mobilize."

"Yes, mage, there is," Ruzik snarled. "If you have the ears to listen and the mind to hear."

Algarik raised his eyebrows but kept silent, nodding for the stonecutter to continue.

"I was desolate, alone," Ruzik sighed. "So, I carved a marble likeness of my beloved Zaminah, capturing her grace and beauty. I shaped a heart out of red jasper and placed it in her chest." He hung his head, grasping his hair with his hands. "I was faceting the topaz quartz for her eyes when the Maüli returned. Attracted by the red jasper, the spirit embraced the statue, animating it with her ferocity."

"It broke my heart to see her face ravaged once more by despair and torment," Ruzik said in a voice just above a whisper. "I thought I could save her, return her soul to peace and Lady Muralia, but her anger was too strong. My only option was to try and survive long enough for her rage to dissipate so that I could soothe the Maüli."

Ruzik raised his eyes and focused on the mage. "She was the flower of my garden, the blossom of my love, and they ruined her. The only thing left that I could do for her was to wait. I encased myself in crystal, hoping that in time, I would be able to free her. But then you came and awakened me, taking me from my home and my beloved and asking me to recreate the monster that still roams the quarry. You know not what you ask."

Algarik gazed at the stonemason, allowing his story to settle in his mind before responding. He scrubbed at his face with both hands to stave off the exhaustion.

"We have not encountered any Maüli here." Algarik shook his head. "If there are any, they will be in the lands of the Askári, and we are headed to Yezmarantha. We should be reasonably safe."

Ruzik gave a short laugh. "How many did the Garanth slaughter in Askári-bai? How many souls were torn from their bodies to allow the demon essences to create the Arkmuln? No Mage, there are Maüli out there, and they will swarm to the red jasper from wherever they are. If you command me to do this, I must obey. Know that I advise against it. You will not be able to control them, nor will I."

The mage pondered the idea of a Maüli army and saw advantages in it. With his magic, he was confident that he could control the Maüli despite Ruzik's misgivings. Stones of red ore were all firestones and filled with similar characteristics. They were projective energy, passionate, and fierce. Algarik grinned; this army would be unstoppable and under his control. The ruby in his amulet was more potent a firestone than red jasper, and Algarik knew that he could channel the rage of the spirits to battle.

"Do it," Algarik commanded the sculptor. "Also inform Marik. I will return to Aromberk Fortress to collect a few things and to rest. You have three days. We march on the fourth day for Yezmarantha."

chapter 22: To Harness the Wind

Sénna eyed the man-shaped target Anéton had sketched on the bulkhead. She squinted, closing one eye as she raised the throwing knife. With a grunt, she hurled the narrow blade towards her target. The knife sank in at the drawing's throat. Sénna expected a satisfying *thunk*, but instead, she heard a strangled cry from behind her.

"Laylur's beast!" Cédron swore.

Spinning around, Sénna looked at Cédron, who had gone completely pale. "What is it? What happened?"

"I—they—" Cédron swallowed and shook his head, looking at his hand.

Cédron held a palm-sized slab of polished beryl that he'd been using to scry with his Uncle Roväen, who'd gone with the Sumäeri team to check out the city of Zaveen. They'd gone into the silent city to investigate the reports of the murdered priestesses from the Temple of Orwaena. Sénna couldn't fathom such a grisly end for the fabled priestesses, but Cédron's expression confirmed the news.

The fortress city of Zaveen was ancient and thought to be impenetrable. The temple was said to have been established by the moon daughter Orwaena for her priestesses. It was the only temple in Muralia dedicated to the warrior goddess. The Priestesses of Orwaena were renowned for their skill and craftsmanship in designing weapons and armor.

The city sat nestled within the western Zahili desert's red hills, mounds filled with the black metal zolenium and topped with red sands. Working this unbreakable metal was a skill only the Priestesses of Orwaena could master, requiring dedication to learning the craft coupled with innate talent in metal forging and craftsmanship. Blades made by the Priestesses of Orwaena wouldn't break, and armor woven with the light, tensile metal could repel any blow.

To protect this invaluable resource, the goddess built her fortress city into the stone of the hills, her walls snaking around the hillsides' natural contours. Zaveen's defenses had never been breached or her thick walls broken by siege. The fact that both the temple and the small town supporting it appeared abandoned from above in the airship piqued the Sumäeri warriors' curiosity. Sénna knew she wasn't alone in holding out hope that the reports were exaggerations and that the priestesses were safe deep within their mines.

Everyone on deck gathered around Cédron to witness what Roväen projected through the stones. Sénna didn't hesitate to look into the stone that he held out in front of him. The room the Sumäeri entered was cavernous, with all sorts of zolenium weapons hanging on walls, stacked in racks, and laid out on tables.

Roväen lowered the angle of the bracelet he wore. Everyone on the airship surrounding Cédron's stone gasped. Sénna felt her last meal rise in her throat. She swallowed and turned away, walking to the rail of the airship. She leaned over the side and vomited. She wasn't alone.

Roväen's scry showed the floor of the citadel littered with slain priestesses. From the eldest Doyäenne to the child acolytes, none survived. Blood from the mutilated bodies dried in thin rivulets down the stairs to the exterior doors. Who could have defeated so many priestesses of the warrior goddess within their demesnes? There were no bodies of foes among the red-clad corpses. Sénna couldn't imagine any force so powerful that they could oppose the Priestesses of Orwaena and not suffer even a single casualty.

"We will scour the rest of the temple to see if there are any survivors," Roväen said through the stone. "I'm not optimistic."

"Be back before Lord Shamar sets," Cédron warned. "We don't know who did this and if they are still in the area. We should be far away before dark."

Roväen nodded, and the scry connection broke. Sénna watched Cédron shove the polished beryl into the pouch at his hip with shaking hands. Anéton noticed as well and put an arm around his friend's shoulders, speaking in low tones. She couldn't hear Anéton's words, but she watched Cédron shake then nod his head, a slight smile breaking through the horror of the scry.

"All right, everyone," Anéton called, clapping his hands to get their attention. "They will be back soon, and we will need to be ready to lift off. Cybél, would you run out to the Sumäeri over the hill there? They are feeding the läeniers from Zaveen's ozryk herds. Tell them we need to have the raptors ready to go in an hour."

Cybél nodded and gathered her skirts to run down the gangplank to the dunes below. Anéton turned to those who remained on deck.

"I want two teams," he said, looking at the circle of faces surrounding him. "We need lookouts just in case we get some unwanted visitors, and we need to get the harnesses ready for the läeniers. Let's go, folks. We have a lot of work to do."

"I still think we should have been there to honor the priestesses," Sénna muttered to Cybél.

Sénna and Cybél knelt on the main deck, their backs to the forecastle, weaving reinforcements into ropes forming a rigging ladder hanging over the side of the ship. Sturdy railings rimmed the main deck except for the narrow gap for the gangplank and ladder. Sénna sat near the opening with one end of the rigging rope spread out in front of her, and Cybél sat nearer the mainmast with the bulk of the frayed rope bunched up between them.

Cybél sighed and nodded. Her delicate hands twisted the hemp and spliced it into the rungs that had snapped when the landing party scrambled up too quickly after their gruesome discovery in Zaveen. They'd raced back to the airship, grim and tense. Although Sénna understood that the Sumäeri created a massive release of energy, returning the priestesses' life forces to Lady Muralia, she would like to have witnessed it.

"I have a hard time believing they would expend their Árk'äezhi for a mass burial when there are so many other dangers we could be facing," Sénna said. She jutted out her jaw and twisted the hemp in her hand with short, fierce gestures. "What if they missed some? What if they become Maüli?"

Cybél dropped her hands. "There's been so much death already, and the Sumäeri are saying that Táksabai was just a small battle. I can't imagine the number of Maüli that may be around Táksabai." She swallowed and lowered her eyes. "Nearly the entire city was lost; our homes, our families, our futures." Cybél grasped the rope, shaking her head. "We have a bigger job now. We have to support Cédron, so the rest of our world doesn't suffer the same fate. I know it feels wrong to leave without ceremony, but we have to hurry. That mage will set the Great Demon free if we don't."

Sénna sighed and shrugged her shoulders. "I know. So much about it just seems hurried. My grandmother would tell me stories of Maüli and their destructive power. I just think it's a possibility, and we need to be prepared for it. It also seems wrong to put all our hopes into that half-Shäeli—"

"Sénna," Cybél chided. "You have no place saying such things. It is your mixed heritage that makes you and your family special. Cédron is no different."

Sénna huffed and narrowed her eyes at the young demon coming up on deck from below.

"I'd have a lot more confidence in him if he knew what he was doing," she said under her breath.

Cédron stood in front of Sénna, his arms crossed over his chest. "You speak of Maüli like you have experience with them," he said, narrowing his eyes. "Have you ever actually faced one?"

Sénna shifted from her hips to her knees, then stood to face Cédron. "No, but I—"

"Well, I have," Cédron interrupted, poking her sternum with a finger. "And I've never been so terrified and helpless in my life. When it comes to Maüli, no preparation will help. I suggest you don't tell stories you know nothing about."

Cédron turned on his heel and joined Rováen and Säeshi as they passed by the girls and took up positions in the center of the deck. The elder Shäeli caught Sénna's eyes, and she felt heat rise in her cheeks. Sénna sat back down on the deck, lowered her gaze to her work, and tried to ignore the discomfort of his attention. She crossed her legs on the deck, seeking a more comfortable position. The heat of Lord Shamar's rays on her ears and shoulders kept the flush from receding. Sénna scowled and put her hands to her cheeks to cool them.

"Well, *I* have confidence in him," Cybél said, returning to her work. "I won't believe that I've lost Myknét and my grandmother and my home for nothing."

Sénna shrugged and set down her rope to watch the Shäeli. She didn't think she'd ever get used to the silver-haired warriors with sparkling, gem-colored eyes and green foliage tattoos covering all but their faces. Rováen pulled out a windstone, nearly half the size of his palm, and held it out to Cédron. He began explaining something to the young man about the stone, but Sénna couldn't quite hear his words. She scooted closer to the opening in the railing and towards the group, pretending to pull the rope out to disentangle it.

Rováen laid his hands on Cédron's shoulders. "You're going to need to clear your mind. I know with recent events that will be difficult, but you cannot access the windstone's Árk'äezhi energy if you don't."

Säeshi pulled her cousin to the deck. They sat in a loose circle with their legs crossed. Säeshi moved to Cédron's side, and he flinched. She closed her eyes and took several slow, deep breaths before opening her eyes and looking at Cédron.

"The windstone is a different sort of energy than either the firestone or the aquastone," she said, adjusting her legs and leaning towards Cédron. "The windstone embodies mental and spiritual energy. It is softer, quieter, and represents a state of being that only transforms perception. It doesn't truly change anything. There are three main ways to use the windstone: one is to harness, shape, or move the wind; another is to create an illusion of something that either isn't there or isn't in the specific location it appears to be in, and last to move things from one place to another. This last one is the most difficult power to learn, and it's perilous, so don't try it until after you've mastered the other two aspects. Understood?"

Sénna saw Cédron swallow and nod his head. His face was pale, and he wiped his palms on his pants, but his eyes never left Säeshi's. Sénna wondered what the woman had meant by illusion. Certainly, the stone's energy couldn't trick her mind into seeing something that wasn't there, could it?

Manipulating the wind was to be expected. Cédron had already demonstrated that ability when he'd called the winds to cushion his fall off the cliffs. Sénna wondered how strong the wind would have to be to move something from one place to another. Cédron could move light objects like feathers or leaves, but a person or the ship?

Sénna shook her head and snorted. Fortunately, the Sumäeri warriors' läeniers were pulling the vessel and directing its course so that Cédron could focus on other aspects of the windstone's Árk'äezhi.

Rovaen began instructing Cédron on how to focus his thoughts through the stone's energy and think of what he wanted the others to see. As Cédron concentrated, Anéton and Tóran wandered over to the group from the galley below, each bearing a meatroll in their hands and chewing like a herd of mijáko.

"What's going on over here?" Anéton smiled at Cybél and nudged Tóran to join him in an elaborate bow to the young ladies.

Sénna scowled at the two young legionnaires and noticed that Cédron was also frowning at them. She raised her eyebrows. Maybe the young demon was simply annoyed at the distraction to his concentration, or perhaps he was also interested in Cybél and bothered by the competition. She smirked. The lot of them were wasting their time. Their adolescent charms wouldn't overcome Cybél's heartbreak at losing Myknét.

"We're helping Cédron master more properties of the

windstone's Árk'äezhi," Rováen said over his shoulder. He turned to face the newcomers and waved them into the circle. "He will need to be prepared to align with the sacred windstone as soon as he gets it, so he has much to learn. Join us if you like, but keep quiet while he concentrates."

Tóran raised a meatroll in salute and sank to the deck with his legs crossed. Anéton smiled one last time at the ladies and joined the circle. Sénna watched Cédron close his eyes and start his deep breathing once again. The elderly Shäeli ran his nephew through several exercises, including blowing rope pieces and a cloak around the deck.

Rováen then had Cédron concentrate on making their little circle invisible to Sénna and Cybél. Sénna perked up, but Cybél showed no interest in the magical demonstration and kept her head bent towards the netting. Sénna leaned against the bulkhead, waiting for nothing to happen. She felt her heart nearly stop when the group sitting on the deck shimmered and disappeared.

"Where did they go?" Sénna grasped the railing of the ship with white knuckles and scoured the deck with her eyes. "What happened to them?"

Sénna heard Rováen chuckle just to her left. "We are still here, but Cédron has hidden our images from sight. Not a bad effort, lad."

"It's a lot like using the bloodstone to make myself invisible," Cédron's voice said. "I've had that mastered for Tides."

"Indeed," Rováen growled.

The group shimmered into view, and Sénna stared at them with wide eyes. "Did you see that?" she asked Cybél, who shrugged and kept her eyes on her hands and the netting.

Sénna couldn't help but find this demonstration fascinating. What she wouldn't do for such a skill; the ability to become invisible. Sénna thought of all the places she could go, the information she could gather, the value she could bring to her father's Gróshan. The thought of earning her father's approval tightened her throat. She blinked her stinging eyes and returned to repairing the netting. She wasn't a magic wielder, never would be, and would never have her father's blessing to become one of his spies.

Säeshi smiled at Cédron. She pulled a delicate silver chain from her pouch and laid it on the deck. Sénna thought the silver pendant was shaped like a letter and had a pale blue stone mounted in the center, but she couldn't get close enough to see without appearing too interested in the group's conversation. Sénna's ears pricked at Säeshi's following words.

"I want you to try and move this necklace from here over to Tóran." Säeshi pointed to the legionnaire, who was brushing flakes of pastry off his chest.

Cédron cocked his head sideways. "How do I do that? I could use the wind to blow it towards Tóran, but I don't see how I can just make it appear there."

Rováen smiled and looked at Säeshi, who shrugged her shoulders and nodded.

"Try this," he said to Cédron. "See the necklace around Tóran's throat. Feel what it would feel like, the weight of it, the cold metal against his skin, all of it. Then reach for it like it's already there."

"It's not his style," Anéton shoved Tóran with his shoulder and grinned. "But, I'm sure it will be very fetching."

Tóran grimaced and nudged his comrade in the side with his elbow. "Knock it off, or I'll throw you over the side."

Sénna glanced through the railings at the distant ground below. The vast desert stretched as far as the eye could see in every direction. The only features breaking up the reddish sands were the river they followed and the far distant hills. It was so different from the teeming city of Táksabai, the place she'd never been allowed to leave.

Beneath the airship, a cluster of sharp rocks jutted from

the ground like tusks from the wild beasts she'd seen in books. She shuddered. A fall from this height would give way too much time to contemplate the unpleasant landing. She turned away from her morbid thoughts and watched as Cédron squeezed his eyes shut and tried visibly to relax.

Sénna kept her eyes on the necklace, the netting in her lap forgotten. A drop of moisture splashed onto the pendant, and she glanced at Cédron. His face was a mask of effort, his body rigid, and beads of sweat rolled down his temples.

Säeshi's laugh pealed across the deck. She grasped Cédron's shoulders and shook him gently. "You must clear your mind, and you must relax. The Árk'äezhi must flow through you, and through the stone, you can't push it. You are blocking it with all this effort."

Sénna kept her eyes on the scene. Cédron's eyes were wide, and he gulped before nodding at his cousin. He took another deep breath and closed his eyes. Sénna watched his shoulders relax and his breathing slow. Then, without warning, the necklace simply disappeared.

Across the deck, Tóran let out a strangled cry. The necklace hung around his throat, a red line of blood forming around the tiny links from the force expended to wrap it around his neck. Tóran gripped the chain and yanked it away from his throat, tossing it onto the deck at Cédron's feet.

"I'm going to try not to take that demonstration of power personally," Tóran growled, glaring at his brother.

Cédron sighed and slumped his shoulders. He looked up at the other two Shäeli and shook his head. "I can't focus. I just—I can't get the power right. I have too much, and I can't control it. People get hurt around me. I just don't think I'm ready."

"That's why we're practicing, lad," Rováen said. "You are progressing well, but you can't expect to master this on your first try."

Cédron looked towards the sky and blinked his eyes. "I *have* to learn quickly. Everything and everyone depends on me."

Sénna raised her eyebrows and glanced from one Shäeli to the other. Cédron was right. The fate of their world depended on him, and he was right to worry. She had similar doubts about his abilities. Her skin prickled at the thought of him failing in his quest, and she rubbed her arms furiously with her hands to dispel the sensation.

Sénna looked over at the legionnaires. Anéton had eyes only for the meatroll in his hand and chewed with loud, smacking noises. Tóran scrutinized Cédron with an odd expression on his face. Sénna thought it was a combination of fascination and disgust, which would make sense for a Harmólin Legionnaire faced with a Shäeli demon. Those hatreds ran long and deep.

Roväen stood Cédron up and walked him towards the stern of the airship with Säeshi. "Now, let's see if you can manage something a little trickier. I want you to use Räeshun to see if you can use the wind to steer the ship towards the opposite side of the river below us. Säeshi will be right here if you feel you're losing your strength or concentration."

Cédron nodded, his jaw set, and his hand clenched around the staff. Roväen removed the firestone and aquastone from Räeshun's crown and put them in Cédron's pouch before placing the large windstone in the phalanges ringing the staff's top. Räesha's finger bones grasped the smooth yellow stone.

"That'll be quite the trick if he can pull it off," Tóran said. He eyed his brother skeptically and pulled Anéton towards the forecastle and the girls. "He's never been one to focus on any one thing for long."

Anéton pulled a flask from his pouch and pulled the cork. He raised it to Tóran. "I'll drink to that. Did I ever tell you about the time he tried to—"

"Mijáko piles," Sénna coughed and reached for the flask. "What are you drinking? It smells like—"

"It's a spirit called arák I got from Murádit," Anéton

grabbed his bottle and sniffed. "It's a bit strong, yes, but it's tasty."

Sénna coughed again and barked a laugh. "If Murádit made it, you might want to drink with caution. I call that stuff gák because that's the sound you make when you drink it."

Anéton took a large swig and handed the flask to Tóran. The legionnaire tipped the flask to his lips and sniffed, setting it back down again.

"What's in this stuff?" Tóran asked, reeling against the side of the railing as the ship lurched sideways. "It smells awful."

Sénna looked up at the two legionnaires and smiled sweetly. "It's made from fermented cocoa palm sap and anise. Usually, he mixes it with water to dilute it, but I've known him to add husan piss for an extra kick."

Anéton sprayed out the mouthful he'd just taken, hitting Cédron in the back of the neck with the liquid.

"Hey!" Cédron spun around, waving Räeshun in a wild arc.

The bow of the airship followed the staff's swing, causing the vessel to dip deeply to port. Everyone cried out. Hands grabbed whatever was closest and held on. Sénna slid towards the opening and reached for the rope ladder. She wrenched her shoulder as the rope caught on a barrel and snapped tautly. Tóran and Anéton fell sideways and grasped the railings. Cybél clung to the mast, her feet tangled in the netting.

"Cédron!" Rováen yelled over the shrieks and screams. "Calm the winds. The läeniers are tangled up in their ropes."

Sénna pulled herself towards Cybél, hand over hand on the swaying deck. Her fingers rubbed raw on the coarse rope. She saw Cédron and Säeshi holding onto each other and trying to get the winds under control. The läeniers over the side screeched, and their riders barked orders back and forth, trying to untangle the magnificent raptors. The airship tilted starboard, and she slid into Cybél, the netting interlacing both their feet in the rope.

"Mijáko piles!" Sénna cursed and pulled frantically at the netting caught on her boot knife. "Cédron is going to be the death of us all if he isn't more careful!"

The legionnaires gripped the railing and called directions to the riders beneath the airship. Sénna pulled her knife free and sawed at the ropes when the vessel lurched again. She reached for the barrels as she slid by, wincing as splinters gouged her hands. Before she could take a breath, Sénna slid through the open railings and over the side of the ship.

The wind struck her face with such force that she couldn't breathe. Her eyes watered and stung, and her hair whipped out behind her like a banner. Her heart hammering in her chest was the only other thing Sénna could feel besides the bite of the air on her skin. She saw the river below winding through the desert like a ribbon of blue silk against the reddish sands and wondered if it would be a quicker death to hit the soft sand or the hard water.

Sénna knew death awaited her and felt a level of relief. She would be joining her mother and Myknét in Lady Muralia's bosom. This was a better fate than watching Laylur destroy her world a little at a time. Sénna closed her eyes and faced her last moments with all the dignity she could muster.

When the pain hit her, it was unexpected. Her belly struck a hardened surface that knocked what little air she'd been able to inhale out of her chest. Sénna felt strong hands gripping her arm as she slid to one side. She opened her eyes and gasped. All around her were the soft golden feathers and leather straps of a läenier. The rider pulled her up onto the saddle in front of him and pulled her against his chest.

"Got you," the rider yelled into her ear. "You're safe now. I'll get you back up to the airship once it stabilizes."

Sénna nodded. When she got back to the airship, she was going to kill Cédron. The läenier banked towards the east.

With Lord Shamar at their backs, the desert spread out before them like a waving sea of red and brown. Sénna marveled at its beauty. She'd never been beyond the borders of Askári-bai, let alone halfway across their world. The raptor's wings beat in a steady rhythm as it strove to gain the height needed to return her to the airship.

Far below, a cluster of black shapes broke away from the rocks and moved towards the river. Sénna tapped the thigh of the rider she sat in front of and pointed. The Sumäeri turned to follow the direction of her finger and gave a strangled cry. He lurched forward into Sénna's back, a black arrow sunk into the back of his shoulder.

chapter 23: Torus Knot

"No!" Cédron cried as Sénna slid through the railing.

Cédron leaped toward the opening, reaching for Sénna's leg but got tangled in the rope netting. She spun away from him and plunged towards the desert below. Her scream filled the air, adding to the cacophony of shrieks made by the flailing läeniers trying to stabilize the airship.

Cybél helped untangle his foot, and he crouched to spring after her. Rough hands shoved him onto the deck and held him. Räeshun spun out of his hands across the wooden planks.

"You can't go after her yourself," Tóran yelled, pinning

him to the ground. "One of the riders will catch her."

Cédron shoved his brother off and sat up. He crawled to the railing of the ship and peeked overboard. Sénna was still flailing in mid-air, but he could see one of the Sumäeri diving his raptor towards her. He held his breath until she was safe on the läenier's back, then cried out as her rescuer fell to the side, a black arrow piercing his shoulder. More bolts filled the air, followed by screams of pain as they found their marks.

Anéton raced to Cybél's side and leaned out over the railing. He gasped, jumping back as an arrow whizzed past his cheek.

"There are Hazzara out there! Look!" He pointed toward the dark shapes racing across the desert floor on four-legged reptilian beasts with long tails and elongated jaws filled with sharp teeth.

Cédron gaped at the terrifying creatures and didn't immediately notice that their riders were launching arrows at the läeniers. "What are those things?"

Tóran stepped up to the railing and looked over; Räeshun held slack in his left hand. "They are called alzaytan, *sand devils* to the Yezman. Their hide is like armor, teeth like swords, and see the ball on the end of that long tail? Like a weighted whip. We can't defeat these creatures."

Cédron stared at his brother and blinked a few times. "How…how do you know all that?"

Tóran stared down at the indestructible beasts and slowly shook his head from side to side, a vertical crease forming between his brows. His right hand gripped the railing until his knuckles showed white.

"I'm not sure," he whispered and blinked his eyes, handing Räeshun back to Cédron.

Anéton knelt and grabbed Cybél's shoulders. "Get below. It's too dangerous for you up here." He turned to Roväen, who stood behind him near the mast. "Does this ship have any weapons or defenses?"

Cybél gave him a very pointed look and snorted before turning to go below decks. "I'll get my simples and bandages. I can at least be useful that way."

Anéton grinned and bowed, then turned his attention back to the advancing Hazzara.

Cédron slid across the deck towards his uncle, skidding into him as Rovāen helped Säeshi to her feet. "Uncle, what can we do?"

The airship stabilized as several of the läeniers disconnected their straps and turned to face the Hazzara. Six raptors kept the ship sailing east, but their speed slackened, and the vessel lost altitude, sinking towards the desert floor. Cédron felt the familiar prickle on the back of his neck and down his spine. The Hazzara were getting closer, and their arrows more accurate as the ship lowered into range.

Cédron raised Räeshun and increased the wind's lift, pulling the ship and her läenier escort higher and farther. Still, the Hazzara simply targeted the Wing of riders sweeping above them. Cédron watched the wounded läeniers and their riders fall aside, leaving fewer targets for the many Hazzara to find. He dropped Räeshun to the deck and tore at the ties on the pouch at his hip. The ship slowed and sank again despite the efforts of the few raptors still attached to its hull.

Cédron pulled out the sacred firestone and closed his eyes. He took three deep breaths before opening his eyes and aiming the stone at the main body of the attackers. Fire shot from the gem in his hands and struck the riders' center, tossing several into the air and scattering the rest.

"That's the way!" Anéton whooped next to him. "Blast them all to the abyss."

Cédron aimed his firestone and shot more pulses of red energy. The riders and their monstrous alzaytan burned at the impact but quickly rolled in the sand, extinguishing the flames before they could do much damage.

"Mijáko piles," Cédron cursed and wiped the sweat off

his face with his forearm. "I'm not doing enough damage. Those alzaytan have thicker hide than Garanth bulls!"

"Just keep at it," Rovaen squeezed his nephew's shoulder. "At least rolling in the sand keeps them from shooting at us. We're getting a little too close—"

"What should I do?" Cédron interrupted his uncle. "I can't shoot at the Hazzara and keep the ship aloft and out of range."

Behind them, Tóran picked up the bone staff off the deck and gave her a twirl. "It's too bad this thing won't work for me. I don't seem to be much help."

Cédron turned from the railing and stared at his brother. He saw something flicker behind Tóran's eyes that made his chest tighten. Could it be Tóran's disdain of what he'd always professed to feel for magic? He'd never known Tóran to covet any magical power; instead, he'd always shunned that aspect of Cédron's being.

Narrowing his eyes, Cédron looked harder at his brother's face. He saw a hunger there he didn't recognize. Cédron reached for Räeshun, but Rovaen pulled him back just as a pair of arrows hissed past his nose.

"Never mind Räeshun," his uncle spun him toward the railing of the sinking ship. "They're getting too close. Blast them!"

Cédron raised the firestone and launched fireballs into the oncoming Hazzara. He wasn't doing enough damage to make much of a difference. The black-clad Hazzara continued to advance, wounding more of their Sumäeri escort with each volley of arrows. The wounded Sumäeri and läeniers limped from the attack to the far side of the airship, keeping its hull between themselves and the onslaught of arrows.

The uninjured riders performed what aid they could to their raptors mid-air, and the injured stoically held on to their mounts until they could find a safe place to land and treat their injuries. Cédron's respect for their determination and strength blossomed into near worship. He could never be as brave as these fierce warriors. Across the deck of the airship, Roväen, Säeshi, and Anéton strapped on their weapons.

"Shoot from the stern," Roväen instructed Säeshi, who was buckling her strap of bolts to her back. He adjusted his own bolt strap and brandished his compound bow. "I'll shoot from the bow. Anéton, I want you to protect Cédron."

The legionnaire adjusted his sword belt low across his hips and patted the sash around his waist where Cédron knew he hid a brace of throwing knives. "Nobody will get close enough to touch him unless they've killed me first."

Cédron turned to his friend with a strained smile. "We know you have a hard head. How about the rest of you? Feeling invincible today?"

Anéton grinned. He spotted Cybél coming up from the hold carrying her basket of herbs and strips of cloth. "If not, perhaps she can patch me up enough to get through the day."

Cédron glanced at Cybél and shook his head. "Just try not to get killed today, ok?"

Anéton drew his sword and brandished it. The ship was now low enough to see the eyes in the otherwise covered faces of their enemies. Cédron raised the firestone again and shot a pulse into the group nearest the ship. The blast halted their progress, and as Cédron raised the stone for another shot, he heard a pop and whistle of air. Both young men turned and looked up. An arrow pierced the silk balloon, which began deflating. No amount of energy from Lord Shamar's rays would keep them aloft.

"Laylur's beast!" Cédron swore and cupped his hands over his mouth. "We're going down," he yelled at the Wingleader and pointed at the sagging silks. "Get yourselves detached before we hit the ground!"

The Wingleader looked where Cédron pointed up to the punctured balloon and nodded, then whistled instructions to his companions. The ship tilted and lurched as the raptors were untied from their straps. With the läeniers gone, the vessel sank rapidly towards the sand.

Wrapping his arm around the railing, Cédron turned to his companions. "Grab onto something. It's going to be a hard landing."

Cédron gripped the sacred firestone close to his chest and hooked one leg around the railing. Anéton lunged towards Cybél, securing her to the mast with a loose end of the mooring line snaking across the deck. At the bow, Cédron saw Rováen twist his left arm and leg around one of the lines running from the bow to the mast while he continued to fire his deadly bolts into the oncoming Hazzara. He didn't have time to check on Säeshi before the ship plowed sideways into a rocky ridge covered with sand, sending a gritty, red wave over the deck and jarring his shoulder against the bars of the railing where he'd wedged himself.

The Hazzara were upon them in an instant. He raised the firestone, but Anéton knocked him back. The legionnaire hurled himself at the lead alzaytan, swinging his sword not at the tough hide but at the reins and then at the straps holding the saddle. The rider slid sideways and landed on his back in the sand with a thud and breathless curse.

Anéton spun around and did the same to the following two alzaytan and their riders. They were too close now to use their arrows, so Anéton dodged the curved swords swinging at him as he slashed past them. He whooped his war cry and continued to cut through the enemy.

On the airship, Cédron reconsidered his approach. Fireballs weren't effective against these alzaytan and their Hazzara riders. The only other thing he could think of was some of the deeper magic of the firestone. He trusted Anéton to protect him for the few minutes it would take him to access his Árk'äezhi and focus it through the sacred stone.

Cédron cleared his mind and slowed his racing heartbeat. The warmth started around his heart, spreading through his chest and down his arms into the stone. The firestone burst into brilliant light, radiating scorching heat well beyond the confines of the airship. He heard rather than saw his uncle gathering everyone off the ship and herding them behind the outcropping of stone that created the berm they'd struck upon landing. Anéton returned to his side and screamed a challenge to the Hazzara, now advancing on foot.

Seeing that the rest of his companions were safe, Cédron focused on the heat of the stone's powerful Árk'äezhi. The sands began to shimmer. He heard full-throated bellows of distress from the alzaytan and shrieks from their riders. Cédron focused his thoughts and forced the heat forward into the red sands.

Shaping the idea in his mind first, he gave his Árk'äezhi direction. The sands in front of him began to swirl. The heat shimmered in Lord Shamar's light, blinding the Hazzara and their beasts. The spiraling sands rose and took form. Cédron smiled. The beings took on the details of the Caravan Master's shape and strength, expanding in size to gargantuan proportions.

The sands continued to heat as they formed, the dense red becoming a translucent rose color that maintained the brilliant light of the stone's magical energy. The glass giants solidified into seven replicas of Caravan Master Shozin Chezak standing twenty feet above the airship's side. Cédron nodded and felt the power of his Árk'äezhi explode through his chest.

Cédron felt himself rise into the air with the strength of his Árk'äezhi, the flame tattoos on his chest scorching his skin as the sacred firestone's energy melded with his intentions. The behemoth Shozin-shaped creatures advanced upon the Hazzara and their alzaytan mounts, herding them against the stone berm in front of the airship. The black-clad warriors screamed and swung at the glass warriors with their curved swords, striking sparks in Lord Shamar's light as the metal blades slid along their adamantine bodies.

The feeling of power swelled in Cédron's mind. His awareness expanded beyond the confines of their minor skirmish into the minds and hearts of his enemies. He could feel their anger, their fear, and, in one of the men, his excitement. Cédron focused his attention on the one Hazzara, who seemed to welcome his strength and power.

The leader faced Cédron's glass warriors and seemed to share his growing feeling of power and invincibility instead of fear. The two of them rose higher above the battle, and Cédron could feel a connection between them. He felt the heat in his chest rise, the burning making it impossible for him to draw breath.

Prickles of fear raced up his spine and exploded into sparks in his mind. Looming in his mind's eye were the Hazzara's eyes, black as coal and fathomless as the abyss. He could hear his adversary's laughter in his ears, taunting and tormenting him.

Cédron felt his control slipping over both his Árk'äezhi and his focus. He reached deep inside, seeking strength and the reassurance of Räeshun, whose ever-present guidance and wisdom had never failed to assuage his insecurities. He found only emptiness and silence. Räesha wasn't with him; he couldn't feel her presence. His lungs labored for breath as he tried to calm his racing thoughts.

The dark eyes again filled his mind, and he saw the brilliant red glow of the Hazzara's firestone beneath them. The stone nestled within the intricate weaving of a torus knot, just like the one his Uncle Algarik wore. Cédron felt the energy of his Árk'äezhi flowing from his body and the marks of the deities on his chest cool. He focused on the glass warriors to hold back the wave of helplessness that threatened to crash over him. His creations had surrounded and imprisoned the Hazzara and their mounts.

Cédron saw the seven figures weave their arms together, forming an impenetrable fortress around their enemies. Their cage shrank as the glass men squeezed in around their quarry. Cédron could feel his strength slipping, ebbing as laughter from the black-eyed Hazzara wormed its way into his thoughts. The farther he intruded, the more it disrupted his concentration.

The Hazzara's firestone began to pulse, its glow causing the glass warriors to gleam with an ominous vermillion cast. Cédron poured all of his focus into the glass prison woven by his creatures. The Hazzara's firestone flared one last time. The seven leviathans exploded into a shower of glittering red sand.

The blast shot Cédron backward, away from his enemy. He struck his head on the ship's wooden hull and slid to the desert floor.

chapter 24: Betrayal

Sénna watched the airship crash from her vantage point on the raptor with her rescuer. She winced at the impact and tucked her head into her companion's shoulder as a spray of red sands blew into the air around them. Despite her sinking heart, the spicy muskiness of the rider's body struck her. Its familiarity confused her for a moment as she tried to place it.

The smell brought a fleeting memory of when her grandmother took her to the Varkáras Caravan on its annual arrival in Táksabai. She'd been fascinated by the large, round berries that were so dark purple that they seemed black. *Jäebuticaba* or something similar, Sénna couldn't remember.

What she did remember was their sharp, spicy flavor. She glanced up at the rider's face, and he raised an eyebrow. She shook her head and turned forward. The berries must have been from Samshäeli because that was precisely how he smelled.

The rider pulled the black arrow from his shoulder and pressed on the wound with his other hand to slow the bleeding. They circled out of the Hazzara's bow range and headed toward camp and safety. With a loud shriek, the läenier banked sharply to the left to avoid the bright vermillion light radiating from near the airship. Sénna gripped the läenier's golden feathers so tightly her fingers ached, but the golden raptor didn't seem to notice.

Sénna craned her neck to find the source of the red glow. She wasn't surprised to find Cédron floating within a swirling vortex of red sands. Fascinated, she watched the sands take shape. Once assembled, they converged upon the Hazzara and their beasts. Sénna yanked the feathers to guide the raptor towards the injured läeniers, and riders clustered behind the airship, but the man at her back nudged her leg with his.

"What?" she yelled over the wind that ripped the words from her mouth. She turned and saw her rescuer's silver brows knit, his emerald eyes slits as he glared at something on the ground,

"What is he doing?" the rider yelled, jutting his chin towards a figure running away from behind the airship.

Sénna shook her billowing hair back, blinking the water from her stinging eyes. "No, he wouldn't!" She gasped and leaned back into her rider's chest. Heat flashed in her chest at the betrayal she witnessed below her. "Can we follow him?"

The rider's lips were tight, his eyes sharp facets of the jewel they resembled. He nodded and nudged the raptor with his knees, turning the beast back towards the glowing light.

The dark-haired figure racing across the red sands below them still wore the Harmólin Legion's overtunic and had a long, bone staff strapped across his back. Sénna watched him plow through the sands with his sturdy legs, increasing the distance between himself and the airship with each stride.

Cédron would be sick to learn that his brother had betrayed him.

Sénna knew Tóran had no interest in or ability to wield the staff's power. He had to be taking it to someone else, but who? She couldn't believe that he'd be working with the rogue mage Algarik, but she couldn't be sure of anything at this point. Tóran hadn't said much about his imprisonment at the Garanth encampment.

Tóran might have been compelled to switch sides by the demon, possibly by a spell or—

Her insides went cold. What if he'd been converted into some form of Arkmuln? Maybe become possessed by demon energy in some way? The implications sent a chill down her spine. Regardless of what motivated Tóran to spirit away with Räeshun, she had to stop him.

"Can you get us closer to him?" Sénna felt the words rip from her lips, but the rider nodded. He shifted his weight.

Lord Shamar was high in the sky, his brilliant light glaring off the hot sands blinding her as the läenier banked away from the airship to face the open desert. The raptor shrieked as it homed in on its prey, causing Tóran to slow and look over his shoulder at them. His eyes glittered blue in the light. Sénna snatched the reins from the rider's grip, jerking the läenier's head aside. She had to get them away from those eyes.

Sénna tried to close her own eyes, to reject the sparkling deep blue that had replaced Tóran's warm brown ones, but she was magnetized. She couldn't pull her gaze away and gasped when Tóran smiled. There was no warmth in that face, no feeling. He turned and continued to race away from the airship, breaking their connection and allowing Sénna to take a breath.

"We have to get to Cédron!" She lashed the raptor's reins and tried to turn its head towards the airship.

"No," the rider argued. "We need to get Räeshun. We can't lose her again."

Sénna shook her head and pulled on the reins harder. "He can get her with his Árk'äezhi and the windstone. I've seen it. We have to tell him that Tóran has her."

The rider behind her grunted and pulled the reins out of her hands. "Then, you'll have to quit annoying Shäelan, or she'll dump us off."

The rider leaned in closer to her, taking back the reins and resting his chest on Sénna's back. The warm solidness of his body soothed her rising panic, as did his competence in handling the raptor. He turned the läenier towards the airship and gasped. She glanced up and felt her chest squeeze her heart into stillness.

Two figures floated above a colossal cage of man-shaped glass that corralled the Hazzara and their terrifying mounts. One was Cédron, cradling a firestone next to his body; the other was one of the Hazzara. The black-clad man wielded the same kind of red-stoned amulet she'd seen on the leader of the men who'd captured her.

Sénna shielded her eyes from the blinding red glow surrounding the two figures. She could feel her companion stiffen and squeeze his raptor with his knees. She didn't know what was happening between Cédron and the Hazzara, but it didn't look right. The heat of their magic muted even Lord Shamar's rays. Sénna watched Cédron shrivel under the other man's force.

"Get up, Cédron! Remember who you are!" Sénna screamed.

Sénna saw Anéton pacing the tilted deck, seeking a way to reach his friend. He cupped his hands around his mouth and yelled something at Cédron, but she couldn't hear his words over the howling wind. She doubted Cédron could either.

She glanced over at the Hazzara. The turbaned man threw his head back and laughed. She couldn't see his mouth—the black fabric of his headpiece covered it—but there was no mistaking his movement.

"Can we do anything to help?" she asked the Sumäeri rider.

The rider shook his head, banking Shäelan behind Cédron and his adversary. "It's too dangerous. I can't risk—"

The explosion blew the raptor sideways, rolling her wings almost vertical and nearly dumping off her riders. Sénna screamed and flung herself onto the raptor's neck, gripping feathers with white knuckles. The Sumäeri yelled at her to hold on as he pulled the reins tight and flattened himself over her.

Shäelan shrieked in pain and protest, flopping back horizontally and awkwardly beating her wings. Sénna could feel the erratic rhythm of her flapping and the raptor's tense body beneath her. Then she saw the blood.

"Shäelan is injured!" She pointed towards the golden underside of the wings and chest.

Shäelan's rider had already steered her towards the other wounded. "Hold on; she may not be able to land without causing more damage."

Sénna looked down, scouring the desert floor for a safe place to land. Beyond the confrontation by the airship, the remaining Wing of healthy läeniers hovered above the wounded, guarding and protecting them from both enemies and the brutal heat of the deity's rays. Sénna could see Cybél weaving in among the injured with her basket of bandages and simples. Roväen and Säeshi patrolled the sands below, repelling any Hazzara that might get through Cédron's glass cage.

The läenier plummeted towards the sand, and Sénna's stomach flopped. She tore handfuls of golden feathers from Shäelan's neck when her rider flung himself sideways, pulling them both off the raptor into the sands just before impact. He wrapped his arms and legs around her body and twisted mid-air, landing on his back. She felt his chest compress as they hit the ground. Rolling off, she turned to find her rescuer motionless, his eyes wide and glazed.

"No, no, no, you can't die," Sénna moaned and felt along his chest for broken bones. She loosened the strings to his leather breastplate and saw the faint pulse in his neck.

Sénna cried out and sank her head on his chest when he began working his mouth, trying to get air into his lungs. She lifted her head and turned at the shushing sound of feet running in the sand towards her. Cybél fell to her knees beside the Sumäeri.

"Where is he injured?" She began probing the rider's blood-soaked shoulder with her delicate fingers.

The rider batted her hands away. "I'm fine," he gasped, groaning as he sat up. He turned his head toward his läenier. "Shäelan took the brunt of the explosion and the impact. Tend to her first."

Sénna shook her head as the rider rolled onto his knees and got his legs beneath himself to stand. She stood and offered him her arm when he wavered, his knees buckling. She felt the heat rise in her cheeks as he smiled at her and nodded his thanks. His breath came in shallow gasps. Sénna would ask Cybél to help her bandage his shoulder wound and bind the chest to support his cracked ribs once they treated his raptor.

The rider collapsed at Shäelan's head. The golden läenier lay on her side; one wing tucked beneath it and the other twitching feebly. The rider cradled her head in his lap and stroked between her eyes, crooning softly. Sénna felt the sting of tears in her eyes.

Sénna blinked away the moisture and cleared her throat. "Will she be okay, Cybél?"

The young healer completed her inventory of the wounds and nodded. "There are glass shards embedded in her chest here, and there may be internal damage. She's injured some muscles with that hard landing, but she should be fine with rest. I'll need some water for a poultice and tincture."

Sénna nodded and pulled the flask from her hip. She handed it to Cybél, who poured water and glittering red powder from her basket into the small wooden bowl in her hand. Shäelan squawked feebly and lolled her head to one side. The light of her golden eye clouded and dimmed.

"Shäelan!" her rider cried, a tear spilling down his hardened cheek as he buried his head in the läenier's feathered topknot. He stroked the down along her neck and sang softly, his voice cracking and off-key. *"Stay strong and true; your grace and bravery know no bounds. Stay with me...."*

Sénna felt her throat constrict as she watched the man grieve. Cybél's fingers flew over the raptor's injuries; then, she urged the great beast to drink the remainder of her tincture. Sénna watched her work, blinking as Cybél's fingers glowed soft pink. She gasped, causing the healer to glance over her shoulder.

"What are you doing?" Sénna gasped.

"I'm giving her a draught that will ease her breathing," Cybél shrugged, dropping her bowl and shifting her hands out of Sénna's view.

"But that glow—" Sénna began.

Cybél stood. "Just Lord Shamar's light," she said over her shoulder, spots of pink blooming on her high cheeks. "I'm sure it just caught the sparkle of some residual powder on my fingers."

Sénna glanced at the daytime deity and back to her friend, who was wiping her hands on her skirts. Sénna narrowed her eyes, putting her hands on her slim hips. She opened her mouth to say she wasn't buying Cybél's explanation about the strange glow when the läenier shifted and rose to her feet. Her rider cried out, hugging her muscular neck as Shäelan tossed her head and pranced in a circle.

"That was nothing short of miraculous," Sénna breathed. She raised an eyebrow as Cybél finished packing her supplies.

Cybél smiled and shook her head. "No, her wounds were shallow. The poultice cleaned them, and the tincture eased the shock from the pain, that's all."

Sénna stared at her friend for a long moment, then exhaled. She approached the rider and held out her right arm. "I am Sénna Kráal. I thank you for catching me and for bringing me safely back."

The rider clasped her forearm. "Roshäen, rider of Shäelan, and it was my pleasure."

Sénna felt her pulse beat faster as the Sumäeri warrior smiled at her. His emerald eyes were tight with worry and pain, but she saw the warmth and humor in them. Her cheeks flushed again, and she pressed her lips together. She wouldn't tolerate the foolishness of these rogue emotions, certainly not for a Shäeli. Sénna pulled her arm away and nodded, avoiding Roshäen's eyes.

"I need to get to Cédron and tell him about his brother." Her voice cracked, and she cleared her throat. "My thanks to you as well, Shäelan." Sénna met the wounded raptor's amber eye and bowed. She turned and began walking towards the chaos and destruction surrounding the airship.

Squawks of injured läeniers rose above the subdued moaning of the wounded Sumäeri, who rode them. Sénna scanned the sea of golden feathers and silver hair, searching for the compromise between them that was Cédron. His blond hair was nowhere in sight.

Sénna spotted Rovären and Säeshi cleaning wounds and applying poultices, aided by a few uninjured Sumäeri. The astringent odor of herbs nearly masked the coppery smell of blood. Sénna wrinkled her nose and turned towards the airship.

The thick mast that held the mainsail lay in splinters

across the deck; its blunt tip jammed into the sand. The silk sails were shredded and blowing in the breeze. Sparkling shards of rose-colored glass glittered across the sands, evidence of the Árk'äezhi's destructive power.

Sénna's heart sank when she noticed the gaps torn between the planks in the hull. How would they get to Taboriz? What if more Hazzara attacked them?

Sénna slogged through the sand to the bow of the airship and froze. Severed limbs and other body parts of both Hazzara and their alzaytan mounts lay scattered across the ground. Their still-seeping blood turned the red sands a dark crimson. The breeze shifted direction, and the stench of blood and voided bowels reached her nose.

"Laylur's beast!" She turned away and retched.

Sénna eventually caught her breath and began investigating the airship. It laid off-center against a rock berm, tilting to starboard. Sénna wove her way through broken boards to the lower deck. She found the stairs that led to the forecastle and held onto the rail as she navigated the leaning steps.

Cédron knelt next to Anéton's prone, nearly-naked body. Blood pooled on the deck near the fallen legionnaire's piled clothing and trickled across the planks. Sénna took a breath to call out but halted when she saw Cédron's tattoos flare to life. They cast an eerie glow over Anéton's drawn features. The demon had his hands over his friend's chest, the windstone clenched tightly in his right fist. His eyes were closed, and his forehead wrinkled in concentration.

Sénna saw wet streaks down his cheeks and felt a stab of sorrow in her chest. She had no quarrel with Anéton. He was loud, obnoxious, and flirtatious but ultimately harmless. As she watched Cédron slowly move the windstone above his friend's body, she saw tiny shards of glass rise from Anéton's skin where they'd been embedded.

"How are you doing that?" Sénna asked, her eyes wide as she followed the movement of his hands.

Cédron didn't open his eyes. He continued to move his hands down Ancton's figure, pulling shards as he made his way from stomach to legs. Sénna could see open wounds on the legionnaire's face, chest, and arms that continued to seep blood. Anéton groaned and turned his head.

Cédron's hands faltered, and the glow diminished with the loss of his concentration. Sénna knelt beside Anéton across from Cédron and began staunching the deeper wounds with the discarded shirt. She realized Cédron wasn't pulling the shards from his friend's body; they simply appeared above it.

"How do you—" she began.

"It's the windstone's Árk'äezhi," Cédron sighed. Scan completed, he looked at Sénna. "It allows me to move things from one place to another." He put the yellow stone into his pouch and pulled out the firestone. He closed his eyes. "The firestone will help me speed up his healing. I'm glad you're okay. I'm sorry for...." He shook his head. "Well, for everything."

Sénna rocked back on her heels; her legs clasped tightly in her arms. She thought of all the things she thought she knew about magic wielders. They were destructive, power-hungry, and corrupt. She watched more wounds close. Cédron's Árk'äezhi wasn't only destructive power; it was healing. It was going to save this young man's life.

"I-I didn't realize your Árk'äezhi could heal," Sénna breathed. She touched the closed wound. Anéton's skin was hot and dry, not the clammy heat of infection. "Maybe you're not completely evil."

Cédron glanced at her with a wry smile. "Hmm, we shall see. This isn't the first time I've nearly killed him. I don't know why he sticks around."

Sénna caught the strain in his voice and looked at him. His eyes were the soft green of moss, warmer than the clear emerald of Roshäen's eyes. They seemed out of place with his drawn features. Cédron was close to Anéton, much like brothers, Sénna mused.

The thought struck Sénna like a knife in the chest, remembering why she'd sought Cédron out. She felt a pang of sadness for him, knowing that she was about to compound his pain a thousand-fold. She waited, watching him complete his task.

The breeze shifted, increasing in strength. Sénna shivered, spotting Lord Shamar near the horizon. The night would soon be upon them, making tracking nearly impossible. She blew out a deep breath.

"Cédron, you need to hurry," Sénna swallowed hard, wincing as she spoke her next words. "It's Tóran. He's stolen Räeshun and escaped with the remaining Hazzara."

chapter 25: Zaroon Quarry

Tóran was speaking. He could feel his mouth shaping words and felt the rumble and vibration in his throat. He listened. It sounded like his voice, yet not his voice. The words spoken were familiar but remained just outside his understanding. Tóran felt his head nod up and down once. He got to his feet and began walking. He stumbled, weaving slightly. It was disorienting to be watching and listening to himself from a distance within his mind.

Tóran felt awareness of his true self in a remote corner of his brain, relegated there by an entity more potent than his own. Then, a terrible certainty struck him, a cold prickling in the back of his neck that spread like sharp, jagged blades through his veins. He put a hand on the smooth marble wall to hold himself upright.

That demon put something in his head when he was unconscious. He must have. But why hadn't anyone noticed? Why hadn't *he* noticed it? The Arkmuln had either white or sparkling blue eyes. Tóran's eyes were brown, and Cédron would have spotted it. He felt his head shake from side to side.

"What's the matter with you?" A man came up from behind, grabbed Tóran by the arm, and spun him around to face him.

The man's skin was dark bronze, and his close-cropped hair was black. He didn't have the burnt umber skin of Shozin, but he was likely Yezman. He wore a black turban with a loose flap of fabric dangling on the left side, nearly touching his shoulder. Tóran knew the flap was to cover the man's face from blowing sands. The man glared at him with piercing, dark-brown eyes. It felt like his eyes were a gateway into his soul rather than the mirror of the world Tóran always imagined eyes to be.

The man shook him again. "I asked you a question."

"Nothing, I'm fine. Headache."

Tóran felt his head shake. The presence that occupied the more significant portion of his awareness began to search. In the dark corners of his mind, he could see sparkling blue liquid flowing around the rest of his thoughts, filling in holes, nooks, and crannies. Tóran retreated deeper inside his mind. He didn't think he could overpower whatever force had infiltrated him. Neither did he want to alert it to his growing presence.

The world grew dark when Tóran closed his eyes. He felt his chest rise and fall with deep breaths. The sparkling liquid oozed around his head, searching, seeking, preparing to destroy the last remnants of his personality. He retreated further up, further in, relinquishing control to the interloper.

The man in front of Tóran turned and motioned for him to follow. Tóran felt his tense body relax and take another deep breath. He felt the smooth stone floor beneath his feet. It wasn't cold as he'd expected. He swept his gaze upwards, noting the white-and-rose crystalline walls that had striations crisscrossing them at regular intervals like slashing claw marks.

Tóran remembered Shozin telling him about the marble and quartz quarries near Yezmarantha and the grids that marked the stone for cutting. The ceiling rose over forty feet high, with the marks etched on the walls clear to the top. The air was dry with no discernable scents. A fine mist of powdered stone permeated his nostrils despite trying to breathe solely through his mouth.

Tóran figured the Zaroon Quarry was the only logical place he could be. He couldn't remember how he'd gotten there; in fact, he didn't remember anything after holding Räeshun for Cédron during the Hazzara attack on the airship. It felt as if he'd been struck in the head by Lord Shamar's lightning the moment the staff touched his hand.

Tóran squirmed and instantly retracted his consciousness back into the recesses of his mind. Every time he experienced an emotion, the intruder in his conscious mind noticed. He could sense the other's presence and recognized the sharpening of internal focus. He would have to be mindfully strategic of his thoughts and feelings if he wanted his awareness to survive.

Military tactics were one of Tóran's strengths. He would observe, learn what he could, then try to get Räeshun and escape. He had hazy visions of handing the staff to a red-robed mage when he arrived. The guilt at that thought made his chest hurt.

Tóran knew Cédron would be headed for Taboriz, even if he'd been slowed down by the Hazzara attack. Tóran snorted, wishing he'd paid closer attention during his cartography lessons. He remembered that the Zaroon Quarry was near Taboriz, but he wasn't sure which direction the city lay from his current location.

Located in the Zahili Desert just west of Taboriz, the quarry was famed for its prized rose quartz and creamy marble. His father Kásuin had imported slabs of the rose quartz for the baths inside the castle at Dúlnat. He felt a stab of guilt at the thought of his father, but he quickly squelched it. Tóran vaguely remembered something about the quarry being closed by a curse, but he couldn't remember specifics. Curses didn't matter because he was going to get out of there long before anything could happen.

Cédron and his companions would be fixing the airship or finding another method of getting into the city. Tóran remembered enough geography to know that the Räenetti River flowed near Taboriz. Tributaries of the river funneled water around the city, making it like an island in the center of the desert.

The water created a port for shipping goods to and from the city. If he could figure out a way to get to the river, he'd only have to let it carry him to Taboriz. His musings were interrupted when his companion stopped at a narrow, stone archway. The man bowed slightly and waved his hand for Tóran to go inside.

"You will find food, a basin for washing, clean clothes, and a bed," the man was saying as he pointed out the various items. "Algarik will be here soon and will certainly want to speak with you."

Tóran's head nodded. The man turned, leaving the chamber and allowing Tóran time to search for an exit besides the one he'd just used. Nothing. Spying a plate of pastries and sliced fruits, he sat and began to eat. The small, dense cakes made with fruit were unfamiliar but delicious. He would wash and sleep when he finished eating. He knew he'd need to keep his body in good shape for what he had to do.

Algarik had escaped Aromberk Fortress, weak and barely able to maintain control of the rinzar, his monstrous winged mount. Laylur's anger at Algarik's recent failings had been tremendous and his punishment severe.

Algarik knew the risks when he agreed to free the Great Demon from his prison in the abyss, but he had never considered the possibility of being thwarted. Algarik was the most powerful mage in the guild, even though he still only wore red and not white. The idea of failure hadn't crossed his mind. Until now.

Cédron was alive. How the boy had survived Wézija's grasp was beyond comprehension. True, the boy's powers were great but should be insignificant against an immortal. Laylur's fury was tempered only with Algarik's report of the success with the stone army. Ruzik's warning of uncontrolled stone soldiers inhabited by the vicious Maüli spirits was well-founded.

Marik scried him in a panic after nearly a third of the Hazzara escort had been torn to shreds by the vengeful spirits. The promise that these soldiers would cut a swath across Samshäeli had appeased Laylur's ire, so the demon had let Algarik live. Tasked with capturing or killing his nephew, Algarik pored through everything he had at his disposal at the Zaroon Quarry that might lure the boy to him.

A knock at the door stirred Algarik from his morbid thoughts. He stormed across the stone floor of his spartan chamber, robes snapping around his legs to answer the timid knock. His eyes caught the glint of white bone from the strange staff resting against the wall, and he grabbed it. Irritation at the disturbance added to mounting frustrations at his continued inability to decipher the markings on Cédron's unique talisman.

The euphoria he'd felt when Tóran arrived at the Zaroon

Quarry with the staff quickly dissipated. Two days of research and spells had revealed nothing, and he was running out of time. Algarik maintained a firm grip on the strange staff as he pulled the lever in the door that started the gears moving. Growling at its slow progress, Algarik slammed the butt of the talisman on the ground as the door slid open.

"What, in Our Lady's name, do you want?" the mage snarled at the terrified boy trembling just outside the doorway.

"The Old Man has asked for you to join him in his chambers," the lad squeaked, his eyes wide. His copper skin paled in the light of the glowstones.

"Bah, I don't have time for this!" Algarik roared, causing the waif to hunch his shoulders until they nearly touched his ears. "Tell him that I'll see him on my way out."

The mage reached for the lever to shut the door, but the boy reached out a trembling hand.

"He insisted that you come now" the lad's voice shook, but he held the lever firmly.

"Did he now?" Algarik purred. The tic in his left cheek jumped, pulling at the long scar and warping his expression into a sneer.

Algarik's eyes narrowed at the child's subtle defiance. He watched the young boy shift his feet uncomfortably. The mage could see it took every ounce of willpower the boy had to look him in the eyes. He nodded affirmatively.

"No."

The boy opened his mouth to protest, but Algarik was faster. He whipped his right hand out of his robes, the ruby ring glowing malevolently as he shot forth a blast of fire from the stone. The searing heat blew back the boy's dark hair from his face, but the flames arched around his wiry body, leaving him unscathed.

Shocked, Algarik stepped back from the child, unsure what unseen power the lad possessed that would defy his own. He glanced at the boy's eyes and saw a similar shock reflected in his dark irises. The energy hadn't come from the child. Algarik let out a sharp cry as his left hand suddenly burned.

The etched staff in his hand glowed white-hot, causing him to drop it. The protective magic identified, Algarik tilted his head to one side and regarded first his visitor, then the staff. The boy was in shock, his Adam's apple bobbing with trepidation.

"Come here, Boy," Algarik ordered. "I want to try something."

The lad spared the mage one horrified glance and turned, sprinting back down the corridor as fast as his scrawny legs could carry him.

Algarik sighed and pulled the lever that closed the door. He stared warily at the staff, now dark on the stone floor. Gingerly, he picked it up and carried it over to his table. He lit several of the large candles along the shelf above the workbench to brighten the room. He ignored the ebony obelisk that occupied the corner of his desk and the old scraps of metal and leather that had once been mechanized lighting that now held the candles.

The mage pondered the markings again, the tic in his cheek jumping in growing agitation. He'd recognized some of the etchings but couldn't place their origin. The staff appeared to be bone, indicating Meq'qan culture, but the markings were all wrong for that.

For centuries, the Meq'qan had utilized the bones of their dead for decorating their homes and temples. He had seen priestesses bearing chalices made from their predecessors' skulls and the macabre splendor of charnel houses with their festoons and chandeliers made from the remains of their deceased. The Meq'qan wasted nothing, but the mage didn't think that the priestesses to Lady Muralia had the power to infuse a staff with such energy. Only a deity had such power—or a demon.

Algarik scrutinized the bones. The markings were so

delicately wrought along the top that they barely seemed to be etched at all. It was almost as if the bones were tattooed. The mage stiffened and inhaled sharply. He picked up the staff gently and twisted it around in his fingers, noting how the foliage markings ran the entire length of the bones. These were the bones of a Sumäeri warrior.

The impossibility of such a feat caused his head to throb. His breath sped up with his heartbeat. The Great Demon wouldn't have done this. The only other possibility was—but that was impossible.

The deities hadn't interfered in the world since the Great Betrayal. This staff could be hundreds of Tides old. But in all his Tides of study, Algarik had never heard of it. Could it have been created recently? If so, who was the Sumäeri who had sacrificed their life? More importantly, how did it come to be in Cédron's possession?

The mage glanced around the room. The ancient Shäeli scrolls Algarik had been painstakingly deciphering littered the workbench. Tides ago, White Mage Bín Nétar charged him with the task of learning how to activate the Rod of Shouman should the need arise, and the scrolls were the only source of information that Algarik had been able to find. They spoke of how the Rod of Shouman harnessed the energy of the daytime deity, Lord Shamar's lightning, which was the deity's way of replenishing his mate's life force.

Lightning strikes were the primary source of Lady Muralia's strength to maintain her hold on the demon who was now worming his way free of his prison. Nothing in the scrolls instructed him on how to harness that energy with the Rod of Shouman. The collection must be incomplete, but he no longer had access to the Mages Guild in Táksabai.

Algarik abandoned his translation of the scrolls to ponder how to access the bone staff's power. He paced the room. If it were indeed a creation of the deities, which was the only feasible answer, then maybe Lord Shamar's lightning could entice a response from it. A grin spread across the mage's disfigured face. He walked over to the glass case that housed the Rod of Shouman, keeping it safe from damage or falling into the wrong hands.

Grinning wider, Algarik chuckled at the irony of it all. Pulling the torus knot from beneath the folds of his robes, he closed his eyes and activated the ruby at its center. The stone throbbed in its setting, the blinding light causing everything except the spidery veins running along the inside of Algarik's eyelids to disappear in a wash of vermillion brilliance.

The mage raised his hands and whispered, *"maftah."* The glass surrounding the rod burst into flame, each grain of sand combusting internally as the heat evaporated its existence. Algarik ran hands through his silvering hair, relieving the tingle that his charged Árk'äezhi had stirred up. He brushed sparks from his fingertips on his robes and reached for the legendary rod.

The Shäeli scrolls revealed that the Rod of Shouman required a stone to activate it, calling forth the "fire from the skies" as its power. The mage knew Cédron had the firestone he needed for the rod, and he also knew the boy wasn't far away. He would take the Rod of Shouman and the bone staff with him when he collected Cédron to hand him over to the Great Demon. Algarik wouldn't let the boy slip away again.

As if reading his thoughts, the little black obelisk on his desk wobbled and shifted. The bony statue sprouted a long, pointed tail and a pair of horns as it came to life. Rickety legs with cloven hooves elongated from the obelisk base, and a couple of arms grabbed the long tail. The creature crooned and began preening the tail with its curved talons.

"I bring a message," the evil little imp hissed, its long tongue darting in and out of its mouth. "You must begin it *now.*"

Chapter 26: Scrying Stones

"What are you doing up here?" Sénna puffed as she flopped down on the rock next to Cédron at the top of the berm above the airship. She gulped air into her lungs.

He didn't answer. Sénna glanced over at him sideways, wiping a bead of sweat from her temple. His moss-green eyes seemed to glow from the light of the bonfire far below. With a sigh, he turned to look at her. Sénna could see the dark smudges beneath his swollen eyes.

"Same as you, I guess," he said in a flat voice. "Just trying to find a place to think."

Sénna nodded. That was why she'd climbed to the top of

the rocks that sheltered their ship and her crew.

Darkness enveloped the camp, and a large bonfire burned in the hollow between the damaged airship and the berm of rocks that shielded the flames from the wind. The wounded läeniers and their riders had all been treated and settled with food and the promise of rest. The raptors picked clean the bodies of the fallen alzaytan and their riders, but they needed more meat to feed the entire Wing. There were no villages nearby, and Sénna wasn't sure what kind of desert animal would satiate the full complement of ravenous läeniers.

Sénna leaned back on her hands and stared up at the sky, awash with brilliant stars. Orwaena's rose hues illuminated the eastern edge of the desert as she began her ascent to join the pinpricks in the heavens that were her subjects. A breeze blew her dark hair off her face, bringing with it the scent of desert grasses and just the faintest hint of smoke from the meat roasting over the fires below.

"I suppose I owe you an apology," Sénna said, nudging Cédron with her shoulder.

Cédron turned to look at her, one eyebrow raised. "An apology from you?"

Sénna felt the heat rise to her cheeks and was grateful for the darkness. "I've been unfair and ungrateful to you because you're a magic-wielding demon. I do have a good reason for distrusting you, though," she shrugged with a sigh.

Cédron gave a snort and half-smile but said nothing.

"A mage killed my mother," she said. "He befriended her to gain access to her raptor breeding notes. He used her information to create a terrifying winged monster, then set the stables and offices on fire. He destroyed her entire section of the Laborers Guild and the team who worked with her."

Cédron sat quietly for a few moments, staring up at the stars. "I'm very sorry for your loss. And I agree; you are wise to mistrust anyone who wields powerful magic." He opened his mouth to say more, and his breath hitched in his throat. He picked up a stone and rubbed his thumb across its rough surface.

"A mage also killed my mother and dearest friend. At the time, I thought I caused the explosion that killed them and several others, but I learned later that it was my Uncle Algarik. I have been hunting him ever since," he said, throwing the rock far out into the desert.

Sénna leaned forward and put her elbows on her knees and her chin on her fists. "The mage who killed my mother wore the red robes of the Mages Guild, but he also wore the same sort of amulet as the Hazzara leader you faced today."

Cédron's lips became a thin, white line. Sénna saw his temple pulse as he gritted his teeth several times before turning to her.

"I doubt that is a coincidence," he said, his eyes cast down. "I suspect that mage and the one I hunt are the same. I fought him and the monstrous rinzar he'd created from some sort of raptor, which confirms to me that he's the one who killed your mother. He may also be responsible for the abnormal enhancements on those alzaytan ridden by the Hazzara."

Sénna shuddered. The Sumäeri warriors had been fortunate to have suffered no casualties in the skirmish against the Hazzara. The blast of Árk'äezhi energy that ended the fighting had killed several black-clad fighters and their beasts, leaving two wounded alzaytan along with the läeniers. The few surviving Hazzara fled with Torán across the dunes.

Sénna glanced to where the beasts were being held and shook her head. The alzaytan were terrifying with their armor-plated skin and two rows of short spikes that circled the head, running down both sides of the neck. She understood the Shäeli belief against unnecessary killing, but these creatures would likely attack them as soon as their injuries allowed them to. The sound of their tails swishing across the sand was a warning, as were their sharp whines and occasional grating shrieks.

"What do you think Trilläen and the rest will do with them?" Sénna asked, nodding toward the alzaytan. She wrapped her arms around her legs and placed her chin on her knees.

Cédron was silent. He pulled his legs up and mirrored her position, heaving a sigh. "I don't know. I don't know about anything anymore. I was so sure that I could get the Sceptre of Kulari and face Laylur, but I know now that I'm not strong enough."

Sénna tilted her head as she looked at his profile in the firelight. "What makes you think that?"

Moisture welled up in Cédron's eyes, and he bit down hard on his lower lip. Hot tears streamed down his cheeks, and he swiped at them savagely. "Because I've lost everything that made this quest important. I have no one left. Algarik killed my mother and my best friend before I left Dúlnat. My father has been missing since the Garanth attack on Dúlnat and is probably dead. My Shäeli cousins have lost half of their family because of me and now—"

"But you've defeated the Hazzara how many times already?" Sénna asked. "At least three times that Anéton has talked about." She reached up to touch his shoulder, but he shook her off.

"And now my brother, the last member of my family, has betrayed me and taken Räeshun. How can I face her sisters now? How can I continue when I'm nothing without her?" His voice cracked, and he buried his face in his knees.

Sénna felt an uncomfortable tension in her chest. She'd never quite believed the story of the Sumäeri warrior who had fallen in battle protecting Cédron from her people and been transformed by the goddess Orwaena to continue to serve him in his quest. She saw the tightness of his shoulders and heard the honest despair in his voice.

Maybe that was why the staff made her feel so uncomfortable; because she'd recently been a living, breathing person. Sénna understood the pain of loss, but she also knew what was at stake should Laylur be freed from the abyss.

"You have to keep going," she said. "You have the support and weapons from the Mages Guild and all of us to help you. Having the Sumäeri warriors supporting you has to count for something. Even I've gained a little respect for you and your abilities, so what's your problem?"

"Don't you see?" Cédron raised his head and snarled at her. "Everyone around me ends up dead. Without Räeshun to temper and focus my power, I'll cause more harm than good. I'll turn out to be just like my Uncle Algarik. The next time I have to use my Ark'äezhi, I may not control it completely. You will all die, and it will be my fault."

Sénna stared at him for a long moment, then shrugged. "Nobody gets out alive. We're all going to die one day; either it will be now at your hands, later after Laylur and his minions destroy our world, or after long and peaceful lives. What matters now are the choices we have. You are choosing to quit. I am not."

"I'm not choosing to quit," he snapped. "I'm choosing not to be the cause of any more death."

"Hmm," Sénna stared at the black dunes silhouetted against the red light of Orwaena's moon as she rose into the sky. "And yet you were able to defeat that Hazzara mage today *without* the help of your staff or anyone else."

"And I nearly killed Anéton – again!" He pounded the hard ground with his fist. "You know, the last time I used my power to help, it got me killed. The Shäeli don't trust me to do what they need me to do. Maybe they're right."

"What do you mean, 'it got you killed'?" Sénna asked, frowning at her companion. "You look very much alive to me." She pinched his arm and laughed at him when he flinched.

Cédron sighed. He clasped his arms around his knees and stared at the fire below them. "We were in a Meq'qan village. The tribesmen were preparing for battle when the women and children were attacked by urluks, predators of Molonark whose quills are filled with a blood-poisoning toxin. I used the sacred stones to cleanse the toxins and save the villagers, but I forced the Árk'äezhi from the attending priestesses for the power to do it. The Sumäeri learned of my abuse of power and bound me with wicker. They drained the life and the Árk'äezhi from my body. Only the intervention of Lady Muralia saved me. She returned my soul to my body and charged me with this quest. I still don't know if she was right to do so. I'm a monster."

Sénna took a breath to retort but stopped as a fist-sized creature swooped past her head, chittering as it banked around.

"Mijáko piles," she swore as she ducked. "What in Our Lady's Name is that?"

Cédron squinted in the dusk and stood. "It's coming back," he said.

Sénna raised her arm over her head to protect it from the flying creature. She flinched as it landed on her forearm, squeaking and grinding as it folded its leathery wings.

"It's one of Mage Kiel's diclurues," she exclaimed, holding the creature up. "And look, it bears a message." Sénna pulled the tiny scroll from the underside of the diclurue's belly and unrolled it. "It's a message from Mage Kiel," she said.

"What news from Táksabai?" Cédron asked, sitting next to her and crossing his legs.

"He writes, 'only cryptic mentions of windstone in archives, but we did come across this passage: The Aruzzi guard the windstone with the ferocity of their eggs.' We don't know what that means, but thought we should pass it along," she read.

Sénna folded the paper and handed it to Cédron. She turned the mechanical diclurue over and pressed the orange stone embedded in the body. She'd worked out that the orange stones emitted an energy that matched the Mages Guild. The gears began turning, and the wings squeaked as they unfolded. Sénna held her hand up as the tiny diclurue launched itself into the air, flitting west toward the dark skyline and Askári-bai.

"Good thing I didn't have a message to return," Cédron snorted, shaking his head. "Besides, I'm beyond any help they could give at this point."

Sénna turned to retort when she heard a piercing whistle followed by shouting. The group was calling for them to return to the camp. She rose to her feet and looked down at Cédron, her hands on her hips.

"Look, you're afraid. I get it," Sénna said and held up a hand to still Cédron's argument. "I'm afraid, also. I don't know why I'm here, but my grandmother said our destinies are intertwined. I can't imagine what I have to do with your magic. All I know is that I don't fit in, and neither do you. We are both outsiders trying to find our place, living lives that feel like lies. I get that. I think we're all afraid, but we've come this far. Right now, you're still wallowing in self-pity. You're a victim, but of what?"

"I'm a victim of my own power," Cédron scrubbed at his face with his hands. "If I use it, I'm too powerful, and people feel threatened. If I don't use it, I'm abandoning the world to Laylur's destruction."

Sénna shook her head. "You're thinking like prey, but you're a predator. Look at the gifts the deities have given you. Not only did you get your cousin, but the marks of the sacred stones are tattooed on your torso. Doesn't that count for something?"

Cédron raised his head. "Yes, but—"

"There is no 'but.' You have a power that no other in Muralia has, but you are wasting it. Until you decide you deserve to have it *and use it,* your ability doesn't matter," she said. "The deities chose you for this quest. They must know what they're doing. It isn't our place to second-guess the gods."

The edge in Sénna's voice surprised even her, and she turned from Cédron. She walked a few steps away, inhaling deep breaths to get her emotions under control. She wasn't sure what frustrated her more: that Cédron had the power and she didn't or that he had the power and wouldn't use it. She took two more deep breaths and decided it was the latter. Cédron had to believe in himself, or their world would collapse under Laylur's wrath.

Sénna returned to Cédron. "Look, you're not alone in this fight. You have friends and what's left of your family in addition to the Sumäeri. You've even won me over. Let's see if we can put all our heads together and come up with a way to get into Taboriz, find that sacred windstone, and get Räeshun back."

She held out her hand and, after a moment, Cédron grasped it and let her pull him to his feet. Together, they walked back toward the campfire. Thinking of her brother Myknét, Sénna sent a quick prayer to Hamra, goddess of birth and death, to watch over her brother's spirit and to the warrior goddess Orwaena to guide her so that her brother's death would have some meaning.

When the two of them arrived at the fire, they were met by Roväen and Trilläen, who bade them join their group and eat. Cédron shook his head, but his uncle shoved a meatroll into his hands with an admonishing look. Sénna gratefully took the mug of steaming adzuki tea and dried fruit from Trilläen. She sat cross-legged next to the Sumäeri captain and across from Roväen and Cédron. The two Shäeli men shared a look between them, and she felt her insides twist.

"Our plans have to change a bit now," Roväen said, rolling up the left sleeve of his shirt. The bracelet with the scrying stone that Sahráron had made him glinted in the firelight. "The Hazzara know who you are and where you are headed. They likely have contacts in Taboriz who will be watching for you. I'm going to try and reach Shozin to see if he has any suggestions."

Cédron chewed his meatroll and swallowed, then nodded. Sénna stared at the glittering emerald embedded in the center of Rovären's bracelet. The green stones in each finger ring began to glow and pulse with the same rhythm as the emerald. Rovären closed his eyes and took several slow, deep breaths.

Sénna understood that this sort of scrying required focused intention on the person sought, but that was the extent of her knowledge. She watched with wide eyes as the emerald's surface shimmered into a form. A moment later, Sahráron's narrow face and freckled nose appeared.

"Rovären!" Sahráron inhaled, her dark eyes sharpening in concern. "What has happened?"

The old Shäeli blinked a few times and smiled slightly before answering. "I must speak with Shozin. Is he with you?"

Sahráron's brows knitted, and she glanced to her side, talking to someone. "I've sent a lad to fetch him. What's going on?"

Rovären shook his head. "I'd prefer to wait for Shozin. Tell me news of the caravan while we wait."

"There isn't much to tell," Sahráron's face fell slightly, and she swallowed. "The devastation after the Garanth attack has overwhelmed the survivors of Táksabai. Shozin sent a group to Dúlnat to search for survivors but has kept the bulk of the caravan here, offering us as work crews to help the city rebuild. We'll stay through Dormantide, then return to the mountains and whatever remains of Dúlnat in early Buddingtide."

Rovären raised his eyebrows. "Has he then? How is the rebuilding process going?"

Sahráron's expression was bleak, and she shook her head. "It will take a lifetime if the city is ever able to recover. The Gróshan have proven themselves extremely useful."

Sénna's despair at hearing about the destruction of her

city lessened as she heard Sahráron talk about her father's efforts. He had organized the return of the city's vulnerable, including orphaned children who couldn't provide for themselves. He converted his remaining warehouses into dormitories and had the caravan women assist with cooking and caring for the young ones who lost their families.

Sénna felt a surge of pride for her father and brother Murádit, whose contributions would only help solidify their credibility with the guilds in the future. Sénna was startled when Shozin's deep voice blasted through the scrying stone.

"I see the desert hasn't swallowed you up yet," the Caravan Master rumbled.

Rováen gave a mirthless chuckle. "Not for lack of trying, I assure you, my friend. We are just outside Taboriz. We've been following the course of the Räenetti River and were attacked earlier today by a group of Hazzara mounted on alzaytan."

"What casualties did you have?" Shozin interrupted, his eyes darting around the stone as if trying to see who was missing behind Rováen.

"Fortunately, none lost their lives. However, some of the Hazzara escaped, and," Rováen closed his eyes for a moment, then took a deep breath. "Torán has betrayed us. He escaped with the fleeing men, and he took Räeshun with him."

There was silence. Rováen's words hung like a miasma, clinging with chilled fingers to all who heard them. Sénna didn't understand how Torán could have betrayed his brother. He was the epitome of the proper legionnaire and had been both courteous and helpful to everyone. This news came as a shock to those back in Askári-bai as much as it had been to those who'd traveled with him.

Shozin cleared his throat. "So, what can I do to help you?"

Rováen looked at Cédron and nodded. "We need a new plan for getting inside Taboriz. The Hazzara must have a lair near the city. We suspect they have spies looking for us. They know who we are and what we are after."

Sénna peeked over at the stone glowing on Rovaen's wrist and watched the Caravan Master rub his bald head. His dark skin was nearly invisible in the evening light.

"I have heard rumors that the Zaroon Quarry is occupied, but not by miners. It may be that they have holed up there. It's remote but still less than a day's ride from the city." Shozin moved his hand to his chin and rubbed the stubble.

"You must find the Market Queen. If it's help you need with locating the windstone, she's the one you need. However, approaching her now will be dangerous. The only side she takes is her own, and she'll do what benefits her the most. You must be prepared to offer something of more value than the Hazzara's offer for both information and safe passage," Shozin said.

Rovaen looked around the group with his eyebrows raised. Sénna looked at Cédron, whose unfocused gaze revealed his hopelessness. Trilläen shifted on his haunches and looked back at the makeshift stable.

"Would a couple of alzaytan be of value, do you think?" Trilläen leaned over Rovaen's stone so that Shozin could hear him.

The Caravan Master's eyes widened. "How did you get a hold of a couple of alzaytan and still have your hands?"

Trilläen grimaced. "The Hazzara were mounted on them. Two alzaytans were wounded but not mortally. They will recover from their injuries in a few days."

Shozin nodded. "That might just do. The tricky part will be presenting yourselves to the Market Queen without being exposed. The qanats are too far to the east to reach quickly."

Shozin turned his head as someone to his side spoke to him. He nodded and faced the stone again, a big grin gleaming on his dark face. "Sahráron has reminded me that the Zholi Festival is in three days. People will be coming to Taboriz in droves. You might be able to slip in with the throngs of festival-goers."

Sénna looked over at Rováen and cocked her head to one side. "Once we enter the city, where do we go? Where will we stay?"

"All excellent questions," Sénna heard Shozin chuckle. "I see one of you is thinking. I believe Queen Marizen is your best bet. However, you will have to be careful. If she doesn't accept your tribute, you will be on your own."

"How are we supposed to do that," Cédron sighed and fell back into the sand with his arms spread wide. "We don't know anything about the city, how it's designed, where to inquire, nothing. I only have the one token Mage Kiel gave me, so I must choose who I speak with very carefully. Anyone we talk to will be suspicious."

Sénna sat up straight and looked at each member of the group in turn. Her yellow Meq'qan eyes gleamed in the firelight. "Leave that to me."

Chapter 27: The Public Baths

Sénna drew the silky ochre headscarf around her face and attached it to the clasp by her ear. The brightly-colored costume was a better disguise than her brother's trousers and tunic, for scores of people wearing their most elegant clothes were entering the city to celebrate the Zholi Festival. Shozin had given her a brief overview of the sacred ceremony so she could discuss it if necessary. Pilgrims, merchants, and families made their way towards the gleaming black pillars that supported the city gates. Sénna fell in behind a group of merchants and tried to look like she belonged.

The filmy pants ballooned around her legs in the breeze,

making her feel nearly naked. She swallowed and glanced around at the men pulling their flat carts stacked with bricks of salt. The men wore only sandals and loincloths wrapped around their middles, pulled up between their legs, and tied at the waist.

The morning was chilly, Lord Shamar's rays still thin in the desert air, but the laborers' dark backs glistened with sweat as they inched their heavy loads toward the gate. Sénna pulled at the halter top, conscious of her bare midriff. She sighed and dropped her hands. She blended with every other Yezman girl that walked toward the city walls.

RovÄen had used his Shäeli talent of invisibility to raid a small cottage outside Taboriz for the wash hanging on lines. He was very proud of his clothing choice, and the Angäersol twins immediately set to work, altering the halter to fit Sénna's slim figure. They'd fussed over her nearly the entire afternoon, adjusting the clothing, fixing her hair, and convincing her to take one of the small beryl stones so that they could track her if anything went awry.

Sénna had fidgeted in annoyance, but RovÄen thanked her for her patience. The twins still mourned the loss of Räeshun and worried about what Tóran might do with her. Working on Sénna's disguise gave them something else to occupy their thoughts.

Sénna pressed the smooth white beryl stitched into the center of her halter. Säeshi was adamant that she take it so that the twins could track her, but there was no pocket to stash it in, given her current costume. Sénna snorted at the thought and glanced around. Before her, the city of Taboriz rose like an emerald cone in the golden sands of the desert. The city's vast, circular wall curved for miles around the city, whose buildings piled upon each other like a litter of suckling cochäera seeking a teat. The white marble palace sat at the cone's pinnacle, a pearl nestled within the verdant rings of climbing plants that epitomized the concept of hanging gardens.

Marveling at the oasis's lush greenery in the center of the desert, Sénna turned her thoughts to getting inside the imposing gates. She watched the artisans and farmers, whose carts rolled toward the city gates. There were larger flatbeds pulled by thickly-muscled ozryks, the cloven-hoofed pack animals whose two long, spiraling horns gave them an elegant look that contradicted their menial occupations. Their heads tossed, causing the patches of red, cream, and black fur to shimmer in Lord Shamar's early light. Muscles bunched and rippled as they strained against their wagons filled with tall jars of oil or water, rolls of brightly colored fabrics, and baskets filled with various fruits and vegetables.

Families followed behind their carts, occasionally relieving the beasts of excess weight and picking up ozryk droppings. Sénna overheard a father chastising his son for complaining, stating that the Zhoula of Taboriz charged stiff fines for any detritus, human or otherwise, that mucked up her pristine city.

Crack! "Hyaaa!"

A man charged up the road astride one of the fearsome alzaytan, the beast foaming at the mouth as the rider whipped its flank. The reptile's eyes were wide, and it thrashed its long, thick tail. Families and carts scattered to either side of the road.

One of the ozryks pulling a wagon with a young family riding atop reared up on its hind legs, dumping the family and their bundles of cloth onto the road. Their cries mingled with the screams of the beasts, the cacophony adding to the chaos. The smallest of the four children rolled in front of another wagon. Sénna gasped and leaped toward the child, snatching her up just as the massive hoof of the lumbering beast stomped where she lay.

Sénna clasped the toddler to her chest, her heart hammering. She shivered and stepped out of the road to catch her breath. A dark-bearded man wearing a dusty white turban and the worn, homespun clothing of the working class turned towards her and cried out. His long shirt and trousers billowed as he raced toward her with his arms outstretched.

"Kindest of women, bravest flower of the desert," he said, stopping in front of Sénna and bowing formally. "I am most grateful that you have rescued my daughter from harm." He reached for the child, who clasped her arms around his neck and buried her head in his shoulder. "May I offer you a refreshment? Rosewater? Tea?"

Sénna glanced over the man's shoulder at his wife, who was attempting to calm the spooked ozryk while herding the other children and scolding them to gather up their spilled wares.

"Let's get your cart and family settled first," she said, smiling at him and the child.

The two of them returned to the cart, where the woman had succeeded in calming the beast. They had righted the wagon, but the children were struggling to lift the heavy bundles of thick cloth. The man set the little girl into her mother's arms and gave a piercing whistle, causing all children to stop and stand at attention.

"You two," he pointed at the tallest boy and girl who looked to be young teens. "Work together to lift the bundles. Whatever you do, don't break the twine holding the wrapping on it, or we won't get paid by the Master of the Baths."

The children bowed slightly and scampered to the scattered bundles. Sénna noticed a smaller boy grabbing the twine on a package. He looked to be about nine, his arms still skinny with sharp elbows. His face scrunched up as he strained to lift it. The string stretched, cutting into the flesh of his hands, but the cloth didn't move.

"Here you, what are you doing?" The man whirled upon the little boy, ripping the bulky package out of his hands. "Go and help your maman with the baby."

The boy's lower lip trembled for a moment, then his jaw tightened. "I want to be helpful to you, Baba. Maman can handle the baby."

The man rested his hands on his hips and sighed. "You can best help me by keeping out of the way, Raziz."

Raziz hung his head, shoulders drooping like a flower bereft of water. He turned and shuffled his feet in the red sand heading back towards his mother.

Sénna's eyes followed the boy for a long moment before joining the rest of the family. Waving her over, the man's eyes crinkled with his grin.

"Lady Muralia blessed me with good children," he sighed and shook his head, watching the young Raziz. "But my little one has already lost me a week's profit with his 'help.'"

Sénna nodded, feeling the familiar ache in her chest. She recognized the little boy's heartbreak, recalling vividly her father's disappointment and anger at her attempts to spy for him. Sénna reached for the bundle lifted towards her by the girl and marveled at how heavy it was. She grunted and raised it to her shoulder before thrusting it into the waiting hands of the boy on the wagon.

"Beautiful and strong," the merchant's black eyes sharpened. "I mistook you for a vazurgan lady with your fine clothing and confident air."

Sénna hunched her shoulders at the comparison to nobility but continued to lift the dense bales. Her grandmother would have been proud of the merchant's recognition of her status, but she needed to blend in with the masses. She cast her eyes downward and shuffled her feet.

Red sand stained her toes through the sandals, the leather straps weaving from her ankles to mid-calf. It was a narrow rope she walked. Sénna needed to be elegant enough not to be questioned too carefully but not so lowly to be a target of unscrupulous men. She already sketched the outline of a story should she be stopped.

"I thank you for the compliment," Sénna bowed, feeling a trickle of sweat course down her middle as she began her lie. "My sister and I lived in Zaveen, but…." She dropped her eyes.

"That would explain your Meq'qan eyes. Acolytes for the temple are welcomed from all lands if memory serves." The merchant tossed the final bundle to his son and knelt before her, his sharp eyes softening. "Word of the tragedy there created a well of eternal sorrow, of which mine is but a cup. How can I be of service?"

Sénna clenched her fists, digging her nails into the flesh of her palms. Tears sprang into her eyes. She glanced up at the merchant and gave a tremulous smile. "I thank you for your kindness. My sister and I were separated during the attack. I hope to find out if she made it here to Taboriz."

"Ah," the merchant stood, a wide grin splitting his face. "Then you must come with us. The public baths are the best place to hear gossip and news. Help us deliver our towels, and you can slip inside while I settle accounts with the Master of the Baths. If there is news of your sister or anything else you want to know, you'll hear it there."

The air inside the bathhouse was so humid that Sénna could see the swirls of perfumed water droplets as she followed the merchant and his family into the main lobby. Sweat poured down her temples, and her pants stuck to her thighs. The scent of rosewater and orange blossom hovered above the pungent smells of sandalwood oil and body odor.

Sénna and the older children each bore a wrapped bundle of towels balanced upon their heads, with the merchant and his wife each managing three. The little ones held hands, Raziz tethered to his mother's skirts by a string to prevent him from slipping away again.

"Welcome, Anzen," a slim, well-dressed man with shiny copper skin welcomed the merchant. "My patrons are clamoring for your soft towels after the washing ladies ruined an entire shipment." He clapped his heavily-ringed hands together and directed the two young men summoned to unload and stack the bales of towels for inspection.

Anzen bowed, touching his fingers to his forehead before sweeping his open palm out toward the Master of the Bath. "Your compliments are a song of rain in the desert of my heart."

Anzen smiled and nodded to his wife, who arranged the children on the cushions lining the wall where they settled down to wait while the men bartered. A servant brought a tray filled with zaimat. The children squealed in delight, falling upon the crunchy round dumplings drizzled with honey. Raziz shoved three in his mouth before his mother scolded him, wiping the sticky drool from his chin.

Sénna slid down the smooth, rose quartz walls, reveling in the coolness of the stone against her sweating skin. She glanced around, drinking in the lush greenery that grew up the walls and the flowering vines that wove their way across the ceiling. The vertical gardens of Taboriz were the stuff of legend in the chilly, damp West of Askári-bai. Verdant growth clung to the sides of nearly every building, making the capital city of Yezmarantha a glowing emerald in the muted landscape of sand.

The soft pink hues of the quartz walls complemented the vertical gardens without overwhelming them. The tiles on the floor wove a black pathway of hematite amidst the white curves of marble. Both were cool, but Sénna thought the hematite tiles absorbed more heat and preferred to sit on the white tiles. Between the bartering counter and the entrance was a fountain with an Aruzzi statue in the center. The mythical avian stood with its wings outspread; its seven feathered tails curled around it like an aura.

Sénna's observations were cut short at the sharp tone of the merchant.

"What do you mean they are unsuitable, Zaran?" Anzen fumed, face red above his dark beard as he faced off with the

Master of the Baths. "I make the softest, thickest towels in all of Yezmarantha. They are worth twice what you are offering."

Zaran, the Master of the Baths, raised his sharply-arched brows high above his triangular eyes. He sucked his cheeks beneath prominent cheekbones and raised his pointed nose as if smelling something distasteful.

"These towels are filthy," he sniffed. "They look as if you've dragged them through the streets. Perhaps I could use some of them in the public bathing areas, but certainly not in the private vazurgan chambers."

"You, you strutting faróc!" Anzen sputtered, pulling a fresh, white towel from the bale. "Show me filth, my blind friend."

Zaran glared down his long nose at the plush fabric. Pulling the corner from Anzen's hand, he parted a line of thick weaving and pointed. "There, deceiver. Sand from the streets. Do you deny it?"

Sénna stood and craned her neck to see the offending filth. Anzen stared at the single grain of red sand wedged inside the towel's tight weave. His face went pale, and he folded the cloth before putting it back into the open wrap of the bale.

Sénna felt a flush rise in her cheeks at the blatant unfairness. The family nearly lost a child when that alzaytan rider stormed past them, dumping their wares into the street. Now they would lose their livelihood as well.

The family stood. Sénna noted their somber expressions and joined them. Anzen's lips were tight as he accepted the small handful of flecksun coins from Zaran. His shoulders slumped as he led his family towards the entrance. Sénna saw a flash of smugness on Zaran's face, and her blood boiled. She opened her mouth, but Anzen placed his hand on her arm, shaking his head.

"I cannot antagonize him if I want his business in the future," Anzen sighed, watching the Master of the Baths direct one of his workers to take the money chest to his private quarters. Other young men began distributing the towels to the lower-level public bath.

"But it was only *one* grain of sand!" Sénna hissed, glancing over her shoulder to see if Zaran heard her. "He's cheating you."

Anzen swallowed, watching his young family ahead of him. "Yes, but my wife is a rare gem and can stretch my earnings until our next batch is ready." He grabbed Sénna's hand and patted it. "Do not let our troubles dim your radiance."

Anzen smiled and looked around. "Down there is the public bathing area," he pointed to a wide corridor on the left. "The private vazurgan bathing chambers are straight ahead. Go, listen, and find your sister." He dropped her hand and ushered his family down the corridor toward the exit.

Sénna shifted from one foot to the other, wiping her sweating palms on her sheer yellow pants. A group of men entered through the foyer and headed straight towards her. She glanced around, trying to find something that would give her a purpose. She spied a pitcher of water by one of the doors to a private room and grabbed it. Turning to take the glazed clay pitcher to the fountain for a refill, she ran into one of the men. He grabbed her arms to steady her as she wobbled.

"Please forgive my clumsiness, fair one," the young man smiled at her.

Sénna kept her head down and her tell-tale Meq'qan eyes hooded beneath her lashes. She mumbled something soft and unintelligible and moved to go past the men. The young man gripped her arm harder.

"Won't you tell me your name?" His smile widened.

Sénna felt her heart beat faster in her chest. Her hand gripped the smooth handle of the pitcher. If she swung it at his head, he would probably let go of her arm, but she didn't think she'd make it past the rest of the men. She swallowed.

Her hand gripped the handle so tightly that her knuckles showed white. One of the men noticed her trembling and put a hand on his friend's shoulder.

"Leave her be," he said. "Can't you see you're terrifying the poor girl?"

The man kept his grip on her arm another moment; then, he dropped it with a sharp laugh.

"Of course, my friend," he grinned at his companions and shrugged. As the group made their way down the corridor to the vazurgan chambers, he turned and called back. "Bring us that pitcher when you've refilled it."

Sénna leaned against the wall and closed her eyes, willing her heartbeat to slow. How was she going to get information if she had to wait on these men like a servant? She reached the fountain and plunged the pitcher into its pool, hoping to find another servant who could take the water to the men. She placed the full pitcher on the rim of the basin and sat down. She waited for several minutes, but when no other servants appeared, she sighed heavily and picked up the pitcher.

Brushing through the beaded curtains into the private chamber, Sénna nearly dropped the vessel. Standing before her were two naked men. A manservant dressed only in a loincloth applied scented oil to the first man's body. The second man stood with his legs spread and arms outstretched. His attendant scraped the scented oil off his skin with a curved blade that both strigiled and exfoliated as he swiped the wooden instrument along the flesh.

The other three men were already lounging in effervescent water that emitted a delicate, floral scent. The men were talking and took no notice of her. She found a table with colorful glasses on the far wall next to the stand of towels. As she filled the glasses, she heard "bone staff" and froze. Pouring as slowly as she could, she cocked her head to catch more of the men's conversation.

"...will be coming with the stone army. He'll know what

to do with it." A bald man scratched his thick, black beard and punched the shoulder next to him. "The Zaouni warriors won't be able to stand against it. The royal family won't know what hit them, eh?"

Laughter and splashing. Sénna's blood pounded in her head. The pitcher slipped in her sweating grip, smashing into a thousand colorful shards on the tile floor.

"Mijáko piles!" The strigiled man swore. "She's heard you!"

The three men in the pool vaulted out and moved to corner her. Sénna stepped back over the shattered vessel and edged along the wall. The first man leered at her, edging around the table.

"Ah, the dainty freesia," the man licked his bottom lip and narrowed his eyes at her. "It is said that sweet nectar hides beneath the freesia's petals. Give us a taste."

Sénna swallowed and fingered the beryl nestled in her halter. She didn't like the glint in the man's eyes. She edged to the left, keeping watch on the other two men dripping water onto the marble floor.

The man to her left barked a laugh. "I have just the tool to pollinate this flower."

Sénna felt heat scorch her cheeks as the man grasped a part of his body that she wished had remained hidden. He lunged at her, reaching for her with his free hand, and stepped on the broken pitcher. He let out a scream and grasped his foot.

Blood welled around the shard that protruded from the arch of his foot. Jumping away from the fragments, he crashed into the first man, causing them both to wobble. The two men slipped on the water-slick marble and careened into the third man, tumbling them all to the ground.

The two oiled and exfoliated men shoved the servants aside to help their companions.

"Never mind us," the first man growled. "She heard our plans."

One of the men crouched, his oiled muscles straining as he moved toward Sénna. "Forget tasting the nectar," he cracked his knuckles. "This flower needs to be plucked."

Sénna feinted to the left, then ducked to the right, going under the man's arm and behind the group. The two manservants stepped out of her way, bowing so low she could see the silvery lash scars striating their deep bronze backs.

Sénna grasped the closest manservant by the shoulders and raised him with a shake. "Help me," she pleaded. "How can I get out of here?"

The young man flinched, glancing at the still-tangled men. Mischief glinted in his black eyes. "Go through the curtain across from the pool, then right. I will slow them down." He reached for the curved strigil and brandished it. "Zalid," he called to his companion. "Help me with this."

Sénna glanced at the towels that shimmered with the grime scraped from the mens' bodies and wrinkled her nose. The second manservant, Zalid, grabbed the towels and flipped them onto the floor, oil side down. She didn't think the strigil would be very threatening, but the vazurgan men would have a hard time keeping their footing on the wet, oily floor. Sénna raced through the beaded curtain into the hallway.

Bath patrons filled the corridor, laden with the soft towels and chatting amiably. She moved to the left, but a careworn woman herding several young children blocked her way. She had to get to Cédron and the others and warn them, but there was no angling through this group. They seemed determined to thwart her every effort to get past them.

Pushing through the women, Sénna stumbled into a room filled with sweet smoke. Men sat in circular groups around hookahs; the colorful glass water bowls offset their hoses' black snaking coils that extended from the hookah to the wooden mouthpieces. Several men withdrew the mouthpieces, exhaling the blue smoke as she burst in on them.

"What are you doing, young lady?" a middle-aged gentleman stood, his expression a mixture of consternation and concern. "This room is for—"

Sénna leaped over the cushions and grasped the glass hookah, wrenching all the hoses from the mouths in the circle. She turned and hurled it towards her pursuers, who'd spotted her in the smoking room. Her aim was off. Rather than striking the leader, the glass hookah smashed into one of the blazesand containers near the doorway, shattering the terra cotta pot. Charcoal from the hookah landed in the blazesand and ignited. The explosion destroyed the stone columns of the entrance and sent shards of tile and marble into the faces of patrons and pursuers alike.

Sénna didn't stick around to watch but sprinted across the smoking room and into another corridor. Shouts from behind made her pulse race, and she looked around, seeking an alternate route. A movement down the hallway to her left caught her eye, and she turned her head in time to see a door close. She hurried down the smaller corridor and halted in front of the door. The sign on the door identified the room as Zaran's office. The thought of entering caused a watery feeling in her knees, but her pursuers were getting closer. She eased the door open and crept inside.

Sénna peeked into the gloom of the darkened office and spotted a small figure rifling through a chest. She heard the jingle of coins and the snap of the chest's lid. Down the corridor, she heard men's voices. She recognized Zaran's silky wheedle and sent a quick prayer to Hamra that his companions weren't the men she'd just escaped.

The voices got louder as the men approached. Her hands felt like ice. She slipped past the chest and was knocked to the floor as the fleeing thief ran into her. Sénna rolled to her feet and lunged, grabbing the thief by the front of his vest.

"Ow! Hey, let me go!" a shrill voice cried. The little body wiggled, but Sénna's grip was firm. "Let go! They'll kill me if they find me!"

Sénna shook the thief, clapping her hand over his mouth. "Shh, stop your racket, or they'll kill us both. We have to hide." She turned the person around to face her, keeping her hand firmly over his mouth. "I'm going to remove my hand now. Stay silent."

Eyes wide, the thief nodded. Sénna pulled her hand away from the face and gasped. "Raziz! What are you doing here?"

The boy hunched his shoulders and gulped. He stuck the pouch of flecksun coins into the pack he wore on his hip and jutted his chin. "Zaran cheated my father. I'm just taking what he owes us."

Sénna sucked in her breath. She admired the lad's spirit and sense of outrage, but stealing from the Master of the Baths? "Raziz, they will kill you and me too. I look like your accomplice!"

Voices and footsteps echoed in the hallway, growing louder. Sénna turned around, peering in the gloomy chamber for a place to hide but found none. Her heart stopped when Zaran and his companions opened the door, spilling the light of the corridor onto their guilty faces.

"Laylur's beast!" Zaran swore, his pointed eyebrows lost in his hairline. "What is going on here?"

chapter 28: To Catch A Spy

The sands of the Zahili Desert rippled and shimmered like a flowing red ocean of heat. The breeze blowing from the east brought little relief from the sweltering heat. Läenshi peeled her tunic away from her damp skin and flapped it in the air, hoping to cool the sweat pouring rivulets between her breasts and down the thick muscles of her back. Dry, hot air scorched her nose and throat as she breathed, making her long for the cool, fragrant air of Samshäeli. The foliage tattoos covering her skin glistened green with her perspiration.

Läenshi missed her home and family but knew she could

never return to Samshäeli. The choking grief that had been her constant companion since her parents' deaths wrapped tendrils around her throat, squeezing and burning with the dry air. The discomfort of the heat and her memories only made the growing sense of unease tickling the back of her mind more pronounced.

Juläen sensed her growing turmoil. The fierce raptor paced, extending and retracting his golden wings halfway as if trying to decide whether to escape to the air or remain with his rider. The other läeniers of their Wing shifted and ruffled their feathers in response.

"Be at peace, my friend," she murmured, stroking the sensitive ridge bone between the läenier's eyes. "I'm sure it's nothing."

Juläen crooned and nudged her shoulder with his curved beak, his subtle request for more attention. Läenshi grinned and rubbed his beak, running her thumbs up along the ridge and over the spikey orange top feathers that sprang back into position as soon as her hands passed them.

Läenshi had already fed the beast, eaten some dried fruit and nuts from her pack, and checked her gear twice before seeking the solace of her raptor. He nestled in a shallow hollow on the outskirts of the roost the Wing had made in the warm sands near the crashed airship. Läenshi began humming as she groomed Juläen's wings, shoving her dark thoughts away for the moment. The tightness in her chest and the unease remained.

"So, you feel it too."

Läenshi whirled with a cry and crouched into a defensive position. The dagger she'd whipped from her hip glinted in the golds and oranges of Lord Shamar's light. Her heart pounded, and her muscles tensed.

Her slender twin, Säeshi, stood with palms outstretched and a slight smile on her lips. "You do feel it, don't you?"

Läenshi straightened and sheathed her dagger. "Yes, but I can't name the source. I just have this feeling...." She shook her head. "Do you think it's Räeshun? I've been edgy since that young Askári soldier stole her."

Säeshi placed her hands on Läenshi's shoulders. "I can sense several energies but not Räeshun's. I haven't been able to sense her Árk'äezhi since...." She swallowed hard and squeezed her sister's shoulder. "I get traces of things surrounding us - layers of them - but I don't want to transform around the Askári. They are already uncertain about us."

Läenshi felt her chest tighten. She hesitated for a moment, then straightened her shoulders. "What things?"

Säeshi bit her lower lip. "I can feel the flow of Árk'äezhi from the people of Taboriz like a slow current coursing deep beneath the sands. Layering above it is discordant energy, like jagged red spikes, stabbing and twisting its way through the city's core. It feels like danger, but not directly to us."

Säeshi pressed her fingers into her temples. She paced a few steps then stood dead still, her aquamarine eyes troubled. "Hovering above it all is a growing feeling that something has happened to Sénna. I don't sense anything specific to her or any pain, just this feeling of—"

"Unease." Läenshi nodded and crossed her arms over her chest. "We are alone. I'll open my mind to yours. Show me Sénna."

Säeshi held Läenshi's hands as her twin shimmered and blurred. She felt her form shrinking and hardening into the palm-sized polished beryl that Sénna now carried. The Árk'äezhi of the stone and her heart pulsed twice then stopped. The beryl went dark. Läenshi poured her own Árk'äezhi to enhance the energy detected by her sister. Säeshi, in the form of the white stone, remained cold and dark. Läenshi released her grip on her sister, and Säeshi's willowy form reappeared, gasping and holding her throat.

"Sénna," she gasped, falling to her knees. "We have to get to her!"

Cold slapped Sénna's bare midriff as her body hit the water. She shuddered and cried out, inhaling water through the silk bag tied around her head. Rough hands gripped her wrists, pulling her along a chilly current. Sénna's lungs ached for air, causing her body to spasm and jerk in panic. The hands clamped harder, wrenching her shoulders and forcing her through a now-rushing stream. Her head throbbed, and she saw sparkles of light behind her lids.

Sénna's final thoughts were of her father. She wished she'd gained his trust and been able to serve him. At least her captors couldn't hold her for ransom. Cédron wasn't around to rescue her this time, either.

A jolt of desperation ripped through her at the thought of Cédron. She wiggled and thrust her body into her captor's torso. Sénna's strength had gone with the air. The spots in her eyes snapped and popped as the man pulled her out of the water, ripping off the hood.

Sénna found herself draped over her captor's shoulder. He stood on a landing next to the churning channel of an aqueduct. The smooth sandstone walls had sconces filled with blazesand. Sénna marveled at their brilliant flickers of green and blue. Their light reflected from the water and danced merrily on the smooth walls, reminding her of the bathhouse in Táksabai. A pang of homesickness stabbed her chest, causing tears to spring into her eyes. It was likely that she'd never see the baths or any other part of her city again. Two tears spilled down her cheeks and onto the flagstone floor.

"Put her with that street urchin," Zaran snapped at the man holding her.

The journey through the aqueduct hadn't washed the acrid scent of stale body odor from her captor's clothing. She gagged, then felt the man grasp her around the waist and fling her through the air. She landed on her shoulder and cracked the side of her head against the smooth sandstone wall. Sénna coughed to force the remaining liquid out of her lungs.

Through blurred vision, Sénna spied Raziz crumpled in a heap next to the wall to her right. Blood trickled down the left side of his face from a cut above his eye. His left eye was swollen, giving him a lopsided appearance. His skin was a sickly pallor, but his chest raised and lowered with each breath. She cried out in relief and gathered the crumpled ball into her arms. She pulled the boy tight to her chest, feeling the steady beat of his heart.

"What are you going to do with us?" Sénna croaked through her stinging throat.

The man who'd thrown her shrugged and looked at Zaran. The Master of the Baths glared at the two of them and pulled the boy's leather pouch from his shirt. The jingle of flecksun coins caused Raziz to stir. His eyelids fluttered.

"Normally, thieves lose a hand," his smile was as cold as his voice. "However, I require small bodies with nimble fingers.

The lackey pulled Raziz to his feet and held the boy's arm as he wobbled. Zaran turned, forcing the two captives to follow him along a circular sandstone corridor that housed a colossal metal screw. The fourteen-foot-wide gleaming blades corkscrewed upwards from below, dumping water into the vast pool.

Far below them, the rushing water swirled as it entered the cavern at the base of the screw. The second set of turning blades lifted water ever higher as they rotated, dumping into multiple channels high above them. The circulating air was fresh, tinged with the terra that the rain brought from the desert. She inhaled then coughed, expelling the last of the water from her lungs.

Zaran led the way to the far side of the screw, where levers extended from a wall of gears. Sénna watched the gears mesh and turn the screws causing the water to continue its inexorable climb towards the far-distant top. The water came from the desert qanats and was lifted by this spire to the tallest part of the city, the Zhoula's palace. From there, it flowed down the aqueducts that crisscrossed the city. She wiped her eyes.

"Here we are, my little imps," Zaran stopped at the box, faced his prisoners, and pulled out a rod with a crescent-shaped end. He thrust it at Raziz. "Now, use this to loosen the gears along the bottom of this wall." He squatted down and jabbed a long finger towards the spoked wheels in the contraption.

Raziz eyed the tool and the gears, his jaw dropping.

"You want me to stick my hand in there?" Raziz gasped, his voice rising. "It'll cut off my fingers or maybe even my whole hand!"

Zaran grabbed Raziz by his shirtfront and shook him. "Your hand is already forfeit, you little thief. Now, take this and turn the inside nut six times to the left." He thrust the tool into the boy's hand and shoved him towards the wall of gears.

Sénna inhaled and held her breath. The gears ground around each other in a relentless circuit, with only a few seconds between the spokes as they completed their rotation. Even if Raziz could get his hand in the tiny hole and be able to turn the tool, he wouldn't be able to rotate the nut more than once or twice before his hand would be trapped and torn off. There had to be a better option. She glanced around but saw nothing that inspired her. What she needed was more time to think.

"What would blocking water from the upper echelons of the city accomplish other than cause the sewers to back up?" she asked, looking up the length of the screw. She scratched the back of her neck as she pondered.

Zaran's head jerked towards her. His eyes narrowed, and then his thin lips twisted into a sneer. "Very clever, girl.

However, you're not quite correct." He motioned towards the levers and pointed. "These control where the water is released, not the gears. The gears move the screw, yes, but beneath the city are gates that regulate water flow from the qanats, with other gates in the palace that distribute the lifted water from the palace down the aqueducts. If this mechanism breaks down, the city's lower levels will flood because the water from the desert qanats will have nowhere else to go. Consider it a design flaw."

"Wouldn't flooding the lower levels destroy your baths?" Sénna asked, memorizing the instruction chart by the levers with her head tilted sideways.

Zaran gave a mirthless laugh and nudged his companion, who leered at her. "The baths are unimportant," Zaran said. "We are about to reshape Yezman society, and indeed, the very composition of life on Muralia."

As he spoke, Zaran crossed his arms over his chest, and the left sleeve of his robe pulled back from his wrist. Sénna spotted the tattoo revealed on the inside of his left arm: a coiled snake with its head up and fangs ready to strike.

It was a sinister design for a merchant, but Sénna knew that Zaran was more than just the proprietor of the local baths. She also knew he was smart enough not to keep two witnesses around. She took a breath to ask another question, but he held his hand up.

"I don't have time for your foolishness, girl." He turned back to Raziz and shoved him closer to the wall. "Loosen that nut now, boy."

Raziz looked at Sénna with eyes so wide the whites showed all around his dark-brown irises. The man behind him pulled a sharp, curved blade and poked him in the back. Raziz swallowed audibly and faced the gears. Sénna watched his eyes track the timing and pattern of the mechanism, then dart his hand in quickly, giving the tool two turns before pulling it out again. A bead of sweat rolled down his cheek. He bit his lower lip when the gears spiraled back around. He thrust his hand back in and turned once, twice, then let out a scream.

Raziz pulled his hand out of the hole. A chunk of skin and muscle dangled from the outside of his hand just below the pinky. Blood welled from the wound and dripped down his arm. The gears clanked and began grinding, hesitating in their smooth pattern.

"You imbecile!" Zaran shrieked. "You've dropped the tool inside the housing. Now we'll never get it out again!"

The two men shoved the boy aside and tried to peer down into the shaft, banging their heads together in their haste. Sénna saw her opportunity. She grabbed the lackey's sword hand and twisted it sideways, yanking as hard as she could. It struck Zaran in the thigh. The blade sank deep—a line of vermillion stained and clashed with the burnt orange fabric of his silken trousers.

The knife-wielding man was momentarily stunned, trapped behind Zaran. The wounded Zaran writhed on the narrow floor and cursed his companion. Sénna wrapped her yellow scarf around Raziz's hand.

"Hurry, we have to get out of here," Sénna whispered, pulling at the little boy.

They ran until they hit the end of the corridor. Two hallways stretched left and right with no markings to indicate the direction they should take. Sénna hauled Raziz towards the left passage. He shook his head and pulled her to a halt.

"We need to go that way," he said, pointing to the right.

Sénna peered down the gloomy hallway lit by only a couple sconces of blazesand placed at distant intervals. "Why that way? What's down there?"

Raziz smiled at her through the pain in his hand. "My Dadaji."

Sénna frowned at the unfamiliar word. Raziz grabbed her wrist with his good hand and pulled her down the right passage. She stumbled into his shoulder, and he grunted but held her hand firmly and continued away from the spiraling screw and the faint shouts of their captors.

They ran, Sénna following the boy blindly as he turned down this corridor and that until they reached a rusted, iron-wrought gate. The scents of frying food and dirty clothes wafted through the bars. They were at once the most delightful and repulsive smells Sénna had ever encountered together, and her stomach warred with itself between hunger and nausea.

"Faugh, where are we?" She covered her nose and mouth with her hand.

Raziz raised his eyebrows at her and shrugged. "The shanty, but…" he looked at her soiled ochre halter and rents in her gauzy pants and rubbed his nose. "People are going to notice you. We'll need to grab something to throw over your fancy clothes."

Sénna looked down at herself and snorted. "Okay, but don't get caught this time."

Raziz grinned and pushed open the gate. He scampered through ahead of her, looking in both directions before waving her to follow. She stepped onto the narrow sand lane, winding through brightly-colored awnings where merchants hawked their wares.

Läenshi crouched along the outside wall of Taboriz, watching the crowds of festival-goers entering the city. The Zholi Festival brought pilgrims from as far away as Zaveen to honor the deities. They clogged the entrance to Taboriz as Zaouni guards searched each cart for unauthorized weapons. Läenshi clicked her tongue and frowned. There was no way they could get through the gate unnoticed.

The carved hematite pillars and gate to the city yawned above the crowds, their black and lapis lazuli mosaics offering a counterpoint to the beige and red sandstone of the surrounding walls. She looked up and gauged the height — about 100 feet. It was nearly as high as the great trees of Suläeri that formed the city's foundation, within whose boughs nestled several levels of homes and businesses.

Läenshi nodded at Säeshi and Rováen. They could scale this wall; the carving and mosaics offered excellent handholds. However, the trio remained invisible only when connected to Rováen and his ability to hide them with his gift.

Rováen followed her line of sight and shook his head. "We can't risk discovery, and I don't think rescuing Sénna can wait until nightfall."

Läenshi glanced again at her sister. "What do you sense?"

Säeshi closed her eyes and took a slow, deep breath. She turned her head slowly from left to right, then stared at her companions with wide eyes. "I sense a strong current of energy. It's hidden or," she frowned and rubbed her forehead, "…or maybe it's hiding. I can't tell the difference. Either way, something is obscuring her. I don't know if the Hazzara got here ahead of us and are laying a trap or if it's something else entirely."

Rováen twisted the hair in his beard. "Well, we can't go after both the Hazzara and Sénna. Just stay vigilant, and hopefully, we won't run afoul of any of their tricks before we—"

The sound of laughter interrupted his comment. Rováen's gaze followed a group of women returning from the river with baskets laden with washing balanced on their heads. Their bright-colored woven dresses offset their dark skin. Their laughter made him smile, and he nodded in their direction. "Let's slip in with them. They're unlikely to get a second glance from the guards."

There were two guards, one on either side of the gate. They wore the Zaouni uniform, billowing red trousers bound with a gold sash at the waist and curved swords dangling off their left hips. Each man wore a red headpiece trimmed with gold. Their leather breastplates covered the sternum and bore the emblem of Lord Shamar rising from the East. Both guards carried a spear with a curved blade at the end.

Läenshi looked at her sister, who nodded. Roväen gripped the hand of each niece and activated his Árk'äezhi. The three of them wavered like heat rising above the sands as they disappeared from view. Connected by Roväen's power, the three slunk around the city wall towards the gate and crept behind the chattering group.

The women smelled of sweet oils and fresh sweat; doing laundry in the desert heat was brutal work. Their lively chatter covered the footfalls of the trio following in their wake. The group slowed as they approached the gate and the guards.

The guard at the left post gave them a cursory glance and waved the washing women through the gate. The other guard spat through gap teeth at the feet of the woman directly in front of Säeshi. The group stopped.

"Pay the merchant fee, whore," he sneered and held his spear out to block their way.

The woman steadied the heavy basket on her head with one hand and placed her other on her hip. "I am not selling anything; this is my laundry."

The guard barked a laugh and stepped closer, inflating his chest. "These are the sheets from your whoring bed. Consider it a business expense." He leered at her, the space between his teeth making his appearance almost comical.

Läenshi saw the malicious glint in the guard's eye. The man harbored some resentment towards the woman and was using his position to get even. She hated such abuse of power. A flush of anger swept through her, and she pulled the dagger at her hip awkwardly with her left hand. She felt Roväen squeeze her fingers.

"Whatever his vendetta with the woman is, it isn't our business," he whispered into her ear.

"But he is blocking our way and is looking for trouble," she hissed back. "I'm happy to give it to him."

Läenshi started to pull away, but Roväen pulled her back. "Wait."

A second woman stepped up next to the harassed laundress. Her yellow dress complemented the flash in her amber eyes.

"Is this the man you told us about?" She jutted her chin towards the belligerent guard. "The one who couldn't do his business with you?"

The other guard laughed. "So, that night of unbridled passion with three beautiful ladies who couldn't get enough of you was an exaggeration?"

The gap-toothed guard's face flushed dusky maroon. "She put something in my wine—"

"How dare you blame your impotence on her, filthy pig!" a third woman cried as she stepped up behind the other two. "Extorting money for your inability to perform is against the Market Queen's rules. Let us pass unmolested, or we'll report you to her."

The second guard moved closer to his companion. "You don't want to get on the wrong side of *her*! Let them pass. Next time you visit the brothel, drink less wine."

The first guard growled deep in his chest but stepped back. His black eyes narrowed as they followed the women passing into the city gates. Läenshi felt the tension in her shoulders relax, and she, Rováen, and Säeshi crept into the city behind the women. The dust swirls stirred by their footfalls went unnoticed by the guards.

Taboriz was a mountain island built in concentric rings from a base covering nearly eighteen miles around its perimeter. Surrounding the outside of the city was a canal diverted directly from the Räenetti River. The channel accommodated both local fishing fleets and the three-masted shipping vessels that transported cargo to and from the capital of Yezmarantha.

Docks and warehouses rimmed the river along the wall's outer ring—brothels and pubs filled in the occasional gaps between guild offices and crew's quarters. The inner rings decreased in size, with walls four feet thick separating each ascending level. The second ring made up the bazaar, and living quarters for the Market Queen and her laborers, while the third held the shops and homes of merchants and artisans and the Zaouni Warriors' barracks. The top ring belonged to the Zhoula's palace.

Taboriz was an emerald nestled in the center of the Zahili Desert. Läenshi marveled at the vertical gardens that sprouted over every surface, creating a lush, refreshing atmosphere in the otherwise arid heat. She couldn't imagine the city using water from the canal to feed the gardens, so where did it come from in the desolate Zahili Desert? A squeeze of her hands brought her attention back to their task.

"This way," Roväen tugged his nieces toward the south.

They left the public thoroughfare, with its wide sandstone streets lined with glass blazesand containers. They ducked into a narrow alley filled with ramshackle lean-to's attached to the wall. Laundry crisscrossed above them like billowing rainbow clouds. The sound of children's laughter drifted from above them along the flat rooftops.

Roväen pulled them along until they reached a courtyard too small for a fountain. The smell of filth and refuse stung their nostrils. Flies swarmed over suspicious piles decaying against the walls. Läenshi held her breath, but she could taste the foulness in the dry air on her tongue. The pained look on Säeshi's face betrayed similar disgust. The courtyard was empty except for the tunnel snakes they'd disturbed on their way through the alley. Roväen let go of the twins, and the three shimmered into visibility.

"Säeshi," Roväen said, turning to face her. "What can you sense? Can you tell which direction we must go to find Sénna?"

Läenshi gripped her sister's hands in her own, and the two women activated their magic. Säeshi's body shrank and darkened into a wizened old woman with blackened teeth. Läenshi poured her Ärk'äezhi into her sister's and felt the familiar tug of magic pulling her towards the central market area. She opened her eyes.

"She's not far," Läenshi breathed and let go of Säeshi's hands. "We need to get into the bazaar."

Säeshi grasped her sister's arm and held her back. "Wait, we need a plan. Do not underestimate that woman. Whoever she is, she has great strength."

Läenshi nodded. "I felt it too. We'll be careful, but we need to hurry. I can feel Sénna nearby."

"Are you ready?" Rovären asked and held out his hands.

The three now-invisible Shäeli crept back through the alley, disrupting a swarm of gnats swirling around the garden wall. Grinning, Läenshi reached out and pulled a small, round zambutan from its vine. She broke the soft shell with her teeth and popped the white fruit into her mouth, spitting out the seed. The Yezman were famous for their glass, but Läenshi thought perhaps their most remarkable feat was these hanging gardens that provided nourishment from the very walls.

The three Shäeli made their way into the broad stone street that led towards the ring's entry gate. They wandered down the sand flagstones, avoiding carts pulled by sturdy ozryks and dodging the occasional squad of Zaouni that patrolled the streets. It took longer than anticipated to reach the bazaar, and Läenshi's nerves jangled.

The open square was nearly half a mile across and almost the same distance wide. Vendor stalls were set up in orderly rows with their wares overflowing and spilling into the walkways. Flats of vegetables and fruits vyed with buckets of brilliantly colored flowers and baskets of spices shaped into colorful spikes. The savory scent of meat grilled with cumin and garlic filled the air. Läenshi inhaled and sighed.

Hundreds of people filled the square, haggling with vendors over their purchases and gathering their food for the day. A stall frying stuffed pastries boasted the densest crowd, and Läenshi's gaze lingered as they continued past. Women wearing brightly-colored silk dresses with filmy scarves and men sporting wildly patterned tunics swam before the trio in a riot of color and scent. Läenshi felt her energy falter and noticed that she and her companions seemed to shimmer in Lord Shamar's punishing heat.

"Rovä̈en, focus!" Läenshi hissed.

"I am," Rovä̈en growled. "Something is interfering with my Árk'ä̈ezhi."

Her uncle's grip on her hands tightened, but their bodies shimmered. The harder they grasped, the more slippery their hands became. Läenshi's heart raced, and she glanced around. A group of four men wearing grey, loose-fitting robes encircled the Shä̈eli. Darker grey trousers peeked from beneath the knee-length robe's hem. Läenshi saw their sharp, black eyes focused on them, and her breath caught in her throat. The three fully visible Shä̈eli stood erect and faced the men.

Sä̈eshi stepped forward with her hands outstretched and palms up. "We are not a threat to you or your people. We are searching for a member of our group."

"Ah, you silver-haired demons," said a rich contralto voice behind the men. "If that were so, you would not have utilized your Shä̈eli tricks."

Two of the grey-clad men stepped aside, and a middle-aged woman with startling green eyes and a brilliantly patterned headwrap that enhanced the bronze glow of her skin stepped forward. Around her neck was strung a necklace of pulsing yellow stones.

"We weren't…how did you…?" Läenshi sputtered.

Rovä̈en leaned towards her and whispered into her ear. "Windstone necklace; she used it to break through my illusion."

The woman's grin lit her entire face. "Yes, but it wasn't necessary. I am Anzeri. I serve the market as the peacekeeper." She nodded to her companions. "They noticed the sand stirred up behind the group of women entering the gate. They followed but told me they weren't certain we had interlopers until a zambutan seed appeared from nowhere and struck one of them in the shoulder."

Läenshi felt her face flush at Rovären's sharp glance at her.

"Betrayed by my appetite." She shrugged and eased her right hand toward the blade hidden in the small of her back. She didn't make it.

Without a word, the four men stripped the Shäeli of their weapons. Anzeri's smile hardened, and she placed her hands on her hips. Läenshi spun away from the group, sweeping her powerful leg behind one man, and knocking him to the ground before whirling into the second and wrapping her bulging arm around his throat.

Läenshi turned to face Anzeri and gasped. The remaining two men had their knives to Säeshi and Rovären's throats. Anzeri gave a curt nod, and Läenshi watched drops of blood pool around the blades as they sank into the soft flesh of their hostages.

"No!" Läenshi gave a strangled cry.

Anzeri's hand went up, and the men pulled back their weapons. She gave Läenshi a pointed look, and the Sumäeri warrior released the man's neck. Läenshi raised her hands and stepped back. The man she'd held captive glared at her and grasped her wrists, binding them securely with twine pulled from a pocket inside his billowing robe.

"Now, Lady of the Green Tattoos, unless you'd like my companions to finish pruning the vines of your kinsmen's throats, I suggest you come with us." Anzeri turned and took several steps toward a narrow alley between the food vendors.

Rovären lifted his chin and called after her. "Where are you taking us?"

Anzeri turned back, her grin matching the mischief in her green eyes. "The Market Queen, Marizen Grozen, will decide your fate."

Chapter 30: Traitor's Plan

The wind whipped Tóran's hair into his face and he blinked, causing the tears to stream down his cheeks. The black turbans that he and his companions wore protected head and face, leaving their eyes vulnerable to the sting of the glaring sands. He lowered his head, focusing on the leather reins he held tightly in his grip.

The rough, reptilian hide and curved horns of the alzaytan gleamed in the afternoon light. In contrast, the pulsing blue crystals lining the harnesses cast their calming glow over the beasts, ensuring their obedience. Tóran felt the alzaytan's muscles ripple beneath his legs, expanding and contracting as it ran. The shushing of the herd's claws driving through the sand beat an erratic rhythm below the whistles and hoots of the men surrounding him.

Ten black-clad Hazzara rode from their lair in the Zaroon Quarry toward a rendezvous point just outside the city gates of Taboriz. A small group of spies awaited them, charged with infiltrating this advanced group into the palace. The remainder of their forces would storm the city once they neutralized the Zaouni.

Events of the past few days had unfolded in a blur of faces and fear for Tóran. The effort of participating in the plot to slaughter the ruling family of Taboriz and subdue the city while maintaining his semi-conscious watchfulness took a toll on him. His skin felt stretched too tightly across his bones, and his eyes sunken deep into his skull. Tóran's movements were methodical but slow. He felt the eyes of the Hazzara behind him hot between his shoulder blades.

Despite his best efforts to fit in, Tóran knew he'd aroused some suspicions. The battle raging in his body between himself and whatever entity had infiltrated it continued. The awkward dance of advance and retreat, of uninhibited enthusiasm and self-conscious withholding, hadn't gone unnoticed.

Tóran glanced sideways at the man riding next to him. The bones showing beneath the skin of his knuckles and the stiffness of his shoulders belied the man's attempt to appear casual and relaxed. They were watching him, not trusting the façade he'd displayed. He had the grim satisfaction of knowing they would underestimate him.

The shadows spread out long ahead of them as the daytime deity angled towards the rising dunes to the west. At dawn, the Festival of Zholi would begin in earnest. The Zaouni would be preoccupied with enforcing order among the population and protecting the royal family as they participated in the sacred rituals.

Tóran had never heard of the Zhoula of Taboriz and was

intrigued by the idea that a woman could effectively rule the city of nearly half a million residents. The very concept of a matriarchal system mystified him completely, for Askári-bai was a male-dominated society.

The idea of eradicating the Zhoula of Taboriz and her family filled the back of his throat with bile. Fighting warriors in battle was honorable. Sneaking into bed chambers at night and slaughtering women and children in their sleep was not. Tóran felt the heat rise in his chest.

The ache in his head spread to the temples, causing his eyes to throb. He had to figure out a way to overcome this demon inside before it killed him. He gritted his teeth and slapped the flanks of his lizard mount with his reins. The sooner they got to the city, the sooner he could figure out a plan.

The great walled city of Taboriz rose out of the shimmering heat in the distance like a verdant mirage. Nestled in the center, the white palace dome gleamed like a pearl in the emerald city's vertical gardens. Tóran marveled at the lush vegetation thriving in the arid barrenness of Yezmarantha. The desert had some water somewhere, he mused, or they wouldn't be able to feed the dense population.

The leader of their group reined in his alzaytan. The beast bellowed in agitation and swung the sharp bony protrusions lining his head and neck back and forth as if trying to free himself of the restraining glow of the crystals lining his harness.

"Halt! Wait here," the leader of their group held up his fist, wheeling his beast around to face the group. "I'll ride on ahead and locate our men. They should have been waiting here for us."

A low buzz of grumbling rose from the men as they circled their beasts to keep them from biting each other or their riders. The creatures gnashed their teeth, snapping at each other as they jostled around the sands. The riders tugged on the reins, hard-pressed to keep the alzaytans in check. The two posted on either side of Tóran wheeled sideways, then back around, not letting him out of their sight. The entire group of Hazzara bristled with weapons that glinted in the fading light,

Tóran squinted toward the city. He saw the thin masts of fishing boats lined up along the wharf, just across the river from his position. The docks were quiet with no longshoremen offloading barges, no fishermen selling their day's catch, and no street urchins scraping their living by pickpocketing passers-by.

The entity in Tóran's mind coalesced into a rubbery coating, fixing itself to the folds and creases of his brain. The groping tendrils massaged his memories, discarding the irrelevant images and probing deeper for a recognition buried within the deepest recesses of his mind. He felt the entity access the memory of Shozin's scry, informing them that tomorrow began the Zholi Festival. He knew that thousands of Yezman citizens were preparing themselves for the holy rituals that would start at dawn.

"It's too quiet," Tóran muttered under his breath, his eyes darting around the pier and towards the city walls. "The festival begins tomorrow, doesn't it?"

One Hazzara weaved his beast close to Tóran, who ducked the spiked ball at the end of the agitated alzaytan's swishing tail. The creature reared up on its hind legs, nearly tossing the man to the ground. The Hazzara yanked the reins, bowing the reptile's thick neck and causing it to whimper in pain. He pulled the ruby amulet from his neck with one hand and sent a pulse of energy into the blue quartz mounted in the harness. The stones flared, brightening the glow of the obedience spell over the alzaytan.

"Yes, Zholi begins at dawn," he grunted, struggling with his mount while keeping an eye on Tóran.

"Where are the festival-goers?" Tóran's brows furrowed, sensing the stab of cold fear at the base of his neck. "It is barely dusk, and the gates are already closed." He turned and looked back at his companions. "Could they have known we were coming?"

The man got his alzaytan under control and squinted at Tóran. "Ah, Askári, your mind is as swift as your prized racing husan." He spat a blob of blackroot in the sand and grinned. "Sadly, you, like your people, flow west with Lord Shamar, sinking into the horizon and the darkness of night."

Tóran blinked. He looked at the man, who only shook his head and kicked his mount into prowling in a complete circle around the small group. Shozin Chezak had demonstrated the Yezman language of formality, cautioning their group to be wary of flowery words that disguised threats or insults. He wasn't sure, but it sounded like the Hazzara just called him an imbecile. He glanced around at the other Hazzara and saw the tell-tale crinkling at the eyes. The fabric from the face coverings hid the sly grins behind them.

"The eve of Zholi is time for fasting and prayer," said another man, apparently taking pity on the foreigner's ignorance.

Tóran snorted, grimacing. He nodded his thanks to his comrade and returned his gaze to the silent city.

A gentle breeze blew across the desert sands, billowing their clothing and cooling their skin. The floral scents wafting from the gardens of Taboriz replaced the stench of onions and stale sweat from his companions. Jasmine and honeysuckle and orange blossom teased his nose as he turned his head toward the city. The murmuring of the men obscured the sound of the families approaching from the desert.

Tóran's alzaytan screamed and bucked, startled by the appearance of a child screeching as he raced ahead of his friends. The five children ran around the small group of mounted Hazzara, tossing a fist-sized bag of seeds between them. One lad jumped to block the bag on his chest as it bounced to his knees. He raised his knee and bounded the sack to his ankle before kicking it across to his companion. Two more bags arched across the group, defying both gravity and the nervous animals.

Several more of the alzaytan stomped and squealed, tossing their horns as a defense against the airborne object. More people followed the children. An extended family of parents, elders, and infants in arms came into view, halting at the sight of the terrifying beasts and their ominous riders.

"Forgive us, friends," a middle-aged man stepped forward, his palms outstretched and his homespun beige pants billowing in the breeze. "We did not mean to interrupt you. Here, you scamps," he called to the boys kicking the sack back and forth. "Come now and leave these men alone before their beasts skewer your hides."

Tóran reined in his alzaytan and glanced at the other men. He caught the pressed lips on the face of the one who nodded to the other and felt his skin prickle. They drew curved blades from the sashes at their hips. The two riders closest to the group of adults swung their beasts around and kicked their haunches. The alzaytan screamed and plunged forward.

A wave of nausea crashed over Tóran with the blood of the first victim. He wiped the drops from his eyes and stared down at the corpse. Grey bowels slithered from the gash in the man's midsection, the sand soaking up blood and fluids like a parched flower. Tóran felt his brain contract and tighten as the entity took over. He closed his eyes and clenched every muscle in his body, but the strain of recent days had taken its toll.

Tóran felt a cool tingling spread from the base of his skull down his spine. The numbing substance coursed through his body, deadening sensation from his awareness. In seconds, he had no control of his body, and his conscious thought screamed in anguish before retreating into the dark recesses of his brain. Tóran unsheathed his sword and kicked his heels into his alzaytan's flank.

Children screamed and scattered as he approached, his blade raised high. Tóran felt the demon inside his head swell with joy as it forced his body to do unspeakable things. His consciousness retreated away from his eyes, trying to escape the truth of what his body was doing. He felt the muscles contract as he swung his sword downward. His hand jarred as the metal struck bone. He felt his heart pounding with excitement. The flush of bloodlust rose in his cheeks. With an anguished cry, Tóran huddled in the corner of his awareness, shutting himself off from the atrocities.

The slaughter took mere minutes. As his heartbeat slowed, Tóran cautiously stretched his awareness. The demon was still too powerful for him to overtake, but he could see through his eyes a carnage that would normally have caused him to weep. He had to get this thing in his mind under control before the heinousness of his actions overwhelmed him.

Several of his Hazzara companions hefted corpses onto their shoulders. Two Hazzara pulled several long spears from the saddles. Tóran watched them mount the bodies on the pikes and stick them into the sand. It was a macabre display of artistry and form. Stepping back, he joined his companions in admiring their work.

A circle of grotesque puppets stood in the sand. One had a spear point where its head should have been; others tilted off-balance from missing limbs. Only the sound of the restless alzaytan disrupted the stillness of the dead. The men retrieved their beasts and, after wiping their blades, mounted and waited as the leader approached from the city.

"I see you kept yourselves entertained," the rider said, bringing his snarling alzaytan to a halt in the middle of the group. "The city has been sealed for the night. The Zaouni spotted the wreckage of the airship and a Wing of läeniers on the outskirts of town. They're monitoring them. The city is on alert for strangers. We'll make for the safehouse our spies use just inside the western gate."

"Is there any threat to our plans?" asked a bearded man to Tóran's right.

"Yes," the leader said curtly. "So, we'll need to adapt."

"We'll have to wait until tomorrow when the Zholi Festival is over," the gnarled old man slapped the table with his arthritic hand, the fingers twisted and swollen. He peered at the group with bleary eyes and grimaced. "The Zaouni are on full alert, and they've sequestered the Zhoula and her family in the palace. She won't perform the rituals of the festival for fear of the Shäeli raptors camped outside the city."

"But we have our mandate!" shouted the Hazzara leader. "I cannot speak for you, but I do not wish to cross the Great Demon."

The elderly spy scratched at the wispy, white beard that hung nearly to his waist and blinked several times. "You will not defy Laylur with a delay; you will increase your chances of success. Jump in now with everyone watching, and not only will you not reach the royal family, but you will be caught, exposed as traitors, and summarily killed."

Tóran snagged a zamboosa from the breakfast tray held by the spy's wife and took a bite. His mouth exploded with saliva as savory juices of spiced meat wrapped in flakey pastry slid over his tongue. He nodded his thanks to the woman whose teeth shone like pearls against her sepia skin.

Tóran stepped out of the twelve-foot square living space occupied by the six members of the spy's family and squatted on his haunches. Leaning back against the stone wall of the hut, he tried to calm his racing heart.

The presence of the Shäeli raptors confirmed that Cédron was near. The idea of his brother both warmed his insides and caused his head to pound. The battle raging in his mind eased with the tiny flame of hope that thoughts of Cédron ignited in his soul.

Lord Shamar rose above the desert in the east, the tall dunes of sand spreading shadows like long fingers reaching toward him. Above, a flimsy awning made from threadbare fabric fluttered against its frame. It fanned the sharp scents of spices piled in multi-colored cones on the mats toward him. On his right stood rows of the tall terra-cotta jars filled with the fragrant oil the Yezman used for everything from hair tonic to fire starter.

The angry voices faded as Tóran took slow, deep breaths and calmed his mind. He took another bite, his attention torn between enjoying the best zamboosa he'd ever eaten and the anticipation of possibly regaining control of his mind.

Experimenting, Tóran brought to the fore the memory of Cédron clasping his arm before the tournament. He recalled their excitement when plotting the succession of the regency. He remembered his brother's radiant joy at being reunited after his capture by the Garanth. As he focused on the memories and the warm feelings they brought, he could feel the invader in his mind shrinking and pulling back. It helped. He'd found a way to defeat – or at least neutralize – the being in his head.

Tóran pinched a finger-full of the deep red powder from the cone closest to him. He sniffed and sprinkled it on the last bite of his pastry. The heat from the spice cleared both his sinuses and his mind. He had to get to Cédron and warn him before the Hazzara could execute their scheme. He needed a plan.

Tóran remembered Shozin telling them about the Market Queen when they discussed this trip before leaving Táksabai. That might be a way to reach Cédron. Tóran stood, brushed the crumbs from his breakfast off his chest, and went back inside.

"...be getting our men into position, so they are ready," the leader of the group continued arguing with the spy.

The old man shook his head, his beard swinging like a pendulum. "You will need to get the Market Queen's blessing to get into the aqueducts. The Zaouni guard the main ones, but the queen's men could lead you to the cisterns beneath the city. That's where the screw that supplies water to the city is – and it's right below the palace."

"Or," Tóran interjected, grabbing one of the stuffed dates displayed on the counter and popping it into his mouth. "a small group of us could take this opportunity to kill that Shäeli lad and stop the threat against our Master." He chewed deliberately, turning his head to meet the eyes of each man. "Which do you think carries more weight with the Great Demon, killing a family of weak women or slicing the throat of the Shäeli bastard that has thwarted our Master's plans again and again?"

The men glanced at each other, muttering under their breath. Their leader stiffened and snapped his head in Tóran's direction.

"I haven't forgotten that the young Shäeli is your brother," the leader drawled, his shrewd eyes raking the legionnaire as he considered. "Perhaps you are right, though. We do have time, and we could maximize our efforts by splitting up."

The Hazzara leader pulled a carved pipe from the folds of his sash and went to the canisters lining the back wall. He lifted a lid and picked out a dried leaf, crumbling it into the pipe's bowl. One of the younger boys scurried over to the hearth and pulled a long twig from the flames. The ember glowed red in the dim light of the room. The boy held out the stick for the Hazzara, who took it solemnly and bowed to the boy. Giggling, the boy scampered back to the huddle of children hiding behind their mother.

The smoldering twig ignited the dry leaf with only a few hard pulls on the pipe stem. The leader inhaled the fragrant smoke and blew it leisurely through his nostrils. He surveyed his men with narrowed eyes and puffed away for several minutes. Nodding, he pulled the pipe out of his mouth and pointed the stem at the four men to Tóran's left.

"You four will take the alzaytan and go after the Shäeli brat. Capture him or kill him; it's all the same to me," he ordered and turned to the two men next to him. "You two will accompany me to visit the Market Queen. Go and fetch one of the smaller chests of coins hitched to my saddlebags and meet me by the southern gate."

Pivoting on his heel, he faced Tóran. "You will go with the rest of the men to the public bathhouse at the west gate. The proprietor is a friend of mine. Zaran may be able to get you into the inner workings of the water screw and aqueduct doors. You all know what to do."

Tóran's breath hitched in his chest, and beads of sweat coursed down the center of his back. He nodded curtly and exited the humble home. This was not at all what he'd planned. Sure, the men would split up, but it looked like their leader had not underestimated him after all. Now, it didn't matter if Cédron stayed with the läenier Wing or went to appeal to the Market Queen. He was in danger either way, and there was no one to warn him.

Tóran wracked his brain for ideas as he followed the other Hazzara westward down the street. He looked to the right and left, seeking anything that would provide a distraction. Neither an escape nor a method of disposing of his custodians appeared. The narrow alleys that branched off from the main thoroughfare were dim, making it impossible to see if they extended to the next street or ended in an interior courtyard.

Tóran fell back, letting the men get a few steps ahead of him. When the distance stretched to several feet, he ducked into one of the more crowded alleyways. Children with wide eyes and smudged faces skittered out of his way. The smell of urine and unwashed bodies was overpowering in the narrow space.

Tóran jogged several feet down the alley, dodging the ramshackle shelters of the poverty-stricken families and the row of beggars whose alms cups sat beside limbs red and swollen with oozing scabs and flesh-eating infections. He turned his eyes away. The poor and injured in Dúlnat were never left to fend for themselves on the street.

The alley changed direction and turned uphill, leaving the shanties behind. Tóran followed a flagstone street past homes belonging to proper merchants, no more shacks leaning against the walls. It ended in a courtyard where washing festooned the walls like jewel-toned banners. Women sang as they stirred the laundry with wooden paddles over an enormous cauldron filled with boiling water. Something caustic in the steaming water caused him to cough.

Startled at the appearance of a stranger dressed in black, the women ceased their singing. Banding together, they advanced on the legionnaire in a line. They sent one little girl running into the house. The women bore no weapons, but their stern, unyielding expressions made Tóran's legs weak. He raised his hands, palms up.

"Greetings, fair ones. Forgive my intrusion. I have lost my way." He spoke softly, not moving from his pose or position as the women approached.

One woman stepped forward. Obviously in charge, this woman wore a cobalt blue shift woven with brilliant yellow and orange in a bold, angular pattern complemented by the tall cobalt headwrap that framed her face. The woman's expression was cold and wary, but her tawny eyes held a warmth that allowed Tóran to expel the breath he'd been holding.

"What or who is it you seek, stranger?" the woman asked in a deep, throaty voice.

Tóran bowed formally then knelt on one knee. "I humbly seek Market Queen Marizen Grozen. I bring her a warning."

The woman's full lips curved into a slight smile. Her

companions tittered but maintained their defensive postures. She grasped his open hands and pulled him to his feet, inclining her head toward him.

"I am Tazien Grozen. What is your message for my husband's mother?" She arched one brow, cocking her head to the right.

Tóran tried to swallow, but his throat was too dry. He pulled his damp palms from her grasp and wiped them on his trousers. His answer was crucial. It could determine the fates of not only himself but those of Cédron and his companions. Lying could get him strung up by his innards. Telling the truth would get his throat slit if the Hazzara found him. He took a deep breath and let it out, lowering his eyes to the ground.

Tóran raised his head and squared his shoulders. "The Market Queen is in danger. The Hazzara are going to offer her an enormous bribe to gain access to the aqueducts. She cannot accept this gift. They plan to murder the Zhoula and the royal family."

Tazien laughed, a rich and resonant sound like the gong in his father's dining hall that summoned guests to their seats.

"You must be very new to our land if you believe that my husband's mother is in any danger," Tazien said. Her amber eyes glittered like topaz in the blazesand that illuminated the courtyard. "Her protection is second only to the Zhoula's. There is no danger to either of them."

"But—" Tóran began.

Tazien waved him away with a negligent hand. "Leave us now, and do not return. I will not be so forgiving of your next intrusion."

Tóran stood rooted to his spot, his mouth opening and closing as he tried to formulate an argument that might persuade Tazien to change her mind. His chest tightened, and he heard the throbbing of his blood in his ears.

The fear awoke the sleeping creature in his brain. He felt

the sluggish oozing of its form begin to inch out of the recesses of his mind. No, he could not let it take over! Pain exploded in Tóran's head, causing him to grab the sides of his skull and cry out. He dropped to his knees, writhing.

Tazien snapped her fingers. Two of her companions grabbed the legionnaire under the arms and raised him to his feet. He felt the iron of their grips and could not resist their pull as they marched him towards one of the archways. The agony in his head sharpened, causing his vision to blur. He gritted his teeth, trying to hold back the bile that burned the back of his throat.

"What shall we do with him, mistress?" one of the women asked Tazien, pausing just inside the breezeway.

The copper skin of Tazien's forehead creased into dark lines as she frowned. "Put him with the others for now. We will discuss what to do with the lot of them after the festival."

Tóran heard the clink of a key turning in a lock and the creak of hinges. The women propelled him forward before letting go of his arms. The door slammed behind him and was locked. He heard gasps through the haze of pain and saw three figures across the small room stand and move towards him.

"Well, traitor," said a familiar voice. "Tell us what you've done with Räeshun, and we'll kill you quickly. Play games, and you will beg for death long before you receive its blessing."

Chapter 31: The Market Queen

The windstone pulsed in Lord Shamar's light as Cédron held it high above his head. He felt the flow of his Árk'äezhi through his fingers as the wind pushed sand over the bow of the damaged airship, still poking through the makeshift dune. Shadows stretched out long from the tall mast standing sentinel atop the sand hiding the rest of the ship, the lone marker identifying its location.

Cédron shaded his eyes, wiping the sweat along his forehead as he surveyed his work. Turning east, he scanned the horizon towards Taboriz. Still no sign of anyone leaving the city and heading back towards their encampment. He paced back and forth in front of the new dune and sighed. Hours crawled as he waited for word from his uncle and cousins who'd gone to rescue Sénna.

Waiting was challenging, even painful for Cédron. It brought back the same feelings of helplessness and worry he'd suffered during his confinement in Dúlnat. The Askári people he lived among had always been wary of his existence. When his demonic powers manifested last Dormantide, his parents sequestered him for his safety. Cédron grimaced, the pang of grief ripping through his chest at the memories of his life's tragedy.

Kasúin and Maräera were gone now, and he was nobody's captive. Cédron shook the pestering thoughts out of his head and looked around for other things he could do to keep his mind off those in Taboriz. Dwelling on the past wouldn't help him now.

Laughter and shouts caught his ear from the Sumäeri camp. He envied Anéton's ability to rustle up a game of Sénur among the bored länier riders and find the patience to teach them the intricacies of the dice game. His friend had traveled halfway across Muralia, carrying the pyramidal dice and the carved aventurine charm his mother had made him. Cédron snorted. Anéton never missed an opportunity to gamble. He turned and made his way towards the raucous game.

"Has Anéton robbed you of all your coins yet?" Cédron grinned at the circle of Sumäeri warriors as he nudged his way next to his friend. "He's a terrible cheat."

Anéton gasped and looked at Cédron, his face a mask of feigned horror. "Betrayed by my best friend!" The legionnaire clasped a hand to his chest as if struck, then leaned towards the circle. "This guy has neither luck nor ability. I can beat him with my eyes closed, and he resents my superior skill."

Cédron shoved his shoulder against Anéton's and laughed with the rest of the group. A pile of glinting flecksun coins rose in front of Anéton, but it wasn't much higher than those of the riders.

"I see you've learned both discretion and humility," Cédron said, nodding at the blue coins.

Anéton turned his head to look at his friend, tapping his temple with a forefinger. "I am not very smart, but I do know that being outnumbered two-hundred to one justifies the occasional loss."

Jeers and laughter rose from the riders, along with a few pieces of flatbread thrown at Anéton's head. He ducked and laughed with the group, then pointed across the circle at the next man to throw the dice. Trilläen grabbed the handful of dice but didn't toss them.

"It grows late," he said, looking at the two from Dúlnat then up to the deity lowering himself from the sky.

The Sumäeri captain excused himself from the game and indicated that Cédron should accompany him with a sideways nod. Anéton raised an eyebrow, and Cédron nodded. The legionnaire gathered his flecksun coins and shoved them into his pack. He followed Cédron and Trilläen as they walked back toward the camouflaged airship.

"Have you any word from Roväen or the twins?" Trilläen asked.

Swallowing against the tightness in his throat, Cédron shook his head. "No, and this silent waiting is unbearable."

Cédron looked up to find Trilläen staring at him with his bright, amethyst eyes. "I agree. What does your device show you?"

Cèdron pulled out the diptych compass Sahráron made him and lifted the ivory-and-lapis lid. He willed the instrument to show him his uncle. The inside cover of the compass was dark for a moment, then the inky black wavered. Roväen's face shimmered into view, his lips pursed tight, and his eyes downcast.

Behind him, the twins marched with their hands behind their backs. Each Shäeli had a Yezman guard herding them with grips on their arms or shoulders. The drops of sweat clinging to Cèdron's neck chilled and shivered down his spine. He could feel the blood draining from his face.

"They have been captured by the Yezman," Cèdron croaked. He cleared his throat and held the compass for the others to see.

Trilläen squinted and moved closer. "Those aren't Zaouni. It looks like civilians have taken them." He stood straight and nodded to Cèdron and Anèton. "I could have my Wing do a sweep for them, but I fear that might look like a hostile move, and it could jeopardize any rescue attempts. It's bad enough some of my läeniers have fed from the domestic herds just outside the city walls."

"You're right," Anèton said. He frowned and fingered his sash, touching the tops of each of the throwing knives he kept hidden there. "What if we posed as pilgrims for the Zholi Festival? We could use that contraption of yours to track them. However," he scrubbed at the back of his neck. "You two will stick out like pearls in obsidian. You will need disguises, or you'll never convince the guards that you're pilgrims."

Cèdron glanced eastward, where the top curve of Lord Shamar was barely visible above the dunes and shivered. "It's getting dark and chilly. We can at least wear cloaks and hope for the best." He rummaged in his pouch and pulled out the scalloped shell. "With luck, we'll find allies that can assist us."

A quarter of an hour later, Captain Villinäes had organized watches and got the three of them aboard a läenier headed for Taboriz. Cédron used the windstone to create a gentle sand spiral ahead of them to hide their approach. The swirling sand, coupled with the lowering of Lord Shamar in the sky, kept the läenier and her burden unseen until they landed on the main road leading to the western gates. Trilläen thanked the rider and dismissed her back to the Wing.

The three cloaked "pilgrims" scurried through the western gates of Taboriz with the last of the authentic revelers. They blended easily with the rough laborers returning to their homes from the narrow harbor in the river that wreathed the city like a lapis lazuli necklace. The Zaouni guards, poised to shove the gates closed and secure the wall for the night, gave the group no more than a cursory glance.

Anèton led them down the main thoroughfare then ducked into one of the narrower side streets lined with awnings and shanties. "That was almost too easy. What do you think, should we head deeper into the city or search around the perimeter?"

Trilläen leaned around the corner building and looked back towards the gate. "We may be fine as long as there isn't a curfew in the city for the festival. There aren't many people on the streets now." He put a hand on Cèdron's shoulder. "What does your gadget tell you?"

Cèdron pulled the compass from the sash at his waist and opened the lid. He closed his eyes, imagining his uncle and cousins. They were seated in a small room with a pale light somewhere. The dial on the base of the compass swung to their right, angling towards the harbor.

Cèdron snapped the lid shut and stowed the compass back into the sash, pointing towards the road heading south. "We go this way."

Sénna woke to the homey scent of warm flatbread and beans with overtones of coriander and cumin that promised a simple but tasty breakfast. Her stomach rumbled, and she rolled over, sitting up. She smiled at Raziz, who lay curled up on the carpet beside her. His long eyelashes cast shadows on his cheek as Lord Shamar's rays poured in from the gap between the wooden shutters.

Tapestries depicting scenes of Yezman dancers or battle scenes hung on most of the clay brick walls, and pierce-work bronze lanterns decorated the beams stretching across the ceiling. The cloak she'd worn last night lay draped across the burgundy sofa pillow that stretched the length of the wall behind her. The scent of spices and baking bread caused a pang of homesickness in Sénna's chest.

The sound of shrieks and laughter startled Sénna and woke Raziz. He yawned, rubbing his eyes, and squinted in the direction of the noise. His older sister charged into the room, squealing and jumping onto the sitting pillows. The hem of her jade dress swirled around her ankles, showing the worn toes on her leather slippers. Their older brother Caliz careened through the door after her, his bony knees peeping through a hole in his pants. He lunged toward his sister and tripped over Raziz's stretching form.

"I've got you, Zah—" Caliz cried, then gasped as he hit the thick carpets.

Zahna stuck out her tongue and lept from the pillows. Bouncing over her prone brothers, she stopped in the archway between the rooms. "Dadaji says to come to breakfast." Then she twirled away in a flash of green impudence.

Caliz picked himself up and scowled at his little brother. "I would have caught her if you hadn't sprawled across the whole room."

Raziz winked at Sénna, then turned towards his brother and bowed. "My most humble apologies, honored brother, wisest of the wise, strongest of the strong, and I don't only mean your smell."

Caliz's pacified expression flushed, and he rounded on his little brother. "You little beast, I'll—"

Raziz giggled and darted behind Sénna. "You'll have to catch me first, and you'll have to go through her."

Sénna was rescued from the crashing waves of sibling

rivalry by the appearance of a wizened and bent man carrying a steaming pot of tea. The aroma of mint filled the room, and she felt her stomach protest its emptiness.

The withered man smiled at her, creases in his leathery cheeks nearly obscuring his eyes, which twinkled behind round, wire-rimmed spectacles. "I am Razelf Grozen. Forgive my rambunctious grandchildren. They have yet to master the art of hospitality."

Razelf waved the children into the eating area, glaring at each of the boys as they passed before bowing deeply to Sénna. "You are welcome to our humble home. May you blossom and thrive here like the desert rose that you so closely resemble."

Sénna could feel the heat creep up her cheeks and scorch her ears. Having two older brothers, she was more accustomed to teasing than flattery. She inclined her head and swallowed hard, trying to get her complexion under control.

"M-my name is Sénna Králl. I-I am in your debt, sir," she stammered, brushing her sweaty hands on the sides of her thighs.

"And mine," Raziz piped up, poking his head from behind Sénna and puffing out his scrawny chest. "I rescued her from Zaran and brought her here, Dadaji."

Razelf scratched his head, causing a few wispy white strands to wave in the air. "Indeed, your adventure yesterday and our men catching those Shäeli intruders have nearly overshadowed the excitement of the Zholi Festival. Your parents are quite upset with you, young scamp," Razelf said. He shook a wavering finger at Raziz, who grinned and shrugged his shoulders.

Sénna caught her breath at the man's mention of Shäeli intruders. They had to be from Trilläen's Wing. Some of them must have come looking for her when she didn't return. She took several slow, deep breaths to get her racing heart under control.

"Don't the Shäeli trade with the merchants of Taboriz?" Sénna asked, keeping her face neutral and her voice as inflectionless as she could.

Razelf's rheumy eyes peered at her. He squinted at her face and shook his head. "You're no Shäeli. You have the look of the Askári - hmm, and the yellow eyes of the Meq'qan, but…." He shuffled towards the low table and offered one of the square cushions to Sénna. "We're not going to puzzle all this out on an empty stomach. Let us hear your story over some food."

Sénna barely tasted the spiced beans slathered in yogurt or the fresh flatbread. She ran through several different stories she could tell, but none of them had any ring of authenticity. She knew Raziz's Dadaji would see the truth, despite his low vision. All grandparents seem to have an acute sensitivity to deception.

"I recently escaped an attack on Táksabai by the Garanth army. They razed our fields and city, leaving only death and destruction. Those I'm with include the Shäeli Sumäeri. We came to request assistance from the Zhoula and her Zaouni Warriors. We were attacked in the desert just west of here by another enemy. Men mounted on alzayten wearing black clothing and red amulets assailed us, damaging our ship and wounding several of our members. My companions called them Hazzara." Sénna paused, twisting a strand of brown hair around her first finger.

Razelf took a bite of his honeyed flatbread and nudged Raziz, who was squirming in his seat. He passed the boy the stuffed dates then waved her to continue.

Sénna inhaled and eased her breath out slowly. "I came here to try and find a way to approach the Zhoula and encountered Raziz and his family." She smiled at the little boy whose sticky hands were dripping honey all over his clothes. "They suggested I go to the bathhouse, which I did. There, I stumbled into more of the Hazzara and overheard them conspiring against the Zhoula and her family. I escaped them at first, but then Zaran captured us."

"May the mites of a thousand shezaki infest his armpits," Raziz mumbled as he sucked his fingers.

Razelf looked at his grandson over the rims of his spectacles and frowned. "Raziz, it is both unwise and ill-mannered to speak so disparagingly of your elders."

Raziz opened his mouth and took a deep breath, ready to protest, but his Dadaji held up a hand. "However, in this case, I must agree with your sentiment."

Sénna watched the boy's argument deflate as giggles broke out all around the table. She laughed as well, but she could hear the hysterical note in her voice. It was fortunate that Razelf didn't punish them for what they did to Zaran, but that didn't mean she'd completed her task. Sénna still desperately needed to warn the Zhoula about the Hazzara's threat. The men spoke like the attack on the city would be sooner rather than later, but she didn't know how much time she had.

Sénna found the savory breakfast and mint tea the best food she'd had in days, but they soured in her stomach as she thought about facing the Hazzara again, especially alone and in this unfamiliar city. She had to return to Cédron and the others with her news.

Together, they would need to rescue the captured Shäeli. Then they could decide to either stay and fight or flee for a safer haven, but the longer it took to find them, the fewer options would be available.

"Can you help me find my friends so that we can warn your rulers?" Sénna asked. She dipped her hands into the brass bowl of water and wiped them on the little towel laid next to it. "The attack could come anytime. I don't want either my friends or your Zhoula caught by surprise."

Razelf harrumphed and pointed to the tiny bowls at each place setting. The two older children complied and dipped their fingers. Raziz was still sucking the last of the honey when his grandfather grabbed the tiny towel and dipped a corner into the bowl. He proceeded to wipe Raziz's face and fingers while the boy squirmed and writhed on his cushion.

"I can't help you with that," he said, placing his bony hand on her forearm when her face fell. "But perhaps my spouse can. She is in the markets, which are filters for all the information in Taboriz."

Raziz jumped up from his cushion and grabbed Sénna's hand, tugging her to her feet. "Come on. I'll take you to her!"

"I'll go with you," Razelf said, rocking forward and using the table as leverage to ease his creaking legs into a standing position. "You two stay here and clean up."

Caliz and Zahna groaned, but their Dadaji's brows furrowed above his spectacles. The children hopped to their feet and began clearing the plates before he could admonish them further. Razelf led Sénna and Raziz through the cozy home, beneath beaded curtains, into the foyer where the leaded glass in the wooden front door cast colorful beams of light onto the floor and walls. Raziz let go of Sénna's hand and raced to open the door.

"May you exit our home with your thirst slaked, your hunger abated, and your heart filled with gladness," Raziz bowed and waved Sénna over the threshold.

Razelf hobbled behind Sénna and whacked Raziz softly on the back of his head. "Quit showing off. If you wanted to impress us, you should have used your manners at the table."

Raziz grinned and rubbed his hair back into place. The three of them made their way through the narrow, flagstone streets. A myriad of awnings of all colors and patterns hung from the stone walls casting paltry shade from Lord Shamar's harsh rays. Men and women lounged in their doorways beneath the awnings.

The men sat in circles smoking hookahs. The women ground flour, mended clothing, tended children, and performed countless other domestic tasks outside in the morning air before the sweltering heat of the day drove them indoors.

The air was already hot and dry, and Sénna could feel the skin inside her nostrils burn and crack. She opened her mouth to breathe, then closed it again. The acrid smells of animal and human urine were overwhelming. She tried not to gag.

Sénna wrapped her thin, yellow scarf around her face as a buffer and took shallow breaths. It was still damp from its washing and cooled the air she breathed through it. The flagstones warmed her feet through the flimsy suede slippers she had worn into the city. She prayed their destination wasn't far.

Raziz led them through the second wall's open gate and into the market level. The change felt to Sénna like slipping into a soothing pool. The walls inside the second level and all subsequent levels rising to the palace teemed with lush greenery. Climbing plants, flowers, even fruits, and vegetables poked through the vertical gardens' leaves and vines.

The temperature dropped several degrees, and the humidity due to the plant life was enough for Sénna to remove the scarf from her face. She inhaled deeply and sighed, smiling. Orange blossom, jasmine, and vanilla wafted above the soil's earthier scents and what could only be ozryk dung used for fertilizer.

The market stretched along both sides of the street, with vendors hawking their wares under awnings and tents that clung to walls in every shape and color imaginable. Sénna marveled at the jewel-toned pyramids of powdered pigments used for dying fabrics and the tall cones of spices in shallow bowls.

Glass canisters filled with blazesand lined both sides of the street, their glow muted in Lord Shamar's morning light. Pierced metal lanterns and colorful carpets hung on every available wall, hook, or makeshift display possible. Bins crammed onto rickety tables overflowed with ripe succulents, nuts, fresh and dried fruits, and flowers. Sénna had never considered such abundance possible in the desert.

"What do you think of our city?" Razelf asked, glancing sidelong at Sénna as they followed the little boy. "Is it anything like your home in Táksabai?"

Sénna snorted and shook her head. "No, nothing like my home. There, everything is gray and brown. We have machines and technologies that do much of our work for us, but we don't have the warmth or the palette of colors here."

Sénna reached out and touched a broad, waxy leaf on the wall and lifted it to find tiny round clusters of white fruits. She looked at Razelf and raised an eyebrow. He smiled and nodded, so she picked one and popped it into her mouth. The taut skin broke between her teeth, bursting into a sweet-tart juice with soft, fleshy meat. Sénna closed her eyes and chewed, swallowing reluctantly.

"The ancient Yezman must have been brilliant engineers to create methods of both cooling and feeding their people," Sénna said. She wiped a drop of juice escaping her lips and licked her finger. "I could live here for the fresh food alone, and the vibrancy of colors almost makes up for this intolerable heat."

Razelf smiled, exposing the three teeth left in his deep purple gums. "Taboriz is a rare gem. We are prosperous and safe. Our Zaouni warriors are fierce and respected far and wide. I know you are worried about these Hazzara, but they will have difficulty launching an attack from the outside."

Sénna pursed her lips, thinking of Zaran. "They won't be coming from outside."

"We're here!" Raziz said. He grabbed Sénna's hand again and tugged her through the archway in the street and into a large, square courtyard. "Look, there is my Naniji."

Sénna's eyes followed the boy's finger. Blossoming orange and lemon trees in painted porcelain pots lined the stone courtyard walls at even intervals. The walls rose two stories, with the second story open to the courtyard by a walkway bordered by lacework railings. Archways led to additional rooms on both levels, all filled with people coming and going, fetching and carrying. The center of the stone courtyard held an enormous fountain with several layers of water spraying up and around the tiled pool.

Beyond the fountain sat a shriveled woman with a jade-colored scarf wrapped around her head. Her leathery jowls hung in drapes above a voluminous jade and yellow dress. The circular platform that held her seat was raised several feet off the ground and over-filled with cushions. Attendants whizzed to and from the woman like twillings, whose wings beat so fast they were nearly invisible.

Sénna gaped as the woman's cackle rang out, echoing across the courtyard, followed by the crack of a whip. Raziz's Naniji was holding court. Sénna recognized the postures of supplicants, bowing and entreating, the advisors leaning in to offer opinions, and the guards posted on both sides of each archway on both levels.

Raziz dragged Sénna in front of the crone, displacing a middle-aged couple negotiating the price of the wagon load of dutars and sitars. The long-necked, two-stringed instruments appeared to be well-crafted, at least to Sénna's practiced eye. The woman plucked a tune demonstrating the lute's pure tone while her partner scowled at Raziz and continued to make his pitch.

"You hear the pure notes of the strings and the resonance of the bowl. You will not find a more elegant sound, one that will elicit the strains of Hamra's agony when she learns of Laylur's betrayal," the merchant said.

Raziz stepped in front of the man, bowing low and pulling Sénna over with him. "Wise and kind Naniji," he began, dropping his eyes to the pillows that held the woman's sandalled feet. "We come to you, humble servants, with important news." He rose and pulled Sénna upright. "My companion and I—"

"What is that noise?" The ancient woman's brows knitted

together, creating crevices between eyes that cascaded down her nose. "What happened to the music?"

An attendant with a jewel-toned headdress accentuating her high cheekbones knelt on a cushion at the woman's side and whispered into her ear, waving towards the musician. The ancient woman nodded, and the attendant pulled the merchant and his musician further from the platform to complete their business.

The crone peered down again at Raziz and Sénna. "Oh, it's my silken-tongued Raziz, is it? Are you here to charm me out of more sweets?"

The tips of the little boy's ears turned pink, and he grinned. "Not this time, Naniji. We have to get a message to the Zhoula. There are bad men—"

A young girl raced through the courtyard, leaping high over the neat pile of dutars. Her soft slippers skidded on the smooth marble floor, and she slid into Raziz's shoulder. He lurched forward, nearly smashing his face in his Naniji's lap. Sénna reached out to steady him. Raziz turned to face his assailant.

"Hey, watch where you're—" Raziz began, then stopped, his lips twisting sideways like he'd swallowed something bitter. "Oh, it's just you. What are you doing here?"

The girl drew herself up and looked down her very straight nose at Raziz, who stood a few inches shorter than she did. Several black coils escaped the purple and blue scarf holding her locs off her face. The girl turned from Raziz with a delicate "humph" and knelt at the woman's feet.

"Queen Marizen, may your eternal benevolence shine upon our markets," the girl touched her fingers to her lips, then her forehead, before extending them towards the Market Queen. "My father bade me request an audience with you. Foreigners bearing the shell of the seeker arrived at our door late last night. They have asked for sanctuary and information. Will you see them?"

The girl made it through her speech in a single breath and

inhaled when she'd finished. She opened her mouth to speak again, but Marizen put up a hand to stop her.

"Tell your father to bring me the foreigners, child," Marizen rubbed her chin, causing a few white whiskers to waver between her fingers. "Three groups of foreigners in one day is too many for coincidence."

The girl bowed her head to the floor then stood. Turning gracefully, she walked a few steps away from Marizen and Raziz, then put her fingers to her lips. A piercing whistle filled the courtyard, causing many to cringe and stick fingers into their ears.

Cédron woke to the aroma of cinnamon, cardamom, and pepper. He inhaled, shaking Anéton awake, and got to his feet. Trilläen stood by the bead curtain separating their sleeping quarters from the merchant's kitchen. He handed a mug of steaming tea to Cédron and Anéton, squatting down to speak without the merchant overhearing them.

"Our host sent his daughter to request an audience with Marizen, the Market Queen. Apparently, they are beholden to her in some way," he said, glancing over his shoulder at the clattering of dishes in the kitchen.

Anéton rolled to his feet and raised his cup in salute. "A fine start to a fine morning. Tea, good food, and an audience with the one person with whom we need to speak. Well done, my friend."

Cédron sipped his tea, hoping it would soothe the twisting of his innards. "We still don't know where Sénna, Rováen, and the twins are or if they are safe. We can only hope that this Market Queen person will accept the alzaytan as an offering and help us. What happens if she doesn't?"

Trilläen stood. "There's no point in worrying about what we have no control over. Let's take our challenges one at a time." He held back the beads for his companions to go through. "Breakfast awaits."

Baizen, the silk and textile merchant who responded to their appeal with the pilgrim's shell, beamed at his guests and waved them to the table laden with terra-cotta plates and stacks of warm flatbread. Bowls of nuts, figs, and dates nestled between pitchers of honey and cream.

"Come, my foreign friends. May you find both your stomachs and your minds satiated at my table," he sat cross-legged upon the long roll cushion beneath the low table.

"You don't have to invite me twice," Anéton said, flopping next to Baizen and snagging two rounds of the flatbread, slathering them with honey.

Cédron's nerves made his stomach turn, but he couldn't offend his host. He smiled and sat at the table, grabbing a date and a few nuts. He nibbled on his snack, only half-listening as Trilläen engaged their host in discussing the scarves and fabrics the merchant wove for the women of Taboriz. Cédron's eyes glazed at comparing hemp and cotton fiber tensile strengths and the appropriate blend of silk. He barely tasted the peppery tea that burned his throat but filled his belly with a pleasant warmth.

"…could hold a man and some of our acrobats use our scarves for aerial displays at the Zhoula's palace. My eldest dau—"

Baizen's comment was interrupted by a shrill whistle. Their host's jaws clamped shut, and he stood. "It is time," he said. "Queen Marzien has agreed to our audience."

A middle-aged man with greying temples swept into the courtyard. The metallic threads of his embroidered jacket glinted in Lord Shamar's light, making it glow against his bronze skin. Behind him came two pale-skinned travelers, one whose legionnaire jacket was almost as dirty-brown as his hair and the other with golden hair that vied with the older man's jacket for greater brilliance. A third silver-haired form stepped from behind Cédron, his amethyst eyes scanning the courtyard.

Sénna gasped, her heart pounding in her chest. "Cédron! Anéton! Trilläen! What has happened? Why are you here?" She skirted around Raziz and the older man to grasp each of their hands, her wide eyes bouncing from one to the other.

Cédron pulled her from Anéton, who began looking around at the people gathered. He stepped closer, looking her up and down with his dark green eyes. "When you didn't return, Rováen and the twins went looking for you. They never returned. Have you seen them?"

Sénna stiffened. She opened her mouth to answer, then clamped it shut. Sénna pulled her arms free of Cédron's grip but held his hand as she pulled him towards the Market Queen. Two guards on either side of the circular dais stepped between the foreigners and Marizen, their hands on the pommels of the curved swords at their hips, their faces stern. Raziz hissed at Sénna, and she froze.

"Queen Marizen, we humbly ask your indulgence. The Shäeli you have captured are part of our group. We have come to warn the Zhoula and her family of a plot to murder them." Sénna bowed low and pulled Cédron with her, glaring at Anéton to do the same. Trilläen was already on his knees. "We ask for your assistance in gaining an audience with her."

"That's what I was trying to tell you, Naniji!" Raziz cried, pulling at a tassel hanging off one of the long cushions.

Queen Marizen sat back on her pillows and pulled a long-stemmed pipe from the folds of her silk skirts. The woman with the yellow headdress leaned behind the dais and pulled a stick of smoking incense from the brass holder. She held the burning end into the pipe's bowl until the leaf lit.

Marizen sucked her cheeks deep into her sunken face and blew several plumes of fragrant vapor into the air. Sénna held her breath and sent a prayer to Orwaena. Raziz promised her that his Naniji would help, but it now appeared that she might have other plans.

Marizen tapped the bowl of her pipe on the side of the dais, loosening the leaf to allow more air. She held the bowl in her hand and pointed the long stem at the foreigners. "I may help you, but first, I need to hear the entire story."

The Market Queen cackled and coughed before sticking the pipe back in her mouth and sucking. She blew a few more clouds of smoke, then nodded. She pointed a bony finger at one of her attendants. "Bring me our prisoners."

chapter 32: A Reckoning

Two men approached from the opposite side of the square with Rovären and the twins. Behind them, two men carried Tóran, who appeared to be unconscious.

"Tóran!" Cédron ran to his brother, who was deposited unceremoniously on the ground at the woman's feet. "What happened to him? How did he come to be here?" Cédron looked at Rovären. "Did he have Räeshun with him?"

Läenshi turned her head to the side and spat. "No, the traitor handed our sister over to Algarik."

Cédron felt the world spin. He couldn't get a breath out at the thought of his beloved Räeshun in the hands of the rogue mage. He fell back onto the ground. His hands splayed on the flagstones, grounding him.

"We have to get her back," he gasped, looking up at Queen Marizen. Cédron stood, reeling slightly, then bowed to the Market Queen. "I am Cédron Varkáras of Dúlnat. I humbly offer two subdued alzaytan in exchange for your assistance."

Queen Marizen lifted her brows. "And what do you ask, in return for the alzaytan?"

"I seek the sacred windstone," Cédron announced, straightening his shoulders. "I have been chosen to assemble the Sceptre of Kulari and—"

"No, we need an audience with the Zhoula to warn her of the Hazzara attack—" Sénna interrupted, stepping in front of Cédron and bowing to the crone.

Läenshi and Säeshi jostled Sénna and Cédron to face Queen Marizen. "But first, we need to find the rogue mage Algarik and recover our sister."

Arguments ensued as the factions vied for Marizen's attention. Cédron's face flushed as he tried to yell above the twins and Sénna to get Rovaën's attention. A piercing whistle cut through the commotion and silenced the chaos. Queen Marizen stood.

"Silence!" she commanded.

Cédron was impressed with the authority she wielded within such a withered and shrunken frame. He glanced at the twins. Säeshi had a grip on Trilläen's arm, and Läenshi looked mutinous, but everyone ceased their arguments. Queen Marizen grabbed the gnarled walking stick next to her cushions and hobbled her way down the dais. She stood by Tóran.

The legionnaire groaned and rolled over onto his back. Cédron gasped. His brother's left cheek was purple, and the skin around his left eye was swollen. Dried blood coated a nasty wound to his temple. In his efforts to get the Market Queen to hear him, Cédron missed the signs of Tóran's recovery.

"Where am I?" Tóran croaked. He sat up, his hands clasping his head. "What happened?"

Läenshi bent down and grabbed him by the shirt, her muscles straining as she pulled him to his feet. She spun him to face Cédron and Marizen, pulling his arms up behind his back. Tóran winced, then squinted at Cédron.

"Cédron!" he took a step towards his brother, but Läenshi pulled his arms, holding him back. "I'm so sorry. I'm so—"

"Why did you take Räeshun to Algarik?" Cédron interrupted his brother. The heat and chill of anger and fear battled back and forth in his body, neither gaining the upper hand. He grabbed Tóran by the shoulders and shook him. "How could you betray me?"

"It wasn't me," Tóran slumped, his eyes closed. He looked at Säeshi. "Please, will you show him?"

Roväen clasped Cédron's arm, shaking his head at Tóran. "No, but I will tell him. The demon infected Tóran with a parasite during his captivity. The creature took over his mind. Tóran has managed to overcome much of the creature's power, but he remains compromised and a threat."

"That doesn't matter now," Tóran said. He looked at Marizen. "I came here with a group of men known as Hazzara. We got in through the public baths. Our mission was to destroy the Zaouni and the Zhoula."

The men and women surrounding Marizen gasped, chattering at once at Tóran's announcement. Cédron's jaw dropped. His brother had been forced to work with their enemies by a demon implanted in his head. He felt a deep sadness at what Tóran has had to endure since his capture. He had little basis for conceiving the horrors his brother had faced. Cédron was looking at a stranger.

Marizen surveyed the exchange between her guests and pounded her stick on the flagstones. "O unwary twillings, you warble so eloquently on the bough, filling yourselves with your rightness, until the serpent among you casts you upon the ground and devours you and all around you." She shook her head. "You have all come here for different reasons. The only thing that is clear to me is that you *all* pose a threat to our peaceful city. I do not accept your tribute. You must leave my city."

"But wait, what about the threat to the Zhoula?" Sénna asked, pulling Raziz with her as she knelt before Marizen. "We have to warn her of the Hazzara."

Marizen squinted at Sénna, who had Raziz's hand clasped in hers. "May the delicate bud of your youth blossom into the wisdom of the flower. Be seen, be beautiful, but do not speak out of turn. You have befriended my Raziz, but that doesn't lessen your threat. We will tell the Zaouni of your visit. They will protect the Zhoula."

The Market Queen's guards surrounded the group, blocking Marizen from view. The circle grew tighter, squeezing the foreigners close together.

"Do not defy us, or it will be difficult for you to return to the desert from whence you came," Anzeri chided. She clapped her hands, and Cédron felt his wrists locked into restraints.

Sweat beaded along Cédron's hairline. The last time he'd been restrained, his kin drained the Árk'äezhi from his body. The memories caused him to hyperventilate. He looked at Rováen and Anéton with wide eyes, but they both looked away. Nobody was fighting. Even the twins had the slumped shoulders of defeat.

Marizen's guards herded them toward the iron gate. Tóran stumbled into Cédron, knocking him off balance. Cédron grasped his brother's arm, holding them both from falling over. When Cédron's fingers touched Tóran's skin, a jolt of Árk'äezhi shot from Cédron's hand to Tóran's flesh. The tattoos surrounding Cédron's heart flared to life, responding to the creature inhabiting Tóran's mind.

"Laylur's beast! Marizen gasped, echoing the whispers of those surrounding her. "What is happening?"

The men and women escorting them out of the courtyard turned, encircling the group with weapons drawn. The Sumäeri closed in around Cédron, their postures protective. Cédron couldn't tell if they were ready to intervene between the guards or Tóran, but it didn't matter which. They were there for him, willing to risk their lives for him, and that was what mattered.

Beneath his fingers, Tóran sank to his knees. His face twisted in pain. When Tóran opened his eyes, they glittered dark blue.

"Tóran!" Cédron gasped, shaking his brother's arm. "What's happening?"

Tóran dropped his head, pounding both forehead and fists on the flagstone street. "I can't let it take over again!" he cried, roaring and clawing at his braid. "Get it out or kill me. Please!"

Cédron gaped as Tóran yanked his braid to the side, exposing a hole in the base of his skull just above the neck. The slit was no bigger than a thumbnail, hidden just inside Tóran's hairline. A sparkling dribble of dark blue ooze rimmed the lip of the incision. Whatever that thing was, it occupied the inside of his brother's skull. Cédron felt sick.

"I-I don't know what to do," Cédron stammered. He looked at Sénna, then at Rováen, but both just returned blank stares.

Säeshi touched Cédron's shoulder. "Use a windstone. It's the only thing that might get that thing out of Tóran without killing him."

Cédron pulled the palm-sized yellow stone from his pouch and nodded at his cousin. "Hold him down for me," he ordered, nodding at the Sumäeri. "Wait, I need a container. I don't want anyone else infected from touching it."

Nobody moved.

Sénna darted through the gate and returned a moment later carrying one of the bulky blazesand canisters. "Will this work? We don't know what that thing will do, so maybe the sand will neutralize it." She looked at Raziz and the guards surrounding her. "Can one of you show me how to open this lid?"

One of Marizen's guards turned the dial on the lid and pressed the hollow in the center, springing the top open. The glow of the blazesand made Cédron squint. He saw several inches of open space in the jar and prayed to Hamra it would hold the entity in Tóran's head. He nodded to the Sumäeri, who turned the legionnaire face-down. Läenshi and Säeshi each grabbed an arm, while Rováen and Trilläen stretched out Tóran's legs and straddled them.

"Give them room," Marizen commanded her guards. "Be ready if something goes awry."

The guards stepped back but kept their weapons raised and ready. Cédron felt the pressure of every eye on him as he closed his eyes and accessed his Árk'äezhi. He took a deep breath and focused on relocating the gooey blue entity in his brother's skull into the blazesand canister.

Warmth spread through his chest, down his arms, and through his hands into Tóran's skull. Cédron held the windstone over the incision, and the other hand cupped Tóran's forehead off the stones. He focused his energy on siphoning the creature from the base of the skull.

Cédron let out a long breath and let his shoulders relax as the glittering blue sludge flowed slowly from the incision. It didn't relocate from the skull to the canister as he envisioned, making his progress slow. The entity resisted Cédron's pull, forcing him to increase the Árk'äezhi strength. Tóran moaned and tried to roll over, but the Sumäeri held him fast.

"Keep going," Säeshi grunted, pressing down on Tóran's writhing shoulder. "I can sense it getting weaker."

Rováen and Trilläen both nodded at him, their knuckles white as they pressed Tóran's thighs to the ground. Cédron clenched his jaw and poured his magical energy through the windstone and into his brother's head, activating the relocation principle of the windstone. The resistance he felt was elastic, like he was pulling a rope taut before it snapped. Tóran struggled and screamed in pain.

Cédron's hand began to tremble. He was running out of Árk'äezhi fighting with the creature and couldn't get it free of his brother's body. Sweat beaded on his upper lip, and he took a deep breath. Bearing down, Cédron pulled energy from the source in his heart and felt the burn as it coursed through his blood. Tóran's screams muted behind the rushing of the power flowing out of him.

Above Tóran's head, a floating ball of dense, dark blue muck wriggled and oozed in midair. Sénna hovered with the blazesand canister, waiting for the last of the filaments to pull free of Tóran's head. Grunting with effort, Cédron raised the stone, tugging the last of the entity in a thin string. Tóran's agonized screams increased until, with a *snap,* the creature released his hold on Tóran.

"Got it," Sénna cried as she shoved the lid over the blue entity, forcing it into the blazesand container.

Tóran collapsed, his face pressed against the flagstones, breathing heavily. He rolled over, panting with the effort.

"We have to stop them," he grunted, trying to sit up.

Cédron squatted next to him. "Stop who?"

The canister in Sénna's hands emitted a high-pitched whine and began vibrating. She gasped, placing the canister on the ground, and backed away as it glowed bright blue. Seconds later, the jar exploded, raining blazesand and fine blue glitter over everyone assembled. Anzeri threw herself over the diminutive Marizen, protecting the Market Queen from the debris.

"Don't let it touch your skin," Tóran cried, covering his head with his arms.

Cédron stood, sweeping his arm in an arc and using the windstone to whip a stiff breeze through the courtyard. He circled his hand, creating a slow cyclone, trapping the sparkling blue sand in its grip. He lifted his hand, expelling the feeble hurricane into the air where it dissipated far above the city.

Cédron turned back to Tóran. "Who do we need to stop?"

"The Hazzara," Tóran stared up at his brother with wide, haunted eyes. "They're going to—"

An explosion shook the ground, causing vases and planters to topple and break. A dark plume of smoke rose from the west end of the city. Shrieks and screams from the Yezman in the courtyard added to the chaos. Cédron looked down at his brother. Tóran sat with his head in his hands. Cédron bent toward his brother, barely able to hear his words.

"We're too late."

chapter 33: Unintended Consequences

Algarik circled his rinzar above the thousands of stationary stone figures, still no further south than when he'd left them. He gnashed his teeth together, fighting the pulsing ache in his temple. Four days and Ruzik hadn't completed infusing their breastplates with the red jasper medallions. Were the deities conspiring against him from their lofty realm?

When he'd arrived in Aromberk Fortress, he found no fresh food in the kitchens, no cooks, and only one guard for his solitary prisoner. Tormenting that forsaken soul gave him a few moments of pleasure, but then the prisoner lost consciousness. Algarik hoped his brother would live long enough for more torture.

Algarik stayed in Aromberk Fortress only long enough to rest, feed his rinzar and retrieve his silver wand. He fitted the torus knot holding his ruby firestone into the prongs at the end of the talisman. The silver would amplify the stone's power and allow him to control Ruzik's creations once they'd attracted the Maüli to inhabit them.

Now, as his rinzar spiraled to land, Algarik scrubbed his face, erasing the fatigue and frustration of his journey. He shivered from the cold, his cloak and gloves inadequate for the high elevation and wind chill of flying. As the rinzar neared the bare ground of Nuriak's Cauldron, the acrid air seeped into his lungs, causing him to cough. He hated traveling among the acidic pools and bubbling geysers of this barren stretch of land.

"Well met," Marik hailed him from his tent on the outskirts of the standing army. "How did you find Aromberk Fortress? Was the food up to your standard?"

Algarik took a deep breath and let it out his nose before turning to face Marik. The journeymage had a pleasant smile fixed on his face, one that didn't reach the eyes that fluttered upwards, showing only the whites. Marik's knit cap maintained its usual smushed position, awkward and loose on his head. Algarik clenched his fists, restraining the urge to alter his agent's features.

"As usual, the food was adequate, the prisoner was miserable, and I return to you rested and ready to march on Samshäeli," Algarik smiled through a clenched jaw. "How much longer until Ruzik has the soldiers ready to march?"

Marik's eyes rolled up and fluttered. "Oh, I believe they're ready," he said, turning to face the man in question. "He wanted to wait for you to return before moving them too far – something about harnessing Maüli energy being more than he could manage alone – something to that effect. I assume you're prepared to handle the angry spirits should they inhabit the warriors?"

"I have no doubt," Algarik said, turning away from his agent and striding towards Ruzik.

Algarik's eyes narrowed as he approached the Yezman sculptor. Ruzik's attention was focused on the facial features of one of his stone soldiers. As Algarik watched, the sculptor's hands caressed the warrior's face, smoothing the stone and repairing gouges as if the rock were soft clay. He raised his eyebrows. The man had some natural talent, but he also had some latent Árk'äezhi that Algarik wasn't aware of heretofore. He would have to watch the sculptor more carefully.

"Ruzik," Algarik called in greeting. "The day is half over already. Are we ready to march?"

Ruzik ran a loving finger down his creation's cheek, pinching the chin into a quick cleft, then turned. "Ah, our fearless leader returns. I await your command, O Great One," Ruzik bowed.

Algarik smirked. If only the man meant half the words that spewed from his lips. He wasn't fooled; Ruzik hated and resented him for removing him from his fate and forcing this labor upon him. Still, Laylur had given Algarik the power to reanimate the sculptor, so he'd used it. He hoped he wouldn't regret that decision.

"I command you to get this army moving southwest," Algarik snarled, squeezing his hands into fists so tightly that his fingernails drew blood in the fleshy parts of his palms. "I want to engage the Shäeli before they have time to prepare for the onslaught."

Ruzik raised an eyebrow. "You know my misgivings, mage. We should head east to avoid the angry spirits as long as possible. Do you have a way to control this army when the Maüli roaming from the battle in Askári-bai join it?"

Algarik pulled the wand from his cloak. "This silver wand, coupled with the ruby, should keep them in check. We will head west first, then south to Samshäeli once we have our Maüli. Move them out."

Ruzik bowed, touching his fingers to his forehead. "As you command," he said.

Algarik strode back to the encampment where Marik and his contingent of two hundred Hazzara and their stolen husan packed and prepared to leave. The Hazzara moved efficiently, dropping and folding tents in seconds, with the camp obliterated from sight within half an hour.

Ruzik mounted his husan and rode directly behind the Hazzara, leading his stone soldiers. Marik and the Hazzara spurred their husan into a canter. Ruzik followed suit, and Algarik heaved a sigh, closing his eyes in gratitude when the stone soldiers picked up the pace to match. A swirling dust cloud grew around the army as the soldiers trudged quickly over the wasteland that was Molonark. The Hazzara had their turbans to cover their faces from the dust and poisoned air. The stone soldiers needed no such accouterments.

High above the army, Algarik scouted ahead astride his rinzar. The Tawaki Chasm route was clear, with no sign of opposition from the Tawaki or the Askári coming from Lake Juláni. He circled and flew back to the army, pulling some dried meat from his pouch. The rinzar smelled the flesh and squawked, turning its head sideways and snapping at the mage.

"Silence, you ungrateful wretch," Algarik growled and zapped the rinzar's neck with a thin line of fire from his finger.

The raptor shrieked and shook its head, continuing on its course. The long day was uneventful, even dull astride the rinzar. The army below marched without ceasing, and the Hazzara escort demonstrated their dedication to duty with the uninterrupted ride. These men were hardened to the rigors of travel and battle. Algarik was pleased with the results of his investment with Zen Hazad, the Old Man of the desert, to train these men; they had proven themselves many times over in his eyes.

Lord Shamar's trek through the skies neared its end, and Orwaena's scarlet hues painted the eastern horizon. The army crossed the Tawaki Chasm and was within thirty leagues of the Garanth lands. Tomorrow, they would skirt the northern edges of Askári-bai and have the highest likelihood of attracting Maüli. Algarik planned to land shortly and camp. He would need a good meal and rest if he were to be at full strength tomorrow for the challenges he would face.

The haze below darkened in the enveloping dusk. Algarik gazed ahead for a spot to camp. His body and mind both ached from the strain of travel and maintaining his spell on the rinzar. The husan and Hazzara were also weary, and their pace slowed. The dust cloud surrounding the army settled.

Algarik scrubbed his face and ran his fingers through his hair. He reached for his flask and took two deep swallows. The liquor burned his throat but helped to clear the throbbing in his temple. He heard a grating noise like fingernails on stone and cast about for the source. Below, some of the stone soldiers in the trailing right flank broke ranks. Their shrieks assaulted Algarik's ears even high above them.

As he watched, more stone soldiers twitched, their extremities jerking and faces animating. He watched spellbound as their jaws opened and screams erupted from their mouths. More and more soldiers broke ranks, surging forward and overrunning their comrades. Algarik scanned the leading edge for Ruzik's colorful turban among the sea of black-clad Hazzara. The sculptor was turned in the saddle watching with wide eyes as his creations moved of their own accord.

It took several minutes for the reality of what he was witnessing to sink into Algarik's fatigued mind. The jasper in the soldiers' chests attracted Maüli. But they were too far east to draw the Maüli from Askári-bai. So what Maüli were joining with the jasper? Algarik thought for a moment, then dropped his head into his hands. These were the tormented souls of the slaughtered Garanth from his initial strike at the beginning of Suntide. The Garanth spirits were powerful, and he knew he wouldn't be able to control them.

Algarik watched the dust cloud stir up higher from where he circled high above as more angry spirits melded with the stone. Their shrieks blended with the cries of terror from the Hazzara and their husan. The stone army bore down on their human escort, crushing men and beasts indiscriminately. Ruzik's blue turban dodged among the soldiers, his body holding a glow of light Algarik had never seen before.

"Laylur's beast," Algarik swore, digging the silver wand from his cloak. "Ruzik can't hold them all."

Channeling what strength he had through the silver wand and into his firestone, Algarik poured his Árk'äezhi into the front line of soldiers. The stone figures wavered, the Maüli inside them writhing in torment. They shrieked their defiance and burst through his line of energy. Wave upon wave of stone warriors trampled the scores of Hazzara, whose firestones were woefully inadequate against the raging Garanth spirits.

Algarik slumped in the saddle, his energy spent and his chest heaving. The silver wand was hot to the touch, but his firestone was cold, depleted. The army continued its rush southward, charging ahead toward any and all life they could end in their righteous rage. They could run without stopping, without direction, without him. He spied Ruzik galloping behind the army, his Árk'äezhi glowing around him like a halo. The soldiers still respected him as their creator, but Algarik wasn't sure how much control the sculptor had over the Maüli.

Algarik felt the cold certainty of fate in his bones. He'd unleashed a force upon the land that was too great to control. They would slaughter everyone and everything in their path until Muralia was an empty husk, starting with Yezmarantha. He stared at the dust cloud diminishing on the horizon and began to chuckle. Then he began to laugh, a full-body, deep, belly laugh.

Algarik had inadvertently set into motion events that would accomplish the Great Demon's wishes. It was his ultimate goal – the torment and destruction of life. Wiping tears of laughter from his eyes, Algarik nudged the rinzar toward the ground. The beast began a slow, downward spiral. He continued to chuckle as he landed and reinforced the binding spell upon it.

Algarik built a fire and ate the dried meat and fruit in his pack. He raised his flask and toasted the scores of corpses littering the ground a hundred yards beyond his camp. He'd lost all of his Hazzara today, but they were a fitting tribute to the Great Demon's plan. Rising to his feet, Algarik walked toward the carnage that was what remained of his men.

The scent of human excrement mingled with the metallic tang of blood. Algarik pulled the end of his turban down and wrapped it over his nose and mouth. It didn't quell the stench, but it dampened it enough to allow him to walk among the dead until he found what he was seeking. It didn't take long. Algarik spotted the knit cap first. It still clung to Marik's head, bent and distorted as his agent's skull. Marik's eyes stared sightlessly toward the mangled corpse of the husan draped over his body.

"A fitting end to a thorn in my side," Algarik raised his flask again and took a swallow. He turned and made his way back to his small campfire and stretched his legs toward the warmth of the fire. "Tonight, I will sleep better than I have in a sennight."

chapter 34: News from the Desert

The rumble from the explosion caused Sénna's heart to race as she scanned the skyline seeking the source of the danger.

"Naniji, Naniji!"

Sénna turned toward the high-pitched call just as Raziz's sister Zahna careened through the iron gate, racing toward the Market Queen. The little girl's amber face was ashen, and tears glistened in tracks down her cheeks.

"Naniji, they destroyed the Zaouni armory!" Zahna cried, throwing herself into her grandmother's arms. "Papan went to help, but there are men in black turbans everywhere. They chased Papan and Caliz. I'm so scared." Zahna buried her sobs in Marizen's chest, her hands gripping the silk of Marizen's dress with white knuckles.

Sénna felt her knees buckle. Hazzara. They were here in the city. She looked at Cédron, whose pale skin had a sheen of sweat covering it. They both turned to Tóran as he staggered to his feet. He leaned to one side, his hand on his temple, then stood straight.

"They are headed for the palace to kill the Zhoula and her family," he said, lips compressed in a frown. "We have to protect them."

Anzeri stepped forward, her finger in Tóran's chest. "What is their plan? What do you know?"

Sénna took a step back in the face of the woman's fury. She watched Tóran's face flush, then go pale as he nodded.

"Our advance group came in through the baths. The owner is a sympathizer to the Hazzara cause. They destroyed the Zaouni armory as a distraction, hoping to pull as many guards from the palace as possible. Another group is making their way to the palace to hide until tonight. They plan to kill the Zhoula and her family after they've retired for the night," Tóran said, giving Rováen a pleading look. "I tried to warn you; I'm sorry."

Läenshi raised her hand to strike Tóran, but Rováen held her back. "You were compromised. We need to know everything. Tell us what you can."

Tóran swallowed and nodded. "There were three groups: one to destroy the armory, one sent into the desert to find and kill Cédron, and mine to sabotage the aqueducts and water apparatus. The second wave would sneak into the city after the explosion. They have places to hide during the Zholi Festival rituals today. They will attack the Zhoula and her family once they've gone to bed."

"Laylur's beast, such cowardice!" cursed Trilläen, glaring at Tóran.

Marizen stepped into the ring of foreigners, still holding

the clinging girl to her chest. "So, Zaran of the golden tongue has betrayed the city," she mused, stroking Zahna's shoulders.

"What will happen if these men sabotage the water screw or its gates?" Marizen turned to face Anzeri, her eyebrows raised into the folds of her forehead.

Anzeri frowned. "They will at least disrupt the water flow throughout the city. Depending on what damage they cause, the entire city will either be without water or immensely flooded."

"Zaran has already attempted to sabotage the gates releasing the water from the city, flooding the lower level of the city," Sénna said, and Raziz, at her side, nodded. "He took us into the inner workings at the screw's base and forced Raziz to loosen the bolts that hold the gears in place."

"The controls at the bathhouse level control the gates allowing water in from the qanats. If they are stuck open, the city will flood as the screw can't raise the water that quickly," Anzeri said, rubbing her temple with one calloused hand. "What we need is to contain these Hazzara and neutralize them without harming our citizens and all the pilgrims here for the festival."

"What we need first is to send someone to the airship to alert my Wing and bring them here," said Trilläen, pacing back and forth between Tóran and the twins. "Several of my riders and their läeniers are still recovering, and others went hunting. Läerei is out in the desert, gathering herbs. They won't be expecting an attack—"

"Cybél is still there," Anéton gasped. "We have to get her – I mean them – to safety."

Voices rose in disparate conversation as ideas were thrown in and tossed out. Sénna struggled to make sense of the racket and reconcile what she knew into a plan. The destruction of the armory was a distraction but not an immediate threat. The Zaouni would investigate, leaving the palace open for infiltration by the Hazzara, who weren't supposed to strike until after dark.

Thousands of pilgrims celebrating Zholi would soon clog the streets to hang their colorful mosaics and prepare for the feasts at dusk. The Hazzara could slip through the city unnoticed in the crowds. However, so could they. If Marizen could get a group to warn the Zhoula, then trap the Hazzara in the palace, perhaps they could find a way to defeat them. An idea started to form in Sénna's mind, and she placed a hand on Raziz's shoulder to get his attention.

"Can you get your Naniji to speak with me?" she asked, bending low so those surrounding them couldn't overhear.

Raziz's cheeks dimpled, and his eyes had a mischievous twinkle. "She'll do anything for me," he puffed out his chest. "I'm her favorite."

"No, you're not," Zahna sniffed, extricating herself from her grandmother's silk. "You're a flea on the bottom of a—"

"Silence, all of you," Marizen commanded. She narrowed her eyes at Rováen and pointed to his hand. "What sorcery have you brought into my city, Shäeli?"

Sénna glanced down at the elderly Sumäeri's right hand and gasped. The large stone on his wrist held the wavering image of a woman, another Sumäeri, with a hot pink streak in her silver hair.

"Läerei!" gasped Säeshi, falling to her knees at her uncle's side.

Läenshi grasped Rováen's hand and pulled it close. "She's scrying. Be quiet so we can hear her."

Rováen held up his hand, lifting the flat, palm-sized green stone nestled at his wrist so that everyone could see his niece's face.

"Tell me what has happened," he said to the image in the stone.

Läerei's image in the stone pursed her lips and nodded. "There is an army headed south from Molonark," she said. "They have crossed the Sharäedan River and are now headed into the Kha'san Valley."

"An army? What army?" Trilläen asked, stepping next to Roväen, momentarily blocking Sénna's view. "How do you know this?"

Läerei's grim smile didn't reach her eyes. "We captured four Hazzara this morning. They were seeking Cédron. It took some convincing, but I was able to learn their plans. You must get to the Zhoula and her family."

Roväen nodded. "We have captured one ourselves and are aware of the plan against the Zhoula. What of this other army? Where are they headed? Who are they?"

Sénna saw Läerei's eyes darken. "They number at least fifty thousand. It is not *who* they are. It is *what* they are. They are an army carved from stone and inhabited by Maüli spirits. They're moving at a swift pace with no sign of stopping. That's all I know."

Roväen's shoulders slumped. Sénna saw several heads bow under the weight of this news. She looked at Raziz and Zahna and clenched her fists. Even if the city of Taboriz could hold off the Hazzara, they wouldn't survive the onslaught of this new threat. They would slaughter all the families that traveled to Taboriz to celebrate Zholi.

Marizen stepped closer to the group, her cane thumping on the stones as she walked. Anzeri stayed close to her side, her fingers splaying and clenching. The old queen quirked her lips at Sénna, then faced Roväen.

"It is said that we must suspect the unknown, for one cannot always see the thorns hidden beneath the petals of the foreign flower. However, it appears that a strain of rot lies in the roots of our most exalted blossoms," Marizen scratched at the spindly whiskers along her chin. "We don't know how insidious the blight in our society is, and neither does the Zhoula. Nor is she aware of the danger posed to her by these Hazzara."

Marizen clapped her hands, her bracelets clinking like tiny cymbals on her wrists. "My people," she raised her voice above the babble, and instantly the courtyard was silent. "Today, we celebrate Zholi, our most holy festival. You hear that we also face the destruction of our city. My leaders will mobilize our gangs to begin evacuating the city of Taboriz. Take the citizens through the qanats in the desert to avoid running afoul of the stone army. Take only food and supplies for the journey north. We have until Lord Shamar rises tomorrow to save our people."

The Market Queen placed her hand on her hip and squinted toward the palace. "Our beloved Zhoula needs to be warned. She will send the Zaouni to investigate the explosion," she said. Placing both hands on the head of the cane, Marizen leaned over to Raziz. "Anzeri will lead our new friends to the palace to meet with the Zhoula. I want you to go with them and report back to me immediately with whatever plan they come up with."

Sénna felt the wave of heat radiating from her little friend as he straightened his shoulders and nodded. The hissing of whispered conversations became a buzz of activity as orders and counter orders flew about the courtyard. Anzeri rounded up the visitors to Taboriz and gave them a quick inspection.

"This won't do," she frowned, looking at the group. Anzeri stalked over to a chest and rifled through stacks of fabric, pulling out several bundles of silky cloth. "Wrap these around your hair and shoulders," she ordered Sénna, tossing her a startling bright green scarf. She passed a brilliant blue and purple bundle to Roväen and Trilläen. "These tunics should hide your tattoos. And for you," she turned to face the twins. "Only the finest silks to present you to our Zhoula. She will be very pleased to welcome Sumäeri."

Sénna wrapped her scarf around her hair and helped Anzeri disguise Säeshi and Läenshi in the exquisite wrap-around dresses. Satisfied with the final inspection, she led them to the gate.

"Keep your weapons handy," she warned. "We won't be able to tell friend from foe once we leave this gate."

425

Chapter 35: The Zhoula's Palace

Sénna shrugged the guard's hand off her shoulder as he attempted to shove her through the gate. There was no reason for his roughness. Tensions were high. She could see it in the set of everyone's shoulders, in the shifting of their eyes. The joyous, celebratory vibe the city held this morning had morphed into an almost palpable panic.

Everywhere she looked, the pilgrims dressed in their finery for the Zholi Festival should have been laughing and adding their handcrafted glass to the temple's mosaics. Instead, they clustered in tight groups, clutching their children to their chests. Rather than waves of worshipers dancing toward the temples, the flow of humanity was decidedly toward the city gates and the water.

The air felt chilly and oppressive despite the heat. Sénna wiped her sweating palms on her thighs and stuck close to the Shäeli as the group made their way up the flagstone streets to the Zhoula's palace. Citizens cast dark looks in their direction as the suspicious and superstitious alike attempted to explain the mysterious threat to their city. Smoke from the explosion and subsequent fire obscured Lord Shamar's morning rays while forcing Taboriz's inhabitants to wrap their faces to breathe.

"Stay close to me," Anzeri instructed her charges as they approached the palace guards. "I will do the talking."

Sénna caught Läenshi palming one of her short knives, hiding it in the billowing silk of her dress. She raised an eyebrow, and Läenshi grimaced.

"I've met a group of Zaouni already," she whispered. Läenshi rolled her shoulders and cracked her knuckles. "I was not impressed with their level of integrity."

Sénna nodded, swallowing against the tightness in her throat. The breeze continued to blow smoke from the armory toward them, making her eyes burn. The arsenal sat just below the palace and was now swarming with Zaouni. The men raced around in red-gold blurs, tending the wounded, fighting the still-burning fire, and interrogating every passer-by.

"Halt," a guard challenged Anzeri as she approached the gates to the palace.

A second and third Zaouni detached themselves from the fire line and stood by the guard, all bristling with their black zolenium weapons and suspicious eyes. Läenshi pushed Sénna and Säeshi behind her as she stepped next to Anzeri. Trilläen and Anéton flanked the women on either side, their postures taut and their gazes wary.

Anzeri held her palms open and bowed low. "May the strength of your arms match the courage of your hearts, fearless Zaouni. I bring travelers to our city to speak with the Zhoula. They have information on the events of this morning that may help us defend our city."

"They may not bring weapons into the palace," the first Zaouni said, frowning at the swords hanging from the men's belts.

The Sumäeri and Askári men glanced at each other, then at Anzeri, who nodded. Buckles jingled, and loosened belts fell. Sénna kept her eyes on Läenshi, whose blade now nestled snugly against her tattooed hip.

The first guard reached for Tóran's belt. "Your weapons will remain with us until—"

A fast-moving shadow blanketed the city, blotting out Lord Shamar's light. The Zaouni ducked, and the people cried out in fear. A shriek from above made Sénna's heart thrill as she craned her neck upward. The läenier Wing had arrived. Golden raptors alighted on the walls surrounding the upper echelon of Taboriz, some clinging to the gate towers and others remaining aloft to ride patrols over the panicked city. Two raptors circled to land in the courtyard inside the palace gate.

The Zaouni circled the two läeniers and their riders, weapons drawn and lowered. Läerei slid off her beast, grinning at the warriors. Lord Shamar's light glinted off the pink streak in her hair as she held her hands up for Cybél to dismount. The second Sumäeri seemed familiar and wore the Wingleader's shoulder knot above his bandaged shoulder. Sénna squinted, gasping when she recognized Roshäen, the rider who'd suffered the arrow to the shoulder when he rescued her in the desert. The new arrivals exited the palace gates and approached their friends.

Trilläen waved to his riders. "Roshäen, Läerei, well met," he called, smiling. "My newest Wingleader and head tactical officer," he introduced the riders to Anzeri and the Zaouni, who held their weapons at the ready. "They will inform your Zhoula of the situation brewing in the north."

Anzeri nodded and conferred with the guards, who agreed to escort the group to the Zhoula's chamber. Cybél ran to Sénna, embracing her before stepping back to inspect her.

"What happened to you?" Cybél cried. Her eyes lingered on the bruises around Sénna's arms and temple.

Sénna shook her head. "I'm fine. My friend Raziz here kept me safe from any real harm."

Raziz stepped forward with an impudent smile that split his entire face. "The desert rose pales in comparison to your delicate beauty, fair one," he placed his right hand over his heart and bowed low.

"Don't listen to this scamp," Sénna giggled, ruffling Raziz's dark hair. "He'd charm the poison from the fangs of an azp."

"Come, we can see the Zhoula now," Anzeri ushered the group through the gate and the palace doors.

Anéton and Cédron held back, allowing the group of warriors to precede them. They turned to Sénna, Cybél, and the twins.

"Just like old times, isn't it?" Anéton grinned and nudged Cédron's shoulder. "Hazzara, enemy armies, danger lurking around every corner." He lowered his voice to a dramatic level. "And, as always, you ladies can count on us to protect you and keep you from harm."

Sénna rolled her eyes, and she heard Säeshi snort.

"Is he always like that?" Säeshi asked, covering her mouth to stifle her laughter.

Before she could answer, Cédron punched his friend's upper arm.

"He's hopeless but ultimately harmless," he grinned at Anéton's mock-outrage.

Anéton patted the sash around his middle, smirking. "They took my sword, but not my real weapons. I just want you to know I won't leave your side and will protect you with my life," he said in a conspiratorial whisper.

"Hmm, yes, I'm sure we *all* feel much safer now," Sénna said, her sarcasm not lost on anyone in the group.

They continued down the wide corridors where colorful tile mosaic patterns in lapis, gold, malachite, and onyx offset the white marble walls. Arched, two-story windows filled with colorful leaded glass depicted scenes of past conflicts, heroes, and deities in all their radiant glory. A side table with a clay bowl filled with glass balls caught Sénna's eye as she passed. Each ball appeared to have a tiny flower blooming inside the glass, as if they'd been dipped in molten glass at their peak of beauty, freezing the blossom forever in its clear sarcophagus.

"Fascinating," Cédron whispered near her ear. "Sorry," he apologized when Sénna flinched.

As they moved through the palace, Sénna inhaled the fragrances from the many bouquets of vibrant flowers placed at regular intervals along the corridors and the undertone of sumac and cumin wafting up from the kitchens beneath the main floor. The palace was grander than her father's and even the wealthiest merchants of Táksabai. The intricately woven carpets alone were likely more valuable than anything else on which she'd ever trod. Sénna shook her head; she wasn't used to this level of opulence. If their situation weren't so dire, she'd enjoy the palace's many wonders much more. She hoped the palace and its treasures survived the coming battle.

Anzeri and the Zaouni ushered them into the throne room, a vast, towering space filled with geometrically shaped mosaics lining the walls in blue and white, leaving the green malachite tiles to compete with the onyx and white marble on the floor. Her father's entire house could have filled this space. Men filled the room, dressed in long, flowing robes in a kaleidoscope of colors, while the Zhoula's high-level courtiers sat on a dais, shimmering in their cream and gold silks.

Sénna's nostrils flared as she passed the men, whose skin

glistened from the scented oils of sandalwood and myrrh. Several of the women had kohl smudged around their eyes, giving them a smoky look at odds with the lighter oils of orange blossom and jasmine that shimmered on their bodies. The fabric wrapped around their heads ranged from solid jewel tones to complicated geometric designs. Sénna plucked self-consciously at her stained halter.

Several Zaouni stood ranged behind the Zhoula, who sat at the center of the long table. Behind them, mounted on the wall, were a pair of unique weapons. Two glittering black zolenium blades were mounted on spokes radiating from a leaded glass sphere the size of a man's fist. The edges opposed each other, designed to slice as they spun. Sénna wondered if they were hand-held or throwing weapons. She remembered a similar weapon she'd found in Mage Kiel's bag during the siege of Táksabai and stepped in for a closer look.

A cough from Anzeri brought her attention back to the Zhoula, who rose from the table, her headdress a cloud of gold and scarlet that accentuated her high cheekbones and amber eyes. She wore a long, split-leg dress and breastplate, both of golden hues. Instead of kohl around her eyes, she had a thin line of blue paste made from crushed lapis lazuli.

"Ah, Anzeri, Eyes of My City and Sister of My Hearth," the Zhoula said, rising to her feet and silencing the room. "What have you brought me?"

Anzeri stepped forward, arranging the foreigners before the throne. "Great Mother of the Desert and Protector of Taboriz, may your reign be long and peaceful," she bowed low. "I bring you travelers from the lands of Askári-bai and Samshäeli. They come without gifts of riches but with information. They would speak with you about the recent attack and a threat facing our city."

The Zhoula gazed down at the group for a long moment. Sénna felt the urge to squirm under the leader's intense gaze. Her eyes were so similar to her grandmother's, filled with wisdom and knowledge despite being decades Am'aranth's junior. The Zhoula clapped her hands, the golden bangles on her wrists jingling with the movement.

"My Brothers and Sisters," the Zhoula addressed the courtiers and petitioners. "I leave you in the very competent hands of my council. Please, continue your discussions and preparations for assisting those killed, injured, and displaced in today's disaster."

Sénna adjusted her legs on the floor cushion and felt the tingle of blood return to her lower extremities. She was used to sitting in chairs, not on a hard floor with only a thin pad. Her legs and buttocks had fallen asleep. She squirmed, trying to remain unobtrusive, but Rováen winked at her.

"We've worked out all but the minor details, so it shouldn't be much longer," he whispered, leaning into her shoulder. "Besides, I don't think Tóran can stand much more attention."

Sénna shifted her gaze to the legionnaire, who stood sweating and shifting his weight in front of the Zhoula. The leader of Taboriz stood half a head above Tóran, firing question after question as she tried to understand his role in the fiasco facing her city.

"So, this Algarik has a stone army fueled by raging Maüli that will be here in two days or less," she said, putting a hand on her hip. "And these Hazzara have infiltrated my city, blown up my warriors and munitions—"

"And are hiding within the palace, waiting to kill you and your family," Tóran sighed, rubbing his temples with his thumbs. "You need to evacuate the palace before it's too late."

Whispers erupted to her right, and Sénna turned her head to see Cybél, Läerei, Roshäen, and Trilläen with their heads together in a tight huddle. Cybél's hands made short, quick gestures near her lap as she appeared to try and explain something to them. Sénna leaned to her left, but their voices were too low to catch.

On the dais, the Zhoula snorted. "My Zaouni will handle the Hazzara."

"My Lady, the Hazzara have spies within the palace, they have magic, and they have Algarik, who is not empty-handed." Tóran glanced at Cédron and hung his head, his cheeks flushing. "He bears two magical talismans, my brother's staff of bone and a rod of iron. Together, they make him invincible."

To her right, Sénna heard Cédron give a strangled gasp. Sénna had difficulty forgiving such betrayal despite learning the story of Tóran's demon infestation. The iron rod was something different. She'd heard Mage Kíel discussing it with his journeymage. She closed her eyes, trying to remember the conversation.

Mage Kíel had been upset that someone had stolen the Rod of Shouman from a secret vault beneath the Mages Guild. It needed one of the sacred stones to harness – what had he called it – fire from the skies? She remembered that term because it was familiar. She'd read it before when deciphering the Yezman scrolls they'd been working on before they departed from Táksabai. The fire from the skies was a metaphor for Lord Shamar's lightning. But it wasn't Cédron's firestone that was needed; she remembered Mage Kíel impressing upon her, it was the sacred windstone that harnessed Lord Shamar's Árk'äezhi.

Sénna rose, wavering as the tingles in her legs threatened to drop her back to her knees.

"I learned of this rod of iron in Táksabai," she said, bowing to the Zhoula as an apology for the interruption. "Algarik stole the Rod of Shouman from the Mages Guild. It is powerless unless he has the sacred windstone to activate it."

"The sacred windstone has been hidden for centuries," the Zhoula said, crossing her arms over her chest and drumming her fingers on her biceps.

"It is my quest to find the windstone," Cédron said, rising and stepping next to his brother. "I have been charged by the goddess Orwaena to find all the sacred stones and assemble the Sceptre of Kulari. Algarik is just a symptom of a greater evil that threatens Muralia. The Great Demon is behind Algarik and all the other tragedies that have befallen the peoples of our world. I must find it before Algarik does."

The Zhoula gazed at the brothers with calm, amber eyes. Sénna couldn't read any emotion behind the woman's impassive expression. After several silent moments, she clapped her hands.

"Najeriz, Light of My Days, step forward, please," she commanded, nodding to a young woman behind her right side.

The young woman faced her Zhoula and knelt. Her blue and green silk gown pooled around her slippered feet. Over her cloud of dark hair, she wore a small but intricately wrapped headband of blue and silver with matching silver hoop earrings that caught the light from the blown glass necklace at her throat. The colored glass spiraled in the hollow between her collar bones and had three holes on one side. The Zhoula grasped her hands, pulling the woman to her feet. They faced each other; their identical sepia skin and profiles said it all.

"This is my daughter, Najeriz," the Zhoula said, introducing her to Cédron. "She is learned in our ancient lores and histories. Perhaps she can help you begin your search for the windstone. I suggest you go to the libraries." Turning to her daughter, the Zhoula smiled. "Daughter, you will fulfill your sacred role and help this foreigner find what he seeks."

Säeshi stood and walked to Cédron's side. "I would like to accompany you," she said to Cédron and Najeriz. "I have some skill at finding hidden things.”

The Zhoula’s eyes narrowed briefly, then she nodded. Sénna saw her fingers squeeze the princess’s shoulder. Najeriz smiled, nodding at her guests.

Rováen stepped up to Cédron’s other side, clapping a hand over his nephew’s shoulders. “Looks like it’s just the four of us then,” he said, grinning. “Let’s get started, as those stone Maüli make me nervous.”

Najeriz nodded her head. “Come then, O Seekers of Knowledge, let us see if we can find what has been lost for so many Tides.” Najeriz glided down the dais and through the open archway toward the central corridor.

Tóran shifted back and forth, then addressed the Zhoula again. “There is the final group of Hazzara dispatched to sabotage your water system. I need to intercept them and fix the aqueduct gates before they flood the city.”

The Zhoula pursed her lips. “That screw and the aqueducts are the lifeblood of the city. Do you know how to stop them?”

Tóran rocked back on his heels and ran his hand through his hair. “I know how to kill the Hazzara, as long as I can catch them by surprise. I am not entirely sure how to fix your aqueduct gates—”

“I do,” Sénna interrupted. “Raziz and I were captured by Zaran and taken to the operation center at the base. I memorized the schematic of the door levers while Raziz tried to loosen the bolts. He dropped the tool they gave him before he could do any major damage.”

The Zhoula clasped her hands in front of her, knuckles white as she squeezed her hands together. “I would prefer to keep my subjects away from the dangers of the screw and its mechanisms, but I also don’t know if I can trust you to fulfill your promise.”

Tóran hung his head and nodded. “I understand. I have much to atone for and no reason for you to trust me. Perhaps Sénna should accompany me. She bears no love for me and will ensure I do not betray my word – again."

The Zhoula turned to face Sénna. "You are willing to do this, to accompany this traitor and risk your life in the mechanisms of the water screw?"

Sénna swallowed and nodded. "My Lady, if we lose this battle here, Laylur will have nobody to stand in his way from taking over the entire world. I must do what I can, even if it means working with some unsavory characters." Her lips twitched, and she punched Tóran in the shoulder. "Don't screw this up and kill me, or *I'll* become the most terrifying Maüli you've ever seen."

Sénna turned her attention back to the Zhoula as Trilläen, Läerei, Läenshi, Roshäen, and Cybél approached the dais. They bowed, and Trilläen stepped forward.

"My Lady, we also would like to contribute to the safety of you and your citizens. I offer my läenier Wing to the defense of the city. My friends here have a unique suggestion for defending the city if you have a moment to indulge them."

The Zhoula nodded, and Cybél stepped forward. "My Lady, we need to visit the women's quarters."

chapter 36: Splitting Up

Läenshi followed Anzeri, who led the small group through the blue-and-white-striped arches towards the women's quarters. She nudged her sister Läerei.

"What's with Anéton?" she whispered, nodding toward the young legionnaire whose tight shoulders hunched almost protectively over Cybél walking next to him.

Läerei snorted. "Isn't it obvious? He's besotted — and she wants nothing to do with him."

"Hmm," Läenshi sighed. "He's been flirting shamelessly with every female we've encountered, so I didn't realize he might actually have feelings for someone."

Läenshi narrowed her eyes, noting how Anéton's fingers alternately clenched and brushed the back of Cybél's hand. Läerei was right, but this was not the time for unrequited romance or the emotional complications accompanying it. They had a mission to accomplish and very little time. If they couldn't get the resources they needed from the Zhoula's women, they'd be hard-pressed to stave off the Hazzara and their stone army.

Anzeri led them down the long corridor and through the mosaic-tiled grand courtyard filled with fountains and flowering trees. The jasmine and orange blossom scents mingled with cardamom and saffron wafting from the kitchen to their right. Läenshi's stomach rumbled, earning her a sharp look from her sister.

"What? Flatbread and tea weren't much breakfast, and that was hours ago," Läenshi patted her rippled belly with a grin.

Anzeri led the group up the sweeping staircase on the far side of the courtyard. They rose to a wide landing that angled off to the left and right. Anzeri turned to the left.

"The women's quarters are this way," she said, stopping to give Anéton an appraising look. "I'm not sure you would be welcome, Askári. We don't normally allow men in this wing, only eunuchs."

Anéton's face blanched, and he shifted his weight. Läenshi grinned at his discomfort.

"I swore…" Anéton's voice cracked. He cleared his throat. "I swore to protect these women, and I will not leave their sides."

Anzeri raised her eyebrows and glanced at the Angäersol sisters. Läerei looked at the Askári couple and shrugged.

"Who are we to deny to such a brave warrior," she smiled, taking the sting out of her words.

"We will need him to help carry bolts of fabric, if nothing else," Cybél said, patting his arm. "If we are to succeed, we will also need a wagon.

Anzeri stopped and turned. "Bolts of fabric to stop an army?" she asked, eyebrows disappearing into the fabric of her headdress. "You must enlighten me."

"Before we get too bound up in my idea, we need first to see if we can accomplish it," Cybél stated, her cheeks flushing. "Are we near the women's quarters yet?"

Anzeri pressed her lips together and nodded. "Through here," she said and waved them down another wide corridor with walls of intricately engraved stone that opened to the courtyard below.

They halted before tall double doors with brass hinges and filigree designs. Anzeri opened the doors wide, and the troupe followed her into the brightly lit room. Pierced brass and glass lamps hung from the ceiling, filling the room with their colorful light. Long pillows lined the walls with thick, round cushions thrown in between, giving the room a comfortable feel. Low tables filled with dried fruits and nuts dotted the remaining floor space.

Läenshi stopped. Lounging along the pillows were scores of women of all ages, ranging from early teens to ancient crones. The lively chatter that they'd heard through the closed door ceased immediately upon their entry, and Läenshi felt the weight of all their eyes upon them. One middle-aged woman in a silken peach wrap-around dress pointed at Anéton.

"How dare you defile our sacred space?" she hissed, her eyes narrowed.

Cybél stepped forward, curtseying. "Please excuse our rude interruption, my ladies. We are here on an urgent matter. The palace will soon be under attack, and we need—"

A hail of satin slippers bombarded the group, mostly Anéton, who stepped between Cybél and the palace women. At his approach, the women's screams rose, followed by more shoes flying in his direction. The legionnaire ducked, raising his left arm over his head and tucking Cybél into his shoulder with his right.

"This is insane!" he yelled at Anzeri. "Tell them we're trying to protect them."

Anzeri ducked behind her arms. "I don't think they care. Like I said, no men in the women's quarters."

Slipper storm depleted, the women rose and began pushing the group back out through the door, squealing and shrieking as they shoved. Cybél stepped out of Anéton's protective arm and stomped her foot.

"Stop this!" she yelled, thrusting the women back away from her. "You are in danger. We are trying to save your lives."

The peach-clad woman rose to her full height, her tightly-coiled braids glinting with gems in the lamplight. "Such arrogance to think you are superior to our Zaouni. Begone," she said and waved her hand dismissively before turning away.

Läenshi sucked in a breath. These women would be dead by this time tomorrow. So many lives were just beginning. They could force the women to give up their fabric, but that would waste time. She considered options for salvaging the rest of the citizens of Taboriz as the heavy wooden doors slammed behind them.

Läenshi breathed through the knot of tension that squeezed her chest, rotating her shoulders and neck. Perhaps Trilläen was wrong, and the läenier Wing should go to Samshäeli and protect their homeland from the invading army. Still, if the stone army attacked Taboriz first, the Wing would be needed here to prevent the stone soldiers from moving north.

Anzeri stalked ahead of the group, her boots clicking on the marble floor as she walked to the head of the stairs. She stopped and crossed her arms over her chest, leaning against the mosaic wall.

"You won't find any help among the other women here, either. Tell me your plan, and I'll see if I can find other resources that might work."

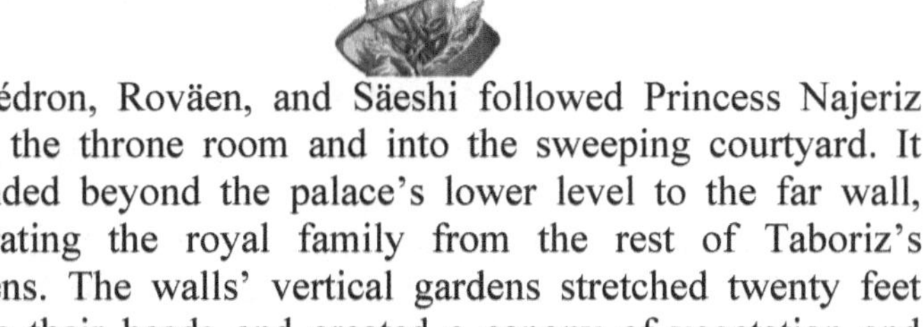

Cédron, Rovāen, and Säeshi followed Princess Najeriz from the throne room and into the sweeping courtyard. It extended beyond the palace's lower level to the far wall, separating the royal family from the rest of Taboriz's citizens. The walls' vertical gardens stretched twenty feet above their heads and created a canopy of vegetation and fruit vines that protected them from Lord Shamar's blistering heat.

"Our great library is the pride of Yezmarantha, attracting scholars from every land across Muralia," Najeriz said, pointing at the domed building nearly a quarter-mile away. "It is the center of learning for science, medicine, and Árk'äezhi studies. Students have contributed to many great engineering feats, from the screw that brings water from the desert's qanats to the vertical gardens that feed our citizens. The true genius of our scholars is the aquaponic system that converts all our wastewater into potable stores. In case of a drought, we have vast stores of water in cisterns beneath the desert that we can access."

Säeshi wrinkled her nose. "Are you telling us that the aqueducts that carry away sewage from your public toilets and baths contribute to the drinking water?" Her face took on a greenish pallor. She reached for the leather water pouch hanging from her shoulder, pulled the cork, and poured the water onto the ground.

Najeriz laughed and took the pouch, pouring the last few drops into her mouth, then wiped it with the back of her hand, bangles glinting in Lord Shamar's light. "The water is safe to drink, I assure you. However, you are correct. Our wastewater flows into the marshes outside the city. There are plants and fish that, well, for lack of a better term, 'eat' the waste materials and transform them into food that nourishes the plants."

Najeriz shrugged, a flush of pink to her cheeks. "I apologize for my primitive explanation. My tutor explained that other creatures inhabit the water. They are too small to be seen with our eyes. They also contribute to the conversion of the water, but I always had difficulty in grasping that concept."

Cédron marveled anew at the tall, verdant walls. The famous Maräera Gardens of Dúlnat were exquisite but only ornamental. The scholars of Taboriz discovered how to create beauty, function, and practicality for all its citizens. The Askári could learn much from the Yezmen.

"I'm hoping to see the gardens depicted in the murals of Shozin's wagon," Roväen said, and Cédron nodded.

"Truly, your vertical gardens are a feat of brilliant engineering, but what about your glass gardens?" Cédron asked, craning his neck to see past one of the gates to a private courtyard. "I have a friend from Taboriz whose eyes glaze over whenever he thinks of them. I'd love to see them while I'm here if that's possible."

Princess Najeriz smiled, deepening the dimple in her left cheek. "If the vertical gardens are the gown that clothes Taboriz, the glass gardens are her crown. They fill the complex that houses the library, so you are in luck, my new friends."

They continued down dusty, stone streets filled with men wearing embroidered tunics and women in jewel-toned wraps bustling to close their shops and homes against the coming invasion. As they passed, the citizens all bowed and touched their foreheads as their princess walked among them, smiling and acknowledging their reverence.

Najeriz paused at one of the human-sized earthenware jars that lined the street. A boxy apparatus attached to the side featured a small slit and knob. The princess slid a flecksun coin into the slot and turned the knob.

Internal metal gears turned, emitting several clicks and then *ping*. Najeriz held out her hand for Säeshi's water pouch, grinning. Säeshi hesitated only a moment before handing it to the princess. Najeriz held the mouthpiece beneath a spout and turned another dial. Clean water poured from the jar, filling the pouch. She handed the bag to Säeshi with a twitch to her lip.

"You will not find sweeter, clearer water anywhere in Yezmarantha," Najeriz said, challenging Säeshi. "Try it."

Säeshi raised an eyebrow and eyed the pouch. She handed it to Cédron.

"I can't get past the idea that you're asking me to drink fish excrement," Säeshi said, shaking her head with a grimace. "You try it. At least if it's toxic, your aquastone can cleanse it from your body."

Rovüen snorted and shook his head.

Cédron grasped the pouch. His mouth went dry, and he tried to swallow. Säeshi was right, he could transmute any toxin in the water with the aquastone, but that didn't curb his trepidation. He wasn't sure he wanted to drink human waste converted through fish waste, either. He glanced at Najeriz, whose amber eyes glinted with mischief and challenge.

Cédron took a deep breath and held it before bringing the pouch to his lips and pouring a small mouthful of water. The liquid touched his tongue, sparking his salivary glands into wakefulness. The refreshing sweetness of the water shocked him. His eyes flew open, and he drank deeper.

"She's right," he gasped, handing the pouch to his uncle, who shook his head. Cédron passed the container to his cousin. "I've never tasted sweeter water."

Säeshi grabbed the pouch with narrowed eyes. "Either that or you're incredibly susceptible to suggestion from a pretty woman," she said with a snort and hung the bag over her shoulder. "I'm not thirsty."

Najeriz laughed and led them through the twenty-foot, red-and-white-striped arches that lined the palace's outer wall, then down the cascading stairs to the lower level of the palace grounds. They skirted the citrus orchard, dodging the workers picking or pushing carts filled with fruit for the evacuation. Lord Shamar's rays beat on the glistening skin of the laborers, who whistled despite the heat and heavy work. Cédron wondered what had prompted Shozin Chezak to leave this magnificent city for the cold reaches of Dúlnat nestled within the Monhádi Mountains of Askári-bai.

The small group made their way past more buildings with courtyards and countless fountains, some filled with marble statues of the fabled Aruzzi or frolicking children. Others boasted impossible-colored glass sculptures of flowers spouting water in stunning bouquets of shimmering light. All caused Cédron to catch his breath and drink in the breathtaking beauty of the city. Najeriz turned down a street that angled to their left and through a series of vined trellises. When they reached the end of the shaded lane, the road dead-ended at a campus so colorful and bright that all three foreigners had to shield their eyes.

"Welcome to our arts and sciences complex," Princess Najeriz spread her arms out wide. "The library is beyond the great fountain over there."

Cédron followed Najeriz's finger and spotted a lake filled with glass shells, balls, flowers, and fountains. Some of the blown-glass sculptures extended scores of feet into the air. The lake itself appeared to be molten metal rather than water. The shimmering surface reflected the light of the sparkling glass in silver monochrome.

"It's beautiful," Säeshi gasped, her hand over her chest as she turned slowly, taking in the blown-glass flowers. She walked to the edge of the lake and bent down near the shimmering silver liquid. "These flowers are like your necklace," she said, turning to Najeriz. "Were they created by the same artist?"

Najeriz fingered the fluted glass pendant at her throat with a wistful smile. "This piece has been passed down in my family for generations. The original artist has been forgotten, but not its purpose."

"It serves a purpose?" Cédron asked, stepping closer to inspect the golden glass flower that blossomed from the princess's chain.

Najeriz waved her hand dismissively. "Well, there's an old legend that this necklace can summon the Aruzzi in a time of need or some such nonsense, but it's just a story. It's still nice to contemplate, though."

Cédron saw Säeshi stiffen. She held her hand out, her fingers trembling slightly as she slowly turned in a circle. Rováen's eyebrows raised in question, and she nodded slightly. Rováen glanced at Najeriz and pursed his lips. Cédron opened his mouth to ask what Säeshi had sensed, but Rováen gave him a warning shake of the head.

Following the princess, the group gazed toward the island garden of glass flowers and trees in the center of the silver lake. Arching above the sculpture of a nest filled with mottled eggs stood a tall tree with emerald branches. Three multi-hued glass Aruzzi statues perched protectively over the nest, their long, orange, and turquoise tail feathers fanning out behind them in a brilliant display.

"The Aruzzi colors are so vibrant," Säeshi said, pacing the shoreline. "Are they accurate?"

Princess Najeriz smiled and nodded. "Yes, the Aruzzi are protectors of Árk'äezhi. Like the Rohíti, they embody all colors to represent all peoples. They shelter their young as the next generation of guardians, protecting both our people and our access to wind Árk'äezhi."

The fierce raptors were more massive than the läeniers of the Sumäeri Wing and far more powerful. Sénna related the histories of the Aruzzi during their journey. Cédron had been impressed with the idea that each fiery tail could lash out and destroy a city and how they were strong enough to carry full-grown towren in each three-taloned claw. He looked at the eggs, so vulnerable in their nest. The translucent glass gave the observers the impression of tiny Aruzzi chicks nestled inside the shells waiting to hatch. One of the eggs was opaque and gleamed a brighter gold than the others.

"That one must be a dud," Cédron pointed at the opaque egg with a grin. "It doesn't have a hatchling inside."

Najeriz looked at him sharply, then smiled with a breezy laugh. "Well-spotted, my friend! Indeed, there are times when some eggs do not hatch. Or, perhaps an apprentice crafted that particular egg. It was so long ago that we have forgotten. Look, the library is just beyond the lake. If there is any information on the windstone, it will be among the scrolls in those hallowed halls."

Sénna led Tóran through the palace and back down into the bustling city. Carts laden with household goods and multiple generations followed behind lumbering towren as the citizens left their homes. The two foreigners passed rows of copper bowls three feet in diameter filled with colorful glass mosaics laid out for the Zholi Festival, sitting untouched in the wake of the city-wide evacuation.

"How much farther is the entrance to the screw?" Tóran asked, wiping sweat from his brow with his sleeve. "I feel like I'm about to melt."

Sénna turned and regarded him, consciously schooling her features into a neutral expression. "The only entrance I know is through the public baths in the vazurgan section of town. It's just below the palace, another block or so."

Zaran's public bathhouse was nearly deserted when they arrived. The door was opened by one of the manservants who'd assisted her previously. His eyes widened in recognition.

"Ah, the fair desert flower," he smiled, his teeth bright against his dusky skin. "What mischief do you bring to us today? We are not open for business."

Sénna smiled and clasped the young man's arm. "You are Zalid, right? Thank you for opening the doors to us. We need to get inside. There is a rumor of a plot to sabotage the water supply system, and we need to stop it."

Zalid bowed, waving the two guests inside, locking the door behind them. "You know the way?" he asked, stowing the large key in the pocket of his baggy pants.

Sénna shook her head. "No, Zaran covered my head when he took me to the lower level of the water screw. Can you help us find access?"

Zalid frowned. "That is ill news, indeed. If the water screw or aqueduct gates are damaged, it would be disastrous. Yes, I will show you the way."

The young man turned and led them to the left, down several flights of stairs, and into a rough-hewn tunnel beneath the baths. The air was cool and damp, almost musty. Sénna wrinkled her nose.

"I don't remember this smell," she mused. She looked at the black mold filling the crevices in the walls. "Also, they pulled me through the water at one point."

"Yes, Zaran took you to the control center," Zalid said, ducking as the ceiling lowered and the passageway narrowed from both sides. "The gates are closed now until midday, so the way is dry."

Sénna exhaled and noticed Tóran's shoulders relax at the news. They followed Zalid through more twists and turns in the passageway before reaching a cast-iron door with a wheel in the center. Zalid grasped the outer rim of the spoked hoop, wrenching it to the left. His muscles bulged, and he grunted, but the wheel grated and gave him only an inch of movement. The thin fabric of his tunic clung to his sweating chest and back.

"Let me take the other side," Tóran offered, stepping to Zalid's right.

The two young men strained and puffed, but the wheel

wouldn't budge.

"I'm not sure what's blocking the mechanism," Zalid scratched his chin, examining the wheel. "There isn't a lock, and there is no rust. This makes no sense."

Sénna looked at the wheel and its spokes. "What if you had something to lever between the spokes – would that give you enough torque to wrench it free?"

Tóran's face lit up. "Yes, and I have just the thing."

The legionnaire unbuckled his sword belt and thrust the sword and scabbard between the spokes. Together, the two men heaved the blade downward. The wheel ground and squealed before breaking free. Tóran fell forward into Zalid's shoulder, and they both tumbled onto the ground.

"Well, that loosened it," Sénna giggled as the two young men scrambled to their feet.

Zalid examined the wheel again. "I wonder what was holding it. There is nothing visible—"

"Perhaps some sort of magic?" Tóran asked, his face pale and sweating. "If the Hazzara have already been here, perhaps they put some sort of binding spell on it."

Sénna inhaled, and Zalid's eyes widened. She hadn't considered that, and clearly, neither had Zalid. If Tóran was correct, then they could already be too late to save the city. Zalid pulled the door open, and they charged through to the control center. Sénna recognized the box with the multiple levers, all exactly as she'd seen them during her previous visit.

"Nothing has changed," she mused, looking at the control box. "Zaran increased water flow to the city by opening all the gates from the palace with this lever," Sénna pointed to the far left. "And, if I remember correctly, this center lever manages the water from the qanats, and the one to the far right controls the gates to the lower city and the harbor."

"Yes, but these are stuck with the gates open," Zalid said, trying to pull the center two upward. "Again, nothing is holding them in place, but they won't move. What sorcery is this?"

Tóran grimaced. "The Hazzara kind. Have they locked the water gates open, so the water comes in from the qanats, travels up the screw to the palace, and sluices down the aqueducts through the city? These levers control the intake water, right?"

Zalid nodded. "The gates at the top of the screw are still open, but we can't control them from here. These Hazzara must be planning to lock them from the top of the screw. There is another control box up there."

"We need to close the intake gates so that the screw doesn't become flooded at the lower level," Tóran said. "If we can't move the levers, what if we destroyed the ropes holding the gates open?"

Zalid scratched his chin and nodded. "These gates control the intake flow on the west side of the screw, but not the east, from where most of the water comes. It might be enough to slow the flooding."

Tóran unsheathed his sword and nodded to Zalid, who knelt to allow the former legionnaire onto his shoulders. Standing, Zalid lifted Tóran high enough to slice through the ropes on the pulleys. Gate after gate slammed closed as they worked until they'd sealed all the gates controlling the water flow into the city center.

"What about the higher gates?" Tóran asked as he slid off Zalid's shoulders. "If we leave them open, will it still cause a problem?"

Sénna felt a sharp stab of panic and let out the breath she'd been holding. "Yes, we have to prevent them from sending the water from the palace into the city. Zalid, can you help us reach the top?"

Zalid nodded. "There is a lift. Come, let's hope they haven't frozen that as well."

Sénna and Tóran followed Zalid around the base of the water screw and over to an open cage attached to a chain. Zalid stepped into the lift and motioned for them to join him.

Once inside, Zalid thrust the lever on the wall forward. The chain clanked, and the enclosure shuddered. Beneath them, Sénna saw the tops of cogwheel gears begin to move. The cage groaned and wobbled, then began to raise. The chain links caught the gears' teeth directly to their right, pulling the chain down and lifting the cage.

"Ingenious," Tóran peeked through the bars of the lift to the turning mechanism beneath them.

Zalid snorted a laugh. "Necessity encourages invention, especially after hiking the distance up the water screw a few times. The lift was the only way we could get to the top and still have the breath to work."

Sénna nodded. She remembered climbing narrow stairs to the rafters inside her father's mansion and how hard it had been when she was younger. The lift raised them to the top of the water screw after only a few minutes. The cage rattled to a stop, and Zalid locked it in place.

"The controls are on the far side," he said, leading them around the blades that sloshed water into the waiting aqueduct lines.

Sénna had her eyes on the network of stone channels leading from the screw and didn't see Zalid stop in front of her. She slammed into his back, bouncing back a step into Tóran's chest.

"Hey, what's going—"

Zalid spun around, grasping her arms. "Don't look," he hissed. His face was pale in the light of the blazesand sconces that flickered on the walls.

Behind her, she heard Tóran unsheath his sword. She stepped back, and her foot slipped. Zalid's hands held her up, but she spied the crimson rivulets coursing along the floor.

"Laylur's beast!" she swore and stepped gingerly out of the bloody pool soaking her slipper.

Tóran stepped past her, forcing Zalid to step aside. Beyond the manservant lay a score of Zaouni, their throats slit. Smears of blood from the passageway indicated that several of the bodies had been killed elsewhere and dragged into this chamber to hide the evidence of Hazzara infiltration.

"They're already in the palace," Sénna gasped. "We have to tell the Zhoula."

"The Hazzara have gone from here. You warn the Zhoula," Tóran said. "I'll try to repair these gates." He sheathed his sword and stepped over the bodies to reach the control box.

Sénna watched the screw turn, dumping gallons of water into the aqueducts branching off toward the central city. The gates were locked above the stone channels, allowing the rushing water to fill the conduits with no regulation.

Zalid hurried to Tóran's side. Together, they threw their weight into the levers, trying to pull the gates down. They didn't budge.

"Mijáko piles," Tóran swore, slamming his fist into the wall. "How can I fix this?" He paced back and forth, wiping his hands on his thighs. He turned to Zalid. "What if I destroyed the gears beneath here manually as I did below? Would that lower the gates?"

Zalid rubbed his chin, his eyes tracing the path of the water should the gears not turn. "Yes, but then the palace will flood. I don't know if that is better."

Sénna's mind raced. If the Hazzara were already in the palace, the Zhoula and her family could already be dead. They'd slaughtered many Zaouni, and who knew how many other warriors littered the corridors of the palace?

"Flooding the palace may be the better option," Sénna said, pinching her lower lip as she thought. "Even if the Zhoula is already dead, you can drown the Hazzara before they infiltrate the rest of the city. They are expecting the water to wipe out the citizens of Taboriz. The Hazzara will wait out the flooding in the palace."

Zalid's eyes widened. "No, look here." He pointed to the

main gears, then to another mechanism. "These work together. If you destroy this one, the palace's gates will lower, stopping the flow from this pool, but you will flood this room. You will drown."

Sénna swallowed against the lump in her throat. She looked at Tóran, who stared at her for a long moment, then at Zalid. He let out a long, slow breath.

"It is a risk I am willing to take," he said. "Beyond the betrayal, I have committed atrocities that do not bear discussing." Tóran looked at his feet, then back at his companions. "Sacrificing myself for a greater cause is better than I deserve."

Chapter 37: Taboriz Under Siege

Algarik flew his rinzar over the lush green forest of Samshäeli's western border. He'd spent the morning scouring the northern border, making way southwest along the treeline, seeking evidence that his stone army had infiltrated the Shäeli lands. The long stretches of the Rabe'en Plains to the west remained pristine, with no indication that a stone army of fifty thousand plus had tramped through its waving sativa fields. Algarik started to feel the first tendrils of panic curling up his spine. How could he have lost an entire army?

The night before, as he'd settled to rest, the army headed

due south. Algarik knew that the western lands of Askári-bai thronged with more enraged Maüli after the battle at Táksabai, but there wouldn't be the raw, unspoiled bodies of their enemies. The guardians had annihilated the Garanth, who themselves created scores of Arkmuln. The civilians in Samshäeli wouldn't have the same appeal to the Maüli, who wanted revenge. No, Algarik realized with a pang in his stomach, the army would be drawn south to Taboriz, where his remaining Hazzara were preparing to engage the Zaouni Warriors.

Algarik yanked the reins with his right hand, pulling his beast's head westward. The rinzar tossed his head and snapped at the rider, causing discomfort, but Algarik was prepared. He shot a thin stream of red energy into the rinzar's skull, reinforcing the obedience spell and adding a jolt of Árk'äezhi with a promise of pain should the raptor continue to resist him. They flew south over the sativa fields, keeping Samshäeli's lush greenery on the left. He rode for two more days without any sign of his army. As Algarik neared the Sharäedan River, he caught sight of the telltale signs of the stone army's passage.

Vast swaths of grains lay trampled, cutting a gash across the golden fields like a wound. He was still miles from Taboriz, but the trajectory of the army's passage confirmed that they made for Yezmarantha and not Samshäeli. Algarik suffered a momentary pang of regret for the Yezmen; they were not his intended target. Taboriz was an ancient and beautiful city filled with priceless relics and treasures that would be a tragedy to lose to the ravages of war.

Algarik patted the saddle where the two talismans were tied. He'd already retrieved priceless spoils from the battle at Táksabai. The Rod of Shouman was a powerful item; he only needed Cédron's firestone to activate its potent magic. He was confident the bone staff lashed to the rod was equally magical, but he couldn't access the staff's Árk'äezhi. The mage grimaced and drummed his fingers on his thigh.

He had to find that boy and get the sacred firestone and aquastone before Cédron could discover and align with the windstone. The lad was becoming far too powerful for comfort.

There was also the legend of the flute that summoned the Aruzzi. That was one item that Algarik couldn't afford to let slip through his fingers. If he could get his hands on that talisman, he could bend the guardians of wind Árk'äezhi to his will. That would strengthen his position and merit in the eyes of the Great Demon. It would be worth reaching Taboriz ahead of the stone army and capturing the Zhoula. The fabled instrument was reportedly under the stewardship of the royal family. He dug his heels into the rinzar's side. He had to hurry.

Despite moving without rest, the stone army still only covered maybe a score of leagues from when Lord Shamar rose in the east until Hamra, the third moon, set in the west. Algarik pushed his gargantuan rinzar past its reserves. The raptor became more recalcitrant the longer it went without food or rest. Algarik felt the same way. It was a battle of wills that, as long as the mage had his firestone, he could win. But only just. Algarik knew he'd have to either release his creation or kill it once he landed. He'd spent most of his energy maintaining the rinzar's obedience spells, but now they were both depleted of strength.

Algarik wavered in the saddle. They'd flown all night, and he was chilled and bone-weary. Lord Shamar's first orange-gold light silhouetted the dunes to the east as the rinzar crossed the Räenetti River and into the desert lands of Yezmarantha. He angled his beast straight into the daytime deity's warming rays and closed his eyes. Algarik knew by the time he reached the capital city of Taboriz that he would have to lose his cloak and gloves to the sweltering desert heat. Still, for now, he enjoyed the sensation of melting ice as his extremities recovered a modicum of feeling.

By midday, the jewel-toned towers of Taboriz's palace sparkled in Lord Shamar's downward gaze. The lush green city promised respite from the arid heat and much-needed rest before the coming battle. Algarik kneed his beast's long neck, intending for the rinzar to fly toward the vazurgan district. Instead, the raptor screeched, its hunting cry tearing the air with rage. It swooped down toward the desert just outside the western gate.

No amount of tugging of the reins or dribble of power from the ruby could dissuade the beast from its current trajectory. Looking ahead, Algarik spied what appeared to be a display of puppets on sticks. As the rinzar approached, he saw that the tableau was much more macabre. An extended family from the eldest grandmother to the youngest child danced on spikes, their bodies already gouged and torn from the earlier attentions of desert scavengers.

Algarik made one last attempt to redirect his mount, but he'd already pushed the rinzar too far. The raptor landed on its feet, spreading its wings to their full width, and snapped the worn leather strap holding the saddle across his chest. Algarik leaped backward, rolling down the blue-black feathers before crashing into the sand. He got to his feet, gagging at the fetid stench wafting from his mount's underside.

The rinzar plucked a woman from a spike that held her high above the sand. There was no spraying of blood as the raptor tore into her still-tender stomach, dragging her cold entrails in its beak. Algarik knew the rinzar was starving and would devour this careful display of Hazzara power, for he recognized the craftsmanship of the metal shafts. This tableau was the handiwork of his Hazzara, serving as a warning to any who dared enter the city.

Now there was a decision to make. Algarik watched the

rinzar consume the corpses, leaving scant flesh on broken bones. In a matter of minutes, the raptor would begin looking for fresh meat, and Algarik knew he wasn't safe from its voracious hunger. He edged toward the raptor's tailfeathers, skirting around the western wall towards the gate. The sound of ripping flesh and crunching bones forced Algarik to grind his teeth together. If he could make it to the gate before the rinzar finished gorging on the corpses, he could escape.

The vazurgan section would be the best place for him to go. Algarik knew Zaran would be holed up safely in his offices at the bathhouse. He would go there right after he found some food. His mouth watered at the thought of the fresh pastries filled with spices and melted cheese made by the old women with their street carts. How long had it been since he'd had a hot meal? He closed his eyes as he thought about the savory juices from the roasted meat and licked his lips.

Algarik's eyes shot open. He looked around. The air around him was still. It took a moment to realize that his alarm was due to a lack of sound rather than an alert to one. Where was the rinzar? He spun around, but the beast was nowhere to be seen. Shards of broken bones and spears were all that remained of the family. He glanced up and froze.

The rinzar sped toward him from the sky like an arrow loosed from a bow. Part of Algarik's mind processed the flawless angle and speed of the predator, while another portion remained in stunned shock. The rinzar angled his lower body and reached toward the mage with his talons. Algarik flattened himself on the ground as the raptor swiped at his shoulders. The curved claws raked the center of his back but couldn't gain purchase in his skin or robes. The rinzar shrieked its frustration and circled back for another pass.

Algarik ran for cover. He'd expended all of his Árk'äezhi the previous two days, keeping the beast obedient to his needs. Now, he had nothing with which to defend himself. The mage scoured the sand around him, praying to Orwaena that his Hazzara might have dropped a spear, a blade, anything to fend off the terror that now stalked him from the sky. There was nothing; no rocks bigger than his fist, no abandoned weapons, and no magic. Wait, there was one thing that might work.

Buried deep within the folds of his cloak, Algarik carried an ebony statue the size of his extended hand. He hated calling upon the curse-bound imp for aid, for the creature relished tormenting his Master. The vile little beast would make him pay for the assistance, but there was no other choice. The rinzar was banking around for another pass. Algarik dug his hand into the deep pockets of his cloak and pulled out the black obelisk. He set it on the ground at his feet.

"Come forth," Algarik summoned his minion with a wave of his ruby ring.

The obelisk vibrated in the sand, wavering and wobbling as first a pointed tail, then cloven hooves popped out the bottom. Within seconds, rickety legs and an emaciated torso appeared. With a final rattle, the obelisk's pointed tip turned into a head with spiked hair and a pointed chin. The little demon glared at its Master with glittering black eyes that were slits in Lord Shamar's brilliant light.

"Why do you disturb my slumber?" it hissed, shooting out its long tongue as if tasting the air.

Algarik took a breath, but the rinzar's screech drowned out anything he might have said. A dark shadow blanketed the sands as the raptor swooped down, talons outstretched. The mage cowered into a ball next to the stone wall surrounding Taboriz, trying to make himself a smaller target for the raptor.

The imp craned its neck to spy the predator and let out a strangled squeak. "Can't you control your beast?"

Algarik gnashed his teeth together; his hands balled into

fists. He hated to admit weakness to this despicable creature.

"My situation has changed since we left Aromberk Fortress, and I don't have time to give you an update," he said through his teeth. "Stop that thing before it kills me, or we both suffer."

The imp's tongue lashed out between its sharp teeth as it watched the rinzar's flight. The black-winged behemoth wheeled around with another shriek and prepared for another pass. The imp waved its hand, barely lifting the fingers in an upwards motion like a bored vazurgan dismissing a servant. The rinzar spun backward as if a blast of air had struck him. It cartwheeled twice before shaking its head and fanning out its tail feathers. The rinzar's baleful yellow eyes bored into Algarik's as it swooped northward.

Algarik felt the tense muscles in his shoulders relax, and he let out a long breath. It galled him to lose his finest creation, but if he could get his hands on that fabled flute, he could summon the Aruzzi and bend them to his will. That would be more than ample compensation. He stood and turned to make his way to the gate.

"I believe thanks are in order," the imp said. It preened its tail with its tongue and claws. "I've saved your life again, and now you're in my debt."

Algarik pursed his lips and snorted. "Yes, and I'm sure I won't hear the end of it any time soon." He took a deep breath and exhaled slowly, keeping his eyes closed until his lungs were empty. Opening his eyes, he turned to the imp with a slight bow and smiled. "I am grateful to you for saving my life," he said, though the words dripped like venom from his mouth. "And I am indebted to you. I'm sure you will find a way for me to make amends."

The tiny demon grinned, its sharp teeth glinting in the daylight. "You are correct on all counts, mage. I will have to consider how to redeem my due. For now, I will bide my time. Taboriz is a beautiful but dangerous place. Perhaps you will need to up the ante before we're done."

"Don't count on it," Algarik grimaced and stuffed the now-solid obelisk back into his robes. He retrieved his bag and both talismans from the remains of the shredded saddle and made his way to the western gate.

Lord Shamar's rays gleamed off the city's stone outer wall, warming Algarik's skin and forcing him to squint in the brightness. Two Zaouni guarded the gate, and Algarik felt a prickle of sweat along his forehead. He couldn't fight these men if they denied him entrance; he had no strength left.

"Hold," ordered the first guard, blocking Algarik from the entrance to the city. "State your purpose in Taboriz."

"I'm an artisan," Algarik lied, pulling the two staffs from his back and unwrapping them. "I make unique walking sticks."

The guard pulled Räeshun from Algarik's grip, twisting it to examine all sides. The second Zaouni joined the first one, his eyebrows raised as his companion held up the bone staff.

"Odd composition for a walking staff, old man," he said.

Algarik felt a flush in his cheeks and inhaled slowly through his nose. "Your vazurgan are always looking for something new and extraordinary. I try to accommodate that," he gave a stiff smile.

The first guard put the staff down and looked at his companion, who shrugged. "Twenty flecksun for the peddler's fee and you may enter," he said, holding out his hand. "Though you may not find many vazurgan left in the city."

"Twenty? That's pretty steep for a peddler's fee, isn't it?" Algarik sputtered, gathering up his staffs and wrapping them in their leather bindings.

The guards shifted into defensive positions, hands on the pommels of their scimitars. "Our city is under siege," the first one said, his eyes narrowing as he watched the mage. "If you wish us no ill will, you will pay the fee and enter. Otherwise…"

Algarik raised his hands in obeisance and pulled a pouch from inside the folds of his cloak. It jingled as he shook out a score of the blue coins stamped with the Yezman symbol of the Aruzzi. He held them out to the Zaouni, who placed them in a small chest before letting the mage enter the city.

Once through the gates, Algarik hurried through the harbor's wide, sandy streets toward the lush, green gates of the vazurgan districts. The dry heat coupled with the strenuous walk caused his legs to chafe, increasing his discomfort. Rivulets of sweat coursed down his spine and temples. He slowed his walk as he approached the carved stone entrance to the higher level and looked around.

The Zaouni had said the city was under siege, and it appeared that many of the businesses were closed. As he watched, he noted that the fishermen going out had their families with them. It looked more like an evacuation than a siege. His Hazzara must have begun their attack closer to the palace.

Algarik sighed with relief as he crossed into the vazurgan district with its vertical gardens and cool, fresh air. He turned left and strode towards the central bathhouse, hoping that tensions hadn't progressed too far for him to enjoy a quick bath. His crimson robes were filthy from his journey, and he yearned for a soak in the scented water and a haircut. The heat in this miserable place was too much for his long hair and full beard.

Algarik found the bathhouse and banged on the door. He stepped back in surprise at the sudden opening.

"Go away; we're closed," Zaran snapped without looking at his patron.

The Master of the Baths half-turned and swung the door closed. Algarik blocked it with his hand, the impact hard enough to cause the stained-glass ovals to shimmy.

"Let me enter, Zaran," Algarik growled, shoving the door back open and stepping inside. "I've traveled far and long to get here. I need a bath, fresh clothes, and food."

Zaran's jaw dropped as he recognized his visitor. "A-Algarik," he stuttered, blinking his eyes. The Master of the Baths clasped his hands together and bowed low. "What brings you to my humble establishment, O great mage of the north? How can I be of service?"

Algarik's face darkened. He hated the Yezmen's propensity for flowery speech. "I just told you; I need a bath, fresh clothing, and food. Call your men to attend to me."

Zaran swallowed, his throat bobbing briefly with the action. "I, um, well, you see, I don't have any men right now. We've begun our siege of the city and the Hazzara—"

"So, it's begun? That's why the peasants were leaving," Algarik mused as he followed Zaran into the reception area of the bathhouse. His leisurely soak in the scented waters would have to wait. "Tell me what is happening now. Where is the Zhoula?"

Zaran blinked again. "Th-the Zhoula is at the palace, I imagine. The Hazzara have destroyed the Zaouni armory and barracks, which pulled most of the warriors from the city and palace to fight the fire and tend to the wounded."

Algarik smiled and rubbed his hands on his thighs, trying to dry the moisture. "So, the Zhoula is vulnerable."

The mage scratched his chin through his beard and walked around the small fountain, thinking. The long counter he sauntered past was laden with trays of untouched food and drink for the bath's absent guests. Clay pitchers sweating from iced rose water and platters of savory zamboosa and sweet zaimat tempted Algarik. He scooped up a handful of zamboosa, popping one into his mouth. He grimaced. It was dry. Algarik could taste the chili and cumin, but the spices burned the back of his throat without moisture.

"Where are my Hazzara now?" Algarik coughed. Particles of the flaky crust flew from his lips as he spoke.

Zaran's brows furrowed, and he steepled his fingers. "There is a band sabotaging the aqueducts to flood the city. Another contingent is scouring the city for any remaining

Zaouni. They are working their way from the palace toward the gates. The last group is positioned in the palace with orders to kill the Zhoula and her family."

"No, they must not kill her or her family," Algarik growled. He grabbed Zaran by the front of his gold-embroidered tunic. The metallic threads bent and poked his fist as Algarik crumpled the fabric in his hands. "We must capture her alive. She has something I want."

Zaran's eyes were wide, and he swallowed audibly. "I-I can try to get a message—"

"We don't have time for that," Algarik snapped, grabbing a piece of zaimat and sucking the honey from his fingers. He guzzled a quick glass of rosewater and poured another. "Take me to the palace. We need to find the Zhoula and the princess before they are harmed or killed."

"But – but, it's too late," Zaran sputtered, fingering a necklace of beads with shaking fingers. "The Hazzara were dispatched early this morning."

Algarik leaned in close to the Master of the Baths, his nose inches from the trembling man's face.

"Then you'd better hurry," he said. "If the Zhoula and princess are already dead, I'll take my frustration out on your hide."

chapter 38: Fire and Water

Sénna tore back through the corridor with Zalid right behind her. She hated leaving Tóran alone to figure out the levers of the water screw, but she had no choice. The Zhoula and her family could already be dead. Her heels pounded the marble floor through her thin slippers, her toes gripping the flimsy leather to keep from slipping as she rounded another corner.

"No, this way," Zalid called to her, beckoning her down the opposite corridor.

Sénna skidded on the floor, her feet sliding out from under her on the smooth stone. She dropped her hand to the marble and pushed herself back up, launching toward Zalid and the wooden door at the end of the hallway. He held it open, and they charged up the circular stairwell, Zalid just ahead of her.

"Where does this take us?" Sénna asked between ragged breaths.

Zalid puffed for a moment, then paused at the landing before another wooden door. "These are servant's stairs. They use these back ways to move through the palace unobserved. The vazurgan like to think we're invisible until they need us." He grimaced and pushed open the door.

The corridor they entered brought them through the abandoned kitchens where scattered food and upturned crockery suggested a hasty retreat. Zalid led her through the dining area where long, narrow tables and benches stood empty of food or company.

"I thought you worked at the baths. Did you work here at the palace also?" Sénna asked as she jogged along behind her companion.

Zalid hunched his shoulders and turned to peek at her, a sheepish grin on his face. "I once loved a man who was one of the finest chefs in the land. I learned many ways to get around the palace unseen during my time with him." He slowed his pace to a walk and stepped up to another door. Listening first, he pushed it open a crack, peeking through to the left and right.

"All clear, let's go," he said. Zalid pulled Sénna through the door and into the brightly lit room.

Sénna recognized the chamber in which the Zhoula had spoken to her small group. She heard voices coming from the adjacent throne room, raised voices. They held their breath and listened at the door, both exhaling visibly at the Zhoula's voice. Sénna opened the door and nearly ran into a Zaouni guard.

"Forgive my interruption," Sénna knelt at the feet of the startled matriarch who'd spun around at the noise.

Zalid prostrated himself next to her, blocking the Zaouni, whose curved sword sang as he pulled it from the metal clip on his hip.

"The Hazzara have already entered the palace and killed several Zaouni," Sénna said, looking up at the Zhoula. "You must evacuate the palace immediately."

The Zhoula raised her eyebrows and waved away the Zaouni's blade. "Where are they now?"

Zalid raised his head slightly but didn't look at his Zhoula's face. "We found nearly a score of Zaouni murdered in the palace control room for the screw. They got in through Master Zaran's bathhouse in the vazurgan sector."

The Zhoula gazed down at the servant and waved him to his feet. "Stand, and give me your name."

Zalid and Sénna both stood. Zalid rocked back and forth on his feet, ducking his head.

"I am called Zalid," he said softly and cleared his throat. "I work at Master Zaran's public baths."

"And you let these Hazzara in to sabotage my water screw?" the Zhoula asked, her lips pursed.

Sénna flinched at the flash in the Zhoula's eyes. She recognized that look. It was the same disappointed expression her grandmother had given her on so many occasions. Her throat tightened. It reminded her so much of home and her family – and her many failings. She glanced sideways at Zalid, not envying the man who'd roused his Zhoula's ire.

"I-I did not know their intentions, my Zhoula," Zalid prostrated himself again at her feet. "Please forgive my incompetence."

The Zhoula snorted and shook her head. "Get up, Zalid. I cannot hold you accountable for your employer's treachery." She looked at Sénna. "What of the Askári lad? Was he able to repair the sabotage?"

Sénna shook her head. "The Hazzara had already damaged the mechanisms and locked them magically. Zalid and Tóran were able to raise the gates to the city but not lower them again. He is working on locking the gates inside the palace so that the flooding is contained here and not risk the entire city."

The Zaouni holding the scimitar inhaled sharply. "There are women and children here. They will perish if we do not evacuate."

The Zhoula nodded. "Exactly. We have little time. If the Hazzara are already here, they are remaining hidden for now." She put her hands on her hips and paced back and forth.

Sénna looked around, noticing the rest of the occupants of the room for the first time. A contingent of Zaouni with gold breastplates and shining headgear stood before the throne. High-ranking Zaouni by the size of the red plumage sprouting from their helmets.

Behind the Zaouni stood a familiar face. Sénna inhaled and waved at Roshäen, who stood with his arms crossed and forehead creased.

"Have the Sumäeri brought the läenier Wing to defend the city?" Sénna asked the Zhoula.

"We don't want their kind here," the Commander of the Zaouni boomed, stepping towards the Zhoula. "We have defended Taboriz for generations; we will continue to do so."

Sénna saw Roshäen's face darken, and her insides dropped along with her jaw. How could the Zaouni refuse assistance in the middle of a crisis? They'd lost how many men and weapons in the explosion earlier and—

"We are not trying to usurp your position," Roshäen seethed through clenched teeth. "We simply want to support you and help you salvage your city."

Sénna turned to the Zhoula, whose lips were a thin line. "My Lady, I don't know how many more Zaouni have been killed here in the castle, but it seems like you could use all the help you could get. We need to evacuate—"

"Do you presume to instruct me, child?" the Zhoula's amber eyes flashed at Sénna.

Sénna's cheeks flushed hot, and she took a deep breath, choking on the spittle that sucked down her windpipe. "No," she coughed and took another deep breath. "But we have very little time before the water floods the palace."

"And even less time before another five thousand alzaytan-mounted Hazzara arrive from the Zaroon Quarry," Roshäen growled. He crossed his arms over his chest. "What would you have us do, my Lady?"

The Zhoula turned and walked to the wall behind her long table. She reached up and pulled down the two circular weapons mounted on the wall. She attached one to each hip, sliding the mosaic glass spheres into silk holsters built into the wide belt that hugged her hips.

"What do you call those weapons?" Sénna asked, her eyes not leaving the curved, black blades.

The Zhoula's lips curled as she pulled one free and held it up. "These are zagala blades," she said. "They are very lethal – especially to the wielder if they don't know what they're doing."

Gripping the sphere, she pressed the center with her thumb. A click was all the warning given before the blades whirred blindingly in the Zhoula's hand. She raised her hand, swirling the edges in a circular dance as she twirled, stopping inches from Sénna's nose.

"The device inside spins the zolenium blades with a torque that cannot easily be slowed. I can wield them myself, or I can fling them at an opponent." She pressed her thumb in the center of the sphere, and the blades slowed to a stop. The Zhoula re-attached the weapon to her hip. "I prefer the control of holding them myself, so I am limited to close combat. Still, I have been known to decapitate a target from over fifty paces away."

Sénna nodded, duly impressed. Her respect and admiration for the matriarch increased with each word the

Zhoula spoke. With clipped speech and similar gestures, the Zhoula dispatched the courtiers in the room to quickly gather their families and necessities and report to the kitchens.

"Marozna," the Zhoula turned to face her high commander with hands on her hips. "I expect you to cooperate with and accept assistance from our Shäeli friends. Do not let your pride cloud your judgment."

The Zaouni High Commander flushed dark crimson and ground his teeth. He gave a curt nod to the Zhoula, turned smartly on his heel, and stormed from the room. The lesser commanders followed in his wake, exiting in a crimson tide of feathers and cloaks.

Roshäen held his palm out in respect and nodded his head. "We will begin patrols over the city and keep you apprised of any new threats, my Lady," he said. He smiled and winked at Sénna before he retreated from the throne room.

The Zhoula watched him leave before turning back to Sénna and Zalid. "Now, we must make haste to the women's quarters and get the rest of my people free of the castle," she said. She turned to her personal guard. "You men go with Zalid to the dining room. Remove the legs from all the long tables and bring them into the kitchens. Move quickly; lives depend on it."

Zalid nodded and waved to the guards. He strode back to the door they'd just entered and disappeared with the Zaouni. Sénna wondered what the Zhoula wanted with kitchen tables, but she didn't have time to ask before the Zhoula grasped her wrist and pulled her down the corridor. Sénna remembered that Cybél had requested to meet with the castle's women and wondered if her friend was still there.

The Zhoula stopped at the filigree double doors with brass hinges and shoved them open simultaneously. Inside, scores of women bustled children and oldsters into groups and grabbed cloaks and packs.

"I see you have again anticipated my commands, Dezeen," the Zhoula nodded at the middle-aged matron in a muted, brown and cream-striped silk wrap who approached her.

Dezeen smiled before ducking her head and kneeling at her Zhoula's feet. "The Princess suggested we prepare for the worst before she left with the foreigners," she said and rose at the Zhoula's touch on her shoulder. "We are ready to follow you wherever we must go."

"Come," the Zhoula commanded. "We must evacuate the palace immediately. There is no time to gather more than the necessities, and we have a long journey ahead of us."

Sénna watched as Dezeen organized the women to assist the elderly and children in an orderly fashion. The room emptied behind the Zhoula in a matter of moments. Sénna turned as Dezeen closed the double doors behind them and scooped up a young boy whose thumb was planted firmly in his mouth.

The group made no sound other than the rustling of silks and the shuffling of feet. Everyone held their breath, scanning the tiled corridors with wide eyes, expecting an attack from any quarter. Even the little ones were silent, sensing the tension in the hips and shoulders of those who carried them.

The Zhoula led the group of nearly three-score into the dining hall, where the tables had been disassembled and stood lined up along one wall. The Zhoula nodded at the guards and turned to face her charges.

"Enemies called Hazzara have killed many of my Zaouni and are taking over the palace. They have sabotaged our aqueduct system and plan to flood the city. One of our allies is saving the city by rerouting the water to flow only to the palace. Our doors are shut and locked, trapping them inside, but we must evacuate before the waters reach this level."

The fear and panic held at bay for the short walk ruptured from the small crowd, with querying voices protesting the abandonment of their home. The Zhoula raised her hands, silencing the group.

"There is no time to debate," she said, turning to her Zaouni. "Take these tables through the kitchens. Zalid, show them the door to the aqueducts leading to the eastern quadrant. The tables are balsa wood and will float us down the aqueducts until we reach the outer gates. Everyone grab a pouch of dried meat and fruit and a container of blazesand. We will have to go underground and follow the qanat tunnels through the desert to Samshäeli. The Shäeli have assured me they will provide sanctuary for us until the battle is over."

Zalid nodded to his companions, and the men picked up the score of long, narrow tables. He led them through the kitchens and into a small antechamber with an enormous stone cistern filled with water. On the chamber's far side stood a wooden door with a lever on the wall. Zalid placed his table into the cistern and motioned for the other guards to do the same. He stood next to the lever and nodded to the Zhoula.

The Zhoula stepped up two feet onto the rim of the cistern and faced the crowd.

"I want one Zaouni in the front and the back of each table with the blazesand so you can see in the tunnels. Load the children and their caregivers first, then the oldsters. I will take the last table," she said, stepping down so that the Zaouni could begin loading.

In the scramble to load the tables with people and keep them from capsizing in the cistern, Sénna didn't consciously recognize the thrumming that buzzed in the back of her mind. It wasn't until the thrum became nearly a roar that she inhaled and turned around. Water streamed toward them from the main palace corridors, rising to her ankles in moments.

"The flooding has begun," the Zhoula said, her voice rising above the whimpers and cries of frightened women and children. "Hurry, get them aboard and open that gate."

Zalid nodded, and as the first full table reached the gate, he pulled the lever to open it. The gate wouldn't budge. He pulled with both hands, then hung using his entire body weight, but the lever didn't move. Behind her, Sénna heard the splash of running feet. She turned to spot Zaran and half a dozen Hazzara, weapons drawn, entering the kitchens and surrounding the cistern.

"Well, well," Zaran grinned and clapped his hands like a child receiving a sugary treat. "It appears I have located the crown jewel. My Lady, if you will come with me?"

The Zhoula gripped the spheres at her hips and pressed her thumbs into the glass, releasing the blades to spin. "I'm not going anywhere with you, traitor," she snarled and turned towards him.

The Hazzara surrounding Zaran plunged toward the Zhoula as her zolenium blades arched toward the Master of the Baths. One angled his scimitar towards her arm while another reached out with a vicious kick. The Zhoula's blade sliced through the pommel of the first man's scimitar, taking part of his hand with it. The second man's kick connected with the Zhoula's thigh, dropping her to one knee. She swung her swirling blades and spun on her knee, bringing the lethal black metal through the second man's thigh.

The Zaouni jumped from their makeshift boats to defend their Zhoula. The civilians hunkered down on the floating tables, whimpering and crying as the skirmish blossomed around them. Sénna ducked away from the Zhoula's side and raced toward Zalid. That door needed to open, or everyone in the room would perish. She didn't know if the Hazzara had noticed that the water level in the room had already risen above her ankles, but she doubted it.

"Zalid, can you get that lever down?" Sénna jumped and grasped the lever above Zalid's, using her entire body weight to pull it.

It didn't budge.

A child let out a wail in the boat nearest to her. Sénna dropped from the lever and reached over to comfort the child. She spotted the container of blazesand and pulled it from the bow of the improvised raft.

"Zalid, can you get through to the kitchen?' she asked. "There is coal stored beneath the stoves. I need you to get it." Sénna grabbed a second container of blazesand, placing them both at the base of the hatch.

Zalid glanced at the fighting and grimaced, then nodded. He ducked around the back of the cistern and edged his way toward the kitchens. Sénna lost track of him as the fighting between the Zaouni and Hazzara edged closer to her position. She prayed to Orwaena that the Zaouni would hold off their enemies long enough for her to help them all escape, or the future of Taboriz would be lost.

Sénna crouched along the full cistern, water splashing over the sides on her head and shoulders as the terrified courtiers shied away from the swinging blades of friend and foe. There were more Hazzara now than Zaouni, and the floor was slippery with both water and blood. The cries of fear from the children and the battle between the warriors echoed in the great chamber, making it difficult for Sénna to think. She had to figure out a way to get that trap door open and free the rafts. If Zalid couldn't get her the coals, then—

Something hard knocked against Sénna's shoulder, rolling her sideways. She crouched and sprang to her feet, ready to leap over the cistern's lip and into the water if need be. She glanced down at the object that struck her and gasped. The golden helmet of a Zaouni rolled toward her. The red spray of feathers bristled from the fixture on the top, while a darker crimson stain trickled from the man's severed neck. Black eyes stared fixedly at the ceiling. Sénna felt the contents of her stomach rise.

"Sénna, take this," Zalid cried, thrusting the silver trencher filled with hot coals at her middle. "I'll watch your—aah."

A red flower of blood blossomed beneath the hilt of a knife sunk deep in Zalid's left side just below his ribs. Sénna shoved Zalid onto the floor, his back propped against the cistern wall. She looked into his eyes and saw agony.

"I think I can stop the bleeding, but it will hurt," she said.

Zalid gritted his teeth and nodded. Sénna pulled off the sash wrapped around Zalid's waist and wrapped the end of it around her hand. She grabbed a piece of hot coal with one hand and the hilt of the knife with the other. She glanced at Zalid. His full lips were pressed so tight they were a white line. He nodded.

Sénna pulled the knife free and thrust the burning coal into the wound. Zalid's scream reverberated throughout the room. She pulled the coal away from the injury to see if it had cauterized, but before she could see the damage, a blade flashed down toward her forearm. Behind her, she heard the Zhoula shriek her war cry. Sénna couldn't explain why, but she ducked just as the spinning zolenium blades of the Zhoula's weapon whizzed into the Hazzara's sword arm, slicing it above the elbow and skimming just above Sénna's shoulder. The zagala blades crashed into the floor and rolled to a stop.

Zalid grunted, lurching to his feet. He raised his blade and plunged it into the Hazzara's chest. The man fell dead at his feet.

"You figure out how to get those trap doors open," he hissed through gritted teeth. "I must defend my Zhoula."

Sénna looked over and marveled at the matriarch, whose remaining zolenium zagala blazed like a dark star as she twirled it around, keeping her enemies at bay. Enemies surrounded her, and the ring of black-clad men shrunk closer and tighter with each moment. Zalid lurched forward, striking two men from behind and giving the Zhoula some room to maneuver, but he was weak. His blows didn't kill his opponents; they only alerted them to his presence.

"Drop your weapon, boy," Zaran's cold, thin voice

commanded. "Do as I say, or I'll kill you here and lash your brothers when I return to the bathhouse."

Zalid pressed the heel of his palm into the leaking wound, breathing heavily. Sénna could see the sweat glistening on the back of his neck. His shoulders were tight, and she spotted the tremor in his grip of the sword, but he didn't release the weapon.

"I'm through taking orders from you, traitor," Zalid snarled and lunged at his employer.

Zaran knocked the tip of Zalid's blade aside with a bored gesture of his hand. He stepped up to where Zalid hunched over his wound and slapped the young man across the face. Zalid toppled and lost his grip on the sword. Zaran picked it up and held the tip at Zalid's throat.

"You and your brothers are my property," Zaran said, his silky voice smooth. "You do what I tell you, or I will kill you." He pressed the tip of the blade into Zalid's throat right at the top of the collar bone. A thin line of blood welled around the metal, and he withdrew the weapon. "Your blood isn't worth soiling my blade," Zaran spat.

"His blood is worth ten times what yours is," the Zhoula's voice rang out behind him. "Step away from the young man if you want to live."

Sénna's breath caught in her throat as she watched the Zhoula rise and weave between the scattered bodies, her zagala spinning in her right hand. The Zhoula was bloody and her dress torn, but she held her chin high, raising her weapon to Zaran's throat. The Master of the Baths curled his lip and sneered but backed up a step.

A movement behind the Zhoula caught Sénna's attention, and she glanced over. A Hazzara eased his way behind the Zhoula, a throwing blade raised. The man aimed and pulled his arm back.

"No!" Sénna screamed and stood, reaching toward the matriarch.

Zalid looked up at her cry and saw the danger. He

grabbed the Zhoula's hips and pulled her towards him, lifting himself and rotating their positions with the same movement. The throwing knife struck him in the back, sinking deep into his body. Zalid dropped to his knees as the Zhoula turned to catch him. She eased him to the floor with one hand, holding her spinning blade out to the side to avoid catching it on his body.

"I apologize for touching your royal self, my Lady," Zalid croaked.

Sénna crawled toward Zalid, tears filling her eyes and blinding her to the horrors through which she moved. Two more Zaouni stepped up to either side of their Zhoula, lowering their weapons and keeping the Hazzara at a small distance. Sénna saw the pink bubbles foaming around the corners of Zalid's mouth as he panted for air. The blade must have punctured a lung. Her chest constricted with the knowledge that he had only a moment left. She placed a pale hand on Zalid's cheek.

"You are so brave," she whispered, caressing his face and wiping at the foam.

Zalid's eyelids fluttered, and he turned his head to face her. "Free...the...people...." The air whistled as he spoke. Sénna blinked away more tears and grasped his hand in hers. She squeezed his fingers, but he dropped her hand and pointed. "Go..."

The Zhoula reached over, closed Zalid's fixed eyes, and nodded. "He deserved better. Go, get those doors open and help my people get clear of the palace," she said, standing up and straddling the fallen servant.

Sénna wiped her face in the crook of her elbow and staggered back to the trap doors. She picked up one of the containers of blazesand and threw it on the ground to break the clay container. The jar bounced and rolled on its side. If she couldn't ignite the blazesand with the coals, she couldn't get those doors open, and they would all perish in this wet and bloody room.

Across from her, Zaran and his men had the Zhoula and her warriors surrounded again. Sénna swallowed the thick lump in her throat. She had to hurry. Grabbing the long silver bowl filled with charcoal, she hunched over and blew on the coals. They flared bright orange, and tiny flames licked up from the center. She placed the trencher in front of the canisters as a Zaouni shuffled in front of her. He fought with a Hazzara, and the two of them grunted and wrestled for position.

The Zaouni stepped back to get a better position and more torque to push his opponent forward. His heel connected with the trencher, sending hot coals flying into the air. They struck the doors and fell between the cistern wall and the floor. Sénna's heart sank. She stared at the pale, frozen faces of the women and children in the rafts and shook her head.

"No, no, no, no," she gasped, trying to scoop up the burning pieces.

It was no use. The coals were scattered beneath the boards of the trap doors and the flooring. Sénna wanted to scream and cry and lash out at the unfairness of the gods. They'd gotten her this far and yet, Zalid was dead, and all these innocent women and children would join him in a matter of moments. Behind her, she heard Zaran's laughter. Sénna spun around in time to see two Hazzara tackle the Zhoula as she launched her blades towards Zaran.

The Master of the Baths sidestepped the zagala, clapping his hands as the weapon spun harmlessly past and hit the side of the cistern. It fell to the floor at Sénna's feet. The Hazzara grasped the Zhoula by each arm and held her fast as Zaran sauntered up to her.

"And so it ends for you and your people," he smirked, rubbing his hands together. "I've always wanted to knock you off your pedestal…."

Sénna turned away from the vile man and his vitriol. She had one last idea for freeing the people huddling on the rafts.

Moving very slowly so as not to capture the attention of the Hazzara, who were now stacking the bodies of the Zaouni along one wall, Sénna reached for the zagala. She eased herself to her feet and eyed the clay blazesand canisters stacked at the base of the trap doors. She pressed the depression in the center of the sphere, and the blades began to spin. Closing her eyes, she sent a prayer to all the goddesses and flung the weapon towards the blazesand.

The zolenium blades sliced through the glass like a knife rendering fat. The blazesand sprayed across the back wall and trickled down between the door and the floor. The explosive sand struck the pieces of hot coals an instant later, and the entire back wall exploded outward. Water sprayed and wood splintered. The cistern's water roiled and rocked before sluicing towards the open waterway, propelling the rafts into the aqueducts and away from the doomed palace.

Chapter 39: Ingenious Deception

Princess Najeriz led her small group towards the library, around the quicksilver lake and its tableau of glass flowers and Aruzzi nest. Cédron followed behind, loathe to turn his back on the glowing Aruzzi egg. He felt drawn to it for some unfathomable reason.

"Come, my friend," Najeriz called. She waved toward the library as the bangles on her wrist glinted in Lord Shamar's light. "The wellspring of knowledge cannot be extinguished, even by the evil that threatens our fair city. Together, we will find the answers to your questions."

Cédron gave her a weak smile and shifted his gaze to

Säeshi, who appeared reluctant to leave the glass gardens.

"Do you feel it also?" Cédron murmured to his cousin as he caught up to her.

Säeshi gave him a sharp look; then, he saw her eyes dart back toward the Aruzzi nest before returning to him. She rubbed her forehead with one hand and closed her eyes.

"I do. I can't quite identify it, though," Säeshi said, a slight pucker forming between her delicate brows. "Whatever Árk'äezhi is at work here, it confounds my ability."

Cédron rubbed the back of his neck and pulled the rolled message from Mage Kiel from his pouch. He re-read the note and glanced back to the nest of eggs, frowning. Could it be? He folded the letter again and placed it in his pouch.

Säeshi knelt on the cobbled street, her face raised to the daytime deity's light and her eyes closed. Cédron wondered if having her gift obscured by an outside force was uncomfortable as she tried to focus her energy on identifying the phenomenon. Roväen and Najeriz returned to them, Roväen squatting at Säeshi's side while Najeriz pulled at Cédron's arm.

"We must scour the library before the enemy overtakes the city," the princess hissed in Cédron's ear, her fingers gripping his arm. "Once the siege begins, the Zaouni will seal the walls, and none will be able to enter or exit. Your chance to find information on the windstone will be lost."

Cédron pried the princess's fingers from his arm and faced her. "There is a strong Árk'äezhi force here. It could be a threat to you and your citizens. We need to identify it first."

"No, you must leave it alone!" Najeriz cried, grasping at his sleeve and reaching toward Roväen. "Do not awaken the guardians!"

Säeshi's eyes snapped open, and she stared at Najeriz. "Guardians? What do you mean?"

Cédron grasped the princess's hands in his and turned her

to face him. Roväen stepped next to him, frowning. They fired questions at Najeriz.

"Tell me what you know."

"Are they dangerous?"

"Can we defeat them?"

"Can they defend the city?"

Najeriz sighed and slumped her shoulders. "I cannot tell you. I am sworn to secrecy."

Cédron scowled and dropped Najeriz's hands. He turned, took three steps to Säeshi, and knelt at her side.

"What do you sense?" he asked, not daring to touch his cousin as she focused her energy.

Säeshi spread her arms, palms out like a ward. She rotated her body, swinging her palms and sensing the air surrounding them. She held her hands toward the island of Aruzzi and stopped.

"It's there, on the island. Whatever it is, it's strong," she said, opening her eyes. "I can't break through it to identify it. Try using your little windstone."

Cédron pulled the small sphene crystal from his pouch. Its yellow depths glittered in Lord Shamar's light. Closing his eyes, Cédron reached his awareness out and into the stone, accessing the windstone's properties. It was the simplest of windstone properties; the removal of mirage. He'd practiced it hundreds of times with Roväen on the airship. Something was hidden, and he had to remove the veil.

Tendrils of awareness crept through the stone and out toward the Aruzzi nest. Cédron could sense the Árk'äezhi himself now. It felt like a thick membrane that warped and twisted as he tried to break through. It was elastic, giving at his touch without compromising. Sweat popped along his hairline and upper lip. He pushed harder, forcing his energy through the stone and into each of the Aruzzi eggs as he searched.

Moving from the sphere of mirage and into the sphere of

movement, Cédron rolled each egg with his mind and magic, examining each one individually with the combined Árk'äezhi of his body and the sphene stone. His energy reached for the flawed golden egg and hit a solid wall. Cédron was nearly knocked backward with the resistant force. He roared and gripped the stone until the rough edges tore through the flesh of his fingers.

Cédron felt Roväen's hands on his shoulders, his energy pouring into him. Säeshi placed her hands on his forearms, joining her Árk'äezhi to theirs.

"You must enter the third sphere," Roväen's voice barely registered in Cédron's awareness as he concentrated. "You must find clarity – the egg is not what it appears to be."

Cédron's eyes widened. Of course, he was trying to unmask the egg. He thought about the shell, how it seemed dense and ugly, not the pure, translucent color of the other eggs. That's because it wasn't an egg. The second that thought struck his mind, Cédron let go of his effort, released his fight with the foreign Árk'äezhi, and let the awareness wash over him. In his mind's eye, he peeled back the shell, tore open the thick membrane, and pulled out—

"It's the sacred windstone," he gasped, falling forward onto his hands.

"No!" Najeriz shrieked and jumped on his back. "You cannot take our sacred windstone; you will leave us unprotected and exposed."

Roväen pulled Najeriz from Cédron's back and set her on the cobbled stone of the street. "If we do not get the sacred windstone, there will be no world left for you to protect, princess," he said. He held her hands together to prevent her from attacking Cédron again. "Tell me how to get the stone from the island. We can't cross the quicksilver."

Cédron tore his eyes away from the Aruzzi nest to look at Najeriz. The princess set her jaw and glared back, her topaz eyes flashing as she narrowed her gaze.

"It is forbidden," she hissed. "I have sworn a vow, and I

will not break it."

Säeshi put her hand over Cédron's, covering the yellow glow of the sphene with her fingers. "The second sphere," she said, nodding toward the nest of eggs. "Just like you did with the necklace."

Cédron nodded and closed his eyes. He willed the sacred stone to move, to appear at his side. He felt the sweat running down his spine and pooling in the small of his back. Najeriz's cries assaulted his ears, making it difficult to concentrate.

"I can't do it," he grunted, looking at Säeshi and trying to force down the rising panic that tightened his chest, making it hard to breathe.

"You can," she breathed and closed her eyes. "Still your mind, breathe deeply, and focus. Put everything except moving the stone out of your mind. Nothing else matters."

"But—"

"Just do what she says," Roväen interrupted his protests. "We're running out of time."

Cédron felt the tension in his chest tighten, robbing him of breath. Säeshi's grip on his hand tightened, and he felt the cooling wave of her energy flow through his fingers and into his body. The band around his ribs loosened, and he inhaled a long, slow breath. He pictured the sacred windstone nestled in his hand. In his mind, he reached for the fist-sized yellow gem and felt its warmth on his palm. He opened his eyes.

In his outstretched hand lay the rough-cut stone. Its inner light shone golden as if he held a piece of Lord Shamar himself. His breath hitched in his chest, and Säeshi gasped.

"You did it," Säeshi said, grinning and hugging him. "Now, let's get out of here—"

"It's too late," Najeriz snarled. She pulled herself from Roväen's grip and stood facing the Aruzzi island. "The guardians of the stone have awakened. We will not survive."

The ground shook, causing the quicksilver lake to vibrate, its surface chopping like waves in a summer storm. The sand between the street's mosaic tiles jumped, reminding Cédron of a swarm of ubrick beetles. The screech emanating from the island shredded the air, causing everyone to cover their ears from the onslaught. Cédron stared at the island, and his jaw dropped. The glass Aruzzi shook out their wings and craned their long necks, seeking the egg stolen from their custody.

The tallest Aruzzi spotted Cédron with the sacred windstone still resting in his outstretched hand. The Aruzzi shrieked and launched itself into the air, its seven tails fanning out beneath it like feathered whips. The fabled beast spread its wings, the faceted feathers bursting into shards of light as Lord Shamar's rays struck them. The group was momentarily blinded before they could shield their eyes.

The other three Aruzzi followed their leader. The sky was filled with colorful, glass predators as the Aruzzi launched into the air and turned to attack the small group. The sand and tiles on the ground sparked and glimmered from the refracted light of their wings. Cédron felt the hair on the back of his neck raise.

Raising the sacred windstone high above his head, Cédron visualized a whirlwind capturing the Aruzzi and holding them from their intended quarry. His heart sank as the glass raptors cut through his mini-tornado, their talons outstretched to retrieve the stone from his grasp. The lead Aruzzi screeched its defiance as it swooped toward Cédron's head. He ducked and rolled away, stopping at the edge of the quicksilver lake.

"Quick, use the windstone to relocate," Roväen yelled. He grabbed Najeriz and Säeshi, pulling them into the foliage of the nearest wall. "I'll try to keep the ladies out of their sight."

Cédron blinked, his mind working feverishly to comprehend his uncle's instructions. Relocate? How could he— and then it struck him. Move his body like he'd moved the necklace across the airship – like he'd pulled the shards of glass from Anéton's chest. Cédron closed his eyes and took a deep breath. He imagined himself across the lake and opened his eyes. There was almost no sensation accompanying the transition. One second, he was with his companions, and the next, he was across the silver liquid on the island.

"Ha, it worked!" Cédron whooped, jumping into the air and waving at his uncle.

The lead Aruzzi cocked its head, shrieking as the arrow of raptors turned and angled toward the island. Cédron gulped and closed his eyes, changing his location. When he appeared on the top of the library roof, he felt his stomach sink to his feet as the arrow of Aruzzi bore straight for his position. They weren't fooled. Cédron glanced about, seeking a safe haven, but there wasn't one.

"You have to align with the windstone," Rovään called. "Once you have its power, perhaps you can control the glass Aruzzi."

Cédron closed his eyes and focused on the windstone's properties. He could feel the shimmer of Árk'äezhi between himself and the stone as waves of magic rolled off its smooth surface, coating his hand. He could feel a tendril of the stone's Árk'äezhi connected to the glass Aruzzi but knew he couldn't break the bond without damaging or destroying the guardians. Cédron continued to move his location, casting images of himself into opposite places from his destination, but the Aruzzi unerringly followed his energetic signature. They were getting faster at anticipating his moves and closer with each jump.

"I can't access its full power without destroying their guardians," Cédron cried, slamming his fist into a fig tree as he roared his frustration. "Säeshi, can you sense anything that will help?"

The Sumäeri warrior closed her eyes and reached out with her right hand toward the Aruzzi, wrapping the fingers of her left hand around the princess's golden necklace.

Cédron continued his constant jumping but felt drained. He knew he couldn't keep moving like this much longer. The Aruzzi would catch him sooner rather than later. He sent a prayer to Orwaena, asking for help in besting his foes without harming them. They were guarding the windstone as they'd been designed to do, and it wasn't his place to destroy them for it.

"Cédron," Säeshi called, waving between the vines and flowers of the vertical garden wall. "I have an idea. Come back here."

A moment later, Cédron stood buried between the leaves and vines of the wall with his cousin and companions. He cocked his head to hear Säeshi over the shrieks of the Aruzzi who sought him.

"I think there is a connection between the egg, or the windstone, and the princess's necklace. See how it glows?" Säeshi pulled the offending jewelry out from Najeriz's throat, turning it for full effect. "I believe that the glass Aruzzi are just extensions of the windstone's magic. The princess did say this bauble summoned the Aruzzi. Try focusing the windstone's energy through the necklace."

The Aruzzi circled above the building, homing in on his location but unable to find him among the foliage scaling the walls. Najeriz stared at Cédron with wide eyes, the glow from the fluted necklace flickering in her amber eyes as he wrapped his fingers around the fluted glass. Cédron closed his eyes and focused on the windstone's signature Árk'äezhi, channeling it through his body and into the necklace.

Najeriz gasped as the fluted necklace glowed bright gold. The Aruzzi circling above cried out in their staccato shrieks, responding to the increase in magical energy. Cédron could feel the connection between the glass guardians and the windstone like a tightly woven yet elastic braid. It was flexible but felt impervious to outside influences, like the stone's eggshell and the glass Aruzzi had been forged from the same plug.

The connection between the glass egg, guardians, and the necklace had a different feel. Cédron likened it in his mind to the glass balls on display in the throne room. The balls held the perfect blossoms of delicate flowers in their centers while surrounded by another layer of molten glass that formed the ball.

Clearly, there were two levels of magical application to the windstone. The first was likely the creation of the eggshell and the Aruzzi guardians. Cédron felt the second level was filled with the wielder's intention to protect the windstone from discovery and removal. He couldn't figure out how to separate the two strands of energy that were inextricably bound together.

"I can't shake the guardians," Cédron exploded. His outburst caused a startled squeak from Najeriz and caused Roväen and Säeshi to glance at him with raised eyebrows. "I can't get out of here with the windstone without destroying their connection to it."

Roväen twisted his fingers in his beard, his brows knitted together for several moments. Cédron peeked between the leaves he hid behind and held his breath as the Aruzzi's circles became tighter and closer. He knew if he couldn't align with the windstone's power, he wouldn't be able to wield it in the Scepter of Kulari and stop Laylur. He had to devise a plan to both extricate himself with the windstone and not destroy its protectors in the process.

"Can you destroy the glass Aruzzi?" Roväen asked, flicking his eyes from the circling threat to his nephew and back.

Cédron swallowed and rubbed the back of his neck. "Maybe if I blasted them with firestone energy," he said slowly. "I just don't want to do that. Maybe I could distract them long enough to escape?" He looked at Najeriz and shrugged his shoulders.

The princess stared back at him with wide eyes. "You would destroy the guardians? What kind of demon are you?"

she asked, scooching back away from him.

Cédron felt a twinge in his guts. What kind of demon, indeed. That was the point of this quest – to prove that he could handle the power of the sacred stones without becoming the monster so many expected him to be. He wasn't his Uncle Algarik, nor did he succumb to his ancestress Laräeth's appetites.

From the moment his demonic powers manifested, his only ambition was to help people and wield his Árk'äezhi to benefit all Muralians. He understood the prejudices against him, but he also resented never being allowed to show who he was, what he strove to achieve. He was tired of always being on the defensive.

"I don't want to destroy the guardians," Cédron said with a heavy sigh as he addressed the frightened princess. "But I do need to align with the windstone and get back to the palace."

Säeshi fingered the necklace and turned it around on its cable. "Princess, this flower appears to have holes along this side," she said, squinting at the row of puckered glass. "If you blew on the end, could you play this like an instrument?"

Princess Najeriz clamped her mouth shut, her lips a tight line. She glowered at Cédron before turning her attention back to Säeshi. "How could you know that?"

Säeshi released the necklace and put her hand on the princess's shoulder. "You hinted earlier that it summoned the Aruzzi. Perhaps it can also encourage them to disperse?" She shook Najeriz's shoulder. "You must try, princess."

"No," Najeriz said. She crossed her arms over her chest and set her jaw. "My sacred duty is to guard the Aruzzi, not to manipulate them. I will not do it."

Cédron looked at his kinsmen and saw the uncompromising determination in their eyes. They understood what was at stake, even if the princess did not. He would have to destroy the Aruzzi. His heart heavy,

Cédron swapped the windstone for the firestone in the pouch at his side and nodded. He stepped out from the covering foliage and raised the firestone above his head.

The four Aruzzi shrieked in defiance at his appearance, diving toward him with terrifying speed, talons outstretched. Cédron felt the fire Árk'äezhi swell in his chest, expanding his ribcage and prickling the fire tattoos surrounding his heart. The power built until he felt he couldn't contain it any longer. Cédron raised the stone and shot a blast of fire into the chest of the raptor at the arrow's apex.

The fireball hit the glass bird and exploded, sending a wave of power that nearly knocked him off his feet. The wind blew his hair into his face, simultaneously blocking his view and protecting his eyes from the brilliant burst of colored light the impact caused. Cédron raised his arm to protect his face from the tiny shards of shattered glass, but there weren't any. He lowered his arm and gasped. The Aruzzi assembled into a new arrow formation with a different raptor at its head and came toward the group.

"Mijáko piles!" Cédron swore. "Now, what do we do?"

"Run!" yelled Roväen, turning toward the fountain.

Cédron herded his companions in front of him, facing them toward the fountain while wondering if the glass Aruzzi claws were as sharp as the real ones. He thought again of the connection between the guardians and the stone, bringing the glass balls again to mind. As he lurched toward the fountain, holding his breath against the talons he knew would soon rake across his back, Cédron had a thought.

"I have a—" Cédron began but was pulled to the ground by Roväen.

Two Aruzzi swooped down, swiping with their claws exactly where his shoulders had been a split second before his uncle pulled him to the flagstones. The raptors screamed their frustration and the hairs inside Cédron's ears quivered and itched. He covered his ears with both hands and got to his knees.

Shoving the firestone back into the pouch, Cédron pulled the aquastone. "Get to that building on the far side of the fountain," he yelled to his companions. "I'm going to try something else."

Säeshi and Rovären both nodded and grabbed the mulish Najeriz, propelling her past the fountain and underneath the building's archway. Cédron raised the aquastone toward the fountain. If fire wouldn't work, perhaps water might. He wondered if encasing himself in a bubble of water would cover him enough to block the magic of the windstone and sever or at least dull the connection between the guardians and their charge.

Cédron closed his eyes, waving the aquastone in a circular motion between his body and the fountain. The water in the fountain responded. Cédron found himself inside a sphere of water and raised the stone to shoulder height. The bubble of water lifted into the air, taking him with it. The Aruzzi swiveled their heads back and forth, tongues flicking outside their beaks like snakes tasting the air. As he guided his water sphere past the fountain and above his friends, he watched the Aruzzi begin a grid-pattern search from his last position, working a grid toward the island.

Cédron felt his eyes sting with relief. It was working. He siphoned some of his Árk'äezhi to pull Rovären, Säeshi, and Najeriz into a second globe of water. Lifting the two spinning orbs of glittering water filled with people, Cédron visualized the palace rooftop and shot forward. The second sphere followed directly behind him, and the Aruzzi continued to circle the island, seeking the missing egg without success. When the mythical creatures were out of his sight, Cédron allowed himself a small breath of relief.

Glancing below, Cédron marveled at the network of aqueducts snaking away from the trough that spread around the tip of the water screw. Waterways angled down in every direction, allowing water to flow throughout the city. The screw turned inexorably, but after watching for a moment, Cédron realized that there was no water splashing into the trough and down the aqueducts. The stone was bone dry. That couldn't be right.

The swirling water spun the group toward the back of the palace, and Cédron heard Säeshi cry out. He turned to see what had alarmed her and followed her pointing finger to a dry aqueduct filled with several boats of people. The rafts were stranded in the empty troughs, though several men shoved from behind to slide the wooden barges down. Cédron wasn't sure what they were doing or why they'd gotten themselves into the aqueducts, but based on the strained expressions on their faces, he figured these people were attempting to escape the palace. What was happening inside that would spur these families to such drastic measures?

A shadow crossed above Cédron, and he ducked, causing the spheres to waver and drop. Säeshi and Najeriz let out short screams at the sudden change in direction. Cédron looked up to find the greasy, black underbelly of Algarik's rinzar. The blood in Cédron's veins turned to shards of ice. He felt the prickling throughout his limbs and torso. If Algarik were in the palace, that would explain the exodus of the families. That also meant that the Zhoula was in grave danger.

Cédron focused his intention and steered the water spheres to the trough at the top of the screw. As they landed, the water broke apart and rushed down the aqueduct holding the family barges. He hoped the men would hear the surging water and jump into the boats before they floated away, but he didn't have time to do more than hope. He had to get to the Zhoula and protect her and the city from his Uncle Algarik.

chapter 40: Facing the Hazzara

"Push!" Sénna yelled at the three Zaouni, heaving the wooden table through the dry aqueduct.

"It's too dry," grunted the warrior closest to her. He stood, wiping the sweat beading his forehead beneath the red headdress. "We need to get the screw moving again and water flowing, or we'll be stuck here like fárocs in a cage."

Sénna's hands slipped off her hips and fell to her sides. She looked at the drawn, tight faces of the vazurgan families she was trying to save and blew out a long breath. There had to be a way to get these people to the safety of the qanats. They just needed a propellant of some sort.

"What about oil?" Sénna asked the Zaouni with the roped hair. "Would that allow the wood to slide down the stone?"

The warrior pulled his thick locs out of his eyes, tied them into a knot at the back of his head, and put the feathered headdress back on. He shook his head and patted the curved edge of the aqueduct with his palm.

"No," he sighed. He looked at Sénna with sad amber eyes. "The stone is porous. The oil would work for a moment but would soak into the stone, making it soft and compromising its integrity. We can't risk it with the weight of all our children."

Sénna slumped back against the edge of the aqueduct, crossing her arms over her chest and frowning. They needed the water from the screw, but they'd locked the doors to prevent flooding the city. They had to leave them closed to drown their enemies in the palace. She ran her fingers through her hair, pulling the sticky tendrils from her face and gasping as she snagged them on knots.

The children on the tables-turned-barges were whining. Their mothers tried soothing them with little songs and games, but Sénna could hear the strain in their voices. They were afraid, and the children sensed it. Two Zaouni walked past, each pulling water canisters from their belts. She reached out and grasped the closest warrior's forearm as he passed her.

"Excuse me, what do you th—"

An explosion rocked the aqueduct. Sénna dropped her arm and looked to the west, where a black cloud of smoke rose into the hazy air. The gate was damaged, and she could see black shapes swarming into the city, heading toward the docks. The acrid scent of the smoke scorched her throat, causing her and the families to cough.

The city walls protected the inlet below her, housing the fishing fleets and merchant ships, but now the vessels were vulnerable. If the Hazzara destroyed them, the citizens of Taboriz would suffer for Tides until they could rebuild.

Sénna felt indignant heat flush through her.

Screams and coughs filled the air as the women and children huddled in the center of the boats. The aqueducts shivered as more minor explosions popped throughout the city, followed by the cries from the wounded. The Zaouni scrambled toward the gate, trying to cut off the Hazzara advance, but they were outnumbered. Sénna could see the Hazzara teeming through the narrow streets and overrunning the red and gold warriors.

The city was doomed. Before Lord Shamar set this evening, Taboriz would be lost, and all her history and culture wiped away like it never existed. Sénna looked out over the vertical gardens' green walls, then raised her eyes to the domes filled with stained glass and shook her head. Centuries of knowledge and art couldn't be destroyed like this. There had to be a way to save at least some of the people. She turned her head to watch the terrified families and groaned.

Sénna pulled her fingers through her hair again, the knotted ends forcing her head back as she raked her fingers viciously through, breaking strands haphazardly. She opened her eyes to the afternoon sky and gasped. Above the city floated three swirling spheres of water. Each globe housed a figure, the third ball holding two people. The Zaouni next to her followed her gaze and gave a yell.

"Enemies in the sky!" he cried, pulling the bow from across his shoulders and nocking an arrow.

Sénna grabbed his arm. "Wait, I don't think they're enemies. Look!" She pointed as the balls floated closer. "Isn't that your princess in the last orb?"

The Zaouni squinted his black eyes and nodded. "Hold!" he cried and lowered his weapon.

"What devilry imprisons her in the water?" he asked. The warrior grabbed Sénna by the shoulders and shook her. "Is she in danger?"

Sénna smiled faintly and shook her head, relief washing

through her knees making them buckle. She gripped the stone rim of the aqueduct and steadied herself.

"It is Cédron's Árk'äezhi that lifts them into the air in the water balls. He already controls fire and water; he must have found the sacred windstone," she said, shaking off the warrior's hands and turning to watch the spheres as they floated toward the palace roof.

The children's cries turned to gasps of wonder. The vazurgan families followed the progress of the floating orbs of water as they sailed overhead and up to the palace. Sénna felt a nagging push in the back of her mind as she watched Cédron, Säeshi, Rovä en, and Princess Najeriz hover over the main building. Cédron would have to release all that water to escape the spheres, and that water would have to go somewhere.

As she watched, Sénna saw Cédron turn and glance down at her. He waved once and pointed to the blocked aqueduct door below him. Sénna nodded and gave him a thumbs-up, then clapped her hands three times.

"Everyone get on the rafts," she yelled, pointing to the tables stuck in the dry stone channel. "We're going to get an influx of water in a moment that should propel us down to the eastern gate."

The six Zaouni surrounding the families raced to corral the scattered children and heave them onto the barges. Women gathered their silken skirts and scarves, tucking them beneath their legs as they crowded together. Above, Sénna heard a loud splash, followed by two more in quick succession. Glancing up, she spotted Cédron standing at the blasted door to the screw, inspecting the damage. Rovä en and the women joined him as the water from their orbs cascaded down the refugees' dry channel.

"Hold on!" Sénna yelled, jumping onto the closest table and sliding her fingers into the narrow space between slats in the wood. "It's going to be bumpy."

The water roared down the aqueduct and hit Sénna's raft

with a crash. The wood lifted into the air, threatening to flip end over end. Sénna grabbed the Zaouni closest to her. He was a massive man with biceps larger than her torso. Her pale hands were dwarfed against his enormous forearms, like a tiny snowflake against a mahogany fence post. She heaved them both back to the edge of the table, shifting the weight and lowering the wooden barge to nearly level on the wave of water.

"Quick thinking, young lady," the warrior grinned and grabbed at his chest. "I am not a strong swimmer."

Sénna laughed. "Glad to—" she began.

Their raft crashed into the table ahead of it, knocking Sénna into the Zaouni's muscular back. She bounced off his shoulders and fell off the raft. Bubbles filled her nose as she plunged into the water. Sénna held her breath as she tumbled head over heels in the narrow channel of the aqueduct. The initial wave of water passed through the three tables, lifting and carrying them down the aqueduct channels toward the eastern gate.

Sénna's head popped above the water, and she shook her head. The rafts were much heavier than she was, gaining momentum as they rode the waves down toward the city's eastern gate. As the water rushed downward, Sénna spotted a corner in the aqueduct. Her stomach tightened. She reached out both arms to hold the water, trying to gain some control of her descent but was pummeled into the side of the channel. Approaching the corner, the Zaouni aboard the rafts all leaned away from the turn, successfully navigating their barges into their new direction.

Sending a prayer to Hamra, Sénna tucked herself into a ball as she neared the corner, increasing her speed. She hit the stone corner with a force that launched her over the side of the aqueduct. Screaming, she flailed her arms in a futile effort to slow her fall. She landed on a green and white striped canopy above a tobacco shop and rolled down the canvas before sliding to the cobbled street with a grunt.

Groaning, Sénna eased herself to her feet. She pulled off her green scarf and wrung it out, waving the thin material in the air to dry it a bit. Modesty required she wrap it around her slim hips to combat the sheerness of her pants from the water. She looked toward the aqueduct, spotting the last of the barges as it sailed around the corner behind the third wall and toward the eastern gate.

Relief washed over her, and she doubled over to hold her weakened knees. The children were safe, but what about the Zhoula? Had Zaran killed the ruler of Taboriz? What about Tóran? No water filled the city streets, so perhaps he'd been successful, but had he survived? Sénna couldn't answer her questions standing in the middle of the road. Cédron and his companions were in the palace – that would be the best place to look for answers. Heaving a sigh, Sénna began the trek up the cobbled streets toward the glittering white marble tower.

Läenshi sat atop the wagon in a seat nearly as ancient as the woman beside her. Market Queen Marizen cracked the whip, eliciting deep brays from the team of four ozryks pulling the laden cart. They tossed their heads, their horns piercing the sky like two-pronged forks.

"May the Zhoula's alzaytan feast on your innards," Marizen cursed at the ambling beasts, spitting past the blackroot gritted between her teeth.

Läenshi grinned and shook her head. "They are pulling over a hundred rolls of fabric," she said. "This wagon must weigh nearly three-thousand pounds."

"That's no excuse," Marizen grumbled, but she tucked the whip beneath the bench seat. "Those black-clad fárocs from the desert will ruin my business if we don't stop them."

Cybél leaned forward from the back of the wagon and squeezed Läenshi's shoulder. The Sumäeri turned around and followed Cybél's gaze toward the harbor.

In the city below, scores of men wearing black with black turbans swarmed the city's pier and lower level. The smoke from their explosions still curled into the air above the wreckage of the gate and stone wall. The colorful rubble of shattered mosaic tiles littered the streets, making it difficult for the alzaytans to navigate the shards with their soft-pad feet.

"We have to hurry," Cybél gasped, her eyes large in her pale face. "Where is your sister? Does she have her potions ready?"

Läenshi put her fingers to her lips and let out a piercing whistle. An answering staccato whistle reverberated above the stone walls. She glanced ahead and waved to the läenier rider perched atop the wall, keeping watch. He pointed forward and whistled again, this time in a trill that swooped from low to high. Läenshi grinned and nodded.

"She's just ahead with the rest of the Wing. They're anxious to get started," she said and patted Cybél's hand.

The ozryks clipped along the narrow street, swerving to avoid the scattered brass pots a merchant toppled in his haste to leave his premises. Marizen tugged their tall horns away from the striped awnings that hung down over doorways and shop stalls and cracked her whip again. Läenshi looked at her companion and noted the ancient woman's tight jaw and gnarled fingers gripping the reins.

"Cybél's plan will work," she said to Marizen. "My sister is a master with potions."

"Hmph, we'll see," Marizen squinted up at the tall Sumäeri woman. "If they don't, we won't have to worry about it for long." She spat again and grinned up at Läenshi with her blackened teeth.

The narrow street opened into a thoroughfare wide enough that two wagons could drive abreast. Laundry lines and colorful awnings stretched from building to building like a canopy overhead. The fabric filtered Lord Shamar's light, easing some of the tension between Läenshi's brows. She hoped her confidence in her sister Läerei's abilities wasn't misplaced. Cybél's plan, however unorthodox, did have its merits—provided everything worked as planned.

Behind them, three more wagons loaded with more rolls of fabric and the blazesand canisters rocked and creaked as they sped to keep up with Marizen. The wagons angled up toward the Zaouni quadrant and their training grounds. After a short delay from a broken wheel, accompanied by such eloquent swearing by the Market Queen that Läenshi's ears burned, the lead wagon pulled through an arched gate made of red-and-white-checkered stones.

Läenshi scanned the courtyard area for Trilläen and found him surrounded by a knot of the tall Zaouni. His silver hair glimmered like a diamond surrounded in onyx as the group of men converged over a table. Marizen slapped the reins and allowed the ozryks to charge forward, yanking their heads back as they reached the men.

"You there," Marizen called. She waved an imperious finger at Captain Villinäes and the Zaouni leaders. "Get these carts unloaded and the rolls to all those flying beasties."

Trilläen straightened and turned, a bemused look on his face. He glanced at Läenshi, who shrugged before turning his attention to Marizen.

"Great Lady," he said, bowing. "How can I be of service?"

Marizen spat blackroot out of the side of her mouth and put her tiny, gnarled hands on her hips. "I told you, get these carts unloaded."

Läenshi swallowed a laugh as her captain's eyebrows raised so high into his bangs that they disappeared.

"Queen Marizen has spoken," one of the Zaouni warriors clapped him on the back and grinned. "We'd better get busy."

Once the Zaouni and Läenier riders were informed of

their task, the offloading took less than ten minutes. Each läenier held two rolls of fabric. The riders or warriors unrolled the damp material and tied a heavy blazesand canister to the end. When both Wings of riders were ready, the Wingleaders whistled and gave the signal to rise.

Läenshi found her sister and Cybél fussing over the last of the rolls. Läerei used a broad brush to paint her toxin onto the fabric held by a couple of riders, who then waved the silken material in the breeze to dry it some before rolling it up.

"Are you sure it will work?" Cybél twisted a strand of her titian hair around her fingers as she watched the riders attach the canister to the end of the roll.

Läerei ran fingers through the blue stripe in her hair and frowned, then brightened as she saw her sister join them. "Läenshi, just in time. We will show these Hazzara the pride of our family and the ferocity of the Sumäeri."

Läenshi bit her lower lip. "You sound just like father." She touched the blue stripe in her sister's hair. "You've captured the sapphire blue of father's eyes."

Läerei's smile faded, and she gripped her sister's arm. "He would be proud of what we're accomplishing together. Both our parents would."

"I miss them so," sighed Läenshi.

Läerei nodded. "We will avenge their deaths when we defeat these desert devils. The Näenji Council has much to answer for."

"So, how are we going to neutralize these Hazzara?" Läenshi asked. She watched the thousands of men snaking their way through the streets of the lower city.

Läerei pulled Cybél closer and wrapped a wiry arm around the Askári woman's slim shoulders. "For a simpering beauty, this one has a surprisingly sharp and devious mind," Läerei grinned at her friend. "I think we should keep her. Just enhance the properties of the liquid I coated the fabric with, and we'll give the city a show."

Läenshi shrugged and jumped back onto the wagon. She raised her arms and closed her eyes, encompassing the entire courtyard filled with läeniers burdened with heavy fabric. She slowed her breath, feeling her heartbeat and the blood pulsing through her body. Sinking deeper, Läenshi imagined the flowing energy coursing through the ground, the river of Árk'äezhi that made up Lady Muralia's terran form. She reached for that connection, siphoning the energy of the deity's magic and shaping it to her intention.

Opening her eyes, Läenshi guided the sparkling motes of energy erupting from her palms toward the fabric. As she encompassed the material with her power, the properties of the substance revealed themselves to her.

"Oh ho, linseed oil! Now I see what you have in mind," Läenshi laughed, shooting her sister a grin.

The glittering energy turned red as the sparks left her fingers and fused with the many rolls of fabric. The air shimmered with her magic, muting the light from Lord Shamar above them. When the linseed oil had all been expanded and enhanced, Läenshi dropped her hands and doused her Árk'äezi.

"That will be a terrible way to die," Läenshi said, facing her sister and Cybél.

"Yes, it will," Läerei said. Her face was impassive, her shoulders and jaw both set, but her eyes sparkled.

Läenshi cast one last glance over her shoulder at the doomed Hazzara and allowed her sister to link her arm and Cybél's in her own and lead them toward the läenier Wing.

"Show-off," Läenshi snorted.

chapter 41: Victory and Defeat

Sénna's side ached from running. She grabbed her side, blowing out hard to relieve the pain, but kept going. The thin soles of her slippers barely protected her feet from the hot cobblestones as she made her way to the palace. The press of humanity trying to leave the city thinned as she made her way to the palace.

Sénna had sprinted through the last two gates and into the Vazurgan District. Catching her breath, she swept her gaze toward the western entrance and gasped. Thousands of black-clad Hazzara, some mounted on their fierce alzaytans, swarmed the gate and the city's lower level. She thought of the advance group of Hazzara sent to the palace to kill the Zhoula and hoped that the ruler had survived her wounds. She didn't know how many more of the enemy had infiltrated the castle.

Sénna's thoughts shifted to Tóran. He'd succeeded in sabotaging the water screw and flooding the palace in the effort to thwart the Hazzara's plans, but she didn't know if he survived the sharp metal blades of the screw. She hoped he did – he'd proven himself worthy of forgiveness, and it would be a shame to lose such an accomplished warrior. Cédron's face floated into her mind, and she grimaced. He would be devastated at the loss of his brother should Tóran not survive. She shook those thoughts from her mind and looked out over the city.

Citizens of Taboriz continued to stream from the southern gate toward the desert. Sénna wondered where they would find shelter. Did they have underground places they could hide until the danger was past? She couldn't see the eastern gate, but she hoped the women and children she'd helped escape the palace had made it safely out of the city. The influx of water was sufficient to propel them through the last two interior gates and out into the desert. She hoped they would find their way into the safety of the qanats. The underground water system ran beneath the desert sands in a continual northeastern rise toward the hills of Samshäeli, where they would find sanctuary.

Sénna took one last deep breath, turned, and jogged toward the palace. The streets were mostly empty now, with one lone wagon clattering toward her from the ruins of the Zaouni armory. She spared it a glance as she jogged past, then did a double-take. Atop the wagon were Marizen and Anzeri. Sénna waved to the women, who pulled the reins and slowed the canter of the ozryks. Once brought to a halt, the beasts tossed their two-pronged horns and stamped sideways.

"What news from the Zaouni?" Sénna asked, shading her

eyes from Lord Shamar's brilliant light.

Anzeri frowned down at Sénna. "We lost many of our warriors. Those remaining prepare now to defend the city with the Sumäeri. The läenier Wings and your friend have a rather unorthodox plan."

Queen Marizen cackled and waggled a finger at Sénna. "Your friend has a devious mind. If her plan works, it will save the city without risking more of our warriors."

"What plan is this? I wasn't able to hear the specifics," Sénna said. She wiped the sweat from her forehead with the now-grimy green scarf.

Marizen coughed and spat blackroot onto the cobbles. "Jump up here, girl; we'll watch together."

"Yes, join us," Anzeri smiled. She reached down to assist Sénna up the side of the wooden wagon to the bench seat. "If this plan doesn't work, at least we'll be mounted and ready to flee the city before the Hazzara overrun it completely."

Sénna settled herself next to Anzeri, and Marizen whipped the reins, spurring the skittish ozryks back into motion. They angled up the streets toward the palace, branching off before the gates to a promontory overlooking the western quadrant. They ducked the overhanging vines laden with clusters of purple fruits as they entered the courtyard. Sénna and Anzeri both plucked handfuls as they passed beneath the arch, grinning at each other in their single-mindedness.

"And now we wait," clucked Marizen, tying the reins to the hitch protruding from the wall.

The city below them spread out like a lush carpet, with black rot worming its way upward at the edge. Behind them, faint whistles carried on the breeze, and Sénna ducked involuntarily as the shadow of the Wing flew overhead. Looking up, she spied the läeniers burdened with rolls of fabric.

"Mijáko piles!" Sénna snorted. "What are they doing, defeating the Hazzara by broadening their fashion sense?"

She dropped her head into her hands and shook it from side to side.

Marizen screeched a laugh and rolled backward on the bench, nearly toppling into the bed.

Anzeri nudged Sénna in the ribs. "Watch."

Sénna raised her head and watched the Wings spread out over the western quadrant of the city. The Wingleaders whistled and gestured their instructions to each other as the raptors jockeyed for position. She spotted Läerei as she flew overhead, grinning at the warrior's flushed cheeks and fierce expression. Sénna had come to respect the Angäersol women during her journey with them. Not only for their unwavering dedication to the Sumäeri Order but for the love they had for one another despite their differences. Sénna's own losses seemed paltry compared to theirs, and yet they managed to move forward, always the next mission to accomplish. She felt a little ashamed for the self-pity she'd indulged in and for the disdain she'd shown them earlier.

A loud whistle jerked Sénna from her thoughts, and she gazed upwards. As one, the läeniers and their riders screamed their war cries and launched forward. The first Wing angled down toward the advancing Hazzara and flung their rolls of fabric. The colorful ribbons of cloth streamed out behind the bulky canisters of blazesand attached to the material's leading edge.

"And so it begins," cackled Marizen, clapping her hands and rocking back and forth.

Sénna glanced over at Anzeri, whose hands bunched the silk of her tunic with white knuckles. Sénna turned her gaze back over the city. The streaming fabric coursed down the various narrow streets, sometimes catching on the awnings sticking out from windows and covering doorways but mostly blanketing the advancing Hazzara. Blazesand containers tipped as they landed, dumping the fiery sand onto the ground. Although the alzaytans struggled and panicked beneath the covering, Sénna couldn't see why covering their enemies in cloth would stop them.

"Come on, come on," Anzeri chanted, bunching more silk into her spasming fists.

Sénna looked at her companions and back to the streets now covered in colorful stripes of writhing cloth. "What's supposed to happen?"

Marizen stopped her laughing and rocking, her expression going slack. Anzeri pursed her lips, her cheeks pale.

"They coated the cloth in a flammable oil," she said, frowning as she stood. "The blazesand was supposed to ignite the fabric, but it's not working."

Sénna stood with Anzeri, watching in horror as the Hazzara fought their way free of the different ribbons of cloth and untangled their alzaytans. A knot in her stomach rose to clamp icy fingers around her chest. The sweat pooling between her breasts turned cold, and she shivered.

"They will overrun the city and the palace," Sénna gasped and sat down hard on the wooden bench, her mind spinning as she considered and discarded various escape options.

They were too high to reach any of the main gates before the Hazzara would catch them. The aqueducts were dry again so that they couldn't escape via the water system. Perhaps they could slide down the blades of the water screw. Sénna looked at the ancient Market Queen and sighed, deflated. Marizen didn't look like she would survive the rigors of escape, even if they had a viable option. No, they would stand and fight. And die. Or worse. Sénna dropped her head back into her hands, closing her eyes. She took a deep breath and nearly choked when Anzeri whooped and jumped next to her.

"What is it? What's happening?" Sénna raised her head and looked out at the city, now a wall of flames.

Drums beat, vibrating the ground and the cart. Zaouni Warriors chanted as they advanced, some clashing swords upon shields while others shot flaming arrows into the saturated cloth, blanketing their enemies. Ribbon after ribbon of colorful fabric blossomed into flame as the burning arrows ignited the linseed oil. The shrieks of men and beasts roiling beneath the cloth turned Sénna's stomach, in direct opposition to the enticing scent of roasted meat wafting up from the carnage below.

"It's working," Anzeri cried. She gasped, sitting hard on the wagon bench, and pointed to the street directly below them. "Look, some of the Hazzara have escaped the flames."

The women turned to watch the grim-faced enemy charge up the street. Smoke rose from the group as some garments were still flaming, but it didn't faze the determined Hazzara. Sénna held her breath, both from the tension and the need to quell her stomach. Anzeri grabbed her hand and squeezed it. Sénna squeezed back. The Hazzara advanced, one of the men smiling as he spotted the women frozen on the wagon.

Anzeri swallowed audibly and cleared her throat. "My Queen, I am sorry for not protecting you—"

A shriek from above cut the apology short. Sénna's breath released in a whoosh as the läeniers swooped down overhead. She looked up to see Läenshi and Läerei weave their Árk'äezhi together. Läerei launched a glowing green vial at the advancing Hazzara. Läenshi waved her hands, increasing the vial in both size and luminosity before it crashed to the ground and sprayed the Hazzara in its liquid.

Behind the wagon, the rumbling of quick-marching feet shook the ground. A squad of gold-breasted, red-feathered Zaouni charged past and formed a barrier in front of the wagon. At a command from the leader, flaming arrows were nocked and loosed towards the enemy. As the first arrow struck the green liquid, the air around the wagon seemed to suck down into the city and the Hazzara. Sénna couldn't get a breath. One second later, the force from the explosion of energy toppled both the warriors standing their ground and the women atop the wagon.

Sénna ignored the bruises and splinters in her knees to crawl over to Queen Marizen and roll the tiny woman onto her back.

"Queen Marizen, are you alright?" Sénna gasped, feeling the still woman's neck for a pulse.

Anzeri crawled over and cradled the ancient woman's head in her lap, tears streaming down her cheeks. "My Queen, forgive me." She dropped her head, tears splashing onto Marizen's forehead.

"You're leaking, Anzeri," Marizen croaked, wiping Anzeri's tears from her forehead. "Or have the rains started early this Tide?"

The usually stoic Anzeri collapsed over her matriarch with a final laughing sob and wiped her eyes. "No, my Queen, the rains haven't begun. Are you injured?"

Marizen closed her eyes and took a few breaths. Sénna continued to explore her body with practiced fingers, finding no apparent breaks or tightness in the body indicative of swelling. Sénna was grateful for the long hours she'd spent under Cybél's medical tutelage on the airship. She looked at Anzeri and shrugged, shaking her head.

"I seem to be fine," the elderly woman groaned and reached for Sénna's hand. "Pull me up, my girl."

Sénna eased Marizen up while Anzeri lifted her gently from behind, settling the woman's back against her chest. They watched as the Sumäeri and Zaouni neutralized the last of the Hazzara threat to their city, tossing black-clad bodies into the raging infernos, simultaneously destroying their enemies and cleansing the streets.

"We should get back to the palace," Anzeri said, helping Sénna lift Marizen to her unsteady feet and set her back on the bench.

The ozryks were tangled in their harnesses from the blast of energy. Sénna jumped out to straighten the leather straps, dodging the sharp tines of their horns as she unstrapped and re-buckled the leather. As she climbed back aboard the wagon, she spotted a cloud off to the northwest. Shading her eyes, she squinted against the glare to identify what caused the sand to stir so violently.

"Is that a sandstorm approaching?" Sénna asked, pointing towards the disturbance.

Anzeri and Marizen both twisted on the bench to follow her finger. Anzeri gasped, and Marizen exhaled a long gust of wind through filled cheeks.

"Zaran told us—no, taunted us—with news of a stone army of Maüli. They will be here before nightfall," Anzeri said in a toneless voice. "We will not survive them."

Sénna felt the elation from watching their allies defeat the Hazzara deflate and turn to dust. She had desperately wanted the rumors of a stone army inhabited by angry spirits of the dead to have remained an inconceivable hoax. Looking out over the desert, the proof of their impending doom stirred a deep-seated horror in her chest. Sénna was torn between wanting to hide in a corner and race to the palace. Her sense of duty won over her fear.

"We have to get to the palace and warn them," Sénna said, handing the reins to Marizen.

It was a longshot, Sénna knew, but she held out hope that Cédron had gained enough power—and confidence—to stop the catastrophe. She assumed that he'd acquired the windstone when she spotted him using his formidable powers above the palace. She wondered if he needed the Rod of Shouman to access the stone's magic or if he could do that on his own. Either way, their fates lay in that young man's hands, and she prayed to Orwaena that he'd found the courage to use his power.

Marizen wheeled the cart around and cracked the reins across the ozryk's backs. The wagon jerked as the beasts bolted back up the hill. The staccato clicking of their nails on the stones pounded in Sénna's head, providing an uncomfortable counter-beat to her racing heart. She wasn't sure what they would find when they reached the palace. The

Zhoula had been badly injured in the fight over their escape. Sénna hoped the matriarch would survive her wounds, but she couldn't be sure. She didn't know what kind of healers or medicines they had here in Taboriz. Perhaps if she could find Cybél and have her look at the Zhoula's wounds—

"Laylur's beast, what is that creature?" Anzeri gasped. Her bronze cheeks were pale and drawn as she stared into the sky with wide eyes.

Sénna followed Anzeri's gaze and felt the tiny spark of optimism she'd nurtured in her mind fizzle and die. Perched atop one of the palace's high, green walls was a black-feathered raptor so large they could seat three airships on its back. The beast's baleful yellow eyes were hooded in Lord Shamar's light, but Sénna recognized it. She'd seen it once before, Tides ago.

"It's a rinzar," Sénna whispered and wrapped her arms tight around her chest, holding herself together against the painful emotions assaulting her.

Memories filled her mind. Her breath came in short pants, and she felt her palms prickle with sweat – she was living the panic and fear for herself and her mother once again. Sénna felt her mother thrusting her notes into a much-younger Sénna's arms and commanding her to run. She felt the heat of the flames, and her lungs burned from the scorching smoke. And then there was the laughter.

The magic-wielder with the red amulet incinerated the Laborers Guild in Táksabai, slaughtering everyone still working and all their animals, then flew away on this monster shrieking with glee as everything surrounding her burned. No, she wouldn't succumb to the terror. It wasn't here now. Sénna clamped down on her thoughts, forcing them into the past where they belonged. She had different options now. This time, she wouldn't run away.

"What's a rinzar, and why is it perched on the palace wall?" Marizen snorted through her nose, her lips pursed in disapproval or the raptor's choice of eyries.

Sénna closed her eyes and took a deep breath. When she opened her eyes again, she focused on her companions. "It is the beast ridden by the vilest mage in Muralia. That mage hunts Cédron. We have to warn him."

Marizen raised the reins again, but Anzeri pulled them to the right. "No, we can't drive straight to the palace. What if that thing spots us and raises the alarm?"

"Where would you have me go, Daughter of My House?" the Market Queen nodded to Anzeri and held the stamping beasts in check.

Anzeri stood and turned, her vibrant green headwrap capturing the flecks of hazel in her eyes as she scoured the city with her gaze. "Drive the wagon down this street to our right and follow it behind the main entrance of the palace. A servant's entrance on the lower level will allow us access to a staircase that opens above the throne room. Perhaps we can see what the situation is before we announce ourselves to those inside."

Sénna swallowed hard and nodded. She didn't know if the Zoula had perished from Zaran's attack, if Algarik held the palace or if Cédron still lived. Regardless of what they would find, caution was the wisest choice.

The wagon groaned as Marizen turned it down the narrow street, navigating between upturned carts, household goods, and clothes strewn haphazardly in the street after the inhabitant's hasty evacuation. The scent of rancid oil and rotting food wafted from the pile of shattered pottery in a corner between buildings where several large jars had rolled off their transport and smashed against the cobblestones of the street. Sénna covered her face with her scarf and allowed herself only shallow breaths.

After several turns, ever angling up towards the palace, Anzeri raised her palm in a halting motion. Marizen reined in the ozryks, and the wagon rattled to a stop. They could see the domed top of the palace curve above the wall beneath which they sat. Sénna spied the sturdy vines that wove up the wall filled with clusters of fruits. She followed the climbing tendrils up and over the courtyard to where it connected with the palace dome's bottom edge and formed a plan.

"Let me go in first," Sénna said to her companions. "I have many Tides of experience slipping unseen into small places and gathering information. The Zhoula may already be dead, and this city can't afford to lose two of its leaders today."

Anzeri placed her hand on Sénna's forearm and squeezed gently. "You remember your way to the throne room?"

Sénna gave a wan smile. "I've had a chance to use the servant's back stairs and hallways already and the opportunity to learn my way around the palace. I'll be fine."

Anzeri nodded. "May Lord Shamar's blessing be upon you," she said and turned to Marizen. "We must return to the city and help with the evacuation of our people. I hope to see you on the other side of this chaos, my friend."

Sénna nodded, then leaped from the wagon, reaching for the corded vines. She pulled herself up, hand over hand, her lithe form gliding up the overgrown wall with practiced ease. Reaching the top of the wall, she looked up to find the glass piping holding the vertical garden angled steeply toward the adjacent rooftop, overhanging a courtyard below.

Leaning out onto the glass aquaponic system, Sénna stretched her hands to reach the next cluster of climbing vines. She sprang upward with a grunt, but the pressure from the launch drove her right foot through the pipe.

"Mijáko piles," Sénna cursed under her breath and pulled her foot free.

Glancing down, she saw that she'd broken through one of the circular holes from which the plants grew. She now stood three inches farther from her goal. Heat flared through her as the frustration spiked. She wrapped her scarf around her right fist and punched the pipe at eye level. She broke through the glass, sending a shower of dirt into her eyes and down her halter.

"That was stupid," Sénna gritted her teeth and pulled herself up on the jagged edge of the pipe, then laughed. "Or brilliant."

Sénna reached up with her swathed fist and smashed another spot on the pipe trellis. Grinning, she pulled herself higher and stuck her foot on the pipe below. Up and up, Sénna climbed, reaching the windows just below the highest domed roof after several minutes. The leaded glass windows were locked – but wait – she spied a hole in the third window from her position.

Sénna inched her way across the wall, glancing down occasionally to ensure nobody had spotted her. She still wore the yellow garments that, although dirty, would still be very visible against the green vines and purple fruits across which she made her way. She reached the broken window, and her heart sank. The opening was big enough for her leg but wouldn't allow her body, slender though she was. The lead piping was cracked and weak, but Sénna didn't think she could break it with her fists.

"Now what, genius?" Sénna muttered to herself, glancing around for ideas.

Sénna pulled herself just a couple of inches higher on the vines, still leaning back, and tugged at them. They held.

"You can do this," she said, blowing short breaths through rounded lips to gear herself up for the feat she was about to attempt. "You have to – everyone is counting on you. Don't screw this up."

Sénna's heart continued to hammer her chest, and the sweat on her palms made her hold on the vines slippery. She wiped one hand, then the other, on her thighs. With a deep inhale and prayer to Hamra for her life, she bunched her legs and jumped backward. Sénna's grip on the vines held as her feet left the windowsill and back into the air a few feet. As she swung back toward the window, she flexed her feet so that her heels would strike the windows first.

The glass shattered, and she felt the lead piping give way beneath the thin sole of her slipper. Her left ankle burned as the glass tore through the skin. She landed in a colorful shower of glass shards and twisted metal. She tucked and rolled, springing to her feet a short distance away.

The carpet she landed on was thick, both cushioning her fall and masking the sound of her entrance. Thick, embroidered pillows lined the walls, extending their entire length. Brass and glass lanterns hung haphazardly along the ceiling, casting light on the shelves of books that filled the room. It was a private reading room, she thought with some envy. If she survived the coming battle, she'd ask permission to spend some time among these volumes.

Sénna tiptoed her way to the door and peeked out. Two staircases, one to her left and the other on the far wall across the room, were empty of guards from Hazzara or Zaouni. She made her way down to the next level and found herself on a landing with an open balcony. Corridors extended to either side and around the throne room below. The space was empty of courtiers and looked like it could easily house an entire läenier Wing.

Glancing to either side, Sénna found doors that presumably went to various bedrooms. The hallway was carpeted and decorated with paintings and small tables with floral arrangements, so Sénna knew she was not in the servants' quarters. She hurried down the corridor to her left, seeking the tell-tale seams in the wall indicating a hidden door to the servant's back stairs.

Voices echoed up from the gallery below, causing Sénna to stop. She dropped to the floor, crawling toward the balcony, and peeked through the carved rails at the terrifying scene unfolding below her. Zaran led two black-clad Hazzara carrying the Zhoula's body, followed by another Hazzara with his blade extended into the back of his prisoner.

"No!" Sénna gasped, clapping her hand over her mouth.

Chapter 42: Transfer of Power

Sénna froze. Below her, Tóran limped ahead of his captor. Soaking wet and disheveled, he struggled to walk, hunched over a seeping wound in his midsection. Sénna felt her chest constrict, and she exhaled slowly. Cédron was somewhere in the palace preparing to confront Algarik, and she knew he wasn't ready to find his brother a hostage.

A rustling and movement in the corner to her left caught her attention. Sénna tore her gaze from Tóran in time to spot a hidden door slide open behind a mosaic pillar. Princess Najeriz peeked from around the opening and started into the room. Behind her, Sénna could see moving shadows, presumably Cédron and the two Sumäeri. Sénna doubted that the princess could remain silent if she spotted her mother's corpse. Could Cédron, if he saw that his brother was a captive? Could she do anything to prevent them from getting captured as well?

Sénna looked back toward Algarik and Tóran. The mage's attention was on Zaran, whose nasal speech she could hear, but his words were indistinct. She inched away from the edge of the balcony and waved her hand back and forth along the floor, hoping it would be enough movement to capture the princess's attention. Najeriz was looking the wrong way. Sénna blew an exasperated breath through her nostrils and scooted back faster, rising to her feet once she reached the cover of the pillar.

"Psst, Najeriz," Sénna whispered as loud as she dared, waving her hand to capture the princess's attention. "Najeriz, over here."

Sénna's knees nearly gave way when the princess looked up. Najeriz's eyes widened, and her jaw dropped as she crouched back behind the pillar.

"What are you doing here?" Najeriz whispered, glancing back toward the hidden doorway and waving her companions out.

Sénna slipped across the corridor on tiptoes, darting like a shadow from one pillar to the next until she reached her friends. She pulled the princess's left shoulder away from the scene below and nodded to Cédron, Rováen, and Säeshi, who had just snuck out of the hidden doorway.

"Algarik is below," Sénna whispered, leaning into the circle of bodies to keep her voice inaudible to those below. "He has Zaran and at least three Hazzara with him."

Cédron nodded, patting the pouch hanging at his hip. "I have the sacred windstone. Did you see if he held the Rod of Shouman?"

Sénna closed her eyes and took a deep breath, letting it out slowly as she carefully chose her words. She opened her eyes and looked at each person for a moment before resting her gaze on Cédron. She swallowed.

"I—" Sénna cleared her throat. "I didn't notice what he was carrying." She looked down at her feet for a second, then back up at her friend. "He—"

"Mother, no!" Najeriz cried from the edge of the balcony, where she leaned over, her hand gripping the creaking banister.

Sénna gasped, watching Najeriz race down the corridor to the sweeping staircase. She grabbed Cédron by the shoulders and shook him, getting his attention.

"Hide, get back into that door before Algarik sends his men up here, and all is lost," she said.

"But the princess—" Cédron began.

"Is lost to us," Sénna hissed and spun him around, propelling Cédron back toward the hidden door.

Rováen nodded and ushered Cédron and Säeshi into the hidden alcove and slid the door shut. He turned to Sénna and grabbed her arm.

"You were about to tell us what Algarik had?" he asked, raising an eyebrow.

Sénna nodded, her weight shifting from one foot to the other as she looked at each of her companions in the gloom.

"The Zhoula is dead. Algarik has her body down there and removed the golden circlet from her headdress. He's not wearing it, but I'm sure he isn't planning on handing it to Najeriz either," Sénna said. She clasped and unclasped her hands in a twisting motion as she continued to shift from side to side.

Säeshi placed two steadying hands on Sénna's shoulders, halting her motion. "What is it you are not saying?" she asked. Her pale aqua eyes bored into Sénna's golden gaze.

Sénna dropped her head, breaking the connection, and swallowed again. She looked at Cédron. "Tóran survived his mission to sabotage the water screw, but he was injured. I don't know how severely." She looked at Rováen and raised her shoulders. "Algarik has him captive down there with the Zhoula's body."

Cédron and Säeshi both inhaled. Roväen's posture slumped, and he shook his head.

"He will use Tóran as leverage to get to Cédron," Roväen sighed. He squatted, gripping his head in his hands. "This complicates things."

Cédron felt the hairs on the back of his neck raise. Algarik held his wounded brother prisoner, and he was helpless to change that. The heat of his frustration rose from his belly to his ears. There had to be a way to save Tóran. He couldn't lose his brother after losing so much already. Cédron turned and stalked away from his companions, pacing in a tight circle.

"I have the windstone, firestone, and aquastone, but Algarik has both Räeshun and the Rod of Shouman," Cédron muttered. He combed his fingers through sweaty, golden hair. "I have to get those talismans away from him."

Roväen shook his head. "We don't know if he has the talismans with him."

Sénna snorted. "What kind of evil mage would he be if he came all this way to take over or destroy the city and left his best weapons at home? No, he's got them, I'm sure of it."

"Regardless, his power is still formidable without them," Säeshi smiled sadly at her cousin. "And we don't know how severe Tóran's injuries are. We may not be able to help him."

The ache in Cédron's chest sharpened and his breath caught in his throat. They were right. He might lose Tóran regardless of the outcome of his confrontation with Algarik. He had to decide his next step. With Najeriz also now a captive and the Zhoula dead, the mage would move to take over leadership of Taboriz, if not destroy the city outright. He couldn't let that happen. There were too many innocent lives at stake.

"Algarik wants me," Cédron said, continuing his four-step circle in their cramped, hidden space. "He also wants the firestone, which I have. If memory serves, he believes that the firestone activates the Rod of Shouman—"

"But it's the windstone that does that," Sénna interrupted, then dropped her head in silent apology.

"Right, so we have to exploit his ignorance of how the rod works," Cédron said. He lifted Sénna's chin with his fingers to smile at her. "Something that we have you to thank for."

Sénna blushed, and Cédron dropped his hand, feeling a flush of his own. He couldn't tell if she was unaccustomed to compliments or if there was a deeper meaning to her coloring, but he didn't have time now to think about it. He had to rescue Tóran and Räeshun, then get the Rod of Shouman away from his uncle.

"I have the beginning of an idea," Cédron said. He rubbed his temples with his fingers then looked at his Uncle Rováen. "But I don't think you're going to like it."

Rováen's eyes narrowed. "What do you have in mind?"

Cédron pulled the three sacred stones from his pouch, handing the windstone to his uncle and the aquastone to Säeshi. He shoved the firestone back into the satchel and secured the strings. Taking a deep breath, Cédron straightened his shoulders.

"Algarik has Tóran and knows that I'll be willing to give anything to have him back," he began, his green eyes tight as he spoke. "Algarik believes he needs the sacred firestone for the Rod of Shouman, so that's what he'll likely want. I'm going to give it to him."

Säeshi gasped. "No, you can't do that!"

Cédron closed his eyes and shook his head. "I have to. There's no other way." He looked at Sénna. "If I keep his attention focused on our negotiations, do you think you can get Räeshun from him?"

"I'm certain that I can," Sénna said. She twisted a lock of her brown hair around a finger and pulled it out again. "I can try to get both talismans if you like. Pilfering is a skill that I've honed to an art form."

Cédron grinned and shook his head. "I'm sure your skills are formidable, but I think I want Algarik to keep the Rod of Shouman, at least for now. We don't know what will happen when he activates it with the wrong stone. Maybe it won't work at all. If I can keep him occupied with it and the firestone, then you get Räeshun," he turned to look at his uncle and cousin. "And you two can try and secure Tóran and Najeriz," Cédron said, nodding at Roväen and Säeshi.

Säeshi opened the pouch at her hip and picked through its contents, pulling out a small vial of orange liquid. "Läerei's restorative potion. She gave each of the Sumäeri a dose when we left Samshäeli. I still have mine, and it might help Tóran if I can safely get him to drink it."

Cédron felt his knees buckle from relief. He gripped his cousin's shoulder and squeezed. "Anything you can do to help save him is appreciated – and yes, I know –" he held up one hand, "you may not be able to save him. But if anyone has a healing potion that could work, it will be Läerei."

Their various strategies solidified, the small group eased their way out of the hidden alcove and slid the door shut. Sénna slithered off toward the staircase on the opposite side of the balcony from their current position. She'd come up from behind Algarik while Säeshi and Roväen took up posts behind the pillars at the top of the closest stairs. They would follow behind Cédron once he'd shifted Algarik's attention away from Tóran and Najeriz.

Cédron patted the bulge in his pouch as reassurance. He had the one thing he was most certain Algarik would demand. If the mage wanted something else, he'd be disappointed. Cédron felt a hollow pang in his chest. If

Algarik wanted something else and Cédron had nothing else to give, then he would lose his brother along with the city. No, he couldn't afford to think like that. Cédron swallowed the yawning chasm of fear that opened out in front of him as he began to descend the staircase.

Movement from across the chamber caught Cédron's attention. Two Hazzara guards marched through the hallway at the end of the balcony on which he stood and headed toward the back staircase behind Sénna. If they caught her, his plans would fail, and they'd lose their chance to save Tóran and Räeshun.

Cédron whipped the firestone from his pouch and poured the Árk'äezhi from his heart through the stone's properties. A fireball shot across the open balcony, striking and shattering the mosaic's colorful tiles near their heads. The Hazzara turned their attention to Cédron, running back up the stairs and around the balcony with weapons drawn. Cédron hurled more fireballs at the oncoming men, setting fire to the priceless tapestries lining the stone walls.

The Hazzara dodged three more blasts as they advanced, their own firestone talismans peeking from inside the torus knots of their pendants. Their stones glowed as they accessed their power, and Cédron gathered all the Árk'äezhi he could muster for a final assault. His chest burned as the activated firestone poured energy through his body. Cédron lifted the firestone and felt the sharp bite of a whip twist his legs below the knee and pull him off his feet.

Cédron twisted around as he fell, channeling all his energy toward this new threat. The blast of fire shot from the stone in his hands and into this new Hazzara's chest. The man didn't budge. Cédron squinted his eyes and saw that this mage also wore a torus knot talisman and redirected Cédron's magic around him like a stone in a brook. When he'd expended all his energy, the Hazzara grinned and approached Cédron unscathed. His clothes weren't even warm.

"Well, it looks like my search is over," the Hazzara said.

The mage waved his hand, and the leather from the whip cut deeper into Cédron's shins. The initial jab was unexpected and sharp. Cédron cried out before he could guard himself. He clamped his jaws together and gritted his teeth; he wasn't going to give these men the satisfaction of showing them any fear or pain. The three Hazzara converged upon his position and circled him.

Cédron noted their differences. One was fit with several scars running down his cheek and shoulder, indicating some wartime service. *Avoid fighting that one.* The second mage was older but whip-thin, with cheekbones sharp as razors and ruthless eyes. *This man would be the brains behind the assault on the city.* The third Hazzara was muscular with vacant eyes. *And, of course, there's the brawn,* Cédron sighed and twisted himself into a sitting position, his legs still bound by the whip.

"I need to speak with Algarik," Cédron said to his sharp-featured captor. "I have something he wants."

The Hazzara smiled, showing perfect teeth with only slight staining from blackroot. "Yes, you do. Let's give it to him."

Cédron struggled to stand just as the muscular Hazzara grabbed him around the waist and threw him over his massive shoulder. From his new vantage point, Cédron could see down the back stairs and spotted Sénna crouched behind a tall vase, her eyes wide as he caught her gaze. He closed his eyes and nodded his head, willing her to understand that he was ok with this slight change in plans. He opened his eyes, and she nodded back, staying put and watching.

"Well, boy, it appears our little game of *asátto hunts mijáko* has finally concluded," Algarik said. He turned from the throne to face his nephew. "I can't say that I've enjoyed chasing you all over Muralia, but I'm pleased to have had a chance to get to know your friend here a bit better."

Cédron's captor plopped him unceremoniously onto the

tiles and stepped back. Cédron's jaw clenched as Algarik pulled Räeshun and the Rod of Shouman from where they leaned against the throne's arm. Räeshun's tattoos remained dark as the mage swung her toward Cédron's head.

"He's quite stubborn, this friend of yours," Algarik sneered, waving Räeshun in a wide circle and bringing her crown to touch his nephew's chest. "He won't activate or show any sign of life unless *he* chooses to do so. Who was he? A Sumäeri, clearly, but why give his allegiance to you? And who created him?"

Algarik pressed the crown against Cédron's chest with each question, bruising his sternum and forcing the young man to focus on what answers he could give that would keep Algarik engaged.

"Orwaena created that staff at the Sumäeri's request upon death," Cédron said. He swallowed the lump that clogged his throat.

"Liar!" Algarik hissed, pushing his face inches from Cédron's nose. "The deities haven't interfered in the happenings of Muralia for several ages. Where did you get this talisman?"

Cédron shrugged. "Looks like you have something more powerful anyway," Cédron said, jutting his chin toward the Rod of Shouman. "What's that, and what are you planning to do with it?"

Algarik barked a laugh and turned, setting Räeshun down across the arms of the throne and turning back to Cédron. "This is the Rod of Shouman we discussed in Dúlnat if you remember," Algarik said, holding the staff upright in his hand. "Said to harness Lord Shamar's fire. I will use its power to bring Taboriz to its knees and return my Master to our world."

"Yeah, how is your Master? Pretty annoyed at your last failure, wasn't he?" Cédron scoffed, watching Sénna inch down the staircase behind Algarik. "Were you punished too severely? You don't seem to have suffered much."

"You know nothing of my suffering, boy," Algarik snarled. He grabbed Cédron by the shoulder and propelled him toward the wall where Najeriz sat cradling her mother's head in her lap. Three armed Hazzara guarded her and a very pale Tóran.

"Perhaps I can return the favor," Algarik said. "Your traitor brother here hasn't fared too well since he left my service, but I do want to thank him for bringing your staff to me for inspection and providing me with information on your plans."

Tóran looked up at Algarik, loathing clear in his brown eyes. "And for all that, Cédron will still defeat you again. Your Master will send you to the abyss for eternity, and that will be the end of all your machinations."

Algarik smiled, the scar on his left cheek twisting his lips into a sneer. "Not this time."

The mage swung the Rod of Shouman, striking Tóran's face and knocking him to the floor. Blood welled from the swelling cut on Tóran's cheek, and he groaned, holding the wound in his stomach. Najeriz whimpered and pulled her mother's corpse close to her chest. Cédron clenched his teeth and his fists, holding his anger in check as Sénna reached for Räeshun. The three Hazzara guards were busy watching the action with Algarik and didn't spot her slip around the throne and behind one of the hanging tapestries.

"He's right, you know," Cédron said, kneeling at his brother's side and dabbing the blood with his shirtsleeve. "You will spend eternity in the abyss with nobody to mourn you or even miss you."

"Perhaps, and perhaps not," Algarik crooned. He bent to grab Cédron's shoulder. "You see, I have everything I need to bring him back and nobody to stand in my way. Your Árk'äezhi remains weak and untrained without your bone staff, and the resistance of the Sumäeri and Zaouni is insignificant against my stone army."

Algarik slid his fingers beneath the strap of Cédron's

pouch and pulled it off his shoulder. He reached inside and pulled out the sacred firestone, placing it in the holder at the end of the iron rod. The firestone in his torus knot amulet burst into red fire, activating the sacred stone in the rod. The room glowed in scarlet light. Algarik turned away from Cédron and strode towards the side window that opened over the city.

"My stone army will purge the city of all who oppose me before I send them on to Samshäeli. My Master already has a hold on the Näenji Council. The world will be his before the first snows of Dormantide," the mage announced as he raised the iron rod toward the heavens.

Cédron held his breath, waiting to see how the firestone responded to the rod. The iron remained dark, but the firestone gleamed in the evening gloom. Tóran's groans pulled his attention from the mage.

"You have to stop him, no matter the cost," Tóran croaked. He grabbed Cédron's jerkin, his hands shaking as they balled the leather in his grip.

Cédron pulled his brother into a tight embrace and raised him to his feet. "I have a plan," he whispered into Tóran's ear. "Säeshi and Roväen are waiting for me to distract Algarik so they can get you and Najeriz to safety. Be ready."

Tóran pulled back from their embrace and held his brother at arm's length. "You've grown into a man this Tide," he said; a slight smile cracked the drying blood on his cheek. "Father would be proud of you."

"Father will be proud of both of us," Cédron corrected him. "We will find him together once this is over."

Tóran nodded and winced, grasping at the wound in his abdomen. "Yes, when this is over, and I can stand straight again."

Cédron's heart skipped a beat as he noted the spread of blood seeping freely through Tóran's shirt. He pulled off his shirt and handed it to Tóran.

"Press this to that wound and try to slow the bleeding,"

Cédron urged his brother.

"Very impressive," Algarik called from the window. "I see you've aligned with two of the four stones already. Too bad you won't have the opportunity to find the rest of them."

The mage swung the Rod of Shouman toward Cédron. The power of the firestone struck Cédron in the back, knocking him away from his brother. The three Hazzara left their post by Najeriz and surrounded Cédron, weapons lowered and pointed at his chest. The muscular man grinned as he cracked his knuckles.

"No, he's mine," Algarik warned, stopping their advance. "You three watch the door – I don't want any more surprises."

The three Hazzara leered at Cédron one last time, then jogged across the great room to the main doors, closing them behind as they exited. Despite the pain in his back, Cédron grinned. He felt the firestone's powers were inconsistent and unfocused in the rod. Algarik couldn't completely control the firestone's magic. Algarik also didn't know how disciplined Cédron's skills were without the assistance of a talisman.

Closing his eyes and taking a deep breath, Cédron dove deep into his mind, opening the door to his vast stores of Árk'äezhi. He felt the tattoos surrounding his heart flare to life, the flames licking his chest as he activated the element of fire. Spreading his hands open in front of him, Cédron shaped a huge fireball between his palms. He launched the ball straight at Algarik, who stumbled back into the throne, his clothes bursting into flames. His screams echoed throughout the cavernous palace and allowed Cédron a moment to breathe and look around.

Säeshi and Roväen sprinted from their hiding space and took charge of Tóran and Najeriz. The princess was unwilling to leave her mother's body, but Roväen put his arm around her shoulders and steered the princess toward Säeshi. Across the room, Sénna raced toward Cédron with

Räeshun in one hand.

Cédron looked back at the writhing and screaming mage, whose shrieks had taken on a new tone. They were lower, less piercing, and – was it possible? Cédron took a step towards his uncle, who rose from where he'd fallen against the throne. The fire still licked at his robes, but his screams had turned into laughter. Algarik waved the rod over his clothing, pulling the flames into the firestone and charging it with Cédron's energy.

The mage raised the rod and pointed it at Cédron. The blast lifted Cédron off his feet. He felt the breath explode from his lungs as he struck the wall. He tried to inhale, but the searing pain across his back prevented it.

"Here, take her," Sénna said. She shoved Räeshun into his hands as she helped him to his feet.

Cédron swayed and gripped her shoulder, slamming Räeshun's butt on the floor to hold himself steady. "Thanks, see if you can help me get the other stones for her," he wheezed, holding one arm across his chest.

"Right," Sénna nodded and sprang toward the Sumäeri.

The Hazzara outside the throne room rushed in at the sound of all the commotion, with weapons drawn. The scarred warrior flung a knife at Sénna's back as she ran. Cédron watched helplessly, unable to catch enough breath to call out a warning. Säeshi must have felt their presence, for she turned and gasped.

Sénna dove to one side, tumbling on the carpet twice before hitting her stride again. She slid sideways past the throne and bumped up against the wall by Najeriz. The knife struck a bowl of glass balls, shattering the clay and sending the orbs rolling across the floor.

Cédron breathed a shallow sigh of relief and turned back to Algarik. The mage was advancing on him, the firestone a malevolent gleam in the tip of the iron rod. Cédron hesitated, not sure what to do. He couldn't attack Algarik without assistance; he didn't have the stamina to use his own

Árk'äezhi alone. He glanced at Sénna, who held out her hands for the other sacred stones. Accepting them from Säeshi and Roväen, she turned to Cédron.

Algarik spotted her at the same time and let fly a burst of red power. Sénna flew into the air.

"Sénna!" Cédron grunted, waving Räeshun towards her.

Sénna twisted mid-air and tossed the windstone and aquastone towards the bone staff as she fell. Räeshun flared to life, the tattoos along her shaft glowing brilliant white light. Finger bones reached for the airborne stones, capturing and locking them into the crown. Cédron felt the rush of power through the gems, down Räeshun's shaft, and into his body. He swung the staff and blew, the yellow glow of the windstone cushioning Sénna's headlong fall, so she drifted softly to the floor.

Cédron turned to face his uncle. Räeshun's image entered his mind.

"You cannot beat him with strength," Räeshun said in his mind. "You must keep him unbalanced."

Cédron nodded and activated the aquastone. He focused on having Algarik's thoughts flow in and out of his mind like waves. Algarik's face twisted as he struggled to use the Rod of Shouman, which flickered and went dark.

"You think your little tricks will stop me, boy?" Algarik roared, advancing on the small group huddled by the wall. "I'll whittle your strength and support away piece by piece. Then, when you're all alone and devastated with the understanding that I've taken everyone from you, I'll show you what *real* power looks like."

Cédron staggered toward his friends, Räeshun held in front of him like a shield. Every step, every breath seared through his body like a lance, but he had to stop Algarik from harming his family. Looking ahead, he saw Säeshi pouring the healing elixir into Tóran's mouth. Roväen stepped in front of them, his sword drawn. The mage ignited the firestone in the rod again, sending out a large burst of energy. The fireball was weak and exploded before it reached the small group. It had enough force to scatter everyone except Najeriz, who remained grounded by her grip on her mother's body.

Algarik hovered over the princess, who glared up at him with fierce eyes and a defiant set to her chin.

"You killed our Zhoula, my mother. You will pay for this insult to our city," Najeriz swore through clenched teeth.

Algarik smiled down at her. "Ah, little twilling, your city is mine to do with as I choose." He held up the Zhoula's golden circlet and twirled it on his index finger. "I have eliminated its leadership, and my army will soon raze it to the ground. I will rebuild it into a tribute worthy of my Master."

"You haven't eliminated all the leadership," Najeriz stood over her mother's body, facing the mage. "I am Princess Najeriz, rightful Zhoula of Taboriz."

Algarik laughed and executed a short bow. "Your Highness, it pleases me to no end to be able to reunite you with your mother."

The firestone in the tip of the Rod of Shouman flared to life as the mage raised it and sent a fireball towards the princess's chest.

"No!"

Cédron turned toward the outcry and felt the air leave his body again. Tóran dropped the empty orange vial, shoving Säeshi to one side. He leaped over Rováen's shoulders and flung himself in front of Najeriz. The burst of red fire struck Tóran in the middle of his chest, throwing his body into the princess. They both hit the floor, their bodies motionless. Tóran's eyes stared at nothing.

Chapter 43: Aligning With the Windstone

Cédron felt his world tilt sideways. He leaned on Räeshun to keep from falling, but the staff slipped sideways across the marble floor. He crashed to his knees, the impact jarring his bruised ribs and adding to the jagged wound he could feel tearing through his chest.

"Tóran!" Cédron's voice cracked, the high-pitched sound both foreign and familiar.

Cédron staggered to his feet and crumpled next to his brother's body. The tears in his eyes blurred his vision, but not enough to blind him to the truth. Tóran was gone, just like his mother, father, best friend Zariun, and cousins. They were all gone. He'd failed them all. Failed to protect them, failed to stop Laylur, and failed to stop the war that was now raging outside the city gates. Everything they'd suffered and died for was all for nothing.

Cédron bowed his head, blinking the tears from his eyes, and sent a prayer to Hamra to watch over his brother's soul and to Orwaena to set him a place at her warrior's table. Tóran's eyes caught the last of Lord Shamar's rays, the light reflecting his empty gaze. Cédron reached out and closed Tóran's eyes.

Absolute fury overtook Cédron, and he swung Räeshun in a wide circle, sweeping Algarik off his feet with the sudden impact. He lunged at Algarik and ripped the torus knot amulet off his neck. He flung it across the room toward Säeshi and Rováen.

"You've taken everything from me," Cédron snarled. He ignored the tears streaming down his cheeks. He was consumed by the molten anger burning in his chest.

"Not quite everything, boy," Algarik smirked and rose to his feet. "There are still a few loose ends to tidy up." He glanced at the Sumäeri before looking at Cédron. "Once I destroy the city and enslave your Sumäeri friends here, I'll return to Aromberk Fortress, where my dear brother rots away in a cell. It will give me great pleasure to tell him how I killed both his sons before releasing the Great Demon upon the world. He will suffer for eternity with that knowledge."

Cédron turned away from the mage, his shoulders hunched. He took a deep breath and uncurled, twisting as he stood and swinging Räeshun with the power of his rage. The bone crown smashed into Algarik's jaw, lifting the mage off his feet before he crashed down on the far side of the throne.

"Not if I kill you first," Cédron roared. He twirled Raishun in his hand before swinging the crown into Algarik's shoulder.

Algarik reached up with his hand, blocking the swing and grasping Räeshun's shaft just below the skull. The mage gripped the bone and rose to his feet, holding Cédron's weapon at bay. Cédron pushed back, but Algarik had both height and weight on him.

"Get that rod," Rováen ordered the women and charged toward Algarik, sword raised.

The mage kicked Cédron in the stomach, causing his grip to loosen. Algarik twisted Räeshun, snapping Cédron's wrist. He thrust the bone end behind him, plunging it into Rováen's middle as the Sumäeri advanced. Räeshun flared to life, her tattoos gleaming in the dusky room. Räeshun's ethereal form appeared, cradling Rováen in her lap as she eased him down to the floor.

"Get the Rod of Shouman away from that mage," Räeshun's shade ordered her sister.

Cédron gasped; he forgot the pain in his wrist as his uncle sank to the floor. He felt like it took Rováen forever to fall. Algarik's crow of triumph echoed behind Rováen's grunt of pain and Räeshun's instructions. Cédron felt like he was floating in the thermal baths in Dúlnat; all sound and sensation was murky and underwater. He looked up to see Sénna and Säeshi charge toward Algarik, Säeshi with her straight blade raised high.

Before Säeshi's blade fell, Cédron found Räeshun's face inches from his own. He could hear her voice but couldn't understand her words. Everything was surreal. Sounds echoed. He felt nothing; his mind and body were numb from pain and loss. Let this be his end. He had no reason to continue this pointless quest. Laylur could have Muralia and let it burn. Cédron no longer cared. He wanted only to join the rest of his family in death's release.

Aquamarine eyes swam before him, annoying as the buzzing in his ears with their persistence.

"Cédron, you need to focus!" Räeshun's voice blared inside his head, clearing the indistinct buzz.

Cédron shook his head and sharpened his gaze. "Räeshun, help me," he pleaded with her image.

"Use the windstone," Räeshun said, pulling memories from his mind of his earlier lessons. "Keep them safe."

Cédron nodded. He reached for the windstone in Räeshun's crown, pulling it carefully so as not to jar the staff that still penetrated Rováen's midsection. He held the sacred stone to his forehead, visualizing different images of Sénna and Säeshi all around the room. He directed these thoughts into Algarik's mind, causing the mage to see enemies all around him. Algarik shot fireballs into mirage after mirage, allowing Sénna and Säeshi to harass him with their constant but unexpected jabs.

"Enough of this," Algarik roared and slammed the end of the Rod of Shouman onto the marble floor.

The sacred firestone glowed vermillion in the darkening room as Algarik raised his left hand, pulling the power from his ruby ring and channeling it into the rod.

"I call upon Lord Shamar to rain fire from the skies," Algarik cried. He raised both arms to the heavens.

The Rod of Shouman gleamed in the light of the firestones, and a bolt of lightning shot down outside the window, raising the hair on the back of Cédron's neck. The stained-glass windows imploded, sending tiny fragments of glass in all directions. The smell of ozone filled the room, igniting the firestone set on the end of the talisman. The firestone's energy flared, causing Cédron to shade his eyes. As quickly as the magic flared, it dissipated, leaving the room charged with latent energy.

"Cédron, catch!" Säeshi yelled. She tossed the silver torus knot amulet toward him.

Algarik lunged, grabbing for the amulet before it could reach its intended target. Sénna sprang simultaneously from the opposite direction, twisting the Rod of Shouman from Algarik's grip and sliding it across the floor to Cédron. He swapped the firestone in the rod with the windstone.

The latent energy in the room coalesced, enveloping Cédron and the Rod of Shouman with its yellow light. Wind whipped through the throne room. Cédron felt the stone's power pour through him, lifting him into the air. He sent images of hordes of Zaouni running into the palace for Algarik to fend off. The mage launched fireballs at ghosts while Sénna and Säeshi moved Roväen and Najeriz behind the throne to safety.

Moving to the second sphere of windstone magic, Cédron willed the broken glass from the window to fly toward the mage, cutting and gouging him as he fought off the imaginary warriors attacking his mind. Cédron felt the power of the windstone swell inside his chest and cried out as the tattoos blossomed across his back and shoulders. He opened his eyes, triumphant at the spirals of wind now holding him aloft.

The windstone's power grew, clearing both Cédron's perception and his vision. He spied Algarik below him on the palace floor, but he no longer saw a man. With his unobscured perception, Cédron saw the truth of Algarik's existence: a soul shredded from Tides of sorcery, betrayal, and murder that fluttered feebly within the mage's physical shell.

Beyond the palace, Cédron saw through the gates into the desert, where the glowing red forms of thousands of stone soldiers began their assault on the city. Walls crumbled, houses fell, and the remaining inhabitants of Taboriz who hadn't evacuated the city prayed for their salvation. As Cédron turned his attention from the army, a bright, gleaming form rose into view. It stood back from the stone warriors yet appeared to harness them.

Cédron focused his energy on this individual. He was human but different – he had a power that Cédron didn't recognize. The man radiated energy that muted the anger of the Maüli inhabiting the stone soldiers, channeling it into the destruction of stone and not life. Cédron felt his heart swell. Despite the devastating loss he'd suffered, hope blossomed in his mind. His path cleared in his mind; neutralize Algarik, recruit this new ally and begin reconstruction on the city.

Looking beyond Yezmarantha's borders with this new sense, Cédron could see the entire globe. He felt as if he were viewing Muralia from Lord Shamar's celestial seat. He spied undulations on the planet's surface and knew them to be weak spots where Laylur's minions exploited Lady Muralia's weakness. He could see the black of the abyss and the vacuum of Laylur's prison sucking the world into its depths.

Casting his gaze north toward Molonark, Cédron saw only a black void instead of a land filled with Garanth villages and Aromberk Fortress. He knew that was where the world was weakest – that was where Laylur was working on his escape. Cédron had to stop the Great Demon, but he still had one sacred stone to acquire. He would need to hurry, for he could see Laylur's power destroying the wards on his prison.

Cédron raised the Rod of Shouman, the spiraling vortices lifting him just outside the broken window. Lightning filled the sky, striking the stone with jagged bolts that coursed down the shaft. Cédron felt the rod absorb the lightning's energy, filling the talisman with the deities' Árk'äezhi. He felt invincible, omnipotent, and filled with a vengeance for everything that Algarik had taken from him.

"Algarik," Cédron called to the rogue mage, relieving him of the mirages he'd been fighting. "In your lust for power, you didn't learn how to access it properly. The fire in the skies is auratic power, so the windstone must harness it. The windstone shows us the truth of who we are, not the lie we create. I see you. I see what you have become."

"And do you see your death at my hands, boy?" Algarik cursed. He whipped an inferno of fire with his amulet and thrust it toward Cédron.

Cédron swept the rod down like a clap of thunder, quelling the mage's spell. He raised his left hand and twirled it once, capturing Algarik in a sphere of water. The mage's amulet burned at his chest, evaporating the water spell and dropping Algarik to the ground. The mage raised his hands, preparing a fireball with the Árk'äezhi left in his amulet and ruby ring. The energy formed then sputtered out. Algarik roared as he circled his hands, trying to capture the magic he needed.

"The truth is more powerful than your deception," Cédron called to him, still hovering by the high window. "Your lifetime of evil has taken a toll. I see the torn and ragged soul you have become. There is not enough power in your amulet to hold your Árk'äezhi together. The only one who doesn't realize this truth is you."

Cédron lowered himself back into the room where he hovered above his uncle. "You murdered my family, took my life from me, and nearly destroyed our world. Each of these crimes comes with a cost, and your atonement is now."

"You don't have the power to kill me, boy," Algarik sneered. He pulled a wand from his robes and placed his ruby ring in the tip of it. "You are undisciplined, untrained and—"

"I am not the one who demands retribution, Uncle Algarik," Cédron glided down and grasped the neck of the mage's robes with his free hand.

Raising the Rod of Shouman, Cédron captured the last of Lord Shamar's evening rays in the light of the windstone. The rod gleamed, adding strength to Cédron's body and pulling him and his burden skyward. The image of the deity's demand filled his mind as he ascended higher into the twilight sky.

Algarik groaned and writhed in Cédron's grasp. "Release me, boy," he cried. "The heat, it's searing my innards."

Orwaena's red orb crested the dunes to the east as Lord Shamar's burnt orange light exited the skies to the west. Algarik twisted and snarled in his grasp, trying to escape, but Cédron's body was imbued with the celestial power of the deities. Algarik's feeble protests were insignificant to

Cédron's current mission.

A piercing whistle emanated from the rogue mage. Below, an answering shriek halted Cédron's flight. He glanced down and spotted a shadow the size of a house lift from a perch in the city's vazurgan section. The rinzar beat its mighty wings, reaching its Master in seconds and knocking Cédron into a spin as it angled past. Algarik slipped from his grasp and tumbled through the air, landing on the raptor's back as it circled beneath him.

Cédron inhaled, closing his eyes. His downward motion ceased, and he hovered high above the palace. Algarik, astride his monstrous beast, flew west toward the stone army and what remained of his Hazzara forces.

Cédron turned to face the west, where his last light tucked into darkness as the glowing daylight orb fell beneath the horizon. Cédron raised the rod and pulled lightning from the clouds. Cédron felt his Árk'äezhi flow through the talisman, focused through the windstone.

The beam of light struck the rinzar's tail feathers. Embers erupted in the raptor's tail, creeping upward, slowly engulfing the beast and its rider. The rinzar's shriek and Algarik's agonized cry stopped short as the smoldering embers devoured man and beast. Within seconds, only a puff of grey ash swirled in the breeze.

Cédron's extremities felt leaden, and his mind buzzed. Algarik was gone, and he wanted to feel relief, but the only emotion Cédron could muster was emptiness. He ached for oblivion – away from the pain of loss, disappointment, and tragedy—an escape from the daunting task that yawned out before him. The past hour overwhelmed him, draining the last dregs of energy in his body. Utterly exhausted, Cédron collapsed.

chapter 44: Maüli

Säeshi pulled free of Rovaen's arms and raced to Cédron. He still clutched the Rod of Shouman in his left hand. Cédron rolled over and groaned.

"He's all right," Säeshi cried. "All that Árk'äezhi has left him weak."

Sénna and Najeriz joined Säeshi around Cédron, all marveling at the golden tattoos still glowing across his back and shoulders. Säeshi traced the swirls and whorls etched into his left shoulder with her index finger. The skin was smooth and cool to her touch, not what she expected. After channeling the Árk'äezhi of the deities, she anticipated some residual trace.

"How are you feeling?" Säeshi asked.

Cédron rolled onto his back. "I just need to catch my breath."

Sénna scowled, crossing her arms across her chest. "We don't have time for you to lay around. The city is crumbling around the west sector, and it won't take long for that stone army to make its way up here to the palace."

Roväen grunted as he pulled Räeshun from his stomach. Säeshi turned, her knees buckling when she saw the blood welling from her uncle's wound.

"What have you done?" Säeshi gasped, lurching back to Roväen's side and pressing her hand against the ragged hole. "You're going to die."

Roväen batted her hand away and placed a lodestone over his injury. "This will stop the bleeding. We can worry about healing me more thoroughly later."

The lodestone absorbed the blood from the wound while Sénna and Najeriz tore strips of silk from the princess's robes as bandages. They pressed a thick pad of cloth over the stone and tied it securely around Roväen's waist. Säeshi helped her uncle to his feet, keeping her firm grip on his arm. He'd lost a lot of blood and was weak despite his protests to the contrary.

Roväen took a step toward Cédron, his fingers gripping Säeshi's arm so tightly they pressed divots into her skin. She didn't mind the pain. Säeshi guided Roväen's steps to her cousin.

Cédron opened his eyes and gasped, lurching to his feet. "Uncle Roväen, you're injured. Let me use the firestone—"

"No, there isn't time," Roväen grunted. He pulled the rod from Cédron's grip and handed it to Säeshi.

"Cédron and I are both weak; we can't protect Räeshun and the Rod of Shouman. We need to keep our resources safe." He turned to Najeriz and placed a hand on her delicate shoulder. "I am so sorry for your loss. We need to try and stop that army to prevent greater tragedy."

"And I need to prepare my mother for a proper burial," Najeriz said, jutting her chin and crossing her arms.

"If we don't do something soon, the Zhoula will be buried with the rest of us under the rubble of the palace," Sénna said through clenched teeth. She paced back and forth between the throne and the bodies of Tóran and the Zhoula. "Can't we just put them somewhere for safekeeping? Nobody is going to take them." She looked at Najeriz and narrowed her eyes, her hands on her hips. "What are you hiding?"

Najeriz gasped and clapped her hands to her mouth. Säeshi and Rováen stepped closer, concern creasing their brows.

"What is it?" Säeshi asked, setting the rod and Räeshun across the arms of the throne. "Are you injured?"

Najeriz waved them away. "No, Sénna is right – and wrong. The reality of our situation just hit me. My mother is dead; that makes me Zhoula now." She picked up the thin, golden circlet worn in her mother's headwrap and broke it in half. She stuck one of the semi-circles through the braids at her temples so that it rested across her forehead.

"I know what we need to do," Najeriz brandished the other half of the circlet and walked behind the throne. She looked at Sénna and shrugged one shoulder. "You are very perceptive. I haven't told you everything."

Säeshi recognized the door they'd entered during their first encounter with the Zhoula. Najeriz led them through that small antechamber to the back of the room where a glass sculpture of an Aruzzi stood perched, wings outstretched, on a pedestal. The princess stuck the sheared end of the circlet into the pedestal's base and turned it like a key. The Aruzzi clicked and hummed as gears rotated the statue sideways. Behind the glass figure, a hidden panel slid aside, exposing a narrow set of curving stairs.

"Follow me," Najeriz said and led the way into the

hidden staircase.

Säeshi glanced at Roväen. He grinned at her raised eyebrow and nodded toward the talismans. She grabbed them. Cédron sagged against the doorway and waved for her to precede him.

"I'll cover our retreat," he said.

Säeshi shook her head and snorted. "Sure."

The group followed the princess up the narrow, winding staircase until they reached a door. Najeriz used the circlet key to open this door, hesitating for a breath before pushing it open. Säeshi wondered what caused the princess to pause, stepping closer to her in case of danger.

The room inside was nothing like the rest of the palace. It was circular and open, easily as big as the throne room, with a ceiling two stories above them. Columns of marble were attached to the skeletal arches of the roof. The columns and ceiling bricks were blue and white stripes, while the floor was tiled with the blue, green, and white mosaics used inside the palace. Säeshi walked the thirty paces to the nearest column and gazed down.

Below, the city burned along the wharf nearest the western gate. The buildings destroyed by the stone army lay twisted and broken like silhouettes of corpses against the flames' orange glow. Water that encircled the city gleamed in Orwaena's vermillion light around to the east.

"Cédron and I will rest here," Roväen said, breathless from the climb. "We can recover a bit while we decide our next step."

Säeshi nodded and handed the Rod of Shouman to her uncle. Roväen pressed one hand to his bandages and used the iron rod as a crutch. Another crash and subsequent wail brought her attention back to the western side of the city.

"They're razing it to the ground," Sénna gasped. She leaned out over the platform with her right arm around a column for balance.

"Yes, and we have few Zaouni left to stop them," Najeriz

sighed. "Not that they could. No, we need more help."

Najeriz pulled her glass necklace from beneath the silken scarf wrapped around her shoulders and neck. She walked over to the southeastern quadrant of the room and faced the desert and rising moon. Raising the fluted flower ornament to her lips, she blew into the glass bell. Her fingers played over the holes, creating a haunting melody that echoed across the desert.

"What help did you just summon?" Rováen asked, turning from Cédron to face Najeriz.

The princess lowered her necklace and faced the group, raising her chin. "Long have the rulers of Taboriz held a position of trust and friendship with the Aruzzi of the desert. We protect each other's secrets and vulnerabilities. The ruler of Taboriz is present at the hatching of new Aruzzi, and they preside over the rituals of succession here." Najeriz glided to the section facing the southwest. "They need to know what we are facing. I hope that the Aruzzi can assist us, but if not, at least they will know we fell protecting them."

Säeshi stepped next to Sénna, following her gaze toward Orwaena's rising moon, not knowing if the Aruzzi would hear their summons and, if so, whether they would come. Taboriz would not survive long under the onslaught of the stone army. Most of the inhabitants had gotten clear of the city before the attack, but thousands remained trapped, and more lost their lives each minute.

Säeshi wondered what the Aruzzi could do against the enraged and bloodthirsty Maüli. Could they help? The Aruzzi were the guardians of wind Árk'äezhi, but it would take a tremendous amount of air current to slow the stone warriors. Perhaps the Aruzzi would simply bring a sandstorm to cover the city, allowing the survivors to start a new settlement elsewhere. Her thoughts were interrupted by a loud screech.

"That was fast," Sénna said. They both turned toward the center of the room, glancing into the sky.

Above the circular eyrie hovered two läeniers. They circled the round tower once, then folded their wings to squeeze through the open columns to land side-by-side in the center of the room.

"We saw the lightning strikes," Läenshi called. Her thighs bulged as she slid down the side of her raptor and strode to her twin. She embraced Säeshi, who still gripped Räeshun in her other hand. Läenshi released her sister, then spotted Cédron and Rovären leaning against the column. "What happened?" she gasped.

Rovären lurched forward and clasped forearms with Roshäen, who'd slid off his raptor to join them.

"Cédron aligned with the windstone and has destroyed Algarik," Rovären sighed. "However, the Árk'äezhi needed for such a feat drained him. He is exhausted. I haven't fared much better," he grunted and leaned against the wall.

Läenshi nodded, her eyes noting the wound in her uncle's midsection. She frowned.

"You need a healer," Läenshi said, pacing the room and looking out at the city. "The temple of Azria is too far away, but maybe that Askári girl can help. We'll get you to her shortly. Will you be alright for a little bit?"

Rovären smiled wanly and nodded. "We have more important things to worry about than my old carcass."

Säeshi snorted and shook her head. "Everything is a priority right now, even your old carcass, Uncle Rovären."

Roshäen spotted Sénna and hurried to her side, dropping to a knee and grasping her hand.

"I'm pleased to see you well," he touched his forehead to Sénna's fingers, then rose. "How can we serve you?"

Säeshi's lips twitched at the blush raging across Sénna's cheeks, visible even in the faint light of the moon.

"The stone army is imbued with Maüli spirits. I can sense their anger, their despair. They are unstoppable, bent on destroying the city and taking as many lives as they can. I don't know how we can salvage Taboriz or her people,"

Säeshi sighed, shaking her head.

Najeriz faced the newcomers and stepped forward. "I have summoned the Aruzzi, but I don't know how long it will take them to get here or how many will come. I also don't know if they can help us."

The shadows shortened as the red moon rose higher. The vermillion light brightened as Orwaena cleared the dunes and tallest buildings behind them. It took Säeshi another moment to realize that a secondary light source kindled in the room. Holding Räeshun out in front of her, she gasped at the tattoos gleaming white. In another moment, her sister's form materialized.

"There is only one way to defeat the Maüli," Räesha's ethereal form said, turning to make eye contact with each member of the group. "I was once a Maüli and Cédron very nearly lost me. It took soothing from the aquastone. With a group this big, we will need all the sacred stones and each other to have sufficient Árk'äezhi to attempt this."

Rovä́en cast a doubting glance at Cédron. "He doesn't have the strength—"

"I will give him the strength he needs," Räesha interrupted, then turned to her sisters. "I need each of you to help." When they nodded, Räesha turned to Cédron. "Lie down." When Cédron lay on his back, Räesha turned to Säeshi. "Lay my bones across his chest."

Säeshi hurried to Cédron and placed the bone staff over his body, stepping back as Räesha melded into her bones, then sinking further into the young man's form. Cédron's tattoos flared to life. He sucked in a deep breath and sat up, his eyes luminous in the twilight.

"What do I need to do?" he asked.

Räesha extricated herself from his form and stood smiling down at her cousin. "It's time to work," Räesha said, floating just above the group. "We have to remove the Maüli from the stone army before they wipe out the entire city."

Sénna frowned and crossed her arms. "They've destroyed

much of the city already, and they will make their way here before long."

Cédron blinked and shook his head. "No, wait." He rubbed his temples with his fingers and shook his head again. "I saw someone holding them back," he said. He stepped to the western quadrant of the building and looked over the city. "There is someone out there who has some kind of hold or power over them. Not control, but influence. Can we find him?"

Räesha closed her eyes and was silent for a moment. Säeshi wondered if she was checking to see what sort of power the man had that remained undetected from her own talent or if her sister's essence could communicate with the man.

"Yes, perhaps he can help," Räesha's shade said. "You will need to work together. Cédron, take the Rod of Shouman. Roväen, please hold my staff with the firestone and aquastone attached. Säeshi and Läenshi, I'll need you both to work with the sculptor."

Najeriz inhaled. "Sculptor? Do you mean the rumors are true? That mage brought back Ruzik Ozan to create that army? I thought Zaran was making that up just to scare us."

"Who is Ruzik Ozan?" Sénna asked.

Najeriz closed her eyes and exhaled. "He was a renowned sculptor over a century ago. His story is a tragic one and a cautionary tale. I was not aware that this Algarik had the power of necromancy."

Cédron turned to face the princess. "Not necromancy, per se." He rotated his neck in a circle and rubbed the back of his head. "The sense I got from my brief contact with him was one of reanimation from stasis, not death. Regardless, we need to work with him." Cédron turned to his cousins. "Can you locate him?"

Säeshi tore her gaze from Räesha and looked at Cédron, the lines of a frown formed between her brows. "Yes, I can. But first, I'd like you to be very clear about what you want us to do with him. I'm not convinced that this is a good idea."

Läenshi took her sister's hand and nodded in agreement. "Please help us understand your plan. We don't want to make things any worse for the people of Taboriz," she said, nodding at Najeriz. "They've already suffered so much."

Cédron shuffled his feet and looked over at Räesha, then at Roväen.

"Räesha has a unique perspective on the world," he began, swallowing hard and clearing his throat. "She can sense things on an energetic level," Cédron said. "I mean, she can see how their Árk'äezhi is responding to the different influences of the stones and—"

"What our cousin is trying to say," Räesha interrupted. "Is that you need to trust me to know what I'm doing. Things change with our source's energy, and I need to be free to adjust what I'm doing. I need you to find this sculptor and help him enhance his hold over the stone army. I will try to pull the Maüli from them and set them free."

The twins looked at each other and nodded. "Ok, we'll trust you," Läenshi said, looking at her older sister's spirit and not at Cédron. "Let me find him."

Säeshi saw Cédron's shoulders sag. She marveled at how the young man continued to struggle with his immense powers. The deities chose one who was not arrogant, but she wasn't sure he had the confidence to fulfill the task for which he'd been selected. Indecision plagued him. Without Räeshun's guidance, she wasn't sure Cédron would have the strength to face Laylur.

Säeshi released Läenshi's hand and held her palm out like she was feeling a wall. She moved her hand sideways, rotating her body to follow as she turned to the west. She continued turning until she'd hit the northwest corner of the city. She could feel the heat of the sculptor's energy radiating from that quadrant. Säeshi held her position for a few more seconds, then opened her eyes.

"He is just inside the western gate, on the north edge of the shanty district. The stone army is tearing through it, leaving no survivors," Säeshi whispered. "I can sense his power weakening."

Najeriz gasped and grabbed Cédron by the shoulders. "You must hurry. Please, save my people!"

Roshäen stepped up to Cédron. "We can take you there on our läeniers. It isn't far, so they can carry a few of us."

Cédron nodded and turned to Säeshi. "Lead the way."

Läenshi grabbed her sister's hand, pulling her to her raptor and climbing onto Juläen's back before reaching a hand down for her sister and Cédron. Roshäen helped Sénna and Roväen astride Shäelan, urging her skyward with a series of whistles.

Najeriz shielded her eyes as the läeniers rose into the air. "I'll bring help as soon as it arrives," she called, waving after them.

Cédron waved his acknowledgment and turned to face his next challenge. He hoped he was strong enough to do what Räesha required of him. He remained weak from his battle with Algarik, and his thoughts swam with images of his uncle's body shredding under the truth of the windstone. He shook his head and tried to clear his mind. He needed to focus.

Juläen dipped his wing to the right and banked slightly north of the western gate. Below, they could see the shanty quadrant burning. The reek of scorched refuse blended with burning wood and charred flesh. It turned Cédron's stomach. Screams rose above the roar of the fire and crashing of collapsing buildings. The stone soldiers were destroying everything in their path with their misplaced vengeance.

The läeniers flew over an open square that held a fountain

in the center. There was no water in the fountain, only a man sitting cross-legged atop the sculpture of an Aruzzi with its wings outstretched. The man seemed to float on the Aruzzi's head. Cédron squinted and saw that the man's eyes were closed, and his hands were together at heart level with his fingers steepled.

"Get his attention, Shäelan," Roshäen ordered his raptor.

The läenier circled the man's silent form, screeching a war cry as she angled towards his face. The man's eyes flew open, as did his mouth. He toppled from the statue and righted himself, stepping out of the fountain and prostrating himself in supplication.

Juläen and Shäelan landed in the square, their claws scrabbling on the cobblestones as they came to a halt. The riders slid down, assisting their passengers before facing the prone sculptor.

"Ruzik Ozan?" Sénna stepped forward and touched the man on the shoulder. "We are here to help you with the army."

Ruzik raised to his knees, glancing with narrowed eyes at the newcomers. "Help how?" he asked. He stood, noting the talismans held by Cédron and Rovä en. "How do you know my name?"

Säeshi stepped forward, holding her palms up in the traditional greeting. "May the tranquility of Lady Muralia bring peace to your heart and purpose to your hands."

Ruzik touched his fingers to his forehead and swept his arm out as he bowed. "May the light of the Shäeli never dim and the strength of your arms bear you to victory." He straightened, fixing Säeshi with a penetrating stare. "You are a foreigner, yet you know our ways. Why should I trust you?"

"Because if you don't, your Maüli will destroy the entire city," Läenshi said, stepping next to her sister.

Ruzik scowled. "They're not *my* Maüli," the sculptor spat. "They are an abomination. One that Algarik created, and I'm trying to mitigate."

"And we're here to help you," Säeshi said again. "I am Säeshi Angäerol, and this is my twin Läenshi. Our sister Räeshun bears two sacred elemental stones, and our cousin Cédron has the windstone."

Ruzik shook his head. "The Maüli are not of this plane and are not subject to the power of the stones. I don't see how you can help."

Räesha materialized from her staff form and floated toward the sculptor. "I was once Maüli, only briefly, but I understand the twisted nature of their anger. I think I can heal them and release them to Lady Muralia. Will you help us undo the damage you've caused to their souls?" Räesha asked, hovering right in front of Ruzik's frozen face.

Cédron shook his head and snorted. The poor man didn't have a chance with Räesha using his superstitions against him. There was no way he wouldn't help if it meant atonement with the deities for his part in creating this army and restitution for their damages.

"Wh-what—wh-who are you?" Ruzik stuttered, staring wide-eyed at Räesha's shade.

"I was once a Sumäeri warrior," Räesha's tattoos gleamed upon her translucent form for a brief second then dimmed. "I died defending this young man, for there is a prophecy among my people that foretold his coming. He is the one to bring balance to Muralia. When I died, Orwaena honored my plea to continue this fight and allowed me to transform into the staff so that I may assist Cédron. I now need your help as well."

Räesha's spirit turned sideways and opened her arm to welcome her sisters into the small circle. "My sisters can locate and enhance Árk'äezhi. They will help you maintain your hold on the stone figures while I attempt to sever the Maüli from them."

Ruzik's face grayed, and beads of sweat formed across his upper lip as it quivered. "B-but if you release the Maüli, they will attack us all, and my soldiers will—" he gasped, looking toward the city with wide eyes. "There will be no survivors."

Sénna cocked her head to one side. "You are concerned for the stone soldiers? They are your creations, yes?" She stepped closer to the sculptor. "How did the Maüli come to animate them?"

Ruzik swallowed, his bronze cheeks paling to ashen brass. "It is the jasper. The Maüli were attracted to the redstone. I don't know what will happen to my men if I try to remove it from their chests."

"So, the army is like your children," Sénna mused. She crossed her arms over her chest as she paced. "And the Maüli have infiltrated the stone bodies."

Säeshi laid a hand on Ruzik's shoulder. "Be at peace, friend. My sister's power is connected to the deities. She will be able to soothe their anger and release them to Lady Muralia's bosom. There they will find rest, and your stone warriors will be as they once were."

"And if she can't," Läenshi said, shrugging one shoulder as she grinned. "We'll all die fighting them anyway. You have nothing to lose by working with us."

Ruzik stared at Läenshi for a moment before closing his slack jaw and nodding. Cédron turned away to hide his smile. He'd learned over the past sennight that if Säeshi's gentle nature didn't convince someone, Läenshi would step in with a more energetic persuasion. The sculptor would cooperate with their efforts; now, it was up to him. He and Räeshun would have to soothe the Maüli spirits and induce them to return to the celestial plane. He took a deep breath and let it out.

"Are we ready then?" Cédron asked, looking at the sculptor and the Sumäeri flanking him.

Läenshi placed her hand on Ruzik's other shoulder and nodded to her sister. They each kept a hand on the sculptor's shoulder and reached out with their free hand. Roväen planted Räeshun's tip on the stones at the fountain's base and took his position in front of Ruzik, next to Läenshi. Cédron completed the circle standing between his uncle and Säeshi, with the Aruzzi statue's wings arching protectively over the small gathering.

As one, the group closed their eyes and focused on their respective tasks. Cédron held the Rod of Shouman ready, waiting for Räesha's signal. Roväen held Räeshun steady with one hand, his free hand gripping Cédron's shoulder. Cédron felt his uncle's fingers squeeze gently, and he wondered if Roväen's touch was support or warning.

Cédron felt a twinge of panic. His hold over the windstone was tenuous, having just aligned with the sacred stone. What if his powers spiraled out of control again? What if he caused more damage, killed more people? Would Roväen make the same decision as to when Cédron's abilities pushed beyond his conscious awareness in the Meq'qan village?

Bile burned the back of Cédron's throat. He felt his knees turn to liquid at the enormity of the task before him. He wasn't ready. He couldn't do it. He wasn't strong enough. Cédron's vision filled with tiny sparkling lights as his breathing sped up.

"Breathe," Roväen murmured next to him, squeezing his shoulder again. "You're going to be fine. We're all here for you."

Cédron opened his eyes and found his uncle's aqua gaze on him. He saw only love and confidence in Roväen's eyes this time. He took a deep breath and nodded, smiling weakly before closing his eyes and concentrating. With his free hand, he grasped Räeshun's shaft and felt his cousin's shade emerge.

In his mind's eye, he watched Räesha soar over the stone army, singing a siren's song of anger that blended sharp notes with their discordant energy. From Räesha's perspective, Cédron could see the jagged red energy surging over the stone soldiers' forms, like a serrated haze hovering above the army. Räesha's spirit sailed overhead, harmonizing their power with the Árk'äezhi of the firestone held firmly in the phalanges forming her crown.

Cédron guided the firestone's Árk'äezhi through the staff and over the army with Räesha's guidance. He felt the instant the Maüli energy connected fully with their wave of magic. The shock of rage and vengeance surged through him, causing his heart to race and his skin to burn. The tattoos surrounding his heart flared to life.

"We have their attention now," Räesha's voice filled his mind. "Now, ease your Árk'äezhi toward the aquastone. We need to soothe them."

Cédron concentrated on the cooling azure energy of the aquastone, wrenching his mind from the desire for blood flooding his veins. The Maüli were powerful, and there were so many of them. He felt his lungs labor as he struggled to breathe. Räesha's energy started to pull away from him. The change was subtle at first; then, he felt her essence slip from his mind.

"Don't leave me!"

Cédron's anguished cry rang out over the city. He felt the ripple of Árk'äezhi blow his hair back, but he couldn't lose focus, or he'd lose Räesha. Reaching with his mind, he grasped on to her energy, holding her hands in his tight grip.

"Fight it," he gasped, begging his cousin not to succumb to the call of the Maüli.

Räesha's shade wavered, shimmering in his mind as he poured every ounce of Árk'äezhi he had into keeping her form and their intention stable. He felt the misery of her grief and righteous fury over the loss of her sister and her parents. She was slipping into the chaos of madness. Cédron watched as the Maüli rose from the ranks of the stone soldiers and swarmed his cousin's soul. They swirled around her ethereal form, filling them both with their furor and torment.

Cédron stood frozen in horror as Räesha's face elongated, her jaw extending into a screech of hatred and torture. He felt his grip on her Árk'äezhi fracture and dissipate. Räesha's shade succumbed to the Maüli's rage, joining them in their single-minded thirst for blood and revenge. His mind was catapulted out of sync with Räesha's awareness as she rejected him and their mission.

Cédron's senses slammed into his body, his pounding heart and thundering pulse roaring in his ears, still not drowning out the shriek of the Maüli's triumph. He opened his eyes to his uncle's face, all color drained and a fixed look of shock registering in his eyes. Räeshun was cold and dark; Cédron could sense no essence of life within her bones.

"Räesha, no!" Cédron gasped and sank to his knees. "She's gone."

chapter 45: Aruzzi

Sénna gaped as she watched the tableau of people in the fountain waver and collapse. An audible shriek rose from the Maüli inhabiting the stone soldiers, echoing across the desert. She clapped her hands over her ears and sank to her knees. The sound pierced her head and tore at her heart as she felt the spirit's anger and despair. Now she understood Cédron's reaction to her story when she told it back on the airship. He'd faced a Maüli and found no pleasure in reliving the experience, if only in a tale.

Even as a child, Sénna's fascination with Maüli legends hadn't prepared her for the force of their anger. She'd loved the creeping sensation of bumps raised along her flesh as her grandmother spun the yarns. Still, Sénna never fully appreciated the terror of what facing a Maüli must have been like for those retelling the tales.

Sénna closed her eyes, trying to remember how the heroes of those old myths had beaten the specters. There had to be a way of separating the shades from the stone soldiers and weakening their power; if only she could remember it. Images of women and men clad in flowing purple robes chanting and sprinkling salt came to her mind. Her eyes flew open, and she gasped.

"I know what to do," Sénna said, standing and turning to Roshäen. "We have to get to the Market Queen."

Roshäen looked toward his fallen friends and back to Sénna. "Shouldn't we help them?"

"Mijáko piles!" Sénna swore and grabbed the rider by the arm, pulling him toward his läenier. "We are, and we don't have much time. Let's go."

Roshäen grabbed his riding straps and pulled himself aboard his raptor, reaching down to help Sénna up behind him. "Where to?"

"Fly toward the western docks," Sénna said, wrapping her arms around his waist. "Queen Marizen and Anzeri are in a wagon headed from the palace toward the pier."

Shäelan's legs bunched as she launched herself into the air. Sénna squeezed Roshäen's chest, eliciting a grunt from the warrior. As the raptor beat her mighty wings, gaining altitude, Sénna eased her grip on the rider's body. She felt Roshäen shift his weight, and Shäelan responded to his touch. The raptor angled her body westward, soaring above the city of Taboriz and the chaos below.

Sénna scanned the various streets as they flew overhead, many clogged with the still-smoldering bodies of the Hazzara or rubble from toppled buildings. The stone army worked its way toward the center of the city, a swath of destruction in its wake. Here and there, the servants of Azria carried the wounded toward their temple, specters in blue against the sable dust of rubble and red stains of blood.

Several streets over, they spotted the wagon. The ozryks tossed their tall horns as they picked their way through the clotted street. Sénna tapped Roshäen's arm and pointed toward the wagon.

"There they are," she said. "Find a place to land that won't spook the ozryks."

Roshäen nodded and shifted his weight. Shäelan banked to the right and angled toward an open square to land. Sénna slid down her leg as soon as the raptor touched the cobblestones and raced to the wagon.

"Queen Marizen, Anzeri," she cried, racing toward the wagon. Sénna waved, her ribs visible as she panted. "I need your help to stop the stone army."

Marizen pulled the reins and halted the ozryks. "Such blunt and coarse speech from this delicate flower," she said to Anzeri then turned to Sénna. "Tell me, child, does your tongue get you into trouble where you're from?"

Sénna grimaced. "You don't know the half of it," she muttered, then felt her cheeks flush. "I mean, Queen Marizen, please forgive my intrusion. I beseech the kindness of your heart and the generosity of your folk. The Maüli inhabiting the stone army have overwhelmed my companions. I may have a solution but will need salt from your warehouses."

Anzeri barked a laugh. "I see your idea if the old stories are true, but you will need more help than we can give. I suggest you put a salt perimeter around the army, but you may need to salt the stone as well. You will need oil so that the salt can adhere to the stone and create the incentive for the Maüli to flee."

Sénna nodded. "Is there a temple to Hamra nearby? I believe the acolytes can help guide the separated Maüli back to Lady Muralia if there are enough of them."

Queen Marizen pursed her lips. "Not lightly do the

servants of Hamra leave their demesnes. You will need to convince them of the need and prove that it outweighs their mandate to ease the transition of those recently deceased from the army's destruction."

Sénna twisted a lock of her brown hair around her finger and nodded. "I can guarantee that their assistance will lessen their overall burden. If we can't stop the Maüli, there won't be anyone left to assist the souls."

Anzeri looked at Queen Marizen, who nodded. "Hamra's temple is down that street, then over two to the north. We will get the supplies you need. Where shall we meet?" Anzeri asked.

Sénna collapsed to her knees; her head bowed as she wiped the tears of relief from her cheeks. She touched her forehead to the cobblestone street, then raised her eyes to the cart.

"Thank you," Sénna exhaled, then cleared her throat. "Without the help of the Market Queen, Taboriz would be lost."

Marizen cackled and reached for Sénna's hand. The girl stood and placed her hand in Marizen's bony grasp.

"You tell that Zhoula who it is that saved her city," Marizen grinned, showing her blackened teeth. "I will expect to be fairly compensated when this is over."

Sénna heard Anzeri's snort and grinned. "It will be as you command, Queen Marizen."

Anzeri whistled and cracked her reins, startling the ozryks into motion. Marizen dropped Sénna's hand as the wagon lurched forward. With one final nod from Anzeri, Sénna turned and sprinted down the identified street towards Hamra's temple, leaving Roshäen to return to his Wing.

The temple dedicated to Hamra was a low sandstone structure, only three regular stories high. Wings to the left and right covered sweeping staircases leading deep underground, while the main entrance led to the receiving area. Carved obelisks stood sentry beside the stairs, engraved with the images of births and deaths that Hamra oversaw. The second-story exterior exhibited bas-relief sculptures of Hamra as a midwife and as a reaper. Men and women dressed in the plum robes of Hamra's followers carried stretcher after stretcher of bodies from the main hall and down the stairs to the wings. Each corpse was wrapped entirely from head to toe in gauze.

Sénna swallowed hard and jogged up the stone steps into the main reception hall, dodging the followers and their grim burdens. She reached the open area and edged along the rough walls veined with copper and turquoise. There was no room to walk as bodies in various stages of preparation lined the floor. Men and women in robes varying in shade from lavender to deep plum teemed throughout the area, singing prayers, wrapping corpses, and hauling bodies for interment. The scent of death covered the room like a thick blanket with tattered, acrid edges.

Sénna scanned the room for signs of anyone in charge. She spotted a short, plump woman whose imperious gestures and deep purple robes identified her as someone of rank. Sénna picked her way toward the woman and knelt at her feet once she reached her.

"Priestess of Hamra," Sénna began, touching her forehead to the stone floor at the woman's feet. "I implore the help, generosity, and compassion of the acolytes of Hamra. I come from the western gate where the stone army infused with Maüli has decimated the city's entire quadrant. Queen Marizen's people are gathering their salts to—"

"Stand, child," the woman interrupted, lifting Sénna to her feet. "I am sorry for your troubles, but my people are overwhelmed with the needs of our services. I cannot spare any to assist you."

Sénna felt the breath leave her body as if she'd been punched. Her mouth opened and shut as she tried to convince her frozen chest to inhale. The priestess turned on her heel and stepped away, but Sénna grabbed a handful of her silky plum robes.

"Wait," Sénna gasped, her breathing still ragged. "The Maüli are razing the city. There will be none left by morning. Please…"

The priestess looked at the hand holding her robes and then into Sénna's face. Sénna was surprised to see tears filling the woman's hazel eyes. Sénna released the woman's robes and knelt again. This time, the woman grasped her by the shoulders and lifted her.

"Who are you, child?" the priestess asked, her eyes narrowing as she examined Sénna. "Where do you come from, and how is it that you are here during this tragic time?"

Sénna cleared her throat and raised her chin, grinding her teeth to keep it from trembling. "I am Sénna Králl of Askáribai. My companions and I came here to meet with the Zhoula. We are helping the Zaouni against the forces that now threaten this city, but we are unable to stand against the Maüli."

"And what do you think the acolytes of Hamra can do for you against these Maüli?" the woman asked, her eyebrows raised nearly to the dusting of silvery down that covered her head.

Sénna wiped her sweating hands along her thighs. "My grandmother told my brothers and me stories of Maüli when we were children. I always loved the way they raised bumps along my arms. In those stories, the only weapons that worked against the Maüli were salt and incantations by the followers of Hamra. We cannot destroy the Maüli, but with your help, we can release them to Lady Muralia."

The priestess clucked her tongue and shook her head. "I am Zulina, High Priestess of Hamra for Taboriz. I have followed the goddess's teachings for the past 50 Tides and have never seen any reference to incantations against Maüli. Those stories your grandmother told you were exactly that – stories. Now, go in peace, child, but go."

"Priestess Zulina, wait!" Sénna jumped in front of the

retreating woman. "My grandmother was a Priestess of Hamra for her Meq'qan tribe. Her stories were always instructive, not just entertainment. Besides, if we can't stop the Maüli, no acolytes will be left to sing and prepare the dead. Taboriz will become an open graveyard."

Priestess Zulina puckered her full lips into a frown, adding lines to her forehead and mouth that competed with the crinkles at her eyes. A flush deepened the copper sheen in the woman's cheeks. She placed her hands on ample hips and leaned toward Sénna.

"What would you have me do, girl?" Priestess Zulina hissed, glancing around at the acolytes buzzing around them in a hive of activity. "Shall we just abandon our posts and mandate to sing to the Maüli as they slaughter us all? Even if we are to die today, we can assist as many souls as possible before we do."

Sénna observed the priestess, noting the sweat beading on her forehead and the flush in her dusky cheeks.

"Priestess Zulina, your wisdom and leadership have guided this temple for decades," Sénna said, placing her hand on the priestess's forearm. "My wish is that your life and leadership continues, giving you time to train hundreds more in their service to Hamra." She leaned in toward the priestess's ear and whispered, "I know the words to the incantation we need if you have not had the opportunity to learn it."

Priestess Zulina gasped, raising herself to her full height, several inches below Sénna's chin. "You dare insult me, child?"

Sénna pursed her lips and stuck her hands on her slim hips. "No, Priestess Zulina. There is no way that every priestess, even a high priestess, can learn *all* the lore dedicated to Hamra. There is no shame in gaps in learning. But if you and your followers don't help us, we will all perish. We are running out of time."

A twitch at the corner of Priestess Zulina's mouth was the

only answer Sénna received. The priestess turned and clapped her hands. All movement and talking in the hall ceased; all eyes were on the short woman.

"My children," Zulina's rich contralto echoed in the enormous hall. "Our mandate has shifted. We have an opportunity to prevent deaths in our city rather than just process them. This young Meq'qan woman will guide us in challenging the Maüli attacking our city. She believes, and has convinced me, that we can invoke the rites of passage to ease the specters from the stone bodies they inhabit and ease their way to Lady Muralia's peace."

Sénna clasped her hands behind her back, twisting her fingers at the uncomfortable attention, then stepped forward. "My grandmother was a Meq'qan Priestess of Hamra. She taught me the chant we need. The Market Queen Marizen is gathering salt to trap the Maüli's progress and encourage them to exit the stone. We need to meet them at the western gate, so we must hurry."

The wagons raced toward the western gate, filled with acolytes of Hamra and one hoarse Meq'qan girl. Sénna spent the journey singing the incantation for the priests and priestesses, teaching them the tones and inflections needed to make the spell work. By the time they reached the läenier Wings at the western gate, she could barely squeak her instructions to Anzeri and the Sumäeri waiting for her.

"Salt," Sénna croaked, then cleared her throat. "Salt repels Maüli – they may leave the stone bodies and then be susceptible to the invocations of Hamra's acolytes. They will try to soothe the spirits back to Lady Muralia."

Anzeri stepped forward. "We have plenty of salt but couldn't get many jars of oil. We don't have enough to cover the entire army. I don't know how we're going to get the salt to stick to the soldiers."

The Sumäeri huddled together, throwing out ideas and discarding them. The Angäersol sisters were muted in their animation, all still reeling from losing Räesha to the Maüli. Sénna glanced over to the fountain where Cédron sat with the sculptor and his uncle. Roväen's injury prevented him from moving, and Sénna was surprised to see Cybél tending to him. She remembered how Cybél's hands glowed when helping her grandmother and hoped the woman's simples and remedies might hold some miraculous cure. Sénna had heard sailors tell stories about the slow, painful death of a gut wound, and she frowned. Cédron would be devastated if he lost his uncle now.

Sénna was shaken from her thoughts by the whipping wind of the läenier Wing landing to the east. The raptors settled inside the western gate a reasonable distance from the milling stone army. Many of the Maüli had escaped their stone vessels to trap Räesha and now raged through the city in their ethereal forms, terrorizing the fleeing Yezman. Those stone soldiers with Maüli still bound to them continued their destruction to the south, flattening the harbor area and destroying warehouses. If anyone survived this siege, there would be precious little in supplies to feed them.

The Angäersol sisters stepped up next to Sénna, creating a united front to face Trilläen and his riders.

"Our Wing is here to help," Trilläen called, sliding down from the raptor. "What can we do?"

Sénna turned to her companions, her eyebrows raised in question.

Läenshi and Läerei smiled and nodded. Läerei tossed her hot pink braid over her shoulder, then waved Trilläen and Anzeri into their group.

"We need a way to get the Maüli to evacuate the stone soldiers. Oil would have worked, but it is too heavy, and we don't have enough of it. I propose we try mixing some black-seed with the salt. The läeniers can drop the jars of salt and blackseed among the soldiers. When the salt mixes with the blackseed on impact, they should explode. The black-seed has an adhesive quality that should cause the salt to stick to the stone soldiers sufficiently to expel the specters," Läerei said, looking at the different faces in the group. "If it doesn't work, we're all dead anyway."

Anzeri pursed her full lips and frowned. "I am not familiar with black-seed or how it works. Can you guarantee we aren't gambling our only viable resource?"

Läerei nodded and faced the Yezman woman. "Black-seed is a purifier, and it is also incendiary. When black-seed is heated, it becomes sticky. We used black-seed to coat the Arkmuln outside Táksabai, freeing the people of their demonic infestations. It wasn't a pleasant operation, but it was effective. It is our best and only option here. We will need the Zaouni to ignite the black-seed with flaming arrows."

Läenshi nodded. "Juläen and I will get the message to the Zaouni; then we will return. The Zaouni will be ready." She turned and sprinted to her raptor.

Anzeri nodded and waved to her people to unload the jars from the wagons. Läerei and Säeshi opened the sacks of black-seed. Cédron stood in the fountain behind her and raised the Rod of Shouman. Wind rose from his fulcrum of power, pulling the black-seed from the bags and into the vortex spinning overhead. He guided the seeds over the hundreds of salt jars, easing the breeze and allowing the black-seed to settle on top of the salt.

Sénna ducked as the massive Wing of raptors lifted into the air and swooped past in lines of four, the läeniers grabbing the jars as they glided over the wagons. Trilläen and Roshäen whistled for their Wings to array into a double-wedge formation as they spread out in the sky above. Trilläen pumped his fist and whistled one last time as he led the scores of raptors over the stone army.

The läeniers dumped the black-seed over the advancing

stone army. From their positions on the remaining rooftops of the lower city, the Zaouni rained a shower of flaming arrows upon the soldiers. Sénna watched with rapt attention as the glittering black particles mushroomed around the soldiers, causing the stone to sparkle in Orwaena's fading light. Azria's cerulean hue brightened the eastern horizon as she followed her sister across the sky. Sénna prayed that the healing light would assist the acolytes of Hamra with their spells.

The men and women from Hamra's temple arrayed themselves in a semicircle around the fountain. As the Maüli tore themselves from their stone forms, the chorus of voices raised in song. At first, Sénna only heard the cacophony between the angry shrieks of the specters and the early chanting of the spell, but as the magic grew in strength, the singers overpowered the Maüli. Sénna exhaled, letting her tense shoulders fall. Her plan had worked. The Maüli retreated and appeared to begin their transition into the heavens, where they would be reunited with Lady Muralia's essence.

Behind the singing, as an undertone, Sénna could hear as well as sense a bass thrumming. It rolled and swelled, reminding her of the waves rolling in and crashing against the walls around Táksabai. She turned and looked out over the city, and her blood turned to ice. The stone army stood frozen in their destruction, but the swell of spirits rising above them grew until they blotted out the stars. The booming rise of shrieks crashed over the air as thousands of Maüli raced toward the group as inexorably as the tide.

Sénna held her breath. There was nothing she could do to stem this cresting surge of angry spirits bearing down upon them. The servants of Hamra raised their voices, but they'd seen their doom and the strain was audible. The chant became disjointed, the harmony disrupted, and ultimately overwhelmed by the siren call of the Maüli. Sénna closed her eyes and whispered a prayer to Hamra, begging the goddess to watch over her father, brother, and grandmother. She'd never see them again in this world and possibly not the next. What if she became Maüli, joining this murderous cloud of spirits raging across the land?

A cry arose in the air. The shrieks that sounded like a clarion above her were not the sharp, jagged cries of the Maüli. Sénna opened her eyes and gaped at the array of colorful, gleaming feathers the flock of Aruzzi displayed as they swooped past. The fabled guardians formed a circle around the remaining people on the ground and spread their wings. The rainbow of colors shimmered in Azria's light, the barrier formed by the Aruzzi effecting a sea wall against the crashing wave of Maüli. The incensed specters hit the wall of wind Árk'äezhi enhanced by the Aruzzi and sheared off, regrouping at a distance behind the western gate.

Hamra's followers and Cédron's small group, heartened by the timely arrival of the Aruzzi, increased their efforts. Cédron raised the Rod of Shouman, calling down Lord Shamar's lightning as the mighty chorus of singers continued the invocation behind him. Sénna felt the thrum of undercurrent to the singing and looked around. She spied the Sumäeri ranged around the fountain, all with tears streaming down their cheeks. She followed their gaze to the circle of Aruzzi and realized that the deep hum emitted from the chests of the golden raptors.

Blinking away her tears, Sénna gasped to see a brilliant light rising in the south. Streaks of lightning arched across the skies, striking the rod in Cédron's hand and fragmenting across the city. The rays of Lord Shamar pierced the night, dimming Azria's blue hues as the deity altered his usual trajectory and added his power to the rod. Sénna's jaw dropped as she watched the swirling wind surround and raise Cédron above the fountain.

The lightning arcing from the windstone in his talisman became a solid blanket covering the city of Taboriz in its power. The shrieks of the Maüli lessened as their anger calmed and their forms dissolved into glittering particles. With a wave of the Rod of Shouman, Cédron directed the residual energy of the Maüli southward, soothing the spirits back to the source of creation.

Sénna felt her chest ache as she watched the vortex of wind slow, easing Cédron to the fountain and his companions. She thought of her initial unfairness towards him when he used his power to free Myknét's spirit and again when he saved their group from Wézija. Perhaps all magic wielders weren't evil. Cédron had undoubtedly proven his desire to do good in the world. She smiled and shook her head. Someday, that annoying Shäeli demon might even be strong enough to take on Laylur. She'd had her doubts, but today she felt nothing but pride in her friend's success.

The light from Lord Shamar faded as the deity resumed his path, returning the world to Azria's cerulean tones. Looking around, Sénna compared the ravaged city to the shipwrecks along the coastline; bare skeletons of broken spars and shattered hulls. Taboriz was in shambles, all of the poorest districts flattened, and the wealthier laborer and merchant areas in the second and third tiers devastated by the stone army's passing. Still, the Maüli were gone, and they had Ruzik Ozan and his now-inert stone army to help rebuild. Sénna skipped toward the fountain with a light heart to share the triumph of the moment with her friends.

The scene that welcomed her sank her spirits. Roväen lay prone just outside the fountain with his head resting in Cédron's lap. The wound in his middle seeped through the bandages, and his ordinarily translucent skin carried a gray pallor. The Angäersol women and the sculptor surrounded him as Cybél pulled the dressing from the wound to administer a new poultice.

Sénna gasped at the jagged and puckering wound. Blood and sections of Roväen's insides spilled over his abdomen. She looked at Cédron, whose drawn, pale face was a frozen mask of grief.

"Uncle Roväen, you cannot leave me," Cédron's voice cracked as he stroked his uncle's hair. "I can't do this without you. You've got to let us heal you."

Roväen shook his head. "I carry a burden on my soul that I cannot heal in this life," he said, looking at those surrounding him. "I've lost my brother, sister, and nieces. The Näenji Council has been corrupted from the inside, and, of course, I've lost your trust. You must be free to make your own decisions. I can't do much more here to help, but maybe I can help from the other side."

"But what about Sahráron?" Cédron cried. "She loves you and is waiting for you to build a life with her."

"I cannot stay, even though my love for her is as deep as forever. I will always be with you, guiding you, and supporting you," Roväen said, patting Cédron's hand. "I need your help one last time. I want to say goodbye to Sahráron, and I don't have enough Árk'áezhi to reach her on my own."

Cédron nodded. Tears coursed down his cheeks as he placed his hands on his uncle's shoulders. The Angäersol sisters knelt around Roväen, their faces stoic, and put their hands along his body. Roväen held up his right hand, activating the stones in the bracelet and ring array that Sahráron made him. Sénna watched as the gemcutter's thin face appeared on the smooth stone's surface.

"My love," Roväen smiled, clearing his throat. "Cédron has aligned with the sacred windstone and killed Algarik. We are all safe for now."

Sahráron smiled at Roväen. "Then, you will be coming home soon?"

Roväen nodded. "Soon, my—"

Roväen's hand dropped to his chest, his eyes fixed. Cédron grasped his uncle's wrist and held the gemstone to his eye level, staring at Sahráron's drawn features. His eyes were wide and filled with tears.

"What is it?" Sahráron asked. "What has happened?"

Cédron opened his mouth, but he couldn't speak. Sénna couldn't make out what the gemcutter said next, but Cédron just shook his head. Säeshi scooted next to Cédron and looked into the scrying stone.

"Algarik wounded Rováen earlier this evening. We tended the wound and wrapped it, but he wouldn't allow us to heal him properly. He still managed to help Cédron stop the stone army, release the thousands of Maüli, and save the city. We didn't realize the wound was mortal. I'm so sorry," Säeshi said, holding back her sobs until she saw Sahráron's nod.

"I will see you in the stars, my love," Sahráron said as the gem's face darkened.

Sénna felt tears sting her eyes and her throat constrict. Rováen was a good man. He'd been one of the kindest, wisest, and most compassionate men she'd ever met. It surprised her to realize how much she'd come to depend upon his stabilizing presence and sense of humor.

The Angäersol sisters stood, Säeshi and Läenshi each putting a hand on Cédron's shoulders.

"We must prepare him for burial," Säeshi said, holding out her other hand to the young man. "We'll take him back to the palace."

Cédron gently lowered Rováen's head to the ground and stood. Sénna marveled at the body. Everything about Rováen that made him special, unique, and vibrant was simply gone. She'd never thought about it before and had been too distraught to notice with Myknét's death. But looking at Rováen now, the concept that the body was just a vessel struck home. With Rováen's living essence gone, the corpse was just an empty shell, almost disassociated from the person he'd been. The thought brought Sénna a level of peace, for all that essential Árk'äezhi that was Rováen lived on, just not in this body.

Läerei put two fingers to her mouth and gave a piercing

whistle. Several moments later, three läeniers landed – only one with a rider, Roshäen. He surveyed the scene and nodded solemnly.

"We will escort you all back to the palace," he placed his fist over his heart then opened his palm as a sign of respect for the fallen. "We have lost the best of us today."

Chapter 46: Reconstruction

The next hour felt like a slog through the winter caves above Dúlnat for Cédron. His mind was numb, his body a wooden puppet going through motions that had no meaning. He knew that if he thawed even a little to feel the anguish he felt from losing both Rováen and Tóran, the despair of the abyss would swallow him whole.

Cédron helped Roshäen carry Rováen's body into the palace throne room, where he found Zhoula Najeriz sitting between her mother and Tóran's bodies. Najeriz motioned for them to place their last fallen hero next to Tóran. Staring at the waxen faces of the two men he loved most, Cédron felt a chest-sized hole tear through his body.

The emptiness filled Cédron's mind, allowing the unbearable blackness to overtake him. He'd failed them. Despite aligning with three of the four sacred stones, his powers hadn't been sufficient to save what mattered most. There was no point in finishing this quest – he wasn't strong enough to face Laylur. The Great Demon would ravage the world anyway. Cédron didn't want to be around to see that. He closed his eyes and sighed, walking away from his remaining friends and standing at the window that looked out over the smoldering city.

"I'm so sorry," Sénna said. She laid a hand on his arm.

Cédron swallowed against the tightness in his throat and nodded, patting her fingers. "It should have been me, not Tóran," he said, clearing his throat.

Sénna stood silent for a moment, then turned to face him. "I blame myself for Myknét's death. If I hadn't been spying on those Hazzara, he'd be alive, and Cybél would be happily by his side," she sighed, nodding her head. "I understand the feelings you—"

"You don't understand anything," Cédron snarled, yanking his arm away. "You lost your brother because you foolishly thought you could be a spy for your father. Well, who is the bigger fool?"

Sénna's golden eyes widened, then she looked down. "You're right. I was a fool," she said. "I was a fool to try and be someone I'm not. I've spent my entire life trying to be a spy for my father, to earn his approval, and I've paid a heavy price for that foolishness. I need to find my own way now, a way independent of my father's wishes and my grandmother's expectations. But your way was destined for you. You weren't foolish; you were inspired and guided to this quest."

Cédron's voice raised, causing the others in the room to turn his direction. "Laylur's beast! I listened to the Meq'qan Seeress and foolishly thought this prophecy meant I could heal the world. Instead, I've lost my entire family. Cities have been destroyed, and thousands have died, and with all my power, I couldn't stop it."

"But the prophecy—" Sénna began.

"That prophecy was wrong or misinterpreted," Cédron shouted. "That prophecy calls for someone born of all the races who can bring them all together. I only meet half of those criteria. Yes, I have the blood of all the races, but I'm not the Child of Muralia. I'm the descendant of Laräeth the Betrayer! It's my destiny to destroy the world. Can't you all see that?" Cédron turned away from his friends and faced the window, his arms crossed over his heaving chest.

Najeriz stood and stepped away from her mother's body, striding across the room until she was shoulder-to-shoulder with Cédron. She mirrored his posture, her arms folded across her chest.

"I, too, have lost my family," Najeriz began, her voice just above a whisper. "My Zaouni were decimated, and my city destroyed. I do not feel ready to step into my mother's slippers. They are too big for me."

Najeriz turned to face Cédron. "I can spend days listing reasons why I am not fit to be Zhoula, but that will not rebuild my city or feed my people. The role of Zhoula has fallen to me today, just as the prophecy has fallen to you. We both have the same choice: to wallow in self-pity and bemoan our lot or find the single, most compelling reason why we *can* succeed," she said. She placed a hand on Cédron's shoulder, her bangles jingling against the leather. "Look around; you will find that neither of us is alone in our challenges. The fastest way to success is to accept the help that is offered."

Cédron turned away from the window, surprised to find himself surrounded by the remaining Angäersol sisters, Sénna, Cybél, Anéton, Trilläen, and Roshäen. Outside, he heard the shrill cries of the Aruzzi and läenier Wings. His eyes stung. He didn't deserve their trust or their support.

"Yes, you do," Sénna punched him in the shoulder.

Cédron's eyes opened wide. "You can hear my thoughts?" he gasped, staring into Sénna's golden eyes.

Sénna snorted and shook her head. "No, but your expression was easy to read."

Cédron clenched his teeth against the arguments bubbling up from his chest. He looked around the room and saw the conviction of belief in his companions' eyes. Cédron felt the pang of fear in his chest.

"But what if I can't do it?" Cédron looked at each of his friends in turn. "What if I cause one of you to die next?"

Läenshi stepped forward. "Do you think that you have any control over our fates? You are powerful, but do we not have the power to make our own decisions? Follow whom we choose?" she asked.

"Besides," Anéton said, punching Cédron's shoulder. "You need me around to keep you in line."

The tattoos along Räeshun's bones gleamed in the dim light as her spirit emerged from the staff. "I will never leave your side," she said. "Thank you all for rescuing me from the Maüli so I can complete my quest."

Trilläen cleared his throat, and Räesha's shade turned to face him. They stared silently at each other for a moment, and Sénna was surprised to see tears in the stoic warrior's eyes. Trilläen cleared his throat again, and the moment passed. He clapped his hands twice.

"Excellent," he said, turning to the entrance to the throne room. "Now that we have that established, we have new business to attend to."

The sculptor, Ruzik Ozan, walked into the throne room flanked by two grim-faced Zaouni. One held the cord binding Ruzik's hands and the other his drawn sword. The warriors brought Ruzik to Najeriz and forced him to his knees.

Najeriz stood silently, watching the sculptor, whose eyes never left the floor. Cédron wondered what punishment she was formulating for the man who'd created the stone army. He couldn't fathom what she must be feeling, weighing the depth of his crime toward her city and people against the miracle of his existence.

"Stand, Ruzik Ozan," Najeriz commanded. "Face your Zhoula like the proud Yezman you are."

Ruzik shook his head, his face stubbornly toward the ground. "Fair and just Zhoula, you do not deserve to have the very air you breathe besmirched by my filth. My crimes against your people are too heinous to bear. I implore you to slay me at once for the atrocities I have committed."

Cédron's eyebrows raised when he saw the corners of Najeriz's lips tilt upward. "We agree that you have violated the vows you made at your mastery acceptance not to use your power and talent for evil. However, I cannot sacrifice the gift of your service out of a sense of vengeance. You will spend the rest of your days in service to Taboriz, utilizing your vast talents to rebuilding the city and helping her people."

Ruzik spat on the marble floor. "I will not," he said, the bitter lines of his face twisting, ravaging his features. "I have already been torn from my eternal life, forced against my will to create an army that has destroyed my brethren, and now you deny me a chance to return to my rest? That is not just punishment. That is torture. Either kill me or release me to the quarry where I can return to my crystal tomb."

Räeshun warmed and glowed in Cédron's hands. Her shade appeared and floated toward the sculptor, who remained kneeling on the floor. Behind Räesha drifted a dark beauty with long, braided hair and a jewel in the center of her forehead. Ruzik gasped when this specter appeared and prostrated himself on the floor.

"Zaminah, my love," he cried, grasping at the ephemeral skirts that eluded his fingers. "My shame has no bounds. I've lost you and any path back to you. Forgive me."

"The man who awakened you destroyed your crystal

tomb," Zaminah said in a breezy voice. "But you may atone for your transgressions by using your creations to rebuild the city. I will watch over you from Lady Muralia's side until we can be together once more."

Räesha's shade hovered above the sculptor. "Ruzik Ozan, the deities have given you great gifts, and you owe it to them and your beloved to right the wrongs done in the name of the Great Demon. Once you have completed your task, if you appease the deities, they will allow you to rejoin Zaminah in Lady Muralia's embrace."

Ruzik held his head in his hands. "I am not worthy of their blessings," he sobbed. He yanked handfuls of shaggy, dark-brown hair in his agony.

"Then become worthy," Zaminah said. She placed a translucent hand upon her beloved's head. "Be the man I knew and loved. I will wait for you."

Ruzik raised his head, his soft brown eyes filled with tears that streamed down his cheeks. He swallowed convulsively and reached out to caress Zaminah's face. His hand passed through the image of her skin, and he dropped his arm.

"I will strive to become worthy of you," Ruzik whispered to Zaminah. "I will build the most magnificent city and dedicate it to you, my love."

"Dedicate yourself and your work to rebuilding Taboriz, and it will be enough," Zaminah sighed. "Goodbye, my love. I will be watching over you."

Zaminah's image shimmered and disappeared, as did Räesha's. Najeriz stepped forward and lifted Ruzik to his feet, dismissing her Zaouni after having them unbind the sculptor's wrists.

"You will use your stone soldiers to help with the rebuilding," Najariz commanded, her air of authority unwavering. "But first, you will assist my Zaouni with the rescue and recovery of my citizens from the destruction your army created. Go, begin your work. You can rest when my people are safe."

Ruzik bowed to his Zhoula and followed the Zaouni out of the throne room and into the night. She turned to Cédron and his companions.

"Next, we must conduct proper burials for our families," she sighed, glancing at the row of bodies lining the floor. "I do not have the time or resources to conduct a traditional funeral for my mother, with the appropriate preparations and processions, so we will have to make do with what's available."

Cédron stepped forward. "I can give them a fire and air burial – burn the bodies and release their essences to Lady Muralia," he said, kneeling before Najeriz. "It may not fulfill your traditions, but my Árk'äezhi is sufficient to free their spirits."

Najeriz closed her eyes and took a deep breath. Cédron noticed her fists clenching and unclenching at her sides. He felt for the young ruler and all the decisions and sacrifices she was forced to make under such terrible circumstances. He hoped his assistance would ease her burden even a little.

"Take the bodies to the courtyard. The Aruzzi are already gathering and can bear witness to my mother's passing," Najeriz said, nodding to the Sumäeri in the room.

Trilläen and Läenshi lifted Rovaen's body, while Cédron and Anéton hefted Tóran. Najeriz nodded at Roshäen and Säeshi, who gently lifted the Zhoula's body and followed the others through the archway into the courtyard. A score of Aruzzi perched atop the many columns surrounding the open courtyard with its lush gardens and central fountain. Three läeniers roosted on glass balls that decorated the northern corner of the park. Najeriz led the procession toward the fountain and pulled a lever artfully disguised in the foliage. The water stopped flowing, and the pedestal in the center raised three feet above the fountain's rim.

"Place them on the pedestal," Najeriz said, stepping back to give the bearers room.

The Aruzzi hummed as the deceased were placed reverently on the pedestal. Najeriz raised the platform another foot, then turned to Cédron.

"You have incantations for burial?" Najeriz asked, her eyes not leaving her mother's form.

"We do," Säeshi said as she and Läenshi stepped next to Cédron. "We have had to perform this ritual too many times since Suntide."

Cédron jumped onto the platform and planted Räeshun on the platform to one side of the Zhoula's head and the Rod of Shouman on the other.

"I've only done this once. I don't know the words to the songs," Cédron said, his voice cracking. "But I can follow along with the melody."

Läerei began the song of power that would ease the soul's transition. Her sisters joined her with their silvery voices. Cédron still didn't understand the words, but he could feel their meaning. He remembered when Roväen sang it for Räesha and tried to hum along. The followers of Hamra arrived from the field and entered the courtyard, offering harmony to their song. Cédron saw Räeshun's white markings glow along the staff in his hands as the melody grew in strength. Räesha's spirit materialized and added her voice to the song.

Above the singers, the firestone in Räeshun's crown glowed, and the mortal remains of the three fallen heroes began to shimmer. Each particle of their bodies glistened as they broke away from the whole, reminding Cédron to activate the windstone in the Rod of Shouman. The tattoos along his shoulder blades tingled as the windstone whipped a gentle swirling breeze above the bodies.

The glittering particles floated with the breeze into the sky with joyful abandon. Even through his tears, Cédron felt the exhilaration of his uncle and brother's release and the promise of their eternal love. He hoped that Najeriz could feel her mother's love in the same sense and find the peace and courage to move forward as ruler of Taboriz.

As the last filaments of power disappeared into the night sky, the Aruzzi ended their song, followed by the priests and priestesses of Hamra. The Sumäeri sang the final chorus, their voices fading into silence. Cédron released a long breath and slumped over the now-empty platform. The rod and staff in his hands stood cold and dark.

"May I be worthy of your sacrifice and love," Cédron whispered as he watched the last of the lights wink out in the night sky.

Below him in the courtyard, the followers of Hamra surrounded their new Zhoula with gentle touches and words of encouragement. Najeriz held her head high, smiling at her subjects, but her eyes were still full. She wasn't fooling anyone. Nor was she alone in her grief. Tears glistened on every face as mourners bade farewell to their fallen loved ones. Now they faced the grim task of burying scores of dead and rebuilding their city.

Cédron jumped down from the dais. He landed next to his cousins and his friends from Dúlnat, who arrived with the priests and priestesses of Hamra. They were huddled in a circle with the läenier Wingleaders as he approached them.

"—and return them before they are discovered and hurt, or worse, killed," Trilläen said, slapping his hand on his thigh.

Läenshi nodded. "We can fly to the crystal bridge and work our way south from there," she said. "That is where Sénna sent them, so they shouldn't be hard to find once they emerge from the qanats in the desert."

"You will need to take food, water, and blankets," Najeriz said, stepping into the circle next to Cédron. "My people will be cold, hungry, and afraid to return." The young Zhoula pulled a ring from her finger and handed it to Säeshi. "Take this as proof of my succession and sending you as my ambassadors. I have summoned Anzeri to the palace to gather supplies. Please see her before you go, and she will provide everything you need. Your raptors will need to hunt – take them to the herds in the northern fields above the salt mines. They may hunt their fill."

The Sumäeri bowed, placing their right fists over their hearts then extending their hands with open palms before running into the palace to find Anzeri. Najeriz surveyed the small group from Askári-bai with a slight frown lining her forehead. Cédron was struck at how her sepia skin and amber eyes glowed in the warm light of the blazesand. The dark dimples in her cheeks reminded him of Zariun, and a stab of loss pierced his chest. He swallowed and cleared his throat.

"Zhoula Najeriz, I—" Cédron began, bowing toward the young Zhoula.

"Yes, about you," Najeriz interrupted, narrowing her eyes at the young man. "You were indeed the harbinger of doom as was foretold. Our world is no longer as it was. Everything we thought we knew was wrong, and we must adapt. Change is coming."

Cédron felt each of her words like a dagger to his heart. He knew he was the cause of all the death and destruction she and her city had suffered. He also knew that he couldn't do anything to alleviate her pain. His only path was forward with the hope that, with a great deal of help from his friends and the people of Muralia, he might prevail against the Great Demon. As Cédron tried to formulate a coherent plea to Najeriz that would salvage some of his credibility in her eyes, she placed a hand on his shoulder.

"Your path is the most difficult of all," she smiled through her tears. "I know what you've lost and what you've gained. More importantly, I know what you still face. You have the support of Yezmarantha. The Aruzzi acknowledge that you have aligned with the sacred windstone and are willing to bear you and your friends to the Tawaki for the terrastone."

Cédron's knees buckled, and he sagged forward, falling

to his knees at Najeriz's feet.

"I-I can't tell you how h-humbled and grateful I am – we are," Cédron stumbled over the words.

"Yes," Anéton and Sénna chimed in simultaneously, also bowing low as the Aruzzi shrieked and flapped their wings.

Najeriz lifted Cédron to his feet, squeezing his hand and smiling. "You will need to rest before you leave—"

"My apologies, Zhoula," Anéton interrupted. "But we must leave as soon as possible. We haven't stopped Laylur, only slowed him down."

Sénna stepped up and bowed. "Besides," she said, grinning. "We couldn't sleep anyway. The thought of riding a fabled Aruzzi thrills us beyond words. We are supremely grateful and indebted to you and them for the generosity."

"You have our blessings," Najeriz smiled, deepening her dimples. She turned to face the colorfully plumed Aruzzi. "We will need four willing to carry these people to the Tawaki Chasm."

Cybél stepped forward and knelt. "Pardon me, Zhoula Najeriz," she said, her eyes on the Zhoula's slippers. "I would like to join the Sumäeri in assisting your people. I am a trained healer and can see to their needs."

Najeriz lifted Cybél and hugged her. "I am truly grateful for your offer, friend Cybél. Please join them and see me when your ministrations to my people are complete."

Cybél nodded and turned to Sénna. "I'm sorry to leave you like this, but I need to go where I can be most helpful. I'm not useful in a fight. I'm a liability. I know that now."

Sénna hugged her friend and held her at arm's length. "In another life, we would have been sisters. Myknét must be so proud of you and how you've found your calling. I know I am, and I wish you well. We will see you again when this is done, and I'm sure you will head your own healing hall by then."

Cybél smiled, and the young women clung to each other for another long moment before Cybél broke away and hurried into the palace to catch up with the Sumäeri.

Anéton watched her go, rubbing his chest. "There goes the love of my life," he sighed.

Cédron and Sénna looked at each other, rolled their eyes, and grinned. "Some things never change." Cédron shrugged.

"Even though they should," Sénna gave an exasperated sigh and threw Anéton a sour glance.

Anéton pretended to wince under her scrutiny then brightened. "Hey, provisions!"

Three young pages from the palace bearing leather packs and the durable clay canisters of water lined up in front of the Zhoula and bowed.

"Provisions for the foreigners," the first young man said, holding out his pack. The other two followed suit.

Najeriz waved the pages to her guests. "It looks as though you are ready to begin your journey. Come, let me introduce you to the Aruzzi."

Cédron shouldered the heavy pack, adjusting the straps as he eyed the stamping Aruzzi watching him with the same intensity. He remembered wearing the glass Aruzzi costume for the festival of Nársham-vu, what seemed like Tides ago, and flushed with shame. He'd done no service to the graceful and fearsome raptors that day.

The turquoise Aruzzi watching him stepped forward, nudging Cédron with her beak, then crooning as he scratched the topknot of feathers. He felt a wave of emotion crash over him – like when terror meets excitement. Cédron felt a moment of overwhelming anticipation that soothed his grief and calmed his nerves. Shocked, he looked into the Aruzzi's keen eye as she winked. There was a connection there – he could sense her emotions.

"Well, my dangerous beauty," Cédron crooned as he continued scratching her head. "Whatever challenges we may face, we will face them together."

About The Author

Mikko Azul lives in the Pacific Northwest, where the majestic beauty of her surroundings feeds her imagination and her soul.

Glossary

<u>Askári-bai</u>

Álraun Bessínos – Anéton's father, Harmolin Legionnaire, husband to Datúra and father to Lúlo and Népita.

Am'aranth Králl – Meq'qan originally from Zig'orman Marsh, Syrán's mother, grandmother to Sénna, Myknét and Múradit.

Ánderan Pól – White Mage and leader of the Táksabai Mage's Guild.

Anéton Bessínos – Harmolin Legionnaire, Cédron's companion, son or Áalraun and Dátura, brother to Népita and Lúlo.

Arák – A distilled spirit made from fermented coco palm sap and anise. Sénna calls it 'gak'

Aréon Kírsis – Harmolin Legionnaire and Tóran's competition in the Warrior's Challenge.

Árk'äezhi – The energetic source of all life and power/magic in Muralia.

Arís Tóque – One of Kásuin Varkáras's elderly counselors in Dúlnat.

Arkmuln – Bodies inhabited by demon spirits. The host can be either living or dead.

Askári – Those people, places or things located in or originating from Askári-bai.

Askári-bai – The western most country in Muralia.

Asátto – The fearsome grassland feline found in Kha'san and Dágon Valleys.

Beréna Kráal – Sénna, Múradit and Myknét's mother, wife to Syrán. Worked in animal husbandry in the Laborer's Guild.

Bín Nétar – Algarik's mentor, white mage of Táksabai's Mage's Guild.

Bórnibos – Innkeeper at Lake Julani.

Cámbor – A tasty, freshwater crustacean averaging about 6" in length.

Captain Sórsen – Captain of the Harmolin Legion in Dúlnat.

Cédron Varkáras – Child of Muralia prophecy. Son of Kásuin Varkáras and Maräera Angäersol.

Cybél Láhta – Myknét's fiancée, granddaughter of Urléen the apothecarist. Healer.

Dágon Valley – Fertile sativa valley between Táksabai

and Támon.

Datúra Bessínos – Anéton, Népita and Lúlo's mother, wife to Álraun.

Dúlnat – Mining town in northern Askári-bai held in regency by the Varkáras family and home to Cédron Varkáras.

Fároc – a flightless fowl and insult indicating fearfulness, spinelessness or weakness.

Firespeak – Scrying through flames.

Gérand Kiél – White Mage at Táksabai's Mage's Guild.

Glowstones – Naturally-occurring stones that can be charged with a person's warmth/energy to provide a long-lasting soft light.

Gordán Varkáras – Kásuin's father, Cédron's grandfather.

Gróshan – Formerly the Thieves' Guild, the Gróshan thrive under Syrán Králl as spies and information brokers.

Guilds of Táksabai – Mage's Guild, Merchant's Guild, Laborer's Guild, Gróshan

Hármolin Legion – Askári-bai's uniformed peacekeeping/defensive forces. Each city has a contingent. They wear blue uniforms with silver overlay bearing the crest of their ruling family.

Húsan – Equines with midnight blue hides/manes and horns on the top and bottom of the snout.

Járrik – Caravan guard killed by Wézija.

Jórrel – Hármolin Legionnaire, once friend now foe of Cédron's.

Kásuin Varkáras – Regent of Dúlnat and proprietor of the Varkáras Caravan. Cédron's father.

Kazan – Bovines that reach 12'-18' in length and 8'-10' in height. Used to haul heavy loads. Massive horns on their heads and the sides of their snouts.

Konárras – The original ruling family of Dúlnat, now kept under a Regency.

Konárras Compass Rose – The family crest for Varkáras family and Hármolin Legion of Dúlnat.

Králl Family Crest – Silver rook wearing golden crown with three points inlaid with gemstones.

Lake Juláni – Large lake east of Dúlnat where Bórnibos runs an inn where Álraun Bessínos likes to gamble.

Lúlo Bessínos – Anéton's younger sister, age 13.

Lótril – The immortal guardians of the Rohíti, keepers of water Árk'äezhi.

Méjok – Medium-sized ovid native to the Rohnádi Mountains of Askári-bai. Larger relative to the mijáko.

Méjok-káo – Largest ovid of Muralia, native to both Sinharkon and Rohnádi Mountain ranges.

Mijáko – Smallest ovid of Muralia. Also an expletive and swear word: *mijáko piles*

Mítyon – Askári city southwest of Táksabai on the Tímin Sea. Tóran's birthplace.

Monsáki – Primates covered in brown fur with long tails.

Murádit Králl – Middle son of Syrán Králl, Sénna's older brother and partner in crime. He runs the husan racetrack and works at the Laborer's Guild.

Myknét Králl – Eldest son of Syrán Králl, Sénna's eldest brother and Hármolin Legionnaire. Betrothed to Cybél Láhta.

Nársham-Vu – Annual Suntide Askári festival honoring the deities and the keepers of Árk'äezhi.

Nek'ka – Am'aranth's blind, silver rook who accesses the spirit world and can translate images to her keeper.

Népita Bessínos – Anéton's youngest sister, age 11.

Orén Fár – Red Journeymage under White Mage Gérand Kiél in Táksabai Mage's Guild.

Pánar – Hármolin Legionnaire, once friend now foe of Cédron's.

Rílek Zúhn – Caravan guard/scout.

Rohíti – legendary rainbow-colored fish, keepers of water Árk'äezhi whose scales have magical properties including healing and invisibility.

Róknaar – A hard-shelled, rock-eating worm that inhabits mountains. They create tunnels by eating through them, then disguise themselves as caves by resting with their mouths open on the mountainside.

Ronhádi Mountains – Chain of mountains that run northwest to southeast from Dúlnat to the Zudian Gorge.

Sahráron Thóren – Famed gem cutter/jeweler with Varkáras Caravan. Rováen's beloved.

Scóurj – Gróshan spy utilized by both Mage Kiél and Gróshan King Syrán.

Sénna Králl – Daughter of Syrán the Gróshan King who, as a spy, joins Cédron's quest.

Sénur – Game played with pyramid-shaped dice.

Shalaen Falls – The Shásti River ends at these falls that flow into the Tímin Sea. Home of Rohíti and Lótril and guarded by Wézija.

Shásti River – River that flows east to west in the north of Muralia, separating Molonark from Askári-bai.

Skáresk – Legendary sword of the Askári used in the battle to defeat Laräeth the Betrayer. This sword holds the sacred firestone in its pommel.

Syrán Králl – The Gróshan King and father of Sénna, Myknét & Murádit. Son of Am'aranth.

Tádim Pass – Popular pass in Ronhádi Range between the twin peaks of Zohír and Zohár.

Táksabai – Capitol city of Askári-bai.

Tália Jungle – Surrounding Mítyon and the southwestern quadrant of Askári-bai.

Támon – Small city west of Dúlnat and south of the Ta'voran Marsh.

Tímin Sea – Forms the western border of Askári-bai.

Tóran Varkáras – Orphan of Mítyon adopted by Kásuin and Maräera. Brother to Cédron and the youngest Hármolin Legionnaire to win the Warrior's Challenge.

Twillings – Tiny birds whose wings move so quickly that they can hover in one spot. In Askári-bai, twillings are earth-toned and in Samshäeli, they are jewel-toned.

Urléen Láhta – The apothecarist of Táksabai and grandmother to Cybél.

Vitrón Varkáras – Ancestral founder of Dúlnat with Konárras King's blessing.

Wézija – Immortal guardian of the Shalaen Falls, the Rohíti and Lótril.

Zohár/Zohír – Twin peaks in the Ronhádi Range comprising the Tadím Pass.

<u>Samshäeli</u>

Árk'äezhi – The magical energy originating from the deities and the birthright of all Muralians.

Auräevya – The Tree of Life, origin of terran Árk'äezhi in Samshäeli and tended by the Wushäen.

Azria – Blue moon daughter and patron deity of healers.

Black-seed – Explosive seeds used by Läerei Angäersol for purification of Arkmuln and Maüli.

Bräentu – Sumäeri Council Guard who murders Räesha. Labradorite (gray) eyes.

Bronäen Sea – Northeastern border of Samshäeli.

Cochäera – Swine sporting long, black topknots of hair and fierce tusks native to Samshäeli.

Doyäenne (f) or **Doyäen** (m) – Leader of the Wushäen who guard and tend Auräevya, the Tree of Life in Suläeri. Amethyst eyes.

Eläeni Angäersol – Matriarch of the current Angäersol family, killed by the Selväen. She was a formidable Sumäeri warrior and had aquamarine eyes.

Ginäeyi Forest – The primary topography of Samshäeli.

Häeris – Messenger to the deities and an annual comet.

Hamra – Violet moon daughter and deity presiding over births and deaths.

Ikäerin – Demon-compromised cart driver in Suläeri, Räesha's accuser. Onyx eyes.

Jäebuticaba – Spicy purple berries grown on the trunks of trees in Samshäeli.

Jäeden – The young Wushäen runner who befriends

Räesha. Jäeden has amber eyes.

Juläen – Läenshi's male läenier.

Kessäeri – Fierce, large and flightless avians with indigo skin and feathers.

Lady Muralia – Mother Goddess of Creation and the embodiment of the world.

Läenier – Golden raptors of Samshäeli ridden by elite Sumäeri warriors. The average läenier stands 12' from claw to topknot with a wingspan of 30+ feet.

Läenshi Angäersol – Twin to Säeshi. Läenshi's power is enhancement of Árk'äezhi. She has a muscular build and sapphire eyes.

Läerei Angäersol – Second eldest Angäersol. Läerei's power is to understand and create natural toxins for weapons. She streaks her hair different colors and has aquamarine eyes.

Lanäe Angäersol – Youngest Angäersol daughter with amethyst eyes whose power was to read plant energy. She became a Wushäen. Demons killed Läenia and framed Räesha for it.

Laräeth the Betrayer – Askári woman who studied in Samshäeli a millennium ago. She abused the power and teachings, starting the War of Betrayal and leading to imbalance of Árk'äezhi.

Laylur – The Great Demon, fallen commander of Lord Shamar's celestial army.

Lord Shamar – Father Creator of the world and embodiment of the sun.

Maräera Angäersol – Cédron's Shäeli mother, niece to Roväen & illicit daughter of Neräena and the Meq'qan guard.

Maüli – Tortured souls of those killed by violence. These souls seek vengeance and are lethal.

Näenji Council – Ruling council of Samshäeli housed at the capitol of Suriyäeh, infiltrated by Laylur's minions and compromised.

Neräena Angäersol – Betrothed to Elder Tomäer Bräegan, sister to Roväen and Maräera's mother. Banished after bearing Maräera, who had duel parentage.

Orwaena – Red moon daughter and patron deity of warriors.

Räebin Angäersol – Patriarch of the Angäersol family. Brother to Roväen, husband to Eläeni, father to Räesha, Läerei, Säeshi, Läenshi and Lanäe. Sapphire eyes and is killed by the Selväen.

Räenetti River – Flows west/east from Datínai to Taboriz.

Räesha Angäersol – Eldest Angäersol daughter with aquamarine eyes. Her power was empathy with animals, making her a natural läenier rider. Lover of Trilläen, she was killed by Bräentu and transformed into the Staff of Fire and Bone (Räeshun) by the deity Orwaena.

Räeshun – After her death and transformation, Räesha became Räeshun, her talisman identity.

Roshäen – Sumäeri Wingleader and rider of Shäelan. He rescues Sénna from the airship fall. Emerald eyes.

Roshäeo – Saurian beasts of burden with flat bills and indigo spotted hide. Native to Samshäeli.

Roväen Angäersol – Cédron's maternal uncle, a Sumäeri warrior whose talent is invisibility. He has sapphire eyes.

Säeshi Angäersol - Twin to Läenshi. Säeshi's power is identification of Árk'äezhi. She has a slender build and sapphire eyes.

Samshäeli – Land in the far east of Muralia and home to the Shäeli peoples. Samshäeli's borders closed after the War of Betrayal and they have a Covenant forbidding interaction with all others.

Selväen – An immortal and neutral elemental creature of wicker that was warped and weaponized by the compromised Näenji Council. The Selväen was sent to destroy the Angäersol family.

Shäelan – The female läenier of Roshäen.

Shäeli – The people of Samshäeli.

Sharäedan River – Flows east/west from the Bronäen Sea to the Shalaen Falls.

Siläeri – Suspended city in the trees, home of the Wushäen who tend Auräevya, the Tree of Life.

Sumäeri – The warriors of Samshäeli.

Suriyäeh – Capitol city of Samshäeli housed in a single, colossal tree in the northeast quadrant. Home to the Näenji Council.

Trilläen Villinäes – Captain of the Sumäeri Council Guard with the ability to track anything. He has amethyst eyes and was officially stripped of his title when he defied the Näenji Council.

Twillings – Tiny jewel-feathered birds whose wings beat so rapidly that they can hover. In Askári-bai, the feathers are earth-toned.

Wing – The unit of fighting läenier riders. A Wing consists of a Wingleader and 100 läeniers and their riders.

Wushäen – Shäeli occupation of those who tend Auräevya in Suläeri. There is a deep-seated conflict between the Wushäen and the Sumäeri.

Yongäen – Räesha's male läenier.

<u>Yezmarantha</u>

Alzaytan – Vicious four-legged reptiles with claws, plated exoskeleton with spiny ridges and long tail with spiked ball on the tip. Only the brave or foolish use them as mounts.

Anzeri – Market Queen's Head of Security. She has bronze skin and clear, green eyes.

Anzen Grozak – Son of the Market Queen Marizen and textile merchant who provides towels to the public bath houses. He is tall, slim with a brown beard, brown eyes and coppery skin.

Aruzzi – Legendary, colorful birds with seven tailfeathers who are keepers of wind Árk'äezhi.

Azp – A poisonous black snake native to Yezmarantha.

Baizen – A Yezman silk textile merchant.

Blazesand – The colorful, flammable sand used in glass jars to illuminate: green, blue or yellow.

Caliz Grozak – Eldest son of Anzen Grozak, brother of Raziz. Age 14.

Dadaji – Yezman word for grandfather.

Dezeen – Matron of the palace women's quarters. Stout, middle-aged woman with brown eyes, close-cropped curls and sepia skin.

Dutar – A long-necked, two-stringed instrument like a lute.

Hazzara – Black-clad assassins of the desert. Trained by Zen Hazad, known as The Shadow.

Laizo Tabriz – Merchant and rival of Ruzik Ozan for both the hand of Zaminah.

Maman – Yezman word for mother.

Marizen Grozak – Elderly Market Queen of Taboriz. She is diminutive and wrinkled but wields tremendous power and influence in the city.

Marozna – High Commander of the Taboriz Zaouni Warriors. He is tall, barrel-chested and pompous. His hair, skin and eyes are all dark brown and he is handsome but not pleasant.

Najeriz – Princess of Taboriz, she has sepia skin, amber eyes and a cloud of long, black hair.

Naniji – Yezman word for grandmother.

Ozryk – Bovine pack animals with two long, straight horns extending 2-2.5' in a V from their heads. Their fur is light gray or dun and they weigh up to a ton.

Papan – Yezman word for father.

Priestesses of Orwaena – Sequestered in their temple in Zaveen, these dedicated women craft zolenium into weapons, artifacts and talismans.

Razelf Grozak – Spouse of Marizen, the Market Queen and Dadaji to Raziz and his siblings. He is a small, frail man with round spectacles, missing teeth, wrinkles and thin hair.

Ruzik Ozan – Fabled sculptor who imprisoned himself in crystal tomb. He was reanimated by Algarik and compelled to create the stone army.

Shezak (pl. Shezaki) – Gargantuan hooved beasts with thick shoulders, heavy heads bearing two large-pronged horns out the front of their foreheads. Ridden by the Zaouni Warriors into battle. These creatures stand 20' at the shoulder and weigh up to three tons.

Shanty – The poor district inside the first wall of Taboriz. Also a lean-to shelter.

Shozin Chezak – Master of the Varkáras Caravan. He is powerfully-built and stands 7' tall, bald with black eyes and sable/burnt umber skin.

Taboriz – Capitol city of Yezmarantha.

Tazien Grozak – Anzen's wife, Raziz's mother. She is a slender woman with sharp features, hazel eyes and full lips. Her skin is tawny and her hair in thick plaits between her shoulders.

Vazurgan – The nobility or elite class of Taboriz.

Yezman – The people of Yezmarantha. Also, anything with Yezmaranthan origin.

Zagala Blades – Circular, hand-held weapon with opposing zolenium blades. Wielded by Zhoula.

Zahili Desert – The topography covering the entirety of Yezmarantha.

Zahna Grozak – Eldest daughter of Anzen Grozak and Raziz's sister. Age 12.

Zaimat – A round, pastry-like dumpling smothered in honey.

Zalid – Slave/manservant in Zaran's bathhouse that becomes Sénna's accomplice.

Zalmek Varkaraz – Yezman lover of Laräeth the Betrayer. They began the Varkáras line.

Zaminah – Ruzik Ozan's murdered betrothed. Her stone statue inhabits her Maüli spirit and guarded the Zaroon Quarry until the Hazzara overran it.

Zamboosa – Fried pastry filled with savory meats and

cheese.

Zaouni Warriors – The defending and peace-keeping force of Taboriz. They wear red feather headdresses and gold breastplates.

Zaran – Master of the public bathhouse, ally of Algarik and traitor to the Zhoula.

Zariun – Cédron's dearest friend and acrobat in the caravan. Killed by Algarik in Dúlnat.

Zaroon Quarry – Ruzik Ozan's workplace and Algarik's Hazzara lair in the Zahili Desert.

Zaveen – The ancient walled fortress city in Yezmarantha's west where the Priestesses of Orwaena have their temple.

Zebrina – Baizen's 12-year-old daughter. She is lanky with a straight nose and long, coiled hair.

Zholi Festival – Yezman colorful festival of mosaics, celebrating the moon daughter's capture and imprisonment of Laylur.

Zhoula – The leader or matriarch of Taboriz.

Zindra – Yezman word for rain.

Zolenium – The strong, black metal mined near Zaveen and worked by the Priestesses of Orwaena.

Zora – Yezman word for dawn.

Zudian Gorge – At the base of the Ronhádi Mountains above the Räenetti River.

Zulina – High Priestess of Hamra in Taboriz. She is short & plump with downy, silver hair cropped short. She has coppery skin with fine wrinkles and warm, brown eyes.

<u>Meq'qan Tribes of Ta'voran and Zig'orman Marshes</u>

Am'aranth – Given to the Askári King of Thieves in arranged marriage. Sénna's grandmother and Priestess Zale'en's younger sister.

Caf'iq – Meq'qan term for leader.

Caf'iq Mak'ki – Leader of the Zig'orman Tribes, spouse of Zale'en and father of Chaq'ta.

Chaq'ta – Son of Zale'en and Mak'ki. A headstrong and shortsighted Meq'qan warrior.

Chem'ewa – One of three survivors of the Ta'voran Marsh massacre.

Dir'iq – One of three survivors of the Ta'voran Marsh massacre. He dies of injuries in Dúlnat.

Falah – A five-pronged fishing spear.

Kha'san Valley – Between the Ronhádi Mountains and Samshäeli's Ginäeyi Forest.

Ma'lok – Member of a remote northern Zig'orman Tribe who reports Hazzara infiltration.

Mashuf – A two-man canoe made of woven reeds.

Meq'qan – The golden-yellow eyed peoples of the marshlands who honor the deities by utilizing bones in their structures and decorations.

Ra'lina – Chaq'ta's six-year-old daughter.

Rabe'en Plains – Between the Zig'orman Marsh and Samshäeli, north of the Sharäedan River.

Ser'aq – Lady Muralia's aquatic steeds who guard her underwater cave.

Tar'iq – One of three survivors of the Ta'voran Marsh massacre. He accompanies Tóran to war against the Garanth.

Tarrada – A four-man fishing skiff made of woven reeds over a bone frame.

Ta'voran Marsh – Located in the northwest corner of Muralia.

Ur'luq – A low-riding reptile of the marshlands with

spiked hide and large teeth.

Vak'ki – Zale'en's priestess whose daughter and grandchildren are poisoned by the urglek spines.

Wakazan – The horned bovines used for burden or war. Average height is 20' at the shoulder and weight approximately 2-3 tons.

Zale'en – High Priestess of the Zig'orman Meq'qan. Mak'ki's wife, Chaq'ta's mother, Am'aranth's elder sister.

<u>Mololark</u>

Algarik Muhr – Born the elder brother of Kásuin Varkáras, he was banished from the family by their father Górdan for practicing forbidden magic and killing a family in the process.

Arkmuln – Bodies inhabited by demon spirits. The bodies can be living or not.

Charknan Geysers – A geographic feature along Molonark's eastern border.

Garanth – Tribal peoples of Molonark. They are muscular, stand 9-12' tall with leathery skin. The males have two horns sprouting from their foreheads. The horns are distinctive to each male and are a source of pride. They speak a guttural language that is incomprehensible to others.

Hareeki – Amphibians that dwell in the lava rivers of the Sinkarkon Range or the scalding waters of the Charknan Geysers.

Kaband – The name of the demon with the Garanth army who captures Tóran.

Levirk Sirkran – Hazzara spy sent by Algarik to Dúlnat. He infiltrates the Hármolin Legion.

Maftaka – The Immortal guardian of fire Árk'äezhi and the northern gate to the abyss in the Sinharkon Range.

Mairk Lerkinan – Algarik's Hazzara Lieutenant at Aromberk Fortress who is in charge of affairs when Algarik is away.

Molonark – The desolate and barren land on Muralia's northern quadrant.

Nuriak's Cauldron – A large cauldera in Molonark west of the Sinharkon Range.

Sinharkon Range – The active volcanic mountain range running along Molonark's northern border.

Tawaki – Subterranean-dwelling peoples of the Tawaki Chasm aligned with the sacred terrastone.

Thoromberk Fortress – Deep in the Sinharkon Range, this stone fortress was built by Tawaki slaves and was once Laräeth the Betrayer's home, it is now Algarik's lair.

Urglek – Large, feliform carnivores of Molonark with long, poisonous quills. They have a laugh-like bark and weigh an average of 120 lbs.

<u>Spells</u>

Maftah – The spell to create a fire or to set something ablaze.

Tezra – The spell to enlarge something.

Maiya am Badaiya – The incantation in Laräeth's codex to free the Great Demon Laylur.

<u>Expletives</u>

Laylur's beast

Méjako piles

Kazan dung

Time

Tide – The equivalent of a year.

Fortnight – A two-week period.

Sennight – A four-week period.

Dormantide – The cold, barren season.

Buddingtide – The warm, rainy season when all things begin to grow.

Suntide – The hot, dry season.

Autumntide – The crisp, harvest season.

Special Thanks

A special thanks must be made to the Kitsap Writers Group, whose insight and criticisms honed this book into a story that I'm very proud of. This collaborative effort not only improved my manuscript but helped me become a better writer. Thank you to Michelle VanBerkom, Roland Boykin, Jerry Hall, Archie Kregear, Denise Moreno, Kristina Anderson Younger, Meghan Skye, Kate Ota, Evan Harris, Jeanne Lewis, and Carrie Lawrence. A very special thank you goes to Paul Hathaway, whose detailed editing and brutal honesty were appreciated beyond measure. My gratitude also goes out to Viveca Shearin and Benjamin Gorman, the fantastic editors and publishers from Not A Pipe Publishing, whose insights and confidence in my work inspire me to grow both as a writer and a person.

www.ingramcontent.com/pod-product-compliance
Lightning Source LLC
Chambersburg PA
CBHW030655190726
48286CB00001B/25